PENGUIN BOOKS

THE GRAPES OF WRATH
Text and Criticism

Peter Lisca is Professor of English at the University of Florida, Gainesville. He has also taught at the Woman's College of the University of North Carolina, and at the University of Washington. He is the author of *The Wide World of John Steinbeck* and numerous articles appearing in *PMLA, Modern Fiction Studies, Twentieth Century Literature,* and various collections of essays.

THE VIKING CRITICAL LIBRARY

JOHN STEINBECK

The Grapes of Wrath

TEXT AND CRITICISM

EDITED BY PETER LISCA
UNIVERSITY OF FLORIDA, GAINESVILLE

PENGUIN BOOKS

Penguin Books Ltd, Harmondsworth,
Middlesex, England
Penguin Books, 625 Madison Avenue,
New York, New York 10022, U.S.A.
Penguin Books Australia Ltd, Ringwood,
Victoria, Australia
Penguin Books Canada Limited, 2801 John Street,
Markham, Ontario, Canada L3R 1B4
Penguin Books (N.Z.) Ltd, 182–190 Wairau Road,
Auckland 10, New Zealand

The Grapes of Wrath first published in the
United States of America by The Viking Press 1939
The Viking Critical Library edition of *The Grapes of Wrath*
first published in the United States of America by The Viking Press 1972
Reprinted 1976
Published in Penguin Books 1977
Reprinted 1977, 1979, 1981, 1982

Library of Congress Cataloging in Publication Data
Steinbeck, John, 1902–1968.
The grapes of wrath.
(The Viking critical library)
Bibliography: p. 869.
I. Title.
[PZ3.S8195Gr38] [PS3537.T3234] 813'.5'2 76-30628
ISBN 0 14 015.508 2

Printed in the United States of America by
The Murray Printing Company, Westford, Massachusetts
Set in Linotype Electra and Janson

EDITOR'S PREFACE

Very few of those who read *The Grapes of Wrath* in 1939 could have foreseen that this book, which dramatized the headlines and newsreels of the day, which seemed so intimately connected with them that its merits were debated not in literary terms but in those of sociological research and political ideology, would continue to be read long after the headlines had been forgotten. True, its depiction of "the establishment" on one side and the dispossessed on the other contributes to its interest for this age of both violent demonstrations against authority and idealistic efforts to aid the impoverished. But if that were all it had to offer, *The Grapes of Wrath* would be shelved with dozens of other "proletarian" novels of the 1930s, to gather dust in an out-of-print edition. What distinguishes this one novel is not only its greater authenticity of detail but also the genius of its author, who, avoiding mere propaganda, was able to raise those details and themes to the level of lasting art, while muting none of the passionate human cry against injustice. Anyone who has used the novel in a classroom can testify to its viability. In fact, the response of students leaves no doubt that as literature *The Grapes of Wrath* is generally experienced more completely today than it was in 1939, when it was much more difficult to dissociate the novel from current events or to see Steinbeck's bold technical experiments as something more than what one critic called "calculated crudities."

Like all true works of art, *The Grapes of Wrath* reaches into universal human experience and hence is capable of communicating even across a chasm of ignorance regarding the definite intellectual and social milieu from which it sprang. Once again like all true art, however, it gains in stature when understood in relation to that milieu. This explains one feature of the present critical edition. The study materials start with three essays expressing various points of view about the conditions depicted in the novel, and they continue with another essay that samples the reactions to the novel in Oklahoma, the state from which the Joads were uprooted. Together these essays compose the first section.

The second section of study materials consists of the most enlightening critical essays devoted to *The Grapes of Wrath* during the years since its publication. As introduction to the section, I have written a history of critical reactions to the novel —not too long an introduction, I hope, but still with sufficient particulars to guide the student further in any direction he may wish to pursue. The essays themselves are presented in chronological order. Several of the best essays are fairly recent, and three are published here for the first time. There has been no effort to represent fully the early critical misreadings of the novel, but one later attack has been included as an example of some persistent arguments against it.

Two hitherto unpublished documents, a letter from Steinbeck to his editor, Pascal Covici, and a suggested interview sent by Steinbeck to his friend, the journalist Joseph Henry Jackson, cast light on the author's intentions. Additional material of interest to students and instructors includes maps of the route followed by the Joads, a Steinbeck chronology, "Topics for Discussions and Papers," and finally a rather full bibliography in which will be found, besides other items, every article about Steinbeck mentioned in this book.

The present text of the novel itself—including pagination—is that of the Penguin Edition, which is standard. All page references to *The Grapes of Wrath* in the essays printed here have been adjusted to that edition or provided by the editor and put in parentheses. Also for the student's convenience, page references in these essays to other essays also printed here have likewise been adjusted to the present edition. Information about the original publication of the essays is contained in the bibliography.

To Malcolm Cowley, Marshall A. Best, and Barbara Burn of The Viking Press I extend my thanks for their confidence, patience, and good advice. My special thanks are due Betty Perez, who, as a graduate student at the University of Florida and my assistant, not only participated in all aspects of this work but also mapped the journey of the Joads and contributed one of the essays.

PETER LISCA

CONTENTS

IV. TWO UNPUBLISHED DOCUMENTS

CHRONOLOGY

1902   John Ernst Steinbeck born on February 27 in Salinas, California. His father, John Ernst, Sr., was a miller and was treasurer of Monterey County; his mother was formerly a schoolteacher. He was the third of four children, and the only son. Grew up in a semi-rural environment.

1919   Graduated from Salinas High School, a good student and athlete.

1920   Enrolled at Stanford University, but attended sporadically, dropping out to work on ranches, farms, and roadbuilding gangs.

1924   Published two stories in *The Stanford Spectator*, "Fingers of Cloud" and "Adventures in Arcademy."

1925   Left Stanford without taking a degree. Went to New York, where he worked briefly as a reporter for the *American* and later as a laborer. Wrote short stories, but could find no publisher.

1926   Returned to California and continued to write, supporting himself by a variety of jobs, including caretaker of an isolated lodge at Lake Tahoe.

1929   Published first novel, *Cup of Gold*, a highly fictionalized biography of Henry Morgan, the buccaneer.

1930   Married Carol Henning and took up residence in a family cottage at Pacific Grove; continued to write, living mostly on a $25-a-month allowance from his father. Met Edward F. Ricketts, commercial marine biologist, who became his close, influential friend and served as model for several of Steinbeck's characters.

1932   Moved to Los Angeles. Published *The Pastures of Heaven*.

1933   Returned to Pacific Grove. Published *To a God Unknown* and the first two parts of *The Red Pony*.

1934   "The Murder" chosen as an O. Henry Prize Story. His mother, Olive Hamilton Steinbeck, died.

1935 Published *Tortilla Flat* and was awarded the Commonwealth Club of California Gold Medal; realized his first financial success as author.

1936 Published *In Dubious Battle* and a series of articles on migrants ("The Harvest Gypsies") in *San Francisco News*. Traveled in Mexico. His father died.

1937 Published *Of Mice and Men*, the first of several of his novels to be chosen by the Book-of-the-Month Club. Also published *The Red Pony* (in three parts). Traveled in Europe. The play *Of Mice and Men* was produced in November and won the Drama Critics Circle Award for that season. Joined migrants in Oklahoma and traveled with them to California.

1938 Published *The Long Valley*, a collection of his short stories, and *Their Blood Is Strong*, a reprint of the migrant articles with a postscript.

1939 Published *The Grapes of Wrath*. Elected to the National Institute of Arts and Letters.

1940 Awarded the Pulitzer Prize for *The Grapes of Wrath*. Cruised the Gulf of California with Ricketts, collecting marine invertebrates. Wrote and helped film *The Forgotten Village*, documentary, in Mexico. Received Social Work Today Award and American Booksellers Association Award.

1941 Published *Sea of Cortez*, with Ricketts, based on materials gathered in the Gulf of California.

1942 Published *The Moon Is Down* (also produced as a play) and *Bombs Away*, a documentary designed to encourage enlistments in the Army Air Corps. Divorced from Carol Henning.

1943 Married Gwyndolen Conger, began residence in New York. Served as European war zone correspondent for the New York *Herald Tribune*.

1944 Wrote film story (unpublished) for *Lifeboat*, 20th Century–Fox. Thom, his first son, was born.

1945 Published *Cannery Row*; published *The Red Pony*, including a fourth part—"The Leader of the People"; published "The Pearl of the World" (same as *The Pearl*) in *Woman's Home Companion*. Wrote film story for *A Medal for Benny*, Paramount.

1946 Awarded the King Haakon (Norway) Liberty Cross for *The Moon Is Down*. Second son, John IV, was born.

1947   Published *The Pearl* and *The Wayward Bus*. Traveled in Russia with the photographer Robert Capa.

1948   Published *A Russian Journal*, with Robert Capa. Elected to American Academy of Arts and Letters. Edward Ricketts died. Divorced from Gwyndolen Conger.

1950   Published *Burning Bright*, later produced as a play. Wrote film story for *Viva Zapata*, 20th Century–Fox. Married Elaine Scott.

1951   Published *The Log from the Sea of Cortez*, containing the narrative portion from *Sea of Cortez* and a tribute to his deceased friend—"About Ed Ricketts."

1952   Published *East of Eden*. Traveled in Europe, sending reports to *Collier's*.

1954   Published *Sweet Thursday*.

1955   *Pipe Dream* (from *Sweet Thursday*) produced, a musical comedy by Rodgers and Hammerstein.

1956   "The Affair at 7, Rue de M——" chosen as an O. Henry Prize Story.

1957   Published *The Short Reign of Pippin IV*.

1958   Published *Once There Was a War*, a collection of his war dispatches.

1961   Published *The Winter of Our Discontent*, his last novel.

1962   Published *Travels With Charley*. Awarded the Nobel Prize for Literature.

1964   Appointed as a Trustee of the John F. Kennedy Memorial Library. Awarded a Press Medal of Freedom and a United States Medal of Freedom.

1965–
1966   From November through April traveled in Europe and the Middle East, reporting his travels in "Letters to Alicia" (*Newsday*).

1966–
1967   From December through May reported from Vietnam on the American involvement, continuing his "Letters to Alicia."

1968   Suffered from coronary disease and died of a severe attack in New York City on December 20.

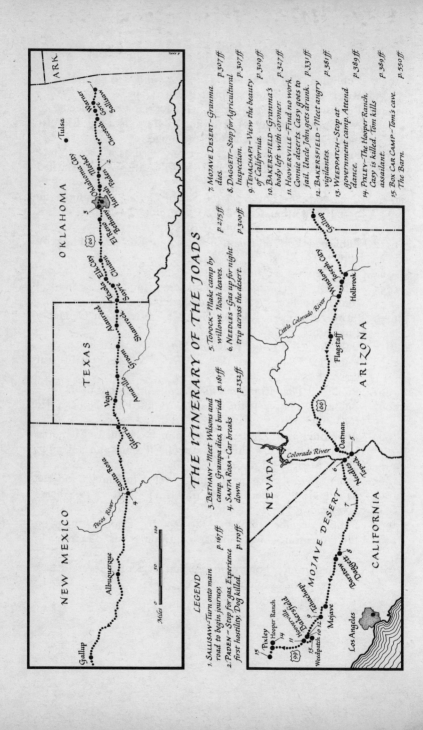

THE ITINERARY OF THE JOADS

LEGEND

1. SALLISAW – Turn onto main
   road to begin journey. p. 161 ff

2. PADEN – Stop for gas. Experience
   first hostility. Dog killed. p. 110 ff

3. BETHANY – Meet Wilsons and
   camp. Grampa dies, is buried. p. 181 ff

4. SANTA ROSA – Car breaks
   down.

5. TOROCK – Make camp by
   willows. Noah leaves. p. 275 ff

6. NEEDLES – Gas up for night
   trip across the desert. p. 253 ff

7. MOJAVE DESERT – Gramma
   dies. p. 307 ff

8. DAGGETT – Stop for Agricultural
   Inspection. p. 307 ff

9. TEHACHAPI – View the beauty
   of California. p. 309 ff

10. BAKERSFIELD – Gramma's
    body left with coroner. p. 327 ff

11. HOOVERVILLE – Find no work.
    Connie deserts. Casy goes to
    jail. Uncle John gets drunk. p. 331 ff

12. BAKERSFIELD – Meet angry
    vigilantes. p. 381 ff

13. WEEDPATCH – Stop at
    government camp. Attend
    dance.

14. PIXLEY – The Hooper Ranch.
    Casy is killed. Tom kills
    assailant. p. 389 ff

15. BOX CAR CAMP – Tom's cave.
    The Barn. p. 550 ff

✿✿

The Grapes of Wrath

The Text

To CAROL who willed this book
To TOM who lived it

Chapter One

TO THE red country and part of the gray country of Oklahoma, the last rains came gently, and they did not cut the scarred earth. The plows crossed and recrossed the rivulet marks. The last rains lifted the corn quickly and scattered weed colonies and grass along the sides of the roads so that the gray country and the dark red country began to disappear under a green cover. In the last part of May the sky grew pale and the clouds that had hung in high puffs for so long in the spring were dissipated. The sun flared down on the growing corn day after day until a line of brown spread along the edge of each green bayonet. The clouds appeared, and went away, and in a while they did not try any more. The weeds grew darker green to protect themselves, and they did not spread any more. The surface of the earth crusted, a thin hard crust, and as the sky became pale, so the earth became pale, pink in the red country and white in the gray country.

In the water-cut gullies the earth dusted down in dry little streams. Gophers and ant lions started small avalanches. And as the sharp sun struck day after day, the leaves of the young corn became less stiff and erect; they bent in a curve at first, and then, as the central ribs of strength grew weak, each leaf tilted downward. Then it was June, and the sun shone more fiercely. The brown lines on the corn leaves widened and moved in on the central ribs. The weeds frayed

3

and edged back toward their roots. The air was thin and the sky more pale; and every day the earth paled.

In the roads where the teams moved, where the wheels milled the ground and the hooves of the horses beat the ground, the dirt crust broke and the dust formed. Every moving thing lifted the dust into the air: a walking man lifted a thin layer as high as his waist, and a wagon lifted the dust as high as the fence tops, and an automobile boiled a cloud behind it. The dust was long in settling back again.

When June was half gone, the big clouds moved up out of Texas and the Gulf, high heavy clouds, rain-heads. The men in the fields looked up at the clouds and sniffed at them and held wet fingers up to sense the wind. And the horses were nervous while the clouds were up. The rain-heads dropped a little spattering and hurried on to some other country. Behind them the sky was pale again and the sun flared. In the dust there were drop craters where the rain had fallen, and there were clean splashes on the corn, and that was all.

A gentle wind followed the rain clouds, driving them on northward, a wind that softly clashed the drying corn. A day went by and the wind increased, steady, unbroken by gusts. The dust from the roads fluffed up and spread out and fell on the weeds beside the fields, and fell into the fields a little way. Now the wind grew strong and hard and it worked at the rain crust in the corn fields. Little by little the sky was darkened by the mixing dust, and the wind felt over the earth, loosened the dust, and carried it away. The wind grew stronger. The rain crust broke and the dust lifted up out of the fields and drove gray plumes into the air like sluggish smoke. The corn threshed the wind and made a dry, rushing sound. The finest dust did not settle back to earth now, but disappeared into the darkening sky.

The wind grew stronger, whisked under stones, carried up straws and old leaves, and even little clods, marking its course as it sailed across the fields. The air and the sky darkened and through them the sun shone redly, and there was a raw sting in the air. During a night the wind raced faster over the land, dug cunningly among the rootlets of the corn, and the corn fought the wind with its weakened leaves until the roots were freed by the prying wind and then each stalk settled wearily sideways toward the earth and pointed the direction of the wind.

The dawn came, but no day. In the gray sky a red sun appeared, a dim red circle that gave a little light, like dusk; and as that day advanced, the dusk slipped back toward darkness, and the wind cried and whimpered over the fallen corn.

Men and women huddled in their houses, and they tied handkerchiefs over their noses when they went out, and wore goggles to protect their eyes.

When the night came again it was black night, for the stars could not pierce the dust to get down, and the window lights could not even spread beyond their own yards. Now the dust was evenly mixed with the air, an emulsion of dust and air. Houses were shut tight, and cloth wedged around doors and windows, but the dust came in so thinly that it could not be seen in the air, and it settled like pollen on the chairs and tables, on the dishes. The people brushed it from their shoulders. Little lines of dust lay at the door sills.

In the middle of that night the wind passed on and left the land quiet. The dust-filled air muffled sound more completely than fog does. The people, lying in their beds, heard the wind stop. They awakened when the rushing wind was gone. They lay quietly and listened deep into the stillness. Then the roosters crowed, and their voices were muffled, and the people stirred restlessly in their beds and wanted the morning. They knew it would take a long time for the dust to settle out of the air. In the morning the dust hung like fog, and the sun was as red as ripe new blood. All day the dust sifted down from the sky, and the next day it sifted down. An even blanket covered the earth. It settled on the corn, piled up on the tops of the fence posts, piled up on the wires; it settled on roofs, blanketed the weeds and trees.

The people came out of their houses and smelled the hot stinging air and covered their noses from it. And the children came out of the houses, but they did not run or shout as they would have done after a rain. Men stood by their fences and looked at the ruined corn, drying fast now, only a little green showing through the film of dust. The men were silent and they did not move often. And the women came out of the houses to stand beside their men—to feel whether this time the men would break. The women studied the men's faces secretly, for the corn could go, as long as something else remained. The children stood near by, drawing figures in the dust with bare toes, and the children sent exploring senses out to see whether men and women would break. The children peeked at the faces of the men and women, and then drew careful lines in the dust with their toes. Horses came to the watering troughs and nuzzled the water to clear the surface dust. After a while the faces of the watching men lost their bemused perplexity and became hard and angry and resistant. Then the women knew that they were safe and that there was no break. Then they asked, What'll we do?

And the men replied, I don't know. But it was all right. The women knew it was all right, and the watching children knew it was all right. Women and children knew deep in themselves that no misfortune was too great to bear if their men were whole. The women went into the houses to their work, and the children began to play, but cautiously at first. As the day went forward the sun became less red. It flared down on the dust-blanketed land. The men sat in the doorways of their houses; their hands were busy with sticks and little rocks. The men sat still—thinking—figuring.

Chapter Two

A HUGE red transport truck stood in front of the little roadside restaurant. The vertical exhaust pipe muttered softly, and an almost invisible haze of steel-blue smoke hovered over its end. It was a new truck, shining red, and in twelve-inch letters on its sides—OKLAHOMA CITY TRANSPORT COMPANY. Its double tires were new, and a brass padlock stood straight out from the hasp on the big back doors. Inside the screened restaurant a radio played, quiet dance music turned low the way it is when no one is listening. A small outlet fan turned silently in its circular hole over the entrance, and flies buzzed excitedly about the doors and windows, butting the screens. Inside, one man, the truck driver, sat on a stool and rested his elbows on the counter and looked over his coffee at the lean and lonely waitress. He talked the smart listless language of the roadsides to her. "I seen him about three months ago. He had a operation. Cut somepin out. I forget what." And she—"Doesn't seem no longer ago than a week I seen him myself. Looked fine then. He's a nice sort of a guy when he ain't stinko." Now and then the flies roared softly at the screen door. The coffee machine spurted steam, and the waitress, without looking, reached behind her and shut it off.

Outside, a man walking along the edge of the highway crossed over and approached the truck. He walked slowly to the front of it, put his hand on the shiny fender, and looked at the *No Riders* sticker on the windshield. For a moment he was about to walk on down the road, but instead he sat on the running board on the side away from the restaurant. He was not over thirty. His eyes were very dark brown and there was a hint of brown pigment in his eyeballs. His cheek bones were high and wide, and strong deep lines cut down his cheeks, in curves beside his mouth. His upper lip was long, and since his teeth protruded, the lips stretched to cover them, for this man kept his lips closed. His hands were hard, with broad fingers and nails as thick and ridged as little clam shells. The space between thumb and forefinger and the hams of his hands were shiny with callus.

The man's clothes were new—all of them, cheap and new. His gray cap was so new that the visor was still stiff and the button still on, not shapeless and bulged as it would be when it had served for a while all the various purposes of a cap— carrying sack, towel, handkerchief. His suit was of cheap gray hardcloth and so new that there were creases in the trousers. His blue chambray shirt was stiff and smooth with filler. The coat was too big, the trousers too short, for he was a tall man. The coat shoulder peaks hung down on his arms, and even then the sleeves were too short and the front of the coat flapped loosely over his stomach. He wore a pair of new tan shoes of the kind called "army last," hob-nailed and with half-circles like horseshoes to protect the edges of the heels from wear. This man sat on the running board and took off his cap and mopped his face with it. Then he put on the cap, and by pulling started the future ruin of the visor. His feet caught his attention. He leaned down and loosened the shoelaces, and did not tie the ends again. Over his head the exhaust of the Diesel engine whispered in quick puffs of blue smoke.

The music stopped in the restaurant and a man's voice spoke from the loudspeaker, but the waitress did not turn him off, for she didn't know the music had stopped. Her exploring fingers had found a lump under her ear. She was trying to see it in a mirror behind the counter without letting the truck driver know, and so she pretended to push a bit of hair to neatness. The truck driver said, "They was a big dance in Shawnee. I heard somebody got killed or somepin. You hear anything?" "No," said the waitress, and she lovingly fingered the lump under her ear.

Outside, the seated man stood up and looked over the cowl of the truck and watched the restaurant for a moment. Then he settled back on the running board, pulled a sack of tobacco and a book of papers from his side pocket. He rolled his cigarette slowly and perfectly, studied it, smoothed it. At last he lighted it and pushed the burning match into the dust at his feet. The sun cut into the shade of the truck as noon approached.

In the restaurant the truck driver paid his bill and put his two nickels' change in a slot machine. The whirling cylinders gave him no score. "They fix 'em so you can't win nothing," he said to the waitress.

And she replied, "Guy took the jackpot not two hours ago. Three-eighty he got. How soon you gonna be back by?"

He held the screen door a little open. "Week-ten days," he said. "Got to make a run to Tulsa, an' I never get back soon as I think."

She said crossly, "Don't let the flies in. Either go out or come in."

"So long," he said, and pushed his way out. The screen door banged behind him. He stood in the sun, peeling the wrapper from a piece of gum. He was a heavy man, broad in the shoulders, thick in the stomach. His face was red and his blue eyes long and slitted from having squinted always at sharp light. He wore army trousers and high laced boots. Holding the stick of gum in front of his lips he called through the screen, "Well, don't do nothing you don't want me to hear about." The waitress was turned toward a mirror on the back wall. She grunted a reply. The truck driver gnawed down the stick of gum slowly, opening his jaws and lips wide with each bite. He shaped the gum in his mouth, rolled it under his tongue while he walked to the big red truck.

The hitch-hiker stood up and looked across through the windows. "Could ya give me a lift, mister?"

The driver looked quickly back at the restaurant for a second. "Didn' you see the *No Riders* sticker on the win'shield?"

"Sure—I seen it. But sometimes a guy'll be a good guy even if some rich bastard makes him carry a sticker."

The driver, getting slowly into the truck, considered the parts of this answer. If he refused now, not only was he not a good guy, but he was forced to carry a sticker, was not allowed to have company. If he took in the hitch-hiker he was automatically a good guy and also he was not one whom any rich bastard could kick around. He knew he was being trapped, but he couldn't see a way out. And he wanted to be a good guy. He glanced again at the restaurant. "Scrunch down on the running board till we get around the bend," he said.

The hitch-hiker flopped down out of sight and clung to the door handle. The motor roared up for a moment, the gears clicked in, and the great truck moved away, first gear, second gear, third gear, and then a high whining pick-up and fourth gear. Under the clinging man the highway blurred dizzily by. It was a mile to the first turn in the road, then the truck slowed down. The hitch-hiker stood up, eased the door open, and slipped into the seat. The driver looked over at him, slitting his eyes, and he chewed as though thoughts and impressions were being sorted and arranged by his jaws before they were finally filed away in his brain. His eyes began at the new cap, moved down the new clothes to the new shoes. The hitch-hiker squirmed his back against the seat in comfort, took off his cap, and swabbed his sweating forehead and chin with it. "Thanks, buddy," he said. "My dogs was pooped out."

"New shoes," said the driver. His voice had the same quality of secrecy and insinuation his eyes had. "You oughtn' to take no walk in new shoes—hot weather."

The hiker looked down at the dusty yellow shoes. "Didn't have no other shoes," he said. "Guy got to wear 'em if he got no others."

The driver squinted judiciously ahead and built up the speed of the truck a little. "Goin' far?"

"Uh-uh! I'd a walked her if my dogs wasn't pooped out."

The questions of the driver had the tone of a subtle examination. He seemed to spread nets, to set traps with his questions. "Lookin' for a job?" he asked.

"No, my old man got a place, forty acres. He's a cropper, but we been there a long time."

The driver looked significantly at the fields along the road where the corn was fallen sideways and the dust was piled on it. Little flints shoved through the dusty soil. The driver said, as though to himself, "A forty-acre cropper and he ain't been dusted out and he ain't been tractored out?"

" 'Course I ain't heard lately," said the hitch-hiker.

"Long time," said the driver. A bee flew into the cab and buzzed in back of the windshield. The driver put out his hand and carefully drove the bee into an air stream that blew it out of the window. "Croppers going fast now," he said. "One cat' takes and shoves ten families out. Cat's all over hell now. Tear in and shove the croppers out. How's your old man hold on?" His tongue and his jaws became busy with the neglected gum, turned it and chewed it. With each opening of his mouth his tongue could be seen flipping the gum over.

"Well, I ain't heard lately. I never was no hand to write, nor my old man neither." He added quickly, "But the both of us can, if we want."

"Been doing a job?" Again the secret investigating casualness. He looked out over the fields, at the shimmering air, and gathering his gum into his cheek, out of the way, he spat out the window.

"Sure have," said the hitch-hiker.

"Thought so. I seen your hands. Been swingin' a pick or an ax or a sledge. That shines up your hands. I notice all stuff like that. Take a pride in it."

The hitch-hiker stared at him. The truck tires sang on the road. "Like to know anything else? I'll tell you. You ain't got to guess."

"Now don't get sore. I wasn't gettin' nosy."

"I'll tell you anything. I ain't hidin' nothin'."

"Now don't get sore. I just like to notice things. Makes the time pass."

"I'll tell you anything. Name's Joad, Tom Joad. Old man is ol' Tom Joad." His eyes rested broodingly on the driver.

"Don't get sore. I didn't mean nothin'."

"I don't mean nothin' neither," said Joad. "I'm just tryin'

to get along without shovin' nobody around." He stopped and looked out at the dry fields, at the starved tree clumps hanging uneasily in the heated distance. From his side pocket he brought out his tobacco and papers. He rolled his cigarette down between his knees, where the wind could not get at it.

The driver chewed as rhythmically, as thoughtfully, as a cow. He waited to let the whole emphasis of the preceding passage disappear and be forgotten. At last, when the air seemed neutral again, he said, "A guy that never been a truck skinner don't know nothin' what it's like. Owners don't want us to pick up nobody. So we got to set here an' just skin her along 'less we want to take a chance of gettin' fired like I just done with you."

" 'Preciate it," said Joad.

"I've knew guys that done screwy things while they're drivin' trucks. I remember a guy use' to make up poetry. It passed the time." He looked over secretly to see whether Joad was interested or amazed. Joad was silent, looking into the distance ahead, along the road, along the white road that waved gently, like a ground swell. The driver went on at last, "I remember a piece of poetry this here guy wrote down. It was about him an' a couple other guys goin' all over the world drinkin' and raisin' hell and screwin' around. I wisht I could remember how that piece went. This guy had words in it that Jesus H. Christ wouldn't know what they meant. Part was like this: 'An' there we spied a nigger, with a trigger that was bigger than a elephant's proboscis or the whanger of a whale.' That proboscis is a nose-like. With a elephant it's his trunk. Guy showed me in a dictionary. Carried that dictionary all over hell with him. He'd look in it while he's pulled up gettin' his pie an' coffee." He stopped, feeling lonely in the long speech. His secret eyes turned on his passenger. Joad remained silent. Nervously the driver tried to force him into participation. "Ever know a guy that said big words like that?"

"Preacher," said Joad.

"Well, it makes you mad to hear a guy use big words. 'Course with a preacher it's all right because nobody would fool around with a preacher anyway. But this guy was funny. You didn't give a damn when he said a big word 'cause he just done it for ducks. He wasn't puttin' on no dog." The driver was reassured. He knew at least that Joad was listening. He swung the great truck viciously around a bend and the tires shrilled. "Like I was sayin'," he continued, "guy that drives a truck does screwy things. He got to. He'd go nuts just settin' here an' the road sneakin' under the wheels. Fella says once that truck skinners eats all the time— all the time in hamburger joints along the road."

"Sure seem to live there," Joad agreed.

"Sure they stop, but it ain't to eat. They ain't hardly ever hungry. They're just goddamn sick of goin'—get sick of it. Joints is the only place you can pull up, an' when you stop you got to buy somepin so you can sling the bull with the broad behind the counter. So you get a cup a coffee and a piece pie. Kind of gives a guy a little rest." He chewed his gum slowly and turned it with his tongue.

"Must be tough," said Joad with no emphasis.

The driver glanced quickly at him, looking for satire. "Well, it ain't no goddamn cinch," he said testily. "Looks easy, jus' settin' here till you put in your eight or maybe your ten or fourteen hours. But the road gets into a guy. He's got to do somepin. Some sings an' some whistles. Company won't let us have no radio. A few takes a pint along, but them kind don't stick long." He said the last smugly. "I don't never take a drink till I'm through."

"Yeah?" Joad asked.

"Yeah! A guy got to get ahead. Why, I'm thinkin' of takin' one of them correspondence school courses. Mechanical engineering. It's easy. Just study a few easy lessons at home. I'm thinkin' of it. Then I won't drive no truck. Then I'll tell other guys to drive trucks."

Joad took a pint of whisky from his side coat pocket. "Sure you won't have a snort?" His voice was teasing.

"No, by God. I won't touch it. A guy can't drink liquor all the time and study like I'm goin' to."

Joad uncorked the bottle, took two quick swallows, recorked it, and put it back in his pocket. The spicy hot smell of the whisky filled the cab. "You're all wound up," said Joad. "What's the matter—got a girl?"

"Well, sure. But I want to get ahead anyway. I been training my mind for a hell of a long time."

The whisky seemed to loosen Joad up. He rolled another cigarette and lighted it. "I ain't got a hell of a lot further to go," he said.

The driver went on quickly, "I don't need no shot," he said. "I train my mind all the time. I took a course in that two years ago." He patted the steering wheel with his right hand. "Suppose I pass a guy on the road. I look at him, an' after I'm past I try to remember ever'thing about him, kind a clothes an' shoes an' hat, an' how he walked an' maybe how tall an' what weight an' any scars. I do it pretty good. I can jus' make a whole picture in my head. Sometimes I think I ought to take a course to be a fingerprint expert. You'd be su'prised how much a guy can remember."

Joad took a quick drink from the flask. He dragged the last smoke from his raveling cigarette and then, with callused thumb and forefinger, crushed out the glowing end. He rubbed the butt to a pulp and put it out the window, letting the breeze suck it from his fingers. The big tires sang a high note on the pavement. Joad's dark quiet eyes became amused as he stared along the road. The driver waited and glanced uneasily over. At last Joad's long upper lip grinned up from his teeth and he chuckled silently, his chest jerked with the chuckles. "You sure took a hell of a long time to get to it, buddy."

The driver did not look over. "Get to what? How do you mean?"

Joad's lips stretched tight over his long teeth for a moment, and he licked his lips like a dog, two licks, one in each direction from the middle. His voice became harsh. "You know what I mean. You give me a goin'-over when I first got in. I seen you." The driver looked straight ahead, gripped the wheel so tightly that the pads of his palms bulged, and the backs of his hands paled. Joad continued, "You know where I come from." The driver was silent. "Don't you?" Joad insisted.

"Well—sure. That is—maybe. But it ain't none of my business. I mind my own yard. It ain't nothing to me." The words tumbled out now. "I don't stick my nose in nobody's business." And suddenly he was silent and waiting. And his hands were still white on the wheel. A grasshopper flipped through the window and lighted on top of the instrument panel, where it sat and began to scrape its wings with its angled jumping legs. Joad reached forward and crushed its hard skull-like head with his fingers, and he let it into the wind stream out the window. Joad chuckled again while he brushed the bits of broken insect from his fingertips. "You got me wrong, mister," he said. "I ain't keepin' quiet about it. Sure I been in McAlester. Been there four years. Sure these is the clothes they give me when I come out. I don't give a damn who knows it. An' I'm goin' to my old man's place so I don't have to lie to get a job."

The driver said, "Well—that ain't none of my business. I ain't a nosy guy."

"The hell you ain't," said Joad. "That big old nose of yours been stickin' out eight miles ahead of your face. You had that big nose goin' over me like a sheep in a vegetable patch."

The driver's face tightened. "You got me all wrong—" he began weakly.

Joad laughed at him. "You been a good guy. You give me a lift. Well, hell! I done time. So what! You want to know what I done time for, don't you?"

"That ain't none of my affair."

"Nothin' ain't none of your affair except skinnin' this here bull-bitch along, an' that's the least thing you work at. Now look. See that road up ahead?"

"Yeah."

"Well, I get off there. Sure, I know you're wettin' your pants to know what I done. I ain't a guy to let you down." The high hum of the motor dulled and the song of the tires dropped in pitch. Joad got out his pint and took another short drink. The truck drifted to a stop where a dirt road opened at right angles to the highway. Joad got out and stood beside the cab window. The vertical exhaust pipe puttered up its barely visible blue smoke. Joad leaned toward the driver. "Homicide," he said quickly. "That's a big word—

means I killed a guy. Seven years. I'm sprung in four for keepin' my nose clean."

The driver's eyes slipped over Joad's face to memorize it. "I never asked you nothin' about it," he said. "I mind my own yard."

"You can tell about it in every joint from here to Texola." He smiled. "So long, fella. You been a good guy. But look, when you been in stir a little while, you can smell a question comin' from hell to breakfast. You telegraphed yours the first time you opened your trap." He spatted the metal door with the palm of his hand. "Thanks for the lift," he said. "So long." He turned away and walked into the dirt road.

For a moment the driver stared after him, and then he called, "Luck!" Joad waved his hand without looking around. Then the motor roared up and the gears clicked and the great red truck rolled heavily away.

Chapter Three

THE concrete highway was edged with a mat of tangled, broken, dry grass, and the grass heads were heavy with oat beards to catch on a dog's coat, and foxtails to tangle in a horse's fetlocks, and clover burrs to fasten in sheep's wool; sleeping life waiting to be spread and dispersed, every seed armed with an appliance of dispersal, twisting darts and parachutes for the wind, little spears and balls of tiny thorns, and all waiting for animals and for the wind, for a man's trouser cuff or the hem of a woman's skirt, all passive but armed with appliances of activity, still, but each possessed of the anlage of movement.

The sun lay on the grass and warmed it, and in the shade under the grass the insects moved, ants and ant lions to set traps for them, grasshoppers to jump into the air and flick their yellow wings for a second, sow bugs like little armadillos, plodding restlessly on many tender feet. And over the grass at the roadside a land turtle crawled, turning aside for nothing, dragging his high-domed shell over the grass. His hard legs and yellow-nailed feet threshed slowly through the grass, not really walking, but boosting and dragging his shell along. The barley beards slid off his shell, and the clover burrs fell on him and rolled to the ground. His horny beak was partly open, and his fierce, humorous eyes, under brows like fingernails, stared straight ahead. He came over the grass leaving a beaten trail behind him, and the hill, which was the highway embankment, reared up ahead of him. For a moment he stopped, his head held high. He blinked and looked up and down. At last he started to climb the embankment. Front clawed feet reached forward but did not touch. The hind feet kicked his shell along, and it scraped on the grass, and on the gravel. As the embankment grew steeper and steeper, the more frantic were the efforts of the land turtle. Pushing hind legs strained and slipped, boosting the shell along, and the horny head protruded as far as the neck could stretch. Little by little the shell slid up the embankment until at last a parapet cut straight across its line of march, the shoulder of the road, a concrete wall four inches high. As though they worked independently the hind legs pushed the shell against the wall. The head upraised and peered over the wall to the broad smooth plain of cement. Now the hands, braced on top of the wall, strained and lifted, and the shell came slowly up and rested its front end on the wall. For a moment the turtle rested. A red ant ran into the shell, into the soft skin inside the shell, and suddenly head and legs snapped in, and the armored tail clamped in sideways. The red ant was crushed between body and legs. And one head of wild oats was clamped into the shell by a front leg. For a long moment the turtle lay still, and then the neck crept out and the old humorous frowning eyes looked about and the legs and tail came out. The back legs went to work, straining like elephant legs, and the shell tipped to an angle so that the front legs could not reach the level cement plain. But higher and higher the hind legs boosted it, until at last the center of balance was reached, the front tipped down, the front legs scratched at the pavement, and it was up. But the head of wild oats was held by its stem around the front legs.

Now the going was easy, and all the legs worked, and the

shell boosted along, waggling from side to side. A sedan driven by a forty-year old woman approached. She saw the turtle and swung to the right, off the highway, the wheels screamed and a cloud of dust boiled up. Two wheels lifted for a moment and then settled. The car skidded back onto the road, and went on, but more slowly. The turtle had jerked into its shell, but now it hurried on, for the highway was burning hot.

And now a light truck approached, and as it came near, the driver saw the turtle and swerved to hit it. His front wheel struck the edge of the shell, flipped the turtle like a tiddly-wink, spun it like a coin, and rolled it off the highway. The truck went back to its course along the right side. Lying on its back, the turtle was tight in its shell for a long time. But at last its legs waved in the air, reaching for something to pull it over. Its front foot caught a piece of quartz and little by little the shell pulled over and flopped upright. The wild oat head fell out and three of the spearhead seeds stuck in the ground. And as the turtle crawled on down the embankment, its shell dragged dirt over the seeds. The turtle entered a dust road and jerked itself along, drawing a wavy shallow trench in the dust with its shell. The old humorous eyes looked ahead, and the horny beak opened a little. His yellow toe nails slipped a fraction in the dust.

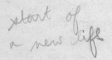
start of
a new life

Chapter Four

WHEN Joad heard the truck get under way, gear climbing up to gear and the ground throbbing under the rubber beating of the tires, he stopped and turned about and watched it until it disappeared. When it was out of sight he still watched the distance and the blue air-shimmer. Thoughtfully he took the pint from his pocket, unscrewed the metal cap, and sipped the whisky delicately, running his tongue inside the bottle neck, and then around his lips, to gather in any flavor that might have escaped him. He said experimentally, "There we spied a nigger—" and that was all he could remember. At last he turned about and faced the dusty side road that cut off at right angles through the fields. The sun was hot, and no wind stirred the sifted dust. The road was cut with furrows where dust had slid and settled back into the wheel tracks. Joad took a few steps, and the flourlike dust spurted up in front of his new yellow shoes, and the yellowness was disappearing under gray dust.

He leaned down and untied the laces, slipped off first one shoe and then the other. And he worked his damp feet comfortably in the hot dry dust until little spurts of it came up between his toes, and until the skin on his feet tightened with dryness. He took off his coat and wrapped his shoes in it and slipped the bundle under his arm. And at last he moved up the road, shooting the dust ahead of him, making a cloud that hung low to the ground behind him.

The right of way was fenced, two strands of barbed wire on willow poles. The poles were crooked and badly trimmed. Whenever a crotch came to the proper height the wire lay in it, and where there was no crotch the barbed wire was lashed to the post with rusty baling wire. Beyond the fence, the corn lay beaten down by wind and heat and drought, and the cups where leaf joined stalk were filled with dust.

Joad plodded along, dragging his cloud of dust behind him. A little bit ahead he saw the high-domed shell of a land turtle, crawling slowly along through the dust, its legs working stiffly and jerkily. Joad stopped to watch it, and his shadow fell on the turtle. Instantly head and legs were withdrawn and the short thick tail clamped sideways into the shell. Joad picked it up and turned it over. The back was brown-gray, like the dust, but the underside of the shell was creamy yellow, clean and smooth. Joad shifted his bundle high under his arm and stroked the smooth undershell with his finger, and he pressed it. It was softer than the back. The hard old head came out and tried to look at the pressing finger, and the legs waved wildly. The turtle wetted on Joad's hand and struggled uselessly in the air. Joad turned it back upright and rolled it up in his coat with his shoes. He could feel it pressing and struggling and fussing under his arm. He moved ahead more quickly now, dragging his heels a little in the fine dust.

Ahead of him, beside the road, a scrawny, dusty willow tree cast a speckled shade. Joad could see it ahead of him, its poor branches curving over the way, its load of leaves tattered and scraggly as a molting chicken. Joad was sweating now. His blue shirt darkened down his back and under his arms. He pulled at the visor of his cap and creased it in the middle, breaking its cardboard lining so completely that it

could never look new again. And his steps took on new speed
and intent toward the shade of the distant willow tree.
At the willow he knew there would be shade, at least one
hard bar of absolute shade thrown by the trunk, since the sun
had passed its zenith. The sun whipped the back of his neck
now and made a little humming in his head. He could not see
the base of the tree, for it grew out of a little swale that held
water longer than the level places. Joad speeded his pace
against the sun, and he started down the declivity. He
slowed cautiously, for the bar of absolute shade was taken.
A man sat on the ground, leaning against the trunk of the
tree. His legs were crossed and one bare foot extended nearly
as high as his head. He did not hear Joad approaching, for he
was whistling solemnly the tune of "Yes, Sir, That's My
Baby." His extended foot swung slowly up and down in the
tempo. It was not dance tempo. He stopped whistling and
sang in an easy thin tenor:

> "Yes, sir, that's my Saviour,
> Je—sus is my Saviour,
> Je—sus is my Saviour now.
> On the level
> 'S not the devil,
> Jesus is my Saviour now."

Joad had moved into the imperfect shade of the molting
leaves before the man heard him coming, stopped his song,
and turned his head. It was a long head, bony, tight of skin,
and set on a neck as stringy and muscular as a celery stalk.
His eyeballs were heavy and protruding; the lids stretched
to cover them, and the lids were raw and red. His cheeks
were brown and shiny and hairless and his mouth full—
humorous or sensual. The nose, beaked and hard, stretched

the skin so tightly that the bridge showed white. There was no perspiration on the face, not even on the tall pale forehead. It was an abnormally high forehead, lined with delicate blue veins at the temples. Fully half of the face was above the eyes. His stiff gray hair was mussed back from his brow as though he had combed it back with his fingers. For clothes he wore overalls and a blue shirt. A denim coat with brass buttons and a spotted brown hat creased like a pork pie lay on the ground beside him. Canvas sneakers, gray with dust, lay near by where they had fallen when they were kicked off.

The man looked long at Joad. The light seemed to go far into his brown eyes, and it picked out little golden specks deep in the irises. The strained bundle of neck muscles stood out.

Joad stood still in the speckled shade. He took off his cap and mopped his wet face with it and dropped it and his rolled coat on the ground.

The man in the absolute shade uncrossed his legs and dug with his toes at the earth.

Joad said, "Hi. It's hotter'n hell on the road."

The seated man stared questioningly at him. "Now ain't you young Tom Joad—ol' Tom's boy?"

"Yeah," said Joad. "All the way. Goin' home now."

"You wouldn' remember me, I guess," the man said. He smiled and his full lips revealed great horse teeth. "Oh, no, you wouldn't remember. You was always too busy pullin' little girls' pigtails when I give you the Holy Sperit. You was all wropped up in yankin' that pigtail out by the roots. You maybe don't recollect, but I do. The two of you come to Jesus at once 'cause of that pigtail yankin'. Baptized both of you in the irrigation ditch at once. Fightin' an' yellin' like a couple a cats."

Joad looked at him with drooped eyes, and then he laughed. "Why, you're the preacher. You're the preacher. I jus' passed a recollection about you to a guy not an hour ago."

"I was a preacher," said the man seriously. "Reverend Jim Casy—was a Burning Busher. Used to howl out the name of Jesus to glory. And used to get an irrigation ditch so squirmin' full of repented sinners half of 'em like to drownded. But not no more," he sighed. "Just Jim Casy now. Ain't got the call no more. Got a lot of sinful idears—but they seem kinda sensible."

Joad said, "You're bound to get idears if you go thinkin' about stuff. Sure I remember you. You use ta give a good meetin'. I recollect one time you give a whole sermon walkin' around on your hands, yellin' your head off. Ma favored you more than anybody. An' Granma says you was just lousy with the spirit." Joad dug at his rolled coat and found the pocket and brought out his pint. The turtle moved a leg but he wrapped it up tightly. He unscrewed the cap and held out the bottle. "Have a little snort?"

Casy took the bottle and regarded it broodingly. "I ain't preachin' no more much. The sperit ain't in the people much no more; and worse'n that, the sperit ain't in me no more. 'Course now an' again the sperit gets movin' an' I rip out a meetin', or when folks sets out food I give 'em a grace, but my heart ain't in it. I on'y do it 'cause they expect it."

Joad mopped his face with his cap again. "You ain't too damn holy to take a drink, are you?" he asked.

Casy seemed to see the bottle for the first time. He tilted

it and took three big swallows. "Nice drinkin' liquor," he said.

"Ought to be," said Joad. "That's fact'ry liquor. Cost a buck."

Casy took another swallow before he passed the bottle back. "Yes, sir!" he said. "Yes, sir!"

Joad took the bottle from him, and in politeness did not wipe the neck with his sleeve before he drank. He squatted on his hams and set the bottle upright against his coat roll. His fingers found a twig with which to draw his thoughts on the ground. He swept the leaves from a square and smoothed the dust. And he drew angles and made little circles. "I ain't seen you in a long time," he said.

"Nobody seen me," said the preacher. "I went off alone, an' I sat and figured. The sperit's strong in me, on'y it ain't the same. I ain't so sure of a lot of things." He sat up straighter against the tree. His bony hand dug its way like a squirrel into his overall pocket, brought out a black, bitten plug of tobacco. Carefully he brushed off bits of straw and gray pocket fuzz before he bit off a corner and settled the quid into his cheek. Joad waved his stick in negation when the plug was held out to him. The turtle dug at the rolled coat. Casy looked over at the stirring garment. "What you got there—a chicken? You'll smother it."

Joad rolled the coat up more tightly. "An old turtle," he said. "Picked him up on the road. An old bulldozer. Thought I'd take 'im to my little brother. Kids like turtles."

The preacher nodded his head slowly. "Every kid got a turtle some time or other. Nobody can't keep a turtle though. They work at it and work at it, and at last one day they get out and away they go—off somewheres. It's like me. I wouldn' take the good ol' gospel that was just layin' there to my hand. I got to be pickin' at it an' workin' at it until I got it all tore down. Here I got the sperit sometimes an' nothin' to preach about. I got the call to lead the people, an' no place to lead 'em."

"Lead 'em around and around," said Joad. "Sling 'em in the irrigation ditch. Tell 'em they'll burn in hell if they don't think like you. What the hell you want to lead 'em someplace for? Jus' lead 'em." The straight trunk shade had stretched out along the ground. Joad moved gratefully into it and squatted on his hams and made a new smooth place on which to draw his thoughts with a stick. A thick-furred yellow shepherd dog came trotting down the road, head low, tongue lolling and dripping. Its tail hung limply curled, and it panted loudly. Joad whistled at it, but it only dropped its head an inch and trotted fast toward some definite destination. "Goin' someplace," Joad explained, a little piqued. "Goin' for home maybe."

The preacher could not be thrown from his subject. "Goin' someplace," he repeated. "That's right, he's goin' someplace. Me—I don't know where I'm goin'. Tell you what—I use ta get the people jumpin' an' talkin' in tongues, an' glory-shoutin' till they just fell down an' passed out. An' some I'd baptize to bring 'em to. An' then—you know what I'd do? I'd take one of them girls out in the grass, an' I'd lay with her. Done it ever' time. Then I'd feel bad, an' I'd pray an' pray, but it didn't do no good. Come the nex' time, them an' me was full of the sperit, I'd do it again. I figgered there just wasn't no hope for me, an' I was a damned ol' hypocrite. But I didn't mean to be."

Joad smiled and his long teeth parted and he licked his lips. "There ain't nothing like a good hot meetin' for pushin' 'em over," he said. "I done that myself."

Casy leaned forward excitedly. "You see," he cried, "I seen it was that way, an' I started thinkin'." He waved his bony big-knuckled hand up and down in a patting gesture. "I got to thinkin' like this—'Here's me preachin' grace. An' here's them people gettin' grace so hard they're jumpin' an' shoutin'. Now they say layin' up with a girl comes from the devil. But the more grace a girl got in her, the quicker she wants to go out in the grass.' An' I got to thinkin' how in hell, s'cuse me, how can the devil get in when a girl is so full of the Holy Sperit that it's spoutin' out of her nose an' ears. You'd think that'd be one time when the devil didn't stand a snowball's chance in hell. But there it was." His eyes were shining with excitement. He worked his cheeks for a moment and then spat into the dust, and the gob of spit rolled over and over, picking up dust until it looked like a round dry little pellet. The preacher spread out his hand and looked at his palm as though he were reading a book. "An' there's me," he went on softly. "There's me with all them people's souls in my han'—responsible an' feelin' my responsibility—an' ever' time, I lay with one of them girls." He looked over at Joad and his face looked helpless. His expression asked for help.

Joad carefully drew the torso of a woman in the dirt, breasts, hips, pelvis. "I wasn't never a preacher," he said. "I never let nothin' get by when I could catch it. An' I never had no idears about it except I was goddamn glad when I got one."

"But you wasn't a preacher," Casy insisted. "A girl was just a girl to you. They wasn't nothin' to you. But to me they was holy vessels. I was savin' their souls. An' here with all that responsibility on me I'd just get 'em frothin' with the Holy Sperit, an' then I'd take 'em out in the grass."

"Maybe I should of been a preacher," said Joad. He brought out his tobacco and papers and rolled a cigarette. He lighted it and squinted through the smoke at the preacher. "I been a long time without a girl," he said. "It's gonna take some catchin' up."

Casy continued, "It worried me till I couldn't get no sleep. Here I'd go to preachin' and I'd say, 'By God, this time I ain't gonna do it.' And right while I said it, I knowed I was."

"You should a got a wife," said Joad. "Preacher an' his wife stayed at our place one time. Jehovites they was. Slep' upstairs. Held meetin's in our barnyard. Us kids would listen. That preacher's missus took a godawful poundin' after ever' night meetin'."

"I'm glad you tol' me," said Casy. "I use to think it was jus' me. Finally it give me such pain I quit an' went off by myself an' give her a damn good thinkin' about." He doubled up his legs and scratched between his dry dusty toes. "I says to myself, 'What's gnawin' you? Is it the screwin'?' An' I says, 'No, it's the sin.' An' I says, 'Why is it that when a fella ought to be just about mule-ass proof against sin, an' all full up of Jesus, why is it that's the time a fella gets fingerin' his pants buttons?'" He laid two fingers down in his palm in rhythm, as though he gently placed each word there side by side. "I says, 'Maybe it ain't a sin. Maybe it's just the way folks is. Maybe we been whippin' the hell out of ourselves for nothin'.' An' I thought how some sisters took to beatin' theirselves with a three-foot shag of bobwire. An' I thought how maybe they liked to hurt themselves, an' maybe I liked to hurt myself. Well, I was layin' under a tree when I figured that out, and I went to sleep. And it come night, an' it was dark when I come to. They was a coyote squawkin' near by. Before I knowed it, I was sayin' out loud, 'The hell with it!

There ain't no sin and there ain't no virtue. There's just stuff people do. It's all part of the same thing. And some of the things folks do is nice, and some ain't nice, but that's as far as any man got a right to say.'" He paused and looked up from the palm of his hand, where he had laid down the words.

Joad was grinning at him, but Joad's eyes were sharp and interested, too. "You give her a goin'-over," he said. "You figured her out."

Casy spoke again, and his voice rang with pain and confusion. "I says, 'What's this call, this sperit?' An' I says, 'It's love. I love people so much I'm fit to bust, sometimes.' An' I says, 'Don't you love Jesus?' Well, I thought an' thought, an' finally I says, 'No, I don't know nobody name' Jesus. I know a bunch of stories, but I only love people. An' sometimes I love 'em fit to bust, an' I want to make 'em happy, so I been preachin' somepin I thought would make 'em happy.' An' then—I been talkin' a hell of a lot. Maybe you wonder about me using bad words. Well, they ain't bad to me no more. They're jus' words folks use, an' they don't mean nothing bad with 'em. Anyways, I'll tell you one more thing I thought out; an' from a preacher it's the most unreligious thing, and I can't be a preacher no more because I thought it an' I believe it."

"What's that?" Joad asked.

Casy looked shyly at him. "If it hits you wrong, don't take no offense at it, will you?"

"I don't take no offense 'cept a bust in the nose," said Joad. "What did you figger?"

"I figgered about the Holy Sperit and the Jesus road. I figgered, 'Why do we got to hang it on God or Jesus? Maybe,' I figgered, 'maybe it's all men an' all women we love;

maybe that's the Holy Sperit—the human sperit—the whole shebang. Maybe all men got one big soul ever'body's a part of.' Now I sat there thinkin' it, an' all of a suddent—I knew it. I knew it so deep down that it was true, and I still know it."

Joad's eyes dropped to the ground, as though he could not meet the naked honesty in the preacher's eyes. "You can't hold no church with idears like that," he said. "People would drive you out of the country with idears like that. Jumpin' an' yellin'. That's what folks like. Makes 'em feel swell. When Granma got to talkin' in tongues, you couldn't tie her down. She could knock over a full-growed deacon with her fist."

Casy regarded him broodingly. "Somepin I like to ast you," he said. "Somepin that been eatin' on me."

"Go ahead. I'll talk, sometimes."

"Well"—the preacher said slowly—"here's you that I baptized right when I was in the glory roof-tree. Got little hunks of Jesus jumpin' outa my mouth that day. You won't remember 'cause you was busy pullin' that pigtail."

"I remember," said Joad. "That was Susy Little. She bust my finger a year later."

"Well—did you take any good outa that baptizin'? Was your ways better?"

Joad thought about it. "No-o-o, can't say as I felt anything."

"Well—did you take any bad from it? Think hard."

Joad picked up the bottle and took a swig. "They wasn't nothing in it, good or bad. I just had fun." He handed the flask to the preacher.

He sighed and drank and looked at the low level of the whisky and took another tiny drink. "That's good," he said.

"I got to worryin' about whether in messin' around maybe I done somebody a hurt."

Joad looked over toward his coat and saw the turtle, free of the cloth and hurrying away in the direction he had been following when Joad found him. Joad watched him for a moment and then got slowly to his feet and retrieved him and wrapped him in the coat again. "I ain't got no present for the kids," he said. "Nothin' but this ol' turtle."

"It's a funny thing," the preacher said. "I was thinkin' about ol' Tom Joad when you come along. Thinkin' I'd call in on him. I used to think he was a godless man. How is Tom?"

"I don' know how he is. I ain't been home in four years."

"Didn't he write to you?"

Joad was embarrassed. "Well, Pa wasn't no hand to write for pretty, or to write for writin'. He'd sign up his name as nice as anybody, an' lick his pencil. But Pa never did write no letters. He always says what he couldn' tell a fella with his mouth wasn't worth leanin' on no pencil about."

"Been out travelin' around?" Casy asked.

Joad regarded him suspiciously. "Didn' you hear about me? I was in all the papers."

"No—I never. What?" He jerked one leg over the other and settled lower against the tree. The afternoon was advancing rapidly, and a richer tone was growing on the sun.

Joad said pleasantly, "Might's well tell you now an' get it over with. But if you was still preachin' I wouldn't tell, fear you get prayin' over me." He drained the last of the pint and flung it from him, and the flat brown bottle skidded lightly over the dust. "I been in McAlester them four years."

Casy swung around to him, and his brows lowered so that his tall forehead seemed even taller. "Ain't wantin' to talk about it, huh? I won't ask you no questions, if you done something bad——"

"I'd do what I done—again," said Joad. "I killed a guy in a fight. We was drunk at a dance. He got a knife in me, an' I killed him with a shovel that was layin' there. Knocked his head plumb to squash."

Casy's eyebrows resumed their normal level. "You ain't ashamed of nothin' then?"

"No," said Joad, "I ain't. I got seven years, account of he had a knife in me. Got out in four—parole."

"Then you ain't heard nothin' about your folks for four years?"

"Oh, I heard. Ma sent me a card two years ago, an' las' Christmus Granma 'sent a card. Jesus, the guys in the cell block laughed! Had a tree an' shiny stuff looks like snow. It says in po'try:

>" 'Merry Christmus, purty child,
> Jesus meek an' Jesus mild,
> Underneath the Christmus tree
> There's a gif' for you from me.'

I guess Granma never read it. Prob'ly got it from a drummer an' picked out the one with the mos' shiny stuff on it. The guys in my cell block goddamn near died laughin'. Jesus Meek they called me after that. Granma never meant it funny; she jus' figgered it was so purty she wouldn' bother to read it. She lost her glasses the year I went up. Maybe she never did find 'em."

"How they treat you in McAlester?" Casy asked.

"Oh, awright. You eat regular, an' get clean clothes, and there's places to take a bath. It's pretty nice some ways. Makes it hard not havin' no women." Suddenly he laughed.

"They was a guy paroled," he said. " 'Bout a month he's
back for breakin' parole. A guy ast him why he bust his
parole. 'Well, hell,' he says. 'They got no conveniences at
my old man's place. Got no 'lectric lights, got no shower
baths. There ain't no books, an' the food's lousy.' Says he
come back where they got a few conveniences an' he eats
regular. He says it makes him feel lonesome out there in the
open havin' to think what to do next. So he stole a car an'
come back." Joad got out his tobacco and blew a brown
paper free of the pack and rolled a cigarette. "The guy's
right, too," he said. "Las' night, thinkin' where I'm gonna
sleep, I got scared. An' I got thinkin' about my bunk, an' I
wonder what the stir-bug I got for a cell mate is doin'. Me
an' some guys had a strang band goin'. Good one. Guy said
we ought to go on the radio. An' this mornin' I didn' know
what time to get up. Jus' laid there waitin' for the bell to
go off."

Casy chuckled. "Fella can get so he misses the noise of a
saw mill."

The yellowing, dusty, afternoon light put a golden color
on the land. The cornstalks looked golden. A flight of swallows swooped overhead toward some waterhole. The turtle
in Joad's coat began a new campaign of escape. Joad creased
the visor of his cap. It was getting the long protruding curve
of a crow's beak now. "Guess I'll mosey along," he said. "I
hate to hit the sun, but it ain't so bad now."

Casy pulled himself together. "I ain't seen ol' Tom in a
bug's age," he said. "I was gonna look in on him anyways. I
brang Jesus to your folks for a long time, an' I never took
up a collection nor nothin' but a bite to eat."

"Come along," said Joad. "Pa'll be glad to see you. He
always said you got too long a pecker for a preacher." He

picked up his coat roll and tightened it snugly about his shoes and turtle.

Casy gathered in his canvas sneakers and shoved his bare feet into them. "I ain't got your confidence," he said. "I'm always scared there's wire or glass under the dust. I don't know nothin' I hate so much as a cut toe."

They hesitated on the edge of the shade and then they plunged into the yellow sunlight like two swimmers hastening to get to shore. After a few fast steps they slowed to a gentle, thoughtful pace. The cornstalks threw gray shadows sideways now, and the raw smell of hot dust was in the air. The corn field ended and dark green cotton took its place, dark green leaves through a film of dust, and the bolls forming. It was spotty cotton, thick in the low places where water had stood, and bare on the high places. The plants strove against the sun. And distance, toward the horizon, was tan to invisibility. The dust road stretched out ahead of them, waving up and down. The willows of a stream lined across the west, and to the northwest a fallow section was going back to sparse brush. But the smell of burned dust was in the air, and the air was dry, so that mucus in the nose dried to a crust, and the eyes watered to keep the eyeballs from drying out.

Casy said, "See how good the corn come along until the dust got up. Been a dinger of a crop."

"Ever' year," said Joad. "Ever' year I can remember, we had a good crop comin', an' it never come. Grampa says she was good the first five plowin's, while the wild grass was still in her." The road dropped down a little hill and climbed up another rolling hill.

Casy said, "Ol' Tom's house can't be more'n a mile from here. Ain't she over that third rise?"

"Sure," said Joad. " 'Less somebody stole it, like Pa stole it."

"Your pa stole it?"

"Sure, got it a mile an' a half east of here an' drug it. Was a family livin' there, an' they moved away. Grampa an' Pa an' my brother Noah like to took the whole house, but she wouldn' come. They only got part of her. That's why she looks so funny on one end. They cut her in two an' drug her over with twelve head of horses and two mules. They was goin' back for the other half an' stick her together again, but before they got there Wink Manley come with his boys and stole the other half. Pa an' Grampa was pretty sore, but a little later them an' Wink got drunk together an' laughed their heads off about it. Wink, he says his house is at stud, an' if we'll bring our'n over an' breed 'em we'll maybe get a litter of crap houses. Wink was a great ol' fella when he was drunk. After that him an' Pa an' Grampa was friends. Got drunk together ever' chance they got."

"Tom's a great one," Casy agreed. They plodded dustily on down to the bottom of the draw, and then slowed their steps for the rise. Casy wiped his forehead with his sleeve and put on his flat-topped hat again. "Yes," he repeated, "Tom was a great one. For a godless man he was a great one. I seen him in meetin' sometimes when the sperit got into him just a little, an' I seen him take ten-twelve foot jumps. I tell you when ol' Tom got a dose of the Holy Sperit you got to move fast to keep from gettin' run down an' tromped. Jumpy as a stud horse in a box stall."

They topped the next rise and the road dropped into an old water-cut, ugly and raw, a ragged course, and freshet scars cutting into it from both sides. A few stones were in the crossing. Joad minced across in his bare feet. "You talk about Pa," he said. "Maybe you never seen Uncle John the time they baptized him over to Polk's place. Why, he got to plungin' an' jumpin'. Jumped over a feeny bush as big as a piana. Over he'd jump, an' back he'd jump, howlin' like a dog-wolf in moon time. Well, Pa seen him, an' Pa, he figgers he's the bes' Jesus-jumper in these parts. So Pa picks out a feeny bush 'bout twicet as big as Uncle John's feeny bush, and Pa lets out a squawk like a sow litterin' broken bottles, an' he takes a run at that feeny bush an' clears her an' bust his right leg. That took the sperit out of Pa. Preacher wants to pray it set, but Pa says, no, by God, he'd got his heart full of havin' a doctor. Well, they wasn't a doctor, but they was a travelin' dentist, an' he set her. Preacher give her a prayin' over anyways."

They plodded up the little rise on the other side of the water-cut. Now that the sun was on the wane some of its impact was gone, and while the air was hot, the hammering rays were weaker. The strung wire on crooked poles still edged the road. On the right-hand side a line of wire fence strung out across the cotton field, and the dusty green cotton was the same on both sides, dusty and dry and dark green.

Joad pointed to the boundary fence. "That there's our line. We didn't really need no fence there, but we had the wire, an' Pa kinda liked her there. Said it give him a feelin' that forty was forty. Wouldn't of had the fence if Uncle John didn' come drivin' in one night with six spools of wire in his wagon. He give 'em to Pa for a shoat. We never did know where he got that wire." They slowed for the rise, moving their feet in the deep soft dust, feeling the earth with their feet. Joad's eyes were inward on his memory. He seemed to be laughing inside himself. "Uncle John was a crazy bastard," he said. "Like what he done with that shoat." He chuckled and walked on.

Jim Casy waited impatiently. The story did not continue. Casy gave it a good long time to come out. "Well, what'd he do with that shoat?" he demanded at last, with some irritation.

"Huh? Oh! Well, he killed that shoat right there, an' he got Ma to light up the stove. He cut out pork chops an' put 'em in the pan, an' he put ribs an' a leg in the oven. He et chops till the ribs was done, an' he et ribs till the leg was done. An' then he tore into that leg. Cut off big hunks of her an' shoved 'em in his mouth. Us kids hung around slaverin', an' he give us some, but he wouldn' give Pa none. By an' by he et so much he throwed up an' went to sleep. While he's asleep us kids an' Pa finished off the leg. Well, when Uncle John woke up in the mornin' he slaps another leg in the oven. Pa says, 'John, you gonna eat that whole damn pig?' An' ne says, 'I aim to, Tom, but I'm scairt some of her'll spoil 'fore I get her et, hungry as I am for pork. Maybe you better get a plate an' gimme back a couple rolls of wire.' Well, sir, Pa wasn't no fool. He jus' let Uncle John go on an' eat himself sick of pig, an' when he drove off he hadn't et much more'n half. Pa says, 'Whyn't you salt her down?' But not Uncle John; when he wants pig he wants a whole pig, an' when he's through, he don't want no pig hangin' around. So off he goes, and Pa salts down what's left."

Casy said, "While I was still in the preachin' sperit I'd a made a lesson of that an' spoke it to you, but I don't do that no more. What you s'pose he done a thing like that for?"

"I dunno," said Joad. "He jus' got hungry for pork.

Makes me hungry jus' to think of it. I had jus' four slices of roastin' pork in four years—one slice ever' Christmus."

Casy suggested elaborately, "Maybe Tom'll kill the fatted calf like for the prodigal in Scripture."

Joad laughed scornfully. "You don't know Pa. If he kills a chicken most of the squawkin' will come from Pa, not the chicken. He don't never learn. He's always savin' a pig for Christmas and then it dies in September of bloat or somepin so you can't eat it. When Uncle John wanted pork he et pork. He had her."

They moved over the curving top of the hill and saw the Joad place below them. And Joad stopped. "It ain't the same," he said. "Looka that house. Somepin's happened. They ain't nobody there." The two stood and stared at the little cluster of buildings.

Chapter Five

THE owners of the land came onto the land, or more often a spokesman for the owners came. They came in closed cars, and they felt the dry earth with their fingers, and sometimes they drove big earth augers into the ground for soil tests. The tenants, from their sun-beaten dooryards, watched uneasily when the closed cars drove along the fields. And at last the owner men drove into the dooryards and sat in their cars to talk out of the windows. The tenant men stood beside the cars for a while, and then squatted on their hams and found sticks with which to mark the dust.

In the open doors the women stood looking out, and behind them the children—corn-headed children, with wide eyes, one bare foot on top of the other bare foot, and the toes working. The women and the children watched their men talking to the owner men. They were silent.

Some of the owner men were kind because they hated what they had to do, and some of them were angry because they hated to be cruel, and some of them were cold because they had long ago found that one could not be an owner unless one were cold. And all of them were caught in something larger than themselves. Some of them hated the mathematics that drove them, and some were afraid, and some worshiped the mathematics because it provided a refuge from thought and from feeling. If a bank or a finance company owned the land, the owner man said, The Bank—or the Company—needs—wants—insists—must have—as though the Bank or the Company were a monster, with thought and feeling, which had ensnared them. These last would take no responsibility for the banks or the companies because they were men and slaves, while the banks were machines and masters all at the same time. Some of the owner men were a little proud to be slaves to such cold and powerful masters. The owner men sat in the cars and explained. You know the land is poor. You've scrabbled at it long enough, God knows.

The squatting tenant men nodded and wondered and drew figures in the dust, and yes, they knew, God knows. If the dust only wouldn't fly. If the top would only stay on the soil, it might not be so bad.

The owner men went on leading to their point: You know the land's getting poorer. You know what cotton does to the land; robs it, sucks all the blood out of it.

The squatters nodded—they knew, God knew. If they could only rotate the crops they might pump blood back into the land.

Well, it's too late. And the owner men explained the workings and the thinkings of the monster that was stronger than they were. A man can hold land if he can just eat and pay taxes; he can do that.

Yes, he can do that until his crops fail one day and he has to borrow money from the bank.

But—you see, a bank or a company can't do that, because those creatures don't breathe air, don't eat side-meat. They breathe profits; they eat the interest on money. If they don't get it, they die the way you die without air, without side-meat. It is a sad thing, but it is so. It is just so.

The squatting men raised their eyes to understand. Can't

we just hang on? Maybe the next year will be a good year. God knows how much cotton next year. And with all the wars—God knows what price cotton will bring. Don't they make explosives out of cotton? And uniforms? Get enough wars and cotton'll hit the ceiling. Next year, maybe. They looked up questioningly.

We can't depend on it. The bank—the monster has to have profits all the time. It can't wait. It'll die. No, taxes go on. When the monster stops growing, it dies. It can't stay one size.

Soft fingers began to tap the sill of the car window, and hard fingers tightened on the restless drawing sticks. In the doorways of the sun-beaten tenant houses, women sighed and then shifted feet so that the one that had been down was now on top, and the toes working. Dogs came sniffing near the owner cars and wetted on all four tires one after another. And chickens lay in the sunny dust and fluffed their feathers to get the cleansing dust down to the skin. In the little sties the pigs grunted inquiringly over the muddy remnants of the slops.

The squatting men looked down again. What do you want us to do? We can't take less share of the crop—we're half starved now. The kids are hungry all the time. We got no clothes, torn an' ragged. If all the neighbors weren't the same, we'd be ashamed to go to meeting.

And at last the owner men came to the point. The tenant system won't work any more. One man on a tractor can take the place of twelve or fourteen families. Pay him a wage and take all the crop. We have to do it. We don't like to do it. But the monster's sick. Something's happened to the monster.

But you'll kill the land with cotton.

We know. We've got to take cotton quick before the land dies. Then we'll sell the land. Lots of families in the East would like to own a piece of land.

The tenant men looked up alarmed. But what'll happen to us? How'll we eat?

You'll have to get off the land. The plows'll go through the dooryard.

And now the squatting men stood up angrily. Grampa took up the land, and he had to kill the Indians and drive them away. And Pa was born here, and he killed weeds and snakes. Then a bad year came and he had to borrow a little money. An' we was born here. There in the door—our children born here. And Pa had to borrow money. The bank owned the land then, but we stayed and we got a little bit of what we raised.

We know that—all that. It's not us, it's the bank. A bank isn't like a man. Or an owner with fifty thousand acres, he isn't like a man either. That's the monster.

Sure, cried the tenant men, but it's our land. We measured it and broke it up. We were born on it, and we got killed on it, died on it. Even if it's no good, it's still ours. That's what makes it ours—being born on it, working it, dying on it. That makes ownership, not a paper with numbers on it.

We're sorry. It's not us. It's the monster. The bank isn't like a man.

Yes, but the bank is only made of men.

No, you're wrong there—quite wrong there. The bank is something else than men. It happens that every man in a bank hates what the bank does, and yet the bank does it. The bank is something more than men, I tell you. It's the monster. Men made it, but they can't control it.

The tenants cried, Grampa killed Indians, Pa killed snakes

for the land. Maybe we can kill banks—they're worse than Indians and snakes. Maybe we got to fight to keep our land, like Pa and Grampa did.

And now the owner men grew angry. You'll have to go.

But it's ours, the tenant men cried. We——

No. The bank, the monster owns it. You'll have to go.

We'll get our guns, like Grampa when the Indians came. What then?

Well—first the sheriff, and then the troops. You'll be stealing if you try to stay, you'll be murderers if you kill to stay. The monster isn't men, but it can make men do what it wants.

But if we go, where'll we go? How'll we go? We got no money.

We're sorry, said the owner men. The bank, the fifty-thousand-acre owner can't be responsible. You're on land that isn't yours. Once over the line maybe you can pick cotton in the fall. Maybe you can go on relief. Why don't you go on west to California? There's work there, and it never gets cold. Why, you can reach out anywhere and pick an orange. Why, there's always some kind of crop to work in. Why don't you go there? And the owner men started their cars and rolled away.

The tenant men squatted down on their hams again to mark the dust with a stick, to figure, to wonder. Their sun-burned faces were dark, and their sun-whipped eyes were light. The women moved cautiously out of the doorways toward their men, and the children crept behind the women, cautiously, ready to run. The bigger boys squatted beside their fathers, because that made them men. After a time the women asked, What did he want?

And the men looked up for a second, and the smolder of

pain was in their eyes. We got to get off. A tractor and a superintendent. Like factories.

Where'll we go? the women asked.

We don't know. We don't know.

And the women went quickly, quietly back into the houses and herded the children ahead of them. They knew that a man so hurt and so perplexed may turn in anger, even on people he loves. They left the men alone to figure and to wonder in the dust.

After a time perhaps the tenant man looked about—at the pump put in ten years ago, with a goose-neck handle and iron flowers on the spout, at the chopping block where a thousand chickens had been killed, at the hand plow lying in the shed, and the patent crib hanging in the rafters over it.

The children crowded about the women in the houses. What we going to do, Ma? Where we going to go?

The women said, We don't know, yet. Go out and play. But don't go near your father. He might whale you if you go near him. And the women went on with the work, but all the time they watched the men squatting in the dust—perplexed and figuring.

The tractors came over the roads and into the fields, great crawlers moving like insects, having the incredible strength of insects. They crawled over the ground, laying the track and rolling on it and picking it up. Diesel tractors, puttering while they stood idle; they thundered when they moved, and then settled down to a droning roar. Snub-nosed monsters, raising the dust and sticking their snouts into it, straight down the country, across the country, through fences, through dooryards, in and out of gullies in straight lines. They did not run on the ground, but on their own roadbeds.

They ignored hills and gulches, water courses, fences, houses.

The man sitting in the iron seat did not look like a man; gloved, goggled, rubber dust mask over nose and mouth, he was a part of the monster, a robot in the seat. The thunder of the cylinders sounded through the country, became one with the air and the earth, so that earth and air muttered in sympathetic vibration. The driver could not control it—straight across country it went, cutting through a dozen farms and straight back. A twitch at the controls could swerve the cat', but the driver's hands could not twitch because the monster that built the tractor, the monster that sent the tractor out, had somehow got into the driver's hands, into his brain and muscle, had goggled him and muzzled him —goggled his mind, muzzled his speech, goggled his perception, muzzled his protest. He could not see the land as it was, he could not smell the land as it smelled; his feet did not stamp the clods or feel the warmth and power of the earth. He sat in an iron seat and stepped on iron pedals. He could not cheer or beat or curse or encourage the extension of his power, and because of this he could not cheer or whip or curse or encourage himself. He did not know or own or trust or beseech the land. If a seed dropped did not germinate, it was nothing. If the young thrusting plant withered in drought or drowned in a flood of rain, it was no more to the driver than to the tractor.

He loved the land no more than the bank loved the land. He could admire the tractor—its machined surfaces, its surge of power, the roar of its detonating cylinders; but it was not his tractor. Behind the tractor rolled the shining disks, cutting the earth with blades—not plowing but surgery, pushing the cut earth to the right where the second row of disks cut it and pushed it to the left; slicing blades shining, polished by the cut earth. And pulled behind the disks, the harrows combing with iron teeth so that the little clods broke up and the earth lay smooth. Behind the harrows, the long seeders —twelve curved iron penes erected in the foundry, orgasms set by gears, raping methodically, raping without passion. The driver sat in his iron seat and he was proud of the straight lines he did not will, proud of the tractor he did not own or love, proud of the power he could not control. And when that crop grew, and was harvested, no man had crumbled a hot clod in his fingers and let the earth sift past his fingertips. No man had touched the seed, or lusted for the growth. Men ate what they had not raised, had no connection with the bread. The land bore under iron, and under iron gradually died; for it was not loved or hated, it had no prayers or curses.

At noon the tractor driver stopped sometimes near a tenant house and opened his lunch: sandwiches wrapped in waxed paper, white bread, pickle, cheese, Spam, a piece of pie branded like an engine part. He ate without relish. And tenants not yet moved away came out to see him, looked curiously while the goggles were taken off, and the rubber dust mask, leaving white circles around the eyes and a large white circle around nose and mouth. The exhaust of the tractor puttered on, for fuel is so cheap it is more efficient to leave the engine running than to heat the Diesel nose for a new start. Curious children crowded close, ragged children who ate their fried dough as they watched. They watched hungrily the unwrapping of the sandwiches, and their hunger-sharpened noses smelled the pickle, cheese, and Spam. They didn't speak to the driver. They watched his hand as it carried food to his mouth. They did not watch him chewing; their eyes followed the hand that held the sandwich. After a while the tenant who could not leave the place came out and squatted in the shade beside the tractor.

"Why, you're Joe Davis's boy!"

"Sure," the driver said.

"Well, what you doing this kind of work for—against your own people?"

"Three dollars a day. I got damn sick of creeping for my dinner—and not getting it. I got a wife and kids. We got to eat. Three dollars a day, and it comes every day."

"That's right," the tenant said. "But for your three dollars a day fifteen or twenty families can't eat at all. Nearly a hundred people have to go out and wander on the roads for your three dollars a day. Is that right?"

And the driver said, "Can't think of that. Got to think of my own kids. Three dollars a day, and it comes every day. Times are changing, mister, don't you know? Can't make a living on the land unless you've got two, five, ten thousand acres and a tractor. Crop land isn't for little guys like us any more. You don't kick up a howl because you can't make Fords, or because you're not the telephone company. Well, crops are like that now. Nothing to do about it. You try to get three dollars a day someplace. That's the only way."

The tenant pondered. "Funny thing how it is. If a man owns a little property, that property is him, it's part of him, and it's like him. If he owns property only so he can walk on it and handle it and be sad when it isn't doing well, and feel fine when the rain falls on it, that property is him, and some way he's bigger because he owns it. Even if he isn't successful he's big with his property. That is so."

And the tenant pondered more. "But let a man get property he doesn't see, or can't take time to get his fingers in, or can't be there to walk on it—why, then the property is the man. He can't do what he wants, he can't think what he wants. The property is the man, stronger than he is. And he is small, not big. Only his possessions are big—and he's the servant of his property. That is so, too."

The driver munched the branded pie and threw the crust away. "Times are changed, don't you know? Thinking about stuff like that don't feed the kids. Get your three dollars a day, feed your kids. You got no call to worry about anybody's kids but your own. You get a reputation for talking like that, and you'll never get three dollars a day. Big shots won't give you three dollars a day if you worry about anything but your three dollars a day."

"Nearly a hundred people on the road for your three dollars. Where will we go?"

"And that reminds me," the driver said, "you better get out soon. I'm going through the dooryard after dinner."

"You filled in the well this morning."

"I know. Had to keep the line straight. But I'm going through the dooryard after dinner. Got to keep the lines straight. And—well, you know Joe Davis, my old man, so I'll tell you this. I got orders wherever there's a family not moved out—if I have an accident—you know, get too close and cave the house in a little—well, I might get a couple of dollars. And my youngest kid never had no shoes yet."

"I built it with my hands. Straightened old nails to put the sheathing on. Rafters are wired to the stringers with baling wire. It's mine. I built it. You bump it down—I'll be in the window with a rifle. You even come too close and I'll pot you like a rabbit."

"It's not me. There's nothing I can do. I'll lose my job if I don't do it. And look—suppose you kill me? They'll just hang you, but long before you're hung there'll be another guy on the tractor, and he'll bump the house down. You're not killing the right guy."

"That's so," the tenant said. "Who gave you orders? I'll go after him. He's the one to kill."

"You're wrong. He got his orders from the bank. The bank told him, 'Clear those people out or it's your job.'"

"Well, there's a president of the bank. There's a board of directors. I'll fill up the magazine of the rifle and go into the bank."

The driver said, "Fellow was telling me the bank gets orders from the East. The orders were, 'Make the land show profit or we'll close you up.'"

"But where does it stop? Who can we shoot? I don't aim to starve to death before I kill the man that's starving me."

"I don't know. Maybe there's nobody to shoot. Maybe the thing isn't men at all. Maybe, like you said, the property's doing it. Anyway I told you my orders."

"I got to figure," the tenant said. "We all got to figure. There's some way to stop this. It's not like lightning or earth-quakes. We've got a bad thing made by men, and by God that's something we can change." The tenant sat in his door-way, and the driver thundered his engine and started off, tracks falling and curving, harrows combing, and the phalli of the seeder slipping into the ground. Across the dooryard the tractor cut, and the hard, foot-beaten ground was seeded field, and the tractor cut through again; the uncut space was ten feet wide. And back he came. The iron guard bit into the house-corner, crumbled the wall, and wrenched the little house from its foundation so that it fell sideways, crushed like a bug. And the driver was goggled and a rubber mask covered his nose and mouth. The tractor cut a straight line on, and the air and the ground vibrated with its thunder. The tenant man stared after it, his rifle in his hand. His wife was beside him, and the quiet children behind. And all of them stared after the tractor.

Chapter Six

THE Reverend Casy and young Tom stood on the hill and looked down on the Joad place. The small unpainted house was mashed at one corner, and it had been pushed off its foundations so that it slumped at an angle, its blind front windows pointing at a spot of sky well above the horizon. The fences were gone and the cotton grew in the dooryard and up against the house, and the cotton was about the shed barn. The outhouse lay on its side, and the cotton grew close against it. Where the dooryard had been pounded hard by the bare feet of children and by stamping horses' hooves and by the broad wagon wheels, it was cultivated now, and the dark green, dusty cotton grew. Young Tom stared for a long time at the ragged willow beside the dry horse trough, at the concrete base where the pump had been. "Jesus!" he said at last. "Hell musta popped here. There ain't nobody livin' there." At last he moved quickly down the hill, and Casy followed him. He looked into the barn shed, deserted, a little ground straw on the floor, and at the mule stall in the corner. And as he looked in, there was a skittering on the floor and a family of mice faded in under the straw. Joad paused at the entrance to the tool-shed leanto, and no tools were there—a broken plow point, a mess of hay wire in the corner, an iron wheel from a hayrake and a rat-gnawed mule collar, a flat gallon oil can crusted with dirt and oil, and a pair of torn overalls hanging on a nail. "There ain't nothin' left," said Joad. "We had pretty nice tools. There ain't nothin' left."

Casy said, "If I was still a preacher I'd say the arm of the Lord had struck. But now I don't know what happened. I been away. I didn't hear nothin'." They walked toward the concrete well-cap, walked through cotton plants to get to it, and the bolls were forming on the cotton, and the land was cultivated.

"We never planted here," Joad said. "We always kept this clear. Why, you can't get a horse in now without he tromps the cotton." They paused at the dry watering trough, and the proper weeds that should grow under a trough were gone and the old thick wood of the trough was dry and cracked. On the well-cap the bolts that had held the pump stuck up, their threads rusty and the nuts gone. Joad looked into the tube of the well and spat and listened. He dropped a clod down the well and listened. "She was a good well," he said. "I can't hear water." He seemed reluctant to go to the house. He dropped clod after clod down the well. "Maybe they're all dead," he said. "But somebody'd a told me. I'd a got word some way."

"Maybe they left a letter or something to tell in the house. Would they of knowed you was comin' out?"

"I don' know," said Joad. "No, I guess not. I didn' know myself till a week ago."

"Le's look in the house. She's all pushed out a shape. Something knocked the hell out of her." They walked slowly toward the sagging house. Two of the supports of the porch roof were pushed out so that the roof flopped down on one end. And the house-corner was crushed in. Through a maze of splintered wood the room at the corner was visible. The front door hung open inward, and a low strong gate across the front door hung outward on leather hinges.

Joad stopped at the step, a twelve-by-twelve timber. "Doorstep's here," he said. "But they're gone—or Ma's dead." He pointed to the low gate across the front door. "If Ma was anywheres about, that gate'd be shut an' hooked. That's one thing she always done—seen that gate was shut." His eyes were warm. "Ever since the pig got in over to Jacobs' an' et the baby. Milly Jacobs was jus' out in the barn. She come in while the pig was still eatin' it. Well, Milly Jacobs was in a family way, an' she went ravin'. Never did get over it. Touched ever since. But Ma took a lesson from it. She never lef' that pig gate open 'less she was in the house herself. Never did forget. No—they're gone—or dead." He climbed to the split porch and looked into the kitchen. The windows were broken out, and throwing rocks lay on the floor, and the floor and walls sagged steeply away from the door, and the sifted dust was on the boards. Joad pointed to the broken glass and the rocks. "Kids," he said. "They'll go twenty miles to bust a window. I done it myself. They know when a house is empty, they know. That's the fust thing kids do when folks move out." The kitchen was empty of furniture, stove gone and the round stovepipe hole in the wall showing light. On the sink shelf lay an old beer opener and a broken fork with its wooden handle gone. Joad slipped cautiously into the room, and the floor groaned under his weight. An old copy of the Philadelphia *Ledger* was on the floor against the wall, its pages yellow and curling. Joad looked into the bedroom—no bed, no chairs, nothing. On the wall a picture of an Indian girl in color, labeled Red Wing. A bed slat leaning against the wall, and in one corner a woman's high button shoe, curled up at the toe and broken over the instep.

Joad picked it up and looked at it. "I remember this," he said. "This was Ma's. It's all wore out now. Ma liked them shoes. Had 'em for years. No, they've went—an' took ever'thing."

The sun had lowered until it came through the angled end windows now, and it flashed on the edges of the broken glass. Joad turned at last and went out and crossed the porch. He sat down on the edge of it and rested his bare feet on the twelve-by-twelve step. The evening light was on the fields, and the cotton plants threw long shadows on the ground, and the molting willow tree threw a long shadow.

Casy sat down beside Joad. "They never wrote you nothin'?" he asked.

"No. Like I said, they wasn't people to write. Pa could write, but he wouldn'. Didn't like to. It give him the shivers to write. He could work out a catalogue order as good as the nex' fella, but he wouldn' write no letters just for ducks." They sat side by side, staring off into the distance. Joad laid his rolled coat on the porch beside him. His independent hands rolled a cigarette, smoothed it and lighted it, and he inhaled deeply and blew the smoke out through his nose. "Somepin's wrong," he said. "I can't put my finger on her. I got an itch that somepin's wronger'n hell. Just this house pushed aroun' an' my folks gone."

Casy said, "Right over there the ditch was, where I done the baptizin'. You wasn't mean, but you was tough. Hung onto that little girl's pigtail like a bulldog. We baptize' you both in the name of the Holy Ghos', and still you hung on. Ol' Tom says, 'Hol' 'im under water.' So I shove your head down till you start to bubblin' before you'd let go a that pigtail. You wasn't mean, but you was tough. Sometimes a tough kid grows up with a big jolt of the sperit in him."

A lean gray cat came sneaking out of the barn and crept

through the cotton plants to the end of the porch. It leaped silently up to the porch and crept low-belly toward the men. It came to a place between and behind the two, and then it sat down, and its tail stretched out straight and flat to the floor, and the last inch of it flicked. The cat sat and looked off into the distance where the men were looking.

Joad glanced around at it. "By God! Look who's here. Somebody stayed." He put out his hand, but the cat leaped away out of reach and sat down and licked the pads of its lifted paw. Joad looked at it, and his face was puzzled. "I know what's the matter," he cried. "That cat jus' made me figger what's wrong."

"Seems to me there's lots wrong," said Casy.

"No, it's more'n jus' this place. Whyn't that cat jus' move in with some neighbors—with the Rances. How come nobody ripped some lumber off this house? Ain't been nobody here for three-four months, an' nobody's stole no lumber. Nice planks on the barn shed, plenty good planks on the house, winda frames—an' nobody's took 'em. That ain't right. That's what was botherin' me, an' I couldn't catch hold of her."

"Well, what's that figger out for you?" Casy reached down and slipped off his sneakers and wriggled his long toes on the step.

"I don' know. Seems like maybe there ain't any neighbors. If there was, would all them nice planks be here? Why, Jesus Christ! Albert Rance took his family, kids an' dogs an' all, into Oklahoma City one Christmas. They was gonna visit with Albert's cousin. Well, folks aroun' here thought Albert moved away without sayin' nothin'—figgered maybe he got debts or some woman's squarin' off at him. When Albert come back a week later there wasn't a thing lef' in his house

—stove was gone, beds was gone, winda frames was gone, an' eight feet of plankin' was gone off the south side of the house so you could look right through her. He come drivin' home just as Muley Graves was goin' away with the doors an' the well pump. Took Albert two weeks drivin' aroun' the neighbors' 'fore he got his stuff back."

Casy scratched his toes luxuriously. "Didn't nobody give him an argument? All of 'em jus' give the stuff up?"

"Sure. They wasn't stealin' it. They thought he lef' it, an' they jus' took it. He got all of it back—all but a sofa pilla, velvet with a pitcher of an Injun on it. Albert claimed Grampa got it. Claimed Grampa got Injun blood, that's why he wants that pitcher. Well, Grampa did get her, but he didn't give a damn about the pitcher on it. He jus' liked her. Used to pack her aroun' an' he'd put her wherever he was gonna sit. He never would give her back to Albert. Says, 'If Albert wants this pilla so bad, let him come an' get her. But he better come shootin', 'cause I'll blow his goddamn stinkin' head off if he comes messin' aroun' my pilla.' So finally Albert give up an' made Grampa a present of that pilla. It give Grampa idears, though. He took to savin' chicken feathers. Says he's gonna have a whole damn bed of feathers. But he never got no feather bed. One time Pa got mad at a skunk under the house. Pa slapped that skunk with a two-by-four, and Ma burned all Grampa's feathers so we could live in the house." He laughed. "Grampa's a tough ol' bastard. Jus' set on that Injun pilla an' says, 'Let Albert come an' get her. Why,' he says, 'I'll take that squirt and wring 'im out like a pair of drawers.'"

The cat crept close between the men again, and its tail lay flat and its whiskers jerked now and then. The sun dropped low toward the horizon and the dusty air was red and golden. The cat reached out a gray questioning paw and touched Joad's coat. He looked around. "Hell, I forgot the turtle. I ain't gonna pack it all over hell." He unwrapped the land turtle and pushed it under the house. But in a moment it was out, headed southwest as it had been from the first. The cat leaped at it and struck at its straining head and slashed at its moving feet. The old, hard, humorous head was pulled in, and the thick tail slapped in under the shell, and when the cat grew tired of waiting for it and walked off, the turtle headed on southwest again.

Young Tom Joad and the preacher watched the turtle go—waving its legs and boosting its heavy, high-domed shell along toward the southwest. The cat crept along behind for a while, but in a dozen yards it arched its back to a strong taut bow and yawned, and came stealthily back toward the seated men.

"Where the hell you s'pose he's goin'?" said Joad. "I seen turtles all my life. They're always goin' someplace. They always seem to want to get there." The gray cat seated itself between and behind them again. It blinked slowly. The skin over its shoulders jerked forward under a flea, and then slipped slowly back. The cat lifted a paw and inspected it, flicked its claws out and in again experimentally, and licked its pads with a shell-pink tongue. The red sun touched the horizon and spread out like a jellyfish, and the sky above it seemed much brighter and more alive than it had been. Joad unrolled his new yellow shoes from his coat, and he brushed his dusty feet with his hand before he slipped them on.

The preacher, staring off across the fields, said, "Somebody's comin'. Look! Down there, right through the cotton."

Joad looked where Casy's finger pointed. "Comin' afoot,"

he said. "Can't see 'im for the dust he raises. Who the hell's comin' here?" They watched the figure approaching in the evening light, and the dust it raised was reddened by the setting sun. "Man," said Joad. The man drew closer, and as he walked past the barn, Joad said, "Why, I know him. You know him—that's Muley Graves." And he called, "Hey, Muley! How ya?"

The approaching man stopped, startled by the call, and then he came on quickly. He was a lean man, rather short. His movements were jerky and quick. He carried a gunny sack in his hand. His blue jeans were pale at knee and seat, and he wore an old black suit coat, stained and spotted, the sleeves torn loose from the shoulders in back, and ragged holes worn through at the elbows. His black hat was as stained as his coat, and the band, torn half free, flopped up and down as he walked. Muley's face was smooth and un-wrinkled, but it wore the truculent look of a bad child's, the mouth held tight and small, the little eyes half scowling, half petulant.

"You remember Muley," Joad said softly to the preacher. "Who's that?" the advancing man called. Joad did not answer. Muley came close, very close, before he made out the faces. "Well, I'll be damned," he said. "It's Tommy Joad. When'd you get out, Tommy?"

"Two days ago," said Joad. "Took a little time to hitch-hike home. An' look here what I find. Where's my folks, Muley? What's the house all smashed up for, an' cotton planted in the dooryard?"

"By God, it's lucky I come by!" said Muley. " 'Cause ol' Tom worried himself. When they was fixin' to move I was settin' in the kitchen there. I jus' tol' Tom I wan't gonna move, by God. I tol' him that, an' Tom says, 'I'm worryin' myself about Tommy. S'pose he comes home an' they ain't nobody here. What'll he think?' I says, 'Whyn't you write down a letter?' An' Tom says, 'Maybe I will. I'll think about her. But if I don't, you keep your eye out for Tommy if you're still aroun'.' 'I'll be aroun',' I says. 'I'll be aroun' till hell freezes over. There ain't nobody can run a guy name of Graves outa this country.' An' they ain't done it, neither."

Joad said impatiently, "Where's my folks? Tell about you standin' up to 'em later, but where's my folks?"

"Well, they was gonna stick her out when the bank come to tractorin' off the place. Your grampa stood out here with a rifle, an' he blowed the headlights off that cat', but she come on just the same. Your grampa didn't wanta kill the guy drivin' that cat', an' that was Willy Feeley, an' Willy knowed it, so he jus' come on, an' bumped the hell outa the house, an' give her a shake like a dog shakes a rat. Well, it took somepin outa Tom. Kinda got into 'im. He ain't been the same ever since."

"Where is my folks?" Joad spoke angrily.

"What I'm tellin' you. Took three trips with your Uncle John's wagon. Took the stove an' the pump an' the beds. You should a seen them beds go out with all them kids an' your granma an' grampa settin' up against the headboard, an' your brother Noah settin' there smokin' a cigareet, an' spittin' la-de-da over the side of the wagon." Joad opened his mouth to speak. "They're all at your Uncle John's," Muley said quickly.

"Oh! All at John's. Well, what they doin' there? Now stick to her for a second, Muley. Jus' stick to her. In jus' a minute you can go on your own way. What they doin' there?"

"Well, they been choppin' cotton, all of 'em, even the

kids an' your grampa. Gettin' money together so they can shove on west. Gonna buy a car and shove on west where it's easy livin'. There ain't nothin' here. Fifty cents a clean acre for choppin' cotton, an' folks beggin' for the chance to chop."

"An' they ain't gone yet?"

"No," said Muley. "Not that I know. Las' I heard was four days ago when I seen your brother Noah out shootin' jack-rabbits, an' he says they're aimin' to go in about two weeks. John got his notice he got to get off. You jus' go on about eight miles to John's place. You'll find your folks piled in John's house like gophers in a winter burrow."

"O.K." said Joad. "Now you can ride on your own way. You ain't changed a bit, Muley. If you want to tell about somepin off northwest, you point your nose straight south-east."

Muley said truculently, "You ain't changed neither. You was a smart-aleck kid, an' you're still a smart aleck. You ain't tellin' me how to skin my life, by any chancet?"

Joad grinned. "No, I ain't. If you wanta drive your head into a pile a broken glass, there ain't nobody can tell you different. You know this here preacher, don't you, Muley? Rev. Casy."

"Why, sure, sure. Didn't look over. Remember him well." Casy stood up and the two shook hands. "Glad to see you again," said Muley. "You ain't been aroun' for a hell of a long time."

"I been off a-askin' questions," said Casy. "What happened here? Why they kickin' folks off the lan'?"

Muley's mouth snapped shut so tightly that a little parrot's beak in the middle of his upper lip stuck down over his under lip. He scowled. "Them sons-a-bitches," he said. "Them dirty sons-a-bitches. I tell ya, men, I'm stayin'. They ain't gettin' rid a me. If they throw me off, I'll come back, an' if they figger I'll be quiet underground, why, I'll take couple-three of the sons-a-bitches along for company." He patted a heavy weight in his side coat pocket. "I ain't a-goin'. My pa come here fifty years ago. An' I ain't a-goin'."

Joad said, "What's the idear of kickin' the folks off?"

"Oh! They talked pretty about it. You know what kinda years we been havin'. Dust comin' up an' spoilin' ever'thing so a man didn't get enough crop to plug up an ant's ass. An' ever'body got bills at the grocery. You know how it is. Well, the folks that owns the lan' says, 'We can't afford to keep no tenants.' An' they says, 'The share a tenant gets is jus' the margin a profit we can't afford to lose.' An' they says, 'If we put all our lan' in one piece we can jus' hardly make her pay.' So they tractored all the tenants off a the lan'. All 'cept me, an' by God I ain't goin'. Tommy, you know me. You knowed me all your life."

"Damn right," said Joad, "all my life."

"Well, you know I ain't a fool. I know this land ain't much good. Never was much good 'cept for grazin'. Never should a broke her up. An' now she's cottoned damn near to death. If on'y they didn' tell me I got to get off, why, I'd prob'y be in California right now a-eatin' grapes an' a-pickin' an orange when I wanted. But them sons-a-bitches says I got to get off—an', Jesus Christ, a man can't, when he's tol' to!"

"Sure," said Joad. "I wonder Pa went so easy. I wonder Grampa didn' kill nobody. Nobody never tol' Grampa where to put his feet. An' Ma ain't nobody you can push aroun', neither. I seen her beat the hell out of a tin peddler with a live chicken one time 'cause he give her a argument. She had the chicken in one han', an' the ax in the other, about to cut its head off. She aimed to go for that peddler with the ax, but she forgot which hand was which, an' she takes after him with the chicken. Couldn' even eat that chicken when she got done. They wasn't nothing but a pair a legs in her han'. Grampa throwed his hip outa joint laughin'. How'd my folks go so easy?"

"Well, the guy that come aroun' talked nice as pie. 'You got to get off. It ain't my fault.' 'Well,' I says, 'whose fault is it? I'll go an' I'll nut the fella.' 'It's the Shawnee Lan' an' Cattle Company. I jus' got orders.' 'Who's the Shawnee Lan' an' Cattle Company?' 'It ain't nobody. It's a company.' Got a fella crazy. There wasn't nobody you could lay for. Lot a the folks jus' got tired out lookin' for somepin to be mad at —but not me. I'm mad at all of it. I'm stayin'."

A large red drop of sun lingered on the horizon and then dripped over and was gone, and the sky was brilliant over the spot where it had gone, and a torn cloud, like a bloody rag, hung over the spot of its going. And dusk crept over the sky from the eastern horizon, and darkness crept over the land from the east. The evening star flashed and glittered in the dusk. The gray cat sneaked away toward the open barn shed and passed inside like a shadow.

Joad said, "Well, we ain't gonna walk no eight miles to Uncle John's place tonight. My dogs is burned up. How's it if we go to your place, Muley? That's on'y about a mile."

"Won't do no good." Muley seemed embarrassed. "My wife an' the kids an' her brother all took an' went to California. They wasn't nothin' to eat. They wasn't as mad as me, so they went. They wasn't nothin' to eat here."

The preacher stirred nervously. "You should of went too. You shouldn't of broke up the fambly."

"I couldn'," said Muley Graves. "Somepin jus' wouldn' let me."

"Well, by God, I'm hungry," said Joad. "Four solemn years I been eatin' right on the minute. My guts is yellin' bloody murder. What you gonna eat, Muley? How you been gettin' your dinner?"

Muley said ashamedly, "For a while I et frogs an' squirrels an' prairie dogs sometimes. Had to do it. But now I got some wire nooses on the tracks in the dry stream brush. Get rabbits, an' sometimes a prairie chicken. Skunks get caught, an' coons, too." He reached down, picked up his sack, and emptied it on the porch. Two cottontails and a jackrabbit fell out and rolled over limply, soft and furry.

"God Awmighty," said Joad, "it's more'n four years sence I've et fresh-killed meat."

Casy picked up one of the cottontails and held it in his hand. "You sharin' with us, Muley Graves?" he asked.

Muley fidgeted in embarrassment. "I ain't got no choice in the matter." He stopped on the ungracious sound of his words. "That ain't like I mean it. That ain't. I mean"—he stumbled—"what I mean, if a fella's got somepin to eat an' another fella's hungry—why, the first fella ain't got no choice. I mean, s'pose I pick up my rabbits an' go off somewheres an' eat 'em. See?"

"I see," said Casy. "I can see that. Muley sees somepin there, Tom. Muley's got a-holt of somepin, an' it's too big for him, an' it's too big for me."

Young Tom rubbed his hands together. "Who got a knife? Le's get at these here miserable rodents. Le's get at 'em."

Muley reached in his pants pocket and produced a large horn-handled pocket knife. Tom Joad took it from him, opened a blade, and smelled it. He drove the blade again and again into the ground and smelled it again, wiped it on his trouser leg, and felt the edge with his thumb.

Muley took a quart bottle of water out of his hip pocket and set it on the porch. "Go easy on that there water," he said. "That's all there is. This here well's filled in."

Tom took up a rabbit in his hand. "One of you go get some bale wire outa the barn. We'll make a fire with some a this broken plank from the house." He looked at the dead rabbit. "There ain't nothin' so easy to get ready as a rabbit," he said. He lifted the skin of the back, slit it, put his fingers in the hole, and tore the skin off. It slipped off like a stocking, slipped off the body to the neck, and off the legs to the paws. Joad picked up the knife again and cut off head and feet. He laid the skin down, slit the rabbit along the ribs, shook out the intestines onto the skin, and then threw the mess off into the cotton field. And the clean-muscled little body was ready. Joad cut off the legs and cut the meaty back into two pieces. He was picking up the second rabbit when Casy came back with a snarl of bale wire in his hand. "Now build up a fire and put some stakes up," said Joad. "Jesus Christ, I'm hungry for these here creatures!" He cleaned and cut up the rest of the rabbits and strung them on the wire. Muley and Casy tore splintered boards from the wrecked house-corner and started a fire, and they drove a stake into the ground on each side to hold the wire.

Muley came back to Joad. "Look out for boils on that jackrabbit," he said. "I don't like to eat no jackrabbit with boils." He took a little cloth bag from his pocket and put it on the porch.

Joad said, "The jack was clean as a whistle—Jesus God,

you got salt too? By any chance you got some plates an' a tent in your pocket?" He poured salt in his hand and sprinkled it over the pieces of rabbit strung on the wire.

The fire leaped and threw shadows on the house, and the dry wood crackled and snapped. The sky was almost dark now and the stars were out sharply. The gray cat came out of the barn shed and trotted miaowing toward the fire, but, nearly there, it turned and went directly to one of the little piles of rabbit entrails on the ground. It chewed and swallowed, and the entrails hung from its mouth.

Casy sat on the ground beside the fire, feeding it broken pieces of board, pushing the long boards in as the flame ate off their ends. The evening bats flashed into the firelight and out again. The cat crouched back and licked its lips and washed its face and whiskers.

Joad held up his rabbit-laden wire between his two hands and walked to the fire. "Here, take one end, Muley. Wrap your end around that stake. That's good, now! Let's tighten her up. We ought to wait till the fire's burned down, but I can't wait." He made the wire taut, then found a stick and slipped the pieces of meat along the wire until they were over the fire. And the flames licked up around the meat and hardened and glazed the surfaces. Joad sat down by the fire, but with his stick he moved and turned the rabbit so that it would not become sealed to the wire. "This here is a party," he said. "Salt, Muley's got, an' water an' rabbits. I wish he got a pot of hominy in his pocket. That's all I wish."

Muley said over the fire, "You fellas'd think I'm touched, the way I live."

"Touched, nothin'," said Joad. "If you're touched, I wisht ever'body was touched."

Muley continued, "Well, sir, it's a funny thing. Somepin

went an' happened to me when they tol' me I had to get off the place. Fust I was gonna go in an' kill a whole flock a people. Then all my folks all went away out west. An' I got wanderin' aroun'. Jus' walkin' aroun'. Never went far. Slep' where I was. I was gonna sleep here tonight. That's why I come. I'd tell myself, 'I'm lookin' after things so when all the folks come back it'll be all right.' But I knowed that wan't true. There ain't nothin' to look after. The folks ain't never comin' back. I'm jus' wanderin' aroun' like a damn ol' graveyard ghos'."

"Fella gets use' to a place, it's hard to go," said Casy. "Fella gets use' to a way a thinkin', it's hard to leave. I ain't a preacher no more, but all the time I find I'm prayin', not even thinkin' what I'm doin'."

Joad turned the pieces of meat over on the wire. The juice was dripping now, and every drop, as it fell in the fire, shot up a spurt of flame. The smooth surface of the meat was crinkling up and turning a faint brown. "Smell her," said Joad. "Jesus, look down an' jus' smell her!"

Muley went on, "Like a damn ol' graveyard ghos'. I been goin' aroun' the places where stuff happened. Like there's a place over by our forty; in a gully they's a bush. Fust time I ever laid with a girl was there. Me fourteen an' stampin' an' jerkin' an' snortin' like a buck deer, randy as a billygoat. So I went there an' I laid down on the groun', an' I seen it all happen again. An' there's the place down by the barn where Pa got gored to death by a bull. An' his blood is right in that groun', right now. Mus' be. Nobody never washed it out. An' I put my han' on that groun' where my own pa's blood is part of it." He paused uneasily. "You fellas think I'm touched?"

Joad turned the meat, and his eyes were inward. Casy, feet

drawn up, stared into the fire. Fifteen feet back from the men the fed cat was sitting, the long gray tail wrapped neatly around the front feet. A big owl shrieked as it went overhead, and the firelight showed its white underside and the spread of its wings.

"No," said Casy. "You're lonely—but you ain't touched."

Muley's tight little face was rigid. "I put my han' right on the groun' where that blood is still. An' I seen my pa with a hole through his ches', an' I felt him shiver up against me like he done, an' I seen him kind of settle back an' reach with his han's an' his feet. An' I seen his eyes all milky with hurt, an' then he was still an' his eyes so clear—lookin' up. An' me a little kid settin' there, not cryin' nor nothin', jus' settin' there." He shook his head sharply. Joad turned the meat over and over. "An' I went in the room where Joe was born. Bed wasn't there, but it was the room. An' all them things is true, an' they're right in the place they happened. Joe come to life right there. He give a big ol' gasp an' then he let out a squawk you could hear a mile, an' his granma standin' there says, 'That's a daisy, that's a daisy,' over an' over. An' her so proud she bust three cups that night."

Joad cleared his throat. "Think we better eat her now."

"Let her get good an' done, good an' brown, awmost black," said Muley irritably. "I wanta talk. I ain't talked to nobody. If I'm touched, I'm touched, an' that's the end of it. Like a ol' graveyard ghos' goin' to neighbors' houses in the night. Peters', Jacobs', Rance's, Joad's; an' the houses all dark, standin' like miser'ble ratty boxes, but they was good parties an' dancin'. An' there was meetin's and shoutin' glory. They was weddin's, all in them houses. An' then I'd want to go in town an' kill folks. 'Cause what'd they take when they tractored the folks off the lan'? What'd they get so their

'margin a profit' was safe? They got Pa dyin' on the groun',
an' Joe yellin' his first breath, an' me jerkin' like a billy goat
under a bush in the night. What'd they get? God knows the
lan' ain't no good. Nobody been able to make a crop for
years. But them sons-a-bitches at their desks, they jus'
chopped folks in two for their margin a profit. They jus'
cut 'em in two. Place where folks live is them folks. They
ain't whole, out lonely on the road in a piled-up car. They
ain't alive no more. Them sons-a-bitches killed 'em." And he
was silent, his thin lips still moving, his chest still panting.
He sat and looked down at his hands in the firelight. "I—I
ain't talked to nobody for a long time," he apologized softly.
"I been sneakin' aroun' like a ol' graveyard ghos'."

Casy pushed the long boards into the fire and the flames
licked up around them and leaped up toward the meat again.
The house cracked loudly as the cooler night air contracted
the wood. Casy said quietly, "I gotta see them folks that's
gone out on the road. I got a feelin' I got to see them. They
gonna need help no preachin' can give 'em. Hope of heaven
when their lives ain't lived? Holy Sperit when their own
sperit is downcast an' sad? They gonna need help. They got
to live before they can afford to die."

Joad cried nervously, "Jesus Christ, le's eat this meat 'fore
it's smaller'n a cooked mouse! Look at her. Smell her." He
leaped to his feet and slid the pieces of meat along the wire
until they were clear of the fire. He took Muley's knife and
sawed through a piece of meat until it was free of the wire.
"Here's for the preacher," he said.

"I tol' you I ain't no preacher."

"Well, here's for the man, then." He cut off another piece.
"Here, Muley, if you ain't too goddamn upset to eat. This
here's jackrabbit. Tougher'n a bull-bitch." He sat back and

clamped his long teeth on the meat and tore out a great bite and chewed it. "Jesus Christ! Hear her crunch!" And he tore out another bite ravenously.

Muley still sat regarding his meat. "Maybe I oughtn' to a-talked like that," he said. "Fella should maybe keep stuff like that in his head."

Casy looked over, his mouth full of rabbit. He chewed, and his muscled throat convulsed in swallowing. "Yes, you should talk," he said. "Sometimes a sad man can talk the sadness right out through his mouth. Sometimes a killin' man can talk the murder right out of his mouth an' not do no murder. You done right. Don't you kill nobody if you can help it." And he bit out another hunk of rabbit. Joad tossed the bones in the fire and jumped up and cut more off the wire. Muley was eating slowly now, and his nervous little eyes went from one to the other of his companions. Joad ate scowling like an animal, and a ring of grease formed around his mouth.

For a long time Muley looked at him, almost timidly. He put down the hand that held the meat. "Tommy," he said.

Joad looked up and did not stop gnawing the meat. "Yeah?" he said, around a mouthful.

"Tommy, you ain't mad with me talkin' about killin' people? You ain't huffy, Tom?"

"No," said Tom. "I ain't huffy. It's jus' somepin that happened."

"Ever'body knowed it was no fault of yours," said Muley. "Ol' man Turnbull said he was gonna get you when ya come out. Says nobody can kill one a his boys. All the folks hereabouts talked him outa it, though."

"We was drunk," Joad said softly. "Drunk at a dance. I don' know how she started. An' then I felt that knife go in

me, an' that sobered me up. Fust thing I see is Herb comin'
for me again with his knife. They was this here shovel leanin'
against the schoolhouse, so I grabbed it an' smacked 'im over
the head. I never had nothing against Herb. He was a nice
fella. Come a-bullin' after my sister Rosasharn when he was
a little fella. No, I liked Herb."

"Well, ever'body tol' his pa that, an' finally cooled 'im
down. Somebody says they's Hatfield blood on his mother's
side in ol' Turnbull, an' he's got to live up to it. I don't know
about that. Him an' his folks went on to California six
months ago."

Joad took the last of the rabbit from the wire and passed
it around. He settled back and ate more slowly now, chewed
evenly, and wiped the grease from his mouth with his sleeve.
And his eyes, dark and half closed, brooded as he looked into
the dying fire. "Ever'body's goin' west," he said. "I got me a
parole to keep. Can't leave the state."

"Parole?" Muley asked. "I heard about them. How do
they work?"

"Well, I got out early, three years early. They's stuff I
gotta do, or they send me back in. Got to report ever' so
often."

"How they treat ya there in McAlester? My woman's
cousin was in McAlester an' they give him hell."

"It ain't so bad," said Joad. "Like ever'place else. They
give ya hell if ya raise hell. You get along O.K. les' some
guard gets it in for ya. Then you catch plenty hell. I got
along O.K. Minded my own business, like any guy would.
I learned to write nice as hell. Birds an' stuff like that, too;
not just word writin'. My ol' man'll be sore when he sees me
whip out a bird in one stroke. Pa's gonna be mad when he
sees me do that. He don't like no fancy stuff like that. He

don't even like word writin'. Kinda scares 'im, I guess. Ever' time Pa seen writin', somebody took somepin away from 'im."

"They didn' give you no beatin's or nothin' like that?"

"No, I jus' tended my own affairs. 'Course you get goddamn good an' sick a-doin' the same thing day after day for four years. If you done somepin you was ashamed of, you might think about that. But, hell, if I seen Herb Turnbull comin' for me with a knife right now, I'd squash him down with a shovel again."

"Anybody would," said Muley. The preacher stared into the fire, and his high forehead was white in the settling dark. The flash of little flames picked out the cords of his neck. His hands, clasped about his knees, were busy pulling knuckles.

Joad threw the last bones into the fire and licked his fingers and then wiped them on his pants. He stood up and brought the bottle of water from the porch, took a sparing drink, and passed the bottle before he sat down again. He went on, "The thing that give me the mos' trouble was, it didn' make no sense. You don't look for no sense when lightnin' kills a cow, or it comes up a flood. That's jus' the way things is. But when a bunch of men take an' lock you up four years, it ought to have some meaning. Men is supposed to think things out. Here they put me in, an' keep me an' feed me four years. That ought to either make me so I won't do her again or else punish me so I'll be afraid to do her again"—he paused—"but if Herb or anybody else come for me, I'd do her again. Do her before I could figure her out. Specially if I was drunk. That sort of senselessness kind a worries a man."

Muley observed, "Judge says he give you a light sentence 'cause it wasn't all your fault."

Joad said, "They's a guy in McAlester—lifer. He studies all the time. He's sec'etary of the warden—writes the warden's letters an' stuff like that. Well, he's one hell of a bright guy an' reads law an' all stuff like that. Well, I talked to him one time about her, 'cause he reads so much stuff. An' he says it don't do no good to read books. Says he's read ever'thing about prisons now, an' in the old times; an' he says she makes less sense to him now than she did before he starts readin'. He says it's a thing that started way to hell an' gone back, an' nobody seems to be able to stop her, an' nobody got sense enough to change her. He says for God's sake don't read about her because he says for one thing you'll jus' get messed up worse, an' for another you won't have no respect for the guys that work the gover'ments."

"I ain't got a hell of a lot of respec' for 'em now," said Muley. "On'y kind a gover'ment we got that leans on us fellas is the 'safe margin a profit.' There's one thing that got me stumped, an' that's Willy Feeley—drivin' that cat', an' gonna be a straw boss on lan' his own folks used to farm. That worries me. I can see how a fella might come from some other place an' not know no better, but Willy belongs. Worried me so I went up to 'im and ast 'im. Right off he got mad. 'I got two little kids,' he says. 'I got a wife an' my wife's mother. Them people got to eat.' Gets madder'n hell. 'Fust an' on'y thing I got to think about is my own folks,' he says. 'What happens to other folks is their look-out,' he says. Seems like he's 'shamed, so he gets mad."

Jim Casy had been staring at the dying fire, and his eyes had grown wider and his neck muscles stood higher. Suddenly he cried, "I got her! If ever a man got a dose of the sperit, I got her! Got her all of a flash!" He jumped to his feet and paced back and forth, his head swinging. "Had a tent one time. Drawed as much as five hundred people ever' night. That's before either you fellas seen me." He stopped and faced them. "Ever notice I never took no collections when I was preachin' out here to folks—in barns an' in the open?"

"By God, you never," said Muley. "People around here got so use' to not givin' you money they got to bein' a little mad when some other preacher come along an' passed the hat. Yes, sir!"

"I took somepin to eat," said Casy. "I took a pair a pants when mine was wore out, an' a ol' pair a shoes when I was walkin' through to the groun', but it wasn't like when I had the tent. Some days there I'd take in ten or twenty dollars. Wasn't happy that-a-way, so I give her up, an' for a time I was happy. I think I got her now. I don' know if I can say her. I guess I won't try to say her—but maybe there's a place for a preacher. Maybe I can preach again. Folks out lonely on the road, folks with no lan', no home to go to. They got to have some kind of home. Maybe—" He stood over the fire. The hundred muscles of his neck stood out in high relief, and the firelight went deep into his eyes and ignited red embers. He stood and looked at the fire, his face tense as though he were listening, and the hands that had been active to pick, to handle, to throw ideas, grew quiet, and in a moment crept into his pockets. The bats flittered in and out of the dull firelight, and the soft watery burble of a night hawk came from across the fields.

Tom reached quietly into his pocket and brought out his

tobacco, and he rolled a cigarette slowly and looked over it
at the coals while he worked. He ignored the whole speech
of the preacher, as though it were some private thing that
should not be inspected. He said, "Night after night in my
bunk I figgered how she'd be when I come home again. I
figgered maybe Grampa or Granma'd be dead, an' maybe
there'd be some new kids. Maybe Pa'd not be so tough.
Maybe Ma'd set back a little an' let Rosasharn do the work.
I knowed it wouldn't be the same as it was. Well, we'll sleep
here I guess, an' come daylight we'll get on to Uncle John's.
Leastwise I will. You think you're comin' along, Casy?"

The preacher still stood looking into the coals. He said
slowly, "Yeah, I'm goin' with you. An' when your folks start
out on the road I'm goin' with them. An' where folks are on
the road, I'm gonna be with them."

"You're welcome," said Joad. "Ma always favored you.
Said you was a preacher to trust. Rosasharn wasn't growed
up then." He turned his head. "Muley, you gonna walk on
over with us?" Muley was looking toward the road over
which they had come. "Think you'll come along, Muley?"
Joad repeated.

"Huh? No. I don't go no place, an' I don't leave no place.
See that glow over there, jerkin' up an' down? That's prob'ly
the super'ntendent of this stretch a cotton. Somebody maybe
seen our fire."

Tom looked. The glow of light was nearing over the hill.
"We ain't doin' no harm," he said. "We'll jus' set here. We
ain't doin' nothin'."

Muley cackled. "Yeah! We're doin' somepin jus' bein'
here. We're trespassin'. We can't stay. They been tryin' to
catch me for two months. Now you look. If that's a car

comin' we go out in the cotton an' lay down. Don't have to go far. Then by God let 'em try to fin' us! Have to look up an' down ever' row. Jus' keep your head down."

Joad demanded, "What's come over you, Muley? You wasn't never no run-an'-hide fella. You was mean."

Muley watched the approaching lights. "Yeah!" he said. "I was mean like a wolf. Now I'm mean like a weasel. When you're huntin' somepin you're a hunter, an' you're strong. Can't nobody beat a hunter. But when you get hunted—that's different. Somepin happens to you. You ain't strong; maybe you're fierce, but you ain't strong. I been hunted now for a long time. I ain't a hunter no more. I'd maybe shoot a fella in the dark, but I don't maul nobody with a fence stake no more. It don't do no good to fool you or me. That's how it is."

"Well, you go out an' hide," said Joad. "Leave me an' Casy tell these bastards a few things." The beam of light was closer now, and it bounced into the sky and then disappeared, and then bounced up again. All three men watched.

Muley said, "There's one more thing about bein' hunted. You get to thinkin' about all the dangerous things. If you're huntin' you don't think about 'em, an' you ain't scared. Like you says to me, if you get in any trouble they'll sen' you back to McAlester to finish your time."

"That's right," said Joad. "That's what they tol' me, but settin' here restin' or sleepin' on the groun'—that ain't gettin' in no trouble. That ain't doin' nothin' wrong. That ain't like gettin' drunk or raisin' hell."

Muley laughed. "You'll see. You jus' set here, an' the car'll come. Maybe it's Willy Feeley, an' Willy's a deputy sheriff now. 'What you doin' trespassin' here?' Willy says. Well, you always did know Willy was full a crap, so you says,

'What's it to you?' Willy gets mad an' says, 'You get off or I'll take you in.' An' you ain't gonna let no Feeley push you aroun' 'cause he's mad an' scared. He's made a bluff an' he got to go on with it, an' here's you gettin' tough an' you got to go through—oh, hell, it's a lot easier to lay out in the cotton an' let 'em look. It's more fun, too, 'cause they're mad an' can't do nothin', an' you're out there a-laughin' at 'em. But you jus' talk to Willy or any boss, an' you slug hell out of 'em an' they'll take you in an' run you back to McAlester for three years."

"You're talkin' sense," said Joad. "Ever' word you say is sense. But, Jesus, I hate to get pushed around! I lots rather take a sock at Willy."

"He got a gun," said Muley. "He'll use it 'cause he's a deputy. Then he either got to kill you or you got to get his gun away an' kill him. Come on, Tommy. You can easy tell yourself you're foolin' them lyin' out like that. An' it all just amounts to what you tell yourself." The strong lights angled up into the sky now, and the even drone of a motor could be heard. "Come on, Tommy. Don't have to go far, jus' fourteen-fifteen rows over, an' we can watch what they do."

Tom got to his feet. "By God, you're right!" he said. "I ain't got a thing in the worl' to win, no matter how it comes out."

"Come on, then, over this way." Muley moved around the house and out into the cotton field about fifty yards. "This is good," he said, "Now lay down. You on'y got to pull your head down if they start the spotlight goin'. It's kinda fun." The three men stretched out at full length and propped themselves on their elbows. Muley sprang up and ran toward the house, and in a few moments he came back and threw a bundle of coats and shoes down. "They'd of taken 'em along just to get even," he said. The lights topped the rise and bore down on the house.

Joad asked, "Won't they come out here with flashlights an' look aroun' for us? I wisht I had a stick."

Muley giggled. "No, they won't. I tol' you I'm mean like a weasel. Willy done that one night an' I clipped 'im from behint with a fence stake. Knocked him colder'n a wedge. He tol' later how five guys come at him."

The car drew up to the house and a spotlight snapped on. "Duck," said Muley. The bar of cold white light swung over their heads and crisscrossed the field. The hiding men could not see any movement, but they heard a car door slam and they heard voices. "Scairt to get in the light," Muley whispered. "Once-twice I've took a shot at the headlights. That keeps Willy careful. He got somebody with 'im tonight." They heard footsteps on wood, and then from inside the house they saw the glow of a flashlight. "Shall I shoot through the house?" Muley whispered. "They couldn't see where it come from. Give 'em somepin to think about."

"Sure, go ahead," said Joad.

"Don't do it," Casy whispered. "It won't do no good. Jus' a waste. We got to get thinkin' about doin' stuff that means somepin."

A scratching sound came from near the house. "Puttin' out the fire," Muley whispered. "Kickin' dust over it." The car doors slammed, the headlights swung around and faced the road again. "Now duck!" said Muley. They dropped their heads and the spotlight swept over them and crossed and recrossed the cotton field, and then the car started and slipped away and topped the rise and disappeared.

Muley sat up. "Willy always tries that las' flash. He done it so often I can time 'im. An' he still thinks it's cute."

Casy said, "Maybe they left some fellas at the house. They'd catch us when we come back."

"Maybe. You fellas wait here. I know this game." He walked quietly away, and only a slight crunching of clods could be heard from his passage. The two waiting men tried to hear him, but he had gone. In a moment he called from the house, "They didn't leave nobody. Come on back." Casey and Joad struggled up and walked back toward the black bulk of the house. Muley met them near the smoking dust pile which had been their fire. "I didn' think they'd leave nobody," he said proudly. "Me knockin' Willy over an' takin' a shot at the lights once-twice keeps 'em careful. They ain't sure who it is, an' I ain't gonna let 'em catch me. I don't sleep near no house. If you fellas wanta come along, I'll show you where to sleep, where there ain't nobody gonna stumble over ya."

"Lead off," said Joad. "We'll folla you. I never thought I'd be hidin' out on my old man's place."

Muley set off across the fields, and Joad and Casy followed him. They kicked the cotton plants as they went. "You'll be hidin' from lots of stuff," said Muley. They marched in single file across the fields. They came to a water-cut and slid easily down to the bottom of it.

"By God, I bet I know," cried Joad. "Is it a cave in the bank?"

"That's right. How'd you know?"

"I dug her," said Joad. "Me an' my brother Noah dug her. Lookin' for gold we says we was, but we was jus' diggin' caves like kids always does." The walls of the water-cut were above their heads now. "Ought to be pretty close," said Joad. "Seems to me I remember her pretty close."

Muley said, "I've covered her with bresh. Nobody

couldn't find her." The bottom of the gulch leveled off, and the footing was sand.

Joad settled himself on the clean sand. "I ain't gonna sleep in no cave," he said. "I'm gonna sleep right here." He rolled his coat and put it under his head.

Muley pulled at the covering brush and crawled into his cave. "I like it in here," he called. "I feel like nobody can come at me."

Jim Casy sat down on the sand beside Joad.

"Get some sleep," said Joad. "We'll start for Uncle John's at daybreak."

"I ain't sleepin'," said Casy. "I got too much to puzzle with." He drew up his feet and clasped his legs. He threw back his head and looked at the sharp stars. Joad yawned and brought one hand back under his head. They were silent, and gradually the skittering life of the ground, of holes and burrows, of the brush, began again; the gophers moved, and the rabbits crept to green things, the mice scampered over clods, and the winged hunters moved soundlessly overhead.

Chapter Seven

IN THE towns, on the edges of the towns, in fields, in vacant lots, the used-car yards, the wreckers' yards, the garages with blazoned signs—Used Cars, Good Used Cars. Cheap transportation, three trailers. '27 Ford, clean. Checked cars, guaranteed cars. Free radio. Car with 100 gallons of gas free. Come in and look. Used Cars. No overhead.

A lot and a house large enough for a desk and chair and a blue book. Sheaf of contracts, dog-eared, held with paper clips, and a neat pile of unused contracts. Pen—keep it full, keep it working. A sale's been lost 'cause a pen didn't work.

Those sons-of-bitches over there ain't buying. Every yard gets 'em. They're lookers. Spend all their time looking. Don't want to buy no cars; take up your time. Don't give a damn for your time. Over there, them two people—no, with the kids. Get 'em in a car. Start 'em at two hundred and work down. They look good for one and a quarter. Get 'em rolling. Get 'em out in a jalopy. Sock it to 'em! They took our time.

Owners with rolled-up sleeves. Salesmen, neat, deadly, small intent eyes watching for weaknesses.

Watch the woman's face. If the woman likes it we can screw the old man. Start' em on that Cad'. Then you can work 'em down to that '26 Buick. 'F you start on the Buick, they'll go for a Ford. Roll up your sleeves an' get to work. This ain't gonna last forever. Show 'em that Nash while I get the slow leak pumped up on that '25 Dodge. I'll give you a Hymie when I'm ready.

What you want is transportation, ain't it? No baloney for you. Sure the upholstery is shot. Seat cushions ain't turning no wheels over.

Cars lined up, noses forward, rusty noses, flat tires. Parked close together.

Like to get in to see that one? Sure, no trouble. I'll pull her out of the line.

Get 'em under obligation. Make 'em take up your time. Don't let 'em forget they're takin' your time. People are nice, mostly. They hate to put you out. Make 'em put you out, an' then sock it to 'em.

Cars lined up, Model T's, high and snotty, creaking wheel, worn bands. Buicks, Nashes, De Sotos.

Yes, sir. '22 Dodge. Best goddamn car Dodge ever made. Never wear out. Low compression. High compression got lots a sap for a while, but the metal ain't made that'll hold it for long. Plymouths, Rocknes, Stars.

Jesus, where'd that Apperson come from, the Ark? And a Chalmers and a Chandler—ain't made 'em for years. We ain't sellin' cars—rolling junk. Goddamn it, I got to get jalopies. I don't want nothing for more'n twenty-five, thirty bucks. Sell 'em for fifty, seventy-five. That's a good profit. Christ, what cut do you make on a new car? Get jalopies. I can sell 'em fast as I get 'em. Nothing over two hundred fifty. Jim, corral that old bastard on the sidewalk. Don't know his ass from a hole in the ground. Try him on that Apperson. Say, where is that Apperson? Sold? If we don't get some jalopies we got nothing to sell.

Flags, red and white, white and blue—all along the curb. Used Cars. Good Used Cars.

Today's bargain—up on the platform. Never sell it. Makes folks come in, though. If we sold that bargain at that price we'd hardly make a dime. Tell 'em it's jus' sold. Take out that yard battery before you make delivery. Put in that dumb cell. Christ, what they want for six bits? Roll up your sleeves—pitch in. This ain't gonna last. If I had enough jalopies I'd retire in six months.

Listen, Jim, I heard that Chevvy's rear end. Sounds like bustin' bottles. Squirt in a couple quarts of sawdust. Put some in the gears, too. We got to move that lemon for thirty-five dollars. Bastard cheated me on that one. I offer ten an' he jerks me to fifteen, an' then the son-of-a-bitch took the tools out. God Almighty! I wisht I had five hundred jalopies. This ain't gonna last. He don't like the tires? Tell 'im they got ten thousand in 'em, knock off a buck an' a half.

Piles of rusty ruins against the fence, rows of wrecks in back, fenders, grease-black wrecks, blocks lying on the ground and a pig weed growing up through the cylinders. Brake rods, exhausts, piled like snakes. Grease, gasoline.

See if you can't find a spark plug that ain't cracked. Christ, if I had fifty trailers at under a hundred I'd clean up. What the hell is he kickin' about? We sell 'em, but we don't push 'em home for him. That's good! Don't push 'em home. Get that one in the Monthly, I bet. You don't think he's a prospect? Well, kick 'im out. We got too much to do to bother with a guy that can't make up his mind. Take the right front tire off the Graham. Turn that mended side down. The rest looks swell. Got tread an' everything.

Sure! There's fifty thousan' in that ol' heap yet. Keep plenty oil in. So long. Good luck.

Lookin' for a car? What did you have in mind? See anything attracts you? I'm dry. How about a little snort a good stuff? Come on, while your wife's lookin' at that La Salle. You don't want no La Salle. Bearings shot. Uses too much oil. Got a Lincoln '24. There's a car. Run forever. Make her into a truck.

Hot sun on rusted metal. Oil on the ground. People are wandering in, bewildered, needing a car.

Wipe your feet. Don't lean on that car, it's dirty. How do you buy a car? What does it cost? Watch the children, now. I wonder how much for this one? We'll ask. It don't cost money to ask. We can ask, can't we? Can't pay a nickel over seventy-five, or there won't be enough to get to California.

God, if I could only get a hundred jalopies. I don't care if they run or not.

Tires, used, bruised tires, stacked in tall cylinders; tubes, red, gray, hanging like sausages.

Tire patch? Radiator cleaner? Spark intensifier? Drop this little pill in your gas tank and get ten extra miles to the gallon. Just paint it on—you got a new surface for fifty cents. Wipers, fan belts, gaskets? Maybe it's the valve. Get a new valve stem. What can you lose for a nickel?

All right, Joe. You soften 'em up an' shoot 'em in here. I'll close 'em, I'll deal 'em or I'll kill 'em. Don't send in no bums. I want deals.

Yes, sir, step in. You got a buy there. Yes, sir! At eighty bucks you got a buy.

I can't go no higher than fifty. The fella outside says fifty.

Fifty. Fifty? He's nuts. Paid seventy-eight fifty for that little number. Joe, you crazy fool, you tryin' to bust us? Have to can that guy. I might take sixty. Now look here, mister, I ain't got all day. I'm a business man but I ain't out to stick nobody. Got anything to trade?

Got a pair of mules I'll trade.

Mules! Hey, Joe, hear this? This guy wants to trade mules. Didn't nobody tell you this is the machine age? They don't use mules for nothing but glue no more.

Fine big mules—five and seven years old. Maybe we better look around.

Look around! You come in when we're busy, an' take up our time an' then walk out! Joe, did you know you was talkin' to pikers?

I ain't a piker. I got to get a car. We're goin' to California. I got to get a car.

Well, I'm a sucker. Joe says I'm a sucker. Says if I don't quit givin' my shirt away I'll starve to death. Tell you what I'll do—I can get five bucks apiece for them mules for dog feed.

I wouldn't want them to go for dog feed.

Well, maybe I can get ten or seven maybe. Tell you what we'll do. We'll take your mules for twenty. Wagon goes with 'em, don't it? An' you put up fifty, an' you can sign a contract to send the rest at ten dollars a month.

But you said eighty.

Didn't you never hear about carrying charges and insurance? That just boosts her a little. You'll get her all paid up in four-five months. Sign your name right here. We'll take care of ever'thing.

Well, I don't know——

Now, look here. I'm givin' you my shirt, an' you took all this time. I might a made three sales while I been talkin' to you. I'm disgusted. Yeah, sign right there. All right, sir. Joe, fill up the tank for this gentleman. We'll give him gas.

Jesus, Joe, that was a hot one! What'd we give for that jalopy? Thirty bucks—thirty-five wasn't it? I got that team, an' if I can't get seventy-five for that team, I ain't a business

man. An' I got fifty cash an' a contract for forty more. Oh,
I know they're not all honest, but it'll surprise you how
many kick through with the rest. One guy come through
with a hundred two years after I wrote him off. I bet you
this guy sends the money. Christ, if I could only get five
hundred jalopies! Roll up your sleeves, Joe. Go out an'
soften 'em, an' send 'em in to me. You get twenty on that
last deal. You ain't doing bad.

Limp flags in the afternoon sun. Today's Bargain. '29 Ford
pickup, runs good.

What do you want for fifty bucks—a Zephyr?

Horsehair curling out of seat cushions, fenders battered
and hammered back. Bumpers torn loose and hanging. Fancy
Ford roadster with little colored lights at fender guide, at
radiator cap, and three behind. Mud aprons, and a big die on
the gear-shift lever. Pretty girl on tire cover, painted in color
and named Cora. Afternoon sun on the dusty windshields.

Christ, I ain't had time to go out an' eat! Joe, send a kid
for a hamburger.

Spattering roar of ancient engines.

There's a dumb-bunny lookin' at that Chrysler. Find out
if he got any jack in his jeans. Some a these farm boys is
sneaky. Soften 'em up an' roll 'em in to me, Joe. You're doin'
good.

Sure, we sold it. Guarantee? We guaranteed it to be an
automobile. We didn't guarantee to wet-nurse it. Now listen
here, you—you bought a car, an' now you're squawkin'. I
don't give a damn if you don't make payments. We ain't got
your paper. We turn that over to the finance company.
They'll get after you, not us. We don't hold no paper. Yeah?
Well you jus' get tough an' I'll call a cop. No, we did not
switch the tires. Run 'im outa here, Joe. He bought a car, an'

now he ain't satisfied. How'd you think if I bought a steak an' et half an' try to bring it back? We're runnin' a business, not a charity ward. Can ya imagine that guy, Joe? Say—looka there! Got a Elk's tooth! Run over there. Let 'em glance over that '36 Pontiac. Yeah.

Square noses, round noses, rusty noses, shovel noses, and the long curves of streamlines, and the flat surfaces before streamlining. Bargains Today. Old monsters with deep up-holstery—you can cut her into a truck easy. Two-wheel trailers, axles rusty in the hard afternoon sun. Used Cars. Good Used Cars. Clean, runs good. Don't pump oil.

Christ, look at 'er! Somebody took nice care of 'er.

Cadillacs, La Salles, Buicks, Plymouths, Packards, Chev-vies, Fords, Pontiacs. Row on row, headlights glinting in the afternoon sun. Good Used Cars.

Soften 'em up, Joe. Jesus, I wisht I had a thousand jalopies! Get 'em ready to deal, an' I'll close 'em.

Goin' to California? Here's jus' what you need. Looks shot, but they's thousan's of miles in her.

Lined up side by side. Good Used Cars. Bargains. Clean, runs good.

Chapter Eight

THE SKY grayed among the stars, and the pale, late quarter-moon was insubstantial and thin. Tom Joad and the preacher walked quickly along a road that was only wheel tracks and beaten caterpillar tracks through a cotton field. Only the unbalanced sky showed the approach of dawn, no horizon to the west, and a line to the east. The two men walked in silence and smelled the dust their feet kicked into the air.

"I hope you're dead sure of the way," Jim Casy said. "I'd hate to have the dawn come and us be way to hell an' gone somewhere." The cotton field scurried with waking life, the quick flutter of morning birds feeding on the ground, the scamper over the clods of disturbed rabbits. The quiet thudding of the men's feet in the dust, the squeak of crushed clods under their shoes, sounded against the secret noises of the dawn.

Tom said, "I could shut my eyes an' walk right there. On'y way I can go wrong is think about her. Jus' forget about her, an' I'll go right there. Hell, man, I was born right aroun' in here. I run aroun' here when I was a kid. They's a tree over there—look, you can jus' make it out. Well, once my old man hung up a dead coyote in that tree. Hung there till it was all sort of melted, an' then dropped off. Dried up, like. Jesus, I hope Ma's cookin' somepin. My belly's caved."

"Me too," said Casy. "Like a little eatin' tobacca? Keeps

ya from gettin' too hungry. Been better if we didn' start so damn early. Better if it was light." He paused to gnaw off a piece of plug. "I was sleepin' nice."

"That crazy Muley done it," said Tom. "He got me clear jumpy. Wakes me up an' says, ' 'By, Tom. I'm goin' on. I got places to go.' An' he says, 'Better get goin' too, so's you'll be offa this lan' when the light comes.' He's gettin' screwy as a gopher, livin' like he does. You'd think Injuns was after him. Think he's nuts?"

"Well, I dunno. You seen that car come las' night when we had a little fire. You seen how the house was smashed. They's somepin purty mean goin' on. 'Course Muley's crazy, all right. Creepin' aroun' like a coyote; that's boun' to make him crazy. He'll kill somebody purty soon an' they'll run him down with dogs. I can see it like a prophecy. He'll get worse an' worse. Wouldn' come along with us, you say?"

"No," said Joad. "I think he's scared to see people now. Wonder he come up to us. We'll be at Uncle John's place by sunrise." They walked along in silence for a time, and the late owls flew over toward the barns, the hollow trees, the tank houses, where they hid from daylight. The eastern sky grew fairer and it was possible to see the cotton plants and the graying earth. "Damn' if I know how they're all sleepin' at Uncle John's. He on'y got one room an' a cookin' leanto, an' a little bit of a barn. Must be a mob there now."

The preacher said, "I don't recollect that John had a fambly. Just a lone man, ain't he? I don't recollect much about him."

"Lonest goddamn man in the world," said Joad. "Crazy kind of son-of-a-bitch, too—somepin like Muley, on'y worse in some ways. Might see 'im anywheres—at Shawnee, drunk, or visitin' a widow twenty miles away, or workin' his place with a lantern. Crazy. Ever'body thought he wouldn't live long. A lone man like that don't live long. But Uncle John's older'n Pa. Jus' gets stringier an' meaner ever' year. Meaner'n Grampa."

"Look a the light comin'," said the preacher. "Silverylike. Didn' John never have no fambly?"

"Well, yes, he did, an' that'll show you the kind a fella he is—set in his ways. Pa tells about it. Uncle John, he had a young wife. Married four months. She was in a family way, too, an' one night she gets a pain in her stomick, an' she says, 'You better go for a doctor.' Well, John, he's settin' there, an' he says, 'You just got a stomickache. You et too much. Take a dose a pain killer. You crowd up ya stomick an' ya get a stomickache,' he says. Nex' noon she's outa her head, an' she dies at about four in the afternoon."

"What was it?" Casy asked. "Poisoned from somepin she et?"

"No, somepin jus' bust in her. Ap—appendick or somepin. Well, Uncle John, he's always been a easy-goin' fella, an' he takes it hard. Takes it for a sin. For a long time he won't have nothin' to say to nobody. Just walks aroun' like he don't see nothin', an' he prays some. Took 'im two years to come out of it, an' then he ain't the same. Sort of wild. Made a damn nuisance of hisself. Ever' time one of us kids got worms or a gutache Uncle John brings a doctor out. Pa finally tol' him he got to stop. Kids all the time gettin' a gutache. He figures it's his fault his woman died. Funny fella. He's all the time makin' it up to somebody—givin' kids stuff, droppin' a sack a meal on somebody's porch. Give away about ever'thing he got, an' still he ain't very happy. Gets walkin' around alone at night sometimes. He's a good farmer, though. Keeps his lan' nice."

"Poor fella," said the preacher. "Poor lonely fella. Did he go to church much when his woman died?"

"No, he didn'. Never wanted to get close to folks. Wanted to be off alone. I never seen a kid that wasn't crazy about him. He'd come to our house in the night sometimes, an' we knowed he come 'cause jus' as sure as he come there'd be a pack a gum in the bed right beside ever' one of us. We thought he was Jesus Christ Awmighty."

The preacher walked along, head down. He didn't answer. And the light of the coming morning made his forehead seem to shine, and his hands, swinging beside him, flicked into the light and out again.

Tom was silent too, as though he had said too intimate a thing and was ashamed. He quickened his pace and the preacher kept step. They could see a little into gray distance ahead now. A snake wriggled slowly from the cotton rows into the road. Tom stopped short of it and peered. "Gopher snake," he said. "Let him go." They walked around the snake and went on their way. A little color came into the eastern sky, and almost immediately the lonely dawn light crept over the land. Green appeared on the cotton plants and the earth was gray-brown. The faces of the men lost their gray-ish shine. Joad's face seemed to darken with the growing light. "This is the good time," Joad said softly. "When I was a kid I used to get up an' walk around by myself when it was like this. What's that ahead?"

A committee of dogs had met in the road, in honor of a bitch. Five males, shepherd mongrels, collie mongrels, dogs whose breeds had been blurred by a freedom of social life, were engaged in complimenting the bitch. For each dog sniffed daintily and then stalked to a cotton plant on stiff legs, raised a hind foot ceremoniously and wetted, then went back to smell. Joad and the preacher stopped to watch, and suddenly Joad laughed joyously. "By God!" he said. "By God!" Now all dogs met and hackles rose, and they all growled and stood stiffly, each waiting for the others to start a fight. One dog mounted and, now that it was accomplished, the others gave way and watched with interest, and their tongues were out, and their tongues dripped. The two men walked on. "By God!" Joad said. "I think that up-dog is our Flash. I thought he'd be dead. Come, Flash!" He laughed again. "What the hell, if somebody called me, I wouldn't hear him neither. 'Minds me of a story they tell about Willy Feeley when he was a young fella. Willy was bashful, awful bashful. Well, one day he takes a heifer over to Graves' bull. Ever'body was out but Elsie Graves, and Elsie wasn't bashful at all. Willy, he stood there turnin' red an' he couldn't even talk. Elsie says, 'I know what you come for; the bull's out in back a the barn.' Well, they took the heifer out there an' Willy an' Elsie sat on the fence to watch. Purty soon Willy got feelin' purty fly. Elsie looks over an' says, like she don't know, 'What's a matter, Willy?' Willy's so randy he can't hardly set still. 'By God,' he says, 'by God, I wisht I was a-doin' that!' Elsie says, 'Why not, Willy? It's your heifer.'"

The preacher laughed softly. "You know," he said, "it's a nice thing not bein' a preacher no more. Nobody use' ta tell stories when I was there, or if they did I couldn' laugh. An' I couldn' cuss. Now I cuss all I want, any time I want, an' it does a fella good to cuss if he wants to."

A redness grew up out of the eastern horizon, and on the ground birds began to chirp, sharply. "Look!" said Joad. "Right ahead. That's Uncle John's tank. Can't see the win'mill, but there's his tank. See it against the sky?" He speeded his walk. "I wonder if all the folks are there." The hulk of the tank stood above a rise. Joad, hurrying, raised a cloud of dust about his knees. "I wonder if Ma—" They saw the tank legs now, and the house, a square little box, unpainted and bare, and the barn, low-roofed and huddled. Smoke was rising from the tin chimney of the house. In the yard was a litter, piled furniture, the blades and motor of the windmill, bedsteads, chairs, tables. "Holy Christ, they're fixin' to go!" Joad said. A truck stood in the yard, a truck with high sides, but a strange truck, for while the front of it was a sedan, the top had been cut off in the middle and the truck bed fitted on. And as they drew near, the men could hear pounding from the yard, and as the rim of the blinding sun came up over the horizon, it fell on the truck, and they saw a man and the flash of his hammer as it rose and fell. And the sun flashed on the windows of the house. The weathered boards were bright. Two red chickens on the ground flamed with reflected light.

"Don't yell," said Tom. "Let's creep up on 'em, like," and he walked so fast that the dust rose as high as his waist. And then he came to the edge of the cotton field. Now they were in the yard proper, earth beaten hard, shiny hard, and a few dusty crawling weeds on the ground. And Joad slowed as though he feared to go on. The preacher, watching him, slowed to match his step. Tom sauntered forward, sidled embarrassedly toward the truck. It was a Hudson Super-Six sedan, and the top had been ripped in two with a cold chisel. Old Tom Joad stood in the truck bed and he was nailing on the top rails of the truck sides. His grizzled, bearded face was low over his work, and a bunch of sixpenny nails stuck out of his mouth. He set a nail and his hammer thundered it in. From the house came the clash of a lid on the stove and the wail of a child. Joad sidled up to the truck bed and leaned against it. And his father looked at him and did not see him. His father set another nail and drove it in. A flock of pigeons started from the deck of the tank house and flew around and settled again and strutted to the edge to look over; white pigeons and blue pigeons and grays, with iridescent wings.

Joad hooked his fingers over the lowest bar of the truck side. He looked up at the aging, graying man on the truck. He wet his thick lips with his tongue, and he said softly, "Pa."

"What do you want?" old Tom mumbled around his mouthful of nails. He wore a black, dirty slouch hat and a blue work shirt over which was a buttonless vest; his jeans were held up by a wide harness-leather belt with a big square brass buckle, leather and metal polished from years of wearing; and his shoes were cracked and the soles swollen and boat-shaped from years of sun and wet and dust. The sleeves of his shirt were tight on his forearms, held down by the bulging powerful muscles. Stomach and hips were lean, and legs, short, heavy, and strong. His face, squared by a bristling pepper and salt beard, was all drawn down to the forceful chin, a chin thrust out and built out by the stubble beard which was not so grayed on the chin, and gave weight and force to its thrust. Over old Tom's unwhiskered cheek bones the skin was as brown as meerschaum, and wrinkled in rays around his eye-corners from squinting. His eyes were brown, black-coffee brown, and he thrust his head forward when he looked at a thing, for his bright dark eyes were failing. His lips, from which the big nails protruded, were thin and red.

He held his hammer suspended in the air, about to drive a set nail, and he looked over the truck side at Tom, looked resentful at being interrupted. And then his chin drove forward and his eyes looked at Tom's face, and then gradually his brain became aware of what he saw. The hammer dropped slowly to his side, and with his left hand he took the nails from his mouth. And he said wonderingly, as though he told himself the fact, "It's Tommy—" And then, still informing himself, "It's Tommy come home." His mouth opened again, and a look of fear came into his eyes. "Tommy," he said softly, "you ain't busted out? You ain't got to hide?" He listened tensely.

"Naw," said Tom. "I'm paroled. I'm free. I got my papers." He gripped the lower bars of the truck side and looked up.

Old Tom laid his hammer gently on the floor and put his nails in his pocket. He swung his leg over the side and dropped lithely to the ground, but once beside his son he seemed embarrassed and strange. "Tommy," he said, "we are goin' to California. But we was gonna write you a letter an' tell you." And he said, incredulously, "But you're back. You can go with us. You can go!" The lid of a coffee pot slammed in the house. Old Tom looked over his shoulder. "Le's surprise 'em," he said, and his eyes shone with excitement. "Your ma got a bad feelin' she ain't never gonna see you no more. She got that quiet look like when somebody died. Almost she don't want to go to California, fear she'll never see you no more." A stove lid clashed in the house again. "Le's surprise 'em," old Tom repeated. "Le's go in like you never been away. Le's jus' see what your ma says." At last he touched Tom, but touched him on the shoulder, timidly, and instantly took his hand away. He looked at Jim Casy.

Tom said, "You remember the preacher, Pa. He come along with me."

"He been in prison too?"

"No, I met 'im on the road. He been away."

Pa shook hands gravely. "You're welcome here, sir."

Casy said, "Glad to be here. It's a thing to see when a boy comes home. It's a thing to see."

"Home," Pa said.

"To his folks," the preacher amended quickly. "We stayed at the other place last night."

Pa's chin thrust out, and he looked back down the road for a moment. Then he turned to Tom. "How'll we do her?" he began excitedly. "S'pose I go in an' say, 'Here's some fellas want some breakfast,' or how'd it be if you jus' come in an' stood there till she seen you? How'd that be?" His face was alive with excitement.

"Don't le's give her no shock," said Tom. "Don't le's scare her none."

Two rangy shepherd dogs trotted up pleasantly, until they caught the scent of strangers, and then they backed cautiously away, watchful, their tails moving slowly and tentatively in the air, but their eyes and noses quick for animosity or danger. One of them, stretching his neck, edged forward, ready to run, and little by little he approached Tom's legs and sniffed loudly at them. Then he backed away and watched Pa for some kind of signal. The other pup was not so brave. He looked about for something that could honorably divert his attention, saw a red chicken go mincing by, and ran at it. There was the squawk of an outraged hen, a burst of red feathers, and the hen ran off, flapping stubby wings for speed. The pup looked proudly back at the men, and then flopped down in the dust and beat its tail contentedly on the ground.

"Come on," said Pa, "come on in now. She got to see you. I got to see her face when she sees you. Come on. She'll yell breakfast in a minute. I heard her slap the salt pork in the pan a good time ago." He led the way across the fine-dusted ground. There was no porch on this house, just a step and then the door; a chopping block beside the door, its surface matted and soft from years of chopping. The graining in the sheathing wood was high, for the dust had cut down the softer wood. The smell of burning willow was in the air, and, as the three men neared the door, the smell of frying side-meat and the smell of high brown biscuits and the sharp smell of coffee rolling in the pot. Pa stepped up into the open doorway and stood there blocking it with his wide short body. He said, "Ma, there's a coupla fellas jus' come along the road, an' they wonder if we could spare a bite."

Tom heard his mother's voice, the remembered cool, calm drawl, friendly and humble. "Let 'em come," she said. "We got a'plenty. Tell 'em they got to wash their han's. The bread is done. I'm jus' takin' up the side-meat now." And the sizzle of the angry grease came from the stove.

Pa stepped inside, clearing the door, and Tom looked in at his mother. She was lifting the curling slices of pork from the frying pan. The oven door was open, and a great pan of high brown biscuits stood waiting there. She looked out the door, but the sun was behind Tom, and she saw only a dark figure outlined by the bright yellow sunlight. She nodded pleasantly. "Come in," she said. "Jus' lucky I made plenty bread this morning."

Tom stood looking in. Ma was heavy, but not fat; thick with child-bearing and work. She wore a loose Mother Hubbard of gray cloth in which there had once been colored flowers, but the color was washed out now, so that the small flowered pattern was only a little lighter gray than the background. The dress came down to her ankles, and her strong, broad, bare feet moved quickly and deftly over the floor. Her thin, steel-gray hair was gathered in a sparse wispy knot at the back of her head. Strong, freckled arms were bare to the elbow, and her hands were chubby and delicate, like those of a plump little girl. She looked out into the sunshine. Her full face was not soft; it was controlled, kindly. Her hazel eyes seemed to have experienced all possible tragedy and to have mounted pain and suffering like steps into a high calm and a superhuman understanding. She seemed to know, to accept, to welcome her position, the citadel of the family, the strong place that could not be taken. And since old Tom and the children could not know hurt or fear unless she acknowledged hurt and fear, she had practiced denying them in herself. And since, when a joyful thing happened, they looked to see whether joy was on her, it was her habit to build up laughter out of inadequate materials. But better than joy was calm. Imperturbability could be depended upon. And from her great and humble position in the family she had taken dignity and a clean calm beauty. From her position as healer, her hands had grown sure and cool and quiet; from her position as arbiter she had become as remote and faultless in judgment as a goddess. She seemed to know that if she swayed the family shook, and if she ever really deeply wavered or despaired the family would fall, the family will to function would be gone.

She looked out into the sunny yard, at the dark figure of a man. Pa stood near by, shaking with excitement. "Come in," he cried. "Come right in, mister." And Tom a little shamefacedly stepped over the doorsill.

She looked up pleasantly from the frying pan. And then her hand sank slowly to her side and the fork clattered to the wooden floor. Her eyes opened wide, and the pupils dilated. She breathed heavily through her open mouth. She closed her eyes. "Thank God," she said. "Oh, thank God!" And suddenly her face was worried. "Tommy, you ain't wanted? You didn' bust loose?"

"No, Ma. Parole. I got the papers here." He touched his breast.

She moved toward him lithely, soundlessly in her bare feet, and her face was full of wonder. Her small hand felt his arm, felt the soundness of his muscles. And then her fingers went up to his cheek as a blind man's fingers might. And her joy was nearly like sorrow. Tom pulled his underlip between his teeth and bit it. Her eyes went wonderingly to his bitten lip, and she saw the little line of blood against his teeth and the trickle of blood down his lip. Then she knew, and her control came back, and her hand dropped. Her breath came out explosively. "Well!" she cried. "We come mighty near to goin' without ya. An' we was wonderin' how in the worl' you could ever find us." She picked up the fork and combed the boiling grease and brought out a dark curl of crisp pork. And she set the pot of tumbling coffee on the back of the stove.

Old Tom giggled, "Fooled ya, huh, Ma? We aimed to fool ya, and we done it. Jus' stood there like a hammered sheep. Wisht Grampa'd been here to see. Looked like somebody'd beat ya between the eyes with a sledge. Grampa would a whacked 'imself so hard he'd a throwed his hip out—like he done when he seen Al take a shot at that grea' big airship the army got. Tommy, it come over one day, half a mile big, an' Al gets the thirty-thirty and blazes away at her. Grampa yells, 'Don't shoot no fledglin's, Al; wait till a growed-up one goes over,' an' then he whacked 'imself an' throwed his hip out."

Ma chuckled and took down a heap of tin plates from a shelf.

Tom asked, "Where is Grampa? I ain't seen the ol' devil."

Ma stacked the plates on the kitchen table and piled cups beside them. She said confidentially, "Oh, him an' Granma sleeps in the barn. They got to get up so much in the night. They was stumblin' over the little fellas."

Pa broke in, "Yeah, ever' night Grampa'd get mad. Tumble over Winfield, an' Winfield'd yell, an' Grampa'd get mad an' wet his drawers, an' that'd make him madder, an' purty soon ever'body in the house'd be yellin' their head off." His words tumbled out between chuckles. "Oh, we had lively times. One night when ever'body was yellin' an' a-cussin', your brother Al, he's a smart aleck now, he says, 'Goddamn it, Grampa, why don't you run off an' be a pirate?' Well, that made Grampa so goddamn mad he went for his gun. Al had ta sleep out in the fiel' that night. But now Granma an' Grampa both sleeps in the barn."

Ma said, "They can jus' get up an' step outside when they feel like it. Pa, run on out an' tell 'em Tommy's home. Grampa's a favorite of him."

"A course," said Pa. "I should of did it before." He went out the door and crossed the yard, swinging his hands high.

Tom watched him go, and then his mother's voice called his attention. She was pouring coffee. She did not look at him. "Tommy," she said hesitantly, timidly.

"Yeah?" His timidity was set off by hers, a curious embarrassment. Each one knew the other was shy, and became more shy in the knowledge.

"Tommy, I got to ask you—you ain't mad?"

"Mad, Ma?"

"You ain't poisoned mad? You don't hate nobody? They didn' do nothin' in that jail to rot you out with crazy mad?"

He looked sidewise at her, studied her, and his eyes seemed to ask how she could know such things. "No-o-o," he said. "I was for a little while. But I ain't proud like some fellas. I let stuff run off'n me. What's a matter, Ma?"

Now she was looking at him, her mouth open, as though to hear better, her eyes digging to know better. Her face looked for the answer that is always concealed in language. She said in confusion, "I knowed Purty Boy Floyd. I knowed his ma. They was good folks. He was full a hell, sure, like a good boy oughta be." She paused and then her words poured out. "I don' know all like this—but I know it. He done a little bad thing a' they hurt 'im, caught 'im an' hurt him so he was mad, an' the nex' bad thing he done was mad, an' they hurt 'im again. An' purty soon he was mean-mad. They shot at him like a varmint, an' he shot back, an' then they run him like a coyote, an' him a-snappin' an' a-snarlin', mean as a lobo. An' he was mad. He wasn't no boy or no man no more, he was jus' a walkin' chunk a mean-mad. But the folks that knowed him didn' hurt 'im. He wasn' mad at them. Finally they run him down an' killed 'im. No matter how they say it in the paper how he was bad—that's how it was." She paused and she licked her dry lips, and her whole face was an aching question. "I got to know, Tommy. Did they hurt you so much? Did they make you mad like that?"

Tom's heavy lips were pulled tight over his teeth. He looked down at his big flat hands. "No," he said. "I ain't like that." He paused and studied the broken nails, which were ridged like clam shells. "All the time in stir I kep' away from stuff like that. I ain' so mad."

She sighed, "Thank God!" under her breath.

He looked up quickly. "Ma, when I seen what they done to our house——"

She came near to him then, and stood close; and she said passionately, "Tommy, don't you go fightin' 'em alone. They'll hunt you down like a coyote. Tommy, I got to thinkin' an' dreamin' an' wonderin'. They say there's a hun-'erd thousand of us shoved out. If we was all mad the same way, Tommy—they wouldn't hunt nobody down—" She stopped.

Tommy, looking at her, gradually drooped his eyelids, until just a short glitter showed through his lashes. "Many folks feel that way?" he demanded.

"I don' know. They're jus' kinda stunned. Walk aroun' like they was half asleep."

From outside and across the yard came an ancient creaking bleat. "Pu-raise Gawd fur vittory! Pu-raise Gawd fur vittory!"

Tom turned his head and grinned. "Granma finally heard I'm home. Ma," he said, "you never was like this before!"

Her face hardened and her eyes grew cold. "I never had my house pushed over," she said. "I never had my fambly stuck out on the road. I never had to sell—ever'thing— Here they come now." She moved back to the stove and dumped the big pan of bulbous biscuits on two tin plates. She shook flour into the deep grease to make gravy, and her hand was white with flour. For a moment Tom watched her, and then he went to the door.

Across the yard came four people. Grampa was ahead, a lean, ragged, quick old man, jumping with quick steps and favoring his right leg—the side that came out of joint. He was buttoning his fly as he came, and his old hands were hav-ing trouble finding the buttons, for he had buttoned the top button into the second buttonhole, and that threw the whole sequence off. He wore dark ragged pants and a torn blue shirt, open all the way down, and showing long gray underwear, also unbuttoned. His lean white chest, fuzzed with white hair, was visible through the opening in his underwear. He gave up the fly and left it open and fumbled with the underwear buttons, then gave the whole thing up and hitched his brown suspenders. His was a lean excitable face with little bright eyes as evil as a frantic child's eyes. A cantankerous, complaining, mischievous, laughing face. He fought and argued, told dirty stories. He was as lecherous as always. Vicious and cruel and impatient, like a frantic child, and the whole structure overlaid with amusement. He drank too much when he could get it, ate too much when it was there, talked too much all the time.

Behind him hobbled Granma, who had survived only because she was as mean as her husband. She had held her own with a shrill ferocious religiosity that was as lecherous and as savage as anything Grampa could offer. Once, after a meeting, while she was still speaking in tongues, she fired both barrels of a shotgun at her husband, ripping one of his buttocks nearly off, and after that he admired her and did not try to torture her as children torture bugs. As she walked she hiked her Mother Hubbard up to her knees, and she bleated her shrill terrible war cry: "Pu-raise Gawd fur vittory."

Granma and Grampa raced each other to get across the broad yard. They fought over everything, and loved and needed the fighting.

Behind them, moving slowly and evenly, but keeping up, came Pa and Noah—Noah the first-born, tall and strange, walking always with a wondering look on his face, calm and puzzled. He had never been angry in his life. He looked in wonder at angry people, wonder and uneasiness, as normal people look at the insane. Noah moved slowly, spoke seldom, and then so slowly that people who did not know him often thought him stupid. He was not stupid, but he was strange. He had little pride, no sexual urges. He worked and slept in a curious rhythm that nevertheless sufficed him. He was fond of his folks, but never showed it in any way. Although an observer could not have told why, Noah left the impression of being misshapen, his head or his body or his legs or his mind; but no misshapen member could be recalled. Pa thought he knew why Noah was strange, but Pa was ashamed, and never told. For on the night when Noah was born, Pa, frightened at the spreading thighs, alone in the house, and horrified at the screaming wretch his wife had become, went mad with apprehension. Using his hands, his strong fingers for forceps, he had pulled and twisted the baby. The midwife, arriving late, had found the baby's head pulled out of shape, its neck stretched, its body warped; and she had pushed the head back and molded the body with her hands. But Pa always remembered, and was ashamed. And he was kinder to Noah than to the others. In Noah's broad face, eyes too far apart, and long fragile jaw, Pa thought he saw the twisted, warped skull of the baby. Noah could do all that was required of him, could read and write, could work and figure, but he didn't seem to care; there was a listlessness in him toward things people wanted and needed. He lived in a strange silent house and looked out of it through calm eyes. He was a stranger to all the world, but he was not lonely.

The four came across the yard, and Grampa demanded, "Where is he? Goddamn it, where is he?" And his fingers fumbled for his pants button, and forgot and strayed into his pocket. And then he saw Tom standing in the door. Grampa stopped and he stopped the others. His little eyes glittered with malice. "Lookut him," he said. "A jailbird. Ain't been no Joads in jail for a hell of a time." His mind jumped. "Got no right to put 'im in jail. He done just what I'd do. Sons-a-bitches got no right." His mind jumped again. "An' ol' Turnbull, stinkin' skunk, braggin' how he'll shoot ya when ya come out. Says he got Hatfield blood. Well, I sent word to him. I says, 'Don't mess around with no Joad. Maybe I got McCoy blood for all I know.' I says, 'You lay your sights anywheres near Tommy an' I'll take it an' I'll ram it up your ass,' I says. Scairt 'im, too."

Granma, not following the conversation, bleated, "Pu-raise Gawd fur vittory."

Grampa walked up and slapped Tom on the chest, and his eyes grinned with affection and pride. "How are ya, Tommy?"

"O.K." said Tom. "How ya keepin' yaself?"

"Full a piss an' vinegar," said Grampa. His mind jumped. "Jus' like I said, they ain't a gonna keep no Joad in jail. I says, 'Tommy'll come a-bustin' outa that jail like a bull through a corral fence.' An' you done it. Get outa my way, I'm hungry." He crowded past, sat down, loaded his plate with pork and two big biscuits and poured the thick gravy over the whole mess, and before the others could get in, Grampa's mouth was full.

Tom grinned affectionately at him. "Ain't he a heller?" he said. And Grampa's mouth was so full that he couldn't even splutter, but his mean little eyes smiled, and he nodded his head violently.

Granma said proudly, "A wicketer, cussin'er man never lived. He's goin' to hell on a poker, praise Gawd! Wants to drive the truck!" she said spitefully. "Well, he ain't goin' ta."

Grampa choked, and a mouthful of paste sprayed into his lap, and he coughed weakly.

Granma smiled up at Tom. "Messy, ain't he?" she observed brightly.

Noah stood on the step, and he faced Tom, and his wide-set eyes seemed to look around him. His face had little expression. Tom said, "How ya, Noah?"

"Fine," said Noah. "How a' you?" That was all, but it was a comfortable thing.

Ma waved the flies away from the bowl of gravy. "We ain't got room to set down," she said. "Jus' get yaself a plate an' set down wherever ya can. Out in the yard or someplace."

Suddenly Tom said, "Hey! Where's the preacher? He was right here. Where'd he go?"

Pa said, "I seen him, but he's gone."

And Granma raised a shrill voice, "Preacher? You got a preacher? Go git him. We'll have a grace." She pointed at Grampa. "Too late for him—he's et. Go git the preacher."

Tom stepped out on the porch. "Hey, Jim! Jim Casy!" he called. He walked out in the yard. "Oh, Casy!" The preacher emerged from under the tank, sat up, and then stood up and moved toward the house. Tom asked, "What was you doin', hidin'?"

"Well, no. But a fella shouldn' butt his head in where a fambly got fambly stuff. I was jus' settin' a-thinkin'."

"Come on in an' eat," said Tom. "Granma wants a grace."

"But I ain't a preacher no more," Casy protested.

"Aw, come on. Give her a grace. Don't do you no harm, an' she likes 'em." They walked into the kitchen together.

Ma said quietly, "You're welcome."

And Pa said, "You're welcome. Have some breakfast."

"Grace fust," Granma clamored. "Grace fust."

Grampa focused his eyes fiercely until he recognized Casy. "Oh, that preacher," he said. "Oh, he's all right. I always liked him since I seen him—" He winked so lecherously that Granma thought he had spoken and retorted, "Shut up, you sinful ol' goat."

Casy ran his fingers through his hair nervously. "I got to tell you, I ain't a preacher no more. If me jus' bein' glad to be here an' bein' thankful for people that's kind and gener- ous, if that's enough—why, I'll say that kinda grace. But I ain't a preacher no more."

"Say her," said Granma. "An' get in a word about us goin' to California." The preacher bowed his head, and the others bowed their heads. Ma folded her hands over her stomach and bowed her head. Granma bowed so low that her nose was nearly in her plate of biscuit and gravy. Tom, lean- ing against the wall, a plate in his hand, bowed stiffly, and Grampa bowed his head sidewise, so that he could keep one mean and merry eye on the preacher. And on the preacher's face there was a look not of prayer, but of thought; and in his tone not supplication, but conjecture.

"I been thinkin'," he said. "I been in the hills, thinkin', almost you might say like Jesus went into the wilderness to think His way out of a mess of troubles."

"Pu-raise Gawd!" Granma said, and the preacher glanced over at her in surprise.

"Seems like Jesus got all messed up with troubles, and He

couldn't figure nothin' out, an' He got to feelin' what the hell good is it all, an' what's the use fightin' an' figurin'. Got tired, got good an' tired, an' His sperit all wore out. Jus' about come to the conclusion, the hell with it. An' so He went off into the wilderness."

"A—men," Granma bleated. So many years she had timed her responses to the pauses. And it was so many years since she had listened to or wondered at the words used.

"I ain't sayin' I'm like Jesus," the preacher went on. "But I got tired like Him, an' I got mixed up like Him, an' I went into the wilderness like Him, without no campin' stuff. Nighttime I'd lay on my back an' look up at the stars; morning I'd set an' watch the sun come up; midday I'd look out from a hill at the rollin' dry country; evenin' I'd foller the sun down. Sometimes I'd pray like I always done. On'y I couldn' figure what I was prayin' to or for. There was the hills, an' there was me, an' we wasn't separate no more. We was one thing. An' that one thing was holy."

"Hallelujah," said Granma, and she rocked a little, back and forth, trying to catch hold of an ecstasy.

"An' I got thinkin', on'y it wasn't thinkin', it was deeper down than thinkin'. I got thinkin' how we was holy when we was one thing, an' mankin' was holy when it was one thing. An' it on'y got unholy when one mis'able little fella got the bit in his teeth an' run off his own way, kickin' an' draggin' an' fightin'. Fella like that bust the holiness. But when they're all workin' together, not one fella for another fella, but one fella kind of harnessed to the whole shebang— that's right, that's holy. An' then I got thinkin' I don't even know what I mean by holy." He paused, but the bowed heads stayed down, for they had been trained like dogs to rise at the "amen" signal. "I can't say no grace like I use' ta say. I'm glad of the holiness of breakfast. I'm glad there's love here. That's all." The heads stayed down. The preacher looked around. "I've got your breakfast cold," he said; and then he remembered. "Amen," he said, and all the heads rose up.

"A—men," said Granma, and she fell to her breakfast, and broke down the soggy biscuits with her hard old toothless gums. Tom ate quickly, and Pa crammed his mouth. There was no talk until the food was gone, the coffee drunk; only the crunch of chewed food and the slup of coffee cooled in transit to the tongue. Ma watched the preacher as he ate, and her eyes were questioning, probing and understanding. She watched him as though he were suddenly a spirit, not human any more, a voice out of the ground.

The men finished and put down their plates, and drained the last of their coffee; and then the men went out, Pa and the preacher and Noah and Grampa and Tom, and they walked over to the truck, avoiding the litter of furniture, the wooden bedsteads, the windmill machinery, the old plow. They walked to the truck and stood beside it. They touched the new pine side-boards.

Tom opened the hood and looked at the big greasy engine. And Pa came up beside him. He said, "Your brother Al looked her over before we bought her. He says she's all right."

"What's he know? He's just a squirt," said Tom.

"He worked for a company. Drove truck last year. He knows quite a little. Smart aleck like he is. He knows. He can tinker an engine, Al can."

Tom asked, "Where's he now?"

"Well," said Pa, "he's a-billygoatin' aroun' the country. Tom-cattin' hisself to death. Smart-aleck sixteen-year-older, an' his nuts is just a-eggin' him on. He don't think of nothin' but girls and engines. A plain smart aleck. Ain't been in nights for a week."

Grampa, fumbling with his chest, had succeeded in buttoning the buttons of his blue shirt into the buttonholes of his underwear. His fingers felt that something was wrong, but did not care enough to find out. His fingers went down to try to figure out the intricacies of the buttoning of his fly. "I was worse," he said happily. "I was much worse. I was a heller, you might say. Why, they was a camp meetin' right in Sallisaw when I was a young fella a little bit older'n Al. He's just a squirt, an' punkin-soft. But I was older. An' we was to this here camp meetin'. Five hunderd folks there, an' a proper sprinklin' of young heifers."

"You look like a heller yet, Grampa," said Tom.

"Well, I am, kinda. But I ain't nowheres near the fella I was. Jus' let me get out to California where I can pick me an orange when I want it. Or grapes. There's a thing I ain't never had enough of. Gonna get me a whole big bunch a grapes off a bush, or whatever, an' I'm gonna squash 'em on my face an' let 'em run offen my chin."

Tom asked, "Where's Uncle John? Where's Rosasharn? Where's Ruthie an' Winfield? Nobody said nothin' about them yet."

Pa said, "Nobody asked. John gone to Sallisaw with a load a stuff to sell: pump, tools, chickens, an' all the stuff we brung over. Took Ruthie an' Winfield with 'im. Went 'fore daylight."

"Funny I never saw him," said Tom.

"Well, you come down from the highway, didn' you? He took the back way, by Cowlington. An' Rosasharn, she's nestin' with Connie's folks. By God! You don't even know

Rosasharn's married to Connie Rivers. You 'member Connie. Nice young fella. An' Rosasharn's due 'bout three-four-five months now. Swellin' up right now. Looks fine."

"Jesus!" said Tom. "Rosasharn was just a little kid. An' now she's gonna have a baby. So damn much happens in four years if you're away. When ya think to start out west, Pa?"

"Well, we got to take this stuff in an' sell it. If Al gets back from his squirtin' aroun', I figgered he could load the truck an' take all of it in, an' maybe we could start out tomorra or day after. We ain't got so much money, an' a fella says it's damn near two thousan' miles to California. Quicker we get started, surer it is we get there. Money's a-dribblin' out all the time. You got any money?"

"On'y a couple dollars. How'd you get money?"

"Well," said Pa, "we sol' all the stuff at our place, an' the whole bunch of us chopped cotton, even Grampa."

"Sure did," said Grampa.

"We put ever'thing together—two hunderd dollars. We give seventy-five for this here truck, an' me an' Al cut her in two an' built on this here back. Al was gonna grind the valves, but he's too busy messin' aroun' to get down to her. We'll have maybe a hunderd an' fifty when we start. Damn ol' tires on this here truck ain't gonna go far. Got a couple of wore out spares. Pick stuff up along the road, I guess."

The sun, driving straight down, stung with its rays. The shadows of the truck bed were dark bars on the ground, and the truck smelled of hot oil and oilcloth and paint. The few chickens had left the yard to hide in the tool shed from the sun. In the sty the pigs lay panting, close to the fence where a thin shadow fell, and they complained shrilly now and then. The two dogs were stretched in the red dust under the truck, panting, their dripping tongues covered with dust. Pa pulled his hat low over his eyes and squatted down on his hams. And, as though this were his natural position of thought and observation, he surveyed Tom critically, the new but aging cap, the suit, and the new shoes.

"Did you spen' your money for them clothes?" he asked. "Them clothes are jus' gonna be a nuisance to ya."

"They give 'em to me," said Tom. "When I come out they give 'em to me." He took off his cap and looked at it with some admiration, then wiped his forehead with it and put it on rakishly and pulled at the visor.

Pa observed, "Them's a nice-lookin' pair a shoes they give ya."

"Yeah," Joad agreed. "Purty for nice, but they ain't no shoes to go walkin' aroun' in on a hot day." He squatted beside his father.

Noah said slowly, "Maybe if you got them side-boards all true on, we could load up this stuff. Load her up so maybe if Al comes in——"

"I can drive her, if that's what you want," Tom said. "I drove truck at McAlester."

"Good," said Pa, and then his eyes stared down the road. "If I ain't mistaken, there's a young smart aleck draggin' his tail home right now," he said. "Looks purty wore out, too."

Tom and the preacher looked up the road. And randy Al, seeing he was being noticed, threw back his shoulders, and he came into the yard with a swaying strut like that of a rooster about to crow. Cockily, he walked close before he recognized Tom; and when he did, his boasting face changed, and admiration and veneration shone in his eyes, and his swagger fell away. His stiff jeans, with the bottoms turned up eight inches to show his heeled boots, his three-inch belt with copper figures on it, even the red arm bands on his blue shirt and the rakish angle of his Stetson hat could not build him up to his brother's stature; for his brother had killed a man, and no one would ever forget it. Al knew that even he had inspired some admiration among boys of his own age because his brother had killed a man. He had heard in Sallisaw how he was pointed out: "That's Al Joad. His brother killed a fella with a shovel."

And now Al, moving humbly near, saw that his brother was not a swaggerer as he had supposed. Al saw the dark brooding eyes of his brother, and the prison calm, the smooth hard face trained to indicate nothing to a prison guard, neither resistance nor slavishness. And instantly Al changed. Unconsciously he became like his brother, and his handsome face brooded, and his shoulders relaxed. He hadn't remembered how Tom was.

Tom said, "Hello, Al. Jesus, you're growin' like a bean! I wouldn't of knowed you."

Al, his hand ready if Tom should want to shake it, grinned self-consciously. Tom stuck out his hand and Al's hand jerked out to meet it. And there was liking between these two. "They tell me you're a good hand with a truck," said Tom.

And Al, sensing that his brother would not like a boaster, said, "I don't know nothin' much about it."

Pa said, "Been smart-alecking aroun' the country. You look wore out. Well, you got to take a load of stuff into Sallisaw to sell."

Al looked at his brother Tom. "Care to ride in?" he said as casually as he could.

"No, I can't," said Tom. "I'll help aroun' here. We'll be—together on the road."

Al tried to control his question. "Did—did you bust out? Of jail?"

"No," said Tom. "I got paroled."

"Oh." And Al was a little disappointed.

Chapter Nine

IN THE little houses the tenant people sifted their belongings and the belongings of their fathers and of their grandfathers. Picked over their possessions for the journey to the west. The men were ruthless because the past had been spoiled, but the women knew how the past would cry to them in the coming days. The men went into the barns and the sheds.

That plow, that harrow, remember in the war we planted mustard? Remember a fella wanted us to put in that rubber bush they call guayule? Get rich, he said. Bring out those tools—get a few dollars for them. Eighteen dollars for that plow, plus freight—Sears Roebuck.

Harness, carts, seeders, little bundles of hoes. Bring 'em out. Pile 'em up. Load 'em in the wagon. Take 'em to town. Sell 'em for what you can get. Sell the team and the wagon, too. No more use for anything.

Fifty cents isn't enough to get for a good plow. That seeder cost thirty-eight dollars. Two dollars isn't enough. Can't haul it all back— Well, take it, and a bitterness with it. Take the well pump and the harness. Take halters, collars, hames, and tugs. Take the little glass brow-band jewels, roses red under glass. Got those for the bay gelding. 'Member how he lifted his feet when he trotted?

Junk piled up in a yard.

Can't sell a hand plow any more. Fifty cents for the weight of the metal. Disks and tractors, that's the stuff now.

Well, take it—all junk—and give me five dollars. You're not buying only junk, you're buying junked lives. And more— you'll see—you're buying bitterness. Buying a plow to plow your own children under, buying the arms and spirits that might have saved you. Five dollars, not four. I can't haul 'em back— Well, take 'em for four. But I warn you, you're buying what will plow your own children under. And you won't see. You can't see. Take 'em for four. Now, what'll you give for the team and wagon? Those fine bays, matched they are, matched in color, matched the way they walk, stride to stride. In the stiff pull—straining hams and buttocks, split-second timed together. And in the morning, the light on them, bay light. They look over the fence sniffing for us, and the stiff ears swivel to hear us, and the black forelocks! I've got a girl. She likes to braid the manes and forelocks, puts little red bows on them. Likes to do it. Not any more. I could tell you a funny story about that girl and that off bay. Would make you laugh. Off horse is eight, near is ten, but might of been twin colts the way they work together. See? The teeth. Sound all over. Deep lungs. Feet fair and clean. How much? Ten dollars? For both? And the wagon— Oh, Jesus Christ! I'd shoot 'em for dog feed first. Oh, take 'em! Take 'em quick, mister. You're buying a little girl plaiting the forelocks, taking off her hair ribbon to make bows, standing back, head cocked, rubbing the soft noses with her cheek. You're buying years of work, toil in the sun; you're buying a sorrow that can't talk. But watch it, mister. There's a premium goes with this pile of junk and the bay horses—so beautiful—a packet of bitterness to grow in your house and to flower, some day. We could have saved you, but you cut us down, and soon you will be cut down and there'll be none of us to save you.

And the tenant men came walking back, hands in their pockets, hats pulled down. Some bought a pint and drank it fast to make the impact hard and stunning. But they didn't laugh and they didn't dance. They didn't sing or pick the guitars. They walked back to the farms, hands in pockets and heads down, shoes kicking the red dust up.

Maybe we can start again, in the new rich land—in California, where the fruit grows. We'll start over.

But you can't start. Only a baby can start. You and me— why, we're all that's been. The anger of a moment, the thousand pictures, that's us. This land, this red land, is us; and the flood years and the dust years and the drought years are us. We can't start again. The bitterness we sold to the junk man—he got it all right, but we have it still. And when the owner men told us to go, that's us; and when the tractor hit the house, that's us until we're dead. To California or any place—every one a drum major leading a parade of hurts, marching with our bitterness. And some day—the armies of bitterness will all be going the same way. And they'll all walk together, and there'll be a dead terror from it.

The tenant men scuffed home to the farms through the red dust.

When everything that could be sold was sold, stoves and bedsteads, chairs and tables, little corner cupboards, tubs and tanks, still there were piles of possessions; and the women sat among them, turning them over and looking off beyond and back, pictures, square glasses, and here's a vase.

Now you know well what we can take and what we can't take. We'll be camping out—a few pots to cook and wash in, and mattresses and comforts, lantern and buckets, and a piece of canvas. Use that for a tent. This kerosene can. Know what that is? That's the stove. And clothes—take all the clothes.

And—the rifle? Wouldn't go out naked of a rifle. When shoes and clothes and food, when even hope is gone, we'll have the rifle. When grampa came—did I tell you?—he had pepper and salt and a rifle. Nothing else. That goes. And a bottle for water. That just about fills us. Right up the sides of the trailer, and the kids can set in the trailer, and granma on a mattress. Tools, a shovel and saw and wrench and pliers. An ax, too. We had that ax forty years. Look how she's wore down. And ropes, of course. The rest? Leave it—or burn it up.

And the children came.

If Mary takes that doll, that dirty rag doll, I got to take my Injun bow. I got to. An' this roun' stick—big as me. I might need this stick. I had this stick so long—a month, or maybe a year. I got to take it. And what's it like in California?

The women sat among the doomed things, turning them over and looking past them and back. This book. My father had it. He liked a book. *Pilgrim's Progress*. Used to read it. Got his name in it. And his pipe—still smells rank. And this picture—an angel. I looked at that before the fust three come —didn't seem to do much good. Think we could get this china dog in? Aunt Sadie brought it from the St. Louis Fair. See? Wrote right on it. No, I guess not. Here's a letter my brother wrote the day before he died. Here's an old-time hat. These feathers—never got to use them. No, there isn't room.

How can we live without our lives? How will we know it's us without our past? No. Leave it. Burn it.

They sat and looked at it and burned it into their memories. How'll it be not to know what land's outside the door? How if you wake up in the night and know—and *know* the willow tree's not there? Can you live without the willow tree? Well, no, you can't. The willow tree is you. The pain on that mattress there—that dreadful pain—that's you.

And the children—if Sam takes his Injun bow an' his long roun' stick, I get to take two things. I choose the fluffy pilla. That's mine.

Suddenly they were nervous. Got to get out quick now. Can't wait. We can't wait. And they piled up the goods in the yards and set fire to them. They stood and watched them burning, and then frantically they loaded up the cars and drove away, drove in the dust. The dust hung in the air for a long time after the loaded cars had passed.

Chapter Ten

WHEN the truck had gone, loaded with implements, with heavy tools, with beds and springs, with every movable thing that might be sold, Tom hung around the place. He mooned into the barn shed, into the empty stalls, and he walked into the implement lean-to and kicked the refuse that was left, turned a broken mower tooth with his foot. He visited places he remembered —the red bank where the swallows nested, the willow tree over the pig pen. Two shoats grunted and squirmed at him through the fence, black pigs, sunning and comfortable. And then his pilgrimage was over, and he went to sit on the doorstep where the shade was lately fallen. Behind him Ma moved about in the kitchen, washing children's clothes in a bucket; and her strong freckled arms dripped soapsuds from the elbows. She stopped her rubbing when he sat down. She looked at him a long time, and at the back of his head when he turned and stared out at the hot sunlight. And then she went back to her rubbing.

She said, "Tom, I hope things is all right in California."

He turned and looked at her. "What makes you think they ain't?" he asked.

"Well—nothing. Seems too nice, kinda. I seen the han'bills fellas pass out, an' how much work they is, an' high wages an' all; an' I seen in the paper how they want folks to come an' pick grapes an' oranges an' peaches. That'd be nice work, Tom, pickin' peaches. Even if they wouldn't let you eat none, you could maybe snitch a little ratty one sometimes. An' it'd be nice under the trees, workin' in the shade. I'm scared of stuff so nice. I ain't got faith. I'm scared somepin ain't so nice about it."

Tom said, "Don't roust your faith bird-high an' you won't do no crawlin' with the worms."

"I know that's right. That's Scripture, ain't it?"

"I guess so," said Tom. "I never could keep Scripture straight sence I read a book name' *The Winning of Barbara Worth.*"

Ma chuckled lightly and scrounged the clothes in and out of the bucket. And she wrung out overalls and shirts, and the muscles of her forearms corded out. "Your Pa's pa, he quoted Scripture all the time. He got it all roiled up, too. It was the *Dr. Miles' Almanac* he got mixed up. Used to read ever' word in that almanac out loud—letters from folks that couldn't sleep or had lame backs. An' later he'd give them people for a lesson, an' he'd say, 'That's a par'ble from Scripture.' Your Pa an' Uncle John troubled 'im some about it when they'd laugh." She piled wrung clothes like cord wood on the table. "They say it's two thousan' miles where we're goin'. How far ya think that is, Tom? I seen it on a map, big mountains like on a post card, an' we're goin' right through 'em. How long ya s'pose it'll take to go that far, Tommy?"

"I dunno," he said. "Two weeks, maybe ten days if we got luck. Look, Ma, stop your worryin'. I'm a-gonna tell you somepin about bein' in the pen. You can't go thinkin' when you're gonna be out. You'd go nuts. You got to think about that day, an' then the nex' day, about the ball game Sat'dy.

That's what you got to do. Ol' timers does that. A new young fella gets buttin' his head on the cell door. He's thinkin' how long it's gonna be. Whyn't you do that? Jus' take ever' day."

"That's a good way," she said, and she filled up her bucket with hot water from the stove, and she put in dirty clothes and began punching them down into the soapy water. "Yes, that's a good way. But I like to think how nice it's gonna be, maybe, in California. Never cold. An' fruit ever'place, an' people just bein' in the nicest places, little white houses in among the orange trees. I wonder—that is, if we all get jobs an' all work—maybe we can get one of them little white houses. An' the little fellas go out an' pick oranges right off the tree. They ain't gonna be able to stand it, they'll get to yellin' so."

Tom watched her working, and his eyes smiled. "It done you good jus' thinkin' about it. I knowed a fella from California. He didn't talk like us. You'd of knowed he come from some far-off place jus' the way he talked. But he says they's too many folks lookin' for work right there now. An' he says the folks that pick the fruit live in dirty ol' camps an' don't hardly get enough to eat. He says wages is low an' hard to get any."

A shadow crossed her face. "Oh, that ain't so," she said. "Your father got a han'bill on yella paper, tellin' how they need folks to work. They wouldn' go to that trouble if they wasn't plenty work. Costs 'em good money to get them han'-bills out. What'd they want ta lie for, an' costin' 'em money to lie?"

Tom shook his head. "I don' know, Ma. It's kinda hard to think why they done it. Maybe—" He looked out at the hot sun, shining on the red earth.

"Maybe what?"

"Maybe it's nice, like you says. Where'd Grampa go? Where'd the preacher go?"

Ma was going out of the house, her arms loaded high with the clothes. Tom moved aside to let her pass. "Preacher says he's gonna walk aroun'. Grampa's asleep here in the house. He comes in here in the day an' lays down sometimes." She walked to the line and began to drape pale blue jeans and blue shirts and long gray underwear over the wire.

Behind him Tom heard a shuffling step, and he turned to look in. Grampa was emerging from the bedroom, and as in the morning, he fumbled with the buttons of his fly. "I heerd talkin'," he said. "Sons-a-bitches won't let a ol' fella sleep. When you bastards get dry behin' the ears, you'll maybe learn to let a ol' fella sleep." His furious fingers managed to flip open the only two buttons on his fly that had been buttoned. And his hand forgot what it had been trying to do. His hand reached in and contentedly scratched under the testicles. Ma came in with wet hands, and her palms puckered and bloated from hot water and soap.

"Thought you was sleepin'. Here, let me button you up." And though he struggled, she held him and buttoned his underwear and his shirt and his fly. "You go aroun' a sight," she said, and let him go.

And he spluttered angrily, "Fella's come to a nice—to a nice—when somebody buttons 'em. I want ta be let be to button my own pants."

Ma said playfully, "They don't let people run aroun' with their clothes unbutton' in California."

"They don't, hey! Well, I'll show 'em. They think they're gonna show me how to act out there? Why, I'll go aroun' a-hangin' out if I wanta!"

Ma said, "Seems like his language gets worse ever' year. Showin' off, I guess."

The old man thrust out his bristly chin, and he regarded Ma with his shrewd, mean, merry eyes. "Well, sir," he said, "we'll be a-startin' 'fore long now. An', by God, they's grapes out there, just a-hangin' over inta the road. Know what I'm a-gonna do? I'm gonna pick me a wash tub full a grapes, an' I'm gonna set in 'em, an' scrooge aroun', an' let the juice run down my pants."

Tom laughed. "By God, if he lives to be two hunderd you never will get Grampa house broke," he said. "You're all set on goin', ain't you, Grampa?"

The old man pulled out a box and sat down heavily on it. "Yes, sir," he said. "An' goddamn near time, too. My brother went on out there forty years ago. Never did hear nothin' about him. Sneaky son-of-a-bitch, he was. Nobody loved him. Run off with a single-action Colt of mine. If I ever run across him or his kids, if he got any out in California, I'll ask 'em for that Colt. But if I know 'im, an' he got any kids, he cuckoo'd 'em, an' somebody else is a-raisin' 'em. I sure will be glad to get out there. Got a feelin' it'll make a new fella outa me. Go right to work in the fruit."

Ma nodded. "He means it, too," she said. "Worked right up to three months ago, when he throwed his hip out the last time."

"Damn right," said Grampa.

Tom looked outward from his seat on the doorstep. "Here comes that preacher, walkin' aroun' from the back side a the barn."

Ma said, "Curiousest grace I ever heerd, that he give this mornin'. Wasn't hardly no grace at all. Jus' talkin', but the sound of it was like a grace."

"He's a funny fella," said Tom. "Talks funny all the time. Seems like he's talkin' to hisself, though. He ain't tryin' to put nothin' over."

"Watch the look in his eye," said Ma. "He looks baptized. Got that look they call lookin' through. He sure looks baptized. An' a-walkin' with his head down, a-starin' at nothin' on the groun'. There *is* a man that's baptized." And she was silent, for Casy had drawn near the door.

"You gonna get sun-shook, walkin' around like that," said Tom.

Casy said, "Well, yeah—maybe." He appealed to them all suddenly, to Ma and Grampa and Tom. "I got to get goin' west. I got to go. I wonder if I kin go along with you folks." And then he stood, embarrassed by his own speech.

Ma looked to Tom to speak, because he was a man, but Tom did not speak. She let him have the chance that was his right, and then she said, "Why, we'd be proud to have you. 'Course I can't say right now; Pa says all the men'll talk tonight and figger when we gonna start. I guess maybe we better not say till all the men come. John an' Pa an' Noah an' Tom an' Grampa an' Al an' Connie, they're gonna figger soon's they get back. But if they's room I'm pretty sure we'll be proud to have ya."

The preacher sighed. "I'll go anyways," he said. "Somepin's happening. I went up an' I looked, an' the houses is all empty, an' the lan' is empty, an' this whole country is empty. I can't stay here no more. I got to go where the folks is goin'. I'll work in the fiel's, an' maybe I'll be happy."

"An' you ain't gonna preach?" Tom asked.

"I ain't gonna preach."

"An' you ain't gonna baptize?" Ma asked.

"I ain't gonna baptize. I'm gonna work in the fiel's, in the green fiel's, an' I'm gonna be near to folks. I ain't gonna try to teach 'em nothin'. I'm gonna try to learn. Gonna learn why the folks walks in the grass, gonna hear 'em talk, gonna hear 'em sing. Gonna listen to kids eatin' mush. Gonna hear husban' an' wife a-poundin' the mattress in the night. Gonna eat with 'em an' learn." His eyes were wet and shining. "Gonna lay in the grass, open an' honest with anybody that'll have me. Gonna cuss an' swear an' hear the poetry of folks talkin'. All that's holy, all that's what I didn' understan'. All them things is the good things."

Ma said, "A-men."

The preacher sat humbly down on the chopping block beside the door. "I wonder what they is for a fella so lonely."

Tom coughed delicately. "For a fella that don't preach no more—" he began.

"Oh, I'm a talker!" said Casy. "No gettin' away from that. But I ain't preachin'. Preachin' is tellin' folks stuff. I'm askin' 'em. That ain't preachin', is it?"

"I don' know," said Tom. "Preachin's a kinda tone a voice, an' preachin's a way a lookin' at things. Preachin's bein' good to folks when they wanna kill ya for it. Las' Christmus in McAlester, Salvation Army come an' done us good. Three solid hours a cornet music, an' we set there. They was bein' nice to us. But if one of us tried to walk out, we'd a-drawed solitary. That's preachin'. Doin' good to a fella that's down an' can't smack ya in the puss for it. No, you ain't no preacher. But don't you blow no cornets aroun' here."

Ma threw some sticks into the stove. "I'll get you a bite now, but it ain't much."

Grampa brought his box outside and sat on it and leaned against the wall, and Tom and Casy leaned back against the house wall. And the shadow of the afternoon moved out from the house.

In the late afternoon the truck came back, bumping and rattling through the dust, and there was a layer of dust in the bed, and the hood was covered with dust, and the headlights were obscured with a red flour. The sun was setting when the truck came back, and the earth was bloody in its setting light. Al sat bent over the wheel, proud and serious and efficient, and Pa and Uncle John, as befitted the heads of the clan, had the honor seats beside the driver. Standing in the truck bed, holding onto the bars of the sides, rode the others, twelve-year-old Ruthie and ten-year-old Winfield, grime-faced and wild, their eyes tired but excited, their fingers and the edges of their mouths black and sticky from licorice whips, whined out of their father in town. Ruthie, dressed in a real dress of pink muslin that came below her knees, was a little serious in her young-ladiness. But Winfield was still a trifle of a snot-nose, a little of a brooder back of the barn, and an inveterate collector and smoker of snipes. And whereas Ruthie felt the might, the responsibility, and the dignity of her developing breasts, Winfield was kid-wild and calfish. Beside them, clinging lightly to the bars, stood Rose of Sharon, and she balanced, swaying on the balls of her feet, and took up the road shock in her knees and hams. For Rose of Sharon was pregnant and careful. Her hair, braided and wrapped around her head, made an ash-blond crown. Her round soft face, which had been voluptuous and inviting a few months ago, had already put on the barrier of pregnancy, the self-sufficient smile, the knowing perfection-look; and her plump body—full soft breasts and stomach, hard hips and buttocks that had swung so freely and provocatively as to invite slapping and stroking—her whole body had become demure and serious. Her whole thought and action were directed inward on the baby. She balanced on her toes now, for the baby's sake. And the world was pregnant to her; she thought only in terms of reproduction and of motherhood. Connie, her nineteen-year-old husband, who had married a plump, passionate hoyden, was still frightened and bewildered at the change in her; for there were no more cat fights in bed, biting and scratching with muffled giggles and final tears. There was a balanced, careful, wise creature who smiled shyly but very firmly at him. Connie was proud and fearful of Rose of Sharon. Whenever he could, he put a hand on her or stood close, so that his body touched her at hip and shoulder, and he felt that this kept a relation that might be departing. He was a sharp-faced, lean young man of a Texas strain, and his pale blue eyes were sometimes dangerous and sometimes kindly, and sometimes frightened. He was a good hard worker and would make a good husband. He drank enough, but not too much; fought when it was required of him; and never boasted. He sat quietly in a gathering and yet managed to be there and to be recognized.

Had he not been fifty years old, and so one of the natural rulers of the family, Uncle John would have preferred not to sit in the honor place beside the driver. He would have liked Rose of Sharon to sit there. This was impossible, because she was young and a woman. But Uncle John sat uneasily, his lonely haunted eyes were not at ease, and his thin strong body was not relaxed. Nearly all the time the barrier of loneliness cut Uncle John off from people and from appetites. He ate little, drank nothing, and was celibate. But underneath, his appetites swelled into pressures until they

broke through. Then he would eat of some craved food until
he was sick; or he would drink jake or whisky until he was
a shaken paralytic with red wet eyes; or he would raven with
lust for some whore in Sallisaw. It was told of him that once
he went clear to Shawnee and hired three whores in one
bed, and snorted and rutted on their unresponsive bodies for
an hour. But when one of his appetites was sated, he was sad
and ashamed and lonely again. He hid from people, and by
gifts tried to make up to all people for himself. Then he
crept into houses and left gum under pillows for children;
then he cut wood and took no pay. Then he gave away any
possession he might have: a saddle, a horse, a new pair of
shoes. One could not talk to him then, for he ran away, or if
confronted hid within himself and peeked out of frightened
eyes. The death of his wife, followed by months of being
alone, had marked him with guilt and shame and had left an
unbreaking loneliness on him.

But there were things he could not escape. Being one of
the heads of the family, he had to govern; and now he had
to sit on the honor seat beside the driver.

The three men on the seat were glum as they drove
toward home over the dusty road. Al, bending over the
wheel, kept shifting eyes from the road to the instrument
panel, watching the ammeter needle, which jerked suspiciously, watching the oil gauge and the heat indicator.
And his mind was cataloguing weak points and suspicious
things about the car. He listened to the whine, which might
be the rear end, dry; and he listened to tappets lifting and
falling. He kept his hand on the gear lever, feeling the turning gears through it. And he had let the clutch out against
the brake to test for slipping clutch plates. He might be a
musking goat sometimes, but this was his responsibility, this

truck, its running, and its maintenance. If something went wrong it would be his fault, and while no one would say it, everyone, and Al most of all, would know it was his fault. And so he felt it, watched it, and listened to it. And his face was serious and responsible. And everyone respected him and his responsibility. Even Pa, who was the leader, would hold a wrench and take orders from Al.

They were all tired on the truck. Ruthie and Winfield were tired from seeing too much movement, too many faces, from fighting to get licorice whips; tired from the excitement of having Uncle John secretly slip gum into their pockets.

And the men in the seat were tired and angry and sad, for they had got eighteen dollars for every movable thing from the farm: the horses, the wagon, the implements, and all the furniture from the house. Eighteen dollars. They had assailed the buyer, argued; but they were routed when his interest seemed to flag and he had told them he didn't want the stuff at any price. Then they were beaten, believed him, and took two dollars less than he had first offered. And now they were weary and frightened because they had gone against a system they did not understand and it had beaten them. They knew the team and the wagon were worth much more. They knew the buyer man would get much more, but they didn't know how to do it. Merchandising was a secret to them.

Al, his eyes darting from road to panel board, said, "That fella, he ain't a local fella. Didn' talk like a local fella. Clothes was different, too."

And Pa explained, "When I was in the hardware store I talked to some men I know. They say there's fellas comin' in jus' to buy up the stuff us fellas got to sell when we get

out. They say these new fellas is cleaning up. But there ain't
nothin' we can do about it. Maybe Tommy should of went.
Maybe he could of did better."

John said, "But the fella wasn't gonna take it at all. We
couldn' haul it back."

"These men I know told about that," said Pa. "Said the
buyer fellas always done that. Scairt folks that way. We jus'
don' know how to go about stuff like that. Ma's gonna be disappointed. She'll be mad an' disappointed."

Al said, "When ya think we're gonna go, Pa?"

"I dunno. We'll talk her over tonight an' decide. I'm sure
glad Tom's back. That makes me feel good. Tom's a good
boy."

Al said, "Pa, some fellas was talkin' about Tom, an' they
says he's parole'. An' they says that means he can't go outside
the State, or if he goes, an' they catch him, they send 'im
back for three years."

Pa looked startled. "They said that? Seem like fellas that
knowed? Not jus' blowin' off?"

"I don' know," said Al. "They was just a-talkin' there, an'
I didn' let on he's my brother. I jus' stood an' took it in."

Pa said, "Jesus Christ, I hope that ain't true! We need
Tom. I'll ask 'im about that. We got trouble enough without
they chase the hell out of us. I hope it ain't true. We got to
talk that out in the open."

Uncle John said, "Tom, he'll know."

They fell silent while the truck battered along. The engine was noisy, full of little clashings, and the brake rods
banged. There was a wooden creaking from the wheels, and
a thin jet of steam escaped through a hole in the top of the
radiator cap. The truck pulled a high whirling column of
red dust behind it. They rumbled up the last little rise while

the sun was still half-face above the horizon, and they bore down on the house as it disappeared. The brakes squealed when they stopped, and the sound printed in Al's head—no lining left.

Ruthie and Winfield climbed yelling over the side walls and dropped to the ground. They shouted, "Where is he? Where's Tom?" And then they saw him standing beside the door, and they stopped, embarrassed, and walked slowly toward him and looked shyly at him.

And when he said, "Hello, how you kids doin'?" they replied softly, "Hello! All right." And they stood apart and watched him secretly, the great brother who had killed a man and been in prison. They remembered how they had played prison in the chicken coop and fought for the right to be prisoner.

Connie Rivers lifted the high tail-gate out of the truck and got down and helped Rose of Sharon to the ground; and she accepted it nobly, smiling her wise, self-satisfied smile, mouth tipped at the corners a little fatuously.

Tom said, "Why, it's Rosasharn. I didn' know you was comin' with them."

"We was walkin'," she said. "The truck come by an' picked us up." And then she said, "This is Connie, my husband." And she was grand, saying it.

The two shook hands, sizing each other up, looking deeply into each other; and in a moment each was satisfied, and Tom said, "Well, I see you been busy."

She looked down. "You do not see, not yet."

"Ma tol' me. When's it gonna be?"

"Oh, not for a long time! Not till nex' winter."

Tom laughed. "Gonna get 'im bore in a orange ranch,

huh? In one a them white houses with orange trees all aroun'."

Rose of Sharon felt her stomach with both her hands. "You do not see," she said, and she smiled her complacent smile and went into the house. The evening was hot, and the thrust of light still flowed up from the western horizon. And without any signal the family gathered by the truck, and the congress, the family government, went into session.

The film of evening light made the red earth lucent, so that its dimensions were deepened, so that a stone, a post, a building had greater depth and more solidity than in the day-time light; and these objects were curiously more individual —a post was more essentially a post, set off from the earth it stood in and the field of corn it stood out against. And plants were individuals, not the mass of crop; and the ragged willow tree was itself, standing free of all other willow trees. The earth contributed a light to the evening. The front of the gray, paintless house, facing the west, was luminous as the moon is. The gray dusty truck, in the yard before the door, stood out magically in this light, in the overdrawn perspective of a stereopticon.

The people too were changed in the evening, quieted. They seemed to be a part of an organization of the unconscious. They obeyed impulses which registered only faintly in their thinking minds. Their eyes were inward and quiet, and their eyes, too, were lucent in the evening, lucent in dusty faces.

The family met at the most important place, near the truck. The house was dead, and the fields were dead; but this truck was the active thing, the living principle. The ancient Hudson, with bent and scarred radiator screen, with grease in dusty globules at the worn edges of every moving part, with hub caps gone and caps of red dust in their places —this was the new hearth, the living center of the family; half passenger car and half truck, high-sided and clumsy.

Pa walked around the truck, looking at it, and then he squatted down in the dust and found a stick to draw with. One foot was flat to the ground, the other rested on the ball and slightly back, so that one knee was higher than the other. Left forearm rested on the lower, left, knee; the right elbow on the right knee, and the right fist cupped for the chin. Pa squatted there, looking at the truck, his chin in his cupped fist. And Uncle John moved toward him and squatted down beside him. Their eyes were brooding. Grampa came out of the house and saw the two squatting together, and he jerked over and sat on the running board of the truck, facing them. That was the nucleus. Tom and Connie and Noah strolled in and squatted, and the line was a half-circle with Grampa in the opening. And then Ma came out of the house, and Granma with her, and Rose of Sharon behind, walking daintily. They took their places behind the squatting men; they stood up and put their hands on their hips. And the children, Ruthie and Winfield, hopped from foot to foot beside the women; the children squidged their toes in the red dust, but they made no sound. Only the preacher was not there. He, out of delicacy, was sitting on the ground behind the house. He was a good preacher and knew his people.

The evening light grew softer, and for a while the family sat and stood silently. Then Pa, speaking to no one, but to the group, made his report. "Got skinned on the stuff we sold. The fella knowed we couldn't wait. Got eighteen dollars only."

Ma stirred restively, but she held her peace.

Noah, the oldest son, asked, "How much, all added up, we got?"

Pa drew figures in the dust and mumbled to himself for a moment. "Hunderd fifty-four," he said. "But Al here says we gonna need better tires. Says these here won't last."

This was Al's first participation in the conference. Always he had stood behind with the women before. And now he made his report solemnly. "She's old an' she's ornery," he said gravely. "I gave the whole thing a good goin'-over 'fore we bought her. Didn' listen to the fella talkin' what a hell of a bargain she was. Stuck my finger in the differential and they wasn't no sawdust. Opened the gear box an' they wasn't no sawdust. Test' her clutch an' rolled her wheels for line. Went under her an' her frame ain't splayed none. She never been rolled. Seen they was a cracked cell in her battery an' made the fella put in a good one. The tires ain't worth a damn, but they're a good size. Easy to get. She'll ride like a bull calf, but she ain't shootin' no oil. Reason I says buy her is she was a pop'lar car. Wreckin' yards is full a Hudson Super-Sixes, an' you can buy parts cheap. Could a got a bigger, fancier car for the same money, but parts too hard to get, an' too dear. That's how I figgered her anyways." The last was his submission to the family. He stopped speaking and waited for their opinions.

Grampa was still the titular head, but he no longer ruled. His position was honorary and a matter of custom. But he did have the right of first comment, no matter how silly his old mind might be. And the squatting men and the standing women waited for him. "You're all right, Al," Grampa said. "I was a squirt jus' like you, a-fartin' aroun' like a dog-wolf.

But when they was a job, I done it. You've growed up good." He finished in the tone of a benediction, and Al reddened a little with pleasure.

Pa said, "Sounds right-side-up to me. If it was horses we wouldn' have to put the blame on Al. But Al's the on'y automobile fella here."

Tom said, "I know some. Worked some in McAlester. Al's right. He done good." And now Al was rosy with the compliment. Tom went on, "I'd like to say—well, that preacher —he wants to go along." He was silent. His words lay in the group, and the group was silent. "He's a nice fella," Tom added. "We've knowed him a long time. Talks a little wild sometimes, but he talks sensible." And he relinquished the proposal to the family.

The light was going gradually. Ma left the group and went into the house, and the iron clang of the stove came from the house. In a moment she walked back to the brooding council.

Grampa said, "They was two ways a thinkin'. Some folks use' ta figger that a preacher was poison luck."

Tom said, "This fella says he ain't a preacher no more."

Grampa waved his hand back and forth. "Once a fella's a preacher, he's always a preacher. That's somepin you can't get shut of. They was some folks figgered it was a good respectable thing to have a preacher along. Ef somebody died, preacher buried 'em. Weddin' come due, or overdue, an' there's your preacher. Baby come, an' you got a christener right under the roof. Me, I always said they was preachers *an'* preachers. Got to pick 'em. I kinda like this fella. He ain't stiff."

Pa dug his stick into the dust and rolled it between his fingers so that it bored a little hole. "They's more to this than is he lucky, or is he a nice fella," Pa said. "We got to figger close. It's a sad thing to figger close. Le's see, now. There's Grampa an' Granma—that's two. An' me an' John an' Ma— that's five. An' Noah an' Tommy an' Al—that's eight. Rosasharn an' Connie is ten, an' Ruthie an' Winfiel' is twelve. We got to take the dogs 'cause what'll we do else? Can't shoot a good dog, an' there ain't nobody to give 'em to. An' that's fourteen."

"Not countin' what chickens is left, an' two pigs," said Noah.

Pa said, "I aim to get those pigs salted down to eat on the way. We gonna need meat. Carry the salt kegs right with us. But I'm wonderin' if we can all ride, an' the preacher too. An' kin we feed a extra mouth?" Without turning his head he asked, "Kin we, Ma?"

Ma cleared her throat. "It ain't kin we? It's will we?" she said firmly. "As far as 'kin,' we can't do nothin', not go to California or nothin'; but as far as 'will,' why, we'll do what we will. An' as far as 'will'—it's a long time our folks been here and east before, an' I never heerd tell of no Joads or no Hazletts, neither, ever refusin' food an' shelter or a lift on the road to anybody that asked. They's been mean Joads, but never that mean."

Pa broke in, "But s'pose there just ain't room?" He had twisted his neck to look up at her, and he was ashamed. Her tone had made him ashamed. "S'pose we jus' can't all get in the truck?"

"There ain't room now," she said. "There ain't room for more'n six, an' twelve is goin' sure. One more ain't gonna hurt; an' a man, strong an' healthy, ain't never no burden. An' any time when we got two pigs an' over a hunderd dollars, an' we wonderin' if we kin feed a fella—" She stopped, and Pa turned back, and his spirit was raw from the whipping.

Granma said, "A preacher is a nice thing to be with us. He give a nice grace this morning."

Pa looked at the face of each one for dissent, and then he said, "Want to call 'im over, Tommy? If he's goin', he ought ta be here."

Tom got up from his hams and went toward the house, calling, "Casy—oh, Casy!"

A muffled voice replied from behind the house. Tom walked to the corner and saw the preacher sitting back against the wall, looking at the flashing evening star in the light sky. "Calling me?" Casy asked.

"Yeah. We think long as you're goin' with us, you ought to be over with us, helpin' to figger things out."

Casy got to his feet. He knew the government of families, and he knew he had been taken into the family. Indeed his position was eminent, for Uncle John moved sideways, leaving space between Pa and himself for the preacher. Casy squatted down like the others, facing Grampa enthroned on the running board.

Ma went to the house again. There was a screech of a lantern hood and the yellow light flashed up in the dark kitchen. When she lifted the lid of the big pot, the smell of boiling side-meat and beet greens came out the door. They waited for her to come back across the darkening yard, for Ma was powerful in the group.

Pa said, "We got to figger when to start. Sooner the better. What we got to do 'fore we go is get them pigs slaughtered an' in salt, an' pack our stuff an' go. Quicker the better, now."

Noah agreed, "If we pitch in, we kin get ready tomorrow, an' we kin go bright the nex' day."

Uncle John objected, "Can't chill no meat in the heat a the day. Wrong time a year for slaughterin'. Meat'll be sof' if it don' chill."

"Well, le's do her tonight. She'll chill tonight some. Much as she's gonna. After we eat, le's get her done. Got salt?"

Ma said, "Yes. Got plenty salt. Got two nice kegs, too."

"Well, le's get her done, then," said Tom.

Grampa began to scrabble about, trying to get a purchase to arise. "Gettin' dark," he said. "I'm gettin' hungry. Come time we get to California I'll have a big bunch a grapes in my han' all the time, a-nibblin' off it all the time, by God!" He got up, and the men arose.

Ruthie and Winfield hopped excitedly about in the dust, like crazy things. Ruthie whispered hoarsely to Winfield, "Killin' pigs *and* goin' to California. Killin' pigs *and* goin'— all the same time."

And Winfield was reduced to madness. He stuck his finger against his throat, made a horrible face, and wobbled about, weakly shrilling, "I'm a ol' pig. Look! I'm a ol' pig. Look at the blood, Ruthie!" And he staggered and sank to the ground, and waved arms and legs weakly.

But Ruthie was older, and she knew the tremendousness of the time. "*And* goin' to California," she said again. And she knew this was the great time in her life so far.

The adults moved toward the lighted kitchen through the deep dusk, and Ma served them greens and side-meat in tin plates. But before Ma ate, she put the big round wash tub on the stove and started the fire to roaring. She carried buckets of water until the tub was full, and then around the tub she clustered the buckets, full of water. The kitchen became a swamp of heat, and the family ate hurriedly, and went out to sit on the doorstep until the water should get hot. They sat looking out at the dark, at the square of light the kitchen lantern threw on the ground outside the door, with a hunched shadow of Grampa in the middle of it. Noah picked his teeth thoroughly with a broom straw. Ma and Rose of Sharon washed up the dishes and piled them on the table.

And then, all of a sudden, the family began to function. Pa got up and lighted another lantern. Noah, from a box in the kitchen, brought out the bow-bladed butchering knife and whetted it on a worn little carborundum stone. And he laid the scraper on the chopping block, and the knife beside it. Pa brought two sturdy sticks, each three feet long, and pointed the ends with the ax, and he tied strong ropes, double half-hitched, to the middle of the sticks.

He grumbled, "Shouldn't of sold those singletrees—all of 'em."

The water in the pots steamed and rolled.

Noah asked, "Gonna take the water down there or bring the pigs up here?"

"Pigs up here," said Pa. "You can't spill a pig and scald yourself like you can hot water. Water about ready?"

"Jus' about," said Ma.

"Aw right. Noah, you an' Tom an' Al come along. I'll carry the light. We'll slaughter down there an' bring 'em up here."

Noah took his knife, and Al the ax, and the four men moved down on the sty, their legs flickering in the lantern light. Ruthie and Winfield skittered along, hopping over the ground. At the sty Pa leaned over the fence, holding the lantern. The sleepy young pigs struggled to their feet, grunting suspiciously. Uncle John and the preacher walked down to help.

"All right," said Pa. "Stick 'em, an' we'll run 'em up and bleed an' scald at the house." Noah and Tom stepped over the fence. They slaughtered quickly and efficiently. Tom struck twice with the blunt head of the ax; and Noah, leaning over the felled pigs, found the great artery with his curving knife and released the pulsing streams of blood. Then over the fence with the squealing pigs. The preacher and Uncle John dragged one by the hind legs, and Tom and Noah the other. Pa walked along with the lantern, and the black blood made two trails in the dust.

At the house, Noah slipped his knife between tendon and bone of the hind legs; the pointed sticks held the legs apart, and the carcasses were hung from the two-by-four rafters that stuck out from the house. Then the men carried the boiling water and poured it over the black bodies. Noah slit the bodies from end to end and dropped the entrails out on the ground. Pa sharpened two more sticks to hold the bodies open to the air, while Tom with the scrubber and Ma with a dull knife scraped the skins to take out the bristles. Al brought a bucket and shoveled the entrails into it, and dumped them on the ground away from the house, and two cats followed him, mewing loudly, and the dogs followed him, growling lightly at the cats.

Pa sat on the doorstep and looked at the pigs hanging in the lantern light. The scraping was done now, and only a few drops of blood continued to fall from the carcasses into the black pool on the ground. Pa got up and went to the pigs and felt them with his hand, and then he sat down again. Granma and Grampa went toward the barn to sleep, and Grampa carried a candle lantern in his hand. The rest of the family sat quietly about the doorstep, Connie and Al and Tom on the ground, leaning their backs against the house wall, Uncle John on a box, Pa in the doorway. Only Ma and Rose of Sharon continued to move about. Ruthie and Winfield were sleepy now, but fighting it off. They quarreled sleepily out in the darkness. Noah and the preacher squatted side by side, facing the house. Pa scratched himself nervously, and took off his hat and ran his fingers through his hair. "Tomorra we'll get that pork salted early in the morning, an' then we'll get the truck loaded, all but the beds, an' nex' morning off we'll go. Hardly is a day's work in all that," he said uneasily.

Tom broke in, "We'll be moonin' aroun' all day, lookin' for somepin to do." The group stirred uneasily. "We could get ready by daylight an' go," Tom suggested. Pa rubbed his knee with his hand. And the restiveness spread to all of them.

Noah said, "Prob'ly wouldn' hurt that meat to git her right down in salt. Cut her up, she'd cool quicker anyways."

It was Uncle John who broke over the edge, his pressures too great. "What we hangin' aroun' for? I want to get shut of this. Now we're goin', why don't we go?"

And the revulsion spread to the rest. "Whyn't we go? Get sleep on the way." And a sense of hurry crept into them.

Pa said, "They say it's two thousan' miles. That's a hell of a long ways. We oughta go. Noah, you an' me can get that meat cut up an' we can put all the stuff in the truck."

Ma put her head out of the door. "How about if we forgit somepin, not seein' it in the dark?"

"We could look 'round after daylight," said Noah. They sat still then, thinking about it. But in a moment Noah got up and began to sharpen the bow-bladed knife on his little worn stone. "Ma," he said, "git that table cleared." And he stepped to a pig, cut a line down one side of the backbone and began peeling the meat forward, off the ribs.

Pa stood up excitedly. "We got to get the stuff together," he said. "Come on, you fellas."

Now that they were committed to going, the hurry infected all of them. Noah carried the slabs of meat into the kitchen and cut it into small salting blocks, and Ma patted the coarse salt in, laid it piece by piece in the kegs, careful that no two pieces touched each other. She laid the slabs like bricks, and pounded salt in the spaces. And Noah cut up the side-meat and he cut up the legs. Ma kept her fire going, and as Noah cleaned the ribs and the spines and leg bones of all the meat he could, she put them in the oven to roast for gnawing purposes.

In the yard and in the barn the circles of lantern light moved about, and the men brought together all the things to be taken, and piled them by the truck. Rose of Sharon brought out all the clothes the family possessed: the overalls, the thick-soled shoes, the rubber boots, the worn best suits, the sweaters and sheepskin coats. And she packed these tightly into a wooden box and got into the box and tramped them down. And then she brought out the print dresses and shawls, the black cotton stockings and the children's clothes —small overalls and cheap print dresses—and she put these in the box and tramped them down.

Tom went to the tool shed and brought what tools were left to go, a hand saw and a set of wrenches, a hammer and a box of assorted nails, a pair of pliers and a flat file and a set of rat-tail files.

And Rose of Sharon brought out the big piece of tarpaulin and spread it on the ground behind the truck. She struggled through the door with the mattresses, three double ones and a single. She piled them on the tarpaulin and brought arm-loads of folded ragged blankets and piled them up.

Ma and Noah worked busily at the carcasses, and the smell of roasting pork bones came from the stove. The children had fallen by the way in the late night. Winfield lay curled up in the dust outside the door; and Ruthie, sitting on a box in the kitchen where she had gone to watch the butchering, had dropped her head back against the wall. She breathed easily in her sleep, and her lips were parted over her teeth.

Tom finished with the tools and came into the kitchen with his lantern, and the preacher followed him. "God in a buckboard," Tom said, "smell that meat! An' listen to her crackle."

Ma laid the bricks of meat in a keg and poured salt around and over them and covered the layer with salt and patted it down. She looked up at Tom and smiled a little at him, but her eyes were serious and tired. "Be nice to have pork bones for breakfas'," she said.

The preacher stepped beside her. "Leave me salt down this meat," he said. "I can do it. There's other stuff for you to do."

She stopped her work then and inspected him oddly, as though he suggested a curious thing. And her hands were crusted with salt, pink with fluid from the fresh pork. "It's women's work," she said finally.

"It's all work," the preacher replied. "They's too much of it to split it up to men's or women's work. You got stuff to do. Leave me salt the meat."

Still for a moment she stared at him, and then she poured water from a bucket into the tin wash basin and she washed her hands. The preacher took up the blocks of pork and patted on the salt while she watched him. And he laid them in the kegs as she had. Only when he had finished a layer and covered it carefully and patted down the salt was she satisfied. She dried her bleached and bloated hands.

Tom said, "Ma, what stuff we gonna take from here?"

She looked quickly about the kitchen. "The bucket," she said. "All the stuff to eat with: plates an' the cups, the spoons an' knives an' forks. Put all them in that drawer, an' take the drawer. The big fry pan an' the big stew kettle, the coffee pot. When it gets cool, take the rack outa the oven. That's good over a fire. I'd like to take the wash tub, but I guess there ain't room. I'll wash clothes in the bucket. Don't do no good to take little stuff. You can cook little stuff in a big kettle, but you can't cook big stuff in a little pot. Take the bread pans, all of 'em. They fit down inside each other." She stood and looked about the kitchen. "You jus' take that stuff I tol' you, Tom. I'll fix up the rest, the big can a pepper an' the salt an' the nutmeg an' the grater. I'll take all that stuff jus' at the last." She picked up a lantern and walked heavily into the bedroom, and her bare feet made no sound on the floor.

The preacher said, "She looks tar'd."

"Women's always tar'd," said Tom. "That's just the way women is, 'cept at meetin' once an' again."

"Yeah, but tar'der'n that. Real tar'd, like she's sick-tar'd."

Ma was just through the door, and she heard his words. Slowly her relaxed face tightened, and the lines disappeared from the taut muscular face. Her eyes sharpened and her shoulders straightened. She glanced about the stripped room. Nothing was left in it except trash. The mattresses which had been on the floor were gone. The bureaus were sold. On the floor lay a broken comb, an empty talcum powder can, and a few dust mice. Ma set her lantern on the floor. She reached behind one of the boxes that had served as chairs and brought out a stationery box, old and soiled and cracked at the corners. She sat down and opened the box. Inside were letters, clippings, photographs, a pair of earrings, a little gold signet ring, and a watch chain braided of hair and tipped with gold swivels. She touched the letters with her fingers, touched them lightly, and she smoothed a newspaper clipping on which there was an account of Tom's trial. For a long time she held the box, looking over it, and her fingers disturbed the letters and then lined them up again. She bit her lower lip, thinking, remembering. And at last she made up her mind. She picked out the ring, the watch charm, the earrings, dug under the pile and found one gold cuff link. She took a letter from an envelope and dropped the trinkets in the envelope. She folded the envelope over and put it in her dress pocket. Then gently and tenderly she closed the box and smoothed the top carefully with her fingers. Her lips parted. And then she stood up, took her lantern, and went back into the kitchen. She lifted the stove lid and laid the box gently among the coals. Quickly the heat browned the paper. A flame licked up and over the box. She replaced the stove lid and instantly the fire sighed up and breathed over the box.

Out in the dark yard, working in the lantern light, Pa and Al loaded the truck. Tools on the bottom, but handy to reach in case of a breakdown. Boxes of clothes next, and kitchen utensils in a gunny sack; cutlery and dishes in their box. Then the gallon bucket tied on behind. They made the bottom of the load as even as possible, and filled the spaces between boxes with rolled blankets. Then over the top they laid the mattresses, filling the truck in level. And last they spread the big tarpaulin over the load and Al made holes in the edge, two feet apart, and inserted little ropes, and tied it down to the side-bars of the truck.

"Now, if it rains," he said, "we'll tie it to the bar above, an' the folks can get underneath, out of the wet. Up front we'll be dry enough."

And Pa applauded. "That's a good idear."

"That ain't all," Al said. "First chance I git I'm gonna fin' a long plank an' make a ridge pole, an' put the tarp over that. An' then it'll be covered in, an' the folks'll be outa the sun, too."

And Pa agreed, "That's a good idear. Whyn't you think a that before?"

"I ain't had time," said Al.

"Ain't had time? Why, Al, you had time to coyote all over the country. God knows where you been this las' two weeks."

"Stuff a fella got to do when he's leavin' the country," said Al. And then he lost some of his assurance. "Pa," he asked. "You glad to be goin', Pa?"

"Huh? Well—sure. Leastwise—yeah. We had hard times here. 'Course it'll be all different out there—plenty work, an' ever'thing nice an' green, an' little white houses an' oranges growin' aroun'."

"Is it all oranges ever'where?"

"Well, maybe not ever'where, but plenty places."

The first gray of daylight began in the sky. And the work was done—the kegs of pork ready, the chicken coop ready to go on top. Ma opened the oven and took out the pile of roasted bones, crisp and brown, with plenty of gnawing meat left. Ruthie half awakened, and slipped down from the box, and slept again. But the adults stood around the door, shivering a little and gnawing at the crisp pork.

"Guess we oughta wake up Granma an' Grampa," Tom said. "Gettin' along on toward day."

Ma said, "Kinda hate to, till the las' minute. They need the sleep. Ruthie an' Winfield ain't hardly got no real rest neither."

"Well, they kin all sleep on top a the load," said Pa. "It'll be nice an' comf'table there."

Suddenly the dogs started up from the dust and listened. And then, with a roar, went barking off into the darkness. "Now what in hell is that?" Pa demanded. In a moment they heard a voice speaking reassuringly to the barking dogs and the barking lost its fierceness. Then footsteps, and a man approached. It was Muley Graves, his hat pulled low.

He came near timidly. "Morning, folks," he said.

"Why, Muley." Pa waved the ham bone he held. "Step in an' get some pork for yourself, Muley."

"Well, no," said Muley. "I ain't hungry, exactly."

"Oh, get it, Muley, get it. Here!" And Pa stepped into the house and brought out a hand of spareribs.

"I wasn't aiming to eat none a your stuff," he said. "I was jus' walkin' aroun', an' I thought how you'd be goin', an' I'd maybe say good-by."

"Goin' in a little while now," said Pa. "You'd a missed us if you'd come an hour later. All packed up—see?"

"All packed up." Muley looked at the loaded truck. "Sometimes I wisht I'd go an' fin' my folks."

Ma asked, "Did you hear from 'em out in California?"

"No," said Muley, "I ain't heard. But I ain't been to look in the post office. I oughta go in sometimes."

Pa said, "Al, go down, wake up Granma, Grampa. Tell 'em to come an' eat. We're goin' before long." And as Al sauntered toward the barn, "Muley, ya wanta squeeze in with us an' go? We'd try to make room for ya."

Muley took a bite of meat from the edge of a rib bone and chewed it. "Sometimes I think I might. But I know I won't," he said. "I know perfectly well the las' minute I'd run an' hide like a damn ol' graveyard ghos'."

Noah said, "You gonna die out in the fiel' some day, Muley."

"I know. I thought about that. Sometimes it seems pretty lonely, an' sometimes it seems all right, an' sometimes it seems good. It don't make no difference. But if ya come acrost my folks—that's really what I come to say—if ya come on any my folks in California, tell 'em I'm well. Tell 'em I'm doin' all right. Don't let on I'm livin' this way. Tell 'em I'll come to 'em soon's I git the money."

Ma asked, "An' will ya?"

"No," Muley said softly. "No, I won't. I can't go away. I got to stay now. Time back I might of went. But not now. Fella gits to thinkin', an' he gits to knowin'. I ain't never goin'."

The light of the dawn was a little sharper now. It paled the lanterns a little. Al came back with Grampa struggling and limping by his side. "He wasn't sleepin'," Al said. "He was settin' out back of the barn. They's somepin wrong with 'im."

Grampa's eyes had dulled, and there was none of the old meanness in them. "Ain't nothin' the matter with me," he said. "I jus' ain't a-goin'."

"Not goin'?" Pa demanded. "What you mean you ain't a-goin'? Why, here we're all packed up, ready. We got to go. We got no place to stay."

"I ain't sayin' for you to stay," said Grampa. "You go right on along. Me—I'm stayin'. I give her a goin'-over all night mos'ly. This here's my country. I b'long here. An' I don't give a goddamn if they's oranges an' grapes crowdin' a fella outa bed even. I ain't a-goin'. This country ain't no good, but it's my country. No, you all go ahead. I'll jus' stay right here where I b'long."

They crowded near to him. Pa said, "You can't, Grampa. This here lan' is goin' under the tractors. Who'd cook for you? How'd you live? You can't stay here. Why, with no-body to take care of you, you'd starve."

Grampa cried, "Goddamn it, I'm a ol' man, but I can still take care a myself. How's Muley here get along? I can get along as good as him. I tell ya I ain't goin', an' ya can lump it. Take Granma with ya if ya want, but ya ain't takin' me, an' that's the end of it."

Pa said helplessly, "Now listen to me, Grampa. Jus' listen to me, jus' a minute."

"Ain't a-gonna listen. I tol' ya what I'm a-gonna do."

Tom touched his father on the shoulder. "Pa, come in the house. I wanta tell ya somepin." And as they moved toward the house, he called, "Ma—come here a minute, will ya?"

In the kitchen one lantern burned and the plate of pork bones was still piled high. Tom said, "Listen, I know Grampa got the right to say he ain't goin', but he can't stay. We know that."

"Sure he can't stay," said Pa.

"Well, look. If we got to catch him an' tie him down, we li'ble to hurt him, an' he'll git so mad he'll hurt himself.

Now we can't argue with him. If we could get him drunk it'd be all right. You got any whisky?"

"No," said Pa. "There ain't a drop a' whisky in the house. An' John got no whisky. He never has none when he ain't drinkin'."

Ma said, "Tom, I got a half a bottle soothin' sirup I got for Winfiel' when he had them earaches. Think that might work? Use ta put Winfiel' ta sleep when his earache was bad."

"Might," said Tom. "Get it, Ma. We'll give her a try anyways."

"I throwed it out on the trash pile," said Ma. She took the lantern and went out, and in a moment she came back with a bottle half full of black medicine.

Tom took it from her and tasted it. "Don' taste bad," he said. "Make up a cup a black coffee, good an' strong. Le's see—says one teaspoon. Better put in a lot, coupla table-spoons."

Ma opened the stove and put a kettle inside, down next to the coals, and she measured water and coffee into it. "Have to give it to 'im in a can," she said. "We got the cups all packed."

Tom and his father went back outside. "Fella got a right to say what he's gonna do. Say, who's eatin' spareribs?" said Grampa.

"We've et," said Tom. "Ma's fixin' you a cup a coffee an' some pork."

He went into the house, and he drank his coffee and ate his pork. The group outside in the growing dawn watched him quietly, through the door. They saw him yawn and sway, and they saw him put his arms on the table and rest his head on his arms and go to sleep.

"He was tar'd anyways," said Tom. "Leave him be."

Now they were ready. Granma, giddy and vague, saying, "What's all this? What you doin' now, so early?" But she was dressed and agreeable. And Ruthie and Winfield were awake, but quiet with the pressure of tiredness and still half dreaming. The light was sifting rapidly over the land. And the movement of the family stopped. They stood about, reluctant to make the first active move to go. They were afraid, now that the time had come—afraid in the same way Grampa was afraid. They saw the shed take shape against the light, and they saw the lanterns pale until they no longer cast their circles of yellow light. The stars went out, few by few, toward the west. And still the family stood about like dream walkers, their eyes focused panoramically, seeing no detail, but the whole dawn, the whole land, the whole texture of the country at once.

Only Muley Graves prowled about restlessly, looking through the bars into the truck, thumping the spare tires hung on the back of the truck. And at last Muley approached Tom. "You goin' over the State line?" he asked. "You gonna break your parole?"

And Tom shook himself free of the numbness. "Jesus Christ, it's near sunrise," he said loudly. "We got to get goin'." And the others came out of their numbness and moved toward the truck.

"Come on," Tom said. "Le's get Grampa on." Pa and Uncle John and Tom and Al went into the kitchen where Grampa slept, his forehead down on his arms, and a line of drying coffee on the table. They took him under the elbows and lifted him to his feet, and he grumbled and cursed thickly, like a drunken man. Out the door they boosted him, and when they came to the truck Tom and Al climbed up, and, leaning over, hooked their hands under his arms and lifted him gently up, and laid him on top of the load. Al untied the tarpaulin, and they rolled him under and put a box under the tarp beside him, so that the weight of the heavy canvas would not be upon him.

"I got to get that ridge pole fixed," Al said. "Do her tonight when we stop." Grampa grunted and fought weakly against awakening, and when he was finally settled he went deeply to sleep again.

Pa said, "Ma, you an' Granma set in with Al for a while. We'll change aroun' so it's easier, but you start out that way." They got into the cab, and then the rest swarmed up on top of the load, Connie and Rose of Sharon, Pa and Uncle John, Ruthie and Winfield, Tom and the preacher. Noah stood on the ground, looking up at the great load of them sitting on top of the truck.

Al walked around, looking underneath at the springs. "Holy Jesus," he said, "them springs is flat as hell. Lucky I blocked under 'em."

Noah said, "How about the dogs, Pa?"

"I forgot the dogs," Pa said. He whistled shrilly, and one bouncing dog ran in, but only one. Noah caught him and threw him up on the top, where he sat rigid and shivering at the height. "Got to leave the other two," Pa called. "Muley, will you look after 'em some? See they don't starve?"

"Yeah," said Muley. "I'll like to have a couple dogs. Yeah! I'll take 'em."

"Take them chickens, too," Pa said.

Al got into the driver's seat. The starter whirred and caught, and whirred again. And then the loose roar of the six cylinders and a blue smoke behind. "So long, Muley," Al called.

And the family called, "Good-by, Muley."

Al slipped in the low gear and let in the clutch. The truck shuddered and strained across the yard. And the second gear took hold. They crawled up the little hill, and the red dust arose about them. "Chr-ist, what a load!" said Al. "We ain't makin' no time on this trip."

Ma tried to look back, but the body of the load cut off her view. She straightened her head and peered straight ahead along the dirt road. And a great weariness was in her eyes.

The people on top of the load did look back. They saw the house and the barn and a little smoke still rising from the chimney. They saw the windows reddening under the first color of the sun. They saw Muley standing forlornly in the dooryard looking after them. And then the hill cut them off. The cotton fields lined the road. And the truck crawled slowly through the dust toward the highway and the west.

Chapter Eleven

THE houses were left vacant on the land, and the land was vacant because of this. Only the tractor sheds of corrugated iron, silver and gleaming, were alive; and they were alive with metal and gasoline and oil, the disks of the plows shining. The tractors had lights shining, for there is no day and night for a tractor and the disks turn the earth in the darkness and they glitter in the daylight. And when a horse stops work and goes into the barn there is a life and a vitality left, there is a breathing and a warmth, and the feet shift on the straw, and the jaws champ on the hay, and the ears and the eyes are alive. There is a warmth of life in the barn, and the heat and smell of life. But when the motor of a tractor stops, it is as dead as the ore it came from. The heat goes out of it like the living heat that leaves a corpse. Then the corrugated iron doors are closed and the tractor man drives home to town, perhaps twenty miles away, and he need not come back for weeks or months, for the tractor is dead. And this is easy and efficient. So easy that the wonder goes out of work, so efficient that the wonder goes out of land and the working of it, and with the wonder the deep understanding and the relation. And in the tractor man there grows the contempt that comes only to a stranger who has little understanding and no relation. For nitrates are not the land, nor phosphates; and the length of fiber in the cotton is not the land. Carbon is not a man, nor salt nor water nor calcium. He is all these, but he is much more, much more; and the land is so much more than its analysis. The man who is more than his chemistry, walking on the earth, turning his plow point for a stone, dropping his handles to slide over an outcropping, kneeling in the earth to eat his lunch; that man who is more than his elements knows the land that is more than its analysis. But the machine man, driving a dead tractor on land he does not know and love, understands only chemistry; and he is contemptuous of the land and of himself. When the corrugated iron doors are shut, he goes home, and his home is not the land.

The doors of the empty houses swung open, and drifted back and forth in the wind. Bands of little boys came out from the towns to break the windows and to pick over the debris, looking for treasures. And here's a knife with half the blade gone. That's a good thing. And—smells like a rat died here. And look what Whitey wrote on the wall. He wrote that in the toilet in school, too, an' teacher made 'im wash it off.

When the folks first left, and the evening of the first day came, the hunting cats slouched in from the fields and mewed on the porch. And when no one came out, the cats crept through the open doors and walked mewing through the empty rooms. And then they went back to the fields and were wild cats from then on, hunting gophers and field mice, and sleeping in ditches in the daytime. When the night came, the bats, which had stopped at the doors for fear of light, swooped into the houses and sailed about through the empty rooms, and in a little while they stayed in dark room corners during the day, folded their wings high, and hung head-down among the rafters, and the smell of their droppings was in the empty houses.

And the mice moved in and stored weed seeds in corners, in boxes, in the backs of drawers in the kitchens. And weasels came in to hunt the mice, and the brown owls flew shrieking in and out again.

Now there came a little shower. The weeds sprang up in front of the doorstep, where they had not been allowed, and grass grew up through the porch boards. The houses were vacant, and a vacant house falls quickly apart. Splits started up the sheathing from the rusted nails. A dust settled on the floors, and only mouse and weasel and cat tracks disturbed it.

On a night the wind loosened a shingle and flipped it to the ground. The next wind pried into the hole where the shingle had been, lifted off three, and the next, a dozen. The midday sun burned through the hole and threw a glaring spot on the floor. The wild cats crept in from the fields at night, but they did not mew at the doorstep any more. They moved like shadows of a cloud across the moon, into the rooms to hunt the mice. And on windy nights the doors banged, and the ragged curtains fluttered in the broken windows.

Chapter Twelve

HIGHWAY 66 is the main migrant road. 66—the long concrete path across the country, waving gently up and down on the map, from the Mississippi to Bakersfield—over the red lands and the gray lands, twisting up into the mountains, crossing the Divide and down into the bright and terrible desert, and across the desert to the mountains again, and into the rich California valleys.

66 is the path of a people in flight, refugees from dust and shrinking land, from the thunder of tractors and shrinking ownership, from the desert's slow northward invasion, from the twisting winds that howl up out of Texas, from the floods that bring no richness to the land and steal what little richness is there. From all of these the people are in flight, and they come into 66 from the tributary side roads, from the wagon tracks and the rutted country roads. 66 is the mother road, the road of flight.

Clarksville and Ozark and Van Buren and Fort Smith on 64, and there's an end of Arkansas. And all the roads into Oklahoma City, 66 down from Tulsa, 270 up from McAlester. 81 from Wichita Falls south, from Enid north. Edmond, McLoud, Purcell. 66 out of Oklahoma City; El Reno and Clinton, going west on 66. Hydro, Elk City, and Texola; and there's an end to Oklahoma. 66 across the Panhandle of Texas. Shamrock and McLean, Conway and Amarillo, the yellow. Wildorado and Vega and Boise, and there's an end of Texas. Tucumcari and Santa Rosa and into the New Mexican mountains to Albuquerque, where the road comes down from Santa Fe. Then down the gorged Rio Grande to Los Lunas and west again on 66 to Gallup, and there's the border of New Mexico.

And now the high mountains. Holbrook and Winslow and Flagstaff in the high mountains of Arizona. Then the great plateau rolling like a ground swell. Ashfork and Kingman and stone mountains again, where water must be hauled and sold. Then out of the broken sun-rotted mountains of Arizona to the Colorado, with green reeds on its banks, and that's the end of Arizona. There's California just over the river, and a pretty town to start it. Needles, on the river. But the river is a stranger in this place. Up from Needles and over a burned range, and there's the desert. And 66 goes on over the terrible desert, where the distance shimmers and the black center mountains hang unbearably in the distance. At last there's Barstow, and more desert until at last the mountains rise up again, the good mountains, and 66 winds through them. Then suddenly a pass, and below the beautiful valley, below orchards and vineyards and little houses, and in the distance a city. And, oh, my God, it's over.

The people in flight streamed out on 66, sometimes a single car, sometimes a little caravan. All day they rolled slowly along the road, and at night they stopped near water. In the day ancient leaky radiators sent up columns of steam, loose connecting rods hammered and pounded. And the men driving the trucks and the overloaded cars listened apprehensively. How far between towns? It is a terror between towns. If something breaks—well, if something breaks we camp right here while Jim walks to town and gets a part and walks back and—how much food we got?

Listen to the motor. Listen to the wheels. Listen with your

ears and with your hands on the steering wheel; listen with
the palm of your hand on the gear-shift lever; listen with
your feet on the floor boards. Listen to the pounding old
jalopy with all your senses; for a change of tone, a variation
of rhythm may mean—a week here? That rattle—that's tap-
·pets. Don't hurt a bit. Tappets can rattle till Jesus comes
again without no harm. But that thudding as the car moves
along—can't hear that—just kind of feel it. Maybe oil isn't
gettin' someplace. Maybe a bearing's startin' to go. Jesus, if
it's a bearing, what'll we do? Money's goin' fast.

And why's the son-of-a-bitch heat up so hot today? This
ain't no climb. Le's look. God Almighty, the fan belt's gone!
Here, make a belt outa this little piece a rope. Le's see how
long—there. I'll splice the ends. Now take her slow—slow,
till we can get to a town. That rope belt won't last long.

'F we can on'y get to California where the oranges grow
before this here ol' jug blows up. 'F we on'y can.

And the tires—two layers of fabric worn through. On'y
a four-ply tire. Might get a hunderd miles more outa her if
we don't hit a rock an' blow her. Which'll we take—a hunderd, maybe, miles, or maybe spoil the tube? Which? A
hunderd miles. Well, that's somepin you got to think about.
We got tube patches. Maybe when she goes she'll only
spring a leak. How about makin' a boot? Might get five hunderd more miles. Le's go on till she blows.

We got to get a tire, but, Jesus, they want a lot for a ol'
tire. They look a fella over. They know he got to go on.
They know he can't wait. And the price goes up.

Take it or leave it. I ain't in business for my health. I'm
here a-sellin' tires. I ain't givin' 'em away. I can't help what
happens to you. I got to think what happens to me.

How far's the nex' town?

I seen forty-two cars a you fellas go by yesterday. Where you all come from? Where all of you goin'?

Well, California's a big State.

It ain't that big. The whole United States ain't that big. It ain't that big. It ain't big enough. There ain't room enough for you an' me, for your kind an' my kind, for rich and poor together all in one country, for thieves and honest men. For hunger and fat. Whyn't you go back where you come from?

This is a free country. Fella can go where he wants.

That's what *you* think! Ever hear of the border patrol on the California line? Police from Los Angeles—stopped you bastards, turned you back. Says, if you can't buy no real estate we don't want you. Says, got a driver's license? Le's see it. Tore it up. Says you can't come in without no driver's license.

It's a free country.

Well, try to get some freedom to do. Fella says you're jus' as free as you got jack to pay for it.

In California they got high wages. I got a han'bill here tells about it.

Baloney! I seen folks comin' back. Somebody's kiddin' you. You want that tire or don't ya?

Got to take it, but, Jesus, mister, it cuts into our money! We ain't got much left.

Well, I ain't no charity. Take her along.

Got to, I guess. Let's look her over. Open her up, look a' the casing—you son-of-a-bitch, you said the casing was good. She's broke damn near through.

The hell she is. Well—by George! How come I didn' see that?

You did see it, you son-of-a-bitch. You wanta charge us four bucks for a busted casing. I'd like to take a sock at you.

Now keep your shirt on. I didn' see it, I tell you. Here— tell ya what I'll do. I'll give ya this one for three-fifty.

You'll take a flying jump at the moon! We'll try to make the nex' town.

Think we can make it on that tire?

Got to. I'll go on the rim before I'd give that son-of-a-bitch a dime.

What do ya think a guy in business is? Like he says, he ain't in it for his health. That's what business is. What'd you think it was? Fella's got— See that sign 'longside the road there? Service Club. Luncheon Tuesday, Colmado Hotel? Welcome, brother. That's a Service Club. Fella had a story. Went to one of them meetings an' told the story to all them business men. Says, when I was a kid my ol' man give me a haltered heifer an' says take her down an' git her serviced. An' the fella says, I done it, an' ever' time since then when I hear a business man talkin' about service, I wonder who's gettin' screwed. Fella in business got to lie an' cheat, but he calls it somepin else. That's what's important. You go steal that tire an' you're a thief, but he tried to steal your four dollars for a busted tire. They call that sound business.

Danny in the back seat wants a cup a water.

Have to wait. Got no water here.

Listen—that the rear end?

Can't tell.

Sound telegraphs through the frame.

There goes a gasket. Got to go on. Listen to her whistle. Find a nice place to camp an' I'll jerk the head off. But, God Almighty, the food's gettin' low, the money's gettin' low. When we can't buy no more gas—what then?

Danny in the back seat wants a cup a water. Little fella's thirsty.

Listen to that gasket whistle.

Chee-rist! There she went. Blowed tube an' casing all to hell. Have to fix her. Save that casing to make boots; cut 'em out an' stick 'em inside a weak place.

Cars pulled up beside the road, engine heads off, tires mended. Cars limping along 66 like wounded things, panting and struggling. Too hot, loose connections, loose bearings, rattling bodies.

Danny wants a cup of water.

People in flight along 66. And the concrete road shone like a mirror under the sun, and in the distance the heat made it seem that there were pools of water in the road.

Danny wants a cup a water.

He'll have to wait, poor little fella. He's hot. Nex' service station. *Service* station, like the fella says.

Two hundred and fifty thousand people over the road. Fifty thousand old cars—wounded, steaming. Wrecks along the road, abandoned. Well, what happened to them? What happened to the folks in that car? Did they walk? Where are they? Where does the courage come from? Where does the terrible faith come from?

And here's a story you can hardly believe, but it's true, and it's funny and it's beautiful. There was a family of twelve and they were forced off the land. They had no car. They built a trailer out of junk and loaded it with their possessions. They pulled it to the side of 66 and waited. And pretty soon a sedan picked them up. Five of them rode in the sedan and seven on the trailer, and a dog on the trailer. They got to California in two jumps. The man who pulled them fed them. And that's true. But how can such courage be, and such faith in their own species? Very few things would teach such faith.

The people in flight from the terror behind—strange things happen to them, some bitterly cruel and some so beautiful that the faith is refired forever.

Chapter Thirteen

THE ancient overloaded Hudson creaked and grunted to the highway at Sallisaw and turned west, and the sun was blinding. But on the concrete road Al built up his speed because the flattened springs were not in danger any more. From Sallisaw to Gore is twenty-one miles and the Hudson was doing thirty-five miles an hour. From Gore to Warner thirteen miles; Warner to Checotah fourteen miles; Checotah a long jump to Henrietta—thirty-four miles, but a real town at the end of it. Henrietta to Castle nineteen miles, and the sun was overhead, and the red fields, heated by the high sun, vibrated the air.

Al, at the wheel, his face purposeful, his whole body listening to the car, his restless eyes jumping from the road to the instrument panel. Al was one with his engine, every nerve listening for weaknesses, for the thumps or squeals, hums and chattering that indicate a change that may cause a breakdown. He had become the soul of the car.

Granma, beside him on the seat, half slept, and whimpered in her sleep, opened her eyes to peer ahead, and then dozed again. And Ma sat beside Granma, one elbow out the window, and the skin reddening under the fierce sun. Ma looked ahead too, but her eyes were flat and did not see the road or the fields, the gas stations, the little eating sheds. She did not glance at them as the Hudson went by.

Al shifted himself on the broken seat and changed his grip

on the steering wheel. And he sighed, "Makes a racket, but I think she's awright. God knows what she'll do if we got to climb a hill with the load we got. Got any hills 'tween here an' California, Ma?"

Ma turned her head slowly and her eyes came to life. "Seems to me they's hills," she said. " 'Course I dunno. But seems to me I heard they's hills an' even mountains. Big ones."

Granma drew a long whining sigh in her sleep.

Al said, "We'll burn right up if we got climbin' to do. Have to throw out some a' this stuff. Maybe we shouldn' a brang that preacher."

"You'll be glad a that preacher 'fore we're through," said Ma. "That preacher'll help us." She looked ahead at the gleaming road again.

Al steered with one hand and put the other on the vibrating gear-shift lever. He had difficulty in speaking. His mouth formed the words silently before he said them aloud. "Ma—" She looked slowly around at him, her head swaying a little with the car's motion. "Ma, you scared a goin'? You scared a goin' to a new place?"

Her eyes grew thoughtful and soft. "A little," she said. "Only it ain't like scared so much. I'm jus' a settin' here waitin'. When somepin happens that I got to do somepin— I'll do it."

"Ain't you thinkin' what's it gonna be like when we get there? Ain't you scared it won't be nice like we thought?"

"No," she said quickly. "No, I ain't. You can't do that. I can't do that. It's too much—livin' too many lives. Up ahead they's a thousan' lives we might live, but when it comes, it'll on'y be one. If I go ahead on all of 'em, it's too much. You got to live ahead 'cause you're so young, but—it's jus' the road goin' by for me. An' it's jus' how soon they gonna wanta eat some more pork bones." Her face tightened. "That's all I can do. I can't do no more. All the rest'd get upset if I done any more'n that. They all depen' on me jus' thinkin' about that."

Granma yawned shrilly and opened her eyes. She looked wildly about. "I got to get out, praise Gawd," she said.

"First clump a brush," said Al. "They's one up ahead."

"Brush or no brush, I got to git out, I tell ya." And she began to whine, "I got to git out. I got to git out."

Al speeded up, and when he came to the low brush he pulled up short. Ma threw the door open and half pulled the struggling old lady out beside the road and into the bushes. And Ma held her so Granma would not fall when she squatted.

On top of the truck the others stirred to life. Their faces were shining with sunburn they could not escape. Tom and Casy and Noah and Uncle John let themselves wearily down. Ruthie and Winfield swarmed down the side-boards and went off into the bushes. Connie helped Rose of Sharon gently down. Under the canvas, Grampa was awake, his head sticking out, but his eyes were drugged and watery and still senseless. He watched the others, but there was little recognition in his watching.

Tom called to him, "Want to come down, Grampa?"

The old eyes turned listlessly to him. "No," said Grampa. For a moment the fierceness came into his eyes. "I ain't a-goin', I tell you. Gonna stay like Muley." And then he lost interest again. Ma came back, helping Granma up the bank to the highway.

"Tom," she said. "Get that pan a bones, under the canvas in back. We got to eat somepin." Tom got the pan and passed it around, and the family stood by the roadside, gnawing the crisp particles from the pork bones.

"Sure lucky we brang these along," said Pa. "Git so stiff up there can't hardly move. Where's the water?"

"Ain't it up with you?" Ma asked. "I set out that gallon jug."

Pa climbed the sides and looked under the canvas. "It ain't here. We must a forgot it."

Thirst set in instantly. Winfield moaned, "I wanta drink. I wanta drink." The men licked their lips, suddenly conscious of their thirst. And a little panic started.

Al felt the fear growing. "We'll get water first service station we come to. We need some gas too." The family swarmed up the truck sides; Ma helped Granma in and got in beside her. Al started the motor and they moved on.

Castle to Paden twenty-five miles and the sun passed the zenith and started down. And the radiator cap began to jiggle up and down and steam started to whish out. Near Paden there was a shack beside the road and two gas pumps in front of it; and beside a fence, a water faucet and a hose. Al drove in and nosed the Hudson up to the hose. As they pulled in, a stout man, red of face and arms, got up from a chair behind the gas pumps and moved toward them. He wore brown corduroys, and suspenders and a polo shirt; and he had a cardboard sun helmet, painted silver, on his head. The sweat beaded on his nose and under his eyes and formed streams in the wrinkles of his neck. He strolled toward the truck, looking truculent and stern.

"You folks aim to buy anything? Gasoline or stuff?" he asked.

Al was out already, unscrewing the steaming radiator cap with the tips of his fingers, jerking his hand away to escape the spurt when the cap should come loose. "Need some gas, mister."

"Got any money?"

"Sure. Think we're beggin'?"

The truculence left the fat man's face. "Well, that's all right, folks. He'p yourself to water." And he hastened to explain. "Road is full a people, come in, use water, dirty up the toilet, an' then, by God, they'll steal stuff an' don't buy nothin'. Got no money to buy with. Come beggin' a gallon gas to move on."

Tom dropped angrily to the ground and moved toward the fat man. "We're payin' our way," he said fiercely. "You got no call to give us a goin'-over. We ain't asked you for nothin'."

"I ain't," the fat man said quickly. The sweat began to soak through his short-sleeved polo shirt. "Jus' he'p yourself to water, and go use the toilet if you want."

Winfield had got the hose. He drank from the end and then turned the stream over his head and face, and emerged dripping. "It ain't cool," he said.

"I don' know what the country's comin' to," the fat man continued. His complaint had shifted now and he was no longer talking to or about the Joads. "Fifty-sixty cars a folks go by ever' day, folks all movin' west with kids an' househol' stuff. Where they goin'? What they gonna do?"

"Doin' the same as us," said Tom. "Goin' someplace to live. Tryin' to get along. That's all."

"Well, I don' know what the country's comin' to. I jus' don' know. Here's me tryin' to get along, too. Think any them big new cars stops here? No, sir! They go on to them yella-painted company stations in town. They don't stop no place like this. Most folks stops here ain't got nothin'."

Al flipped the radiator cap and it jumped into the air with a head of steam behind it, and a hollow bubbling sound came out of the radiator. On top of the truck, the suffering hound dog crawled timidly to the edge of the load and looked over, whimpering, toward the water. Uncle John climbed up and lifted him down by the scruff of the neck. For a moment the dog staggered on stiff legs, and then he went to lap the mud under the faucet. In the highway the cars whizzed by, glistening in the heat, and the hot wind of their going fanned into the service-station yard. Al filled the radiator with the hose.

"It ain't that I'm tryin' to git trade outa rich folks," the fat man went on. "I'm jus' tryin' to git trade. Why, the folks that stops here begs gasoline an' they trades for gasoline. I could show you in my back room the stuff they'll trade for gas an' oil: beds an' baby buggies an' pots an' pans. One family traded a doll their kid had for a gallon. An' what'm I gonna do with the stuff, open a junk shop? Why, one fella wanted to gimme his shoes for a gallon. An' if I was that kinda fella I bet I could git—" He glanced at Ma and stopped.

Jim Casy had wet his head, and the drops still coursed down his high forehead, and his muscled neck was wet, and his shirt was wet. He moved over beside Tom. "It ain't the people's fault," he said. "How'd you like to sell the bed you sleep on for a tankful a gas?"

"I know it ain't their fault. Ever' person I talked to is on the move for a damn good reason. But what's the country comin' to? That's what I wanta know. What's it comin' to? Fella can't make a livin' no more. Folks can't make a livin' farmin'. I ask you, what's it comin' to? I can't figure her out. Ever'body I ask, they can't figure her out. Fella wants to trade his shoes so he can git a hunderd miles on. I can't figure her out." He took off his silver hat and wiped his forehead with his palm. And Tom took off his cap and wiped his forehead with it. He went to the hose and wet the cap through and squeezed it and put it on again. Ma worked a tin cup out through the side bars of the truck, and she took water to Granma and to Grampa on top of the load. She stood on the bars and handed the cup to Grampa, and he wet his lips, and then shook his head and refused more. The old eyes looked up at Ma in pain and bewilderment for a moment before the awareness receded again.

Al started the motor and backed the truck to the gas pump. "Fill her up. She'll take about seven," said Al. "We'll give her six so she don't spill none."

The fat man put the hose in the tank. "No, sir," he said. "I jus' don't know what the country's comin' to. Relief an' all."

Casy said, "I been walkin' aroun' in the country. Ever'-body's askin' that. What we comin' to? Seems to me we don't never come to nothin'. Always on the way. Always goin' and goin'. Why don't folks think about that? They's movement now. People moving. We know why, an' we know how. Movin' 'cause they got to. That's why folks always move. Movin' 'cause they want somepin better'n what they got. An' that's the on'y way they'll ever git it. Wantin' it an' needin' it, they'll go out an' git it. It's bein' hurt that makes folks mad to fightin'. I been walkin' aroun' the country, an' hearin' folks talk like you."

The fat man pumped the gasoline and the needle turned on the pump dial, recording the amount. "Yeah, but what's it comin' to? That's what I want ta know."

Tom broke in irritably, "Well, you ain't never gonna know. Casy tries to tell ya an' you jest ast the same thing over. I seen fellas like you before. You ain't askin' nothin'; you're jus' singin' a kinda song. 'What we comin' to?' You don' wanta know. Country's movin' aroun', goin' places. They's folks dyin' all aroun'. Maybe you'll die pretty soon, but you won't know nothin'. I seen too many fellas like you. You don't want to know nothin'. Just sing yourself to sleep with a song— 'What we comin' to?' " He looked at the gas pump, rusted and old, and at the shack behind it, built of old lumber, the nail holes of its first use still showing through the paint that had been brave, the brave yellow paint that had tried to imitate the big company stations in town. But the paint couldn't cover the old nail holes and the old cracks in the lumber, and the paint could not be renewed. The imitation was a failure and the owner had known it was a failure. And inside the open door of the shack Tom saw the oil barrels, only two of them, and the candy counter with stale candies and licorice whips turning brown with age, and cigarettes. He saw the broken chair and the fly screen with a rusted hole in it. And the littered yard that should have been graveled, and behind, the corn field drying and dying in the sun. Beside the house the little stock of used tires and re-treaded tires. And he saw for the first time the fat man's cheap washed pants and his cheap polo shirt and his paper hat. He said, "I didn' mean to sound off at ya, mister. It's the heat. You ain't got nothin'. Pretty soon you'll be on the road yourse'f. And it ain't tractors'll put you there. It's them pretty yella stations in town. Folks is movin'," he said ashamedly. "An' you'll be movin', mister."

The fat man's hand slowed on the pump and stopped while Tom spoke. He looked worriedly at Tom. "How'd you know?" he asked helplessly. "How'd you know we was already talkin' about packin' up an' movin' west?"

Casy answered him. "It's ever'body," he said. "Here's me that used to give all my fight against the devil 'cause I figgered the devil was the enemy. But they's somepin worse'n the devil got hold a the country, an' it ain't gonna let go till it's chopped loose. Ever see one a them Gila monsters take hold, mister? Grabs hold, an' you chop him in two an' his head hangs on. Chop him at the neck an' his head hangs on. Got to take a screw-driver an' pry his head apart to git him loose. An' while he's layin' there, poison is drippin' an' drippin' into the hole he's made with his teeth." He stopped and looked sideways at Tom.

The fat man stared hopelessly straight ahead. His hand started turning the crank slowly. "I dunno what we're comin' to," he said softly.

Over by the water hose, Connie and Rose of Sharon stood together, talking secretly. Connie washed the tin cup and felt the water with his finger before he filled the cup again. Rose of Sharon watched the cars go by on the highway. Connie held out the cup to her. "This water ain't cool, but it's wet," he said.

She looked at him and smiled secretly. She was all secrets now she was pregnant, secrets and little silences that seemed to have meanings. She was pleased with herself, and she complained about things that didn't really matter. And she demanded services of Connie that were silly, and both of them knew they were silly. Connie was pleased with her too, and filled with wonder that she was pregnant. He liked to think he was in on the secrets she had. When she smiled slyly, he smiled slyly too, and they exchanged confidences in whispers. The world had drawn close around them, and they were in the center of it, or rather Rose of Sharon was in the center of it with Connie making a small orbit about her. Everything they said was a kind of secret.

She drew her eyes from the highway. "I ain't very thirsty," she said daintily. "But maybe I *ought* to drink."

And he nodded, for he knew well what she meant. She took the cup and rinsed her mouth and spat and then drank the cupful of tepid water. "Want another?" he asked.

"Jus' a half." And so he filled the cup just half, and gave it to her. A Lincoln Zephyr, silvery and low, whisked by. She turned to see where the others were and saw them clustered about the truck. Reassured, she said, "How'd you like to be goin' along in that?"

Connie sighed, "Maybe—after." They both knew what he meant. "An' if they's plenty work in California, we'll git our own car. But them"—he indicated the disappearing Zephyr —"them kind costs as much as a good size house. I ruther have the house."

"I like to have the house *an'* one a them," she said. "But 'course the house would be first because—" And they both knew what she meant. They were terribly excited about the pregnancy.

"You feel awright?" he asked.

"Tar'd. Jus' tar'd ridin' in the sun."

"We *got* to do that or we won't never get to California."

"I know," she said.

The dog wandered, sniffing, past the truck, trotted to the puddle under the hose again and lapped at the muddy water. And then he moved away, nose down and ears hanging. He sniffed his way among the dusty weeds beside the road, to the edge of the pavement. He raised his head and looked across, and then started over. Rose of Sharon screamed shrilly. A big swift car whisked near, tires squealed. The dog dodged helplessly, and with a shriek, cut off in the middle, went under the wheels. The big car slowed for a moment and faces looked back, and then it gathered greater speed and disappeared. And the dog, a blot of blood and tangled, burst intestines, kicked slowly in the road.

Rose of Sharon's eyes were wide. "D'you think it'll hurt?" she begged. "Think it'll hurt?"

Connie put his arm around her. "Come set down," he said. "It wasn't nothin'."

"But I felt it hurt. I felt it kinda jar when I yelled."

"Come set down. It wasn't nothin'. It won't hurt." He led her to the side of the truck away from the dying dog and sat her down on the running board.

Tom and Uncle John walked out to the mess. The last quiver was going out of the crushed body. Tom took it by the legs and dragged it to the side of the road. Uncle John look embarrassed, as though it were his fault. "I ought ta tied him up," he said.

Pa looked down at the dog for a moment and then he turned away. "Le's get outa here," he said. "I don' know how we was gonna feed 'im anyways. Just as well, maybe."

The fat man came from behind the truck. "I'm sorry, folks," he said. "A dog jus' don' last no time near a highway. I had three dogs run over in a year. Don't keep none, no more." And he said, "Don't you folks worry none about it. I'll take care of 'im. Bury 'im out in the corn field."

Ma walked over to Rose of Sharon, where she sat, still shuddering, on the running board. "You all right, Rosasharn?" she asked. "You feelin' poorly?"

"I seen that. Give me a start."

"I heard ya yip," said Ma. "Git yourself laced up, now."

"You suppose it might of hurt?"

"No," said Ma. " 'F you go to greasin' yourself an' feelin' sorry, an' tuckin' yourself in a swalla's nest, it might. Rise up now, an' he'p me get Granma comf'table. Forget that baby for a minute. He'll take care a hisself."

"Where is Granma?" Rose of Sharon asked.

"I dunno. She's aroun' here somewheres. Maybe in the outhouse."

The girl went toward the toilet, and in a moment she came out, helping Granma along. "She went to sleep in there," said Rose of Sharon.

Granma grinned. "It's nice in there," she said. "They got a patent toilet in there an' the water comes down. I like it in there," she said contentedly. "Would of took a good nap if I wasn't woke up."

"It ain't a nice place to sleep," said Rose of Sharon, and she helped Granma into the car. Granma settled herself happily. "Maybe it ain't nice for purty, but it's nice for nice," she said.

Tom said, "Le's go. We got to make miles."

Pa whistled shrilly. "Now where'd them kids go?" He whistled again, putting his fingers in his mouth.

In a moment they broke from the corn field, Ruthie ahead and Winfield trailing her. "Eggs!" Ruthie cried. "I got sof' eggs." She rushed close, with Winfield close behind. "Look!" A dozen soft, grayish-white eggs were in her grubby hand. And as she held up her hand, her eyes fell upon the dead dog beside the road. "Oh!" she said. Ruthie and Winfield walked slowly toward the dog. They inspected him.

Pa called to them, "Come on, you, 'less you want to git left."

They turned solemnly and walked to the truck. Ruthie

looked once more at the gray reptile eggs in her hand, and then she threw them away. They climbed up the side of the truck. "His eyes was still open," said Ruthie in a hushed tone.

But Winfield gloried in the scene. He said boldly, "His guts was just strowed all over—all over"—he was silent for a moment—"strowed—all—over," he said, and then he rolled over quickly and vomited down the side of the truck. When he sat up again his eyes were watery and his nose running. "It ain't like killin' pigs," he said in explanation.

Al had the hood of the Hudson up, and he checked the oil level. He brought a gallon can from the floor of the front seat and poured a quantity of cheap black oil into the pipe and checked the level again.

Tom came beside him. "Want I should take her a piece?" he asked.

"I ain't tired," said Al.

"Well, you didn' get no sleep las' night. I took a snooze this morning. Get up there on top. I'll take her."

"Awright," Al said reluctantly. "But watch the oil gauge pretty close. Take her slow. An' I been watchin' for a short. Take a look a the needle now an' then. 'F she jumps to discharge it's a short. An' take her slow, Tom. She's overloaded."

Tom laughed. "I'll watch her," he said. "You can res' easy."

The family piled on top of the truck again. Ma settled herself beside Granma in the seat, and Tom took his place and started the motor. "Sure is loose," he said, and he put it in gear and pulled away down the highway.

The motor droned along steadily and the sun receded down the sky in front of them. Granma slept steadily, and even Ma dropped her head forward and dozed. Tom pulled his cap over his eyes to shut out the blinding sun.

Paden to Meeker is thirteen miles; Meeker to Harrah is fourteen miles; and then Oklahoma City—the big city. Tom drove straight on. Ma waked up and looked at the streets as they went through the city. And the family, on top of the truck, stared about at the stores, at the big houses, at the office buildings. And then the buildings grew smaller and the stores smaller. The wrecking yards and hot-dog stands, the out-city dance halls.

Ruthie and Winfield saw it all, and it embarrassed them with its bigness and its strangeness, and it frightened them with the fine-clothed people they saw. They did not speak of it to each other. Later—they would, but not now. They saw the oil derricks in the town, on the edge of the town; oil derricks black, and the smell of oil and gas in the air. But they didn't exclaim. It was so big and so strange it frightened them.

In the street Rose of Sharon saw a man in a light suit. He wore white shoes and a flat straw hat. She touched Connie and indicated the man with her eyes, and then Connie and Rose of Sharon giggled softly to themselves, and the giggles got the best of them. They covered their mouths. And it felt so good that they looked for other people to giggle at. Ruthie and Winfield saw them giggling and it looked such fun that they tried to do it too—but they couldn't. The giggles wouldn't come. But Connie and Rose of Sharon were breathless and red with stifling laughter before they could stop. It got so bad that they had only to look at each other to start over again.

The outskirts were wide spread. Tom drove slowly and carefully in the traffic, and then they were on 66—the great western road, and the sun was sinking on the line of the road. The windshield was bright with dust. Tom pulled his cap lower over his eyes, so low that he had to tilt his head back to see out at all. Granma slept on, the sun on her closed eyelids, and the veins on her temples were blue, and the little bright veins on her cheeks were wine-colored, and the old brown marks on her face turned darker.

Tom said, "We stay on this road right straight through."

Ma had been silent for a long time. "Maybe we better fin' a place to stop 'fore sunset," she said. "I got to get some pork a-boilin' an' some bread made. That takes time."

"Sure," Tom agreed. "We ain't gonna make this trip in one jump. Might's well stretch ourselves."

Oklahoma City to Bethany is fourteen miles.

Tom said, "I think we better stop 'fore the sun goes down. Al got to build that thing on the top. Sun'll kill the folks up there."

Ma had been dozing again. Her head jerked upright. "Got to get some supper a-cookin'," she said. And she said, "Tom, your pa tol' me about you crossin' the State line——"

He was a long time answering. "Yeah? What about it, Ma?"

"Well, I'm scairt about it. It'll make you kinda runnin' away. Maybe they'll catch ya."

Tom held his hand over his eyes to protect himself from the lowering sun. "Don't you worry," he said. "I figgered her out. They's lots a fellas out on parole an' they's more goin' in all the time. If I get caught for anything else out west, well, then they got my pitcher an' my prints in Washington. They'll sen' me back. But if I don't do no crimes, they won't give a damn."

"Well, I'm a-scairt about it. Sometimes you do a crime, an'

you don't even know it's bad. Maybe they got crimes in California we don't even know about. Maybe you gonna do somepin an' it's all right, an' in California it ain't all right."

"Be jus' the same if I wasn't on parole," he said. "On'y if I get caught I get a bigger jolt'n other folks. Now you quit a-worryin'," he said. "We got plenty to worry about 'thout you figgerin' out things to worry about."

"I can't he'p it," she said. "Minute you cross the line you done a crime."

"Well, tha's better'n stickin' aroun' Sallisaw an' starvin' to death," he said. "We better look out for a place to stop."

They went through Bethany and out on the other side. In a ditch, where a culvert went under the road, an old touring car was pulled off the highway and a little tent was pitched beside it, and smoke came out of a stove pipe through the tent. Tom pointed ahead. "There's some folks campin'. Looks like as good a place as we seen." He slowed his motor and pulled to a stop beside the road. The hood of the old touring car was up, and a middle-aged man stood looking down at the motor. He wore a cheap straw sombrero, a blue shirt, and a black, spotted vest, and his jeans were stiff and shiny with dirt. His face was lean, the deep cheek-lines great furrows down his face so that his cheek bones and chin stood out sharply. He looked up at the Joad truck and his eyes were puzzled and angry.

Tom leaned out of the window. "Any law 'gainst folks stoppin' here for the night?"

The man had seen only the truck. His eyes focused down on Tom. "I dunno," he said. "We on'y stopped here 'cause we couldn' git no further."

"Any water here?"

The man pointed to a service-station shack about a quarter of a mile ahead. "They's water there they'll let ya take a bucket of."

Tom hesitated. "Well, ya 'spose we could camp down 'longside?"

The lean man looked puzzled. "We don't own it," he said. "We on'y stopped here 'cause this goddamn ol' trap wouldn' go no further."

Tom insisted. "Anyways you're here an' we ain't. You got a right to say if you wan' neighbors or not."

The appeal to hospitality had an instant effect. The lean face broke into a smile. "Why, sure, come on off the road. Proud to have ya." And he called, "Sairy, there's some folks goin' ta stay with us. Come on out an' say how d'ya do. Sairy ain't well," he added. The tent flaps opened and a wizened woman came out—a face wrinkled as a dried leaf and eyes that seemed to flame in her face, black eyes that seemed to look out of a well of horror. She was small and shuddering. She held herself upright by a tent flap, and the hand holding onto the canvas was a skeleton covered with wrinkled skin.

When she spoke her voice had a beautiful low timbre, soft and modulated, and yet with ringing overtones. "Tell 'em welcome," she said. "Tell 'em good an' welcome."

Tom drove off the road and brought his truck into the field and lined it up with the touring car. And people boiled down from the truck; Ruthie and Winfield too quickly, so that their legs gave way and they shrieked at the pins and needles that ran through their limbs. Ma went quickly to work. She untied the three-gallon bucket from the back of the truck and approached the squealing children. "Now you go git water—right down there. Ask nice. Say, 'Please, kin we git a bucket a water?' and say, 'Thank you.' An' carry it back together helpin', an' don't spill none. An' if you see stick wood to burn, bring it on." The children stamped away toward the shack.

By the tent a little embarrassment had set in, and social intercourse had paused before it started. Pa said, "You ain't Oklahomy folks?"

And Al, who stood near the car, looked at the license plates. "Kansas," he said.

The lean man said, "Galena, or right about there. Wilson, Ivy Wilson."

"We're Joads," said Pa. "We come from right near Sallisaw."

"Well, we're proud to meet you folks," said Ivy Wilson. "Sairy, these is Joads."

"I knowed you wasn't Oklahomy folks. You talk queer, kinda—that ain't no blame, you understan'."

"Ever'body says words different," said Ivy. "Arkansas folks says 'em different, and Oklahomy folks says 'em different. And we seen a lady from Massachusetts, an' she said 'em differentest of all. Couldn' hardly make out what she was sayin'."

Noah and Uncle John and the preacher began to unload the truck. They helped Grampa down and sat him on the ground and he sat limply, staring ahead of him. "You sick, Grampa?" Noah asked.

"You goddamn right," said Grampa weakly. "Sicker'n hell."

Sairy Wilson walked slowly and carefully toward him. "How'd you like ta come in our tent?" she asked. "You kin lay down on our mattress an' rest."

He looked up at her, drawn by her soft voice. "Come on now," she said. "You'll git some rest. We'll he'p you over."

Without warning Grampa began to cry. His chin wavered and his old lips tightened over his mouth and he sobbed hoarsely. Ma rushed over to him and put her arms around him. She lifted him to his feet, her broad back straining, and she half lifted, half helped him into the tent.

Uncle John said, "He must be good an' sick. He ain't never done that before. Never seen him blubberin' in my life." He jumped up on the truck and tossed a mattress down.

Ma came out of the tent and went to Casy. "You been aroun' sick people," she said. "Grampa's sick. Won't you go take a look at him?"

Casy walked quickly to the tent and went inside. A double mattress was on the ground, the blankets spread neatly; and a little tin stove stood on iron legs, and the fire in it burned unevenly. A bucket of water, a wooden box of supplies, and a box for a table, that was all. The light of the setting sun came pinkly through the tent walls. Sairy Wilson knelt on the ground, beside the mattress, and Grampa lay on his back. His eyes were open, staring upward, and his cheeks were flushed. He breathed heavily.

Casy took the skinny old wrist in his fingers. "Feeling kinda tired, Grampa?" he asked. The staring eyes moved toward his voice but did not find him. The lips practiced a speech but did not speak it. Casy felt the pulse and he dropped the wrist and put his hand on Grampa's forehead. A struggle began in the old man's body, his legs moved restlessly and his hands stirred. He said a whole string of blurred sounds that were not words, and his face was red under the spiky white whiskers.

Sairy Wilson spoke softly to Casy. "Know what's wrong?"

He looked up at the wrinkled face and the burning eyes. "Do you?"

"I—think so."

"What?" Casy asked.

"Might be wrong. I wouldn' like to say."

Casy looked back at the twitching red face. "Would you say—maybe—he's workin' up a stroke?"

"I'd say that," said Sairy. "I seen it three times before."

From outside came the sounds of camp-making, wood chopping, and the rattle of pans. Ma looked through the flaps. "Granma wants to come in. Would she better?"

The preacher said, "She'll jus' fret if she don't."

"Think he's awright?" Ma asked.

Casy shook his head slowly. Ma looked quickly down at the struggling old face with blood pounding through it. She drew outside and her voice came through. "He's awright, Granma. He's jus' takin' a little res'."

And Granma answered sulkily, "Well, I want ta see him. He's a tricky devil. He wouldn't never let ya know." And she came scurrying through the flaps. She stood over the mattresses and looked down. "What's the matter'th you?" she demanded of Grampa. And again his eyes reached toward her voice and his lips writhed. "He's sulkin'," said Granma. "I tol' you he was tricky. He was gonna sneak away this mornin' so he wouldn't have to come. An' then his hip got a-hurtin'," she said disgustedly. "He's jus' sulkin'. I seen him when he wouldn' talk to nobody before."

Casy said gently, "He ain't sulkin', Granma. He's sick."

"Oh!" She looked down at the old man again. "Sick bad, you think?"

"Purty bad, Granma."

For a moment she hesitated uncertainly. "Well," she said

quickly, "why ain't you prayin'? You're a preacher, ain't you?"

Casy's strong fingers blundered over to Grampa's wrist and clasped around it. "I tol' you, Granma. I ain't a preacher no more."

"Pray anyway," she ordered. "You know all the stuff by heart."

"I can't," said Casy. "I don' know what to pray for or who to pray to."

Granma's eyes wandered away and came to rest on Sairy. "He won't pray," she said. "D'I ever tell ya how Ruthie prayed when she was a little skinner? Says, 'Now I lay me down to sleep. I pray the Lord my soul to keep. An' when she got there the cupboard was bare, an' so the poor dog got none. Amen.' That's jus' what she done." The shadow of someone walking between the tent and the sun crossed the canvas.

Grampa seemed to be struggling; all his muscles twitched. And suddenly he jarred as though under a heavy blow. He lay still and his breath was stopped. Casy looked down at the old man's face and saw that it was turning a blackish purple. Sairy touched Casy's shoulder. She whispered, "His tongue, his tongue, his tongue."

Casy nodded. "Get in front a Granma." He pried the tight jaws apart and reached into the old man's throat for the tongue. And as he lifted it clear, a rattling breath came out, and a sobbing breath was indrawn. Casy found a stick on the ground and held down the tongue with it, and the uneven breath rattled in and out.

Granma hopped about like a chicken. "Pray," she said. "Pray, you. Pray, I tell ya." Sairy tried to hold her back. "Pray, goddamn you!" Granma cried.

Casy looked up at her for a moment. The rasping breath came louder and more unevenly. "Our Father who art in Heaven, hallowed be Thy name——"

"Glory!" shouted Granma.

"Thy kingdom come, Thy will be done—on earth—as it is in Heaven."

"Amen."

A long gasping sigh came from the open mouth, and then a crying release of air.

"Give us this day—our daily bread—and forgive us—" The breathing had stopped. Casy looked down into Grampa's eyes and they were clear and deep and penetrating, and there was a knowing serene look in them.

"Hallelujah!" said Granma. "Go on."

"Amen," said Casy.

Granma was still then. And outside the tent all the noise had stopped. A car whished by on the highway. Casy still knelt on the floor beside the mattress. The people outside were listening, standing quietly intent on the sounds of dying. Sairy took Granma by the arm and led her outside, and Granma moved with dignity and held her head high. She walked for the family and held her head straight for the family. Sairy took her to a mattress lying on the ground and sat her down on it. And Granma looked straight ahead, proudly, for she was on show now. The tent was still, and at last Casy spread the tent flaps with his hands and stepped out.

Pa asked softly, "What was it?"

"Stroke," said Casy. "A good quick stroke."

Life began to move again. The sun touched the horizon and flattened over it. And along the highway there came a long line of huge freight trucks with red sides. They rumbled along, putting a little earthquake in the ground, and the standing exhaust pipes sputtered blue smoke from the Diesel oil. One man drove each truck, and his relief man slept in a bunk high up against the ceiling. But the trucks never stopped; they thundered day and night and the ground shook under their heavy march.

The family became a unit. Pa squatted down on the ground, and Uncle John beside him. Pa was the head of the family now. Ma stood behind him. Noah and Tom and Al squatted, and the preacher sat down, and then reclined on his elbow. Connie and Rose of Sharon walked at a distance. Now Ruthie and Winfield, clattering up with a bucket of water held between them, felt the change, and they slowed up and set down the bucket and moved quietly to stand with Ma.

Granma sat proudly, coldly, until the group was formed, until no one looked at her, and then she lay down and covered her face with her arm. The red sun set and left a shining twilight on the land, so that faces were bright in the evening and eyes shone in reflection of the sky. The evening picked up light where it could.

Pa said, "It was in Mr. Wilson's tent."

Uncle John nodded. "He loaned his tent."

"Fine friendly folks," Pa said softly.

Wilson stood by his broken car, and Sairy had gone to the mattress to sit beside Granma, but Sairy was careful not to touch her.

Pa called, "Mr. Wilson!" The man scuffed near and squatted down, and Sairy came and stood beside him. Pa said, "We're thankful to you folks."

"We're proud to help," said Wilson.

"We're beholden to you," said Pa.

"There's no beholden in a time of dying," said Wilson, and Sairy echoed him, "Never no beholden."

Al said, "I'll fix your car—me an' Tom will." And Al looked proud that he could return the family's obligation.

"We could use some help." Wilson admitted the retiring of the obligation.

Pa said, "We got to figger what to do. They's laws. You got to report a death, an' when you do that, they either take forty dollars for the undertaker or they take him for a pauper."

Uncle John broke in, "We never did have no paupers."

Tom said, "Maybe we got to learn. We never got booted off no land before, neither."

"We done it clean," said Pa. "There can't no blame be laid on us. We never took nothin' we couldn' pay; we never suffered no man's charity. When Tom here got in trouble we could hold up our heads. He only done what any man would a done."

"Then what'll we do?" Uncle John asked.

"We go in like the law says an' they'll come out for him. We on'y got a hundred an' fifty dollars. They take forty to bury Grampa an' we won't get to California—or else they'll bury him a pauper." The men stirred restively, and they studied the darkening ground in front of their knees.

Pa said softly, "Grampa buried his pa with his own hand, done it in dignity, an' shaped the grave nice with his own shovel. That was a time when a man had the right to be buried by his own son an' a son had the right to bury his own father."

"The law says different now," said Uncle John.

"Sometimes the law can't be foller'd no way," said Pa.

"Not in decency, anyways. They's lots a times you can't. When Floyd was loose an' goin' wild, law said we got to give him up—an' nobody give him up. Sometimes a fella got to sift the law. I'm sayin' now I got the right to bury my own pa. Anybody got somepin to say?"

The preacher rose high on his elbow. "Law changes," he said, "but 'got to's' go on. You got the right to do what you got to do."

Pa turned to Uncle John. "It's your right too, John. You got any word against?"

"No word against," said Uncle John. "On'y it's like hidin' him in the night. Grampa's way was t'come out a-shootin'."

Pa said ashamedly, "We can't do like Grampa done. We got to get to California 'fore our money gives out."

Tom broke in, "Sometimes fellas workin' dig up a man an' then they raise hell an' figger he been killed. The gov'-ment's got more interest in a dead man than a live one. They'll go hell-scrapin' tryin' to fin' out who he was and how he died. I offer we put a note of writin' in a bottle an' lay it with Grampa, tellin' who he is an' how he died, an' why he's buried here."

Pa nodded agreement. "Tha's good. Wrote out in a nice han'. Be not so lonesome too, knowin' his name is there with 'im, not jus' a old fella lonesome underground. Any more stuff to say?" The circle was silent.

Pa turned his head to Ma. "You'll lay 'im out?"

"I'll lay 'im out," said Ma. "But who's to get supper?"

Sairy Wilson said, "I'll get supper. You go right ahead. Me an' that big girl of yourn."

"We sure thank you," said Ma. "Noah, you get into them kegs an' bring out some nice pork. Salt won't be deep in it yet, but it'll be right nice eatin'."

"We got a half sack a potatoes," said Sairy.

Ma said, "Gimme two half-dollars." Pa dug in his pocket and gave her the silver. She found the basin, filled it full of water, and went into the tent. It was nearly dark in there. Sairy came in and lighted a candle and stuck it upright on a box and then she went out. For a moment Ma looked down at the dead old man. And then in pity she tore a strip from her own apron and tied up his jaw. She straightened his limbs, folded his hands over his chest. She held his eyelids down and laid a silver piece on each one. She buttoned his shirt and washed his face.

Sairy looked in, saying, "Can I give you any help?"

Ma looked slowly up. "Come in," she said. "I like to talk to ya."

"That's a good big girl you got," said Sairy. "She's right in peelin' potatoes. What can I do to help?"

"I was gonna wash Grampa all over," said Ma, "but he got no other clo'es to put on. An' 'course your quilt's spoilt. Can't never get the smell a death from a quilt. I seen a dog growl an' shake at a mattress my ma died on, an' that was two years later. We'll wrop 'im in your quilt. We'll make it up to you. We got a quilt for you."

Sairy said, "You shouldn' talk like that. We're proud to help. I ain't felt so—safe in a long time. People needs—to help."

Ma nodded. "They do," she said. She looked long into the old whiskery face, with its bound jaw and silver eyes shining in the candlelight. "He ain't gonna look natural. We'll wrop him up."

"The ol' lady took it good."

"Why, she's so old," said Ma, "maybe she don't even rightly know what happened. Maybe she won't really know for quite a while. Besides, us folks takes a pride holdin' in. My pa used to say, 'Anybody can break down. It takes a man not to.' We always try to hold in." She folded the quilt neatly about Grampa's legs and around his shoulders. She brought the corner of the quilt over his head like a cowl and pulled it down over his face. Sairy handed her half-a-dozen big safety pins, and she pinned the quilt neatly and tightly about the long package. And at last she stood up. "It won't be a bad burying," she said. "We got a preacher to see him in, an' his folks is all aroun'." Suddenly she swayed a little, and Sairy went to her and steadied her. "It's sleep—" Ma said in a shamed tone. "No, I'm awright. We been so busy gettin' ready, you see."

"Come out in the air," Sairy said.

"Yeah, I'm all done here." Sairy blew out the candle and the two went out.

A bright fire burned in the bottom of the little gulch. And Tom, with sticks and wire, had made supports from which two kettles hung and bubbled furiously, and good steam poured out under the lids. Rose of Sharon knelt on the ground out of range of the burning heat, and she had a long spoon in her hand. She saw Ma come out of the tent, and she stood up and went to her.

"Ma," she said. "I got to ask."

"Scared again?" Ma asked. "Why, you can't get through nine months without sorrow."

"But will it—hurt the baby?"

Ma said, "They used to be a sayin', 'A chile born outa sorrow'll be a happy chile.' Isn't that so, Mis' Wilson?"

"I heard it like that," said Sairy. "An' I heard the other: 'Born outa too much joy'll be a doleful boy.'"

"I'm all jumpy inside," said Rose of Sharon.

"Well, we ain't none of us jumpin' for fun," said Ma. "You jes' keep watchin' the pots."

On the edge of the ring of firelight the men had gathered. For tools they had a shovel and a mattock. Pa marked out the ground—eight feet long and three feet wide. The work went on in relays. Pa chopped the earth with the mattock and then Uncle John shoveled it out. Al chopped and Tom shoveled, Noah chopped and Connie shoveled. And the hole drove down, for the work never diminished in speed. The shovels of dirt flew out of the hole in quick spurts. When Tom was shoulder deep in the rectangular pit, he said, "How deep, Pa?"

"Good an' deep. A couple feet more. You get out now, Tom, and get that paper wrote."

Tom boosted himself out of the hole and Noah took his place. Tom went to Ma, where she tended the fire. "We got any paper an' pen, Ma?"

Ma shook her head slowly, "No-o. That's one thing we didn' bring." She looked toward Sairy. And the little woman walked quickly to her tent. She brought back a Bible and a half pencil. "Here," she said. "They's a clear page in front. Use that an' tear it out." She handed book and pencil to Tom.

Tom sat down in the firelight. He squinted his eyes in concentration, and at last wrote slowly and carefully on the end paper in big clear letters: "This here is William James Joad, dyed of a stroke, old old man. His fokes bured him becaws they got no money to pay for funerls. Nobody kilt him. Jus a stroke an he dyed." He stopped. "Ma, listen to this here." He read it slowly to her.

"Why, that soun's nice," she said. "Can't you stick on somepin from Scripture so it'll be religious? Open up an' git a-sayin' somepin outa Scripture."

"Got to be short," said Tom. "I ain't got much room lef'
on the page."

Sairy said, "How 'bout 'God have mercy on his soul'?"

"No," said Tom. "Sounds too much like he was hung. I'll
copy somepin." He turned the pages and read, mumbling his
lips, saying the words under his breath. "Here's a good short
one," he said. " 'An' Lot said unto them, Oh, not so, my
Lord.' "

"Don't mean nothin'," said Ma. "Long's you're gonna put
one down, it might's well mean somepin."

Sairy said, "Turn to Psalms, over further. You kin always
get somepin outa Psalms."

Tom flipped the pages and looked down the verses. "Now
here *is* one," he said. "This here's a nice one, just blowed full
a religion: 'Blessed is he whose transgression is forgiven,
whose sin is covered.' How's that?"

"That's real nice," said Ma. "Put that one in."

Tom wrote it carefully. Ma rinsed and wiped a fruit jar
and Tom screwed the lid down tight on it. "Maybe the
preacher ought to wrote it," he said.

Ma said, "No, the preacher wan't no kin." She took the jar
from him and went into the dark tent. She unpinned the
covering and slipped the fruit jar in under the thin cold
hands and pinned the comforter tight again. And then she
went back to the fire.

The men came from the grave, their faces shining with
perspiration. "Awright," said Pa. He and John and Noah and
Al went into the tent, and they came out carrying the long,
pinned bundle between them. They carried it to the grave.
Pa leaped into the hole and received the bundle in his arms
and laid it gently down. Uncle John put out a hand and
helped Pa out of the hole. Pa asked, "How about Granma?"

"I'll see," Ma said. She walked to the mattress and looked down at the old woman for a moment. Then she went back to the grave. "Sleepin'," she said. "Maybe she'd hold it against me, but I ain't a-gonna wake her up. She's tar'd."

Pa said, "Where at's the preacher? We oughta have a prayer."

Tom said, "I seen him walkin' down the road. He don't like to pray no more."

"Don't like to pray?"

"No," said Tom. "He ain't a preacher no more. He figgers it ain't right to fool people actin' like a preacher when he ain't a preacher. I bet he went away so nobody wouldn' ast him."

Casy had come quietly near, and he heard Tom speaking. "I didn' run away," he said. "I'll he'p you folks, but I won't fool ya."

Pa said, "Won't you say a few words? Ain't none of our folks ever been buried without a few words."

"I'll say 'em," said the preacher.

Connie led Rose of Sharon to the graveside, she reluctant. "You got to," Connie said. "It ain't decent not to. It'll jus' be a little."

The firelight fell on the grouped people, showing their faces and their eyes, dwindling on their dark clothes. All the hats were off now. The light danced, jerking over the people.

Casy said, "It'll be a short one." He bowed his head, and the others followed his lead. Casy said solemnly, "This here ol' man jus' lived a life an' jus' died out of it. I don' know whether he was good or bad, but that don't matter much. He was alive, an' that's what matters. An' now he's dead, an' that don't matter. Heard a fella tell a poem one time, an' he says 'All that lives is holy.' Got to thinkin', an' purty soon it means more than the words says. An' I wouldn' pray for a ol' fella that's dead. He's awright. He got a job to do, but it's all laid out for 'im an' there's on'y one way to do it. But us, we got a job to do, an' they's a thousan' ways, an' we don' know which one to take. An' if I was to pray, it'd be for the folks that don' know which way to turn. Grampa here, he got the easy straight. An' now cover 'im up and let 'im get to his work." He raised his head.

Pa said, "Amen," and the others muttered, "A-men." Then Pa took the shovel, half filled it with dirt, and spread it gently into the black hole. He handed the shovel to Uncle John, and John dropped in a shovelful. Then the shovel went from hand to hand until every man had his turn. When all had taken their duty and their right, Pa attacked the mound of loose dirt and hurriedly filled the hole. The women moved back to the fire to see to supper. Ruthie and Winfield watched, absorbed.

Ruthie said solemnly, "Grampa's down under there." And Winfield looked at her with horrified eyes. And then he ran away to the fire and sat on the ground and sobbed to himself.

Pa half filled the hole, and then he stood panting with the effort while Uncle John finished it. And John was shaping up the mound when Tom stopped him. "Listen," Tom said. " 'F we leave a grave, they'll have it open in no time. We got to hide it. Level her off an' we'll strew dry grass. We got to do that."

Pa said, "I didn' think a that. It ain't right to leave a grave unmounded."

"Can't he'p it," said Tom. "They'd dig 'im right up, an' we'd get it for breakin' the law. You know what I get if I break the law."

"Yeah," Pa said. "I forgot that." He took the shovel from

John and leveled the grave. "She'll sink, come winter," he said.

"Can't he'p that," said Tom. "We'll be a long ways off by winter. Tromp her in good, an' we'll strew stuff over her."

When the pork and potatoes were done the families sat about on the ground and ate, and they were quiet, staring into the fire. Wilson, tearing a slab of meat with his teeth, sighed with contentment. "Nice eatin' pig," he said.

"Well," Pa explained, "we had a couple shoats, an' we thought we might's well eat 'em. Can't get nothin' for them. When we get kinda use' ta movin' an' Ma can set up bread, why, it'll be pretty nice, seein' the country an' two kags a' pork right in the truck. How long you folks been on the road?"

Wilson cleared his teeth with his tongue and swallowed. "We ain't been lucky," he said. "We been three weeks from home."

"Why, God Awmighty, we aim to be in California in ten days or less.".

Al broke in, "I dunno, Pa. With that load we're packin', we maybe ain't never gonna get there. Not if they's mountains to go over."

They were silent about the fire. Their faces were turned downward and their hair and foreheads showed in the firelight. Above the little dome of the firelight the summer stars shone thinly, and the heat of the day was gradually withdrawing. On her mattress, away from the fire, Granma whimpered softly like a puppy. The heads of all turned in her direction.

Ma said, "Rosasharn, like a good girl go lay down with Granma. She needs somebody now. She's knowin', now."

Rose of Sharon got to her feet and walked to the mattress and lay beside the old woman, and the murmur of their soft voices drifted to the fire. Rose of Sharon and Granma whispered together on the mattress.

Noah said, "Funny thing is—losin' Grampa ain't made me feel no different than I done before. I ain't no sadder than I was."

"It's just the same thing," Casy said. "Grampa an' the old place, they was jus' the same thing."

Al said, "It's a goddamn shame. He been talkin' what he's gonna do, how he gonna squeeze grapes over his head an' let the juice run in his whiskers, an' all stuff like that."

Casy said, "He was foolin', all the time. I think he knowed it. An' Grampa didn' die tonight. He died the minute you took 'im off the place."

"You sure a that?" Pa cried.

"Why, no. Oh, he was breathin'," Casy went on, "but he was dead. He was that place, an' he knowed it."

Uncle John said, "Did you know he was a-dyin'?"

"Yeah," said Casy. "I knowed it."

John gazed at him, and a horror grew in his face. "An' you didn' tell nobody?"

"What good?" Casy asked.

"We—we might of did somepin."

"What?"

"I don' know, but——"

"No," Casy said, "you couldn' a done nothin'. Your way was fixed an' Grampa didn' have no part in it. He didn' suffer none. Not after fust thing this mornin'. He's jus' stayin' with the lan'. He couldn' leave it."

Uncle John sighed deeply.

Wilson said, "We hadda leave my brother Will." The

heads turned toward him. "Him an' me had forties side by side. He's older'n me. Neither one ever drove a car. Well, we went in an' we sol' ever'thing. Will, he bought a car, an' they give him a kid to show 'im how to use it. So the afternoon 'fore we're gonna start, Will an' Aunt Minnie go a-practicin'. Will, he comes to a bend in the road an' he yells 'Whoa' an' yanks back, an' he goes through a fence. An' he yells 'Whoa, you bastard' an' tromps down on the gas an' goes over into a gulch. An' there he was. Didn't have nothin' more to sell an' didn't have no car. But it were his own damn fault, praise God. He's so damn mad he won't come along with us, jus' set there a-cussin' an' a-cussin'."

"What's he gonna do?"

"I dunno. He's too mad to figger. An' we couldn' wait. On'y had eighty-five dollars to go on. We couldn' set an' cut it up, but we et it up anyways. Didn' go a hunderd mile when a tooth in the rear end bust, an' cost thirty dollars to get her fix', an' then we got to get a tire, an' then a spark plug cracked, an' Sairy got sick. Had ta stop ten days. An' now the goddamn car is bust again, an' money's gettin' low. I dunno when we'll ever get to California. 'F I could on'y fix a car, but I don' know nothin' about cars."

Al asked importantly, "What's the matter?"

"Well, she jus' won't run. Starts an' farts an' stops. In a minute she'll start again, an' then 'fore you can git her goin', she peters out again."

"Runs a minute an' then dies?"

"Yes, sir. An' I can't keep her a-goin' no matter how much gas I give her. Got worse an' worse, an' now I cain't get her a-movin' a-tall."

Al was very proud and very mature, then. "I think you got a plugged gas line. I'll blow her out for ya."

And Pa was proud too. "He's a good hand with a car," Pa said.

"Well, I'll sure thank ya for a han'. I sure will. Makes a fella kinda feel—like a little kid, when he can't fix nothin'. When we get to California I aim to get me a nice car. Maybe she won't break down."

Pa said, "When we get there. Gettin' there's the trouble."

"Oh, but she's worth it," said Wilson. "Why, I seen han'-bills how they need folks to pick fruit, an' good wages. Why, jus' think how it's gonna be, under them shady trees a-pickin' fruit an' takin' a bite ever' once in a while. Why, hell, they don't care how much you eat 'cause they got so much. An' with them good wages, maybe a fella can get hisself a little piece a land an' work out for extra cash. Why, hell, in a couple years I bet a fella could have a place of his own."

Pa said, "We seen them han'bills. I got one right here." He took out his purse and from it took a folded orange handbill. In black type it said, "Pea Pickers Wanted in California. Good Wages All Season. 800 Pickers Wanted."

Wilson looked at it curiously. "Why, that's the one I seen. The very same one. You s'pose—maybe they got all eight hunderd awready?"

Pa said, "This is jus' one little part a California. Why, that's the secon' biggest State we got. S'pose they did get all them eight hunderd. They's plenty places else. I rather pick fruit anyways. Like you says, under them trees an' pickin' fruit—why, even the kids'd like to do that."

Suddenly Al got up and walked to the Wilsons' touring car. He looked in for a moment and then came back and sat down.

"You can't fix her tonight," Wilson said.

"I know. I'll get to her in the morning."

Tom had watched his young brother carefully. "I was thinkin' somepin like that myself," he said.

Noah asked, "What you two fellas talkin' about?"

Tom and Al were silent, each waiting for the other. "You tell 'em," Al said finally.

"Well, maybe it's no good, an' maybe it ain't the same thing Al's thinking. Here she is, anyways. We got a overload, but Mr. an' Mis' Wilson ain't. If some of us folks could ride with them an' take some a their light stuff in the truck, we wouldn't break no springs an' we could git up hills. An' me an' Al both knows about a car, so we could keep that car a-rollin'. We'd keep together on the road an' it'd be good for ever'body."

Wilson jumped up. "Why, sure. Why, we'd be proud. We certain'y would. You hear that, Sairy?"

"It's a nice thing," said Sairy. "Wouldn' be a burden on you folks?"

"No, by God," said Pa. "Wouldn't be no burden at all. You'd be helpin' us."

Wilson settled back uneasily. "Well, I dunno."

"What's a matter, don' you wanta?"

"Well, ya see—I on'y got 'bout thirty dollars lef', an' I won't be no burden."

Ma said, "You won't be no burden. Each'll help each, an' we'll all git to California. Sairy Wilson he'ped lay Grampa out," and she stopped. The relationship was plain.

Al cried, "That car'll take six easy. Say me to drive, an' Rosasharn an' Connie and Granma. Then we take the big light stuff an' pile her on the truck. An' we'll trade off ever' so often." He spoke loudly, for a load of worry was lifted from him.

They smiled shyly and looked down at the ground. Pa

fingered the dusty earth with his fingertips. He said, "Ma favors a white house with oranges growin' around. They's a big pitcher on a calendar she seen."

Sairy said, "If I get sick again, you got to go on an' get there. We ain't a-goin' to burden."

Ma looked carefully at Sairy, and she seemed to see for the first time the pain-tormented eyes and the face that was haunted and shrinking with pain. And Ma said, "We gonna see you get through. You said yourself, you can't let help go unwanted."

Sairy studied her wrinkled hands in the firelight. "We got to get some sleep tonight." She stood up.

"Grampa—it's like he's dead a year," Ma said.

The families moved lazily to their sleep, yawning luxuriously. Ma sloshed the tin plates off a little and rubbed the grease free with a flour sack. The fire died down and the stars descended. Few passenger cars went by on the highway now, but the transport trucks thundered by at intervals and put little earthquakes in the ground. In the ditch the cars were hardly visible under the starlight. A tied dog howled at the service station down the road. The families were quiet and sleeping, and the field mice grew bold and scampered about among the mattresses. Only Sairy Wilson was awake. She stared into the sky and braced her body firmly against pain.

Chapter Fourteen

THE western land, nervous under the beginning change. The Western States, nervous as horses before a thunder storm. The great owners, nervous, sensing a change, knowing nothing of the nature of the change. The great owners, striking at the immediate thing, the widening government, the growing labor unity; striking at new taxes, at plans; not knowing these things are results, not causes. Results, not causes; results, not causes. The causes lie deep and simply—the causes are a hunger in a stomach, multiplied a million times; a hunger in a single soul, hunger for joy and some security, multiplied a million times; muscles and mind aching to grow, to work, to create, multiplied a million times. The last clear definite function of man—muscles aching to work, minds aching to create beyond the single need—this is man. To build a wall, to build a house, a dam, and in the wall and house and dam to put something of Manself, and to Manself take back something of the wall, the house, the dam; to take hard muscles from the lifting, to take the clear lines and form from conceiving. For man, unlike any other thing organic or inorganic in the universe, grows beyond his work, walks up the stairs of his concepts, emerges ahead of his accomplishments. This you may say of man—when theories change and crash, when schools, philosophies, when narrow dark alleys of thought, national, religious, economic,

grow and disintegrate, man reaches, stumbles forward, pain-
fully, mistakenly sometimes. Having stepped forward, he
may slip back, but only half a step, never the full step back.
This you may say and know it and know it. This you may
know when the bombs plummet out of the black planes on
the market place, when prisoners are stuck like pigs, when
the crushed bodies drain filthily in the dust. You may know
it in this way. If the step were not being taken, if the
stumbling-forward ache were not alive, the bombs would not
fall, the throats would not be cut. Fear the time when the
bombs stop falling while the bombers live—for every bomb
is proof that the spirit has not died. And fear the time when
the strikes stop while the great owners live—for every little
beaten strike is proof that the step is being taken. And this
you can know—fear the time when Manself will not suffer
and die for a concept, for this one quality is the foundation
of Manself, and this one quality is man, distinctive in the
universe.

The Western States nervous under the beginning change.
Texas and Oklahoma, Kansas and Arkansas, New Mexico,
Arizona, California. A single family moved from the land.
Pa borrowed money from the bank, and now the bank wants
the land. The land company—that's the bank when it has land
—wants tractors, not families on the land. Is a tractor bad? Is
the power that turns the long furrows wrong? If this tractor
were ours it would be good—not mine, but ours. If our tractor turned the long furrows of our land, it would be good.
Not my land, but ours. We could love that tractor then as
we have loved this land when it was ours. But this tractor
does two things—it turns the land and turns us off the land.
There is little difference between this tractor and a tank. The

people are driven, intimidated, hurt by both. We must think about this.

One man, one family driven from the land; this rusty car creaking along the highway to the west. I lost my land, a single tractor took my land. I am alone and I am bewildered. And in the night one family camps in a ditch and another family pulls in and the tents come out. The two men squat on their hams and the women and children listen. Here is the node, you who hate change and fear revolution. Keep these two squatting men apart; make them hate, fear, suspect each other. Here is the anlage of the thing you fear. This is the zygote. For here "I lost my land" is changed; a cell is split and from its splitting grows the thing you hate—"We lost *our* land." The danger is here, for two men are not as lonely and perplexed as one. And from this first "we" there grows a still more dangerous thing: "I have a little food" plus "I have none." If from this problem the sum is "We have a little food," the thing is on its way, the movement has direction. Only a little multiplication now, and this land, this tractor are ours. The two men squatting in a ditch, the little fire, the side-meat stewing in a single pot, the silent, stone-eyed women; behind, the children listening with their souls to words their minds do not understand. The night draws down. The baby has a cold. Here, take this blanket. It's wool. It was my mother's blanket—take it for the baby. This is the thing to bomb. This is the beginning—from "I" to "we."

If you who own the things people must have could understand this, you might preserve yourself. If you could separate causes from results, if you could know that Paine, Marx, Jefferson, Lenin, were results, not causes, you might survive. But that you cannot know. For the quality of owning freezes you forever into "I," and cuts you off forever from the "we."

The Western States are nervous under the beginning change. Need is the stimulus to concept, concept to action. A half-million people moving over the country; a million more restive, ready to move; ten million more feeling the first nervousness.

And tractors turning the multiple furrows in the vacant land.

Chapter Fifteen

ALONG 66 the hamburger stands—Al & Susy's Place—Carl's Lunch—Joe & Minnie—Will's Eats. Board-and-bat shacks. Two gasoline pumps in front, a screen door, a long bar, stools, and a foot rail. Near the door three slot machines, showing through glass the wealth in nickels three bars will bring. And beside them, the nickel phonograph with records piled up like pies, ready to swing out to the turntable and play dance music, "Ti-pi-ti-pi-tin," "Thanks for the Memory," Bing Crosby, Benny Goodman. At one end of the counter a covered case; candy cough drops, caffeine sulphate called Sleepless, No-Doze; candy, cigarettes, razor blades, aspirin, Bromo-Seltzer, Alka-Seltzer. The walls decorated with posters, bathing girls, blondes with big breasts and slender hips and waxen faces, in white bathing suits, and holding a bottle of Coca-Cola and smiling—see what you get with a Coca-Cola. Long bar, and salts, peppers, mustard pots, and paper napkins. Beer taps behind the counter, and in back the coffee urns, shiny and steaming, with glass gauges showing the coffee level. And pies in wire cages and oranges in pyramids of four. And little piles of Post Toasties, corn flakes, stacked up in designs.

The signs on cards, picked out with shining mica: Pies Like Mother Used to Make. Credit Makes Enemies, Let's Be Friends. Ladies May Smoke But Be Careful Where You Lay

Your Butts. Eat Here and Keep Your Wife for a Pet. IITYWYBAD?

Down at one end the cooking plates, pots of stew, potatoes, pot roast, roast beef, gray roast pork waiting to be sliced.

Minnie or Susy or Mae, middle-aging behind the counter, hair curled and rouge and powder on a sweating face. Taking orders in a soft low voice, calling them to the cook with a screech like a peacock. Mopping the counter with circular strokes, polishing the big shining coffee urns. The cook is Joe or Carl or Al, hot in a white coat and apron, beady sweat on white forehead, below the white cook's cap; moody, rarely speaking, looking up for a moment at each new entry. Wiping the griddle, slapping down the hamburger. He repeats Mae's orders gently, scrapes the griddle, wipes it down with burlap. Moody and silent.

Mae is the contact, smiling, irritated, near to outbreak; smiling while her eyes look on past—unless for truck drivers. There's the backbone of the joint. Where the trucks stop, that's where the customers come. Can't fool truck drivers, they know. They bring the custom. They know. Give 'em a stale cup a coffee an' they're off the joint. Treat 'em right an' they come back. Mae really smiles with all her might at truck drivers. She bridles a little, fixes her back hair so that her breasts will lift with her raised arms, passes the time of day and indicates great things, great times, great jokes. Al never speaks. He is no contact. Sometimes he smiles a little at a joke, but he never laughs. Sometimes he looks up at the vivaciousness in Mae's voice, and then he scrapes the griddle with a spatula, scrapes the grease into an iron trough around the plate. He presses down a hissing hamburger with his spatula. He lays the split buns on the plate to toast and heat. He gathers up stray onions from the plate and heaps them on the meat and presses them in with the spatula. He puts half the bun on top of the meat, paints the other half with melted butter, with thin pickle relish. Holding the bun on the meat, he slips the spatula under the thin pad of meat, flips it over, lays the buttered half on top, and drops the hamburger on a small plate. Quarter of a dill pickle, two black olives beside the sandwich. Al skims the plate down the counter like a quoit. And he scrapes his griddle with the spatula and looks moodily at the stew kettle.

Cars whisking by on 66. License plates. Mass., Tenn., R.I., N.Y., Vt., Ohio. Going west. Fine cars, cruising at sixty-five.

There goes one of them Cords. Looks like a coffin on wheels.

But, Jesus, how they travel!

See that La Salle? Me for that. I ain't a hog. I go for a La Salle.

'F ya goin' big, what's a matter with a Cad'? Jus' a little bigger, little faster.

I'd take a Zephyr myself. You ain't ridin' no fortune, but you got class an' speed. Give me a Zephyr.

Well, sir, you may get a laugh outa this—I'll take a Buick-Puick. That's good enough.

But, hell, that costs in the Zephyr class an' it ain't got the sap.

I don' care. I don' want nothin' to do with nothing of Henry Ford's. I don' like 'im. Never did. Got a brother worked in the plant. Oughta hear him tell.

Well, a Zephyr got sap.

The big cars on the highway. Languid, heat-raddled ladies, small nucleuses about whom revolve a thousand accouter-

ments: creams, ointments to grease themselves, coloring matter in phials—black, pink, red, white, green, silver—to change
the color of hair, eyes, lips, nails, brows, lashes, lids. Oils,
seeds, and pills to make the bowels move. A bag of bottles,
syringes, pills, powders, fluids, jellies to make their sexual
intercourse safe, odorless, and unproductive. And this apart
from clothes. What a hell of a nuisance!

Lines of weariness around the eyes, lines of discontent
down from the mouth, breasts lying heavily in little ham-
mocks, stomach and thighs straining against cases of rubber.
And the mouths panting, the eyes sullen, disliking sun and
wind and earth, resenting food and weariness, hating time
that rarely makes them beautiful and always makes them old.

Beside them, little pot-bellied men in light suits and pan-
ama hats; clean, pink men with puzzled, worried eyes, with
restless eyes. Worried because formulas do not work out;
hungry for security and yet sensing its disappearance from
the earth. In their lapels the insignia of lodges and service
clubs, places where they can go and, by a weight of numbers
of little worried men, reassure themselves that business is
noble and not the curious ritualized thievery they know it is;
that business men are intelligent in spite of the records of
their stupidity; that they are kind and charitable in spite of
the principles of sound business; that their lives are rich instead of the thin tiresome routines they know; and that a
time is coming when they will not be afraid any more.

And these two, going to California; going to sit in the
lobby of the Beverly-Wilshire Hotel and watch people they
envy go by, to look at mountains—mountains, mind you, and
great trees—he with his worried eyes and she thinking how
the sun will dry her skin. Going to look at the Pacific Ocean,
and I'll bet a hundred thousand dollars to nothing at all, he

will say, "It isn't as big as I thought it would be." And she will envy plump young bodies on the beach. Going to California really to go home again. To say, "So-and-So was at the table next to us at the Trocadero. She's really a mess, but she does wear nice clothes." And he, "I talked to good sound business men out there. They don't see a chance till we get rid of that fellow in the White House." And, "I got it from a man in the know—she has syphilis, you know. She was in that Warner picture. Man said she'd slept her way into pictures. Well, she got what she was looking for." But the worried eyes are never calm, and the pouting mouth is never glad. The big car cruising along at sixty.

I want a cold drink.

Well, there's something up ahead. Want to stop?

Do you think it would be clean?

Clean as you're going to find in this God-forsaken country.

Well, maybe the bottled soda will be all right.

The great car squeals and pulls to a stop. The fat worried man helps his wife out.

Mae looks at and past them as they enter. Al looks up from his griddle, and down again. Mae knows. They'll drink a five-cent soda and crab that it ain't cold enough. The woman will use six paper napkins and drop them on the floor. The man will choke and try to put the blame on Mae. The woman will sniff as though she smelled rotting meat and they will go out again and tell forever afterward that the people in the West are sullen. And Mae, when she is alone with Al, has a name for them. She calls them shitheels.

Truck drivers. That's the stuff.

Here's a big transport comin'. Hope they stop; take away

the taste of them shitheels. When I worked in that hotel in Albuquerque, Al, the way they steal—ever' darn thing. An' the bigger the car they got, the more they steal—towels, silver, soap dishes. I can't figger it.

And Al, morosely, Where ya think they get them big cars and stuff? Born with 'em? You won't never have nothin'.

The transport truck, a driver and relief. How 'bout stoppin' for a cup a Java? I know this dump.

How's the schedule?

Oh, we're ahead!

Pull up, then. They's a ol' war horse in here that's a kick. Good Java, too.

The truck pulls up. Two men in khaki riding trousers, boots, short jackets, and shiny-visored military caps. Screen door—slam.

H'ya, Mae?

Well, if it ain't Big Bill the Rat! When'd you get back on this run?

Week ago.

The other man puts a nickel in the phonograph, watches the disk slip free and the turntable rise up under it. Bing Crosby's voice—golden. "Thanks for the memory, of sunburn at the shore— You might have been a headache, but you never were a bore—" And the truck driver sings for Mae's ears, you might have been a haddock but you never was a whore—

Mae laughs. Who's ya frien', Bill? New on this run, ain't he?

The other puts a nickel in the slot machine, wins four slugs, and puts them back. Walks to the counter.

Well, what's it gonna be?

Oh, cup a Java. Kinda pie ya got?

Banana cream, pineapple cream, chocolate cream—an' apple.

Make it apple. Wait— Kind is that big thick one?

Mae lifts it out and sniffs it. Banana cream.

Cut off a hunk; make it a big hunk.

Man at the slot machine says, Two all around.

Two it is. Seen any new etchin's lately, Bill?

Well, here's one.

Now, you be careful front of a lady.

Oh, this ain't bad. Little kid comes in late ta school. Teacher says, "Why ya late?" Kid says, "Had a take a heifer down—get 'er bred." Teacher says, "Couldn't your ol' man do it?" Kid says, "Sure he could, but not as good as the bull."

Mae squeaks with laughter, harsh screeching laughter. Al, slicing onions carefully on a board, looks up and smiles, and then looks down again. Truck drivers, that's the stuff. Gonna leave a quarter each for Mae. Fifteen cents for pie an' coffee an' a dime for Mae. An' they ain't tryin' to make her, neither.

Sitting together on the stools, spoons sticking up out of the coffee mugs. Passing the time of day. And Al, rubbing down his griddle, listening but making no comment. Bing Crosby's voice stops. The turntable drops down and the record swings into its place in the pile. The purple light goes off. The nickel, which has caused all this mechanism to work, has caused Crosby to sing and an orchestra to play—this nickel drops from between the contact points into the box where the profits go. This nickel, unlike most money, has actually done a job of work, has been physically responsible for a reaction.

Steam spurts from the valve of the coffee urn. The compressor of the ice machine chugs softly for a time and then stops. The electric fan in the corner waves its head slowly back and forth, sweeping the room with a warm breeze. On the highway, on 66, the cars whiz by.

They was a Massachusetts car stopped a while ago, said Mae.

Big Bill grasped his cup around the top so that the spoon stuck up between his first and second fingers. He drew in a snort of air with the coffee, to cool it. "You ought to be out on 66. Cars from all over the country. All headin' west. Never seen so many before. Sure some honeys on the road."

"We seen a wreck this mornin'," his companion said. "Big car. Big Cad', a special job and a honey, low, cream-color, special job. Hit a truck. Folded the radiator right back into the driver. Must a been doin' ninety. Steerin' wheel went right on through the guy an' lef' him a-wigglin' like a frog on a hook. Peach of a car. A honey. You can have her for peanuts now. Drivin' alone, the guy was."

Al looked up from his work. "Hurt the truck?"

"Oh, Jesus Christ! Wasn't a truck. One of them cut-down cars full a stoves an' pans an' mattresses an' kids an' chickens. Goin' west, you know. This guy come by us doin' ninety— r'ared up on two wheels just to pass us, an' a car's comin' so he cuts in an' whangs this here truck. Drove like he's blin' drunk. Jesus, the air was full a bed clothes an' chickens an' kids. Killed one kid. Never seen such a mess. We pulled up. Ol' man that's drivin' the truck, he jus' stan's there lookin' at that dead kid. Can't get a word out of 'im. Jus' rum-dumb. God Almighty, the road is full a them families goin' west. Never seen so many. Gets worse all a time. Wonder where the hell they all come from?"

"Wonder where they all go to," said Mae. "Come here for gas sometimes, but they don't hardly never buy nothin' else.

People says they steal. We ain't got nothin' layin' around. They never stole nothin' from us."

Big Bill, munching his pie, looked up the road through the screened window. "Better tie your stuff down. I think you got some of 'em comin' now."

A 1926 Nash sedan pulled wearily off the highway. The back seat was piled nearly to the ceiling with sacks, with pots and pans, and on the very top, right up against the ceiling, two boys rode. On the top of the car, a mattress and a folded tent; tent poles tied along the running board. The car pulled up to the gas pumps. A dark-haired, hatchet-faced man got slowly out. And the two boys slid down from the load and hit the ground.

Mae walked around the counter and stood in the door. The man was dressed in gray wool trousers and a blue shirt, dark blue with sweat on the back and under the arms. The boys in overalls and nothing else, ragged patched overalls. Their hair was light, and it stood up evenly all over their heads, for it had been roached. Their faces were streaked with dust. They went directly to the mud puddle under the hose and dug their toes into the mud.

The man asked, "Can we git some water, ma'am?"

A look of annoyance crossed Mae's face. "Sure, go ahead." She said softly over her shoulder, "I'll keep my eye on the hose." She watched while the man slowly unscrewed the radiator cap and ran the hose in.

A woman in the car, a flaxen-haired woman, said, "See if you can't git it here."

The man turned off the hose and screwed on the cap again. The little boys took the hose from him and they upended it and drank thirstily. The man took off his dark, stained hat and stood with a curious humility in front of the screen. "Could you see your way to sell us a loaf of bread, ma'am?"

Mae said, "This ain't a grocery store. We got bread to make san'widges."

"I know, ma'am." His humility was insistent. "We need bread and there ain't nothin' for quite a piece, they say."

" 'F we sell bread we gonna run out." Mae's tone was faltering.

"We're hungry," the man said.

"Whyn't you buy a san'widge? We got nice san'widges, hamburgs."

"We'd sure admire to do that, ma'am. But we can't. We got to make a dime do all of us." And he said embarrassedly, "We ain't got but a little."

Mae said, "You can't get no loaf a bread for a dime. We only got fifteen-cent loafs."

From behind her Al growled, "God Almighty, Mae, give 'em bread."

"We'll run out 'fore the bread truck comes."

"Run out, then, goddamn it," said Al. And he looked sullenly down at the potato salad he was mixing.

Mae shrugged her plump shoulders and looked to the truck drivers to show them what she was up against.

She held the screen door open and the man came in, bringing a smell of sweat with him. The boys edged in behind him and they went immediately to the candy case and stared in— not with craving or with hope or even with desire, but just with a kind of wonder that such things could be. They were alike in size and their faces were alike. One scratched his dusty ankle with the toe nails of his other foot. The other whispered some soft message and then they straightened their arms so that their clenched fists in the overall pockets showed through the thin blue cloth.

Mae opened a drawer and took out a long waxpaper-wrapped loaf. "This here is a fifteen-cent loaf."

The man put his hat back on his head. He answered with inflexible humility, "Won't you—can't you see your way to cut off ten cents' worth?"

Al said snarlingly, "Goddamn it, Mae. Give 'em the loaf."

The man turned toward Al. "No, we want ta buy ten cents' worth of it. We got it figgered awful close, mister, to get to California."

Mae said resignedly, "You can have this for ten cents."

"That'd be robbin' you, ma'am."

"Go ahead—Al says to take it." She pushed the wax-papered loaf across the counter. The man took a deep leather pouch from his rear pocket, untied the strings, and spread it open. It was heavy with silver and with greasy bills.

"May soun' funny to be so tight," he apologized. "We got a thousan' miles to go, an' we don' know if we'll make it." He dug in the pouch with a forefinger, located a dime, and pinched in for it. When he put it down on the counter he had a penny with it. He was about to drop the penny back into the pouch when his eye fell on the boys frozen before the candy counter. He moved slowly down to them. He pointed in the case at big long sticks of striped peppermint. "Is them penny candy, ma'am?"

Mae moved down and looked in. "Which ones?"

"There, them stripy ones."

The little boys raised their eyes to her face and they stopped breathing; their mouths were partly opened, their half-naked bodies were rigid.

"Oh—them. Well, no—them's two for a penny."

"Well, gimme two then, ma'am." He placed the copper cent carefully on the counter. The boys expelled their held breath softly. Mae held the big sticks out.

"Take 'em," said the man.

They reached timidly, each took a stick, and they held them down at their sides and did not look at them. But they looked at each other, and their mouth corners smiled rigidly with embarrassment.

"Thank you, ma'am." The man picked up the bread and went out the door, and the little boys marched stiffly behind him, the red-striped sticks held tightly against their legs. They leaped like chipmunks over the front seat and onto the top of the load, and they burrowed back out of sight like chipmunks.

The man got in and started his car, and with a roaring motor and a cloud of blue oily smoke the ancient Nash climbed up on the highway and went on its way to the west.

From inside the restaurant the truck drivers and Mae and Al stared after them.

Big Bill wheeled back. "Them wasn't two-for-a-cent candy," he said.

"What's that to you?" Mae said fiercely.

"Them was nickel apiece candy," said Bill.

"We got to get goin'," said the other man. "We're droppin' time." They reached in their pockets. Bill put a coin on the counter and the other man looked at it and reached again and put down a coin. They swung around and walked to the door.

"So long," said Bill.

Mae called, "Hey! Wait a minute. You got change."

"You go to hell," said Bill, and the screen door slammed. Mae watched them get into the great truck, watched it lumber off in low gear, and heard the shift up the whining gears to cruising ratio. "Al—" she said softly.

He looked up from the hamburger he was patting thin and stacking between waxed papers. "What ya want?"

"Look there." She pointed at the coins beside the cups— two half-dollars. Al walked near and looked, and then he went back to his work.

"Truck drivers," Mae said reverently, "an' after them shitheels."

Flies struck the screen with little bumps and droned away. The compressor chugged for a time and then stopped. On 66 the traffic whizzed by, trucks and fine streamlined cars and jalopies; and they went by with a vicious whiz. Mae took down the plates and scraped the pie crusts into a bucket. She found her damp cloth and wiped the counter with circular sweeps. And her eyes were on the highway, where life whizzed by.

Al wiped his hands on his apron. He looked at a paper pinned to the wall over the griddle. Three lines of marks in columns on the paper. Al counted the longest line. He walked along the counter to the cash register, rang "No Sale," and took out a handful of nickels.

"What ya doin'?" Mae asked.

"Number three's ready to pay off," said Al. He went to the third slot machine and played his nickels in, and on the fifth spin of the wheels the three bars came up and the jack pot dumped out into the cup. Al gathered up the big hand-ful of coins and went back of the counter. He dropped them in the drawer and slammed the cash register. Then he went back to his place and crossed out the line of dots. "Number three gets more play'n the others," he said. "Maybe I ought to shift 'em around." He lifted a lid and stirred the slowly simmering stew.

"I wonder what they'll do in California?" said Mae.

"Who?"

"Them folks that was just in."

"Christ knows," said Al.

"S'pose they'll get work?"

"How the hell would I know?" said Al.

She stared eastward along the highway. "Here comes a transport, double. Wonder if they stop? Hope they do." And as the huge truck came heavily down from the highway and parked, Mae seized her cloth and wiped the whole length of the counter. And she took a few swipes at the gleaming coffee urn too, and turned up the bottle-gas under the urn. Al brought out a handful of little turnips and started to peel them. Mae's face was gay when the door opened and the two uniformed truck drivers entered.

"Hi, sister!"

"I won't be a sister to no man," said Mae. They laughed and Mae laughed. "What'll it be, boys?"

"Oh, a cup a Java. What kinda pie ya got?"

"Pineapple cream an' banana cream an' chocolate cream an' apple."

"Give me apple. No, wait—what's that big thick one?"

Mae picked up the pie and smelled it. "Pineapple cream," she said.

"Well, chop out a hunk a that."

The cars whizzed viciously by on 66.

Chapter Sixteen

JOADS and Wilsons crawled westward as a unit: El Reno and Bridgeport, Clinton, Elk City, Sayre, and Texola. There's the border, and Oklahoma was behind. And this day the cars crawled on and on, through the Panhandle of Texas. Shamrock and Alanreed, Groom and Yarnell. Then went through Amarillo in the evening, drove too long, and camped when it was dusk. They were tired and dusty and hot. Granma had convulsions from the heat, and she was weak when they stopped.

That night Al stole a fence rail and made a ridge pole on the truck, braced at both ends. That night they ate nothing but pan biscuits, cold and hard, held over from breakfast. They flopped down on the mattresses and slept in their clothes. The Wilsons didn't even put up their tent.

Joads and Wilsons were in flight across the Panhandle, the rolling gray country, lined and cut with old flood scars. They were in flight out of Oklahoma and across Texas. The land turtles crawled through the dust and the sun whipped the earth, and in the evening the heat went out of the sky and the earth sent up a wave of heat from itself.

Two days the families were in flight, but on the third the land was too huge for them and they settled into a new technique of living; the highway became their home and movement their medium of expression. Little by little they settled into the new life. Ruthie and Winfield first, then Al, then

Connie and Rose of Sharon, and, last, the older ones. The land rolled like great stationary ground swells. Wildorado and Vega and Boise and Glenrio. That's the end of Texas. New Mexico and the mountains. In the far distance, waved up against the sky, the mountains stood. And the wheels of the cars creaked around, and the engines were hot, and the steam spurted around the radiator caps. They crawled to the Pecos river, and crossed at Santa Rosa. And they went on for twenty miles.

Al Joad drove the touring car, and his mother sat beside him, and Rose of Sharon beside her. Ahead the truck crawled. The hot air folded in waves over the land, and the mountains shivered in the heat. Al drove listlessly, hunched back in the seat, his hand hooked easily over the cross-bar of the steering wheel; his gray hat, peaked and pulled to an incredibly cocky shape, was low over one eye; and as he drove, he turned and spat out the side now and then.

Ma, beside him, had folded her hands in her lap, had retired into a resistance against weariness. She sat loosely, letting the movement of the car sway her body and her head. She squinted her eyes ahead at the mountains. Rose of Sharon was braced against the movement of the car, her feet pushed tight against the floor, and her right elbow hooked over the door. And her plump face was tight against the movement, and her head jiggled sharply because her neck muscles were tight. She tried to arch her whole body as a rigid container to preserve her fetus from shock. She turned her head toward her mother.

"Ma," she said. Ma's eyes lighted up and she drew her attention toward Rose of Sharon. Her eyes went over the tight, tired, plump face, and she smiled. "Ma," the girl said, "when we get there, all you gonna pick fruit an' kinda live in the country, ain't you?"

Ma smiled a little satirically. "We ain't there yet," she said. "We don't know what it's like. We got to see."

"Me an' Connie don't want to live in the country no more," the girl said. "We got it all planned up what we gonna do."

For a moment a little worry came on Ma's face. "Ain't you gonna stay with us—with the family?" she asked.

"Well, we talked all about it, me an' Connie. Ma, we wanna live in a town." She went on excitedly, "Connie gonna get a job in a store or maybe a fact'ry. An' he's gonna study at home, maybe radio, so he can git to be a expert an' maybe later have his own store. An' we'll go to pitchers whenever. An' Connie says I'm gonna have a *doctor* when the baby's born; an' he says we'll see how times is, an' maybe I'll go to a hospiddle. An' we'll have a car, little car. An' after he studies at night, why—it'll be nice, an' he tore a page outa *Western Love Stories*, an' he's gonna send off for a course, 'cause it don't cost nothin' to send off. Says right on that clipping. I seen it. An', why—they even get you a job when you take that course—radios, it is—nice clean work, and a future. An' we'll live in town an' go to pitchers whenever, an'—well, I'm gonna have a 'lectric iron, an' the baby'll have all new stuff. Connie says all new stuff—white an'— Well, you seen in the catalogue all the stuff they got for a baby. Maybe right at first while Connie's studyin' at home it won't be so easy, but —well, when the baby comes, maybe he'll be all done studyin' an' we'll have a place, little bit of a place. We don't want nothin' fancy, but we want it nice for the baby—" Her face glowed with excitement. "An' I thought—well, I thought maybe we could all go in town, an' when Connie gets his store—maybe Al could work for him."

Ma's eyes had never left the flushing face. Ma watched the structure grow and followed it. "We don' want you to go 'way from us," she said. "It ain't good for folks to break up."

Al snorted, "Me work for Connie? How about Connie comes a-workin' for me? He thinks he's the on'y son-of-a-bitch can study at night?"

Ma suddenly seemed to know it was all a dream. She turned her head forward again and her body relaxed, but the little smile stayed around her eyes. "I wonder how Granma feels today," she said.

Al grew tense over the wheel. A little rattle had developed in the engine. He speeded up and the rattle increased. He retarded his spark and listened, and then he speeded up for a moment and listened. The rattle increased to a metallic pounding. Al blew his horn and pulled the car to the side of the road. Ahead the truck pulled up and then backed slowly. Three cars raced by, westward, and each one blew its horn and the last driver leaned out and yelled, "Where the hell ya think you're stoppin'?"

Tom backed the truck close, and then he got out and walked to the touring car. From the back of the loaded truck heads looked down. Al retarded his spark and listened to his idling motor. Tom asked, "What's a matter, Al?"

Al speeded the motor. "Listen to her." The rattling pound was louder now.

Tom listened. "Put up your spark an' idle," he said. He opened the hood and put his head inside. "Now speed her." He listened for a moment and then closed the hood. "Well, I guess you're right, Al," he said.

"Con-rod bearing, ain't it?"

"Sounds like it," said Tom.

"I kep' plenty oil in," Al complained.

"Well, it jus' didn' get to her. Drier'n a bitch monkey now. Well, there ain't nothin' to do but tear her out. Look, I'll pull ahead an' find a flat place to stop. You come ahead slow. Don't knock the pan out of her."

Wilson asked, "Is it bad?"

"Purty bad," said Tom, and walked back to the truck and moved slowly ahead.

Al explained, "I don' know what made her go out. I give her plenty of oil." Al knew the blame was on him. He felt his failure.

Ma said, "It ain't your fault. You done ever'thing right." And then she asked a little timidly, "Is it terrible bad?"

"Well, it's hard to get at, an' we got to get a new con-rod or else some babbitt in this one." He sighed deeply. "I sure am glad Tom's here. I never fitted no bearing. Hope to Jesus Tom did."

A huge red billboard stood beside the road ahead, and it threw a great oblong shadow. Tom edged the truck off the road and across the shallow roadside ditch, and he pulled up in the shadow. He got out and waited until Al came up.

"Now go easy," he called. "Take her slow or you'll break a spring too."

Al's face went red with anger. He throttled down his motor. "Goddamn it," he yelled, "I didn't burn that bearin' out! What d'ya mean, I'll bust a spring too?"

Tom grinned. "Keep all four feet on the groun'," he said. "I didn' mean nothin'. Jus' take her easy over this ditch."

Al grumbled as he inched the touring car down, and up the other side. "Don't you go givin' nobody no idear I burned out that bearin'." The engine clattered loudly now. Al pulled into the shade and shut down the motor.

Tom lifted the hood and braced it. "Can't even start on her before she cools off," he said. The family piled down from the cars and clustered about the touring car.

Pa asked, "How bad?" And he squatted on his hams.

Tom turned to Al. "Ever fitted one?"

"No," said Al, "I never. 'Course I had pans off."

Tom said, "Well, we got to tear the pan off an' get the rod out, an' we got to get a new part an' hone her an' shim her an' fit her. Good day's job. Got to go back to that las' place for a part, Santa Rosa. Albuquerque's about seventy-five miles on— Oh, Jesus, tomorra's Sunday! We can't get nothin' tomorra." The family stood silently. Ruthie crept close and peered into the open hood, hoping to see the broken part. Tom went on softly, "Tomorra's Sunday. Monday we'll get the thing an' prob'ly won't get her fitted 'fore Tuesday. We ain't got the tools to make it easy. Gonna be a job." The shadow of a buzzard slid across the earth, and the family all looked up at the sailing black bird.

Pa said, "What I'm scairt of is we'll run outa money so we can't git there 't all. Here's all us eatin', an' got to buy gas an' oil. 'F we run outa money, I don' know what we gonna do."

Wilson said, "Seems like it's my fault. This here goddamn wreck's give me trouble right along. You folks been nice to us. Now you jus' pack up an' get along. Me an' Sairy'll stay, an' we'll figger some way. We don't aim to put you folks out none."

Pa said slowly, "We ain't a-gonna do it. We got almost a kin bond. Grampa, he died in your tent."

Sairy said tiredly, "We been nothin' but trouble, nothin' but trouble."

Tom slowly made a cigarette, and inspected it and lighted it. He took off his ruined cap and wiped his forehead. "I got an idear," he said. "Maybe nobody gonna like it, but here she is: The nearer to California our folks get, the quicker they's gonna be money rollin' in. Now this here car'll go twicet as fast as that truck. Now here's my idea. You take out some a that stuff in the truck, an' then all you folks but me an' the preacher get in an' move on. Me an' Casy'll stop here an' fix this here car an' then we drive on, day an' night, an' we'll catch up, or if we don't meet on the road, you'll be a-workin' anyways. An' if you break down, why, jus' camp 'longside the road till we come. You can't be no worse off, an' if you get through, why, you'll be a-workin', an' stuff'll be easy. Casy can give me a lif' with this here car, an' we'll come a-sailin'."

The gathered family considered it. Uncle John dropped to his hams beside Pa.

Al said, "Won't ya need me to give ya a han' with that con-rod?"

"You said your own se'f you never fixed one."

"That's right," Al agreed. "All ya got to have is a strong back. Maybe the preacher don' wanta stay."

"Well—whoever—I don' care," said Tom.

Pa scratched the dry earth with his forefinger. "I kind a got a notion Tom's right," he said. "It ain't goin' ta do no good all of us stayin' here. We can get fifty, a hunderd miles on 'fore dark."

Ma said worriedly, "How you gonna find us?"

"We'll be on the same road," said Tom. "Sixty-six right on through. Come to a place name' Bakersfiel'. Seen it on the map I got. You go straight on there."

"Yeah, but when we get to California an' spread out sideways off this road—?"

"Don't you worry," Tom reassured her. "We're gonna find ya. California ain't the whole world."

"Looks like an awful big place on the map," said Ma.

Pa appealed for advice. "John, you see any reason why not?"

"No," said John.

"Mr. Wilson, it's your car. You got any objections if my boy fixes her an' brings her on?"

"I don' see none," said Wilson. "Seems like you folks done ever'thing for us awready. Don' see why I cain't give your boy a han'."

"You can be workin', layin' in a little money, if we don' ketch up with ya," said Tom. "An' suppose we all jus' lay aroun' here. There ain't no water here, an' we can't move this here car. But s'pose you all git out there an' git to work. Why, you'd have money, an' maybe a house to live in. How about it, Casy? Wanna stay with me an' gimme a lif'?"

"I wanna do what's bes' for you folks," said Casy. "You took me in, carried me along. I'll do whatever."

"Well, you'll lay on your back an' get grease in your face if you stay here," Tom said.

"Suits me awright."

Pa said, "Well, if that's the way she's gonna go, we better get a-shovin'. We can maybe squeeze in a hunderd miles 'fore we stop."

Ma stepped in front of him. "I ain't a-gonna go."

"What you mean, you ain't gonna go? You got to go. You got to look after the family." Pa was amazed at the revolt.

Ma stepped to the touring car and reached in on the floor

of the back seat. She brought out a jack handle and balanced it in her hand easily. "I ain't a-gonna go," she said.

"I tell you, you got to go. We made up our mind."

And now Ma's mouth set hard. She said softly, "On'y way you gonna get me to go is whup me." She moved the jack handle gently again. "An' I'll shame you, Pa. I won't take no whuppin', cryin' an' a-beggin'. I'll light into you. An' you ain't so sure you can whup me anyways. An' if ya do get me, I swear to God I'll wait till you got your back turned, or you're settin' down, an' I'll knock you belly-up with a bucket. I swear to Holy Jesus' sake I will."

Pa looked helplessly about the group. "She sassy," he said. "I never seen her so sassy." Ruthie giggled shrilly.

The jack handle flicked hungrily back and forth in Ma's hand. "Come on," said Ma. "You made up your mind. Come on an' whup me. Jus' try it. But I ain't a-goin'; or if I do, you ain't never gonna get no sleep, 'cause I'll wait an' I'll wait, an' jus' the minute you take sleep in your eyes, I'll slap ya with a stick a stove wood."

"So goddamn sassy," Pa murmured. "An' she ain't young, neither."

The whole group watched the revolt. They watched Pa, waiting for him to break into fury. They watched his lax hands to see the fists form. And Pa's anger did not rise, and his hands hung limply at his sides. And in a moment the group knew that Ma had won. And Ma knew it too.

Tom said, "Ma, what's eatin' on you? What ya wanna do this-a-way for? What's the matter'th you anyways? You gone johnrabbit on us?"

Ma's face softened, but her eyes were still fierce. "You done this 'thout thinkin' much," Ma said. "What we got lef' in the worl'? Nothin' but us. Nothin' but the folks. We come out an' Grampa, he reached for the shovel-shelf right off. An' now, right off, you wanna bust up the folks——"

Tom cried, "Ma, we was gonna catch up with ya. We wasn't gonna be gone long."

Ma waved the jack handle. "S'pose we was camped, and you went on by. S'pose we got on through, how'd we know where to leave the word, an' how'd you know where to ask?" She said, "We got a bitter road. Granma's sick. She's up there on the truck a-pawin' for a shovel herself. She's jus' tar'd out. We got a long bitter road ahead."

Uncle John said, "But we could be makin' some money. We could have a little bit saved up, come time the other folks got there."

The eyes of the whole family shifted back to Ma. She was the power. She had taken control. "The money we'd make wouldn't do no good," she said. "All we got is the family unbroke. Like a bunch a cows, when the lobos are ranging, stick all together. I ain't scared while we're all here, all that's alive, but I ain't gonna see us bust up. The Wilsons here is with us, an' the preacher is with us. I can't say nothin' if they want to go, but I'm a-goin' cat-wild with this here piece a bar-arn if my own folks busts up." Her tone was cold and final.

Tom said soothingly, "Ma, we can't all camp here. Ain't no water here. Ain't even much shade here. Granma, she needs shade."

"All right," said Ma. "We'll go along. We'll stop first place they's water an' shade. An'—the truck'll come back an' take you in town to get your part, an' it'll bring you back. You ain't goin' walkin' along in the sun, an' I ain't havin' you out all alone, so if you get picked up there ain't nobody of your folks to he'p ya."

Tom drew his lips over his teeth and then snapped them open. He spread his hands helplessly and let them flop against his sides. "Pa," he said, "if you was to rush her one side an' me the other an' then the res' pile on, an' Granma jump down on top, maybe we can get Ma 'thout more'n two-three of us gets killed with that there jack handle. But if you ain't willin' to get your head smashed, I guess Ma's went an' filled her flush. Jesus Christ, one person with their mind made up can shove a lot of folks aroun'! You win, Ma. Put away that jack handle 'fore you hurt somebody."

Ma looked in astonishment at the bar of iron. Her hand trembled. She dropped her weapon on the ground, and Tom, with elaborate care, picked it up and put it back in the car. He said, "Pa, you jus' got set back on your heels. Al, you drive the folks on an' get 'em camped, an' then you bring the truck back here. Me an' the preacher'll get the pan off. Then, if we can make it, we'll run in Santa Rosa an' try an' get a con-rod. Maybe we can, seein' it's Sat'dy night. Get jumpin' now so we can go. Lemme have the monkey wrench an' pliers outa the truck." He reached under the car and felt the greasy pan. "Oh, yeah, lemme have a can, that ol' bucket, to catch the oil. Got to save that." Al handed over the bucket and Tom set it under the car and loosened the oil cap with a pair of pliers. The black oil flowed down his arm while he unscrewed the cap with his fingers, and then the black stream ran silently into the bucket. Al had loaded the family on the truck by the time the bucket was half full. Tom, his face already smudged with oil, looked out between the wheels. "Get back fast!" he called. And he was loosening the pan bolts as the truck moved gently across the shallow ditch and crawled away. Tom turned each bolt a single turn, loosening them evenly to spare the gasket.

The preacher knelt beside the wheels. "What can I do?"

"Nothin', not right now. Soon's the oil's out an' I get these here bolts loose, you can he'p me drop the pan off." He squirmed away under the car, loosening the bolts with a wrench and turning them out with his fingers. He left the bolts on each end loosely threaded to keep the pan from dropping. "Ground's still hot under here," Tom said. And then, "Say, Casy, you been awful goddamn quiet the las' few days. Why, Jesus! When I first come up with you, you was makin' a speech ever' half-hour or so. An' here you ain't said ten words the las' couple days. What's a matter—gettin' sour?"

Casy was stretched out on his stomach, looking under the car. His chin, bristly with sparse whiskers, rested on the back of one hand. His hat was pushed back so that it covered the back of his neck. "I done enough talkin' when I was a preacher to las' the rest a my life," he said.

"Yeah, but you done some talkin' sence, too."

"I'm all worried up," Casy said. "I didn' even know it when I was a-preachin' aroun', but I was doin' consid'able tom-cattin' aroun'. If I ain't gonna preach no more, I got to get married. Why, Tommy, I'm a-lustin' after the flesh."

"Me too," said Tom. "Say, the day I come outa McAlester I was smokin'. I run me down a girl, a hoor girl, like she was a rabbit. I won't tell ya what happened. I wouldn' tell no-body what happened."

Casy laughed. "I know what happened. I went a-fastin' into the wilderness one time, an' when I come out the same damn thing happened to me."

"Hell it did!" said Tom. "Well, I saved my money any-way, an' I give that girl a run. Thought I was nuts. I should a paid her, but I on'y got five bucks to my name. She said she didn' want no money. Here, roll in under here an' grab a-holt. I'll tap her loose. Then you turn out that bolt an' I turn out my end, an' we let her down easy. Careful that gasket. See, she comes off in one piece. They's on'y four cylinders to these here ol' Dodges. I took one down one time. Got main bearings big as a cantaloupe. Now—let her down—hold it. Reach up an' pull down that gasket where it's stuck —easy now. There!" The greasy pan lay on the ground between them, and a little oil still lay in the wells. Tom reached into one of the front wells and picked out some broken pieces of babbitt. "There she is," he said. He turned the babbitt in his fingers. "Shaft's up. Look in back an' get the crank. Turn her over till I tell you."

Casy got to his feet and found the crank and fitted it. "Ready?"

"Reach—now easy—little more—little more—right there."

Casy kneeled down and looked under again. Tom rattled the connecting-rod bearing against the shaft. "There she is."

"What ya s'pose done it?" Casy asked.

"Oh, hell, I don' know! This buggy been on the road thirteen years. Says sixty-thousand miles on the speedometer. That means a hunderd an' sixty, an' God knows how many times they turned the numbers back. Gets hot—maybe somebody let the oil get low—jus' went out." He pulled the cotter-pins and put his wrench on a bearing bolt. He strained and the wrench slipped. A long gash appeared on the back of his hand. Tom looked at it—the blood flowed evenly from the wound and met the oil and dripped into the pan.

"That's too bad," Casy said. "Want I should do that an' you wrap up your han'?"

"Hell, no! I never fixed no car in my life 'thout cuttin' myself. Now it's done I don't have to worry no more." He fitted the wrench again. "Wisht I had a crescent wrench," he said, and he hammered the wrench with the butt of his hand until the bolts loosened. He took them out and laid them with the pan bolts in the pan, and the cotter-pins with them. He loosened the bearing bolts and pulled out the piston. He put piston and connecting-rod in the pan. "There, by God!" He squirmed free from under the car and pulled the pan out with him. He wiped his hand on a piece of gunny sacking and inspected the cut. "Bleedin' like a son-of-a-bitch," he said. "Well, I can stop that." He urinated on the ground, picked up a handful of the resulting mud, and plastered it over the wound. Only for a moment did the blood ooze out, and then it stopped. "Bes' damn thing in the worl' to stop bleedin'," he said.

"Han'ful a spider web'll do it too," said Casy.

"I know, but there ain't no spider web, an' you can always get piss." Tom sat on the running board and inspected the broken bearing. "Now if we can on'y find a '25 Dodge an' get a used con-rod an' some shims, maybe we'll make her all right. Al must a gone a hell of a long ways."

The shadow of the billboard was sixty feet out by now. The afternoon lengthened away. Casy sat down on the running board and looked westward. "We gonna be in high mountains pretty soon," he said, and he was silent for a few moments. Then, "Tom!"

"Yeah?"

"Tom, I been watchin' the cars on the road, them we passed an' them that passed us. I been keepin' track."

"Track a what?"

"Tom, they's hunderds a families like us all a-goin' west. I watched. There ain't none of 'em goin' east—hunderds of 'em. Did you notice that?"

"Yeah, I noticed."

"Why—it's like—it's like they was runnin' away from soldiers. It's like a whole country is movin'."

"Yeah," Tom said. "They is a whole country movin'. We're movin' too."

"Well—s'pose all these here folks an' ever'body—s'pose they can't get no jobs out there?"

"Goddamn it!" Tom cried. "How'd I know? I'm jus' puttin' one foot in front a the other. I done it at Mac for four years, jus' marchin' in cell an' out cell an' in mess an' out mess. Jesus Christ, I thought it'd be somepin different when I come out! Couldn't think a nothin' in there, else you go stir happy, an' now can't think a nothin'." He turned on Casy. "This here bearing went out. We didn' know it was goin', so we didn' worry none. Now she's out an' we'll fix her. An' by Christ that goes for the rest of it! I ain't gonna worry. I can't do it. This here little piece of iron an' babbitt. See it? Ya see it? Well, that's the only goddamn thing in the world I got on my mind. I wonder where the hell Al is."

Casy said, "Now look, Tom. Oh, what the hell! So goddamn hard to say anything."

Tom lifted the mud pack from his hand and threw it on the ground. The edge of the wound was lined with dirt. He glanced over to the preacher. "You're fixin' to make a speech," Tom said. "Well, go ahead. I like speeches. Warden used to make speeches all the time. Didn't do us no harm an' he got a hell of a bang out of it. What you tryin' to roll out?"

Casy picked the backs of his long knotty fingers. "They's stuff goin' on and they's folks doin' things. Them people layin' one foot down in front of the other, like you says, they ain't thinkin' where they're goin', like you says—but they're all layin' 'em down the same direction, jus' the same. An' if ya listen, you'll hear a movin', an' a sneakin', an' a rustlin', an'—an' a res'lessness. They's stuff goin' on that the folks doin' it don't know nothin' about—yet. They's gonna come somepin outa all these folks goin' wes'—outa all their farms lef' lonely. They's gonna come a thing that's gonna change the whole country."

Tom said, "I'm still layin' my dogs down one at a time."

"Yeah, but when a fence comes up at ya, ya gonna climb that fence."

"I climb fences when I got fences to climb," said Tom.

Casy sighed. "It's the bes' way. I gotta agree. But they's different kinda fences. They's folks like me that climbs fences that ain't even strang up yet—an' can't he'p it."

"Ain't that Al a-comin'?" Tom asked.

"Yeah. Looks like."

Tom stood up and wrapped the connecting-rod and both halves of the bearing in the piece of sack. "Wanta make sure I get the same," he said.

The truck pulled alongside the road and Al leaned out the window.

Tom said, "You was a hell of a long time. How far'd you go?"

Al sighed. "Got the rod out?"

"Yeah." Tom held up the sack. "Babbitt jus' broke down."

"Well, it wasn't no fault of mine," said Al.

"No. Where'd you take the folks?"

"We had a mess," Al said. "Granma got to bellerin', an' that set Rosasharn off an' she bellered some. Got her head under a mattress an' bellered. But Granma, she was just layin' back her jaw an' bayin' like a moonlight houn' dog. Seems like Granma ain't got no sense no more. Like a little baby. Don' speak to nobody, don' seem to reco'nize nobody. Jus' talks on like she's talkin' to Grampa."

"Where'd ya leave 'em?" Tom insisted.

"Well, we come to a camp. Got shade an' got water in pipes. Costs half a dollar a day to stay there. But ever'body's so goddamn tired an' wore out an' mis'able, they stayed there. Ma says they got to 'cause Granma's so tired an' wore out. Got Wilson's tent up an' got our tarp for a tent. I think Granma gone nuts."

Tom looked toward the lowering sun. "Casy," he said, "somebody got to stay with this car or she'll get stripped. You jus' as soon?"

"Sure. I'll stay."

Al took a paper bag from the seat. "This here's some bread an' meat Ma sent, an' I got a jug a water here."

"She don't forget nobody," said Casy.

Tom got in beside Al. "Look," he said. "We'll get back jus' as soon's we can. But we can't tell how long."

"I'll be here."

"Awright. Don't make no speeches to yourself. Get goin', Al." The truck moved off in the late afternoon. "He's a nice fella," Tom said. "He thinks about stuff all the time."

"Well, hell—if you been a preacher, I guess you got to. Pa's all mad about it costs fifty cents jus' to camp under a tree. He can't see that noways. Settin' a-cussin'. Says nex' thing they'll sell ya a little tank a air. But Ma says they gotta be near shade an' water 'cause a Granma." The truck rattled along the highway, and now that it was unloaded, every part of it rattled and clashed. The side-board of the bed, the cut body. It rode hard and light. Al put it up to thirty-eight miles an hour and the engine clattered heavily and a blue smoke of burning oil drifted up through the floor boards.

"Cut her down some," Tom said. "You gonna burn her right down to the hub caps. What's eatin' on Granma?"

"I don't know. 'Member the las' couple days she's been airy-nary, sayin' nothin' to nobody? Well, she's yellin' an' talkin' plenty now, on'y she's talkin' to Grampa. Yellin' at him. Kinda scary, too. You can almos' see 'im a-settin' there grinnin' at her the way he always done, a-fingerin' hisself an' grinnin'. Seems like she sees him a-settin' there, too. She's jus' givin' him hell. Say, Pa, he give me twenty dollars to hand you. He don' know how much you gonna need. Ever see Ma stand up to 'im like she done today?"

"Not I remember. I sure did pick a nice time to get paroled. I figgered I was gonna lay aroun' an' get up late an' eat a lot when I come home. I was goin' out an' dance, an' I was gonna go tom-cattin'—an' here I ain't had time to do none of them things."

Al said, "I forgot. Ma give me a lot a stuff to tell you. She says don't drink nothin', an' don' get in no arguments, an' don't fight nobody. 'Cause she says she's scairt you'll get sent back."

"She got plenty to get worked up about 'thout me givin' her no trouble," said Tom.

"Well, we could get a couple beers, can't we? I'm jus' a-ravin' for a beer."

"I dunno," said Tom. "Pa'd crap a litter of lizards if we buy beers."

"Well, look, Tom. I got six dollars. You an' me could get a

couple pints an' go down the line. Nobody don't know I got that six bucks. Christ, we could have a hell of a time for ourselves."

"Keep ya jack," Tom said. "When we get out to the coast you an' me'll take her an' we'll raise hell. Maybe when we're workin'—" He turned in the seat. "I didn' think you was a fella to go down the line. I figgered you was talkin' 'em out of it."

"Well, hell, I don't know nobody here. If I'm gonna ride aroun' much, I'm gonna get married. I'm gonna have me a hell of a time when we get to California."

"Hope so," said Tom.

"You ain't sure a nothin' no more."

"No, I ain't sure a nothin'."

"When ya killed that fella—did—did ya ever dream about it or anything? Did it worry ya?"

"No."

"Well, didn' ya never think about it?"

"Sure. I was sorry 'cause he was dead."

"Ya didn't take no blame to yourself?"

"No. I done my time, an' I done my own time."

"Was it—awful bad—there?"

Tom said nervously, "Look, Al. I done my time, an' now it's done. I don' wanna do it over an' over. There's the river up ahead, an' there's the town. Let's jus' try an' get a con-rod an' the hell with the res' of it."

"Ma's awful partial to you," said Al. "She mourned when you was gone. Done it all to herself. Kinda cryin' down inside of her throat. We could tell what she was thinkin' about, though."

Tom pulled his cap down low over his eyes. "Now look here, Al. S'pose we talk 'bout some other stuff."

"I was jus' tellin' ya what Ma done."

"I know—I know. But—I ruther not. I ruther jus'—lay one foot down in front a the other."

Al relapsed into an insulted silence. "I was jus' tryin' to tell ya," he said, after a moment.

Tom looked at him, and Al kept his eyes straight ahead. The lightened truck bounced noisily along. Tom's long lips drew up from his teeth and he laughed softly. "I know you was, Al. Maybe I'm kinda stir-nuts. I'll tell ya about it sometime maybe. Ya see, it's jus' somepin you wanta know. Kinda interestin'. But I got a kind a funny idear the bes' thing'd be if I forget about it for a while. Maybe in a little while it won't be that way. Right now when I think about it my guts gets all droopy an' nasty feelin'. Look here, Al, I'll tell ya one thing—the jail house is jus' a kind a way a drivin' a guy slowly nuts. See? An' they go nuts, an' you see 'em an' hear 'em, an' pretty soon you don' know if you're nuts or not. When they get to screamin' in the night sometimes you think it's you doin' the screamin'—an' sometimes it is."

Al said, "Oh! I won't talk about it no more, Tom."

"Thirty days is all right," Tom said. "An' a hunderd an' eighty days is all right. But over a year—I dunno. There's somepin about it that ain't like nothin' else in the worl'. Somepin screwy about it, somepin screwy about the whole idea a lockin' people up. Oh, the hell with it! I don' wanna talk about it. Look a the sun a-flashin' on them windas."

The truck drove to the service-station belt, and there on the right-hand side of the road was a wrecking yard—an acre lot surrounded by a high barbed-wire fence, a corrugated iron shed in front with used tires piled up by the doors, and price-marked. Behind the shed there was a little shack built of scrap, scrap lumber and pieces of tin. The windows were windshields built into the walls. In the grassy lot the wrecks lay, cars with twisted, stove-in noses, wounded cars lying on their sides with the wheels gone. Engines rusting on the ground and against the shed. A great pile of junk; fenders and truck sides, wheels and axles; over the whole lot a spirit of decay, of mold and rust; twisted iron, half-gutted engines, a mass of derelicts.

Al drove the truck up on the oily ground in front of the shed. Tom got out and looked into the dark doorway. "Don't see nobody," he said, and he called, "Anybody here?"

"Jesus, I hope they got a '25 Dodge."

Behind the shed a door banged. A specter of a man came through the dark shed. Thin, dirty, oily skin tight against stringy muscles. One eye was gone, and the raw, uncovered socket squirmed with eye muscles when his good eye moved. His jeans and shirt were thick and shiny with old grease, and his hands cracked and lined and cut. His heavy, pouting underlip hung out sullenly.

Tom asked, "You the boss?"

The one eye glared. "I work for the boss," he said sullenly. "Whatcha want?"

"Got a wrecked '25 Dodge? We need a con-rod."

"I don't know. If the boss was here he could tell ya—but he ain't here. He's went home."

"Can we look an' see?"

The man blew his nose into the palm of his hand and wiped his hand on his trousers. "You from hereabouts?"

"Come from east—goin' west."

"Look aroun' then. Burn the goddamn place down, for all I care."

"Looks like you don't love your boss none."

The man shambled close, his one eye flaring. "I hate 'im,"

he said softly. "I hate the son-of-a-bitch! Gone home now. Gone home to his house." The words fell stumbling out. "He got a way—he got a way a-pickin' a fella an' a-tearin' a fella. He—the son-of-a-bitch. Got a girl nineteen, purty. Says to me, 'How'd ya like ta marry her?' Says that right to me. An' tonight—says, 'They's a dance; how'd ya like to go?' Me, he says it to me!" Tears formed in his eyes and tears dripped from the corner of the red eye socket. "Some day, by God— some day I'm gonna have a pipe wrench in my pocket. When he says them things he looks at my eye. An' I'm gonna, I'm gonna jus' take his head right down off his neck with that wrench, little piece at a time." He panted with his fury. "Little piece at a time, right down off'n his neck."

The sun disappeared behind the mountains. Al looked into the lot at the wrecked cars. "Over there, look, Tom! That there looks like a '25 or '26."

Tom turned to the one-eyed man. "Mind if we look?"

"Hell, no! Take any goddamn thing you want."

They walked, threading their way among the dead automobiles, to a rusting sedan, resting on flat tires.

"Sure it's a '25," Al cried. "Can we yank off the pan, mister?"

Tom kneeled down and looked under the car. "Pan's off awready. One rod's been took. Looks like one gone." He wriggled under the car. "Get a crank an' turn her over, Al." He worked the rod against the shaft. "Purty much froze with grease." Al turned the crank slowly. "Easy," Tom called. He picked a splinter of wood from the ground and scraped the cake of grease from the bearing and the bearing bolts.

"How is she for tight?" Al asked.

"Well, she's a little loose, but not bad."

"Well, how is she for wore?"

"Got plenty shim. Ain't been all took up. Yeah, she's O.K. Turn her over easy now. Get her down, easy—there! Run over the truck an' get some tools."

The one-eyed man said, "I'll get you a box a tools." He shuffled off among the rusty cars and in a moment he came back with a tin box of tools. Tom dug out a socket wrench and handed it to Al.

"You take her off. Don' lose no shims an' don' let the bolts get away, an' keep track a the cotter-pins. Hurry up. The light's gettin' dim."

Al crawled under the car. "We oughta get us a set a socket wrenches," he called. "Can't get in no place with a monkey wrench."

"Yell out if you want a hand," Tom said.

The one-eyed man stood helplessly by. "I'll help ya if ya want," he said. "Know what that son-of-a-bitch done? He come by an' he got on white pants. An' he says, 'Come on, le's go out to my yacht.' By God, I'll whang him some day!" He breathed heavily. "I ain't been out with a woman sence I los' my eye. An' he says stuff like that." And big tears cut channels in the dirt beside his nose.

Tom said impatiently, "Whyn't you roll on? Got no guards to keep ya here."

"Yeah, that's easy to say. Ain't so easy to get a job—not for a one-eye' man."

Tom turned on him. "Now look-a-here, fella. You got that eye wide open. An' ya dirty, ya stink. Ya jus' askin' for it. Ya like it. Lets ya feel sorry for yaself. 'Course ya can't get no woman with that empty eye flappin' aroun'. Put somepin over it an' wash ya face. You ain't hittin' nobody with no pipe wrench."

"I tell ya, a one-eye' fella got a hard row," the man said. "Can't see stuff the way other fellas can. Can't see how far off a thing is. Ever'thing's jus' flat."

Tom said, "Ya full a crap. Why, I knowed a one-legged whore one time. Think she was takin' two-bits in a alley? No, by God! She's gettin' half a dollar extra. She says, 'How many one-legged women you slep' with? None!' she says. 'O.K.,' she says. 'You got somepin pretty special here, an' it's gonna cos' ya half a buck extry.' An' by God, she was gettin' 'em, too, an' the fellas comin' out thinkin' they're pretty lucky. She says she's good luck. An' I knowed a hump-back in—in a place I was. Make his whole livin' lettin' folks rub his hump for luck. Jesus Christ, an' all you got is one eye gone."

The man said stumblingly, "Well, Jesus, ya see somebody edge away from ya, an' it gets into ya."

"Cover it up then, goddamn it. Ya stickin' it out like a cow's ass. Ya like to feel sorry for yaself. There ain't nothin' the matter with you. Buy yaself some white pants. Ya gettin' drunk an' cryin' in ya bed, I bet. Need any help, Al?"

"No," said Al. "I got this here bearin' loose. Jus' tryin' to work the piston down."

"Don' bang yaself," said Tom.

The one-eyed man said softly, "Think—somebody'd like —me?"

"Why, sure," said Tom. "Tell 'em ya dong's growed sence you los' your eye."

"Where at you fellas goin'?"

"California. Whole family. Gonna get work out there."

"Well, ya think a fella like me could get work? Black patch on my eye?"

"Why not? You ain't no cripple."

"Well—could I catch a ride with you fellas?"

"Christ, no. We're so goddamn full now we can't move. You get out some other way. Fix up one a these here wrecks an' go out by yaself."

"Maybe I will, by God," said the one-eyed man.

There was a clash of metal. "I got her," Al called.

"Well, bring her out, let's look at her." Al handed him the piston and connecting-rod and the lower half of the bearing.

Tom wiped the babbitt surface and sighted along it sideways. "Looks O.K. to me," he said. "Say, by God, if we had a light we could get this here in tonight."

"Say, Tom," Al said, "I been thinkin'. We got no ring clamps. Gonna be a job gettin' them rings in, specially underneath."

Tom said, "Ya know, a fella tol' me one time ya wrap some fine brass wire aroun' the ring to hol' her."

"Yeah, but how ya gonna get the wire off?"

"Ya don't get her off. She melts off an' don't hurt nothin'."

"Copper wire'd be better."

"It ain't strong enough," said Tom. He turned to the one-eyed man. "Got any fine brass wire?"

"I dunno. I think they's a spool somewheres. Where d'ya think a fella could get one a them patches one-eye' fellas wear?"

"I don' know," said Tom. "Le's see if you can fin' that wire."

In the iron shed they dug through boxes until they found the spool. Tom set the rod in a vise and carefully wrapped the wire around the piston rings, forcing them deep into their slots, and where the wire was twisted he hammered it flat; and then he turned the piston and tapped the wire all around until it cleared the piston wall. He ran his finger up and down to make sure that the rings and wire were flush with the wall. It was getting dark in the shed. The one-eyed man brought a flashlight and shone its beam on the work.

"There she is!" said Tom. "Say—what'll ya take for that light?"

"Well, it ain't much good. Got fifteen cents' a new batteries. You can have her for—oh, thirty-five cents."

"O.K. An' what we owe ya for this here con-rod an' piston?"

The one-eyed man rubbed his forehead with a knuckle, and a line of dirt peeled off. "Well, sir, I jus' dunno. If the boss was here, he'd go to a parts book an' he'd find out how much is a new one, an' while you was workin', he'd be findin' out how bad you're hung up, an' how much jack ya got, an' then he'd—well, say it's eight bucks in the part book—he'd make a price a five bucks. An' if you put up a squawk, you'd get it for three. You say it's all me, but, by God, he's a son-of-a-bitch. Figgers how bad ya need it. I seen him git more for a ring gear than he give for the whole car."

"Yeah! But how much am I gonna give you for this here?"

" 'Bout a buck, I guess."

"Awright, an' I'll give ya a quarter for this here socket wrench. Make it twice as easy." He handed over the silver. "Thank ya. An' cover up that goddamn eye."

Tom and Al got into the truck. It was deep dark. Al started the motor and turned on the lights. "So long," Tom called. "See ya maybe in California." They turned across the highway and started back.

The one-eyed man watched them go, and then he went through the iron shed to his shack behind. It was dark inside. He felt his way to the mattress on the floor, and he stretched out and cried in his bed, and the cars whizzing by on the highway only strengthened the walls of his loneliness.

Tom said, "If you'd tol' me we'd get this here thing an' get her in tonight, I'd a said you was nuts."

"We'll get her in awright," said Al. "You got to do her, though. I'd be scared I'd get her too tight an' she'd burn out, or too loose an' she'd hammer out."

"I'll stick her in," said Tom. "If she goes out again, she goes out. I got nothin' to lose."

Al peered into the dusk. The lights made no impression on the gloom; but ahead, the eyes of a hunting cat flashed green in reflection of the lights. "You sure give that fella hell," Al said. "Sure did tell him where to lay down his dogs."

"Well, goddamn it, he was askin' for it! Jus' a pattin' hisself 'cause he got one eye, puttin' all the blame on his eye. He's a lazy, dirty son-of-a-bitch. Maybe he can snap out of it if he knowed people was wise to him."

Al said, "Tom, it wasn't nothin' I done burned out that bearin'."

Tom was silent for a moment, then, "I'm gonna take a fall outa you, Al. You jus' scrabblin' ass over tit, fear somebody gonna pin some blame on you. I know what's a matter. Young fella, all full a piss an' vinegar. Wanta be a hell of a guy all the time. But, goddamn it, Al, don' keep ya guard up when nobody ain't sparrin' with ya. You gonna be all right."

Al did not answer him. He looked straight ahead. The truck rattled and banged over the road. A cat whipped out from the side of the road and Al swerved to hit it, but the wheels missed and the cat leaped into the grass.

"Nearly got him," said Al. "Say, Tom. You heard Connie talkin' how he's gonna study nights? I been thinkin' maybe I'd study nights too. You know, radio or television or Diesel engines. Fella might get started that-a-way."

"Might," said Tom. "Find out how much they gonna sock

ya for the lessons, first. An' figger out if you're gonna study 'em. There was fellas takin' them mail lessons in McAlester. I never knowed one of 'em that finished up. Got sick of it an' left 'em slide."

"God Awmighty, we forgot to get somepin to eat."

"Well, Ma sent down plenty; preacher couldn' eat it all. Be some lef'. I wonder how long it'll take us to get to California."

"Christ, I don' know. Jus' plug away at her."

They fell into silence, and the dark came and the stars were sharp and white.

Casy got out of the back seat of the Dodge and strolled to the side of the road when the truck pulled up. "I never expected you so soon," he said.

Tom gathered the parts in the piece of sacking on the floor. "We was lucky," he said. "Got a flashlight, too. Gonna fix her right up."

"You forgot to take your dinner," said Casy.

"I'll get it when I finish. Here, Al, pull off the road a little more an' come hol' the light for me." He went directly to the Dodge and crawled under on his back. Al crawled under on his belly and directed the beam of the flashlight. "Not in my eyes. There, put her up." Tom worked the piston up into the cylinder, twisting and turning. The brass wire caught a little on the cylinder wall. With a quick push he forced it past the rings. "Lucky she's loose or the compression'd stop her. I think she's gonna work all right."

"Hope that wire don't clog the rings," said Al.

"Well, that's why I hammered her flat. She won't roll off. I think she'll jus' melt out an' maybe give the walls a brass plate."

"Think she might score the walls?"

Tom laughed. "Jesus Christ, them walls can take it. She's drinkin' oil like a gopher hole awready. Little more ain't gonna hurt none." He worked the rod down over the shaft and tested the lower half. "She'll take some shim." He said, "Casy!"

"Yeah."

"I'm takin' up this here bearing now. Get out to that crank an' turn her over slow when I tell ya." He tightened the bolts. "Now. Over slow!" And as the angular shaft turned, he worked the bearing against it. "Too much shim," Tom said. "Hold it, Casy." He took out the bolts and removed thin shims from each side and put the bolts back. "Try her again, Casy!" And he worked the rod again. "She's a lit-tle bit loose yet. Wonder if she'd be too tight if I took out more shim. I'll try her." Again he removed the bolts and took out another pair of the thin strips. "Now try her, Casy."

"That looks good," said Al.

Tom called, "She any harder to turn, Casy?"

"No, I don't think so."

"Well, I think she's snug here. I hope to God she is. Can't hone no babbitt without tools. This here socket wrench makes her a hell of a lot easier."

Al said, "Boss a that yard gonna be purty mad when he looks for that size socket an' she ain't there."

"That's his screwin'," said Tom. "We didn' steal her." He tapped the cotter-pins in and bent the ends out. "I think that's good. Look, Casy, you hold the light while me an' Al get this here pan up."

Casy knelt down and took the flashlight. He kept the beam on the working hands as they patted the gasket gently in place and lined the holes with the pan bolts. The two men strained at the weight of the pan, caught the end bolts, and then set in the others; and when they were all engaged, Tom took them up little by little until the pan settled evenly in against the gasket, and he tightened hard against the nuts.

"I guess that's her," Tom said. He tightened the oil tap, looked carefully up at the pan, and took the light and searched the ground. "There she is. Le's get the oil back in her."

They crawled out and poured the bucket of oil back in the crank case. Tom inspected the gasket for leaks.

"O.K., Al. Turn her over," he said. Al got into the car and stepped on the starter. The motor caught with a roar. Blue smoke poured from the exhaust pipe. "Throttle down!" Tom shouted. "She'll burn oil till that wire goes. Gettin' thinner now." And as the motor turned over, he listened carefully. "Put up the spark an' let her idle." He listened again. "O.K., Al. Turn her off. I think we done her. Where's that meat now?"

"You make a darn good mechanic," Al said.

"Why not? I worked in the shop a year. We'll take her good an' slow for a couple hunderd miles. Give her a chance to work in."

They wiped their grease-covered hands on bunches of weeds and finally rubbed them on their trousers. They fell hungrily on the boiled pork and swigged the water from the bottle.

"I like to starved," said Al. "What we gonna do now, go on to the camp?"

"I dunno," said Tom. "Maybe they'd charge us a extry half-buck. Le's go on an' talk to the folks—tell 'em we're fixed. Then if they wanta sock us extry—we'll move on. The folks'll wanta know. Jesus, I'm glad Ma stopped us this afternoon. Look around with the light, Al. See we don't leave nothin'. Get that socket wrench in. We may need her again."

Al searched the ground with the flashlight. "Don't see nothin'."

"All right. I'll drive her. You bring the truck, Al." Tom started the engine. The preacher got in the car. Tom moved slowly, keeping the engine at a low speed, and Al followed in the truck. He crossed the shallow ditch, crawling in low gear. Tom said, "These here Dodges can pull a house in low gear. She's sure ratio'd down. Good thing for us—I wanta break that bearin' in easy."

On the highway the Dodge moved along slowly. The 12-volt headlights threw a short blob of yellowish light on the pavement.

Casy turned to Tom. "Funny how you fellas can fix a car. Jus' light right in an' fix her. I couldn't fix no car, not even now when I seen you do it."

"Got to grow into her when you're a little kid," Tom said. "It ain't jus' knowin'. It's more'n that. Kids now can tear down a car 'thout even thinkin' about it."

A jackrabbit got caught in the lights and he bounced along ahead, cruising easily, his great ears flopping with every jump. Now and then he tried to break off the road, but the wall of darkness thrust him back. Far ahead bright headlights appeared and bore down on them. The rabbit hesitated, faltered, then turned and bolted toward the lesser lights of the Dodge. There was a small soft jolt as he went under the wheels. The oncoming car swished by.

"We sure squashed him," said Casy.

Tom said, "Some fellas like to hit 'em. Gives me a little

shakes ever' time. Car sounds O.K. Them rings must a broke loose by now. She ain't smokin' so bad."

"You done a nice job," said Casy.

A small wooden house dominated the camp ground, and on the porch of the house a gasoline lantern hissed and threw its white glare in a great circle. Half a dozen tents were pitched near the house, and cars stood beside the tents. Cooking for the night was over, but the coals of the campfires still glowed on the ground by the camping places. A group of men had gathered to the porch where the lantern burned, and their faces were strong and muscled under the harsh white light, light that threw black shadows of their hats over their foreheads and eyes and made their chins seem to jut out. They sat on the steps, and some stood on the ground, resting their elbows on the porch floor. The proprietor, a sullen lanky man, sat in a chair on the porch. He leaned back against the wall, and he drummed his fingers on his knee. Inside the house a kerosene lamp burned, but its thin light was blasted by the hissing glare of the gasoline lantern. The gathering of men surrounded the proprietor.

Tom drove the Dodge to the side of the road and parked. Al drove through the gate in the truck. "No need to take her in," Tom said. He got out and walked through the gate to the white glare of the lantern.

The proprietor dropped his front chair legs to the floor and leaned forward. "You men wanta camp here?"

"No," said Tom. "We got folks here. Hi, Pa."

Pa, seated on the bottom step, said, "Thought you was gonna be all week. Get her fixed?"

"We was pig lucky," said Tom. "Got a part 'fore dark. We can get goin' fust thing in the mornin'."

"That's a pretty nice thing," said Pa. "Ma's worried. Ya Granma's off her chump."

"Yeah, Al tol' me. She any better now?"

"Well, anyways she's a-sleepin'."

The proprietor said, "If you wanta pull in here an' camp it'll cost you four bits. Get a place to camp an' water an' wood. An' nobody won't bother you."

"What the hell," said Tom. "We can sleep in the ditch right beside the road, an' it won't cost nothin'."

The owner drummed his knee with his fingers. "Deputy sheriff comes on by in the night. Might make it tough for ya. Got a law against sleepin' out in this State. Got a law about vagrants."

"If I pay you a half a dollar I ain't a vagrant, huh?"

"That's right."

Tom's eyes glowed angrily. "Deputy sheriff ain't your brother-'n-law by any chance?"

The owner leaned forward. "No, he ain't. An' the time ain't come yet when us local folks got to take no talk from you goddamn bums, neither."

"It don't trouble you none to take our four bits. An' when'd we get to be bums? We ain't asked ya for nothin'. All of us bums, huh? Well, we ain't askin' no nickels from you for the chance to lay down an' rest."

The men on the porch were rigid, motionless, quiet. Expression was gone from their faces; and their eyes, in the shadows under their hats, moved secretly up to the face of the proprietor.

Pa growled, "Come off it, Tom."

"Sure, I'll come off it."

The circle of men were quiet, sitting on the steps, leaning

on the high porch. Their eyes glittered under the harsh light of the gas lantern. Their faces were hard in the hard light, and they were very still. Only their eyes moved from speaker to speaker, and their faces were expressionless and quiet. A lamp bug slammed into the lantern and broke itself, and fell into the darkness.

In one of the tents a child wailed in complaint, and a woman's soft voice soothed it and then broke into a low song, "Jesus loves you in the night. Sleep good, sleep good. Jesus watches in the night. Sleep, oh, sleep, oh."

The lantern hissed on the porch. The owner scratched in the V of his open shirt, where a tangle of white chest hair showed. He was watchful and ringed with trouble. He watched the men in the circle, watched for some expression. And they made no move.

Tom was silent for a long time. His dark eyes looked slowly up at the proprietor. "I don't wanta make no trouble," he said. "It's a hard thing to be named a bum. I ain't afraid," he said softly. "I'll go for you an' your deputy with my mitts —here now, or jump Jesus. But there ain't no good in it."

The men stirred, changed positions, and their glittering eyes moved slowly upward to the mouth of the proprietor, and their eyes watched for his lips to move. He was reassured. He felt that he had won, but not decisively enough to charge in. "Ain't you got half a buck?" he asked.

"Yeah, I got it. But I'm gonna need it. I can't set it out jus' for sleepin'."

"Well, we all got to make a livin'."

"Yeah," Tom said. "On'y I wisht they was some way to make her 'thout takin' her away from somebody else."

The men shifted again. And Pa said, "We'll get movin'

smart early. Look, mister. We paid. This here fella is part a our folks. Can't he stay? We paid."

"Half a dollar a car," said the proprietor.

"Well, he ain't got no car. Car's out in the road."

"He came in a car," said the proprietor. "Ever'body'd leave their car out there an' come in an' use my place for nothin'."

Tom said, "We'll drive along the road. Meet ya in the morning. We'll watch for ya. Al can stay an' Uncle John can come with us—" He looked at the proprietor. "That awright with you?"

He made a quick decision, with a concession in it. "If the same number stays that come an' paid—that's awright."

Tom brought out his bag of tobacco, a limp gray rag by now, with a little damp tobacco dust in the bottom of it. He made a lean cigarette and tossed the bag away. "We'll go along pretty soon," he said.

Pa spoke generally to the circle. "It's dirt hard for folks to tear up an' go. Folks like us that had our place. We ain't shif'less. Till we got tractored off, we was people with a farm."

A young thin man, with eyebrows sunburned yellow, turned his head slowly. "Croppin'?" he asked.

"Sure we was sharecroppin'. Use' ta own the place."

The young man faced forward again. "Same as us," he said.

"Lucky for us it ain't gonna las' long," said Pa. "We'll get out west an' we'll get work an' we'll get a piece a growin' land with water."

Near the edge of the porch a ragged man stood. His black coat dripped torn streamers. The knees were gone from his dungarees. His face was black with dust, and lined where sweat had washed through. He swung his head toward Pa. "You folks must have a nice little pot a money."

"No, we ain't got no money," Pa said. "But they's plenty of us to work, an' we're all good men. Get good wages out there an' we'll put 'em together. We'll make out."

The ragged man stared while Pa spoke, and then he laughed, and his laughter turned to a high whinnying giggle. The circle of faces turned to him. The giggling got out of control and turned into coughing. His eyes were red and watering when he finally controlled the spasms. "You goin' out there—oh, Christ!" The giggling started again. "You goin' out an' get—good wages—oh, Christ!" He stopped and said slyly, "Pickin' oranges maybe? Gonna pick peaches?"

Pa's tone was dignified. "We gonna take what they got. They got lots a stuff to work in." The ragged man giggled under his breath.

Tom turned irritably. "What's so goddamn funny about that?"

The ragged man shut his mouth and looked sullenly at the porch boards. "You folks all goin' to California, I bet."

"I tol' you that," said Pa. "You didn' guess nothin'."

The ragged man said slowly, "Me—I'm comin' back. I been there."

The faces turned quickly toward him. The men were rigid. The hiss of the lantern dropped to a sigh and the proprietor lowered the front chair legs to the porch, stood up, and pumped the lantern until the hiss was sharp and high again. He went back to his chair, but he did not tilt back again. The ragged man turned toward the faces. "I'm goin' back to starve. I ruther starve all over at oncet."

Pa said, "What the hell you talkin' about? I got a han'bill

says they got good wages, an' little while ago I seen a thing in the paper says they need folks to pick fruit."

The ragged man turned to Pa. "You got any place to go, back home?"

"No," said Pa. "We're out. They put a tractor past the house."

"You wouldn' go back then?"

" 'Course not."

"Then I ain't gonna fret you," said the ragged man.

" 'Course you ain't gonna fret me. I got a han'bill says they need men. Don't make no sense if they don't need men. Costs money for them bills. They wouldn' put 'em out if they didn' need men."

"I don' wanna fret you."

Pa said angrily, "You done some jackassin'. You ain't gonna shut up now. My han'bill says they need men. You laugh an' say they don't. Now, which one's a liar?"

The ragged man looked down into Pa's angry eyes. He looked sorry. "Han'bill's right," he said. "They need men."

"Then why the hell you stirrin' us up laughin'?"

" 'Cause you don't know what kind a men they need."

"What you talkin' about?"

The ragged man reached a decision. "Look," he said. "How many men they say they want on your han'bill?"

"Eight hunderd, an' that's in one little place."

"Orange color han'bill?"

"Why—yes."

"Give the name a the fella—says so and so, labor contractor?"

Pa reached in his pocket and brought out the folded handbill. "That's right. How'd you know?"

"Look," said the man. "It don't make no sense. This fella wants eight hunderd men. So he prints up five thousand of them things an' maybe twenty thousan' people sees 'em. An' maybe two-three thousan' folks gets movin' account a this here han'bill. Folks that's crazy with worry."

"But it don't make no sense!" Pa cried.

"Not till you see the fella that put out this here bill. You'll see him, or somebody that's workin' for him. You'll be a-campin' by a ditch, you an' fifty other famblies. An' he'll look in your tent an' see if you got anything lef' to eat. An' if you got nothin', he says, 'Wanna job?' An' you'll say, 'I sure do, mister. I'll sure thank you for a chance to do some work.' An' he'll say, 'I can use you.' An' you'll say, 'When do I start?' An' he'll tell you where to go, an' what time, an' then he'll go on. Maybe he needs two hunderd men, so he talks to five hunderd, an' they tell other folks, an' when you get to the place, they's a thousan' men. This here fella says, 'I'm payin' twenty cents an hour.' An' maybe half a the men walk off. But they's still five hunderd that's so goddamn hungry they'll work for nothin' but biscuits. Well, this here fella's got a contract to pick them peaches or—chop that cotton. You see now? The more fellas he can get, an' the hungrier, less he's gonna pay. An' he'll get a fella with kids if he can, 'cause—hell, I says I wasn't gonna fret ya." The circle of faces looked coldly at him. The eyes tested his words. The ragged man grew self-conscious. "I says I wasn't gonna fret ya, an' here I'm a-doin' it. You gonna go on. You ain't goin' back." The silence hung on the porch. And the light hissed, and a halo of moths swung around and around the lantern. The ragged man went on nervously, "Lemme tell ya what to do when ya meet that fella says he got work.

Lemme tell ya. Ast him what he's gonna pay. Ast him to write down what he's gonna pay. Ast him that. I tell you men you're gonna get fooled if you don't."

The proprietor leaned forward in his chair, the better to see the ragged dirty man. He scratched among the gray hairs on his chest. He said coldly, "You sure you ain't one of these here troublemakers? You sure you ain't a labor faker?"

And the ragged man cried, "I swear to God I ain't!"

"They's plenty of 'em," the proprietor said. "Goin' aroun' stirrin' up trouble. Gettin' folks mad. Chiselin' in. They's plenty of 'em. Time's gonna come when we string 'em all up, all them troublemakers. We gonna run 'em outa the country. Man wants to work, O.K. If he don't—the hell with him. We ain't gonna let him stir up trouble."

The ragged man drew himself up. "I tried to tell you folks," he said. "Somepin it took me a year to find out. Took two kids dead, took my wife dead to show me. But I can't tell you. I should of knew that. Nobody couldn't tell me, neither. I can't tell ya about them little fellas layin' in the tent with their bellies puffed out an' jus' skin on their bones, an' shiverin' an' whinin' like pups, an' me runnin' aroun' tryin' to get work—not for money, not for wages!" he shouted. "Jesus Christ, jus' for a cup a flour an' a spoon a lard. An' then the coroner come. 'Them children died a heart failure,' he said. Put it on his paper. Shiverin', they was, an' their bellies stuck out like a pig bladder."

The circle was quiet, and mouths were open a little. The men breathed shallowly, and watched.

The ragged man looked around at the circle, and then he turned and walked quickly away into the darkness. The dark swallowed him, but his dragging footsteps could be heard a long time after he had gone, footsteps along the road; and a car came by on the highway, and its lights showed the ragged man shuffling along the road, his head hanging down and his hands in the black coat pockets.

The men were uneasy. One said, "Well—gettin' late. Got to get to sleep."

The proprietor said, "Prob'ly shif'less. They's so goddamn many shif'less fellas on the road now." And then he was quiet. And he tipped his chair back against the wall again and fingered his throat.

Tom said, "Guess I'll go see Ma for a minute, an' then we'll shove along a piece." The Joad men moved away.

Pa said, "S'pose he's tellin' the truth—that fella?"

The preacher answered, "He's tellin' the truth, awright. The truth for him. He wasn't makin' nothin' up."

"How about us?" Tom demanded. "Is that the truth for us?"

"I don' know," said Casy.

"I don' know," said Pa.

They walked to the tent, tarpaulin spread over a rope. And it was dark inside, and quiet. When they came near, a grayish mass stirred near the door and arose to person height. Ma came out to meet them.

"All sleepin'," she said. "Granma finally dozed off." Then she saw it was Tom. "How'd you get here?" she demanded anxiously. "You ain't had no trouble?"

"Got her fixed," said Tom. "We're ready to go when the rest is."

"Thank the dear God for that," Ma said. "I'm just a-twit-terin' to go on. Wanta get where it's rich an' green. Wanta get there quick."

Pa cleared his throat. "Fella was jus' sayin'——"

Tom grabbed his arm and yanked it. "Funny what he says," Tom said. "Says they's lots a folks on the way."

Ma peered through the darkness at them. Inside the tent Ruthie coughed and snorted in her sleep. "I washed 'em up," Ma said. "Fust water we got enough of to give 'em a goin'-over. Lef' the buckets out for you fellas to wash too. Can't keep nothin' clean on the road."

"Ever'body in?" Pa asked.

"All but Connie an' Rosasharn. They went off to sleep in the open. Says it's too warm in under cover."

Pa observed querulously, "That Rosasharn is gettin' awful scary an' nimsy-mimsy."

"It's her first," said Ma. "Her an' Connie sets a lot a store by it. You done the same thing."

"We'll go now," Tom said. "Pull off the road a little piece ahead. Watch out for us ef we don't see you. Be off right-han' side."

"Al's stayin'?"

"Yeah. Leave Uncle John come with us. 'Night, Ma."

They walked away through the sleeping camp. In front of one tent a low fitful fire burned, and a woman watched a kettle that cooked early breakfast. The smell of the cooking beans was strong and fine.

"Like to have a plate a them," Tom said politely as they went by.

The woman smiled. "They ain't done or you'd be welcome," she said. "Come aroun' in the daybreak."

"Thank you, ma'am," Tom said. He and Casy and Uncle John walked by the porch. The proprietor still sat in his chair, and the lantern hissed and flared. He turned his head as the three went by. "Ya runnin' outa gas," Tom said.

"Well, time to close up anyways."

"No more half-bucks rollin' down the road, I guess," Tom said.

The chair legs hit the floor. "Don't you go a-sassin' me. I 'member you. You're one of these here troublemakers."

"Damn right," said Tom. "I'm bolshevisky."

"They's too damn many of you kinda guys aroun'."

Tom laughed as they went out the gate and climbed into the Dodge. He picked up a clod and threw it at the light. They heard it hit the house and saw the proprietor spring to his feet and peer into the darkness. Tom started the car and pulled into the road. And he listened closely to the motor as it turned over, listened for knocks. The road spread dimly under the weak lights of the car.

Chapter Seventeen

THE cars of the migrant people crawled out of the side roads onto the great cross-country highway, and they took the migrant way to the West. In the daylight they scuttled like bugs to the westward; and as the dark caught them, they clustered like bugs near to shelter and to water. And because they were lonely and perplexed, because they had all come from a place of sadness and worry and defeat, and because they were all going to a new mysterious place, they huddled together; they talked together; they shared their lives, their food, and the things they hoped for in the new country. Thus it might be that one family camped near a spring, and another camped for the spring and for company, and a third because two families had pioneered the place and found it good. And when the sun went down, perhaps twenty families and twenty cars were there.

In the evening a strange thing happened: the twenty families became one family, the children were the children of all. The loss of home became one loss, and the golden time in the West was one dream. And it might be that a sick child threw despair into the hearts of twenty families, of a hundred people; that a birth there in a tent kept a hundred people quiet and awestruck through the night and filled a hundred people with the birth-joy in the morning. A family which the night before had been lost and fearful might search its goods to find a present for a new baby. In the evening, sitting about the fires, the twenty were one. They grew to be units of the camps, units of the evenings and the nights. A guitar unwrapped from a blanket and tuned—and the songs, which were all of the people, were sung in the nights. Men sang the words, and women hummed the tunes.

Every night a world created, complete with furniture—friends made and enemies established; a world complete with braggarts and with cowards, with quiet men, with humble men, with kindly men. Every night relationships that make a world, established; and every morning the world torn down like a circus.

At first the families were timid in the building and tumbling worlds, but gradually the technique of building worlds became their technique. Then leaders emerged, then laws were made, then codes came into being. And as the worlds moved westward they were more complete and better furnished, for their builders were more experienced in building them.

The families learned what rights must be observed—the right of privacy in the tent; the right to keep the past black hidden in the heart; the right to talk and to listen; the right to refuse help or to accept, to offer help or to decline it; the right of son to court and daughter to be courted; the right of the hungry to be fed; the rights of the pregnant and the sick to transcend all other rights.

And the families learned, although no one told them, what rights are monstrous and must be destroyed: the right to intrude upon privacy, the right to be noisy while the camp slept, the right of seduction or rape, the right of adultery and theft and murder. These rights were crushed, because the little worlds could not exist for even a night with such rights alive.

And as the worlds moved westward, rules became laws, although no one told the families. It is unlawful to foul near the camp; it is unlawful in any way to foul the drinking water; it is unlawful to eat good rich food near one who is hungry, unless he is asked to share.

And with the laws, the punishments—and there were only two—a quick and murderous fight or ostracism; and ostracism was the worst. For if one broke the laws his name and face went with him, and he had no place in any world, no matter where created.

In the worlds, social conduct became fixed and rigid, so that a man must say "Good morning" when asked for it, so that a man might have a willing girl if he stayed with her, if he fathered her children and protected them. But a man might not have one girl one night and another the next, for this would endanger the worlds.

The families moved westward, and the technique of building the worlds improved so that the people could be safe in their worlds; and the form was so fixed that a family acting in the rules knew it was safe in the rules.

There grew up government in the worlds, with leaders, with elders. A man who was wise found that his wisdom was needed in every camp; a man who was a fool could not change his folly with his world. And a kind of insurance developed in these nights. A man with food fed a hungry man, and thus insured himself against hunger. And when a baby died a pile of silver coins grew at the door flap, for a baby must be well buried, since it has had nothing else of life. An old man may be left in a potter's field, but not a baby.

A certain physical pattern is needed for the building of a world—water, a river bank, a stream, a spring, or even a faucet unguarded. And there is needed enough flat land to pitch the tents, a little brush or wood to build the fires. If there is a garbage dump not too far off, all the better; for there can be found equipment—stove tops, a curved fender to shelter the fire, and cans to cook in and to eat from.

And the worlds were built in the evening. The people, moving in from the highways, made them with their tents and their hearts and their brains.

In the morning the tents came down, the canvas was folded, the tent poles tied along the running board, the beds put in place on the cars, the pots in their places. And as the families moved westward, the technique of building up a home in the evening and tearing it down with the morning light became fixed; so that the folded tent was packed in one place, the cooking pots counted in their box. And as the cars moved westward, each member of the family grew into his proper place, grew into his duties; so that each member, old and young, had his place in the car; so that in the weary, hot evenings, when the cars pulled into the camping places, each member had his duty and went to it without instruction: children to gather wood, to carry water; men to pitch the tents and bring down the beds; women to cook the supper and to watch while the family fed. And this was done without command. The families, which had been units of which the boundaries were a house at night, a farm by day, changed their boundaries. In the long hot light, they were silent in the cars moving slowly westward; but at night they integrated with any group they found.

Thus they changed their social life—changed as in the whole universe only man can change. They were not farm men any more, but migrant men. And the thought, the planning, the long staring silence that had gone out to the fields, went now to the roads, to the distance, to the West. That

man whose mind had been bound with acres lived with narrow concrete miles. And his thought and his worry were not
any more with rainfall, with wind and dust, with the thrust
of the crops. Eyes watched the tires, ears listened to the clattering motors, and minds struggled with oil, with gasoline,
with the thinning rubber between air and road. Then a
broken gear was tragedy. Then water in the evening was the
yearning, and food over the fire. Then health to go on was
the need and strength to go on, and spirit to go on. The wills
thrust westward ahead of them, and fears that had once
apprehended drought or flood now lingered with anything
that might stop the westward crawling.

The camps became fixed—each a short day's journey from
the last.

And on the road the panic overcame some of the families,
so that they drove night and day, stopped to sleep in the cars,
and drove on to the West, flying from the road, flying from
movement. And these lusted so greatly to be settled that they
set their faces into the West and drove toward it, forcing
the clashing engines over the roads.

But most of the families changed and grew quickly into
the new life. And when the sun went down——

Time to look out for a place to stop.

And—there's some tents ahead.

The car pulled off the road and stopped, and because
others were there first, certain courtesies were necessary.
And the man, the leader of the family, leaned from the car.

Can we pull up here an' sleep?

Why, sure, be proud to have you. What State you from?

Come all the way from Arkansas.

They's Arkansas people down that fourth tent.

That so?

And the great question, How's the water?

Well, she don't taste so good, but they's plenty.

Well, thank ya.

No thanks to me.

But the courtesies had to be. The car lumbered over the ground to the end tent, and stopped. Then down from the car the weary people climbed, and stretched stiff bodies. Then the new tent sprang up; the children went for water and the older boys cut brush or wood. The fires started and supper was put on to boil or to fry. Early comers moved over, and States were exchanged, and friends and sometimes relatives discovered.

Oklahoma, huh? What county?

Cherokee.

Why, I got folks there. Know the Allens? They's Allens all over Cherokee. Know the Willises?

Why, sure.

And a new unit was formed. The dusk came, but before the dark was down the new family was of the camp. A word had been passed with every family. They were known people—good people.

I knowed the Allens all my life. Simon Allen, ol' Simon, had trouble with his first wife. She was part Cherokee. Purty as—as a black colt.

Sure, an' young Simon, he married a Rudolph, didn' he? That's what I thought. They went to live in Enid an' done well—real well.

Only Allen that ever done well. Got a garage.

When the water was carried and the wood cut, the children walked shyly, cautiously among the tents. And they made elaborate acquaintanceship gestures. A boy stopped near another boy and studied a stone, picked it up, examined it closely, spat on it, and rubbed it clean and inspected it until he forced the other to demand, What you go there?

And casually, Nothin'. Jus' a rock.

Well, what you lookin' at it like that for?

Thought I seen gold in it.

How'd you know? Gold ain't gold, it's black in a rock.

Sure, ever'body knows that.

I bet it's fool's gold, an' you figgered it was gold.

That ain't so, 'cause Pa, he's foun' lots a gold an' he tol' me how to look.

How'd you like to pick up a big ol' piece a gold?

Sa-a-ay! I'd git the bigges' old son-a-bitchin' piece a candy you ever seen.

I ain't let to swear, but I do, anyways.

Me too. Le's go to the spring.

And young girls found each other and boasted shyly of their popularity and their prospects. The women worked over the fire, hurrying to get food to the stomachs of the family—pork if there was money in plenty, pork and potatoes and onions. Dutch-oven biscuits or cornbread, and plenty of gravy to go over it. Side-meat or chops and a can of boiled tea, black and bitter. Fried dough in drippings if money was slim, dough fried crisp and brown and the drippings poured over it.

Those families which were very rich or very foolish with their money ate canned beans and canned peaches and packaged bread and bakery cake; but they ate secretly, in their tents, for it would not have been good to eat such fine things openly. Even so, children eating their fried dough smelled the warming beans and were unhappy about it.

When supper was over and the dishes dipped and wiped, the dark had come, and then the men squatted down to talk.

And they talked of the land behind them. I don' know what it's coming to, they said. The country's spoilt.

It'll come back though, on'y we won't be there.

Maybe, they thought, maybe we sinned some way we didn't know about.

Fella says to me, gov'ment fella, an' he says, she's gullied up on ya. Gov'ment fella. He says, if ya plowed 'cross the contour, she won't gully. Never did have no chance to try her. An' the new super' ain't plowin' 'cross the contour. Runnin' a furrow four miles long that ain't stoppin' or goin' aroun' Jesus Christ Hisself.

And they spoke softly of their homes: They was a little cool-house under the win'mill. Use' ta keep milk in there ta cream up, an' watermelons. Go in there midday when she was hotter'n a heifer, an' she'd be jus' as cool, as cool as you'd want. Cut open a melon in there an' she'd hurt your mouth, she was so cool. Water drippin' down from the tank.

They spoke of their tragedies: Had a brother Charley, hair as yella as corn, an' him a growed man. Played the 'cordeen nice too. He was harrowin' one day an' he went up to clear his lines. Well, a rattlesnake buzzed an' them horses bolted an' the harrow went over Charley, an' the points dug into his guts an' his stomach, an' they pulled his face off an' —God Almighty!

They spoke of the future: Wonder what it's like out there?

Well, the pitchers sure do look nice. I seen one where it's hot an' fine, an' walnut trees an' berries; an' right behind, close as a mule's ass to his withers, they's a tall up mountain covered with snow. That was a pretty thing to see.

If we can get work it'll be fine. Won't have no cold in the winter. Kids won't freeze on the way to school. I'm gonna take care my kids don't miss no more school. I can read good, but it ain't no pleasure to me like with a fella that's used to it.

And perhaps a man brought out his guitar to the front of his tent. And he sat on a box to play, and everyone in the camp moved slowly in toward him, drawn in toward him. Many men can chord a guitar, but perhaps this man was a picker. There you have something—the deep chords beating, beating, while the melody runs on the strings like little footsteps. Heavy hard fingers marching on the frets. The man played and the people moved slowly in on him until the circle was closed and tight, and then he sang "Ten-Cent Cotton and Forty-Cent Meat." And the circle sang softly with him. And he sang "Why Do You Cut Your Hair, Girls?" And the circle sang. He wailed the song, "I'm Leaving Old Texas," that eerie song that was sung before the Spaniards came, only the words were Indian then.

And now the group was welded to one thing, one unit, so that in the dark the eyes of the people were inward, and their minds played in other times, and their sadness was like rest, like sleep. He sang the "McAlester Blues" and then, to make up for it to the older people, he sang "Jesus Calls Me to His Side." The children drowsed with the music and went into the tents to sleep, and the singing came into their dreams.

And after a while the man with the guitar stood up and yawned. Good night, folks, he said.

And they murmured, Good night to you.

And each wished he could pick a guitar, because it is a gracious thing. Then the people went to their beds, and the camp was quiet. And the owls coasted overhead, and the coyotes gabbled in the distance, and into the camp skunks walked, looking for bits of food—waddling, arrogant skunks, afraid of nothing.

The night passed, and with the first streak of dawn the women came out of the tents, built up the fires, and put the coffee to boil. And the men came out and talked softly in the dawn.

When you cross the Colorado river, there's the desert, they say. Look out for the desert. See you don't get hung up. Take plenty water, case you get hung up.

I'm gonna take her at night.

Me too. She'll cut the living Jesus outa you.

The families ate quickly, and the dishes were dipped and wiped. The tents came down. There was a rush to go. And when the sun arose, the camping place was vacant, only a little litter left by the people. And the camping place was ready for a new world in a new night.

But along the highway the cars of the migrant people crawled out like bugs, and the narrow concrete miles stretched ahead.

Chapter Eighteen

THE Joad family moved slowly westward, up into the mountains of New Mexico, past the pinnacles and pyramids of the upland. They climbed into the high country of Arizona, and through a gap they looked down on the Painted Desert. A border guard stopped them.

"Where you going?"

"To California," said Tom.

"How long you plan to be in Arizona?"

"No longer'n we can get acrost her."

"Got any plants?"

"No plants."

"I ought to look your stuff over."

"I tell you we ain't got no plants."

The guard put a little sticker on the windshield.

"O.K. Go ahead, but you better keep movin'."

"Sure. We aim to."

They crawled up the slopes, and the low twisted trees covered the slopes. Holbrook, Joseph City, Winslow. And then the tall trees began, and the cars spouted steam and labored up the slopes. And there was Flagstaff, and that was the top of it all. Down from Flagstaff over the great plateaus, and the road disappeared in the distance ahead. The water grew scarce, water was to be bought, five cents, ten cents, fifteen cents a gallon. The sun drained the dry rocky country, and ahead were jagged broken peaks, the western wall of Arizona. And now they were in flight from the sun and the drought. They drove all night, and came to the mountains in the night. And they crawled the jagged ramparts in the night, and their dim lights flickered on the pale stone walls of the road. They passed the summit in the dark and came slowly down in the late night, through the shattered stone debris of Oatman; and when the daylight came they saw the Colorado river below them. They drove to Topock, pulled up at the bridge while a guard washed off the windshield sticker. Then across the bridge and into the broken rock wilderness. And although they were dead weary and the morning heat was growing, they stopped.

Pa called, "We're there—we're in California!" They looked dully at the broken rock glaring under the sun, and across the river the terrible ramparts of Arizona.

"We got the desert," said Tom. "We got to get to the water and rest."

The road runs parallel to the river, and it was well into the morning when the burning motors came to Needles, where the river runs swiftly among the reeds.

The Joads and Wilsons drove to the river, and they sat in the cars looking at the lovely water flowing by, and the green reeds jerking slowly in the current. There was a little encampment by the river, eleven tents near the water, and the swamp grass on the ground. And Tom leaned out of the truck window. "Mind if we stop here a piece?"

A stout woman, scrubbing clothes in a bucket, looked up. "We don't own it, mister. Stop if you want. They'll be a cop down to look you over." And she went back to her scrubbing in the sun.

The two cars pulled to a clear place on the swamp grass. The tents were passed down, the Wilson tent set up, the Joad tarpaulin stretched over its rope.

Winfield and Ruthie walked slowly down through the willows to the reedy place. Ruthie said, with soft vehemence, "California. This here's California an' we're right in it!"

Winfield broke a tule and twisted it free, and he put the white pulp in his mouth and chewed it. They walked into the water and stood quietly, the water about the calves of their legs.

"We got the desert yet," Ruthie said.

"What's the desert like?"

"I don't know. I seen pitchers once says a desert. They was bones ever'place."

"Man bones?"

"Some, I guess, but mos'ly cow bones."

"We gonna get to see them bones?"

"Maybe. I don' know. Gonna go 'crost her at night. That's what Tom said. Tom says we get the livin' Jesus burned outa us if we go in daylight."

"Feels nicet an' cool," said Winfield, and he squidged his toes in the sand of the bottom.

They heard Ma calling, "Ruthie! Winfiel'! You come back." They turned and walked slowly back through the reeds and the willows.

The other tents were quiet. For a moment, when the cars came up, a few heads had stuck out between the flaps, and then were withdrawn. Now the family tents were up and the men gathered together.

Tom said, "I'm gonna go down an' take a bath. That's what I'm gonna do—before I sleep. How's Granma sence we got her in the tent?"

"Don' know," said Pa. "Couldn' seem to wake her up." He cocked his head toward the tent. A whining, babbling voice came from under the canvas. Ma went quickly inside.

"She woke up, awright," said Noah. "Seems like all night she was a-croakin' up on the truck. She's all outa sense."

Tom said, "Hell! She's wore out. If she don't get some res' pretty soon, she ain' gonna las'. She's jes' wore out. Anybody comin' with me? I'm gonna wash, an' I'm gonna sleep in the shade—all day long." He moved away, and the other men followed him. They took off their clothes in the willows and then they walked into the water and sat down. For a long time they sat, holding themselves with heels dug into the sand, and only their heads stuck out of the water.

"Jesus, I needed this," Al said. He took a handful of sand from the bottom and scrubbed himself with it. They lay in the water and looked across at the sharp peaks called Needles, and at the white rock mountains of Arizona.

"We come through them," Pa said in wonder.

Uncle John ducked his head under the water. "Well, we're here. This here's California, an' she don't look so prosperous."

"Got the desert yet," said Tom. "An' I hear she's a son-of-a-bitch."

Noah asked, "Gonna try her tonight?"

"What ya think, Pa?" Tom asked.

"Well, I don' know. Do us good to get a little res', 'specially Granma. But other ways, I'd kinda like to get acrost her an' get settled into a job. On'y got 'bout forty dollars left. I'll feel better when we're all workin', an' a little money comin' in."

Each man sat in the water and felt the tug of the current. The preacher let his arms and hands float on the surface. The bodies were white to the neck and wrists, and burned dark brown on hands and faces, with V's of brown at the collar bones. They scratched themselves with sand.

And Noah said lazily, "Like to jus' stay here. Like to lay here forever. Never get hungry an' never get sad. Lay in the water all life long, lazy as a brood sow in the mud."

And Tom, looking at the ragged peaks across the river and the Needles downstream: "Never seen such tough mountains. This here's a murder country. This here's the bones of a country. Wonder if we'll ever get in a place where folks can live 'thout fightin' hard scrabble an' rocks. I seen pitchers of a country flat an' green, an' with little houses like Ma says, white. Ma got her heart set on a white house. Get to thinkin' they ain't no such country. I seen pitchers like that."

Pa said, "Wait till we get to California. You'll see nice country then."

"Jesus Christ, Pa! This here *is* California."

Two men dressed in jeans and sweaty blue shirts came through the willows and looked toward the naked men. They called, "How's the swimmin'?"

"Dunno," said Tom. "We ain't tried none. Sure feels good to set here, though."

"Mind if we come in an' set?"

"She ain't our river. We'll len' you a little piece of her."

The men shucked off their pants, peeled their shirts, and waded out. The dust coated their legs to the knee; their feet were pale and soft with sweat. They settled lazily into the water and washed listlessly at their flanks. Sun-bitten, they were, a father and a boy. They grunted and groaned with the water.

Pa asked politely, "Goin' west?"

"Nope. We come from there. Goin' back home. We can't make no livin' out there."

"Where's home?" Tom asked.

"Panhandle, come from near Pampa."

Pa asked, "Can you make a livin' there?"

"Nope. But at leas' we can starve to death with folks we know. Won't have a bunch a fellas that hates us to starve with."

Pa said, "Ya know, you're the second fella talked like that. What makes 'em hate you?"

"Dunno," said the man. He cupped his hands full of water and rubbed his face, snorting and bubbling. Dusty water ran out of his hair and streaked his neck.

"I like to hear some more 'bout this," said Pa.

"Me too," Tom added. "Why these folks out west hate ya?"

The man looked sharply at Tom. "You jus' goin' wes'?"

"Jus' on our way."

"You ain't never been in California?"

"No, we ain't."

"Well, don' take my word. Go see for yourself."

"Yeah," Tom said, "but a fella kind a likes to know what he's gettin' into."

"Well, if you truly wanta know, I'm a fella that's asked questions an' give her some thought. She's a nice country. But she was stole a long time ago. You git acrost the desert an' come into the country aroun' Bakersfield. An' you never seen such purty country—all orchards an' grapes, purtiest country you ever seen. An' you'll pass lan' flat an' fine with water thirty feet down, and that lan's layin' fallow. But you can't have none of that lan'. That's a Lan' and Cattle Company. An' if they don't want ta work her, she ain't gonna git worked. You go in there an' plant you a little corn, an' you'll go to jail!"

"Good lan', you say? An' they ain't workin' her?"

"Yes, sir. Good lan' an' they ain't! Well, sir, that'll get you a little mad, but you ain't seen nothin'. People gonna have a look in their eye. They gonna look at you an' their face says, 'I don't like you, you son-of-a-bitch.' Gonna be deputy sheriffs, an' they'll push you aroun'. You camp on the roadside, an' they'll move you on. You gonna see in people's face how they hate you. An'—I'll tell you somepin. They hate you 'cause they're scairt. They know a hungry fella gonna get food even if he got to take it. They know that fallow lan's a sin an' somebody' gonna take it. What the hell! You never been called 'Okie' yet."

Tom said, "Okie? What's that?"

"Well, Okie use' ta mean you was from Oklahoma. Now it means you're a dirty son-of-a-bitch. Okie means you're scum. Don't mean nothing itself, it's the way they say it. But I can't tell you nothin'. You got to go there. I hear there's three hunderd thousan' of our people there—an' livin' like hogs, 'cause ever'thing in California is owned. They ain't nothin' left. An' them people that owns it is gonna hang on to it if they got ta kill ever'body in the worl' to do it. An' they're scairt, an' that makes 'em mad. You got to see it. You got to hear it. Purtiest goddamn country you ever seen, but they ain't nice to you, them folks. They're so scairt an' worried they ain't even nice to each other."

Tom looked down into the water, and he dug his heels into the sand. "S'pose a fella got work an' saved, couldn' he get a little lan'?"

The older man laughed and he looked at his boy, and his silent boy grinned almost in triumph. And the man said, "You ain't gonna get no steady work. Gonna scrabble for your dinner ever' day. An' you gonna do her with people lookin' mean at you. Pick cotton, an' you gonna be sure the scales ain't honest. Some of 'em is, an' some of 'em ain't. But you gonna think all the scales is crooked, an' you don' know which ones. Ain't nothin' you can do about her anyways."

Pa asked slowly, "Ain't—ain't it nice out there at all?"

"Sure, nice to look at, but you can't have none of it. They's a grove of yella oranges—an' a guy with a gun that got the right to kill you if you touch one. They's a fella, newspaper fella near the coast, got a million acres——"

Casy looked up quickly, "Million acres? What in the worl' can he do with a million acres?"

"I dunno. He jus' got it. Runs a few cattle. Got guards ever'place to keep folks out. Rides aroun' in a bullet-proof car. I seen pitchers of him. Fat, sof' fella with little mean eyes an' a mouth like a ass-hole. Scairt he's gonna die. Got a million acres an' scairt of dyin'."

Casy demanded, "What in hell can he do with a million acres? What's he want a million acres for?"

The man took his whitening, puckering hands out of the water and spread them, and he tightened his lower lip and bent his head down to one shoulder. "I dunno," he said. "Guess he's crazy. Mus' be crazy. Seen a pitcher of him. He looks crazy. Crazy an' mean."

"Say he's scairt to die?" Casy asked.

"That's what I heard."

"Scairt God'll get him?"

"I dunno. Jus' scairt."

"What's he care?" Pa said. "Don't seem like he's havin' no fun."

"Grampa wasn't scairt," Tom said. "When Grampa was havin' the most fun, he come clostest to gettin' kil't. Time Grampa an' another fella whanged into a bunch a Navajo in the night. They was havin' the time a their life, an' same time you wouldn' give a gopher for their chance."

Casy said, "Seems like that's the way. Fella havin' fun, he don't give a damn; but a fella mean an' lonely an' old an' disappointed—he's scared of dyin'!"

Pa asked, "What's he disappointed about if he got a million acres?"

The preacher smiled, and he looked puzzled. He splashed a floating water bug away with his hand. "If he needs a million acres to make him feel rich, seems to me he needs it 'cause he feels awful poor inside hisself, and if he's poor in hisself, there ain't no million acres gonna make him feel rich, an' maybe he's disappointed that nothin' he can do'll make him feel rich—not rich like Mis' Wilson was when she give her tent when Grampa died. I ain't tryin' to preach no sermon, but I never seen nobody that's busy as a prairie dog collectin' stuff that wasn't disappointed." He grinned. "Does kinda soun' like a sermon, don't it?"

The sun was flaming fiercely now. Pa said, "Better scrunch down under water. She'll burn the living Jesus outa you." And he reclined and let the gently moving water flow around his neck. "If a fella's willin' to work hard, can't he cut her?" Pa asked.

The man sat up and faced him. "Look, mister. I don' know ever'thing. You might go out there an' fall into a steady job, an' I'd be a liar. An' then, you might never get no work, an' I didn' warn ya. I can tell ya mos' of the folks is purty mis'able." He lay back in the water. "A fella don' know ever'thing," he said.

Pa turned his head and looked at Uncle John. "You never was a fella to say much," Pa said. "But I'll be goddamned if you opened your mouth twicet sence we lef' home. What you think 'bout this here?"

Uncle John scowled. "I don't think nothin' about it. We're a-goin' there, ain't we? None of this here talk gonna keep us from goin' there. When we get there, we'll get there. When we get a job we'll work, an' when we don't get a job we'll set on our tail. This here talk ain't gonna do no good no way."

Tom lay back and filled his mouth with water, and he spurted it into the air and he laughed. "Uncle John don't talk much, but he talks sense. Yes, by God! He talks sense. We goin' on tonight, Pa?"

"Might's well. Might's well get her over."

"Well, I'm goin' up in the brush an' get some sleep then." Tom stood up and waded to the sandy shore. He slipped his clothes on his wet body and winced under the heat of the cloth. The others followed him.

In the water, the man and his boy watched the Joads disappear. And the boy said, "Like to see 'em in six months. Jesus!"

The man wiped his eye corners with his forefinger. "I shouldn' of did that," he said. "Fella always wants to be a wise guy, wants to tell folks stuff."

"Well, Jesus, Pa! They asked for it."

"Yeah, I know. But like that fella says, they're a-goin' anyways. Nothin' won't be changed from what I tol' 'em, 'cept they'll be mis'able 'fore they hafta."

Tom walked in among the willows, and he crawled into a cave of shade to lie down. And Noah followed him.

"Gonna sleep here," Tom said.

"Tom!"

"Yeah?"

"Tom, I ain't a-goin' on."

Tom sat up. "What you mean?"

"Tom, I ain't a-gonna leave this here water. I'm a-gonna walk on down this here river."

"You're crazy," Tom said.

"Get myself a piece a line. I'll catch fish. Fella can't starve beside a nice river."

Tom said, "How 'bout the fam'ly? How 'bout Ma?"

"I can't he'p it. I can't leave this here water." Noah's wide-set eyes were half closed. "You know how it is, Tom. You know how the folks are nice to me. But they don't really care for me."

"You're crazy."

"No, I ain't. I know how I am. I know they're sorry. But— Well, I ain't a-goin'. You tell Ma—Tom."

"Now you look-a-here," Tom began.

"No. It ain't no use. I was in that there water. An' I ain't a-gonna leave her. I'm a-gonna go now, Tom—down the river. I'll catch fish an' stuff, but I can't leave her. I can't." He crawled back out of the willow cave. "You tell Ma, Tom." He walked away.

Tom followed him to the river bank. "Listen, you god-damn fool——"

"It ain't no use," Noah said. "I'm sad, but I can't he'p it. I got to go." He turned abruptly and walked downstream along the shore. Tom started to follow, and then he stopped. He saw Noah disappear into the brush, and then appear again, following the edge of the river. And he watched Noah growing smaller on the edge of the river, until he disappeared into the willows at last. And Tom took off his cap and scratched his head. He went back to his willow cave and lay down to sleep.

Under the spread tarpaulin Granma lay on a mattress, and Ma sat beside her. The air was stiflingly hot, and the flies buzzed in the shade of the canvas. Granma was naked under a long piece of pink curtain. She turned her old head restlessly from side to side, and she muttered and choked. Ma sat on the ground beside her, and with a piece of cardboard drove the flies away and fanned a stream of moving hot air over the tight old face. Rose of Sharon sat on the other side and watched her mother.

Granma called imperiously, "Will! Will! You come here, Will." And her eyes opened and she looked fiercely about. "Tol' him to come right here," she said. "I'll catch him. I'll take the hair off'n him." She closed her eyes and rolled her head back and forth and muttered thickly. Ma fanned with the cardboard.

Rose of Sharon looked helplessly at the old woman. She said softly, "She's awful sick."

Ma raised her eyes to the girl's face. Ma's eyes were patient, but the lines of strain were on her forehead. Ma fanned and fanned the air, and her piece of cardboard warned off the flies. "When you're young, Rosasharn, ever'thing that happens is a thing all by itself. It's a lonely thing. I know, I 'member, Rosasharn." Her mouth loved the name of her daughter. "You're gonna have a baby, Rosasharn, and that's somepin to you lonely and away. That's gonna hurt you, an' the hurt'll be lonely hurt, an' this here tent is alone in the worl', Rosasharn." She whipped the air for a moment to drive a buzzing blow fly on, and the big shining fly circled the tent twice and zoomed out into the blinding sunlight.

And Ma went on, "They's a time of change, an' when that comes, dyin' is a piece of all dyin', and bearin' is a piece of all bearin', an' bearin' an' dyin' is two pieces of the same thing. An' then things ain't lonely any more. An' then a hurt don't hurt so bad, 'cause it ain't a lonely hurt no more, Rosasharn. I wisht I could tell you so you'd know, but I can't." And her voice was so soft, so full of love, that tears crowded into Rose of Sharon's eyes, and flowed over her eyes and blinded her.

"Take an' fan Granma," Ma said, and she handed the cardboard to her daughter. "That's a good thing to do. I wisht I could tell you so you'd know."

Granma, scowling her brows down over her closed eyes, bleated, "Will! You're dirty! You ain't never gonna get clean." Her little wrinkled claws moved up and scratched her cheek. A red ant ran up the curtain cloth and scrambled over the folds of loose skin on the old lady's neck. Ma reached quickly and picked it off, crushed it between thumb and forefinger, and brushed her fingers on her dress.

Rose of Sharon waved the cardboad fan. She looked up at Ma. "She—?" And the words parched in her throat.

"Wipe your feet, Will—you dirty pig!" Granma cried.

Ma said, "I dunno. Maybe if we can get her where it ain't so hot, but I dunno. Don't worry yourself, Rosasharn. Take your breath in when you need it, an' let it go when you need to."

A large woman in a torn black dress looked into the tent. Her eyes were bleared and indefinite, and the skin sagged to her jowls and hung down in little flaps. Her lips were loose, so that the upper lip hung like a curtain over her teeth, and her lower lip, by its weight, folded outward, showing her lower gums. "Mornin', ma'am," she said. "Mornin', an' praise God for victory."

Ma looked around. "Mornin'," she said.

The woman stooped into the tent and bent her head over Granma. "We heerd you got a soul here ready to join her Jesus. Praise God!"

Ma's face tightened and her eyes grew sharp. "She's tar'd, tha's all," Ma said. "She's wore out with the road an' the heat. She's jus' wore out. Get a little res', an' she'll be well."

The woman leaned down over Granma's face, and she seemed almost to sniff. Then she turned to Ma and nodded quickly, and her lips jiggled and her jowls quivered. "A dear soul gonna join her Jesus," she said.

Ma cried, "That ain't so!"

The woman nodded, slowly, this time, and put a puffy hand on Granma's forehead. Ma reached to snatch the hand away, and quickly restrained herself. "Yes, it's so, sister," the woman said. "We got six in Holiness in our tent. I'll go git 'em, an' we'll hol' a meetin'—a prayer an' grace. Jehovites, all. Six, countin' me. I'll go git 'em out."

Ma stiffened. "No—no," she said. "No, Granma's tar'd. She couldn't stan' a meetin'."

The woman said, "Couldn't stan' grace? Couldn' stan' the sweet breath of Jesus? What you talkin' about, sister?"

Ma said, "No, not here. She's too tar'd."

The woman looked reproachfully at Ma. "Ain't you be-lievers, ma'am?"

"We always been Holiness," Ma said, "but Granma's tar'd, an' we been a-goin' all night. We won't trouble you."

"It ain't no trouble, an' if it was, we'd want ta do it for a soul a-soarin' to the Lamb."

Ma arose to her knees. "We thank ya," she said coldly. "We ain't gonna have no meetin' in this here tent."

The woman looked at her for a long time. "Well, we ain't a-gonna let a sister go away 'thout a little praisin'. We'll git the meetin' goin' in our own tent, ma'am. An' we'll forgive ya for your hard heart."

Ma settled back again and turned her face to Granma, and her face was still set and hard. "She's tar'd," Ma said. "She's on'y tar'd." Granma swung her head back and forth and muttered under her breath.

The woman walked stiffly out of the tent. Ma continued to look down at the old face.

Rose of Sharon fanned her cardboard and moved the hot air in a stream. She said, "Ma!"

"Yeah?"

"Whyn't ya let 'em hol' a meetin'?"

"I dunno," said Ma. "Jehovites is good people. They're howlers an' jumpers. I dunno. Somepin jus' come over me. I didn' think I could stan' it. I'd jus' fly all apart."

From some little distance there came the sound of the beginning meeting, a sing-song chant of exhortation. The words were not clear, only the tone. The voice rose and fell, and went higher at each rise. Now a response filled in the pause, and the exhortation went up with a tone of triumph, and a growl of power came into the voice. It swelled and paused, and a growl came into the response. And now gradually the sentences of exhortation shortened, grew sharper, like commands; and into the responses came a complaining note. The rhythm quickened. Male and female voices had been one tone, but now in the middle of a response one woman's voice went up and up in a wailing cry, wild and fierce, like the cry of a beast; and a deeper woman's voice rose up beside it, a baying voice, and a man's voice traveled up the scale in the howl of a wolf. The exhortation stopped, and only the feral howling came from the tent, and with it a thudding sound on the earth. Ma shivered. Rose of Sharon's breath was panting and short, and the chorus of howls went on so long it seemed that lungs must burst.

Ma said, "Makes me nervous. Somepin happened to me."

Now the high voice broke into hysteria, the gabbling screams of a hyena, the thudding became louder. Voices cracked and broke, and then the whole chorus fell to a sobbing, grunting undertone, and the slap of flesh and the thuddings on the earth; and the sobbing changed to a little whining, like that of a litter of puppies at a food dish.

Rose of Sharon cried softly with nervousness. Granma kicked the curtain off her legs, which lay like gray, knotted sticks. And Granma whined with the whining in the distance. Ma pulled the curtain back in place. And then Granma sighed deeply and her breathing grew steady and easy, and her closed eyelids ceased their flicking. She slept deeply, and snored through her half-open mouth. The whining from the distance was softer and softer until it could not be heard at all any more.

Rose of Sharon looked at Ma, and her eyes were blank with tears. "It done good," said Rose of Sharon. "It done Granma good. She's a-sleepin'."

Ma's head was down, and she was ashamed. "Maybe I done them good people wrong. Granma is asleep."

"Whyn't you ast our preacher if you done a sin?" the girl asked.

"I will—but he's a queer man. Maybe it's him made me tell them people they couldn' come here. That preacher, he's gettin' roun' to thinkin' that what people does is right to do." Ma looked at her hands, and then she said, "Rosasharn, we got to sleep. 'F we're gonna go tonight, we got to sleep." She stretched out on the ground beside the mattress.

Rose of Sharon asked, "How about fannin' Granma?"

"She's asleep now. You lay down an' rest."

"I wonder where at Connie is?" the girl complained. "I ain't seen him around for a long time."

Ma said, "Sh! Get some rest."

"Ma, Connie gonna study nights an' get to be somepin."

"Yeah. You tol' me about that. Get some rest."

The girl lay down on the edge of Granma's mattress. "Connie's got a new plan. He's thinkin' all a time. When he gets all up on 'lectricity he gonna have his own store, an' then guess what we gonna have?"

"What?"

"Ice—all the ice you want. Gonna have a ice box. Keep it full. Stuff don't spoil if you got ice."

"Connie's thinkin' all a time," Ma chuckled. "Better get some rest now."

Rose of Sharon closed her eyes. Ma turned over on her back and crossed her hands under her head. She listened to Granma's breathing and to the girl's breathing. She moved a hand to start a fly from her forehead. The camp was quiet in the blinding heat, but the noises of hot grass—of crickets, the hum of flies—were a tone that was close to silence. Ma sighed deeply and then yawned and closed her eyes. In her half-sleep she heard footsteps approaching, but it was a man's voice that started her awake.

"Who's in here?"

Ma sat up quickly. A brown-faced man bent over and looked in. He wore boots and khaki pants and a khaki shirt with epaulets. On a Sam Browne belt a pistol holster hung,

and a big silver star was pinned to his shirt at the left breast.
A loose-crowned military cap was on the back of his head.
He beat on the tarpaulin with his hand, and the tight canvas
vibrated like a drum.

"Who's in here?" he demanded again.

Ma asked, "What is it you want, mister?"

"What you think I want? I want to know who's in here."

"Why, they's jus' us three in here. Me an' Granma an' my
girl."

"Where's your men?"

"Why, they went down to clean up. We was drivin' all
night."

"Where'd you come from?"

"Right near Sallisaw, Oklahoma."

"Well, you can't stay here."

"We aim to get out tonight an' cross the desert, mister."

"Well, you better. If you're here tomorra this time I'll
run you in. We don't want none of you settlin' down here."

Ma's face blackened with anger. She got slowly to her feet.
She stooped to the utensil box and picked out the iron skillet.
"Mister," she said, "you got a tin button an' a gun. Where I
come from, you keep your voice down." She advanced on
him with the skillet. He loosened the gun in the holster. "Go
ahead," said Ma. "Scarin' women. I'm thankful the men folks
ain't here. They'd tear ya to pieces. In my country you
watch your tongue."

The man took two steps backward. "Well, you ain't in
your country now. You're in California, an' we don't want
you goddamn Okies settlin' down."

Ma's advance stopped. She looked puzzled. "Okies?" she
said softly. "Okies."

"Yeah, Okies! An' if you're here when I come tomorra,

I'll run ya in." He turned and walked to the next tent and banged on the canvas with his hand. "Who's in here?" he said.

Ma went slowly back under the tarpaulin. She put the skillet in the utensil box. She sat down slowly. Rose of Sharon watched her secretly. And when she saw Ma fighting with her face, Rose of Sharon closed her eyes and pretended to be asleep.

The sun sank low in the afternoon, but the heat did not seem to decrease. Tom awakened under his willow, and his mouth was parched and his body was wet with sweat, and his head was dissatisfied with his rest. He staggered to his feet and walked toward the water. He peeled off his clothes and waded into the stream. And the moment the water was about him, his thirst was gone. He lay back in the shallows and his body floated. He held himself in place with his elbows in the sand, and looked at his toes, which bobbed above the surface.

A pale skinny little boy crept like an animal through the reeds and slipped off his clothes. And he squirmed into the water like a muskrat, and pulled himself along like a muskrat, only his eyes and nose above the surface. Then suddenly he saw Tom's head and saw that Tom was watching him. He stopped his game and sat up.

Tom said, "Hello."

" 'Lo!"

"Looks like you was playin' mushrat."

"Well, I was." He edged gradually away toward the bank; he moved casually, and then he leaped out, gathered his clothes with a sweep of his arms, and was gone among the willows.

Tom laughed quietly. And then he heard his name called

shrilly. "Tom, oh, Tom!" He sat up in the water and whistled through his teeth, a piercing whistle with a loop on the
end. The willows shook, and Ruthie stood looking at him.

"Ma wants you," she said. "Ma wants you right away."

"Awright." He stood up and strode through the water to
the shore; and Ruthie looked with interest and amazement at
his naked body.

Tom, seeing the direction of her eyes, said, "Run on now.
Git!" And Ruthie ran. Tom heard her calling excitedly for
Winfield as she went. He put the hot clothes on his cool,
wet body and he walked slowly up through the willows
toward the tent.

Ma had started a fire of dry willow twigs, and she had a
pan of water heating. She looked relieved when she saw him.

"What's a matter, Ma?" he asked.

"I was scairt," she said. "They was a policeman here. He
says we can't stay here. I was scairt he talked to you. I was
scairt you'd hit him if he talked to you."

Tom said, "What'd I go an' hit a policeman for?"

Ma smiled. "Well—he talked so bad—I nearly hit him myself."

Tom grabbed her arm and shook her roughly and loosely,
and he laughed. He sat down on the ground, still laughing.
"My God, Ma. I knowed you when you was gentle. What's
come over you?"

She looked serious. "I don' know, Tom."

"Fust you stan' us off with a jack handle, and now you try
to hit a cop." He laughed softly, and he reached out and patted her bare foot tenderly. "A ol' hell-cat," he said.

"Tom."

"Yeah?"

She hesitated a long time. "Tom, this here policeman—he

called us—Okies. He says, 'We don' want you goddamn Okies settlin' down.' "

Tom studied her, and his hand still rested gently on her bare foot. "Fella tol' about that," he said. "Fella tol' how they say it." He considered, "Ma, would you say I was a bad fella? Oughta be locked up—like that?"

"No," she said. "You been tried— No. What you ast me for?"

"Well, I dunno. I'd a took a sock at that cop."

Ma smiled with amusement. "Maybe I oughta ast you that, 'cause I nearly hit 'im with a skillet."

"Ma, why'd he say we couldn' stop here?"

"Jus' says they don' want no damn Okies settlin' down. Says he's gonna run us in if we're here tomorra."

"But we ain't use' ta gettin' shoved aroun' by no cops."

"I tol' him that," said Ma. "He says we ain't home now. We're in California, and they do what they want."

Tom said uneasily, "Ma, I got somepin to tell ya. Noah— he went on down the river. He ain't a-goin' on."

It took a moment for Ma to understand. "Why?" she asked softly.

"I don' know. Says he got to. Says he got to stay. Says for me to tell you."

"How'll he eat?" she demanded.

"I don' know. Says he'll catch fish."

Ma was silent a long time. "Family's fallin' apart," she said. "I don' know. Seems like I can't think no more. I jus' can't think. They's too much."

Tom said lamely, "He'll be awright, Ma. He's a funny kind a fella."

Ma turned stunned eyes toward the river. "I jus' can't seem to think no more."

Tom looked down the line of tents and he saw Ruthie and Winfield standing in front of a tent in decorous conversation with someone inside. Ruthie was twisting her skirt in her hands, while Winfield dug a hole in the ground with his toe. Tom called, "You, Ruthie!" She looked up and saw him and trotted toward him, with Winfield behind her. When she came up, Tom said, "You go get our folks. They're sleepin' down the willows. Get 'em. An' you, Winfiel'. You tell the Wilsons we're gonna get rollin' soon as we can." The children spun around and charged off.

Tom said, "Ma, how's Granma now?"

"Well, she got a sleep today. Maybe she's better. She's still a-sleepin'."

"Tha's good. How much pork we got?"

"Not very much. Quarter hog."

"Well, we got to fill that other kag with water. Got to take water along." They could hear Ruthie's shrill cries for the men down in the willows.

Ma shoved willow sticks into the fire and made it crackle up about the black pot. She said, "I pray God we gonna get some res'. I pray Jesus we gonna lay down in a nice place."

The sun sank toward the baked and broken hills to the west. The pot over the fire bubbled furiously. Ma went under the tarpaulin and came out with an apronful of potatoes, and she dropped them into the boiling water. "I pray God we gonna be let to wash some clothes. We ain't never been dirty like this. Don't even wash potatoes 'fore we boil 'em. I wonder why? Seems like the heart's took out of us."

The men came trooping up from the willows, and their eyes were full of sleep, and their faces were red and puffed with daytime sleep.

Pa said, "What's a matter?"

"We're goin'," said Tom. "Cop says we got to go. Might's well get her over. Get a good start an' maybe we'll be through her. Near three hunderd miles where we're goin'."

Pa said, "I thought we was gonna get a rest."

"Well, we ain't. We got to go. Pa," Tom said, "Noah ain't a-goin'. He walked on down the river."

"Ain't goin'? What the hell's the matter with him?" And then Pa caught himself. "My fault," he said miserably. "That boy's all my fault."

"No."

"I don't wanta talk about it no more," said Pa. "I can't— my fault."

"Well, we got to go," said Tom.

Wilson walked near for the last words. "We can't go, folks," he said. "Sairy's done up. She got to res'. She ain't gonna git acrost that desert alive."

They were silent at his words; then Tom said, "Cop says he'll run us in if we're here tomorra."

Wilson shook his head. His eyes were glazed with worry, and a paleness showed through his dark skin. "Jus' hafta do 'er, then. Sairy can't go. If they jail us, why, they'll hafta jail us. She got to res' an' get strong."

Pa said, "Maybe we better wait an' all go together."

"No," Wilson said. "You been nice to us; you been kin', but you can't stay here. You got to get on an' get jobs and work. We ain't gonna let you stay."

Pa said excitedly, "But you ain't got nothing."

Wilson smiled. "Never had nothin' when you took us up. This ain't none of your business. Don't you make me git mean. You got to go, or I'll get mean an' mad."

Ma beckoned Pa into the cover of the tarpaulin and spoke softly to him.

Wilson turned to Casy. "Sairy wants you should go see her."

"Sure," said the preacher. He walked to the Wilson tent, tiny and gray, and he slipped the flaps aside and entered. It was dusky and hot inside. The mattress lay on the ground, and the equipment was scattered about, as it had been unloaded in the morning. Sairy lay on the mattress, her eyes wide and bright. He stood and looked down at her, his large head bent and the stringy muscles of his neck tight along the sides. And he took off his hat and held it in his hand.

She said, "Did my man tell ya we couldn' go on?"

"Tha's what he said."

Her low, beautiful voice went on, "I wanted us to go. I knowed I wouldn' live to the other side, but he'd be acrost anyways. But he won't go. He don' know. He thinks it's gonna be all right. He don' know."

"He says he won't go."

"I know," she said. "An' he's stubborn. I ast you to come to say a prayer."

"I ain't a preacher," he said softly. "My prayers ain't no good."

She moistened her lips. "I was there when the ol' man died. You said one then."

"It wasn't no prayer."

"It was a prayer," she said.

"It wasn't no preacher's prayer."

"It was a good prayer. I want you should say one for me."

"I don' know what to say."

She closed her eyes for a minute and then opened them

again. "Then say one to yourself. Don't use no words to it. That'd be awright."

"I got no God," he said.

"You got a God. Don't make no difference if you don' know what he looks like." The preacher bowed his head. She watched him apprehensively. And when he raised his head again she looked relieved. "That's good," she said. "That's what I needed. Somebody close enough—to pray."

He shook his head as though to awaken himself. "I don' understan' this here," he said.

And she replied, "Yes—you know, don't you?"

"I know," he said, "I know, but I don't understan'. Maybe you'll res' a few days an' then come on."

She shook her head slowly from side to side. "I'm jus' pain covered with skin. I know what it is, but I won't tell him. He'd be too sad. He wouldn' know what to do anyways. Maybe in the night, when he's a-sleepin'—when he waked up, it won't be so bad."

"You want I should stay with you an' not go on?"

"No," she said. "No. When I was a little girl I use' ta sing. Folks roun' about use' ta say I sung as nice as Jenny Lind. Folks use' ta come an' listen when I sung. An'—when they stood—an' me a-singin', why, me an' them was together more'n you could ever know. I was thankful. There ain't so many folks can feel so full up, so close, an' them folks standin' there an' me a-singin'. Thought maybe I'd sing in theaters, but I never done it. An' I'm glad. They wasn't nothin' got in between me an' them. An'—that's why I wanted you to pray. I wanted to feel that clostness, oncet more. It's the same thing, singin' an' prayin', jus' the same thing. I wisht you could a-heerd me sing."

He looked down at her, into her eyes. "Good-by," he said.

She shook her head slowly back and forth and closed her lips tight. And the preacher went out of the dusky tent into the blinding light.

The men were loading up the truck, Uncle John on top, while the others passed equipment up to him. He stowed it carefully, keeping the surface level. Ma emptied the quarter of a keg of salt pork into a pan, and Tom and Al took both little barrels to the river and washed them. They tied them to the running boards and carried water in buckets to fill them. Then over the tops they tied canvas to keep them from slopping the water out. Only the tarpaulin and Granma's mattress were left to be put on.

Tom said, "With the load we'll take, this ol' wagon'll boil her head off. We got to have plenty water."

Ma passed the boiled potatoes out and brought the half sack from the tent and put it with the pan of pork. The family ate standing, shuffling their feet and tossing the hot potatoes from hand to hand until they cooled.

Ma went to the Wilson tent and stayed for ten minutes, and then she came out quietly. "It's time to go," she said.

The men went under the tarpaulin. Granma still slept, her mouth wide open. They lifted the whole mattress gently and passed it up on top of the truck. Granma drew up her skinny legs and frowned in her sleep, but she did not awaken.

Uncle John and Pa tied the tarpaulin over the cross-piece, making a little tight tent on top of the load. They lashed it down to the side-bars. And then they were ready. Pa took out his purse and dug two crushed bills from it. He went to Wilson and held them out. "We want you should take this, an' "—he pointed to the pork and potatoes—"an' that."

Wilson hung his head and shook it sharply. "I ain't a-gonna do it," he said. "You ain't got much."

"Got enough to get there," said Pa. "We ain't left it all. We'll have work right off."

"I ain't a-gonna do it," Wilson said. "I'll git mean if you try."

Ma took the two bills from Pa's hand. She folded them neatly and put them on the ground and placed the pork pan over them. "That's where they'll be," she said. "If you don' get 'em, somebody else will." Wilson, his head still down, turned and went to his tent; he stepped inside and the flaps fell behind him.

For a few moments the family waited, and then, "We got to go," said Tom. "It's near four, I bet."

The family climbed on the truck, Ma on top, beside Granma. Tom and Al and Pa in the seat, and Winfield on Pa's lap. Connie and Rose of Sharon made a nest against the cab. The preacher and Uncle John and Ruthie were in a tangle on the load.

Pa called, "Good-by, Mister and Mis' Wilson." There was no answer from the tent. Tom started the engine and the truck lumbered away. And as they crawled up the rough road toward Needles and the highway, Ma looked back. Wilson stood in front of his tent, staring after them, and his hat was in his hand. The sun fell full on his face. Ma waved her hand at him, but he did not respond.

Tom kept the truck in second gear over the rough road, to protect the springs. At Needles he drove into a service station, checked the worn tires for air, checked the spares tied to the back. He had the gas tank filled, and he bought two five-gallon cans of gasoline and a two-gallon can of oil. He filled the radiator, begged a map, and studied it.

The service-station boy, in his white uniform, seemed uneasy until the bill was paid. He said, "You people sure have got nerve."

Tom looked up from the map. "What you mean?"

"Well, crossin' in a jalopy like this."

"You been acrost?"

"Sure, plenty, but not in no wreck like this."

Tom said, "If we broke down maybe somebody'd give us a han'."

"Well, maybe. But folks are kind of scared to stop at night. I'd hate to be doing it. Takes more nerve than I've got."

Tom grinned. "It don't take no nerve to do somepin when there ain't nothin' else you can do. Well, thanks. We'll drag on." And he got in the truck and moved away.

The boy in white went into the iron building where his helper labored over a book of bills. "Jesus, what a hard-looking outfit!"

"Them Okies? They're all hard-lookin'."

"Jesus, I'd hate to start out in a jalopy like that."

"Well, you and me got sense. Them goddamn Okies got no sense and no feeling. They ain't human. A human being wouldn't live like they do. A human being couldn't stand it to be so dirty and miserable. They ain't a hell of a lot better than gorillas."

"Just the same I'm glad I ain't crossing the desert in no Hudson Super-Six. She sounds like a threshing machine."

The other boy looked down at his book of bills. And a big drop of sweat rolled down his finger and fell on the pink bills. "You know, they don't have much trouble. They're so goddamn dumb they don't know it's dangerous. And, Christ Almighty, they don't know any better than what they got. Why worry?"

"I'm not worrying. Just thought if it was me, I wouldn't like it."

"That's 'cause you know better. They don't know any better." And he wiped the sweat from the pink bill with his sleeve.

The truck took the road and moved up the long hill, through the broken, rotten rock. The engine boiled very soon and Tom slowed down and took it easy. Up the long slope, winding and twisting through dead country, burned white and gray, and no hint of life in it. Once Tom stopped for a few moments to let the engine cool, and then he traveled on. They topped the pass while the sun was still up, and looked down on the desert—black cinder mountains in the distance, and the yellow sun reflected on the gray desert. The little starved bushes, sage and greasewood, threw bold shadows on the sand and bits of rock. The glaring sun was straight ahead. Tom held his hand before his eyes to see at all. They passed the crest and coasted down to cool the engine. They coasted down the long sweep to the floor of the desert, and the fan turned over to cool the water in the radiator. In the driver's seat, Tom and Al and Pa, and Winfield on Pa's knee, looked into the bright descending sun, and their eyes were stony, and their brown faces were damp with perspiration. The burnt land and the black, cindery hills broke the even distance and made it terrible in the reddening light of the setting sun.

Al said, "Jesus, what a place. How'd you like to walk acrost her?"

"People done it," said Tom. "Lots a people done it; an' if they could, we could."

"Lots must a died," said Al.

"Well, we ain't come out exac'ly clean."

Al was silent for a while, and the reddening desert swept past. "Think we'll ever see them Wilsons again?" Al asked.

Tom flicked his eyes down to the oil gauge. "I got a hunch nobody ain't gonna see Mis' Wilson for long. Jus' a hunch I got."

Winfield said, "Pa, I wanta get out."

Tom looked over at him. "Might's well let ever'body out 'fore we settle down to drivin' tonight." He slowed the car and brought it to a stop. Winfield scrambled out and urinated at the side of the road. Tom leaned out. "Anybody else?"

"We're holdin' our water up here," Uncle John called.

Pa said, "Winfiel', you crawl up on top. You put my legs to sleep a-settin' on 'em." The little boy buttoned his overalls and obediently crawled up the back board and on his hands and knees crawled over Granma's mattress and forward to Ruthie.

The truck moved on into the evening, and the edge of the sun struck the rough horizon and turned the desert red.

Ruthie said, "Wouldn' leave you set up there, huh?"

"I didn' want to. It wasn't so nice as here. Couldn' lie down."

"Well, don' you bother me, a-squawkin' an' a-talkin'," Ruthie said, " 'cause I'm goin' to sleep, an' when I wake up, we gonna be there! 'Cause Tom said so! Gonna seem funny to see pretty country."

The sun went down and left a great halo in the sky. And it grew very dark under the tarpaulin, a long cave with light at each end—a flat triangle of light.

Connie and Rose of Sharon leaned back against the cab, and the hot wind tumbling through the tent struck the backs of their heads, and the tarpaulin whipped and drummed above them. They spoke together in low tones, pitched to the drumming canvas, so that no one could hear them. When Connie spoke he turned his head and spoke into her ear, and she did the same to him. She said, "Seems like we wasn't never gonna do nothin' but move. I'm so tar'd."

He turned his head to her ear. "Maybe in the mornin'. How'd you like to be alone now?" In the dusk his hand moved out and stroked her hip.

She said, "Don't. You'll make me crazy as a loon. Don't do that." And she turned her head to hear his response.

"Maybe—when ever'body's asleep."

"Maybe," she said. "But wait till they get to sleep. You'll make me crazy, an' maybe they won't get to sleep."

"I can't hardly stop," he said.

"I know. Me neither. Le's talk about when we get there; an' you move away 'fore I get crazy."

He shifted away a little. "Well, I'll get to studyin' nights right off," he said. She sighed deeply. "Gonna get one a them books that tells about it an' cut the coupon, right off."

"How long, you think?" she asked.

"How long what?"

"How long 'fore you'll be makin' big money an' we got ice?"

"Can't tell," he said importantly. "Can't really rightly tell. Fella oughta be studied up pretty good 'fore Christmus."

"Soon's you get studied up we could get ice an' stuff, I guess."

He chuckled. "It's this here heat," he said. "What you gonna need ice roun' Christmus for?"

She giggled. "Tha's right. But I'd like ice any time. Now don't. You'll get me crazy!"

The dusk passed into dark and the desert stars came out in

the soft sky, stars stabbing and sharp, with few points and rays to them, and the sky was velvet. And the heat changed. While the sun was up, it was a beating, flailing heat, but now the heat came from below, from the earth itself, and the heat was thick and muffling. The lights of the truck came on, and they illuminated a little blur of highway ahead, and a strip of desert on either side of the road. And sometimes eyes gleamed in the lights far ahead, but no animal showed in the lights. It was pitch dark under the canvas now. Uncle John and the preacher were curled in the middle of the truck, resting on their elbows, and staring out the back triangle. They could see the two bumps that were Ma and Granma against the outside. They could see Ma move occasionally, and her dark arm moving against the outside.

Uncle John talked to the preacher. "Casy," he said, "you're a fella oughta know what to do."

"What to do about what?"

"I dunno," said Uncle John.

Casy said, "Well, that's gonna make it easy for me!"

"Well, you been a preacher."

"Look, John, ever'body takes a crack at me 'cause I been a preacher. A preacher ain't nothin' but a man."

"Yeah, but—he's—a *kind* of a man, else he wouldn' be a preacher. I wanna ast you—well, you think a fella could bring bad luck to folks?"

"I dunno," said Casy. "I dunno."

"Well—see—I was married—fine, good girl. An' one night she got a pain in her stomach. An' she says, 'You better get a doctor.' An' I says, 'Hell, you jus' et too much.'" Uncle John put his hand on Casy's knee and he peered through the darkness at him. "She give me a *look*. An' she groaned all night, an' she died the next afternoon." The preacher mumbled something. "You see," John went on, "I kil't her. An' sence then I tried to make it up—mos'ly to kids. An' I tried to be good, an' I can't. I get drunk, an' I go wild."

"Ever'body goes wild," said Casy. "I do too."

"Yeah, but you ain't got a sin on your soul like me."

Casy said gently, "Sure I got sins. Ever'body got sins. A sin is somepin you ain't sure about. Them people that's sure about ever'thing an' ain't got no sin—well, with that kind a son-of-a-bitch, if I was God I'd kick their ass right outa heaven! I couldn' stand 'em!"

Uncle John said, "I got a feelin' I'm bringin' bad luck to my own folks. I got a feelin' I oughta go away an' let 'em be. I ain't comf'table bein' like this."

Casy said quickly, "I know this—a man got to do what he got to do. I can't tell you. I can't tell you. I don't think they's luck or bad luck. On'y one thing in this worl' I'm sure of, an' that's I'm sure nobody got a right to mess with a fella's life. He got to do it all hisself. Help him, maybe, but not tell him what to do."

Uncle John said disappointedly, "Then you don' know?"

"I don' know."

"You think it was a sin to let my wife die like that?"

"Well," said Casy, "for anybody else it was a mistake, but if you think it was a sin—then it's a sin. A fella builds his own sins right up from the groun'."

"I got to give that a goin'-over," said Uncle John, and he rolled on his back and lay with his knees pulled up.

The truck moved on over the hot earth, and the hours passed. Ruthie and Winfield went to sleep. Connie loosened a blanket from the load and covered himself and Rose of Sharon with it, and in the heat they struggled together, and held their breaths. And after a time Connie threw off the blanket and the hot tunneling wind felt cool on their wet bodies.

On the back of the truck Ma lay on the mattress beside Granma, and she could not see with her eyes, but she could feel the struggling body and the struggling heart; and the sobbing breath was in her ear. And Ma said over and over, "All right. It's gonna be all right." And she said hoarsely, "You know the family got to get acrost. You know that."

Uncle John called, "You all right?"

It was a moment before she answered. "All right. Guess I dropped off to sleep." And after a time Granma was still, and Ma lay rigid beside her.

The night hours passed, and the dark was in against the truck. Sometimes cars passed them, going west and away; and sometimes great trucks came up out of the west and rumbled eastward. And the stars flowed down in a slow cascade over the western horizon. It was near midnight when they neared Daggett, where the inspection station is. The road was floodlighted there, and a sign illuminated, "KEEP RIGHT AND STOP." The officers loafed in the office, but they came out and stood under the long covered shed when Tom pulled in. One officer put down the license number and raised the hood.

Tom asked, "What's this here?"

"Agricultural inspection. We got to look over your stuff. Got any vegetables or seeds?"

"No," said Tom.

"Well, we got to look over your stuff. You got to unload."

Now Ma climbed heavily down from the truck. Her face was swollen and her eyes were hard. "Look, mister. We got a sick ol' lady. We got to get her to a doctor. We can't wait." She seemed to fight with hysteria. "You can't make us wait."

"Yeah? Well, we got to look you over."

"I swear we ain't got any thing!" Ma cried. "I swear it. An' Granma's awful sick."

"You don't look so good yourself," the officer said.

Ma pulled herself up the back of the truck, hoisted herself with huge strength. "Look," she said.

The officer shot a flashlight beam up on the old shrunken face. "By God, she is," he said. "You swear you got no seeds or fruits or vegetables, no corn, no oranges?"

"No, no. I swear it!"

"Then go ahead. You can get a doctor in Barstow. That's only eight miles. Go on ahead."

Tom climbed in and drove on.

The officer turned to his companion. "I couldn' hold 'em."

"Maybe it was a bluff," said the other.

"Oh, Jesus, no! You should of seen that ol' woman's face. That wasn't no bluff."

Tom increased his speed to Barstow, and in the little town he stopped, got out, and walked around the truck. Ma leaned out. "It's awright," she said. "I didn' wanta stop there, fear we wouldn' get acrost."

"Yeah! But how's Granma?"

"She's awright—awright. Drive on. We got to get acrost." Tom shook his head and walked back.

"Al," he said, "I'm gonna fill her up, an' then you drive some." He pulled to an all-night gas station and filled the tank and the radiator, and filled the crank case. Then Al slipped under the wheel and Tom took the outside, with Pa in the middle. They drove away into the darkness and the little hills near Barstow were behind them.

Tom said, "I don' know what's got into Ma. She's flighty as a dog with a flea in his ear. Wouldn' a took long to look over the stuff. An' she says Granma's sick; an' now she says Granma's awright. I can't figger her out. She ain't right. S'pose she wore her brains out on the trip."

Pa said, "Ma's almost like she was when she was a girl. She was a wild one then. She wasn' scairt of nothin'. I thought havin' all the kids an' workin' took it out a her, but I guess it ain't. Christ! When she got that jack handle back there, I tell you I wouldn' wanna be the fella took it away from her."

"I dunno what's got into her," Tom said. "Maybe she's jus' tar'd out."

Al said, "I won't be doin' no weepin' an' a-moanin' to get through. I got this goddamn car on my soul."

Tom said, "Well, you done a damn good job a pickin'. We ain't had hardly no trouble with her at all."

All night they bored through the hot darkness, and jack-rabbits scuttled into the lights and dashed away in long jolting leaps. And the dawn came up behind them when the lights of Mojave were ahead. And the dawn showed high mountains to the west. They filled with water and oil at Mojave and crawled into the mountains, and the dawn was about them.

Tom said, "Jesus, the desert's past! Pa, Al, for Christ sakes! The desert's past!"

"I'm too goddamn tired to care," said Al.

"Want me to drive?"

"No, wait awhile."

They drove through Tehachapi in the morning glow, and the sun came up behind them, and then—suddenly they saw the great valley below them. Al jammed on the brake and stopped in the middle of the road, and, "Jesus Christ! Look!" he said. The vineyards, the orchards, the great flat valley, green and beautiful, the trees set in rows, and the farm houses.

And Pa said, "God Almighty!" The distant cities, the little towns in the orchard land, and the morning sun, golden on the valley. A car honked behind them. Al pulled to the side of the road and parked.

"I want ta look at her." The grain fields golden in the morning, and the willow lines, the eucalyptus trees in rows.

Pa sighed, "I never knowed they was anything like her." The peach trees and the walnut groves, and the dark green patches of oranges. And red roofs among the trees, and barns —rich barns. Al got out and stretched his legs.

He called, "Ma—come look. We're there!"

Ruthie and Winfield scrambled down from the car, and then they stood, silent and awestruck, embarrassed before the great valley. The distance was thinned with haze, and the land grew softer and softer in the distance. A windmill flashed in the sun, and its turning blades were like a little heliograph, far away. Ruthie and Winfield looked at it, and Ruthie whispered, "It's California."

Winfield moved his lips silently over the syllables. "There's fruit," he said aloud.

Casy and Uncle John, Connie and Rose of Sharon climbed down. And they stood silently. Rose of Sharon had started to brush her hair back, when she caught sight of the valley and her hand dropped slowly to her side.

Tom said, "Where's Ma? I want Ma to see it. Look, Ma! Come here, Ma." Ma was climbing slowly, stiffly, down the back board. Tom looked at her. "My God, Ma, you sick?" Her face was stiff and putty-like, and her eyes seemed to have sunk deep into her head, and the rims were red with weariness. Her feet touched the ground and she braced herself by holding the truck-side.

Her voice was a croak. "Ya say we're acrost?"

Tom pointed to the great valley. "Look!"

She turned her head, and her mouth opened a little. Her fingers went to her throat and gathered a little pinch of skin and twisted gently. "Thank God!" she said. "The fambly's here." Her knees buckled and she sat down on the running board.

"You sick, Ma?"

"No, jus' tar'd."

"Didn' you get no sleep?"

"No."

"Was Granma bad?"

Ma looked down at her hands, lying together like tired lovers in her lap. "I wisht I could wait an' not tell you. I wisht it could be all—nice."

Pa said, "Then Granma's bad."

Ma raised her eyes and looked over the valley. "Granma's dead."

They looked at her, all of them, and Pa asked, "When?"

"Before they stopped us las' night."

"So that's why you didn' want 'em to look."

"I was afraid we wouldn' get acrost," she said. "I tol' Granma we couldn' he'p her. The fambly had ta get acrost. I tol' her, tol' her when she was a-dyin'. We couldn' stop in the desert. There was the young ones—an' Rosasharn's baby. I tol' her." She put up her hands and covered her face for a moment. "She can get buried in a nice green place," Ma said softly. "Trees aroun' an' a nice place. She got to lay her head down in California."

The family looked at Ma with a little terror at her strength.

Tom said, "Jesus Christ! You layin' there with her all night long!"

"The fambly hadda get acrost," Ma said miserably.

Tom moved close to put his hand on her shoulder.

"Don' touch me," she said. "I'll hol' up if you don' touch me. That'd get me."

Pa said, "We got to go on now. We got to go on down."

Ma looked up at him. "Can—can I set up front? I don' wanna go back there no more—I'm tar'd. I'm awful tar'd."

They climbed back on the load, and they avoided the long stiff figure covered and tucked in a comforter, even the head covered and tucked. They moved to their places and tried to keep their eyes from it—from the hump on the comfort that would be the nose, and the steep cliff that would be the jut of the chin. They tried to keep their eyes away, and they could not. Ruthie and Winfield, crowded in a forward corner as far away from the body as they could get, stared at the tucked figure.

And Ruthie whispered, "Tha's Granma, an' she's dead."

Winfield nodded solemnly. "She ain't breathin' at all. She's awful dead."

And Rose of Sharon said softly to Connie, "She was a-dyin' right when we——"

"How'd we know?" he reassured her.

Al climbed on the load to make room for Ma in the seat. And Al swaggered a little because he was sorry. He plumped down beside Casy and Uncle John. "Well, she was ol'. Guess her time was up," Al said. "Ever'body got to die." Casy and Uncle John turned eyes expressionlessly on him and looked at him as though he were a curious talking bush. "Well, ain't they?" he demanded. And the eyes looked away, leaving Al sullen and shaken.

Casy said in wonder, "All night long, an' she was alone." And he said, "John, there's a woman so great with love—she scares me. Makes me afraid an' mean."

John asked, "Was it a sin? Is they any part of it you might call a sin?"

Casy turned on him in astonishment, "A sin? No, there ain't no part of it that's a sin."

"I ain't never done nothin' that wasn't part sin," said John, and he looked at the long wrapped body.

Tom and Ma and Pa got into the front seat. Tom let the truck roll and started on compression. And the heavy truck moved, snorting and jerking and popping down the hill. The sun was behind them, and the valley golden and green before them. Ma shook her head slowly from side to side. "It's purty," she said. "I wisht they could of saw it."

"I wisht so too," said Pa.

Tom patted the steering wheel under his hand. "They was too old," he said. "They wouldn't of saw nothin' that's here. Grampa would a been a-seein' the Injuns an' the prairie country when he was a young fella. An' Granma would a remembered an' seen the first home she lived in. They was too ol'. Who's really seein' it is Ruthie an' Winfiel'."

Pa said, "Here's Tommy talkin' like a growed-up man, talkin' like a preacher almos'."

And Ma smiled sadly. "He is. Tommy's growed way up—way up so I can't get aholt of 'im sometimes."

They popped down the mountain, twisting and looping, losing the valley sometimes, and then finding it again. And the hot breath of the valley came up to them, with hot green smells on it, and with resinous sage and tarweed smells. The crickets crackled along the road. A rattlesnake crawled across the road and Tom hit it and broke it and left it squirming.

Tom said, "I guess we got to go to the coroner, wherever he is. We got to get her buried decent. How much money might be lef', Pa?"

" 'Bout forty dollars," said Pa.

Tom laughed. "Jesus, are we gonna start clean! We sure ain't bringin' nothin' with us." He chuckled a moment, and then his face straightened quickly. He pulled the visor of his cap down low over his eyes. And the truck rolled down the mountain into the great valley.

Chapter Nineteen

ONCE California belonged to Mexico and its land to Mexicans; and a horde of tattered feverish Americans poured in. And such was their hunger for land that they took the land—stole Sutter's land, Guerrero's land, took the grants and broke them up and growled and quarreled over them, those frantic hungry men; and they guarded with guns the land they had stolen. They put up houses and barns, they turned the earth and planted crops. And these things were possession, and possession was ownership.

The Mexicans were weak and fed. They could not resist, because they wanted nothing in the world as frantically as the Americans wanted land.

Then, with time, the squatters were no longer squatters, but owners; and their children grew up and had children on the land. And the hunger was gone from them, the feral hunger, the gnawing, tearing hunger for land, for water and earth and the good sky over it, for the green thrusting grass, for the swelling roots. They had these things so completely that they did not know about them any more. They had no more the stomach-tearing lust for a rich acre and a shining blade to plow it, for seed and a windmill beating its wings in the air. They arose in the dark no more to hear the sleepy birds' first chittering, and the morning wind around the house while they waited for the first light to go out to the dear acres. These things were lost, and crops were reckoned in dollars, and land was valued by principal plus interest, and crops were bought and sold before they were planted. Then crop failure, drought, and flood were no longer little deaths within life, but simple losses of money. And all their love was thinned with money, and all their fierceness dribbled away in interest until they were no longer farmers at all, but little shopkeepers of crops, little manufacturers who must sell before they can make. Then those farmers who were not good shopkeepers lost their land to good shopkeepers. No matter how clever, how loving a man might be with earth and growing things, he could not survive if he were not also a good shopkeeper. And as time went on, the business men had the farms, and the farms grew larger, but there were fewer of them.

Now farming became industry, and the owners followed Rome, although they did not know it. They imported slaves, although they did not call them slaves: Chinese, Japanese, Mexicans, Filipinos. They live on rice and beans, the business men said. They don't need much. They wouldn't know what to do with good wages. Why, look how they live. Why, look what they eat. And if they get funny—deport them.

And all the time the farms grew larger and the owners fewer. And there were pitifully few farmers on the land any more. And the imported serfs were beaten and frightened and starved until some went home again, and some grew fierce and were killed or driven from the country. And the farms grew larger and the owners fewer.

And the crops changed. Fruit trees took the place of grain fields, and vegetables to feed the world spread out on the bottoms: lettuce, cauliflower, artichokes, potatoes—stoop crops. A man may stand to use a scythe, a plow, a pitchfork; but he must crawl like a bug between the rows of lettuce, he must bend his back and pull his long bag between the cotton rows, he must go on his knees like a penitent across a cauliflower patch.

And it came about that owners no longer worked on their farms. They farmed on paper; and they forgot the land, the smell, the feel of it, and remembered only that they owned it, remembered only what they gained and lost by it. And some of the farms grew so large that one man could not even conceive of them any more, so large that it took batteries of bookkeepers to keep track of interest and gain and loss; chemists to test the soil, to replenish; straw bosses to see that the stooping men were moving along the rows as swiftly as the material of their bodies could stand. Then such a farmer really became a storekeeper, and kept a store. He paid the men, and sold them food, and took the money back. And after a while he did not pay the men at all, and saved bookkeeping. These farms gave food on credit. A man might work and feed himself; and when the work was done, he might find that he owed money to the company. And the owners not only did not work the farms any more, many of them had never seen the farms they owned.

And then the dispossessed were drawn west—from Kansas, Oklahoma, Texas, New Mexico; from Nevada and Arkansas families, tribes, dusted out, tractored out. Carloads, caravans, homeless and hungry; twenty thousand and fifty thousand and a hundred thousand and two hundred thousand. They streamed over the mountains, hungry and restless—restless as ants, scurrying to find work to do—to lift, to push, to pull, to pick, to cut—anything, any burden to bear, for food. The kids are hungry. We got no place to live. Like ants scurrying for work, for food, and most of all for land.

We ain't foreign. Seven generations back Americans, and

beyond that Irish, Scotch, English, German. One of our folks in the Revolution, an' they was lots of our folks in the Civil War—both sides. Americans.

They were hungry, and they were fierce. And they had hoped to find a home, and they found only hatred. Okies—the owners hated them because the owners knew they were soft and the Okies strong, that they were fed and the Okies hungry; and perhaps the owners had heard from their grandfathers how easy it is to steal land from a soft man if you are fierce and hungry and armed. The owners hated them. And in the towns, the storekeepers hated them because they had no money to spend. There is no shorter path to a storekeeper's contempt, and all his admirations are exactly opposite. The town men, little bankers, hated Okies because there was nothing to gain from them. They had nothing. And the laboring people hated Okies because a hungry man must work, and if he must work, if he has to work, the wage payer automatically gives him less for his work; and then no one can get more.

And the dispossessed, the migrants, flowed into California, two hundred and fifty thousand, and three hundred thousand. Behind them new tractors were going on the land and the tenants were being forced off. And new waves were on the way, new waves of the dispossessed and the homeless, hardened, intent, and dangerous.

And while the Californians wanted many things, accumulation, social success, amusement, luxury, and a curious banking security, the new barbarians wanted only two things—land and food; and to them the two were one. And whereas the wants of the Californians were nebulous and undefined, the wants of the Okies were beside the roads, lying there to be seen and coveted: the good fields with water to be dug for, the good green fields, earth to crumble experimentally in the hand, grass to smell, oaten stalks to chew until the sharp sweetness was in the throat. A man might look at a fallow field and know, and see in his mind that his own bending back and his own straining arms would bring the cabbages into the light, and the golden eating corn, the turnips and carrots.

And a homeless hungry man, driving the roads with his wife beside him and his thin children in the back seat, could look at the fallow fields which might produce food but not profit, and that man could know how a fallow field is a sin and the unused land a crime against the thin children. And such a man drove along the roads and knew temptation at every field, and knew the lust to take these fields and make them grow strength for his children and a little comfort for his wife. The temptation was before him always. The fields goaded him, and the company ditches with good water flowing were a goad to him.

And in the south he saw the golden oranges hanging on the trees, the little golden oranges on the dark green trees; and guards with shotguns patrolling the lines so a man might not pick an orange for a thin child, oranges to be dumped if the price was low.

He drove his old car into a town. He scoured the farms for work. Where can we sleep the night?

Well, there's Hooverville on the edge of the river. There's a whole raft of Okies there.

He drove his old car to Hooverville. He never asked again, for there was a Hooverville on the edge of every town.

The rag town lay close to water; and the houses were tents, and weed-thatched enclosures, paper houses, a great junk pile. The man drove his family in and became a citizen of Hooverville—always they were called Hooverville. The man put up his own tent as near to water as he could get; or if he had no tent, he went to the city dump and brought back cartons and built a house of corrugated paper. And when the rains came the house melted and washed away. He settled in Hooverville and he scoured the countryside for work, and the little money he had went for gasoline to look for work. In the evening the men gathered and talked together. Squatting on their hams they talked of the land they had seen.

There's thirty thousan' acres, out west of here. Layin' there. Jesus, what I could do with that, with five acres of that! Why, hell, I'd have ever'thing to eat.

Notice one thing? They ain't no vegetables nor chickens nor pigs at the farms. They raise one thing—cotton, say, or peaches, or lettuce. 'Nother place'll be all chickens. They buy the stuff they could raise in the dooryard.

Jesus, what I could do with a couple pigs!

Well, it ain't yourn, an' it ain't gonna be yourn.

What we gonna do? The kids can't grow up this way.

In the camps the word would come whispering, There's work at Shafter. And the cars would be loaded in the night, the highways crowded—a gold rush for work. At Shafter the people would pile up, five times too many to do the work. A gold rush for work. They stole away in the night, frantic for work. And along the roads lay the temptations, the fields that could bear food.

That's owned. That ain't our'n.

Well, maybe we could get a little piece of her. Maybe— a little piece. Right down there—a patch. Jimson weed now. Christ, I could git enough potatoes off'n that little patch to feed my whole family!

It ain't our'n. It got to have Jimson weeds.

Now and then a man tried; crept on the land and cleared a piece, trying like a thief to steal a little richness from the earth. Secret gardens hidden in the weeds. A package of carrot seeds and a few turnips. Planted potato skins, crept out in the evening secretly to hoe in the stolen earth.

Leave the weeds around the edge—then nobody can see what we're a-doin'. Leave some weeds, big tall ones, in the middle.

Secret gardening in the evenings, and water carried in a rusty can.

And then one day a deputy sheriff: Well, what you think you're doin'?

I ain't doin' no harm.

I had my eye on you. This ain't your land. You're trespassing.

The land ain't plowed, an' I ain't hurtin' it none.

You goddamned squatters. Pretty soon you'd think you owned it. You'd be sore as hell. Think you owned it. Get off now.

And the little green carrot tops were kicked off and the turnip greens trampled. And then the Jimson weed moved back in. But the cop was right. A crop raised—why, that makes ownership. Land hoed and the carrots eaten—a man might fight for land he's taken food from. Get him off quick! He'll think he owns it. He might even die fighting for the little plot among the Jimson weeds.

Did ya see his face when we kicked them turnips out? Why, he'd kill a fella soon's he'd look at him. We got to keep these here people down or they'll take the country. They'll take the country.

Outlanders, foreigners.

Sure, they talk the same language, but they ain't the same. Look how they live. Think any of us folks'd live like that? Hell, no!

In the evenings, squatting and talking. And an excited man: Whyn't twenty of us take a piece of lan'? We got guns. Take it an' say, "Put us off if you can." Whyn't we do that?

They'd jus' shoot us like rats.

Well, which'd you ruther be, dead or here? Under groun' or in a house all made of gunny sacks? Which'd you ruther for your kids, dead now or dead in two years with what they call malnutrition? Know what we et all week? Biled nettles an' fried dough! Know where we got the flour for the dough? Swep' the floor of a boxcar.

Talking in the camps, and the deputies, fat-assed men with guns slung on fat hips, swaggering through the camps: Give 'em somepin to think about. Got to keep 'em in line or Christ only knows what they'll do! Why, Jesus, they're as dangerous as niggers in the South! If they ever get together there ain't nothin' that'll stop 'em.

Quote: In Lawrenceville a deputy sheriff evicted a squatter, and the squatter resisted, making it necessary for the officer to use force. The eleven-year-old son of the squatter shot and killed the deputy with a .22 rifle.

Rattlesnakes! Don't take chances with 'em, an' if they argue, shoot first. If a kid'll kill a cop, what'll the men do? Thing is, get tougher'n they are. Treat 'em rough. Scare 'em.

What if they won't scare? What if they stand up and take it and shoot back? These men were armed when they were children. A gun is an extension of themselves. What if they won't scare? What if some time an army of them marches on the land as the Lombards did in Italy, as the Germans did on Gaul and the Turks did on Byzantium? They were land-hungry, ill-armed hordes too, and the legions could not stop them. Slaughter and terror did not stop them. How can you frighten a man whose hunger is not only in his own cramped stomach but in the wretched bellies of his children? You can't scare him—he has known a fear beyond every other.

In Hooverville the men talking: Grampa took his lan' from the Injuns.

Now, this ain't right. We're a-talkin' here. This here you're talkin' about is stealin'. I ain't no thief.

No? You stole a bottle of milk from a porch night before last. An' you stole some copper wire and sold it for a piece of meat.

Yeah, but the kids was hungry.

It's stealin', though.

Know how the Fairfiel' ranch was got? I'll tell ya. It was all gov'ment lan', an' could be took up. Ol' Fairfiel', he went into San Francisco to the bars, an' he got him three hunderd stew bums. Them bums took up the lan'. Fairfiel' kep' 'em in food an' whisky, an' then when they'd proved the lan', ol' Fairfiel' took it from 'em. He used to say the lan' cost him a pint of rotgut an acre. Would you say that was stealin'?

Well, it wasn't right, but he never went to jail for it.

No, he never went to jail for it. An' the fella that put a boat in a wagon an' made his report like it was all under water 'cause he went in a boat—he never went to jail neither. An' the fellas that bribed congressmen and the legislatures never went to jail neither.

All over the State, jabbering in the Hoovervilles.

And then the raids—the swoop of armed deputies on the squatters' camps. Get out. Department of Health orders. This camp is a menace to health.

Where we gonna go?

That's none of our business. We got orders to get you out of here. In half an hour we set fire to the camp.

They's typhoid down the line. You want ta spread it all over?

We got orders to get you out of here. Now get! In half an hour we burn the camp.

In half an hour the smoke of paper houses, of weed-thatched huts, rising to the sky, and the people in their cars rolling over the highways, looking for another Hooverville.

And in Kansas and Arkansas, in Oklahoma and Texas and New Mexico, the tractors moved in and pushed the tenants out.

Three hundred thousand in California and more coming. And in California the roads full of frantic people running like ants to pull, to push, to lift, to work. For every manload to lift, five pairs of arms extended to lift it; for every stomachful of food available, five mouths open.

And the great owners, who must lose their land in an upheaval, the great owners with access to history, with eyes to read history and to know the great fact: when property accumulates in too few hands it is taken away. And that companion fact: when a majority of the people are hungry and cold they will take by force what they need. And the little screaming fact that sounds through all history: repression works only to strengthen and knit the repressed. The great owners ignored the three cries of history. The land fell into fewer hands, the number of the dispossessed increased, and every effort of the great owners was directed at repression. The money was spent for arms, for gas to protect the great holdings, and spies were sent to catch the murmuring of revolt so that it might be stamped out. The changing economy was ignored, plans for the change ignored; and only means to destroy revolt were considered, while the causes of revolt went ôn.

The tractors which throw men out of work, the belt lines which carry loads, the machines which produce, all were increased; and more and more families scampered on the highways, looking for crumbs from the great holdings, lusting after the land beside the roads. The great owners formed associations for protection and they met to discuss ways to intimidate, to kill, to gas. And always they were in fear of a principal—three hundred thousand—if they ever move under a leader—the end. Three hundred thousand, hungry and miserable; if they ever know themselves, the land will be theirs and all the gas, all the rifles in the world won't stop them. And the great owners, who had become through their holdings both more and less than men, ran to their destruction, and used every means that in the long run would destroy them. Every little means, every violence, every raid on a Hooverville, every deputy swaggering through a ragged camp put off the day a little and cemented the inevitability of the day.

The men squatted on their hams, sharp-faced men, lean from hunger and hard from resisting it, sullen eyes and hard jaws. And the rich land was around them.

D'ja hear about the kid in that fourth tent down?

No, I jus' come in.

Well, that kid's been a-cryin' in his sleep an' a-rollin' in his sleep. Them folks thought he got worms. So they give him a blaster, an' he died. It was what they call black-tongue the kid had. Comes from not gettin' good things to eat.

Poor little fella.

Yeah, but them folks can't bury him. Got to go to the county stone orchard.

Well, hell.

And hands went into pockets and little coins came out. In front of the tent a little heap of silver grew. And the family found it there.

Our people are good people; our people are kind people. Pray God some day kind people won't all be poor. Pray God some day a kid can eat.

And the associations of owners knew that some day the praying would stop.

And there's the end.

Chapter Twenty

THE family, on top of the load, the children and Connie and Rose of Sharon and the preacher were stiff and cramped. They had sat in the heat in front of the coroner's office in Bakersfield while Pa and Ma and Uncle John went in. Then a basket was brought out and the long bundle lifted down from the truck. And they sat in the sun while the examination went on, while the cause of death was found and the certificate signed.

Al and Tom strolled along the street and looked in store windows and watched the strange people on the sidewalks.

And at last Pa and Ma and Uncle John came out, and they were subdued and quiet. Uncle John climbed up on the load. Pa and Ma got in the seat. Tom and Al strolled back and Tom got under the steering wheel. He sat there silently, waiting for some instruction. Pa looked straight ahead, his dark hat pulled low. Ma rubbed the sides of her mouth with her fingers, and her eyes were far away and lost, dead with weariness.

Pa sighed deeply. "They wasn't nothin' else to do," he said.

"I know," said Ma. "She would a liked a nice funeral, though. She always wanted one."

Tom looked sideways at them. "County?" he asked.

"Yeah," Pa shook his head quickly, as though to get back to some reality. "We didn' have enough. We couldn' of done it." He turned to Ma. "You ain't to feel bad. We couldn' no matter how hard we tried, no matter what we done. We jus' didn' have it; embalming, an' a coffin an' a preacher, an' a plot in a graveyard. It would of took ten times what we got. We done the bes' we could."

"I know," Ma said. "I jus' can't get it outa my head what store she set by a nice funeral. Got to forget it." She sighed deeply and rubbed the side of her mouth. "That was a purty nice fella in there. Awful bossy, but he was purty nice."

"Yeah," Pa said. "He give us the straight talk, awright."

Ma brushed her hair back with her hand. Her jaw tightened. "We got to git," she said. "We got to find a place to stay. We got to get work an' settle down. No use a-lettin' the little fellas go hungry. That wasn't never Granma's way. She always et a good meal at a funeral."

"Where we goin'?" Tom asked.

Pa raised his hat and scratched among his hair. "Camp," he said. "We ain't gonna spen' what little's lef' till we get work. Drive out in the country."

Tom started the car and they rolled through the streets and out toward the country. And by a bridge they saw a collection of tents and shacks. Tom said, "Might's well stop here. Find out what's doin', an' where at the work is." He drove down a steep dirt incline and parked on the edge of the encampment.

There was no order in the camp; little gray tents, shacks, cars were scattered about at random. The first house was nondescript. The south wall was made of three sheets of rusty corrugated iron, the east wall a square of moldy carpet tacked between two boards, the north wall a strip of roofing paper and a strip of tattered canvas, and the west wall six pieces of gunny sacking. Over the square frame, on untrimmed willow limbs, grass had been piled, not thatched, but heaped up in a low mound. The entrance, on the gunnysack side, was cluttered with equipment. A five-gallon kerosene can served for a stove. It was laid on its side, with a section of rusty stovepipe thrust in one end. A wash boiler rested on its side against the wall; and a collection of boxes lay about, boxes to sit on, to eat on. A Model T Ford sedan and a two-wheel trailer were parked beside the shack, and about the camp there hung a slovenly despair.

Next to the shack there was a little tent, gray with weathering, but neatly, properly set up; and the boxes in front of it were placed against the tent wall. A stovepipe stuck out of the door flap, and the dirt in front of the tent had been swept and sprinkled. A bucketful of soaking clothes stood on a box. The camp was neat and sturdy. A Model A roadster and a little home-made bed trailer stood beside the tent.

And next there was a huge tent, ragged, torn in strips and the tears mended with pieces of wire. The flaps were up, and inside four wide mattresses lay on the ground. A clothes line strung along the side bore pink cotton dresses and several pairs of overalls. There were forty tents and shacks, and beside each habitation some kind of automobile. Far down the line a few children stood and stared at the newly arrived truck, and they moved toward it, little boys in overalls and bare feet, their hair gray with dust.

Tom stopped the truck and looked at Pa. "She ain't very purty," he said. "Want to go somewheres else?"

"Can't go nowheres else till we know where we're at," Pa said. "We got to ast about work."

Tom opened the door and stepped out. The family climbed down from the load and looked curiously at the camp. Ruthie and Winfield, from the habit of the road, took down the bucket and walked toward the willows, where there would be water; and the line of children parted for them and closed after them.

The flaps of the first shack parted and a woman looked out. Her gray hair was braided, and she wore a dirty, flowered Mother Hubbard. Her face was wizened and dull, deep gray pouches under blank eyes, and a mouth slack and loose.

Pa said, "Can we jus' pull up anywheres an' camp?"

The head was withdrawn inside the shack. For a moment there was quiet and then the flaps were pushed aside and a bearded man in shirt sleeves stepped out. The woman looked out after him, but she did not come into the open.

The bearded man said, "Howdy, folks," and his restless dark eyes jumped to each member of the family, and from them to the truck to the equipment.

Pa said, "I jus' ast your woman if it's all right to set our stuff anywheres."

The bearded man looked at Pa intently, as though he had said something very wise that needed thought. "Set down anywheres, here in this place?" he asked.

"Sure. Anybody own this place, that we got to see 'fore we can camp?"

The bearded man squinted one eye nearly closed and studied Pa. "You wanta camp here?"

Pa's irritation arose. The gray woman peered out of the burlap shack. "What you think I'm a-sayin'?" Pa said.

"Well, if you wanta camp here, why don't ya? I ain't a-stoppin' you."

Tom laughed. "He got it."

Pa gathered his temper. "I jus' wanted to know does anybody own it? Do we got to pay?"

The bearded man thrust out his jaw. "Who owns it?" he demanded.

Pa turned away. "The hell with it," he said. The woman's head popped back in the tent.

The bearded man stepped forward menacingly. "Who owns it?" he demanded. "Who's gonna kick us outa here? You tell *me*."

Tom stepped in front of Pa. "You better go take a good long sleep," he said. The bearded man dropped his mouth open and put a dirty finger against his lower gums. For a moment he continued to look wisely, speculatively at Tom, and then he turned on his heel and popped into the shack after the gray woman.

Tom turned on Pa. "What the hell was that?" he asked.

Pa shrugged his shoulders. He was looking across the camp. In front of a tent stood an old Buick, and the head was off. A young man was grinding the valves, and as he twisted back and forth, back and forth, on the tool, he looked up at the Joad truck. They could see that he was laughing to himself. When the bearded man had gone, the young man left his work and sauntered over.

"H'are ya?" he said, and his blue eyes were shiny with amusement. "I seen you just met the Mayor."

"What the hell's the matter with 'im?" Tom demanded.

The young man chuckled. "He's jus' nuts like you an' me. Maybe he's a little nutser'n me, I don' know."

Pa said, "I jus' ast him if we could camp here."

The young man wiped his greasy hands on his trousers. "Sure. Why not? You folks jus' come acrost?"

"Yeah," said Tom. "Jus' got in this mornin'."

"Never been in Hooverville before?"

"Where's Hooverville?"

"This here's her."

"Oh!" said Tom. "We jus' got in."

Winfield and Ruthie came back, carrying a bucket of water between them.

Ma said, "Le's get the camp up. I'm tuckered out. Maybe we can all rest." Pa and Uncle John climbed up on the truck to unload the canvas and the beds.

Tom sauntered to the young man, and walked beside him back to the car he had been working on. The valve-grinding brace lay on the exposed block, and a little yellow can of valve-grinding compound was wedged on top of the vacuum tank. Tom asked, "What the hell was the matter'th that ol' fella with the beard?"

The young man picked up his brace and went to work, twisting back and forth, grinding valve against valve seat. "The Mayor? Chris' knows. I guess maybe he's bull-simple."

"What's 'bull-simple'?"

"I guess cops push 'im aroun' so much he's still spinning."

Tom asked, "Why would they push a fella like that aroun'?"

The young man stopped his work and looked in Tom's eyes. "Chris' knows," he said. "You jus' come. Maybe you can figger her out. Some fellas says one thing, an' some says another thing. But you jus' camp in one place a little while, an' you see how quick a deputy sheriff shoves you along." He lifted a valve and smeared compound on the seat.

"But what the hell for?"

"I tell ya I don' know. Some says they don' want us to vote; keep us movin' so we can't vote. An' some says so we can't get on relief. An' some says if we set in one place we'd get organized. I don' know why. I on'y know we get rode all the time. You wait, you'll see."

"We ain't no bums," Tom insisted. "We're lookin' for work. We'll take any kind a work."

The young man paused in fitting the brace to the valve slot. He looked in amazement at Tom. "Lookin' for work?" he said. "So you're lookin' for work. What ya think ever'-body else is lookin' for? Di'monds? What you think I wore my ass down to a nub lookin' for?" He twisted the brace back and forth.

Tom looked about at the grimy tents, the junk equipment, at the old cars, the lumpy mattresses out in the sun, at the blackened cans on fire-blackened holes where the people cooked. He asked quietly, "Ain't they no work?"

"I don' know. Mus' be. Ain't no crop right here now. Grapes to pick later, an' cotton to pick later. We're a-movin' on, soon's I get these here valves groun'. Me an' my wife an' my kids. We heard they was work up north. We're shovin' north, up aroun' Salinas."

Tom saw Uncle John and Pa and the preacher hoisting the tarpaulin on the tent poles and Ma on her knees inside, brushing off the mattresses on the ground. A circle of quiet children stood to watch the new family get settled, quiet children with bare feet and dirty faces. Tom said, "Back home some fellas come through with han'bills—orange ones. Says they need lots a people out here to work the crops."

The young man laughed. "They say they's three hunderd thousan' us folks here, an' I bet ever' dam' fam'ly seen them han'bills."

"Yeah, but if they don' need folks, what'd they go to the trouble puttin' them things out for?"

"Use your head, why don'cha?"

"Yeah, but I wanta know."

"Look," the young man said. "S'pose you got a job a work, an' there's jus' one fella wants the job. You got to pay 'im what he asts. But s'pose they's a hunderd men." He put down his tool. His eyes hardened and his voice sharpened. "S'pose they's a hunderd men wants that job. S'pose them men got kids, an' them kids is hungry. S'pose a lousy dime'll buy a box a mush for them kids. S'pose a nickel'll buy at leas' somepin for them kids. An' you got a hunderd men. Jus' offer 'em a nickel—why, they'll kill each other fightin' for that nickel. Know what they was payin', las' job I had? Fifteen cents an hour. Ten hours for a dollar an' a half, an' ya can't stay on the place. Got to burn gasoline gettin' there." He was panting with anger, and his eyes blazed with hate. "That's why them han'bills was out. You can print a hell of a lot of han'bills with what ya save payin' fifteen cents an hour for fiel' work."

Tom said, "That's stinkin'."

The young man laughed harshly. "You stay out here a little while, an' if you smell any roses, you come let me smell, too."

"But they is work," Tom insisted. "Christ Almighty, with all this stuff a-growin': orchards, grapes, vegetables—I seen it. They got to have men. I seen all that stuff."

A child cried in the tent beside the car. The young man went into the tent and his voice came softly through the canvas. Tom picked up the brace, fitted it in the slot of the valve, and ground away, his hand whipping back and forth. The child's crying stopped. The young man came out and watched Tom. "You can do her," he said. "Damn good thing. You'll need to."

"How 'bout what I said?" Tom resumed. "I seen all the stuff growin'."

The young man squatted on his heels. "I'll tell ya," he said quietly. "They's a big son-of-a-bitch of a peach orchard I worked in. Takes nine men all the year roun'." He paused impressively. "Takes three thousan' men for two weeks when them peaches is ripe. Got to have 'em or them peaches'll rot. So what do they do? They send out han'bills all over hell. They need three thousan', an' they get six thousan'. They get them men for what they wanta pay. If ya don' wanta take what they pay, goddamn it, they's a thousan' men waitin' for your job. So ya pick, an' ya pick, an' then she's done. Whole part a the country's peaches. All ripe together. When ya get 'em picked, ever' goddamn one is picked. There ain't another damn thing in that part a the country to do. An' then them owners don' want you there no more. Three thousan' of you. The work's done. You might steal, you might get drunk, you might jus' raise hell. An' besides, you don' look nice, livin' in ol' tents; an' it's a pretty country, but you stink it up. They don' want you aroun'. So they kick you out, they move you along. That's how it is."

Tom, looking down toward the Joad tent, saw his mother, heavy and slow with weariness, build a little trash fire and put the cooking pots over the flame. The circle of children drew closer, and the calm wide eyes of the children watched every move of Ma's hands. An old, old man with a bent back came like a badger out of a tent and snooped near, sniffing the air as he came. He laced his arms behind him and joined the children to watch Ma. Ruthie and Winfield stood near to Ma and eyed the strangers belligerently.

Tom said angrily, "Them peaches got to be picked right now, don't they? Jus' when they're ripe?"

" 'Course they do."

"Well, s'pose them people got together an' says, 'Let 'em rot.' Wouldn' be long 'fore the price went up, by God!"

The young man looked up from the valves, looked sardonically at Tom. "Well, you figgered out somepin, didn' you. Come right outa your own head."

"I'm tar'd," said Tom. "Drove all night. I don't wanta start no argument. An' I'm so goddamn tar'd I'd argue easy. Don' be smart with me. I'm askin' you."

The young man grinned. "I didn' mean it. You ain't been here. Folks figgered that out. An' the folks with the peach orchard figgered her out too. Look, if the folks gets together, they's a leader—got to be—fella that does the talkin'. Well, first time this fella opens his mouth they grab 'im an' stick 'im in jail. An' if they's another leader pops up, why, they stick *'im* in jail."

Tom said, "Well, a fella eats in jail anyways."

"His kids don't. How'd you like to be in an' your kids starvin' to death?"

"Yeah," said Tom slowly. "Yeah."

"An' here's another thing. Ever hear a' the blacklist?"

"What's that?"

"Well, you jus' open your trap about us folks gettin' together, an' you'll see. They take your pitcher an' send it all over. Then you can't get work nowhere. An' if you got kids——"

Tom took off his cap and twisted it in his hands. "So we take what we can get, huh, or we starve; an' if we yelp we starve."

The young man made a sweeping circle with his hand, and his hand took in the ragged tents and the rusty cars.

Tom looked down at his mother again, where she sat

scraping potatoes. And the children had drawn closer. He said, "I ain't gonna take it. Goddamn it, I an' my folks ain't no sheep. I'll kick the hell outa somebody."

"Like a cop?"

"Like anybody."

"You're nuts," said the young man. "They'll pick you right off. You got no name, no property. They'll find you in a ditch, with the blood dried on your mouth an' your nose. Be one little line in the paper—know what it'll say? 'Vagrant foun' dead.' An' that's all. You'll see a lot of them little lines, 'Vagrant foun' dead.'"

Tom said, "They'll be somebody else foun' dead right 'longside of this here vagrant."

"You're nuts," said the young man. "Won't be no good in that."

"Well, what you doin' about it?" He looked into the grease-streaked face. And a veil drew down over the eyes of the young man.

"Nothin'. Where you from?"

"Us? Right near Sallisaw, Oklahoma."

"Jus' get in?"

"Jus' today."

"Gonna be aroun' here long?"

"Don't know. We'll stay wherever we can get work. Why?"

"Nothin'." And the veil came down again.

"Got to sleep up," said Tom. "Tomorra we'll go out lookin' for work."

"You kin try."

Tom turned away and moved toward the Joad tent.

The young man took up the can of valve compound and dug his finger into it. "Hi!" he called.

Tom turned. "What you want?"

"I want ta tell ya." He motioned with his finger, on which a blob of compound stuck. "I jus' want ta tell ya. Don' go lookin' for no trouble. 'Member how that bull-simple guy looked?"

"Fella in the tent up there?"

"Yeah—looked dumb—no sense?"

"What about him?"

"Well, when the cops come in, an' they come in all a time, that's how you want ta be. Dumb—don't know nothin'. Don't understan' nothin'. That's how the cops like us. Don't hit no cops. That's jus' suicide. Be bull-simple."

"Let them goddamn cops run over me, an' me do nothin'?"

"No, looka here. I'll come for ya tonight. Maybe I'm wrong. There's stools aroun' all a time. I'm takin' a chancet, an' I got a kid, too. But I'll come for ya. An' if ya see a cop, why, you're a goddamn dumb Okie, see?"

"Tha's awright if we're doin' anythin'," said Tom.

"Don' you worry. We're doin' somepin, on'y we ain't stickin' our necks out. A kid starves quick. Two-three days for a kid." He went back to his job, spread the compound on a valve seat, and his hand jerked rapidly back and forth on the brace, and his face was dull and dumb.

Tom strolled slowly back to his camp. "Bull-simple," he said under his breath.

Pa and Uncle John came toward the camp, their arms loaded with dry willow sticks, and they threw them down by the fire and squatted on their hams. "Got her picked over pretty good," said Pa. "Had ta go a long ways for wood." He looked up at the circle of staring children. "Lord God Almighty!" he said. "Where'd you come from?" All of the children looked self-consciously at their feet.

"Guess they smelled the cookin'," said Ma. "Winfiel', get out from under foot." She pushed him out of her way. "Got ta make us up a little stew," she said. "We ain't et nothin' cooked right sence we come from home. Pa, you go up to the store there an' get me some neck meat. Make a nice stew here." Pa stood up and sauntered away.

Al had the hood of the car up, and he looked down at the greasy engine. He looked up when Tom approached. "You sure look happy as a buzzard," Al said.

"I'm jus' gay as a toad in spring rain," said Tom.

"Looka the engine," Al pointed. "Purty good, huh?"

Tom peered in. "Looks awright to me."

"Awright? Jesus, she's wonderful. She ain't shot no oil nor nothin'." He unscrewed a spark plug and stuck his forefinger in the hole. "Crusted up some, but she's dry."

Tom said, "You done a nice job a pickin'. That what ya want me to say?"

"Well, I sure was scairt the whole way, figgerin' she'd bust down an' it'd be my fault."

"No, you done good. Better get her in shape, 'cause tomorra we're goin' out lookin' for work."

"She'll roll," said Al. "Don't you worry none about that." He took out a pocket knife and scraped the points of the spark plug.

Tom walked around the side of the tent, and he found Casy sitting on the earth, wisely regarding one bare foot. Tom sat down heavily beside him. "Think she's gonna work?"

"What?" asked Casy.

"Them toes of yourn."

"Oh! Jus' settin' here a-thinkin'."

"You always get good an' comf'table for it," said Tom.

Casy waggled his big toe up and his second toe down, and he smiled quietly. "Hard enough for a fella to think 'thout kinkin' hisself up to do it."

"Ain't heard a peep outa you for days," said Tom. "Thinkin' all the time?"

"Yeah, thinkin' all the time."

Tom took off his cloth cap, dirty now, and ruinous, the visor pointed as a bird's beak. He turned the sweat band out and removed a long strip of folded newspaper. "Sweat so much she's shrank," he said. He looked at Casy's waving toes. "Could ya come down from your thinkin' an' listen a minute?"

Casy turned his head on the stalk-like neck. "Listen all the time. That's why I been thinkin'. Listen to people a-talkin', an' purty soon I hear the way folks are feelin'. Goin' on all the time. I hear 'em an' feel 'em; an' they're beating their wings like a bird in a attic. Gonna bust their wings on a dusty winda tryin' ta get out."

Tom regarded him with widened eyes, and then he turned and looked at a gray tent twenty feet away. Washed jeans and shirts and a dress hung to dry on the tent guys. He said softly, "That was about what I was gonna tell ya. An' you seen awready."

"I seen," Casy agreed. "They's a army of us without no harness." He bowed his head and ran his extended hand slowly up his forehead and into his hair. "All along I seen it," he said. "Ever' place we stopped I seen it. Folks hungry for side-meat, an' when they get it, they ain't fed. An' when they'd get so hungry they couldn' stan' it no more, why, they'd ast me to pray for 'em, an' sometimes I done it." He clasped his hands around drawn-up knees and pulled his legs in. "I use ta think that'd cut 'er," he said. "Use ta rip off a prayer an' all the troubles'd stick to that prayer like flies on flypaper, an' the prayer'd go a-sailin' off, a-takin' them troubles along. But it don' work no more."

Tom said, "Prayer never brought in no side-meat. Takes a shoat to bring in pork."

"Yeah," Casy said. "An' Almighty God never raised no wages. These here folks want to live decent and bring up their kids decent. An' when they're old they wanta set in the door an' watch the downing sun. An' when they're young they wanta dance an' sing an' lay together. They wanta eat an' get drunk and work. An' that's it—they wanta jus' fling their goddamn muscles aroun' an' get tired. Christ! What'm I talkin' about?"

"I dunno," said Tom. "Sounds kinda nice. When ya think you can get ta work an' quit thinkin' a spell? We got to get work. Money's 'bout gone. Pa give five dollars to get a painted piece of board stuck up over Granma. We ain't got much lef'."

A lean brown mongrel dog came sniffing around the side of the tent. He was nervous and flexed to run. He sniffed close before he was aware of the two men, and then looking up he saw them, leaped sideways, and fled, ears back, bony tail clamped protectively. Casy watched him go, dodging around a tent to get out of sight. Casy sighed. "I ain't doin' nobody no good," he said. "Me or nobody else. I was thinkin' I'd go off alone by myself. I'm a-eatin' your food an' a-takin' up room. An' I ain't give you nothin'. Maybe I could get a steady job an' maybe pay back some a the stuff you've give me."

Tom opened his mouth and thrust his lower jaw forward, and he tapped his lower teeth with a dried piece of mustard stalk. His eyes stared over the camp, over the gray tents and the shacks of weed and tin and paper. "Wisht I had a sack a Durham," he said. "I ain't had a smoke in a hell of a time. Use ta get tobacco in McAlester. Almost wisht I was back." He tapped his teeth again and suddenly he turned on the preacher. "Ever been in a jail house?"

"No," said Casy. "Never been."

"Don't go away right yet," said Tom. "Not right yet."

"Quicker I get lookin' for work—quicker I'm gonna find some."

Tom studied him with half-shut eyes and he put on his cap again. "Look," he said, "this ain't no lan' of milk an' honey like the preachers say. They's a mean thing here. The folks here is scared of us people comin' west; an' so they got cops out tryin' to scare us back."

"Yeah," said Casy. "I know. What you ask about me bein' in jail for?"

Tom said slowly, "When you're in jail—you get to kinda—sensin' stuff. Guys ain't let to talk a hell of a lot together—two maybe, but not a crowd. An' so you get kinda sensy. If somepin's gonna bust—if say a fella's goin' stir-bugs an' take a crack at a guard with a mop handle—why, you know it 'fore it happens. An' if they's gonna be a break or a riot, nobody don't have to tell ya. You're sensy about it. You know."

"Yeah?"

"Stick aroun'," said Tom. "Stick aroun' till tomorra anyways. Somepin's gonna come up. I was talkin' to a kid up the road. An' he's bein' jus' as sneaky an' wise as a dog coyote, but he's too wise. Dog coyote a-mindin' his own business an' innocent an' sweet, jus' havin' fun an' no harm—well, they's a hen roost clost by."

Casy watched him intently, started to ask a question, and

then shut his mouth tightly. He waggled his toes slowly and, releasing his knees, pushed out his foot so he could see it. "Yeah," he said, "I won't go right yet."

Tom said, "When a bunch a folks, nice quiet folks, don't know nothin' about nothin'—somepin's goin' on."

"I'll stay," said Casy.

"An' tomorra we'll go out in the truck an' look for work."

"Yeah!" said Casy, and he waved his toes up and down and studied them gravely. Tom settled back on his elbow and closed his eyes. Inside the tent he could hear the murmur of Rose of Sharon's voice and Connie's answering.

The tarpaulin made a dark shadow and the wedge-shaped light at each end was hard and sharp. Rose of Sharon lay on a mattress and Connie squatted beside her. "I oughta help Ma," Rose of Sharon said. "I tried, but ever' time I stirred about I throwed up."

Connie's eyes were sullen. "If I'd of knowed it would be like this I wouldn' of came. I'd a studied nights 'bout tractors back home an' got me a three-dollar job. Fella can live awful nice on three dollars a day, an' go to the pitcher show ever' night, too."

Rose of Sharon looked apprehensive. "You're gonna study nights 'bout radios," she said. He was long in answering. "Ain't you?" she demanded.

"Yeah, sure. Soon's I get on my feet. Get a little money."

She rolled up on her elbow. "You ain't givin' it up!"

"No—no—'course not. But—I didn' know they was places like this we got to live in."

The girl's eyes hardened. "You got to," she said quietly.

"Sure. Sure, I know. Got to get on my feet. Get a little money. Would a been better maybe to stay home an' study 'bout tractors. Three dollars a day they get, an' pick up extra money, too." Rose of Sharon's eyes were calculating. When he looked down at her he saw in her eyes a measuring of him, a calculation of him. "But I'm gonna study," he said. "Soon's I get on my feet."

She said fiercely, "We got to have a house 'fore the baby comes. We ain't gonna have this baby in no tent."

"Sure," he said. "Soon's I get on my feet." He went out of the tent and looked down at Ma, crouched over the brush fire. Rose of Sharon rolled on her back and stared at the top of the tent. And then she put her thumb in her mouth for a gag and she cried silently.

Ma knelt beside the fire, breaking twigs to keep the flame up under the stew kettle. The fire flared and dropped and flared and dropped. The children, fifteen of them, stood silently and watched. And when the smell of the cooking stew came to their noses, their noses crinkled slightly. The sunlight glistened on hair tawny with dust. The children were embarrassed to be there, but they did not go. Ma talked quietly to a little girl who stood inside the lusting circle. She was older than the rest. She stood on one foot, caressing the back of her leg with a bare instep. Her arms were clasped behind her. She watched Ma with steady small gray eyes. She suggested, "I could break up some bresh if you want me, ma'am."

Ma looked up from her work. "You want ta get ast to eat, huh?"

"Yes, ma'am," the girl said steadily.

Ma slipped the twigs under the pot and the flame made a puttering sound. "Didn' you have no breakfast?"

"No, ma'am. They ain't no work hereabouts. Pa's in tryin' to sell some stuff to git gas so's we can git 'long."

Ma looked up. "Didn' none of these here have no breakfast?"

The circle of children shifted nervously and looked away from the boiling kettle. One small boy said boastfully, "I did —me an' my brother did—an' them two did, 'cause I seen 'em. We et good. We're a-goin' south tonight."

Ma smiled. "Then you ain't hungry. They ain't enough here to go around."

The small boy's lip stuck out. "We et good," he said, and he turned and ran and dived into a tent. Ma looked after him so long that the oldest girl reminded her.

"The fire's down, ma'am. I can keep it up if you want."

Ruthie and Winfield stood inside the circle, comporting themselves with 'proper frigidity and dignity. They were aloof, and at the same time possessive. Ruthie turned cold and angry eyes on the little girl. Ruthie squatted down to break up the twigs for Ma.

Ma lifted the kettle lid and stirred the stew with a stick. "I'm sure glad some of you ain't hungry. That little fella ain't, anyways."

The girl sneered. "Oh, him! He was a-braggin'. High an' mighty. If he don't have no supper—know what he done? Las' night, come out an' say they got chicken to eat. Well, sir, I looked in whilst they was a-eatin' an' it was fried dough jus' like ever'body else."

"Oh!" And Ma looked down toward the tent where the small boy had gone. She looked back at the little girl. "How long you been in California?" she asked.

"Oh, 'bout six months. We lived in a gov'ment camp a while, an' then we went north, an' when we come back it was full up. That's a nice place to live, you bet."

"Where's that?" Ma asked. And she took the sticks from Ruthie's hand and fed the fire. Ruthie glared with hatred at the older girl.

"Over by Weedpatch. Got nice toilets an' baths, an' you kin wash clothes in a tub, an' they's water right handy, good drinkin' water; an' nights the folks plays music an' Sat'dy night they give a dance. Oh, you never seen anything so nice. Got a place for kids to play, an' them toilets with paper. Pull down a little jigger an' the water comes right in the toilet, an' they ain't no cops let to come look in your tent any time they want, an' the fella runs the camp is so polite, comes a-visitin' an' talks an' ain't high an' mighty. I wisht we could go live there again."

Ma said, "I never heard about it. I sure could use a wash tub, I tell you."

The girl went on excitedly, "Why, God Awmighty, they got hot water right in pipes, an' you get in under a shower bath an' it's warm. You never seen such a place."

Ma said, "All full now, ya say?"

"Yeah. Las' time we ast it was."

"Mus' cost a lot," said Ma.

"Well, it costs, but if you ain't got the money, they let you work it out—couple hours a week, cleanin' up, an' garbage cans. Stuff like that. An' nights they's music an' folks talks together an' hot water right in the pipes. You never seen nothin' so nice."

Ma said, "I sure wisht we could go there."

Ruthie had stood all she could. She blurted fiercely, "Granma died right on top a the truck." The girl looked questioningly at her. "Well, she did," Ruthie said. "An' the cor'ner got her." She closed her lips tightly and broke up a little pile of sticks.

Winfield blinked at the boldness of the attack. "Right on the truck," he echoed. "Cor'ner stuck her in a big basket."

Ma said, "You shush now, both of you, or you got to go away." And she fed twigs into the fire.

Down the line Al had strolled to watch the valve-grinding job. "Looks like you're 'bout through," he said.

"Two more."

"Is they any girls in this here camp?"

"I got a wife," said the young man. "I got no time for girls."

"I always got time for girls," said Al. "I got no time for nothin' else."

"You get a little hungry an' you'll change."

Al laughed. "Maybe. But I ain't never changed that notion yet."

"Fella I talked to while ago, he's with you, ain't he?"

"Yeah! My brother Tom. Better not fool with him. He killed a fella."

"Did? What for?"

"Fight. Fella got a knife in Tom. Tom busted 'im with a shovel."

"Did, huh? What'd the law do?"

"Let 'im off 'cause it was a fight," said Al.

"He don't look like a quarreler."

"Oh, he ain't. But Tom don't take nothin' from nobody." Al's voice was very proud. "Tom, he's quiet. But—look out!"

"Well—I talked to 'im. He didn' soun' mean."

"He ain't. Jus' as nice as pie till he's roused, an' then— look out." The young man ground at the last valve. "Like me to he'p you get them valves set an' the head on?"

"Sure, if you got nothin' else to do."

"Oughta get some sleep," said Al. "But, hell, I can't keep my han's out of a tore-down car. Jus' got to git in."

"Well, I'd admire to git a hand," said the young man. "My name's Floyd Knowles."

"I'm Al Joad."

"Proud to meet ya."

"Me too," said Al. "Gonna use the same gasket?"

"Got to," said Floyd.

Al took out his pocket knife and scraped at the block. "Jesus!" he said. "They ain't nothin' I love like the guts of a engine."

"How 'bout girls?"

"Yeah, girls too! Wisht I could tear down a Rolls an' put her back. I looked under the hood of a Cad' 16 one time an', God Awmighty, you never seen nothin' so sweet in your life! In Sallisaw—an' here's this 16 a-standin' in front of a restaurant, so I lifts the hood. An' a guy comes out an' says, 'What the hell you doin'?' I says, 'Jus' lookin'. Ain't she swell?' An' he jus' stands there. I don't think he ever looked in her before. Jus' stands there. Rich fella in a straw hat. Got a stripe' shirt on, an' eye glasses. We don' say nothin'. Jus' look. An' purty soon he says, 'How'd you like to drive her?' "

Floyd said, "The hell!"

"Sure—'How'd you like to drive her?' Well, hell, I got on jeans—all dirty. I says, 'I'd get her dirty.' 'Come on!' he says. 'Jus' take her roun' the block.' Well, sir, I set in that seat an' I took her roun' the block eight times, an', oh, my God Almighty!"

"Nice?" Floyd asked.

"Oh, Jesus!" said Al. "If I could of tore her down why—I'd a give—anythin'."

Floyd slowed his jerking arm. He lifted the last valve from its seat and looked at it. "You better git use' ta a jalopy," he said, " 'cause you ain't goin' a drive no 16." He put his brace down on the running board and took up a chisel to scrape the crust from the block. Two stocky women, bare-headed and bare-footed, went by carrying a bucket of milky water between them. They limped against the weight of the bucket, and neither one looked up from the ground. The sun was half down in afternoon.

Al said, "You don't like nothin' much."

Floyd scraped harder with the chisel. "I been here six months," he said. "I been scrabblin' over this here State tryin' to work hard enough and move fast enough to get meat an' potatoes for me an' my wife an' my kids. I've run myself like a jackrabbit an'—I can't quite make her. There just ain't quite enough to eat no matter what I do. I'm gettin' tired, that's all. I'm gettin' tired way past where sleep rests me. An' I jus' don' know what to do."

"Ain't there no steady work for a fella?" Al asked.

"No, they ain't no steady work." With his chisel he pushed the crust off the block, and he wiped the dull metal with a greasy rag.

A rusty touring car drove down into the camp and there were four men in it, men with brown hard faces. The car drove slowly through the camp. Floyd called to them, "Any luck?"

The car stopped. The driver said, "We covered a hell of a lot a ground. They ain't a hand's work in this here country. We gotta move."

"Where to?" Al called.

"God knows. We worked this here place over." He let in his clutch and moved slowly down the camp.

Al looked after them. "Wouldn' it be better if one fella went alone? Then if they was one piece a work, a fella'd get it."

Floyd put down the chisel and smiled sourly. "You ain't learned," he said. "Takes gas to get roun' the country. Gas costs fifteen cents a gallon. Them four fellas can't take four cars. So each of 'em puts in a dime an' they get gas. You got to learn."

"Al!"

Al looked down at Winfield standing importantly beside him. "Al, Ma's dishin' up stew. She says come git it."

Al wiped his hands on his trousers. "We ain't et today," he said to Floyd. "I'll come give you a han' when I eat."

"No need 'less you want ta."

"Sure, I'll do it." He followed Winfield toward the Joad camp.

It was crowded now. The strange children stood close to the stew pot, so close that Ma brushed them with her elbows as she worked. Tom and Uncle John stood beside her.

Ma said helplessly, "I dunno what to do. I got to feed the fambly. What'm I gonna do with these here?" The children stood stiffly and looked at her. Their faces were blank, rigid, and their eyes went mechanically from the pot to the tin plate she held. Their eyes followed the spoon from pot to plate, and when she passed the steaming plate up to Uncle John, their eyes followed it up. Uncle John dug his spoon into the stew, and the banked eyes rose up with the spoon. A piece of potato went into John's mouth and the banked eyes were on his face, watching to see how he would react. Would it be good? Would he like it?

And then Uncle John seemed to see them for the first time.

He chewed slowly. "You take this here," he said to Tom. "I ain't hungry."

"You ain't et today," Tom said.

"I know, but I got a stomickache. I ain't hungry."

Tom said quietly, "You take that plate inside the tent an' you eat it."

"I ain't hungry," John insisted. "I'd still see 'em inside the tent."

Tom turned on the children. "You git," he said. "Go on now, git." The bank of eyes left the stew and rested wondering on his face. "Go on now, git. You ain't doin' no good. There ain't enough for you."

Ma ladled stew into the tin plates, very little stew, and she laid the plates on the ground. "I can't send 'em away," she said. "I don' know what to do. Take your plates an' go inside. I'll let 'em have what's lef'. Here, take a plate in to Rosasharn." She smiled up at the children. "Look," she said, "you little fellas go an' get you each a flat stick an' I'll put what's lef' for you. But they ain't to be no fightin'." The group broke up with a deadly, silent swiftness. Children ran to find sticks, they ran to their own tents and brought spoons. Before Ma had finished with the plates they were back, silent and wolfish. Ma shook her head. "I dunno what to do. I can't rob the fambly. I got to feed the fambly. Ruthie, Winfiel', Al," she cried fiercely. "Take your plates. Hurry up. Git in the tent quick." She looked apologetically at the waiting children. "There ain't enough," she said humbly. "I'm a-gonna set this here kettle out, an' you'll all get a little tas', but it ain't gonna do you no good." She faltered, "I can't he'p it. Can't keep it from you." She lifted the pot and set it down on the ground. "Now wait. It's too hot," she said, and she went into the tent quickly so she would not see. Her family sat on the ground, each with his plate; and outside they could hear the children digging into the pot with their sticks and their spoons and their pieces of rusty tin. A mound of children smothered the pot from sight. They did not talk, did not fight or argue; but there was a quiet intentness in all of them, a wooden fierceness. Ma turned her back so she couldn't see. "We can't do that no more," she said. "We got to eat alone." There was the sound of scraping at the kettle, and then the mound of children broke and the children walked away and left the scraped kettle on the ground. Ma looked at the empty plates. "Didn' none of you get nowhere near enough."

Pa got up and left the tent without answering. The preacher smiled to himself and lay back on the ground, hands clasped behind his head. Al got to his feet. "Got to help a fella with a car."

Ma gathered the plates and took them outside to wash. "Ruthie," she called, "Winfiel'. Go get me a bucket a water right off." She handed them the bucket and they trudged off toward the river.

A strong broad woman walked near. Her dress was streaked with dust and splotched with car oil. Her chin was held high with pride. She stood a short distance away and regarded Ma belligerently. At last she approached. "Afternoon," she said coldly.

"Afternoon," said Ma, and she got up from her knees and pushed a box forward. "Won't you set down?"

The woman walked near. "No, I won't set down."

Ma looked questioningly at her. "Can I he'p you in any way?"

The woman set her hands on her hips. "You kin he'p me by mindin' your own childern an' lettin' mine alone."

Ma's eyes opened wide. "I ain't done nothin'—" she began.

The woman scowled at her. "My little fella come back smellin' of stew. You give it to 'im. He tol' me. Don' you go a-boastin' an' a-braggin' 'bout havin' stew. Don' you do it. I got 'nuf troubles 'thout that. Come in ta me, he did, an' says, 'Whyn't we have stew?' " Her voice shook with fury.

Ma moved close. "Set down," she said. "Set down an' talk a piece."

"No, I ain't gonna set down. I'm tryin' to feed my folks, an' you come along with your stew."

"Set down," Ma said. "That was 'bout the las' stew we're gonna have till we get work. S'pose you was cookin' a stew an' a bunch a little fellas stood aroun' moonin', what'd you do? We didn't have enough, but you can't keep it when they look at ya like that."

The woman's hands dropped from her hips. For a moment her eyes questioned Ma, and then she turned and walked quickly away, and she went into a tent and pulled the flaps down behind her. Ma stared after her, and then she dropped to her knees again beside the stack of tin dishes.

Al hurried near. "Tom," he called. "Ma, is Tom inside?"

Tom stuck his head out. "What you want?"

"Come on with me," Al said excitedly.

They walked away together. "What's a matter with you?" Tom asked.

"You'll find out. Jus' wait." He led Tom to the torn-down car. "This here's Floyd Knowles," he said.

"Yeah, I talked to him. How ya?"

"Jus' gettin' her in shape," Floyd said.

Tom ran his finger over the top of the block. "What kinda bugs is crawlin' on you, Al?"

"Floyd jus' tol' me. Tell 'em, Floyd."

Floyd said, "Maybe I shouldn', but—yeah, I'll tell ya. Fella come through an' he says they's gonna be work up north."

"Up north?"

"Yeah—place called Santa Clara Valley, way to hell an' gone up north."

"Yeah? Kinda work?"

"Prune pickin', an' pears an' cannery work. Says it's purty near ready."

"How far?" Tom demanded.

"Oh, Christ knows. Maybe two hundred miles."

"That's a hell of a long ways," said Tom. "How we know they's gonna be work when we get there?"

"Well, we don' know," said Floyd. "But they ain't nothin' here, an' this fella says he got a letter from his brother, an' he's on his way. He says not to tell nobody, they'll be too many. We oughta get out in the night. Oughta get there an' get some work lined up."

Tom studied him. "Why we gotta sneak away?"

"Well, if ever'body gets there, ain't gonna be work for nobody."

"It's a hell of a long ways," Tom said.

Floyd sounded hurt. "I'm jus' givin' you the tip. You don' have to take it. Your brother here he'ped me, an' I'm givin' you the tip."

"You sure there ain't no work here?"

"Look, I been scourin' aroun' for three weeks all over hell, an' I ain't had a bit a work, not a single han'-holt. 'F you wanta look aroun' an' burn up gas lookin', why, go ahead. I ain't beggin' you. More that goes, the less chance I got."

Tom said, "I ain't findin' fault. It's jus' such a hell of a long ways. An' we kinda hoped we could get work here an' rent a house to live in."

Floyd said patiently, "I know ya jus' got here. They's stuff ya got to learn. If you'd let me tell ya, it'd save ya somepin. If ya don' let me tell ya, then ya got to learn the hard way. You ain't gonna settle down 'cause they ain't no work to settle ya. An' your belly ain't gonna let ya settle down. Now—that's straight."

"Wisht I could look aroun' first," Tom said uneasily.

A sedan drove through the camp and pulled up at the next tent. A man in overalls and a blue shirt climbed out. Floyd called to him, "Any luck?"

"There ain't a han'-turn of work in the whole darn country, not till cotton pickin'." And he went into the ragged tent.

"See?" said Floyd.

"Yeah, I see. But two hunderd miles, Jesus!"

"Well, you ain't settlin' down no place for a while. Might's well make up your mind to that."

"We better go," Al said.

Tom asked, "When is they gonna be work aroun' here?"

"Well, in a month the cotton'll start. If you got plenty money you can wait for the cotton."

Tom said, "Ma ain't a-gonna wanta move. She's all tar'd out."

Floyd shrugged his shoulders. "I ain't a-tryin' to push ya north. Suit yaself. I jus' tol' ya what I heard." He picked the oily gasket from the running board and fitted it carefully on the block and pressed it down. "Now," he said to Al, " 'f you want to give me a han' with that engine head."

Tom watched while they set the heavy head gently down

over the head bolts and dropped it evenly. "Have to talk about it," he said.

Floyd said, "I don't want nobody but your folks to know about it. Jus' you. An' I wouldn't of tol' you if ya brother didn' he'p me out here."

Tom said, "Well, I sure thank ya for tellin' us. We got to figger it out. Maybe we'll go."

Al said, "By God, I think I'll go if the res' goes or not. I'll hitch there."

"An' leave the fambly?" Tom asked.

"Sure. I'd come back with my jeans plumb fulla jack. Why not?"

"Ma ain't gonna like no such thing," Tom said. "An' Pa, he ain't gonna like it neither."

Floyd set the nuts and screwed them down as far as he could with his fingers. "Me an' my wife come out with our folks," he said. "Back home we wouldn' of thought of goin' away. Wouldn' of thought of it. But, hell, we was all up north a piece and I come down here, an' they moved on, an' now God knows where they are. Been lookin' an' askin' about 'em ever since." He fitted his wrench to the engine-head bolts and turned them down evenly, one turn to each nut, around and around the series.

Tom squatted down beside the car and squinted his eyes up the line of tents. A little stubble was beaten into the earth between the tents. "No, sir," he said, "Ma ain't gonna like you goin' off."

"Well, seems to me a lone fella got more chance of work."

"Maybe, but Ma ain't gonna like it at all."

Two cars loaded with disconsolate men drove down into the camp. Floyd lifted his eyes, but he didn't ask them about their luck. Their dusty faces were sad and resistant. The sun was sinking now, and the yellow sunlight fell on the Hooverville and on the willows behind it. The children began to come out of the tents, to wander about the camp. And from the tents the women came and built their little fires. The men gathered in squatting groups and talked together.

A new Chevrolet coupé turned off the highway and headed down into the camp. It pulled to the center of the camp. Tom said, "Who's this? They don't belong here."

Floyd said, "I dunno—cops, maybe."

The car door opened and a man got out and stood beside the car. His companion remained seated. Now all the squatting men looked at the newcomers and the conversation was still. And the women building their fires looked secretly at the shiny car. The children moved closer with elaborate circuitousness, edging inward in long curves.

Floyd put down his wrench. Tom stood up. Al wiped his hands on his trousers. The three strolled toward the Chevrolet. The man who had got out of the car was dressed in khaki trousers and a flannel shirt. He wore a flat-brimmed Stetson hat. A sheaf of papers was held in his shirt pocket by a little fence of fountain pens and yellow pencils; and from his hip pocket protruded a notebook with metal covers. He moved to one of the groups of squatting men, and they looked up at him, suspicious and quiet. They watched him and did not move; the whites of their eyes showed beneath the irises, for they did not raise their heads to look. Tom and Al and Floyd strolled casually near.

The man said, "You men want to work?" Still they looked quietly, suspiciously. And men from all over the camp moved near.

One of the squatting men spoke at last. "Sure we wanta work. Where's at's work?"

"Tulare County. Fruit's opening up. Need a lot of pickers."

Floyd spoke up. "You doin' the hiring?"

"Well, I'm contracting the land."

The men were in a compact group now. An overalled man took off his black hat and combed back his long black hair with his fingers. "What you payin'?" he asked.

"Well, can't tell exactly, yet. 'Bout thirty cents, I guess."

"Why can't you tell? You took the contract, didn' you?"

"That's true," the khaki man said. "But it's keyed to the price. Might be a little more, might be a little less."

Floyd stepped out ahead. He said quietly, "I'll go, mister. You're a contractor, an' you got a license. You jus' show your license, an' then you give us an order to go to work, an' where, an' when, an' how much we'll get, an' you sign that, an' we'll all go."

The contractor turned, scowling. "You telling me how to run my own business?"

Floyd said, " 'F we're workin' for you, it's our business too."

"Well, you ain't telling me what to do. I told you I need men."

Floyd said angrily, "You didn' say how many men, an' you didn' say what you'd pay."

"Goddamn it, I don't know yet."

"If you don' know, you got no right to hire men."

"I got a right to run my business my own way. If you men want to sit here on your ass, O.K. I'm out getting men for Tulare County. Going to need a lot of men."

Floyd turned to the crowd of men. They were standing

up now, looking quietly from one speaker to the other. Floyd said, "Twicet now I've fell for that. Maybe he needs a thousan' men. He'll get five thousan' there, an' he'll pay fifteen cents an hour. An' you poor bastards'll have to take it 'cause you'll be hungry. 'F he wants to hire men, let him hire 'em an' write it out an' say what he's gonna pay. Ast ta see his license. He ain't allowed to contract men without a license."

The contractor turned to the Chevrolet and called, "Joe!" His companion looked out and then swung the car door open and stepped out. He wore riding breeches and laced boots. A heavy pistol holster hung on a cartridge belt around his waist. On his brown shirt a deputy sheriff's star was pinned. He walked heavily over. His face was set to a thin smile. "What you want?" The holster slid back and forth on his hip.

"Ever see this guy before, Joe?"

The deputy asked "Which one?"

"This fella." The contractor pointed to Floyd.

"What'd he do?" The deputy smiled at Floyd.

"He's talkin' red, agitating trouble."

"Hm-m-m." The deputy moved slowly around to see Floyd's profile, and the color slowly flowed up Floyd's face.

"You see?" Floyd cried. "If this guy's on the level, would he bring a cop along?"

"Ever see 'im before?" the contractor insisted.

"Hmm, seems like I have. Las' week when that used-car lot was busted into. Seems like I seen this fella hangin' aroun'. Yep! I'd swear it's the same fella." Suddenly the smile left his face. "Get in that car," he said, and he unhooked the strap that covered the butt of his automatic.

Tom said, "You got nothin' on him."

The deputy swung around. " 'F you'd like to go in too, you jus' open your trap once more. They was two fellas hangin' around that lot."

"I wasn't even in the State las' week," Tom said.

"Well, maybe you're wanted someplace else. You keep your trap shut."

The contractor turned back to the men. "You fellas don't want ta listen to these goddamn reds. Troublemakers—they'll get you in trouble. Now I can use all of you in Tulare County."

The men didn't answer.

The deputy turned back to them. "Might be a good idear to go," he said. The thin smile was back on his face. "Board of Health says we got to clean out this camp. An' if it gets around that you got reds out here—why, somebody might git hurt. Be a good idear if all you fellas moved on to Tulare. They isn't a thing to do aroun' here. That's jus' a friendly way a telling you. Be a bunch a guys down here, maybe with pick handles, if you ain't gone."

The contractor said, "I told you I need men. If you don't want to work—well, that's your business."

The deputy smiled. "If they don't want to work, they ain't a place for 'em in this county. We'll float 'em quick."

Floyd stood stiffly beside the deputy, and Floyd's thumbs were hooked over his belt. Tom stole a look at him, and then stared at the ground.

"That's all," the contractor said. "There's men needed in Tulare County; plenty of work."

Tom looked slowly up at Floyd's hands, and he saw the strings at the wrists standing out under the skin. Tom's own hands came up, and his thumbs hooked over his belt.

"Yeah, that's all. I don't want one of you here by tomorra morning."

The contractor stepped into the Chevrolet.

"Now, you," the deputy said to Floyd, "you get in that car." He reached a large hand up and took hold of Floyd's left arm. Floyd spun and swung with one movement. His fist splashed into the large face, and in the same motion he was away, dodging down the line of tents. The deputy staggered and Tom put out his foot for him to trip over. The deputy fell heavily and rolled, reaching for his gun. Floyd dodged in and out of sight down the line. The deputy fired from the ground. A woman in front of a tent screamed and then looked at a hand which had no knuckles. The fingers hung on strings against her palm, and the torn flesh was white and bloodless. Far down the line Floyd came in sight, sprinting for the willows. The deputy, sitting on the ground, raised his gun again and then, suddenly, from the group of men, the Reverend Casy stepped. He kicked the deputy in the neck and then stood back as the heavy man crumpled into unconsciousness.

The motor of the Chevrolet roared and it streaked away, churning the dust. It mounted to the highway and shot away. In front of her tent, the woman still looked at her shattered hand. Little droplets of blood began to ooze from the wound. And a chuckling hysteria began in her throat, a whining laugh that grew louder and higher with each breath.

The deputy lay on his side, his mouth open against the dust.

Tom picked up his automatic, pulled out the magazine and threw it into the brush, and he ejected the live shell from the chamber. "Fella like that ain't got no right to a gun," he said; and he dropped the automatic to the ground.

A crowd had collected around the woman with the broken hand, and her hysteria increased, a screaming quality came into her laughter.

Casy moved close to Tom. "You got to git out," he said. "You go down in the willas an' wait. He didn' see me kick 'im, but he seen you stick out your foot."

"I don' want ta go," Tom said.

Casy put his head close. He whispered, "They'll finger-print you. You broke parole. They'll send you back."

Tom drew in his breath quietly. "Jesus! I forgot."

"Go quick," Casy said. " 'Fore he comes to."

"Like to have his gun," Tom said.

"No. Leave it. If it's awright to come back, I'll give ya four high whistles."

Tom strolled away casually, but as soon as he was away from the group he hurried his steps, and he disappeared among the willows that lined the river.

Al stepped over to the fallen deputy. "Jesus," he said ad-miringly, "you sure flagged 'im down!"

The crowd of men had continued to stare at the uncon-scious man. And now in the great distance a siren screamed up the scale and dropped, and it screamed again, nearer this time. Instantly the men were nervous. They shifted their feet for a moment and then they moved away, each one to his own tent. Only Al and the preacher remained.

Casy turned to Al. "Get out," he said. "Go on, get out—to the tent. You don't know nothin'."

"Yeah? How 'bout you?"

Casy grinned at him. "Somebody got to take the blame. I

got no kids. They'll jus' put me in jail, an' I ain't doin' nothin' but set aroun'."

Al said, "Ain't no reason for——"

"Go on now," Casy said sharply. "You get outa this."

Al bristled. "I ain't takin' orders."

Casy said softly, "If you mess in this your whole fambly, all your folks, gonna get in trouble. I don' care about you. But your ma and your pa, they'll get in trouble. Maybe they'll send Tom back to McAlester."

Al considered it for a moment. "O.K.," he said. "I think you're a damn fool, though."

"Sure," said Casy. "Why not?"

The siren screamed again and again, and always it came closer. Casy knelt beside the deputy and turned him over. The man groaned and fluttered his eyes, and he tried to see. Casy wiped the dust off his lips. The families were in the tents now, and the flaps were down, and the setting sun made the air red and the gray tents bronze.

Tires squealed on the highway and an open car came swiftly into the camp. Four men, armed with rifles, piled out. Casy stood up and walked to them.

"What the hell's goin' on here?"

Casy said, "I knocked out your man there."

One of the armed men went to the deputy. He was conscious now, trying weakly to sit up.

"Now what happened here?"

"Well," Casy said, "he got tough an' I hit 'im, and he started shootin'—hit a woman down the line. So I hit 'im again."

"Well, what'd you do in the first place?"

"I talked back," said Casy.

"Get in that car."

"Sure," said Casy, and he climbed into the back seat and sat down. Two men helped the hurt deputy to his feet. He felt his neck gingerly. Casy said, "They's a woman down the row like to bleed to death from his bad shootin'."

"We'll see about that later. Mike. is this the fella that hit you?"

The dazed man stared sickly at Casy. "Don't look like him."

"It was me, all right," Casy said. "You got smart with the wrong fella."

Mike shook his head slowly. "You don't look like the right fella to me. By God, I'm gonna be sick!"

Casy said, "I'll go 'thout no trouble. You better see how bad that woman's hurt."

"Where's she?"

"That tent over there."

The leader of the deputies walked to the tent, rifle in hand. He spoke through the tent walls, and then went inside. In a moment he came out and walked back. And he said, a little proudly, "Jesus, what a mess a .45 does make! They got a tourniquet on. We'll send a doctor out."

Two deputies sat on either side of Casy. The leader sounded his horn. There was no movement in the camp. The flaps were down tight, and the people in their tents. The engine started and the car swung around and pulled out of the camp. Between his guards Casy sat proudly, his head up and the stringy muscles of his neck prominent. On his lips there was a faint smile and on his face a curious look of conquest.

When the deputies had gone, the people came out of the tents. The sun was down now, and the gentle blue evening light was in the camp. To the east the mountains were still yellow with sunlight. The women went back to the fires that had died. The men collected to squat together and to talk softly.

Al crawled from under the Joad tarpaulin and walked toward the willows to whistle for Tom. Ma came out and built her little fire of twigs.

"Pa," she said, "we ain't goin' to have much. We et so late."

Pa and Uncle John stuck close to the camp, watching Ma peeling potatoes and slicing them raw into a frying pan of deep grease. Pa said, "Now what the hell made the preacher do that?"

Ruthie and Winfield crept close and crouched down to hear the talk.

Uncle John scratched the earth deeply with a long rusty nail. "He knowed about sin. I ast him about sin, an' he tol' me; but I don' know if he's right. He says a fella's sinned if he thinks he's sinned." Uncle John's eyes were tired and sad. "I been secret all my days," he said. "I done things I never tol' about."

Ma turned from the fire. "Don' go tellin', John," she said. "Tell 'em to God. Don' go burdenin' other people with your sins. That ain't decent."

"They're a-eatin' on me," said John.

"Well, don' tell 'em. Go down the river an' stick your head under an' whisper 'em in the stream."

Pa nodded his head slowly at Ma's words. "She's right," he said. "It gives a fella relief to tell, but it jus' spreads out his sin."

Uncle John looked up to the sun-gold mountains, and the mountains were reflected in his eyes. "I wisht I could run it down," he said. "But I can't. She's a-bitin' in my guts."

Behind him Rose of Sharon moved dizzily out of the tent. "Where's Connie?" she asked irritably. "I ain't seen Connie for a long time. Where'd he go?"

"I ain't seen him," said Ma. "If I see 'im, I'll tell 'im you want 'im."

"I ain't feelin' good," said Rose of Sharon. "Connie shouldn' of left me."

Ma looked up to the girl's swollen face. "You been a-cryin'," she said.

The tears started freshly in Rose of Sharon's eyes.

Ma went on firmly, "You git aholt on yaself. They's a lot of us here. You git aholt on yaself. Come here now an' peel some potatoes. You're feelin' sorry for yaself."

The girl started to go back in the tent. She tried to avoid Ma's stern eyes, but they compelled her and she came slowly toward the fire. "He shouldn' of went away," she said, but the tears were gone.

"You got to work," Ma said. "Set in the tent an' you'll get feelin' sorry about yaself. I ain't had time to take you in han'. I will now. You take this here knife an' get to them potatoes."

The girl knelt down and obeyed. She said fiercely, "Wait'll I see 'im. I'll tell 'im."

Ma smiled slowly. "He might smack you. You got it comin' with whinin' aroun' an' candyin' yaself. If he smacks some sense in you I'll bless 'im." The girl's eyes blazed with resentment, but she was silent.

Uncle John pushed his rusty nail deep into the ground with his broad thumb. "I got to tell," he said.

Pa said, "Well, tell then, goddamn it! Who'd ya kill?"

Uncle John dug with his thumb into the watch pocket of

his blue jeans and scooped out a folded dirty bill. He spread it out and showed it. "Fi' dollars," he said.

"Steal her?" Pa asked.

"No, I had her. Kept her out."

"She was yourn, wasn't she?"

"Yeah, but I didn't have no right to keep her out."

"I don't see much sin in that," Ma said. "It's yourn."

Uncle John said slowly, "It ain't only the keepin' her out. I kep' her out to get drunk. I knowed they was gonna come a time when I got to get drunk, when I'd get to hurtin' inside so I got to get drunk. Figgered time wasn' yet, an' then—the preacher went an' give 'imself up to save Tom."

Pa nodded his head up and down and cocked his head to hear. Ruthie moved closer, like a puppy, crawling on her elbows, and Winfield followed her. Rose of Sharon dug at a deep eye in a potato with the point of her knife. The evening light deepened and became more blue.

Ma said, in a sharp matter-of-fact tone, "I don' see why him savin' Tom got to get you drunk."

John said sadly, "Can't say her. I feel awful. He done her so easy. Jus' stepped up there an' says, 'I done her.' An' they took 'im away. An' I'm a-gonna get drunk."

Pa still nodded his head. "I don't see why you got to tell," he said. "If it was me, I'd jus' go off an' get drunk if I had to."

"Come a time when I could a did somepin an' took the big sin off my soul," Uncle John said sadly. "An' I slipped up. I didn' jump on her, an'—an' she got away. Lookie!" he said. "You got the money. Gimme two dollars."

Pa reached reluctantly into his pocket and brought out the leather pouch. "You ain't gonna need no seven dollars to get drunk. You don't need to drink champagny water."

Uncle John held out his bill. "You take this here an' gimme two dollars. I can get good an' drunk for two dollars. I don' want no sin of waste on me. I'll spend whatever I got. Always do."

Pa took the dirty bill and gave Uncle John two silver dollars. "There ya are," he said. "A fella got to do what he got to do. Nobody don' know enough to tell 'im."

Uncle John took the coins. "You ain't gonna be mad? You know I got to?"

"Christ, yes," said Pa. "You know what you got to do."

"I wouldn' be able to get through this night no other way," he said. He turned to Ma. "You ain't gonna hold her over me?"

Ma didn't look up. "No," she said softly. "No—you go 'long."

He stood up and walked forlornly away in the evening. He walked up to the concrete highway and across the pavement to the grocery store. In front of the screen door he took off his hat, dropped it into the dust, and ground it with his heel in self-abasement. And he left his black hat there, broken and dirty. He entered the store and walked to the shelves where the whisky bottles stood behind wire netting.

Pa and Ma and the children watched Uncle John move away. Rose of Sharon kept her eyes resentfully on the potatoes.

"Poor John," Ma said. "I wondered if it would a done any good if—no—I guess not. I never seen a man so drove."

Ruthie turned on her side in the dust. She put her head close to Winfield's head and pulled his ear against her mouth. She whispered, "I'm gonna get drunk." Winfield snorted and pinched his mouth tight. The two children crawled away, holding their breath, their faces purple with the pressure of their giggles. They crawled around the tent and leaped up and ran squealing away from the tent. They ran to the willows, and once concealed, they shrieked with laughter. Ruthie crossed her eyes and loosened her joints; she staggered about, tripping loosely, with her tongue hanging out. "I'm drunk," she said.

"Look," Winfield cried. "Looka me, here's me, an' I'm Uncle John." He flapped his arms and puffed, he whirled until he was dizzy.

"No," said Ruthie. "Here's the way. Here's the way. *I'm* Uncle John. I'm awful drunk."

Al and Tom walked quietly through the willows, and they came on the children staggering crazily about. The dusk was thick now. Tom stopped and peered. "Ain't that Ruthie an' Winfiel'? What the hell's the matter with 'em?" They walked nearer. "You crazy?" Tom asked.

The children stopped, embarrassed. "We was—jus' playin'," Ruthie said.

"It's a crazy way to play," said Al.

Ruthie said pertly, "It ain't no crazier'n a lot of things."

Al walked on. He said to Tom, "Ruthie's workin' up a kick in the pants. She been workin' it up a long time. 'Bout due for it."

Ruthie mushed her face at his back, pulled out her mouth with her forefingers, slobbered her tongue at him, outraged him in every way she knew, but Al did not turn back to look at her. She looked at Winfield again to start the game, but it had been spoiled. They both knew it.

"Le's go down the water an' duck our heads," Winfield suggested. They walked down through the willows, and they were angry at Al.

Al and Tom went quietly in the dusk. Tom said, "Casy

shouldn' of did it. I might of knew, though. He was talkin' how he ain't done nothin' for us. He's a funny fella, Al. All the time thinkin'.'

"Comes from bein' a preacher," Al said. "They get all messed up with stuff."

"Where ya s'pose Connie was a-goin'?"

"Goin' to take a crap, I guess."

"Well, he was goin' a hell of a long way."

They walked among the tents, keeping close to the walls. At Floyd's tent a soft hail stopped them. They came near to the tent flap and squatted down. Floyd raised the canvas a little. "You gettin' out?'

Tom said, "I don' know. Think we better?"

Floyd laughed sourly. "You heard what that bull said. They'll burn ya out if ya don't. 'F you think that guy's gonna take a beatin' 'thout gettin' back, you're nuts. The pool-room boys'll be down here tonight to burn us out."

"Guess we better git, then," Tom said. "Where you a-goin'?"

"Why, up north, like I said."

Al said, "Look, a fella tol' me 'bout a gov'ment camp near here. Where's it at?"

"Oh, I think that's full up."

"Well, where's it at?"

"Go south on 99 'bout twelve-fourteen miles, an' turn east to Weedpatch. It's right near there. But I think she's full up."

"Fella says it's nice," Al said.

"Sure, she's nice. Treat ya like a man 'stead of a dog. Ain't no cops there. But she's full up."

Tom said, "What I can't understan's why that cop was so

mean. Seemed like he was aimin' for trouble; seemed like he's pokin' a fella to make trouble."

Floyd said, "I don' know about here, but up north I knowed one a them fellas, an' he was a nice fella. He tol' me up there the deputies got to take guys in. Sheriff gets seventy-five cents a day for each prisoner, an' he feeds 'em for a quarter. If he ain't got prisoners, he don't make no profit. This fella says he didn' pick up nobody for a week, an' the sheriff tol' 'im he better bring in guys or give up his button. This fella today sure looks like he's out to make a pinch one way or another."

"We got to get on," said Tom. "So long, Floyd."

"So long. Prob'ly see you. Hope so."

"Good-by," said Al. They walked through the dark gray camp to the Joad tent.

The frying pan of potatoes was hissing and spitting over the fire. Ma moved the thick slices about with a spoon. Pa sat near by, hugging his knees. Rose of Sharon was sitting under the tarpaulin.

"It's Tom!" Ma cried. "Thank God."

"We got to get outa here," said Tom.

"What's the matter now?"

"Well, Floyd says they'll burn the camp tonight."

"What the hell for?" Pa asked. "We ain't done nothin'."

"Nothin' 'cept beat up a cop," said Tom.

"Well, we never done it."

"From what that cop said, they wanta push us along."

Rose of Sharon demanded, "You seen Connie?"

"Yeah," said Al. "Way to hell an' gone up the river. He's goin' south."

"Was—was he goin' away?"

"I don' know."

Ma turned on the girl. "Rosasharn, you been talkin' an' actin' funny. What'd Connie say to you?"

Rose of Sharon said sullenly, "Said it would a been a good thing if he stayed home an' studied up tractors."

They were very quiet. Rose of Sharon looked at the fire and her eyes glistened in the firelight. The potatoes hissed sharply in the frying pan. The girl sniffled and wiped her nose with the back of her hand.

Pa said, "Connie wasn' no good. I seen that a long time. Didn' have no guts, jus' too big for his overhalls."

Rose of Sharon got up and went into the tent. She lay down on the mattress and rolled over on her stomach and buried her head in her crossed arms.

"Wouldn' do no good to catch 'im, I guess," Al said.

Pa replied, "No. If he ain't no good, we don' want him."

Ma looked into the tent, where Rose of Sharon lay on her mattress. Ma said, "Sh. Don' say that."

"Well, he ain't no good," Pa insisted. "All the time a-sayin' what he's a-gonna do. Never doin' nothin'. I didn' want ta say nothin' while he's here. But now he's run out——"

"Sh!" Ma said softly.

"Why, for Christ's sake? Why do I got to shh? He run out, didn' he?"

Ma turned over the potatoes with her spoon, and the grease boiled and spat. She fed twigs to the fire, and the flames laced up and lighted the tent. Ma said, "Rosasharn gonna have a little fella an' that baby is half Connie. It ain't good for a baby to grow up with folks a-sayin' his pa ain't no good."

"Better'n lyin' about it," said Pa.

"No, it ain't," Ma interrupted. "Make out like he's dead. You wouldn' say no bad things about Connie if he's dead."

Tom broke in, "Hey, what is this? We ain't sure Connie's gone for good. We got no time for talkin'. We got to eat' an' get on our way."

"On our way? We jus' come here." Ma peered at him through the firelighted darkness.

He explained carefully, "They gonna burn the camp to-night, Ma. Now you know I ain't got it in me to stan' by an' see our stuff burn up, nor Pa ain't got it in him, nor Uncle John. We'd come up a-fightin', an' I jus' can't afford to be took in an' mugged. I nearly got it today, if the preacher hadn' jumped in."

Ma had been turning the frying potatoes in the hot grease. Now she took her decision. "Come on!" she cried. "Le's eat this stuff. We got to go quick." She set out the tin plates.

Pa said, "How 'bout John?"

"Where is Uncle John?" Tom asked.

Pa and Ma were silent for a moment, and then Pa said, "He went to get drunk."

"Jesus!" Tom said. "What a time he picked out! Where'd he go?"

"I don' know," said Pa.

Tom stood up. "Look," he said, "you all eat an' get the stuff loaded. I'll go look for Uncle John. He'd of went to the store 'crost the road."

Tom walked quickly away. The little cooking fires burned in front of the tents and the shacks, and the light fell on the faces of ragged men and women, on crouched children. In a few tents the light of kerosene lamps shone through the canvas and placed shadows of people hugely on the cloth.

Tom walked up the dusty road and crossed the concrete highway to the little grocery store. He stood in front of the screen door and looked in. The proprietor, a little gray man with an unkempt mustache and watery eyes, leaned on the counter reading a newspaper. His thin arms were bare and he wore a long white apron. Heaped around and in back of him were mounds, pyramids, walls of canned goods. He looked up when Tom came in, and his eyes narrowed as though he aimed a shotgun.

"Good evening," he said. "Run out of something?"

"Run out of my uncle," said Tom, "Or he run out, or something."

The gray man looked puzzled and worried at the same time. He touched the tip of his nose tenderly and waggled it around to stop an itch. "Seems like you people always lost somebody," he said. "Ten times a day or more somebody comes in here an' says, 'If you see a man named so an' so, an' looks like so an' so, will you tell 'im we went up north?' Somepin like that all the time."

Tom laughed. "Well, if you see a young snot-nose name' Connie, looks a little bit like a coyote, tell 'im to go to hell. We've went south. But he ain't the fella I'm lookin' for. Did a fella 'bout sixty years ol', black pants, sort of grayish hair, come in here an' get some whisky?"

The eyes of the gray man brightened. "Now he sure did. I never seen anything like it. He stood out front an' he dropped his hat an' stepped on it. Here, I got his hat here." He brought the dusty broken hat from under the counter.

Tom took it from him. "That's him, all right."

"Well, sir, he got couple pints of whisky an' he didn' say a thing. He pulled the cork an' tipped up the bottle. I ain't got a license to drink here. I says, 'Look, you can't drink

here. You got to go outside.' Well, sir! He jus' stepped outside the door, an' I bet he didn't tilt up that pint more'n four
times till it was empty. He throwed it away an' he leaned in
the door. Eyes kinda dull. He says, 'Thank you, sir,' an' he
went on. I never seen no drinkin' like that in my life."

"Went on? Which way? I got to get him."

"Well, it so happens I can tell you. I never seen such
drinkin', so I looked out after him. He went north; an' then
a car come along an' lighted him up, an' he went down the
bank. Legs was beginnin' to buckle a little. He got the other
pint open awready. He won't be far—not the way he was
goin'."

Tom said, "Thank ya. I got to find him."

"You want ta take his hat?"

"Yeah! Yeah! He'll need it. Well, thank ya."

"What's the matter with him?" the gray man asked. "He
wasn't takin' pleasure in his drink."

"Oh, he's kinda—moody. Well, good night. An' if you see
that squirt Connie, tell 'im we've went south."

"I got so many people to look out for an' tell stuff to, I
can't ever remember 'em all."

"Don't put yourself out too much," Tom said. He went
out the screen door carrying Uncle John's dusty black hat.
He crossed the concrete road and walked along the edge of
it. Below him in the sunken field, the Hooverville lay; and
the little fires flickered and the lanterns shone through the
tents. Somewhere in the camp a guitar sounded, slow chords,
struck without any sequence, practice chords. Tom stopped
and listened, and then he moved slowly along the side of the
road, and every few steps he stopped to listen again. He had
gone a quarter of a mile before he heard what he listened for.
Down below the embankment the sound of a thick, tuneless

voice, singing drably. Tom cocked his head, the better to hear.

And the dull voice sang, "I've give my heart to Jesus, so Jesus take me home. I've give my soul to Jesus, so Jesus is my home." The song trailed off to a murmur, and then stopped. Tom hurried down from the embankment, toward the song. After a while he stopped and listened again. And the voice was close this time, the same slow, tuneless singing, "Oh, the night that Maggie died, she called me to her side, an' give to me them ol' red flannel drawers that Maggie wore. They was baggy at the knees——"

Tom moved cautiously forward. He saw the black form sitting on the ground, and he stole near and sat down. Uncle John tilted the pint and the liquor gurgled out of the neck of the bottle.

Tom said quietly, "Hey, wait! Where do I come in?"

Uncle John turned his head. "Who you?"

"You forgot me awready? You had four drinks to my one."

"No, Tom. Don' try fool me. I'm all alone here. You ain't been here."

"Well, I'm sure here now. How 'bout givin' me a snort?"

Uncle John raised the pint again and the whisky gurgled. He shook the bottle. It was empty. "No more," he said. "Wanta die so bad. Wanta die awful. Die a little bit. Got to. Like sleepin'. Die a little bit. So tar'd. Tar'd. Maybe—don' wake up no more." His voice crooned off. "Gonna wear a crown—a golden crown."

Tom said, "Listen here to me, Uncle John. We're gonna move on. You come along, an' you can go right to sleep up on the load."

John shook his head. "No. Go on. Ain't goin'. Gonna res' here. No good goin' back. No good to nobody—jus' a-draggin' my sins like dirty drawers 'mongst nice folks. No. Ain't goin'."

"Come on. We can't go 'less you go."

"Go ri' 'long. I ain't no good. I ain't no good. Jus' a-draggin' my sins, a-dirtyin' ever'body."

"You got no more sin'n anybody else."

John put his head close, and he winked one eye wisely. Tom could see his face dimly in the starlight. "Nobody don' know my sins, nobody but Jesus. He knows."

Tom got down on his knees. He put his hand on Uncle John's forehead, and it was hot and dry. John brushed his hand away clumsily.

"Come on," Tom pleaded. "Come on now, Uncle John."

"Ain't goin' go. Jus' tar'd. Gon' res' ri' here. Ri' here."

Tom was very close. He put his fist against the point of Uncle John's chin. He made a small practice arc twice, for distance; and then, with his shoulder in the swing, he hit the chin a delicate perfect blow. John's chin snapped up and he fell backwards and tried to sit up again. But Tom was kneeling over him and as John got one elbow up Tom hit him again. Uncle John lay still on the ground.

Tom stood up and, bending, he lifted the loose sagging body and boosted it over his shoulder. He staggered under the loose weight. John's hanging hands tapped him on the back as he went, slowly, puffing up the bank to the highway. Once a car came by and lighted him with the limp man over his shoulder. The car slowed for a moment and then roared away.

Tom was panting when he came back to the Hooverville,

down from the road and to the Joad truck. John was coming to; he struggled weakly. Tom set him gently down on the ground.

Camp had been broken while he was gone. Al passed the bundles up on the truck. The tarpaulin lay ready to bind over the load.

Al said, "He sure got a quick start."

Tom apologized. "I had to hit 'im a little to make 'im come. Poor fella."

"Didn' hurt 'im?" Ma asked.

"Don' think so. He's a-comin' out of it."

Uncle John was weakly sick on the ground. His spasms of vomiting came in little gasps.

Ma said, "I lef' a plate a potatoes for you, Tom."

Tom chuckled. "I ain't just in the mood right now."

Pa called, "Awright, Al. Sling up the tarp."

The truck was loaded and ready. Uncle John had gone to sleep. Tom and Al boosted and pulled him up on the load while Winfield made a vomiting noise behind the truck and Ruthie plugged her mouth with her hand to keep from squealing.

"Awready," Pa said.

Tom asked, "Where's Rosasharn?"

"Over there," said Ma. "Come on, Rosasharn. We're a-goin'."

The girl sat still, her chin sunk on her breast. Tom walked over to her. "Come on," he said.

"I ain't a-goin'." She did not raise her head.

"You got to go."

"I want Connie. I ain't a-goin' till he comes back."

Three cars pulled out of the camp, up the road to the highway, old cars loaded with the camps and the people. They clanked up to the highway and rolled away, their dim lights glancing along the road.

Tom said, "Connie'll find us. I lef' word up at the store where we'd be. He'll find us."

Ma came up and stood beside him. "Come on, Rosasharn. Come on, honey," she said gently.

"I wanta wait."

"We can't wait." Ma leaned down and took the girl by the arm and helped her to her feet.

"He'll find us," Tom said. "Don' you worry. He'll find us." They walked on either side of the girl.

"Maybe he went to get them books to study up," said Rose of Sharon. "Maybe he was a-gonna surprise us."

Ma said, "Maybe that's jus' what he done." They led her to the truck and helped her up on top of the load, and she crawled under the tarpaulin and disappeared into the dark cave.

Now the bearded man from the weed shack came timidly to the truck. He waited about, his hands clutched behind his back. "You gonna leave any stuff a fella could use?" he asked at last.

Pa said, "Can't think of nothin'. We ain't got nothin' to leave."

Tom asked, "Ain't ya gettin' out?"

For a long time the bearded man stared at him. "No," he said at last.

"But they'll burn ya out."

The unsteady eyes dropped to the ground. "I know. They done it before."

"Well, why the hell don't ya get out?"

The bewildered eyes looked up for a moment, and then

down again, and the dying firelight was reflected redly. "I don' know. Takes so long to git stuff together."

"You won't have nothin' if they burn ya out."

"I know. You ain't leavin' nothin' a fella could use?"

"Cleaned out, slick," said Pa. The bearded man vaguely wandered away. "What's a matter with him?" Pa demanded.

"Cop-happy," said Tom. "Fella was sayin'—he's bull-simple. Been beat over the head too much."

A second little caravan drove past the camp and climbed to the road and moved away.

"Come on, Pa. Let's go. Look here, Pa. You an' me an' Al ride in the seat. Ma can get on the load. No. Ma, you ride in the middle. Al"—Tom reached under the seat and brought out a big monkey wrench—"Al, you get up behind. Take this here. Jus' in case. If anybody tries to climb up—let 'im have it."

Al took the wrench and climbed up the back board, and he settled himself cross-legged, the wrench in his hand. Tom pulled the iron jack handle from under the seat and laid it on the floor, under the brake pedal. "Awright," he said. "Get in the middle, Ma."

Pa said, "I ain't got nothin' in my han'."

"You can reach over an' get the jack handle," said Tom. "I hope to Jesus you don' need it." He stepped on the starter and the clanking flywheel turned over, the engine caught and died, and caught again. Tom turned on the lights and moved out of the camp in low gear. The dim lights fingered the road nervously. They climbed up to the highway and turned south. Tom said, "They comes a time when a man gets mad."

Ma broke in, "Tom—you tol' me—you promised me you wasn't like that. You promised."

"I know, Ma. I'm a-tryin'. But them deputies— Did you ever see a deputy that didn' have a fat ass? An' they waggle their ass an' flop their gun aroun'. Ma," he said, "if it was the law they was workin' with, why, we could take it. But it *ain't* the law. They're a-workin' away at our spirits. They're a-tryin' to make us cringe an' crawl like a whipped bitch. They tryin' to break us. Why, Jesus Christ, Ma, they comes a time when the on'y way a fella can keep his decency is by takin' a sock at a cop. They're workin' on our decency."

Ma said, "You promised, Tom. That's how Pretty Boy Floyd done. I knowed his ma. They hurt him."

"I'm a-tryin', Ma. Honest to God, I am. You don' want me to crawl like a beat bitch, with my belly on the groun', do you?"

"I'm a-prayin'. You got to keep clear, Tom. The fambly's breakin' up. You got to keep clear."

"I'll try, Ma. But when one a them fat asses gets to workin' me over, I got a big job tryin'. If it was the law, it'd be different. But burnin' the camp ain't the law."

The car jolted along. Ahead, a little row of red lanterns stretched across the highway.

"Detour, I guess," Tom said. He slowed the car and stopped it, and immediately a crowd of men swarmed about the truck. They were armed with pick handles and shotguns. They wore trench helmets and some American Legion caps. One man leaned in the window, and the warm smell of whisky preceded him.

"Where you think you're goin'?" He thrust a red face near to Tom's face.

Tom stiffened. His hand crept down to the floor and felt for the jack handle. Ma caught his arm and held it powerfully. Tom said, "Well—" and then his voice took on a servile whine. "We're strangers here," he said. "We heard about they's work in a place called Tulare."

"Well, goddamn it, you're goin' the wrong way. We ain't gonna have no goddamn Okies in this town."

Tom's shoulders and arms were rigid, and a shiver went through him. Ma clung to his arm. The front of the truck was surrounded by the armed men. Some of them, to make a military appearance, wore tunics and Sam Browne belts.

Tom whined, "Which way is it at, mister?"

"You turn right around an' head north. An' don't come back till the cotton's ready."

Tom shivered all over. "Yes, sir," he said. He put the car in reverse, backed around and turned. He headed back the way he had come. Ma released his arm and patted him softly. And Tom tried to restrain his hard smothered sobbing.

"Don' you mind," Ma said. "Don' you mind."

Tom blew his nose out the window and wiped his eyes on his sleeve. "The sons-of-bitches——"

"You done good," Ma said tenderly. "You done jus' good."

Tom swerved into a side dirt road, ran a hundred yards, and turned off his lights and motor. He got out of the car, carrying the jack handle.

"Where you goin'?" Ma demanded.

"Jus' gonna look. We ain't goin' north." The red lanterns moved up the highway. Tom watched them cross the entrance of the dirt road and continue on. In a few moments there came the sounds of shouts and screams, and then a flaring light arose from the direction of the Hooverville. The light grew and spread, and from the distance came a crackling sound. Tom got in the truck again. He turned around and ran up the dirt road without lights. At the highway he turned south again, and he turned on his lights.

Ma asked timidly, "Where we goin', Tom?"

"Goin' south," he said. "We couldn' let them bastards push us aroun'. We couldn'. Try to get aroun' the town 'thout goin' through it."

"Yeah, but where we goin'?" Pa spoke for the first time. "That's what I want ta know."

"Gonna look for that gov'ment camp," Tom said. "A fella said they don' let no deputies in there. Ma—I got to get away from 'em. I'm scairt I'll kill one."

"Easy, Tom." Ma soothed him. "Easy, Tommy. You done good once. You can do it again."

"Yeah, an' after a while I won't have no decency lef'."

"Easy," she said. "You got to have patience. Why, Tom—us people will go on livin' when all them people is gone. Why, Tom, we're the people that live. They ain't gonna wipe us out. Why, we're the people—we go on."

"We take a beatin' all the time."

"I know." Ma chuckled. "Maybe that makes us tough. Rich fellas come up an' they die, an' their kids ain't no good, an' they die out. But, Tom, we keep a-comin'. Don' you fret none, Tom. A different time's comin'."

"How do you know?"

"I don' know how."

They entered the town and Tom turned down a side street to avoid the center. By the street lights he looked at his mother. Her face was quiet and a curious look was in her eyes, eyes like the timeless eyes of a statue. Tom put out his right hand and touched her on the shoulder. He had to. And then he withdrew his hand. "Never heard you talk so much in my life," he said.

"Wasn't never so much reason," she said.

He drove through the side streets and cleared the town,

and then he crossed back. At an intersection the sign said
"99." He turned south on it.

"Well, anyways they never shoved us north," he said. "We
still go where we want, even if we got to crawl for the
right."

The dim lights felt along the broad black highway ahead.

Chapter Twenty-One

THE moving, questing people were migrants now. Those families which had lived on a little piece of land, who had lived and died on forty acres, had eaten or starved on the produce of forty acres, had now the whole West to rove in. And they scampered about, looking for work; and the highways were streams of people, and the ditch banks were lines of people. Behind them more were coming. The great highways streamed with moving people. There in the Middle- and Southwest had lived a simple agrarian folk who had not changed with industry, who had not formed with machines or known the power and danger of machines in private hands. They had not grown up in the paradoxes of industry. Their senses were still sharp to the ridiculousness of the industrial life.

And then suddenly the machines pushed them out and they swarmed on the highways. The movement changed them; the highways, the camps along the road, the fear of hunger and the hunger itself, changed them. The children without dinner changed them, the endless moving changed them. They were migrants. And the hostility changed them, welded them, united them—hostility that made the little towns group and arm as though to repel an invader, squads with pick handles, clerks and storekeepers with shotguns, guarding the world against their own people.

In the West there was panic when the migrants multiplied

on the highways. Men of property were terrified for their property. Men who had never been hungry saw the eyes of the hungry. Men who had never wanted anything very much saw the flare of want in the eyes of the migrants. And the men of the towns and of the soft suburban country gathered to defend themselves; and they reassured themselves that they were good and the invaders bad, as a man must do before he fights. They said, These goddamned Okies are dirty and ignorant. They're degenerate, sexual maniacs. These goddamned Okies are thieves. They'll steal anything. They've got no sense of property rights.

And the latter was true, for how can a man without property know the ache of ownership? And the defending people said, They bring disease, they're filthy. We can't have them in the schools. They're strangers. How'd you like to have your sister go out with one of 'em?

The local people whipped themselves into a mold of cruelty. Then they formed units, squads, and armed them—armed them with clubs, with gas, with guns. We own the country. We can't let these Okies get out of hand. And the men who were armed did not own the land, but they thought they did. And the clerks who drilled at night owned nothing, and the little storekeepers possessed only a drawerful of debts. But even a debt is something, even a job is something. The clerk thought, I get fifteen dollars a week. S'pose a goddamn Okie would work for twelve? And the little storekeeper thought, How could I compete with a debtless man?

And the migrants streamed in on the highways and their hunger was in their eyes, and their need was in their eyes. They had no argument, no system, nothing but their numbers and their needs. When there was work for a man, ten men fought for it—fought with a low wage. If that fella'll work for thirty cents, I'll work for twenty-five.

If he'll take twenty-five, I'll do it for twenty.

No, me, I'm hungry. I'll work for fifteen. I'll work for food. The kids. You ought to see them. Little boils, like, comin' out, an' they can't run aroun'. Give 'em some windfall fruit, an' they bloated up. Me. I'll work for a little piece of meat.

And this was good, for wages went down and prices stayed up. The great owners were glad and they sent out more handbills to bring more people in. And wages went down and prices stayed up. And pretty soon now we'll have serfs again.

And now the great owners and the companies invented a new method. A great owner bought a cannery. And when the peaches and the pears were ripe he cut the price of fruit below the cost of raising it. And as cannery owner he paid himself a low price for the fruit and kept the price of canned goods up and took his profit. And the little farmers who owned no canneries lost their farms, and they were taken by the great owners, the banks, and the companies who also owned the canneries. As time went on, there were fewer farms. The little farmers moved into town for a while and exhausted their credit, exhausted their friends, their relatives. And then they too went on the highways. And the roads were crowded with men ravenous for work, murderous for work.

And the companies, the banks worked at their own doom and they did not know it. The fields were fruitful, and starving men moved on the roads. The granaries were full and the children of the poor grew up rachitic, and the pustules of pellagra swelled on their sides. The great companies did not know that the line between hunger and anger is a thin line. And money that might have gone to wages went for gas, for guns, for agents and spies, for blacklists, for drilling. On the highways the people moved like ants and searched for work, for food. And the anger began to ferment.

Chapter Twenty-Two

IT WAS late when Tom Joad drove along a country road
looking for the Weedpatch camp. There were few lights
in the countryside. Only a sky glare behind showed the
direction of Bakersfield. The truck jiggled slowly along and
hunting cats left the road ahead of it. At a crossroad there
was a little cluster of white wooden buildings.

Ma was sleeping in the seat and Pa had been silent and
withdrawn for a long time.

Tom said, "I don' know where she is. Maybe we'll wait
till daylight an' ast somebody." He stopped at a boulevard
signal and another car stopped at the crossing. Tom leaned
out. "Hey, mister. Know where the big camp is at?"

"Straight ahead."

Tom pulled across into the opposite road. A few hundred
yards, and then he stopped. A high wire fence faced the road,
and a wide-gated driveway turned in. A little way inside the
gate there was a small house with a light in the window. Tom
turned in. The whole truck leaped into the air and crashed
down again.

"Jesus!" Tom said. "I didn' even see that hump."

A watchman stood up from the porch and walked to the
car. He leaned on the side. "You hit her too fast," he said.
"Next time you'll take it easy."

"What is it, for God's sake?"

The watchman laughed. "Well, a lot of kids play in here. You tell folks to go slow and they're liable to forget. But let 'em hit that hump once and they don't forget."

"Oh! Yeah. Hope I didn' break nothin'. Say—you got any room here for us?"

"Got one camp. How many of you?"

Tom counted on his fingers. "Me an' Pa an' Ma, Al an' Rosasharn an' Uncle John an' Ruthie an' Winfiel'. Them last is kids."

"Well, I guess we can fix you. Got any camping stuff?"

"Got a big tarp an' beds."

The watchman stepped up on the running board. "Drive down the end of that line an' turn right. You'll be in Number Four Sanitary Unit."

"What's that?"

"Toilets and showers and wash tubs."

Ma demanded, "You got wash tubs—running water?"

"Sure."

"Oh! Praise God," said Ma.

Tom drove down the long dark row of tents. In the sanitary building a low light burned. "Pull in here," the watchman said. "It's a nice place. Folks that had it just moved out."

Tom stopped the car. "Right there?"

"Yeah. Now you let the others unload while I sign you up. Get to sleep. The camp committee'll call on you in the morning and get you fixed up."

Tom's eyes drew down. "Cops?" he asked.

The watchman laughed. "No cops. We got our own cops. Folks here elect their own cops. Come along."

Al dropped off the truck and walked around. "Gonna stay here?"

"Yeah," said Tom. "You an' Pa unload while I go to the office."

"Be kinda quiet," the watchman said. "They's a lot of folks sleeping."

Tom followed through the dark and climbed the office steps and entered a tiny room containing an old desk and a chair. The guard sat down at the desk and took out a form.

"Name?"

"Tom Joad."

"That your father?"

"Yeah."

"His name?"

"Tom Joad, too."

The questions went on. Where from, how long in the State, what work done. The watchman looked up. "I'm not nosy. We got to have this stuff."

"Sure," said Tom.

"Now—got any money?"

"Little bit."

"You ain't destitute?"

"Got a little. Why?"

"Well, the camp site costs a dollar a week, but you can work it out, carrying garbage, keeping the camp clean—stuff like that."

"We'll work it out," said Tom.

"You'll see the committee tomorrow. They'll show you how to use the camp and tell you the rules."

Tom said, "Say—what is this? What committee is this, anyways?"

The watchman settled himself back. "Works pretty nice. There's five sanitary units. Each one elects a Central Committee man. Now that committee makes the laws. What they say goes."

"S'pose they get tough," Tom said.

"Well, you can vote 'em out jus' as quick as you vote 'em in. They've done a fine job. Tell you what they did—you know the Holy Roller preachers all the time follow the people around, preachin' an' takin' up collections? Well, they wanted to preach in this camp. And a lot of the older folks wanted them. So it was up to the Central Committee. They went into meeting and here's how they fixed it. They say, 'Any preacher can preach in this camp. Nobody can take up a collection in this camp.' And it was kinda sad for the old folks, 'cause there hasn't been a preacher in since."

Tom laughed and then he asked, "You mean to say the fellas that runs the camp is jus' fellas—campin' here?"

"Sure. And it works."

"You said about cops——"

"Central Committee keeps order an' makes rules. Then there's the ladies. They'll call on your ma. They keep care of kids an' look after the sanitary units. If your ma isn't working, she'll look after kids for the ones that is working, an' when she gets a job—why, there'll be others. They sew, and a nurse comes out an' teaches 'em. All kinds of things like that."

"You mean to say they ain't no cops?"

"No, sir. No cop can come in here without a warrant."

"Well, s'pose a fella is jus' mean, or drunk an' quarrelsome. What then?"

The watchman stabbed the blotter with a pencil. "Well, the first time the Central Committee warns him. And the second time they really warn him. The third time they kick him out of the camp."

"God Almighty, I can't hardly believe it! Tonight the deputies an' them fellas with the little caps, they burned the camp out by the river."

"They don't get in here," the watchman said. "Some nights the boys patrol the fences, 'specially dance nights."

"Dance nights? Jesus Christ!"

"We got the best dances in the county every Saturday night."

"Well, for Christ's sake! Why ain't they more places like this?"

The watchman looked sullen. "You'll have to find that out yourself. Go get some sleep."

"Good night," said Tom. "Ma's gonna like this place. She ain't been treated decent for a long time."

"Good night," the watchman said. "Get some sleep. This camp wakes up early."

Tom walked down the street between the rows of tents. His eyes grew used to the starlight. He saw that the rows were straight and that there was no litter about the tents. The ground of the street had been swept and sprinkled. From the tents came the snores of sleeping people. The whole camp buzzed and snorted. Tom walked slowly. He neared Number Four Sanitary Unit and he looked at it curiously, an unpainted building, low and rough. Under a roof, but open at the sides, the rows of wash trays. He saw the Joad truck standing near by, and went quietly toward it. The tarpaulin was pitched and the camp was quiet. As he drew near a figure moved from the shadow of the truck and came toward him.

Ma said softly, "That you, Tom?"

"Yeah."

"Sh!" she said. "They're all asleep. They was tar'd out."

"You ought to be asleep too," Tom said.

"Well, I wanted to see ya. Is it awright?"

"It's nice," Tom said. "I ain't gonna tell ya. They'll tell ya in the mornin'. Ya gonna like it."

She whispered, "I heard they got hot water."

"Yeah. Now you get to sleep. I don' know when you slep' las'."

She begged, "What ain't you a-gonna tell me?"

"I ain't. You get to sleep."

Suddenly she seemed girlish. "How can I sleep if I got to think about what you ain't gonna tell me?"

"No, you don't," Tom said. "First thing in the mornin' you get on your other dress an' then—you'll find out."

"I can't sleep with nothin' like that hangin' over me."

"You got to," Tom chuckled happily. "You jus' got to."

"Good night," she said softly; and she bent down and slipped under the dark tarpaulin.

Tom climbed up over the tail-board of the truck. He lay down on his back on the wooden floor and he pillowed his head on his crossed hands, and his forearms pressed against his ears. The night grew cooler. Tom buttoned his coat over his chest and settled back again. The stars were clear and sharp over his head.

It was still dark when he awakened. A small clashing noise brought him up from sleep. Tom listened and heard again the squeak of iron on iron. He moved stiffly and shivered in the morning air. The camp still slept. Tom stood up and looked over the side of the truck. The eastern mountains were blue-black, and as he watched, the light stood up faintly behind them, colored at the mountain rims with a washed red, then growing colder, grayer, darker, as it went up overhead, until at a place near the western horizon it merged with pure night. Down in the valley the earth was the lavender-gray of dawn.

The clash of iron sounded again. Tom looked down the line of tents, only a little lighter gray than the ground. Beside a tent he saw a flash of orange fire seeping from the cracks in an old iron stove. Gray smoke spurted up from a stubby smoke-pipe.

Tom climbed over the truck side and dropped to the ground. He moved slowly toward the stove. He saw a girl working about the stove, saw that she carried a baby on her crooked arm, and that the baby was nursing, its head up under the girl's shirtwaist. And the girl moved about, poking the fire, shifting the rusty stove lids to make a better draft, opening the oven door; and all the time the baby sucked, and the mother shifted it deftly from arm to arm. The baby didn't interfere with her work or with the quick gracefulness of her movements. And the orange fire licked out of the stove cracks and threw flickering reflections on the tent.

Tom moved closer. He smelled frying bacon and baking bread. From the east the light grew swiftly. Tom came near to the stove and stretched out his hands to it. The girl looked at him and nodded, so that her two braids jerked.

"Good mornin'," she said, and she turned the bacon in the pan.

The tent flap jerked up and a young man came out and an older man followed him. They were dressed in new blue dungarees and in dungaree coats, stiff with filler, the brass buttons shining. They were sharp-faced men, and they looked much alike. The younger man had a dark stubble beard and the older man a white stubble beard. Their heads and faces were wet, their hair dripped, water stood in drops

on their stiff beards. Their cheeks shone with dampness. Together they stood looking quietly into the lightening east.
They yawned together and watched the light on the hill
rims. And then they turned and saw Tom.

"Mornin'," the older man said, and his face was neither
friendly nor unfriendly.

"Mornin'," said Tom.

And, "Mornin'," said the younger man.

The water slowly dried on their faces. They came to the
stove and warmed their hands at it.

The girl kept to her work. Once she set the baby down
and tied her braids together in back with a string, and the
two braids jerked and swung as she worked. She set tin cups
on a big packing box, set tin plates and knives and forks out.
Then she scooped bacon from the deep grease and laid it on
a tin platter, and the bacon cricked and rustled as it grew
crisp. She opened the rusty oven door and took out a square
pan full of big high biscuits.

When the smell of the biscuits struck the air both of the
men inhaled deeply. The younger said, "Kee-rist!" softly.

Now the older man said to Tom, "Had your breakfast?"

"Well, no, I ain't. But my folks is over there. They ain't
up. Need the sleep."

"Well, set down with us, then. We got plenty—thank
God!"

"Why, thank ya," Tom said. "Smells so darn good I
couldn' say no."

"Don't she?" the younger man asked. "Ever smell anything so good in ya life?" They marched to the packing box
and squatted around it.

"Workin' around here?" the young man asked.

"Aim to," said Tom. "We jus' got in las' night. Ain't had no chance to look aroun'."

"We had twelve days' work," the young man said.

The girl, working by the stove, said, "They even got new clothes." Both men looked down at their stiff blue clothes, and they smiled a little shyly. The girl set out the platter of bacon and the brown, high biscuits and a bowl of bacon gravy and a pot of coffee, and then she squatted down by the box too. The baby still nursed, its head up under the girl's shirtwaist.

They filled their plates, poured bacon gravy over the biscuits, and sugared their coffee.

The older man filled his mouth full, and he chewed and chewed and gulped and swallowed. "God Almighty, it's good!" he said, and he filled his mouth again.

The younger man said, "We been eatin' good for twelve days now. Never missed a meal in twelve days—none of us. Workin' an' gettin' our pay an' eatin'." He fell to again, almost frantically, and refilled his plate. They drank the scalding coffee and threw the grounds to the earth and filled their cups again.

There was color in the light now, a reddish gleam. The father and son stopped eating. They were facing to the east and their faces were lighted by the dawn. The image of the mountain and the light coming over it were reflected in their eyes. And then they threw the grounds from their cups to the earth, and they stood up together.

"Got to git goin'," the older man said.

The younger turned to Tom. "Lookie," he said. "We're layin' some pipe. 'F you want to walk over with us, maybe we could get you on."

Tom said, "Well, that's mighty nice of you. An' I sure thank ya for the breakfast."

"Glad to have you," the older man said. "We'll try to git you workin' if you want."

"Ya goddamn right I want," Tom said. "Jus' wait a minute. I'll tell my folks." He hurried to the Joad tent and bent over and looked inside. In the gloom under the tarpaulin he saw the lumps of sleeping figures. But a little movement started among the bedclothes. Ruthie came wriggling out like a snake, her hair down over her eyes and her dress wrinkled and twisted. She crawled carefully out and stood up. Her gray eyes were clear and calm from sleep, and mischief was not in them. Tom moved off from the tent and beckoned her to follow, and when he turned, she looked up at him.

"Lord God, you're growin' up," he said.

She looked away in sudden embarrassment. "Listen here," Tom said. "Don't you wake nobody up, but when they get up, you tell 'em I got a chancet at a job, an' I'm a-goin' for it. Tell Ma I et breakfas' with some neighbors. You hear that?"

Ruthie nodded and turned her head away, and her eyes were little girl's eyes. "Don't you wake 'em up," Tom cautioned. He hurried back to his new friends. And Ruthie cautiously approached the sanitary unit and peeked in the open doorway.

The two men were waiting when Tom came back. The young woman had dragged a mattress out and put the baby on it while she cleaned up the dishes.

Tom said, "I wanted to tell my folks where-at I was. They wasn't awake." The three walked down the street between the tents.

The camp had begun to come to life. At the new fires the women worked, slicing meat, kneading the dough for the morning's bread. And the men were stirring about the tents and about the automobiles. The sky was rosy now. In front of the office a lean old man raked the ground carefully. He so dragged his rake that the tine marks were straight and deep.

"You're out early, Pa," the young man said as they went by.

"Yep, yep. Got to make up my rent."

"Rent, hell!" the young man said. "He was drunk last Sat'dy night. Sung in his tent all night. Committee give him work for it." They walked along the edge of the oiled road; a row of walnut trees grew beside the way. The sun shoved its edge over the mountains.

Tom said, "Seems funny. I've et your food, an' I ain't tol' you my name—nor you ain't mentioned yours. I'm Tom Joad."

The older man looked at him, and then he smiled a little. "You ain't been out here long?"

"Hell, no! Jus' a couple days."

"I knowed it. Funny, you git outa the habit a mentionin' your name. They's so goddamn many. Jist fellas. Well, sir—I'm Timothy Wallace, an' this here's my boy Wilkie."

"Proud to know ya," Tom said. "You been out here long?"

"Ten months," Wilkie said. "Got here right on the tail a the floods las' year. Jesus! We had *a* time, *a* time! Goddamn near starve' to death." Their feet rattled on the oiled road. A truckload of men went by, and each man was sunk into himself. Each man braced himself in the truck bed and scowled down.

"Goin' out for the Gas Company," Timothy said. "They got a nice job of it."

"I could of took our truck," Tom suggested.

"No." Timothy leaned down and picked up a green walnut. He tested it with his thumb and then shied it at a blackbird sitting on a fence wire. The bird flew up, let the nut sail under it, and then settled back on the wire and smoothed its shining black feathers with its beak.

Tom asked, "Ain't you got no car?"

Both Wallaces were silent, and Tom, looking at their faces, saw that they were ashamed.

Wilkie said, "Place we work at is on'y a mile up the road."

Timothy said angrily, "No, we ain't got no car. We sol' our car. Had to. Run outa food, run outa ever'thing. Couldn' git no job. Fellas come aroun' ever' week, buyin' cars. Come aroun', an' if you're hungry, why, they'll buy your car. An' if you're hungry enough, they don't hafta pay nothin' for it. An'—we was hungry enough. Give us ten dollars for her." He spat into the road.

Wilkie said quietly, "I was in Bakersfiel' las' week. I seen her—a-settin' in a use'-car lot—settin' right there, an' seventy-five dollars was the sign on her."

"We had to," Timothy said. "It was either us let 'em steal our car or us steal somepin from them. We ain't had to steal yet, but, goddamn it, we been close!"

Tom said, "You know, 'fore we lef' home, we heard they was plenty work out here. Seen han'bills askin' folks to come out."

"Yeah," Timothy said. "We seen 'em too. An' they ain't much work. An' wages is comin' down all a time. I git so goddamn tired jus' figgerin' how to eat."

"You got work now," Tom suggested.

"Yeah, but it ain't gonna las' long. Workin' for a nice fella.

Got a little place. Works 'longside of us. But, hell—it ain't gonna las' no time."

Tom said, "Why in hell you gonna git me on? I'll make it shorter. What you cuttin' your own throat for?"

Timothy shook his head slowly. "I dunno. Got no sense, I guess. We figgered to get us each a hat. Can't do it, I guess. There's the place, off to the right there. Nice job, too. Gettin' thirty cents an hour. Nice frien'ly fella to work for."

They turned off the highway and walked down a graveled road, through a small kitchen orchard; and behind the trees they came to a small white farm house, a few shade trees, and a barn; behind the barn a vineyard and a field of cotton. As the three men walked past the house a screen door banged, and a stocky sunburned man came down the back steps. He wore a paper sun helmet, and he rolled up his sleeves as he came across the yard. His heavy sunburned eyebrows were drawn down in a scowl. His cheeks were sunburned a beef red.

"Mornin', Mr. Thomas," Timothy said.

"Morning." The man spoke irritably.

Timothy said, "This here's Tom Joad. We wondered if you could see your way to put him on?"

Thomas scowled at Tom. And then he laughed shortly, and his brows still scowled. "Oh, sure! I'll put him on. I'll put everybody on. Maybe I'll get a hundred men on."

"We jus' thought—" Timothy began apologetically.

Thomas interrupted him. "Yes, I been thinkin' too." He swung around and faced them. "I've got some things to tell you. I been paying you thirty cents an hour—that right?"

"Why, sure, Mr. Thomas—but——"

"And I been getting thirty cents' worth of work." His heavy hard hands clasped each other.

"We try to give a good day of work."

"Well, goddamn it, this morning you're getting twenty-five cents an hour, and you take it or leave it." The redness of his face deepened with anger.

Timothy said, "We've give you good work. You said so yourself."

"I know it. But it seems like I ain't hiring my own men any more." He swallowed. "Look," he said. "I got sixty-five acres here. Did you ever hear of the Farmers' Association?"

"Why, sure."

"Well, I belong to it. We had a meeting last night. Now, do you know who runs the Farmers' Association? I'll tell you. The Bank of the West. That bank owns most of this valley, and it's got paper on everything it don't own. So last night the member from the bank told me, he said, 'You're paying thirty cents an hour. You'd better cut it down to twenty-five.' I said, 'I've got good men. They're worth thirty.' And he says, 'It isn't that,' he says. 'The wage is twenty-five now. If you pay thirty, it'll only cause unrest. And by the way,' he says, 'you going to need the usual amount for a crop loan next year?'" Thomas stopped. His breath was panting through his lips. "You see? The rate is twenty-five cents—and like it."

"We done good work," Timothy said helplessly.

"Ain't you got it yet? Mr. Bank hires two thousand men an' I hire three. I've got paper to meet. Now if you can figure some way out, by Christ, I'll take it! They got me."

Timothy shook his head. "I don' know what to say."

"You wait here." Thomas walked quickly to the house. The door slammed after him. In a moment he was back, and he carried a newspaper in his hand. "Did you see this? Here, I'll read it: 'Citizens, angered at red agitators, burn squatters' camp. Last night a band of citizens, infuriated at the agitation going on in a local squatters' camp, burned the tents to the ground and warned agitators to get out of the county.' "

Tom began, "Why, I—" and then he closed his mouth and was silent.

Thomas folded the paper carefully and put it in his pocket. He had himself in control again. He said quietly, "Those men were sent out by the Association. Now I'm giving 'em away. And if they ever find out I told, I won't have a farm next year."

"I jus' don't know what to say," Timothy said. "If they was agitators, I can see why they was mad."

Thomas said, "I watched it a long time. There's always red agitators just before a pay cut. Always. Goddamn it, they got me trapped. Now, what are you going to do? Twenty-five cents?"

Timothy looked at the ground. "I'll work," he said.

"Me too," said Wilkie.

Tom said, "Seems like I walked into somepin. Sure, I'll work. I got to work."

Thomas pulled a bandanna out of his hip pocket and wiped his mouth and chin. "I don't know how long it can go on. I don't know how you men can feed a family on what you get now."

"We can while we work," Wilkie said. "It's when we don't git work."

Thomas looked at his watch. "Well, let's go out and dig some ditch. By God," he said, "I'm a-gonna tell you. You fellas live in that government camp, don't you?"

Timothy stiffened. "Yes, sir."

"And you have dances every Saturday night?"

Wilkie smiled. "We sure do."

"Well, look out next Saturday night."

Suddenly Timothy straightened. He stepped close. "What you mean? I belong to the Central Committee. I got to know."

Thomas looked apprehensive. "Don't you ever tell I told."

"What is it?" Timothy demanded.

"Well, the Association don't like the government camps. Can't get a deputy in there. The people make their own laws, I hear, and you can't arrest a man without a warrant. Now if there was a big fight and maybe shooting—a bunch of deputies could go in and clean out the camp."

Timothy had changed. His shoulders were straight and his eyes cold. "What you mean?"

"Don't you ever tell where you heard," Thomas said uneasily. "There's going to be a fight in the camp Saturday night. And there's going to be deputies ready to go in."

Tom demanded, "Why, for God's sake? Those folks ain't bothering nobody."

"I'll tell you why," Thomas said. "Those folks in the camp are getting used to being treated like humans. When they go back to the squatters' camps they'll be hard to handle." He wiped his face again. "Go on out to work now. Jesus, I hope I haven't talked myself out of my farm. But I like you people."

Timothy stepped in front of him and put out a hard lean hand, and Thomas took it. "Nobody won't know who tol'. We thank you. They won't be no fight."

"Go on to work," Thomas said. "And it's twenty-five cents an hour."

"We'll take it," Wilkie said, "from you."

Thomas walked away toward the house. "I'll be out in a

piece," he said. "You men get to work." The screen door
slammed behind him.

The three men walked out past the little white-washed
barn, and along a field edge. They came to a long narrow
ditch with sections of concrete pipe lying beside it.

"Here's where we're a-workin'," Wilkie said.

His father opened the barn and passed out two picks and
three shovels. And he said to Tom, "Here's your beauty."

Tom hefted the pick. "Jumping Jesus! If she don't feel
good!"

"Wait'll about 'leven o'clock," Wilkie suggested. "See how
good she feels then."

They walked to the end of the ditch. Tom took off his
coat and dropped it on the dirt pile. He pushed up his cap
and stepped into the ditch. Then he spat on his hands. The
pick arose into the air and flashed down. Tom grunted
softly. The pick rose and fell, and the grunt came at the moment it sank into the ground and loosened the soil.

Wilkie said, "Yes, sir, Pa, we got here a first-grade muck-
stick man. This here boy been married to that there little
digger."

Tom said, "I put in time (*umph*). Yes, sir, I sure did
(*umph*). Put in my years (*umph!*). Kinda like the feel
(*umph!*)." The soil loosened ahead of him. The sun cleared
the fruit trees now and the grape leaves were golden green
on the vines. Six feet along and Tom stepped aside and wiped
his forehead. Wilkie came behind him. The shovel rose and
fell and the dirt flew out to the pile beside the lengthening
ditch.

"I heard about this here Central Committee," said Tom.
"So you're one of 'em."

"Yes, sir," Timothy replied. "And it's a responsibility. All them people. We're doin' our best. An' the people in the camp a-doin' their best. I wisht them big farmers wouldn' plague us so. I wisht they wouldn'."

Tom climbed back into the ditch and Wilkie stood aside. Tom said, "How 'bout this fight (*umph!*) at the dance, he tol' about (*umph*)? What they wanta do that for?"

Timothy followed behind Wilkie, and Timothy's shovel beveled the bottom of the ditch and smoothed it ready for the pipe. "Seems like they got to drive us," Timothy said. "They're scairt we'll organize, I guess. An' maybe they're right. This here camp is a organization. People there look out for theirselves. Got the nicest strang band in these parts. Got a little charge account in the store for folks that's hungry. Fi' dollars—you can git that much food an' the camp'll stan' good. We ain't never had no trouble with the law. I guess the big farmers is scairt of that. Can't throw us in jail —why, it scares 'em. Figger maybe if we can gove'n ourselves, maybe we'll do other things."

Tom stepped clear of the ditch and wiped the sweat out of his eyes. "You hear what that paper said 'bout agitators up north a Bakersfiel'?"

"Sure," said Wilkie. "They do that all a time."

"Well, I was there. They wasn't no agitators. What they call reds. What the hell is these reds anyways?"

Timothy scraped a little hill level in the bottom of the ditch. The sun made his white bristle beard shine. "They's a lot a fellas wanta know what reds is." He laughed. "One of our boys foun' out." He patted the piled earth gently with his shovel. "Fella named Hines—got 'bout thirty thousan' acres, peaches and grapes—got a cannery an' a winery. Well, he's all a time talkin' about 'them goddamn reds.' 'Goddamn reds is drivin' the country to ruin,' he says, an' 'We got to drive these here red bastards out.' Well, they were a young fella jus' come out west here, an' he's listenin' one day. He kinda scratched his head an' he says, 'Mr. Hines, I ain't been here long. What is these goddamn reds?' Well, sir, Hines says, 'A red is any son-of-a-bitch that wants thirty cents an hour when we're payin' twenty-five!' Well, this young fella he thinks about her, an' he scratches his head, an' he says, 'Well, Jesus, Mr. Hines. I ain't a son-of-a-bitch, but if that's what a red is—why, I want thirty cents an hour. Ever'body does. Hell, Mr. Hines, we're all reds.'" Timothy drove his shovel along the ditch bottom, and the solid earth shone where the shovel cut it.

Tom laughed. "Me too, I guess." His pick arced up and drove down, and the earth cracked under it. The sweat rolled down his forehead and down the sides of his nose, and it glistened on his neck. "Damn it," he said, "a pick is a nice tool (*umph*), if you don' fight it (*umph*). You an' the pick (*umph*) workin' together (*umph*)."

In line, the three men worked, and the ditch inched along, and the sun shone hotly down on them in the growing morning.

When Tom left her, Ruthie gazed in at the door of the sanitary unit for a while. Her courage was not strong without Winfield to boast for. She put a bare foot in on the concrete floor, and then withdrew it. Down the line a woman came out of a tent and started a fire in a tin camp stove. Ruthie took a few steps in that direction, but she could not leave. She crept to the entrance of the Joad tent and looked in. On one side, lying on the ground, lay Uncle John, his mouth open and his snores bubbling spittily in his throat. Ma and Pa were covered with a comfort, their heads in, away from the light. Al was on the far side from Uncle John, and his arm was flung over his eyes. Near the front of the tent Rose of Sharon and Winfield lay, and there was the space where Ruthie had been, beside Winfield. She squatted down and peered in. Her eyes remained on Winfield's tow head; and as she looked, the little boy opened his eyes and stared out at her, and his eyes were solemn. Ruthie put her finger to her lips and beckoned with her other hand. Winfield rolled his eyes over to Rose of Sharon. Her pink flushed face was near to him, and her mouth was open a little. Winfield carefully loosened the blanket and slipped out. He crept out of the tent cautiously and joined Ruthie. "How long you been up?" he whispered.

She led him away with elaborate caution, and when they were safe, she said, "I never been to bed. I was up all night."

"You was not," Winfield said. "You're a dirty liar."

"Awright," she said. "If I'm a liar I ain't gonna tell you nothin' that happened. I ain't gonna tell how the fella got killed with a stab knife an' how they was a bear come in an' took off a little chile."

"They wasn't no bear," Winfield said uneasily. He brushed up his hair with his fingers and he pulled down his overalls at the crotch.

"All right—they wasn't no bear," she said sarcastically. "An' they ain't no white things made outa dish-stuff, like in the catalogues."

Winfield regarded her gravely. He pointed to the sanitary unit. "In there?" he asked.

"I'm a dirty liar," Ruthie said. "It ain't gonna do me no good to tell stuff to you."

"Le's go look," Winfield said.

"I already been," Ruthie said. "I already set on 'em. I even pee'd in one."

"You never neither," said Winfield.

They went to the unit building, and that time Ruthie was not afraid. Boldly she led the way into the building. The toilets lined one side of the large room, and each toilet had its compartment with a door in front of it. The porcelain was gleaming white. Hand basins lined another wall, while on the third wall were four shower compartments.

"There," said Ruthie. "Them's the toilets. I seen 'em in the catalogue." The children drew near to one of the toilets. Ruthie, in a burst of bravado, boosted her skirt and sat down. "I tol' you I been here," she said. And to prove it, there was a tinkle of water in the bowl.

Winfield was embarrassed. His hand twisted the flushing lever. There was a roar of water. Ruthie leaped into the air and jumped away. She and Winfield stood in the middle of the room and looked at the toilet. The hiss of water continued in it.

"You done it," Ruthie said. "You went an' broke it. I seen you."

"I never. Honest I never."

"I seen you," Ruthie said. "You jus' ain't to be trusted with no nice stuff."

Winfield sunk his chin. He looked up at Ruthie and his eyes filled with tears. His chin quivered. And Ruthie was instantly contrite.

"Never you mind," she said. "I won't tell on you. We'll pretend like she was already broke. We'll pretend we ain't even been in here." She led him out of the building.

The sun lipped over the mountain by now, shone on the corrugated-iron roofs of the five sanitary units, shone on the gray tents and on the swept ground of the streets between the tents. And the camp was waking up. The fires were burning in camp stoves, in the stoves made of kerosene cans and of sheets of metal. The smell of smoke was in the air. Tent flaps were thrown back and people moved about in the streets. In front of the Joad tent Ma stood looking up and down the street. She saw the children and came over to them.

"I was worryin'," Ma said. "I didn' know where you was."

"We was jus' lookin'," Ruthie said.

"Well, where's Tom? You seen him?"

Ruthie became important. "Yes, ma'am. Tom, he got me up an' he tol' me what to tell you." She paused to let her importance be apparent.

"Well—what?" Ma demanded.

"He said tell you—" She paused again and looked to see that Winfield appreciated her position.

Ma raised her hand, the back of it toward Ruthie. "What?"

"He got work," said Ruthie quickly. "Went out to work." She looked apprehensively at Ma's raised hand. The hand sank down again, and then it reached out for Ruthie. Ma embraced Ruthie's shoulders in a quick convulsive hug, and then released her.

Ruthie stared at the ground in embarrassment, and changed the subject. "They got toilets over there," she said. "White ones."

"You been in there?" Ma demanded.

"Me an' Winfiel'," she said; and then, treacherously, "Winfiel', he bust a toilet."

Winfield turned red. He glared at Ruthie. "She pee'd in one," he said viciously.

Ma was apprehensive. "Now what did you do? You show me." She forced them to the door and inside. "Now what'd you do?"

Ruthie pointed. "It was a-hissin' and a-swishin'. Stopped now."

"Show me what you done," Ma demanded.

Winfield went reluctantly to the toilet. "I didn' push it hard," he said. "I jus' had aholt of this here, an'—" The swish of water came again. He leaped away.

Ma threw back her head and laughed, while Ruthie and Winfield regarded her resentfully. "Tha's the way she works," Ma said. "I seen them before. When you finish, you push that."

The shame of their ignorance was too great for the children. They went out the door, and they walked down the street to stare at a large family eating breakfast.

Ma watched them out of the door. And then she looked about the room. She went to the shower closets and looked in. She walked to the wash basins and ran her finger over the white porcelain. She turned the water on a little and held her finger in the stream, and jerked her hand away when the water came hot. For a moment she regarded the basin, and then, setting the plug, she filled the bowl a little from the hot faucet, a little from the cold. And then she washed her hands in the warm water, and she washed her face. She was brushing water through her hair with her fingers when a step sounded on the concrete floor behind her. Ma swung around. An elderly man stood looking at her with an expression of righteous shock.

He said harshly, "How you come in here?"

Ma gulped, and she felt the water dripping from her chin and soaking through her dress. "I didn' know," she said apologetically. "I thought this here was for folks to use."

The elderly man frowned on her. "For men folks," he said sternly. He walked to the door and pointed to a sign on it: MEN. "There," he said. "That proves it. Didn' you see that?"

"No," Ma said in shame, "I never seen it. Ain't they a place where I can go?"

The man's anger departed. "You jus' come?" he asked more kindly.

"Middle of the night," said Ma.

"Then you ain't talked to the Committee?"

"What committee?"

"Why, the Ladies' Committee."

"No, I ain't."

He said proudly, "The Committee'll call on you purty soon an' fix you up. We take care of folks that jus' come in. Now, if you want a ladies' toilet, you jus' go on the other side of the building. That side's yourn."

Ma said uneasily, "Ya say a ladies' committee—comin' to my tent?"

He nodded his head. "Purty soon, I guess."

"Thank ya," said Ma. She hurried out, and half ran to the tent.

"Pa," she called. "John, git up! You, Al. Git up an' git washed." Startled sleepy eyes looked out at her. "All of you," Ma cried. "You git up an' git your face washed. An' comb your hair."

Uncle John looked pale and sick. There was a red bruised place on his chin.

Pa demanded, "What's the matter?"

"The Committee," Ma cried. "They's a committee—a ladies' committee a-comin' to visit. Git up now, an' git washed. An' while we was a-sleepin' an' a-snorin', Tom's went out an' got work. Git up, now."

They came sleepily out of the tent. Uncle John staggered a little, and his face was pained.

"Git over to that house and wash up," Ma ordered. "We got to get breakfus' an' be ready for the Committee." She went to a little pile of split wood in the camp lot. She started a fire and put up her cooking irons. "Pone," she said to herself. "Pone an' gravy. That's quick. Got to be quick." She talked on to herself, and Ruthie and Winfield stood by, wondering.

The smoke of the morning fires arose all over the camp, and the mutter of talk came from all sides.

Rose of Sharon, unkempt and sleepy-eyed, crawled out of the tent. Ma turned from the cornmeal she was measuring in fistfuls. She looked at the girl's wrinkled dirty dress, at her frizzled uncombed hair. "You got to clean up," she said briskly. "Go right over and clean up. You got a clean dress. I washed it. Git your hair combed. Git the seeds out a your eyes." Ma was excited.

Rose of Sharon said sullenly, "I don' feel good. I wisht Connie would come. I don't feel like doin' nothin' 'thout Connie."

Ma turned full around on her. The yellow cornmeal clung to her hands and wrists. "Rosasharn," she said sternly, "you git upright. You jus' been mopin' enough. They's a ladies' committee a-comin', an' the fambly ain't gonna be frawny when they get here."

"But I don' feel good."

Ma advanced on her, mealy hands held out. "Git," Ma said. "They's times when how you feel got to be kep' to yourself."

"I'm a-goin' to vomit," Rose of Sharon whined.

"Well, go an' vomit. 'Course you're gonna vomit. Ever'-body does. Git it over an' then you clean up, an' you wash your legs an' put on them shoes of yourn." She turned back to her work. "An' braid your hair," she said.

A frying pan of grease sputtered over the fire, and it splashed and hissed when Ma dropped the pone in with a spoon. She mixed flour with grease in a kettle and added water and salt and stirred the gravy. The coffee began to turn over in the gallon can, and the smell of coffee rose from it.

Pa wandered back from the sanitary unit, and Ma looked critically up. Pa said, "Ya say Tom's got work?"

"Yes, sir. Went out 'fore we was awake. Now look in that box an' get you some clean overhalls an' a shirt. An', Pa, I'm awful busy. You git in Ruthie an' Winfiel's ears. They's hot water. Will you do that? Scrounge aroun' in their ears good, an' their necks. Get 'em red an' shinin'."

"Never seen you so bubbly," Pa said.

Ma cried, "This here's the time the fambly got to get decent. Comin' acrost they wasn't no chancet. But now we can. Th'ow your dirty overhalls in the tent an' I'll wash 'em out."

Pa went inside the tent, and in a moment he came out with pale blue, washed overalls and shirt on. And he led the sad and startled children toward the sanitary unit.

Ma called after him, "Scrounge aroun' good in their ears."

Uncle John came to the door of the men's side and looked out, and then he went back and sat on the toilet a long time and held his aching head in his hands.

Ma had taken up a panload of brown pone and was drop-ping spoons of dough in the grease for a second pan when a shadow fell on the ground beside her. She looked over her shoulder. A little man dressed all in white stood behind her —a man with a thin, brown, lined face and merry eyes. He was lean as a picket. His white clean clothes were frayed at the seams. He smiled at Ma. "Good morning," he said.

Ma looked at his white clothes and her face hardened with suspicion. "Mornin'," she said.

"Are you Mrs. Joad?"

"Yes."

"Well, I'm Jim Rawley. I'm camp manager. Just dropped by to see if everything's all right. Got everything you need?"

Ma studied him suspiciously. "Yes," she said.

Rawley said, "I was asleep when you came last night. Lucky we had a place for you." His voice was warm.

Ma said simply, "It's nice. 'Specially them wash tubs."

"You wait till the women get to washing. Pretty soon now. You never heard such a fuss. Like a meeting. Know what they did yesterday, Mrs. Joad? They had a chorus. Singing a hymn tune and rubbing the clothes all in time. That was something to hear, I tell you."

The suspicion was going out of Ma's face. "Must a been nice. You're the boss?"

"No," he said. "The people here worked me out of a job. They keep the camp clean, they keep order, they do everything. I never saw such people. They're making clothes in the meeting hall. And they're making toys. Never saw such people."

Ma looked down at her dirty dress. "We ain't clean yet," she said. "You jus' can't keep clean a-travelin'."

"Don't I know it," he said. He sniffed the air. "Say—is that your coffee smells so good?"

Ma smiled. "Does smell nice, don't it? Outside it always

smells nice." And she said proudly, "We'd take it in honor 'f you'd have some breakfus' with us."

He came to the fire and squatted on his hams, and the last of Ma's resistance went down. "We'd be·proud to have ya," she said. "We ain't got much that's nice, but you're welcome."

The little man grinned at her. "I had my breakfast. But I'd sure like a cup of that coffee. Smells so good."

"Why—why, sure."

"Don't hurry yourself."

Ma poured a tin cup of coffee from the gallon can. She said, "We ain't got sugar yet. Maybe we'll get some today. If you need sugar, it won't taste good."

"Never use sugar," he said. "Spoils the taste of good coffee."

"Well, I like a little sugar," said Ma. She looked at him suddenly and closely, to see how he had come so close so quickly. She looked for motive on his face, and found nothing but friendliness. Then she looked at the frayed seams on his white coat, and she was reassured.

He sipped the coffee. "I guess the ladies'll be here to see you this morning."

"We ain't clean," Ma said. "They shouldn't be comin' till we get cleaned up a little."

"But they know how it is," the manager said. "They came in the same way. No, sir. The committees are good in this camp because they do know." He finished his coffee and stood up. "Well, I got to go on. Anything you want, why, come over to the office. I'm there all the time. Grand coffee. Thank you." He put the cup on the box with the others, waved his hand, and walked down the line of tents. And Ma heard him speaking to the people as he went.

Ma put down her head and she fought with a desire to cry.

Pa came back leading the children, their eyes still wet with pain at the ear-scrounging. They were subdued and shining. The sunburned skin on Winfield's nose was scrubbed off. "There," Pa said. "Got dirt an' two layers a skin. Had to almost lick 'em to make 'em stan' still."

Ma appraised them. "They look nice," she said. "He'p yaself to pone an' gravy. We got to get stuff outa the way an' the tent in order."

Pa served plates for the children and for himself. "Wonder where Tom got work?"

"I dunno."

"Well, if he can, we can."

Al came excitedly to the tent. "What a place!" he said. He helped himself and poured coffee. "Know what a fella's doin'? He's buildin' a house trailer. Right over there, back a them tents. Got beds an' a stove—ever'thing. Jus' live in her. By God, that's the way to live! Right where you stop— tha's where you live."

Ma said, "I ruther have a little house. Soon's we can, I want a little house."

Pa said, "Al—after we've et, you an' me an' Uncle John'll take the truck an' go out lookin' for work."

"Sure," said Al. "I like to get a job in a garage if they's any jobs. Tha's what I really like. An' get me a little ol' cut-down Ford. Paint her yella an' go a-kyoodlin' aroun'. Seen a purty girl down the road. Give her a big wink, too. Purty as hell, too."

Pa said sternly, "You better get you some work 'fore you go a-tom-cattin'."

Uncle John came out of the toilet and moved slowly near. Ma frowned at him.

"You ain't washed—" she began, and then she saw how sick and weak and sad he looked. "You go on in the tent an' lay down," she said. "You ain't well."

He shook his head. "No," he said. "I sinned, an' I got to take my punishment." He squatted down disconsolately and poured himself a cup of coffee.

Ma took the last pones from the pan. She said casually, "The manager of the camp come an' set an' had a cup a coffee."

Pa looked over slowly. "Yeah? What's he want awready?"

"Jus' come to pass the time," Ma said daintily. "Jus' set down an' had coffee. Said he didn' get good coffee so often, an' smelt our'n."

"What'd he want?" Pa demanded again.

"Didn' want nothin'. Come to see how we was gettin' on."

"I don' believe it," Pa said. "He's probably a-snootin' an' a-smellin' aroun'."

"He was not!" Ma cried angrily. "I can tell a fella that's snootin' aroun' quick as the nex' person."

Pa tossed his coffee grounds out of his cup.

"You got to quit that," Ma said. "This here's a clean place."

"You see she don't get so goddamn clean a fella can't live in her," Pa said jealously. "Hurry up, Al. We're goin' out lookin' for a job."

Al wiped his mouth with his hand. "I'm ready," he said.

Pa turned to Uncle John. "You a-comin'?"

"Yes, I'm a-comin'."

"You don't look so good."

"I ain't so good, but I'm comin'."

Al got in the truck. "Have to get gas," he said. He started

the engine. Pa and Uncle John climbed in beside him and the truck moved away down the street.

Ma watched them go. And then she took a bucket and went to the wash trays under the open part of the sanitary unit. She filled her bucket with hot water and carried it back to her camp. And she was washing the dishes in the bucket when Rose of Sharon came back.

"I put your stuff on a plate," Ma said. And then she looked closely at the girl. Her hair was dripping and combed, and her skin was bright and pink. She had put on the blue dress printed with little white flowers. On her feet she wore the heeled slippers of her wedding. She blushed under Ma's gaze. "You had a bath," Ma said.

Rose of Sharon spoke huskily. "I was in there when a lady come in an' done it. Know what you do? You get in a little stall-like, an' you turn handles, an' water comes a-floodin' down on you—hot water or col' water, jus' like you want it—an' I done it!"

"I'm a-goin' to myself," Ma cried. "Jus' soon as I get finish' here. You show me how."

"I'm a-gonna do it ever' day," the girl said. "An' that lady—she seen me, an' she seen about the baby, an'—know what she said? Said they's a nurse comes ever' week. An' I'm to go see that nurse an' she'll tell me jus' what to do so's the baby'll be strong. Says all the ladies here do that. An' I'm a-gonna do it." The words bubbled out. "An'—know what—? Las' week they was a baby borned an' the whole camp give a party, an' they give clothes, an' they give stuff for the baby—even give a baby buggy—wicker one. Wasn't new, but they give it a coat a pink paint, an' it was jus' like new. An' they give the baby a name, an' had a cake. Oh, Lord!" She subsided, breathing heavily.

Ma said, "Praise God, we come home to our own people. I'm a-gonna have a bath."

"Oh, it's nice," the girl said.

Ma wiped the tin dishes and stacked them. She said, "We're Joads. We don't look up to nobody. Grampa's grampa, he fit in the Revolution. We was farm people till the debt. And then—them people. They done somepin to us. Ever' time they come seemed like they was a-whippin' me— all of us. An' in Needles, that police. He done somepin to me, made me feel mean. Made me feel ashamed. An' now I ain't ashamed. These folks is our folks—is our folks. An' that manager, he come an' set an' drank coffee, an' he says, 'Mrs. Joad' this, an' 'Mrs. Joad' that—an' 'How you gettin' on, Mrs. Joad?' " She stopped and sighed. "Why, I feel like people again." She stacked the last dish. She went into the tent and dug through the clothes box for her shoes and a clean dress. And she found a little paper package with her earrings in it. As she went past Rose of Sharon, she said, "If them ladies comes, you tell 'em I'll be right back." She disappeared around the side of the sanitary unit.

Rose of Sharon sat down heavily on a box and regarded her wedding shoes, black patent leather and tailored black bows. She wiped the toes with her finger and wiped her finger on the inside of her skirt. Leaning down put a pressure on her growing abdomen. She sat up straight and touched herself with exploring fingers, and she smiled a little as she did it.

Along the road a stocky woman walked, carrying an apple box of dirty clothes toward the wash tubs. Her face was brown with sun, and her eyes were black and intense. She wore a great apron, made from a cotton bag, over her gingham dress, and men's brown oxfords were on her feet. She saw that Rose of Sharon caressed herself, and she saw the little smile on the girl's face.

"So!" she cried, and she laughed with pleasure. "What you think it's gonna be?"

Rose of Sharon blushed and looked down at the ground, and then peeked up, and the little shiny black eyes of the woman took her in. "I don' know," she mumbled.

The woman plopped the apple box on the ground. "Got a live tumor," she said, and she cackled like a happy hen. "Which'd you ruther?" she demanded.

"I dunno—boy, I guess. Sure—boy."

"You jus' come in, didn' ya?"

"Las' night—late."

"Gonna stay?"

"I don' know. 'F we can get work, guess we will."

A shadow crossed the woman's face, and the little black eyes grew fierce. " 'F you can git work. That's what we all say."

"My brother got a job already this mornin'."

"Did, huh? Maybe you're lucky. Look out for luck. You can't trus' luck." She stepped close. "You can only git one kind a luck. Cain't have more. You be a good girl," she said fiercely. "You be good. If you got sin on you—you better watch out for that there baby." She squatted down in front of Rose of Sharon. "They's scandalous things goes on in this here camp," she said darkly. "Ever' Sat'dy night they's dancin', an' not only squar' dancin', neither. They's some does clutch-an'-hug dancin'! I seen 'em."

Rose of Sharon said guardedly, "I like dancin', squar' dancin'." And she added virtuously, "I never done that other kind."

The brown woman nodded her head dismally. "Well,

some does. An' the Lord ain't lettin' it get by, neither; an' don' you think He is."

"No, ma'am," the girl said softly.

The woman put one brown wrinkled hand on Rose of Sharon's knee, and the girl flinched under the touch. "You let me warn you now. They ain't but a few deep down Jesus-lovers lef'. Ever' Sat'dy night when that there strang ban' starts up an' should be a-playin' hymnody, they're a-reelin' —yes, sir, a-reelin'. I seen 'em. Won' go near, myself, nor I don' let my kin go near. They's clutch-an'-hug, I tell ya." She paused for emphasis and then said, in a hoarse whisper, "They do more. They give a stage play." She backed away and cocked her head to see how Rose of Sharon would take such a revelation.

"Actors?" the girl said in awe.

"No, sir!" the woman exploded. "Not *actors*, not them already damn' people. Our own kinda folks. Our own people. An' they was little children didn' know no better, in it, an' they was pertendin' to be stuff they wasn't. I didn' go near. But I hearn 'em talkin' what they was a-doin'. The devil was jus' a-struttin' through this here camp."

Rose of Sharon listened, her eyes and mouth open. "Oncet in school we give a Chris' chile play—Christmus."

"Well—I ain' sayin' tha's bad or good. They's good folks thinks a Chris' chile is awright. But—well, I wouldn' care to come right out flat an' say so. But this here wasn' no Chris' chile. This here was sin an' delusion an' devil stuff. Struttin' an' paradin' an' speakin' like they're somebody they ain't. An' dancin' an' clutchin' an' a-huggin'."

Rose of Sharon sighed.

"An' not jus' a few, neither," the brown woman went on.

"Gettin' so's you can almos' count the deep-down lamb-blood folks on your toes. An' don' you think them sinners is puttin' nothin' over on God, neither. No, sir, He's a-chalkin' 'em up sin by sin, an' He's drawin' His line an' addin' 'em up sin by sin. God's a-watchin', an' I'm a-watchin'. He's awready smoked two of 'em out."

Rose of Sharon panted, "Has?"

The brown woman's voice was rising in intensity. "I seen it. Girl a-carryin' a little one, jes' like you. An' she play-acted, an' she hug-danced. And"—the voice grew bleak and ominous—"she thinned out and she skinnied out, an'—she dropped that baby, dead."

"Oh, my!" The girl was pale.

"Dead and bloody. 'Course nobody wouldn' speak to her no more. She had a go away. Can't tech sin 'thout catchin' it. No, sir. An' they was another, done the same thing. An' she skinnied out, an'—know what? One night she was gone. An' two days, she's back. Says she was visitin'. But—she ain't got no baby. Know what I think? I think the manager, he took her away to drop her baby. He don' believe in sin. Tol' me hisself. Says the sin is bein' hungry. Says the sin is bein' cold. Says—I tell ya, he tol' me hisself—can't see God in them things. Says them girls skinnied out 'cause they didn' git 'nough food. Well, I fixed him up." She rose to her feet and stepped back. Her eyes were sharp. She pointed a rigid fore-finger in Rose of Sharon's face. "I says, 'Git back!' I says. I says, 'I knowed the devil was rampagin' in this here camp. Now I know who the devil is. Git back, Satan,' I says. An', by Chris', he got back! Tremblin' he was, an' sneaky. Says, 'Please!' Says, 'Please don' make the folks unhappy.' I says, 'Unhappy? How 'bout their soul? How 'bout them dead babies an' them poor sinners ruint 'count of play-actin'?' He jes' looked, an' he give a sick grin an' went away. He knowed when he met a real testifier to the Lord. I says, 'I'm a-helpin' Jesus watch the goin's-on. An' you an' them other sinners ain't gittin' away with it." She picked up her box of dirty clothes. "You take heed. I warned you. You take heed a that pore chile in your belly an' keep outa sin." And she strode away titanically, and her eyes shone with virtue.

Rose of Sharon watched her go, and then she put her head down on her hands and whimpered into her palms. A soft voice sounded beside her. She looked up, ashamed. It was the little white-clad manager. "Don't worry," he said. "Don't you worry."

Her eyes blinded with tears. "But I done it," she cried. "I hug-danced. I didn' tell her. I done it in Sallisaw. Me an' Connie."

"Don't worry," he said.

"She says I'll drop the baby."

"I know she does. I kind of keep my eye on her. She's a good woman, but she makes people unhappy."

Rose of Sharon sniffled wetly. "She knowed two girls los' their baby right in this here camp."

The manager squatted down in front of her. "Look!" he said. "Listen to me. I know them too. They were too hungry and too tired. And they worked too hard. And they rode on a truck over bumps. They were sick. It wasn't their fault."

"But she said——"

"Don't worry. That woman likes to make trouble."

"But she says you was the devil."

"I know she does. That's because I won't let her make people miserable." He patted her shoulder. "Don't you worry. She doesn't know." And he walked quickly away.

Rose of Sharon looked after him; his lean shoulders jerked as he walked. She was still watching his slight figure when Ma came back, clean and pink, her hair combed and wet, and gathered in a knot. She wore her figured dress and the old cracked shoes; and the little earrings hung in her ears.

"I done it," she said. "I stood in there an' let warm water come a-floodin' an' a-flowin' down over me. An' they was a lady says you can do it ever' day if you want. An'—them ladies' committee come yet?"

"Uh-uh!" said the girl.

"An' you jus' set there an' didn' redd up the camp none!" Ma gathered up the tin dishes as she spoke. "We got to get in shape," she said. "Come on, stir! Get that sack and kinda sweep along the groun'." She picked up the equipment, put the pans in their box and the box in the tent. "Get them beds neat," she ordered. "I tell ya I ain't never felt nothin' so nice as that water."

Rose of Sharon listlessly followed orders. "Ya think Connie'll be back today?"

"Maybe—maybe not. Can't tell."

"You sure he knows where-at to come?"

"Sure."

"Ma—ya don' think—they could a killed him when they burned—?"

"Not him," Ma said confidently. "He can travel when he wants—jackrabbit-quick an' fox-sneaky."

"I wisht he'd come."

"He'll come when he comes."

"Ma——"

"I wisht you'd get to work."

"Well, do you think dancin' an' play-actin' is sins an'll make me drop the baby?"

Ma stopped her work and put her hands on her hips. "Now what you talkin' about? You ain't done no play-actin'."

"Well, some folks here done it, an' one girl, she dropped her baby—dead—an' bloody, like it was a judgment."

Ma stared at her. "Who tol' you?"

"Lady that come by. An' that little fella in white clothes, he come by an' he says that ain't what done it."

Ma frowned. "Rosasharn," she said, "you stop pickin' at yourself. You're jest a-teasin' yourself up to cry. I don' know what's come at you. Our folks ain't never did that. They took what come to 'em dry-eyed. I bet it's that Connie give you all them notions. He was jes' too big for his over-halls." And she said sternly, "Rosasharn, you're jest one person, an' they's a lot of other folks. You git to your proper place. I knowed people built theirself up with sin till they figgered they was big mean shucks in the sight a the Lord."

"But, Ma——"

"No. Jes' shut up an' git to work. You ain't big enough or mean enough to worry God much. An' I'm gonna give you the back a my han' if you don' stop this pickin' at your-self." She swept the ashes into the fire hole and brushed the stones on its edge. She saw the committee coming along the road. "Git workin'," she said. "Here's the ladies comin'. Git a-workin' now, so's I can be proud." She didn't look again, but she was conscious of the approach of the committee.

There could be no doubt that it was the committee; three ladies, washed, dressed in their best clothes: a lean woman with stringy hair and steel-rimmed glasses, a small stout lady with curly gray hair and a small sweet mouth, and a mammoth lady, big of hock and buttock, big of breast, muscled like a dray-horse, powerful and sure. And the committee walked down the road with dignity.

Ma managed to have her back turned when they arrived. They stopped, wheeled, stood in a line. And the great woman boomed, "Mornin', Mis' Joad, ain't it?"

Ma whirled around as though she had been caught off guard. "Why, yes—yes. How'd you know my name?"

"We're the committee," the big woman said. "Ladies' Committee of Sanitary Unit Number Four. We got your name in the office."

Ma flustered, "We ain't in very good shape yet. I'd be proud to have you ladies come an' set while I make up some coffee."

The plump committee woman said, "Give our names, Jessie. Mention our names to Mis' Joad. Jessie's the Chair," she explained.

Jessie said formally, "Mis' Joad, this here's Annie Little-field an' Ella Summers, an' I'm Jessie Bullitt."

"I'm proud to make your acquaintance," Ma said. "Won't you set down? They ain't nothin' to set on yet," she added. "But I'll make up some coffee."

"Oh, no," said Annie formally. "Don't put yaself out. We jes' come to call an' see how you was, an' try to make you feel at home."

Jessie Bullitt said sternly, "Annie, I'll thank you to remember I'm Chair."

"Oh! Sure, sure. But next week I am."

"Well, you wait'll next week then. We change ever' week," she explained to Ma.

"Sure you wouldn' like a little coffee?" Ma asked help-lessly.

"No, thank you." Jessie took charge. "We gonna show you 'bout the sanitary unit fust, an' then if you wanta, we'll sign you up in the Ladies' Club an' give you duty. 'Course you don' have to join."

"Does—does it cost much?"

"Don't cost nothing but work. An' when you're knowed, maybe you can be 'lected to this committee," Annie interrupted. "Jessie, here, is on the committee for the whole camp. She's a big committee lady."

Jessie smiled with pride. " 'Lected unanimous," she said. "Well, Mis' Joad, I guess it's time we tol' you 'bout how the camp runs."

Ma said, "This here's my girl, Rosasharn."

"How do," they said.

"Better come 'long too."

The huge Jessie spoke, and her manner was full of dignity and kindness, and her speech was rehearsed.

"You shouldn' think we're a-buttin' into your business, Mis' Joad. This here camp got a lot of stuff ever'body uses. An' we got rules we made ourself. Now we're a-goin' to the unit. That there, ever'body uses, an' ever'body got to take care of it." They strolled to the unroofed section where the wash trays were, twenty of them. Eight were in use, the women bending over, scrubbing the clothes, and the piles of wrung-out clothes were heaped on the clean concrete floor. "Now you can use these here any time you want," Jessie said. "The on'y thing is, you got to leave 'em clean."

The women who were washing looked up with interest. Jessie said loudly, "This here's Mis' Joad an' Rosasharn, come to live." They greeted Ma in a chorus, and Ma made a dumpy little bow at them and said, "Proud to meet ya."

Jessie led the committee into the toilet and shower room.

"I been here awready," Ma said. "I even took a bath."

"That's what they're for," Jessie said. "An' they's the same rule. You got to leave 'em clean. Ever' week they's a new committee to swab out oncet a day. Maybe you'll git on that committee. You got to bring your own soap."

"We got to get some soap," Ma said. "We're all out."

Jessie's voice became almost reverential. "You ever used this here kind?" she asked, and pointed to the toilets.

"Yes, ma'am. Right this mornin'."

Jessie sighed. "Tha's good."

Ella Summers said, "Jes' las' week——"

Jessie interrupted sternly, "Mis' Summers—I'll tell."

Ella gave ground. "Oh, awright."

Jessie said, "Las' week, when you was Chair, you done it all. I'll thank you to keep out this week."

"Well, tell what that lady done," Ella said.

"Well," said Jessie, "it ain't this committee's business to go a-blabbin', but I won't pass no names. Lady come in las' week, an' she got in here 'fore the committee got to her, an' she had her ol' man's pants in the toilet, an' she says, 'It's too low, an' it ain't big enough. Bust your back over her,' she says. 'Why couldn' they stick her higher?'" The committee smiled superior smiles.

Ella broke in, "Says, 'Can't put 'nough in at oncet.'" And Ella weathered Jessie's stern glance.

Jessie said, "We got our troubles with toilet paper. Rule says you can't take none away from here." She clicked her tongue sharply. "Whole camp chips in for toilet paper." For a moment she was silent, and then she confessed. "Number Four is usin' more than any other. Somebody's a-stealin' it. Come up in general ladies' meetin'. 'Ladies' side, Unit

Number Four is usin' too much.' Come right up in meetin'!"

Ma was following the conversation breathlessly. "Stealin' it—what for?"

"Well," said Jessie, "we had trouble before. Las' time they was three little girls cuttin' paper dolls out of it. Well, we caught them. But this time we don't know. Hardly put a roll out 'fore it's gone. Come right up in meetin'. One lady says we oughta have a little bell that rings ever' time the roll turns oncet. Then we could count how many ever'body takes." She shook her head. "I jes' don' know," she said. "I been worried all week. Somebody's a-stealin' toilet paper from Unit Four."

From the doorway came a whining voice, "Mis' Bullitt." The committee turned. "Mis' Bullitt, I hearn what you says." A flushed, perspiring woman stood in the doorway. "I couldn' git up in meetin', Mis' Bullitt. I jes' couldn'. They'd a-laughed or somepin."

"What you talkin' about?" Jessie advanced.

"Well, we-all—maybe—it's us. But we ain't a-stealin', Mis' Bullitt."

Jessie advanced on her, and the perspiration beaded out on the flustery confessor. "We can't he'p it, Mis' Bullitt."

"Now you tell what you're tellin'," Jessie said. "This here unit's suffered a shame 'bout that toilet paper."

"All week, Mis' Bullitt. We couldn' he'p it. You know I got five girls."

"What they been a-doin' with it?" Jessie demanded ominously.

"Jes' usin' it. Hones', jes' usin' it."

"They ain't got the right! Four-five sheets is enough. What's the matter'th 'em?"

The confessor bleated, "Skitters. All five of 'em. We been low on money. They et green grapes. They all five got the howlin' skitters. Run out ever' ten minutes." She defended them, "But they ain't stealin' it."

Jessie sighed. "You should a tol'," she said. "You got to tell. Here's Unit Four sufferin' shame 'cause you never tol'. Anybody can git the skitters."

The meek voice whined, "I jes' can't keep 'em from eatin' them green grapes. An' they're a-gettin' worse all a time."

Ella Summers burst out, "The Aid. She oughta git the Aid."

"Ella Summers," Jessie said, "I'm a-tellin' you for the las' time, you ain't the Chair." She turned back to the raddled little woman. "Ain't you got no money, Mis' Joyce?"

She looked ashamedly down. "No, but we might git work any time."

"Now you hol' up your head," Jessie said. "That ain't no crime. You jes' waltz right over t' the Weedpatch store an' git you some grocteries. The camp got twenty dollars' credit there. You git yourself fi' dollars' worth. An' you kin pay it back to the Central Committee when you git work. Mis' Joyce, you knowed that," she said sternly. "How come you let your girls git hungry?"

"We ain't never took no charity," Mrs. Joyce said.

"This ain't charity, an' you know it," Jessie raged. "We had all that out. They ain't no charity in this here camp. We won't have no charity. Now you waltz right over an' git you some grocteries, an' you bring the slip to me."

Mrs. Joyce said timidly, "S'pose we can't never pay? We ain't had work for a long time."

"You'll pay if you can. If you can't, that ain't none of our business, an' it ain't your business. One fella went away, an' two months later he sent back the money. You ain't got the right to let your girls git hungry in this here camp."

Mrs. Joyce was cowed. "Yes, ma'am," she said.

"Git you some cheese for them girls," Jessie ordered. "That'll take care a them skitters."

"Yes, ma'am." And Mrs. Joyce scuttled out of the door.

Jessie turned in anger on the committee. "She got no right to be stiff-necked. She got no right, not with our own people."

Annie Littlefield said, "She ain't been here long. Maybe she don't know. Maybe she's took charity one time-another. Nor," Annie said, "don't you try to shut me up, Jessie. I got a right to pass speech." She turned half to Ma. "If a body's ever took charity, it makes a burn that don't come out. This ain't charity, but if you ever took it, you don't forget it. I bet Jessie ain't ever done it."

"No, I ain't," said Jessie.

"Well, I did," Annie said. "Las' winter; an' we was a-starvin'—me an' Pa an' the little fellas. An' it was a-rainin'. Fella tol' us to go to the Salvation Army." Her eyes grew fierce. "We was hungry—they made us crawl for our dinner. They took our dignity. They—I hate 'em! An'—maybe Mis' Joyce took charity. Maybe she didn' know this ain't charity. Mis' Joad, we don't allow nobody in this camp to build their-self up that-a-way. We don't allow nobody to give nothing to another person. They can give it to the camp, an' the camp can pass it out. We won't have no charity!" Her voice was fierce and hoarse. "I hate 'em," she said. "I ain't never seen my man beat before, but them—them Salvation Army done it to 'im."

Jessie nodded. "I heard," she said softly, "I heard. We got to take Mis' Joad aroun'."

Ma said, "It sure is nice."

"Le's go to the sewin' room," Annie suggested. "Got two

machines. They's a-quiltin', an' they're makin' dresses. You might like ta work over there."

When the committee called on Ma, Ruthie and Winfield faded imperceptibly back out of reach.

"Whyn't we go along an' listen?" Winfield asked.

Ruthie gripped his arm. "No," she said. "We got washed for them sons-a-bitches. I ain't goin' with 'em."

Winfield said, "You tol' on me 'bout the toilet. I'm a-gonna tell what you called them ladies."

A shadow of fear crossed Ruthie's face. "Don' do it. I tol' 'cause I knowed you didn' really break it."

"You did not," said Winfield.

Ruthie said, "Le's look aroun'." They strolled down the line of tents, peering into each one, gawking self-consciously. At the end of the unit there was a level place on which a croquet court had been set up. Half a dozen children played seriously. In front of a tent an elderly lady sat on a bench and watched. Ruthie and Winfield broke into a trot. "Leave us play," Ruthie cried. "Leave us get in."

The children looked up. A pig-tailed little girl said, "Nex' game you kin."

"I wanta play now," Ruthie cried.

"Well, you can't. Not till nex' game."

Ruthie moved menacingly out on the court. "I'm a-gonna play." The pig-tails gripped her mallet tightly. Ruthie sprang at her, slapped her, pushed her, and wrested the mallet from her hands. "I says I was gonna play," she said triumphantly.

The elderly lady stood up and walked onto the court. Ruthie scowled fiercely and her hands tightened on the mallet. The lady said, "Let her play—like you done with Ralph las' week."

The children laid their mallets on the ground and trooped silently off the court. They stood at a distance and looked on with expressionless eyes. Ruthie watched them go. Then she hit a ball and ran after it. "Come on, Winfiel'. Get a stick," she called. And then she looked in amazement. Winfield had joined the watching children, and he too looked at her with expressionless eyes. Defiantly she hit the ball again. She kicked up a great dust. She pretended to have a good time. And the children stood and watched. Ruthie lined up two balls and hit both of them, and she turned her back on the watching eyes, and then turned back. Suddenly she advanced on them, mallet in hand. "You come an' play," she demanded. They moved silently back at her approach. For a moment she stared at them, and then she flung down the mallet and ran crying for home. The children walked back on the court.

Pigtails said to Winfield, "You can git in the nex' game."

The watching lady warned them, "When she comes back an' wants to be decent, you let her. You was mean yourself, Amy." The game went on, while in the Joad tent Ruthie wept miserably.

The truck moved along the beautiful roads, past orchards where the peaches were beginning to color, past vineyards with the clusters pale and green, under lines of walnut trees whose branches spread half across the road. At each entrance-gate Al slowed; and at each gate there was a sign: "No help wanted. No trespassing."

Al said, "Pa, they's boun' to be work when them fruits gets ready. Funny place—they tell ya they ain't no work 'fore you ask 'em." He drove slowly on.

Pa said, "Maybe we could go in anyways an' ask if they know where they's any work. Might do that."

A man in blue overalls and a blue shirt walked along the edge of the road. Al pulled up beside him. "Hey, mister," Al said. "Know where they's any work?"

The man stopped and grinned, and his mouth was vacant of front teeth. "No," he said. "Do you? I been walkin' all week, an' I can't tree none."

"Live in that gov'ment camp?" Al asked.

"Yeah!"

"Come on, then. Git up back, an' we'll all look." The man climbed over the side-boards and dropped in the bed.

Pa said, "I ain't got no hunch we'll find work. Guess we got to look, though. We don't even know where-at to look."

"Shoulda talked to the fellas in the camp," Al said. "How you feelin', Uncle John?"

"I ache," said Uncle John. "I ache all over, an' I got it comin'. I oughta go away where I won't bring down punishment on my own folks."

Pa put his hand on John's knee. "Look here," he said, "don' you go away. We're droppin' folks all the time— Grampa an' Granma dead, Noah an' Connie—run out, an' the preacher—in jail."

"I got a hunch we'll see that preacher agin," John said.

Al fingered the ball on the gear-shift lever. "You don' feel good enough to have no hunches," he said. "The hell with it. Le's go back an' talk, an' find out where they's some work. We're jus' huntin' skunks under water." He stopped the truck and leaned out the window and called back, "Hey! Lookie! We're a-goin' back to the camp an' try an' see where they's work. They ain't no use burnin' gas like this."

The man leaned over the truck side. "Suits me," he said. "My dogs is wore clean up to the ankle. An' I ain't even got a nibble."

Al turned around in the middle of the road and headed back.

Pa said, "Ma's gonna be purty hurt, 'specially when Tom got work so easy."

"Maybe he never got none," Al said. "Maybe he jus' went lookin', too. I wisht I could get work in a garage. I'd learn that stuff quick, an' I'd like it."

Pa grunted, and they drove back toward the camp in silence.

When the committee left, Ma sat down on a box in front of the Joad tent, and she looked helplessly at Rose of Sharon. "Well—" she said, "well—I ain't been so perked up in years. *Wasn't* them ladies nice?"

"I get to work in the nursery," Rose of Sharon said. "They tol' me. I can find out all how to do for babies, an' then I'll know."

Ma nodded in wonder. "Wouldn' it be nice if the menfolks all got work?" she asked. "Them a-workin', an' a little money comin' in?" Her eyes wandered into space. "Them a-workin', an' us a-workin' here, an' all them nice people. Fust thing we get a little ahead I'd get me a little stove—nice one. They don' cost much. An' then we'd get a tent, big enough, an' maybe secon'-han' springs for the beds. An' we'd use this here tent jus' to eat under. An' Sat'dy night we'll go to the dancin'. They says you can invite folks if you want. I wisht we had some frien's to invite. Maybe the men'll know somebody to invite."

Rose of Sharon peered down the road. "That lady that says I'll lose the baby—" she began.

"Now you stop that," Ma warned her.

Rose of Sharon said softly, "I seen her. She's a-comin' here, I think. Yeah! Here she comes. Ma, don't let her——"

Ma turned and looked at the approaching figure.

"Howdy," the woman said. "I'm Mis' Sandry—Lisbeth Sandry. I seen your girl this mornin'."

"Howdy do," said Ma.

"Are you happy in the Lord?"

"Pretty happy," said Ma.

"Are you saved?"

"I been saved." Ma's face was closed and waiting.

"Well, I'm glad," Lisbeth said. "The sinners is awful strong aroun' here. You come to a awful place. They's wicketness all around about. Wicket people, wicket goin's-on that a lamb'-blood Christian jes' can't hardly stan'. They's sinners all around us."

Ma colored a little, and shut her mouth tightly. "Seems to me they's nice people here," she said shortly.

Mrs. Sandry's eyes stared. "Nice!" she cried. "You think they're nice when they's dancin' an' huggin'? I tell ya, ya eternal soul ain't got a chancet in this here camp. Went out to a meetin' in Weedpatch las' night. Know what the preacher says? He says, 'They's wicketness in that camp.' He says, 'The poor is tryin' to be rich.' He says, 'They's dancin' an' huggin' when they should be wailin' an' moanin' in sin.' That's what he says. 'Ever'body that ain't here is a black sinner,' he says. I tell you it made a person feel purty good to hear 'im. An' we knowed we was safe. We ain't danced."

Ma's face was red. She stood up slowly and faced Mrs.

Sandry. "Git!" she said. "Git out now, 'fore I git to be a sinner a-tellin' you where to go. Git to your wailin' an' moanin'."

Mrs. Sandry's mouth dropped open. She stepped back. And then she became fierce. "I thought you was Christians."

"So we are," Ma said.

"No, you ain't. You're hell-burnin' sinners, all of you! An' I'll mention it in meetin', too. I can see your black soul a-burnin'. I can see that innocent child in that there girl's belly a-burnin'."

A low wailing cry escaped from Rose of Sharon's lips. Ma stooped down and picked up a stick of wood.

"Git!" she said coldly. "Don' you never come back. I seen your kind before. You'd take the little pleasure, wouldn' you?" Ma advanced on Mrs. Sandry.

For a moment the woman backed away and then suddenly she threw back her head and howled. Her eyes rolled up, her shoulders and arms flopped loosely at her side, and a string of thick ropy saliva ran from the corner of her mouth. She howled again and again, long deep animal howls. Men and women ran up from the other tents, and they stood near—frightened and quiet. Slowly the woman sank to her knees and the howls sank to a shuddering, bubbling moan. She fell sideways and her arms and legs twitched. The white eye-balls showed under the open eyelids.

A man said softly, "The sperit. She got the sperit." Ma stood looking down at the twitching form.

The little manager strolled up casually. "Trouble?" he asked. The crowd parted to let him through. He looked down at the woman. "Too bad," he said. "Will some of you help get her back to her tent?" The silent people shuffled their feet. Two men bent over and lifted the woman, one held her under the arms and the other took her feet. They carried her away, and the people moved slowly after them. Rose of Sharon went under the tarpaulin and lay down and covered her face with a blanket.

The manager looked at Ma, looked down at the stick in her hand. He smiled tiredly. "Did you clout her?" he asked.

Ma continued to stare after the retreating people. She shook her head slowly. "No—but I would a. Twicet today she worked my girl up."

The manager said, "Try not to hit her. She isn't well. She just isn't well." And he added softly, "I wish she'd go away, and all her family. She brings more trouble on the camp than all the rest together."

Ma got herself in hand again. "If she comes back, I might hit her. I ain't sure. I won't let her worry my girl no more."

"Don't worry about it, Mrs. Joad," he said. "You won't ever see her again. She works over the newcomers. She won't ever come back. She thinks you're a sinner."

"Well, I am," said Ma.

"Sure. Everbody is, but not the way she means. She isn't well, Mrs. Joad."

Ma looked at him gratefully, and she called, "You hear that, Rosasharn? She ain't well. She's crazy." But the girl did not raise her head. Ma said, "I'm warnin' you, mister. If she comes back, I ain't to be trusted. I'll hit her."

He smiled wryly. "I know how you feel," he said. "But just try not to. That's all I ask—just try not to." He walked slowly away toward the tent where Mrs. Sandry had been carried.

Ma went into the tent and sat down beside Rose of Sharon. "Look up," she said. The girl lay still. Ma gently lifted the blanket from her daughter's face. "That woman's kinda crazy," she said. "Don't you believe none of them things."

Rose of Sharon whispered in terror, "When she said about burnin', I—felt burnin'."

"That ain't true," said Ma.

"I'm tar'd out," the girl whispered. "I'm tar'd a things happenin'. I wanta sleep. I wanta sleep."

"Well, you sleep, then. This here's a nice place. You can sleep."

"But she might come back."

"She won't," said Ma. "I'm a-gonna set right outside, an' I won't let her come back. Res' up now, 'cause you got to get to work in the nu'sery purty soon."

Ma struggled to her feet and went to sit in the entrance to the tent. She sat on a box and put her elbows on her knees and her chin in her cupped hands. She saw the movement in the camp, heard the voices of the children, the hammering of an iron rim; but her eyes were staring ahead of her.

Pa, coming back along the road, found her there, and he squatted near her. She looked slowly over at him. "Git work?" she asked.

"No," he said, ashamed. "We looked."

"Where's Al and John and the truck?"

"Al's fixin' somepin. Had ta borry some tools. Fella says Al got to fix her there."

Ma said sadly, "This here's a nice place. We could be happy here awhile."

"If we could get work."

"Yeah! If you could get work."

He felt her sadness, and studied her face. "What you a-mopin' about? If it's sech a nice place why have you got to mope?"

She gazed at him, and she closed her eyes slowly. "Funny,

ain't it. All the time we was a-movin' an' shovin', I never thought none. An' now these here folks been nice to me, been awful nice; an' what's the first thing I do? I go right back over the sad things—that night Grampa died an' we buried him. I was all full up of the road, and bumpin' and movin', an' it wasn't so bad. But now I come out here, an' it's worse now. An' Granma—an' Noah walkin' away like that! Walkin' away jus' down the river. Them things was part of all, an' now they come a-flockin' back. Granma a pauper, an' buried a pauper. That's sharp now. That's awful sharp. An' Noah walkin' away down the river. He don' know what's there. He jus' don' know. An' we don' know. We ain't never gonna know if he's alive or dead. Never gonna know. An' Connie sneakin' away. I didn' give 'em brain room before, but now they're a-flockin' back. An' I oughta be glad 'cause we're in a nice place." Pa watched her mouth while she talked. Her eyes were closed. "I can remember how them mountains was, sharp as ol' teeth beside the river where Noah walked. I can remember how the stubble was on the groun' where Grampa lies. I can remember the choppin' block back home with a feather caught on it, all criss-crossed with cuts, an' black with chicken blood."

Pa's voice took on her tone. "I seen the ducks today," he said. "Wedgin' south—high up. Seems like they're awful dinky. An' I seen the blackbirds a-settin' on the wires, an' the doves was on the fences." Ma opened her eyes and looked at him. He went on, "I seen a little whirlwin', like a man a-spinnin' acrost a fiel'. An' the ducks drivin' on down, wedgin' on down to the southward."

Ma smiled. "Remember?" she said. "Remember what we'd always say at home? 'Winter's a-comin' early,' we said, when the ducks flew. Always said that, an' winter come when it was ready to come. But we always said, 'She's a-comin' early.' I wonder what we meant."

"I seen the blackbirds on the wires," said Pa. "Settin' so close together. An' the doves. Nothin' sets so still as a dove— on the fence wires—maybe two, side by side. An' this little whirlwin'—big as a man, an' dancin' off acrost a fiel'. Always did like the little fellas, big as a man."

"Wisht I wouldn't think how it is home," said Ma. "It ain't our home no more. Wisht I'd forget it. An' Noah."

"He wasn't ever right—I mean—well, it was my fault."

"I tol' you never to say that. Woudn' a lived at all, maybe."

"But I should a knowed more."

"Now stop," said Ma. "Noah was strange. Maybe he'll have a nice time by the river. Maybe it's better so. We can't do no worryin'. This here is a nice place, an' maybe you'll get work right off."

Pa pointed at the sky. "Look—more ducks. Big bunch. An' Ma, 'Winter's a-comin' early.' "

She chuckled. "They's things you do, an' you don' know why."

"Here's John," said Pa. "Come on an' set, John."

Uncle John joined them. He squatted down in front of Ma. "We didn' get nowheres," he said. "Jus' run aroun'. Say, Al wants to see ya. Says he got to git a tire. Only one layer a cloth lef', he says."

Pa stood up. "I hope he can git her cheap. We ain't got much lef'. Where is Al?"

"Down there, to the nex' cross-street an' turn right. Says gonna blow out an' spoil a tube if we don' get a new one." Pa strolled away, and his eyes followed the giant V of ducks down the sky.

Uncle John picked a stone from the ground and dropped

it from his palm and picked it up again. He did not look at Ma. "They ain't no work," he said.

"You didn' look all over," Ma said.

"No, but they's signs out."

"Well, Tom musta got work. He ain't been back."

Uncle John suggested, "Maybe he went away—like Connie, or like Noah."

Ma glanced sharply at him, and then her eyes softened. "They's things you know," she said. "They's stuff you're sure of. Tom's got work, an' he'll come in this evenin'. That's true." She smiled in satisfaction. "Ain't he a fine boy!" she said. "Ain't he a good boy!"

The cars and trucks began to come into the camp, and the men trooped by toward the sanitary unit. And each man carried clean overalls and shirt in his hand.

Ma pulled herself together. "John, you go find Pa. Get to the store. I want beans an' sugar an'—a piece of fryin' meat an' carrots an'—tell Pa to get somepin nice—anything—but nice—for tonight. Tonight—we'll have—somepin nice."

Chapter Twenty-Three

THE migrant people, scuttling for work, scrabbling to live, looked always for pleasure, dug for pleasure, manufactured pleasure, and they were hungry for amusement. Sometimes amusement lay in speech, and they climbed up their lives with jokes. And it came about in the camps along the roads, on the ditch banks beside the streams, under the sycamores, that the story teller grew into being, so that the people gathered in the low firelight to hear the gifted ones. And they listened while the tales were told, and their participation made the stories great.

I was a recruit against Geronimo——

And the people listened, and their quiet eyes reflected the dying fire.

Them Injuns was cute—slick as snakes, an' quiet when they wanted. Could go through dry leaves, an' make no rustle. Try to do that sometime.

And the people listened and remembered the crash of dry leaves under their feet.

Come the change of season an' the clouds up. Wrong time. Ever hear of the army doing anything right? Give the army ten chances, an' they'll stumble along. Took three regiments to kill a hundred braves—always.

And the people listened, and their faces were quiet with listening. The story tellers, gathering attention into their

444

tales, spoke in great rhythms, spoke in great words because the tales were great, and the listeners became great through them.

They was a brave on a ridge, against the sun. Knowed he stood out. Spread his arms an' stood. Naked as morning, an' against the sun. Maybe he was crazy. I don' know. Stood there, arms spread out; like a cross he looked. Four hunderd yards. An' the men—well, they raised their sights an' they felt the wind with their fingers; an' then they jus' lay there an' couldn' shoot. Maybe that Injun knowed somepin. Knowed we couldn' shoot. Jes' laid there with the rifles cocked, an' didn' even put 'em to our shoulders. Lookin' at him. Head-band, one feather. Could see it, an' naked as the sun. Long time we laid there an' looked, an' he never moved. An' then the captain got mad. "Shoot, you crazy bastards, shoot!" he yells. An' we jus' laid there. "I'll give you to a five-count, an' then mark you down," the captain says. Well, sir—we put up our rifles slow, an' ever' man hoped somebody'd shoot first. I ain't never been so sad in my life. An' I laid my sights on his belly, 'cause you can't stop a Injun no other place—an'—then. Well, he jest plunked down an' rolled. An' we went up. An' he wasn' big—he'd looked so grand—up there. All tore to pieces an' little. Ever see a cock pheasant, stiff and beautiful, ever' feather drawed an' painted, an' even his eyes drawed in pretty? An' bang! You pick him up—bloody an' twisted, an' you spoiled somepin better'n you; an' eatin' him don't never make it up to you, 'cause you spoiled somepin in yaself, an' you can't never fix it up.

And the people nodded, and perhaps the fire spurted a little light and showed their eyes looking in on themselves.

Against the sun, with his arms out. An' he looked big—as God.

And perhaps a man balanced twenty cents between food and pleasure, and he went to a movie in Marysville or Tulare, in Ceres or Mountain View. And he came back to the ditch camp with his memory crowded. And he told how it was:

They was this rich fella, an' he makes like he's poor, an' they's this rich girl, an' she purtends like she's poor too, an' they meet in a hamburg' stan'.

Why?

I don't know why—that's how it was.

Why'd they purtend like they's poor?

Well, they're tired of bein' rich.

Horseshit!

You want to hear this, or not?

Well, go on then. Sure, I wanta hear it, but if I was rich, if I was rich I'd git so many pork chops—I'd cord 'em up aroun' me like wood, an' I'd eat my way out. Go on.

Well, they each think the other one's poor. An' they git arrested an' they git in jail, an' they don' git out 'cause the other one'd find out the first one is rich. An' the jail keeper, he's mean to 'em 'cause he thinks they're poor. Oughta see how he looks when he finds out. Jes' nearly faints, that's all.

What they git in jail for?

Well, they git caught at some kind a radical meetin' but they ain't radicals. They jes' happen to be there. An' they don't each one wanta marry fur money, ya see.

So the sons-of-bitches start lyin' to each other right off.

Well, in the pitcher it was like they was doin' good. They're nice to people, you see.

I was to a show oncet that was me, an' more'n me; an' my life, an' more'n my life, so ever'thing was bigger.

Well, I git enough sorrow. I like to git away from it.

Sure—if you can believe it.

So they got married, an' then they foun' out, an' all them people that's treated 'em mean. They was a fella had been uppity, an' he nearly fainted when this fella come in with a plug hat on. Jes' nearly fainted. An' they was a newsreel with them German soldiers kickin' up their feet—funny as hell.

And always, if he had a little money, a man could get drunk. The hard edges gone, and the warmth. Then there was no loneliness, for a man could people his brain with friends, and he could find his enemies and destroy them. Sitting in a ditch, the earth grew soft under him. Failures dulled and the future was no threat. And hunger did not skulk about, but the world was soft and easy, and a man could reach the place he started for. The stars came down wonderfully close and the sky was soft. Death was a friend, and sleep was death's brother. The old times came back—a girl with pretty feet, who danced one time at home—a horse—a long time ago. A horse and a saddle. And the leather was carved. When was that? Ought to find a girl to talk to. That's nice. Might lay with her, too. But warm here. And the stars down so close, and sadness and pleasure so close together, really the same thing. Like to stay drunk all the time. Who says it's bad? Who dares to say it's bad? Preachers—but they got their own kinda drunkenness. Thin, barren women, but they're too miserable to know. Reformers—but they don't bite deep enough into living to know. No—the stars are close and dear and I have joined the brotherhood of the worlds. And everything's holy—everything, even me.

A harmonica is easy to carry. Take it out of your hip pocket, knock it against your palm to shake out the dirt and pocket fuzz and bits of tobacco. Now it's ready. You can do anything with a harmonica: thin reedy single tone, or chords, or melody with rhythm chords. You can mold the music with curved hands, making it wail and cry like bagpipes, making it full and round like an organ, making it as sharp and bitter as the reed pipes of the hills. And you can play and put it back in your pocket. It is always with you, always in your pocket. And as you play, you learn new tricks, new ways to mold the tone with your hands, to pinch the tone with your lips, and no one teaches you. You feel around—sometimes alone in the shade at noon, sometimes in the tent door after supper when the women are washing up. Your foot taps gently on the ground. Your eyebrows rise and fall in rhythm. And if you lose it or break it, why, it's no great loss. You can buy another for a quarter.

A guitar is more precious. Must learn this thing. Fingers of the left hand must have callus caps. Thumb of the right hand a horn of callus. Stretch the left-hand fingers, stretch them like a spider's legs to get the hard pads on the frets.

This was my father's box. Wasn't no bigger'n a bug first time he give me C chord. An' when I learned as good as him, he hardly never played no more. Used to set in the door, an' listen an' tap his foot. I'm tryin' for a break, an' he'd scowl mean till I get her, an' then he'd settle back easy, an' he'd nod. "Play," he'd say. "Play nice." It's a good box. See how the head is wore. They's many a million songs wore down that wood an' scooped her out. Some day she'll cave in like a egg. But you can't patch her nor worry her no way or she'll lose tone. Play her in the evening, an' they's a harmonica player in the nex' tent. Makes it pretty nice together.

The fiddle is rare, hard to learn. No frets, no teacher.

Jes' listen to a ol' man an' try to pick it up. Won't tell how

to double. Says it's a secret. But I watched. Here's how he
done it.

Shrill as a wind, the fiddle, quick and nervous and shrill.
She ain't much of a fiddle. Give two dollars for her. Fella
says they's fiddles four hundred years old, and they git mel-
low like whisky. Says they'll cost fifty-sixty thousan' dollars.
I don't know. Soun's like a lie. Harsh ol' bastard, ain't she?
Wanta dance? I'll rub up the bow with plenty rosin. Man!
Then she'll squawk. Hear her a mile.

These three in the evening, harmonica and fiddle and
guitar. Playing a reel and tapping out the tune, and the big
deep strings of the guitar beating like a heart, and the harmonica's sharp chords and the skirl and squeal of the fiddle.
People have to move close. They can't help it. "Chicken
Reel" now, and the feet tap and a young lean buck takes
three quick steps, and his arms hang limp. The square closes
up and the dancing starts, feet on the bare ground, beating
dull, strike with your heels. Hands 'round and swing. Hair
falls down, and panting breaths. Lean to the side now.

Look at that Texas boy, long legs loose, taps four times for
ever' damn step. Never seen a boy swing aroun' like that.
Look at him swing that Cherokee girl, red in her cheeks an'
her toe points out. Look at her pant, look at her heave. Think
she's tired? Think she's winded? Well, she ain't. Texas boy
got his hair in his eyes, mouth's wide open, can't get air, but
he pats four times for ever' darn step, an' he'll keep a-going'
with the Cherokee girl.

The fiddle squeaks and the guitar bongs. Mouth-organ
man is red in the face. Texas boy and the Cherokee girl,
pantin' like dogs an' a-beatin' the groun'. Ol' folks stan'
a-pattin' their han's. Smilin' a little, tappin' their feet.

Back home—in the schoolhouse, it was. The big moon sailed off to the westward. An' we walked, him an' me—a little ways. Didn' talk 'cause our throats was choked up. Didn' talk none at all. An' purty soon they was a haycock. Went right to it and laid down there. Seein' the Texas boy an' that girl a-steppin' away into the dark—think nobody seen 'em go. Oh, God! I wisht I was a-goin' with that Texas boy. Moon'll be up 'fore long. I seen that girl's ol' man move out to stop 'em, an' then he didn'. He knowed. Might as well stop the fall from comin', and might as well stop the sap from movin' in the trees. An' the moon'll be up 'fore long.

Play more—play the story songs—"As I Walked through the Streets of Laredo."

The fire's gone down. Be a shame to build her up. Little ol' moon'll be up 'fore long.

Beside an irrigation ditch a preacher labored and the people cried. And the preacher paced like a tiger, whipping the people with his voice, and they groveled and whined on the ground. He calculated them, gauged them, played on them, and when they were all squirming on the ground he stooped down and of his great strength he picked each one up in his arms and shouted, Take 'em, Christ! and threw each one in the water. And when they were all in, waist deep in the water, and looking with frightened eyes at the master, he knelt down on the bank and he prayed for them; and he prayed that all men and women might grovel and whine on the ground. Men and women, dripping, clothes sticking tight, watched; then gurgling and sloshing in their shoes they walked back to the camp, to the tents, and they talked softly in wonder:

We been saved, they said. We're washed white as snow. We won't never sin again.

And the children, frightened and wet, whispered together: We been saved. We won't sin no more.

Wisht I knowed what all the sins was, so I could do 'em.

The migrant people looked humbly for pleasure on the roads.

Chapter Twenty-Four

ON SATURDAY morning the wash tubs were crowded. The women washed dresses, pink ginghams and flowered cottons, and they hung them in the sun and stretched the cloth to smooth it. When afternoon came the whole camp quickened and the people grew excited. The children caught the fever and were more noisy than usual. About mid-afternoon child bathing began, and as each child was caught, subdued, and washed, the noise on the playground gradually subsided. Before five, the children were scrubbed and warned about getting dirty again; and they walked about, stiff in clean clothes, miserable with carefulness.

At the big open-air dance platform a committee was busy. Every bit of electric wire had been requisitioned. The city dump had been visited for wire, every tool box had contributed friction tape. And now the patched, spliced wire was strung out to the dance floor, with bottle necks as insulators. This night the floor would be lighted for the first time. By six o'clock the men were back from work or from looking for work, and a new wave of bathing started. By seven, dinners were over, men had on their best clothes: freshly washed overalls, clean blue shirts, sometimes the decent blacks. The girls were ready in their print dresses, stretched and clean, their hair braided and ribboned. The worried women watched the families and cleaned up the evening dishes. On the platform the string band practiced, surrounded by a double wall of children. The people were intent and excited.

In the tent of Ezra Huston, chairman, the Central Committee of five men went into meeting. Huston, a tall spare man, wind-blackened, with eyes like little blades, spoke to his committee, one man from each sanitary unit.

"It's goddamn lucky we got the word they was gonna try to bust up the dance!" he said.

The tubby little representative from Unit Three spoke up. "I think we oughta squash the hell out of 'em, an' show 'em."

"No," said Huston. "That's what they want. No, sir. If they can git a fight goin', then they can run in the cops an' say we ain't orderly. They tried it before—other places." He turned to the sad dark boy from Unit Two. "Got the fellas together to go roun' the fences an' see nobody sneaks in?"

The sad boy nodded. "Yeah! Twelve. Tol' 'em not to hit nobody. Jes' push 'em out ag'in."

Huston said, "Will you go out an' find Willie Eaton? He's chairman a the entertainment, ain't he?"

"Yeah."

"Well, tell 'im we wanta see 'im."

The boy went out, and he returned in a moment with a stringy Texas man. Willie Eaton had a long fragile jaw and dust-colored hair. His arms and legs were long and loose, and he had the gray sunburned eyes of the Panhandle. He stood in the tent, grinning, and his hands pivoted restlessly on his wrists.

Huston said, "You heard about tonight?"

Willie grinned. "Yeah!"

"Did anything 'bout it?"

"Yeah!"

"Tell what you done."

Willie Eaton grinned happily. "Well, sir, ordinary ent'-tainment committee is five. I got twenty more—all good strong boys. They're a-gonna be a-dancin' an' a-keepin' their eyes open an' their ears open. First sign—any talk or argament, they close in tight. Worked her out purty nice. Can't even see nothing. Kinda move out, an' the fella will go out with 'em."

"Tell 'em they ain't to hurt the fellas."

Willie laughed gleefully. "I tol' 'em," he said.

"Well, tell 'em so they know."

"They know. Got five men out to the gate lookin' over the folks that comes in. Try to spot 'em 'fore they git started."

Huston stood up. His steel-colored eyes were stern. "Now you look here, Willie. We don't want them fellas hurt. They's gonna be deputies out by the front gate. If you blood 'em up, why—them deputies'll git you."

"Got that there figgered out," said Willie. "Take 'em out the back way, into the fiel'. Some a the boys'll see they git on their way."

"Well, it soun's awright," Huston said worriedly. "But don't you let nothing happen, Willie. You're responsible. Don' you hurt them fellas. Don' you use no stick nor no knife or arn, or nothing like that."

"No, sir," said Willie. "We won't mark 'em."

Huston was suspicious. "I wisht I knowed I could trus' you, Willie. If you got to sock 'em, sock 'em where they won't bleed."

"Yes, sir!" said Willie.

"You sure of the fellas you picked?"

"Yes, sir."

"Awright. An' if she gits outa han', I'll be in the right-han' corner, this way on the dance floor."

Willie saluted in mockery and went out.

Huston said, "I dunno. I jes' hope Willie's boys don't kill nobody. What the hell the deputies want to hurt the camp for? Why can't they let us be?"

The sad boy from Unit Two said, "I lived out at Sunlan' Lan' an' Cattle Company's place. Honest to God, they got a cop for ever' ten people. Got one water faucet for 'bout two hundred people."

The tubby man said, "Jesus, God, Jeremy. You ain't got to tell me. I was there. They got a block of shacks—thirty-five of 'em in a row, an' fifteen deep. An' they got ten crappers for the whole shebang. An', Christ, you could smell 'em a mile. One of them deputies give me the lowdown. We was settin' aroun', an' he says, 'Them goddamn gov'ment camps,' he says. 'Give people hot water, an' they gonna want hot water. Give 'em flush toilets, an' they gonna want 'em.' He says, 'You give them goddamn Okies stuff like that an' they'll want 'em.' An' he says, 'They hol' red meetin's in them gov'-ment camps. All figgerin' how to git on relief,' he says."

Huston asked, "Didn' nobody sock him?"

"No. They was a little fella, an' he says, 'What you mean, relief?'

" 'I mean relief—what us taxpayers puts in an' you god-damn Okies takes out.'

" 'We pay sales tax an' gas tax an' tobacco tax,' this little guy says. An' he says, 'Farmers get four cents a cotton poun' from the gov'ment—ain't that relief?' An' he says, 'Railroads an' shippin' companies draws subsidies—ain't that relief?'

" 'They're doin' stuff got to be done,' this deputy says.

" 'Well,' the little guy says, 'how'd your goddamn crops

get picked if it wasn't for us?'" The tubby man looked around.

"What'd the deputy say?" Huston asked.

"Well, the deputy got mad. An' he says, 'You goddamn reds is all the time stirrin' up trouble,' he says. 'You better come along with me.' So he takes this little guy in, an' they give him sixty days in jail for vagrancy."

"How'd they do that if he had a job?" asked Timothy Wallace.

The tubby man laughed. "You know better'n that," he said. "You know a vagrant is anybody a cop don't like. An' that's why they hate this here camp. No cops can get in. This here's United States, not California."

Huston sighed. "Wisht we could stay here. Got to be goin' 'fore long. I like this here. Folks gits along nice; an', God Awmighty, why can't they let us do it 'stead of keepin' us miserable an' puttin' us in jail? I swear to God they gonna push us into fightin' if they don't quit a-worryin' us." Then he calmed his voice. "We jes' got to keep peaceful," he reminded himself. "The committee got no right to fly off'n the handle."

The tubby man from Unit Three said, "Anybody that thinks this committee got all cheese an' crackers ought to jes' try her. They was a fight in my unit today—women. Got to callin' names, an' then got to throwin' garbage. Ladies' Committee couldn' handle it, an' they come to me. Want me to bring the fight in this here committee. I tol' 'em they got to handle women trouble theirselves. This here committee ain't gonna mess with no garbage fights."

Huston nodded. "You done good," he said.

And now the dusk was falling, and as the darkness deep-

ened the practicing of the string band seemed to grow
louder. The lights flashed on and two men inspected the
patched wire to the dance floor. The children crowded
thickly about the musicians. A boy with a guitar sang the
"Down Home Blues," chording delicately for himself, and
on his second chorus three harmonicas and a fiddle
joined him. From the tents the people streamed toward the
platform, men in their clean blue denim and women in their
ginghams. They came near to the platform and then stood
quietly waiting, their faces bright and intent under the light.

Around the reservation there was a high wire fence, and
along the fence, at intervals of fifty feet, the guards sat in the
grass and waited.

Now the cars of the guests began to arrive, small farmers
and their families, migrants from other camps. And as each
guest came through the gate he mentioned the name of the
camper who had invited him.

The string band took a reel tune up and played loudly, for
they were not practicing any more. In front of their tents the
Jesus-lovers sat and watched, their faces hard and contemptuous. They did not speak to one another, they watched
for sin, and their faces condemned the whole proceeding.

At the Joad tent Ruthie and Winfield had bolted what little dinner they had, and then they started for the platform.
Ma called them back, held up their faces with a hand under
each chin, and looked into their nostrils, pulled their ears and
looked inside, and sent them to the sanitary unit to wash their
hands once more. They dodged around the back of the
building and bolted for the platform, to stand among the
children, close-packed about the band.

Al finished his dinner and spent half an hour shaving with

Tom's razor. Al had a tight-fitting wool suit and a striped shirt, and he bathed and washed and combed his straight hair back. And when the washroom was vacant for a moment, he smiled engagingly at himself in the mirror, and he turned and tried to see himself in profile when he smiled. He slipped his purple arm-bands on and put on his tight coat. And he rubbed up his yellow shoes with a piece of toilet paper. A late bather came in, and Al hurried out and walked recklessly toward the platform, his eye peeled for girls. Near the dance floor he saw a pretty blond girl sitting in front of a tent. He sidled near and threw open his coat to show his shirt.

"Gonna dance tonight?" he asked.

The girl looked away and did not answer.

"Can't a fella pass a word with you? How 'bout you an' me dancin'?" And he said nonchalantly, "I can waltz."

The girl raised her eyes shyly, and she said, "That ain't nothin'—anybody can waltz."

"Not like me," said Al. The music surged, and he tapped one foot in time. "Come on," he said.

A very fat woman poked her head out of the tent and scowled at him. "You git along," she said fiercely. "This here girl's spoke for. She's a-gonna be married, an' her man's a-comin' for her."

Al winked rakishly at the girl, and he tripped on, striking his feet to the music and swaying his shoulders and swinging his arms. And the girl looked after him intently.

Pa put down his plate and stood up. "Come on, John," he said; and he explained to Ma, "We're a-gonna talk to some fellas about gettin' work." And Pa and Uncle John walked toward the manager's house.

Tom worked a piece of store bread into the stew gravy on

his plate and ate the bread. He handed his plate to Ma, and she put it in the bucket of hot water and washed it and handed it to Rose of Sharon to wipe. "Ain't you goin' to the dance?" Ma asked.

"Sure," said Tom. "I'm on a committee. We're gonna entertain some fellas."

"Already on a committee?" Ma said. "I guess it's 'cause you got work."

Rose of Sharon turned to put the dish away. Tom pointed at her. "My God, she's a-gettin' big," he said.

Rose of Sharon blushed and took another dish from Ma. "Sure she is," Ma said.

"An' she's gettin' prettier," said Tom.

The girl blushed more deeply and hung her head. "You stop it," she said, softly.

" 'Course she is," said Ma. "Girl with a baby always gets prettier."

Tom laughed. "If she keeps a-swellin' like this, she gonna need a wheelbarra to carry it."

"Now you stop," Rose of Sharon said, and she went inside the tent, out of sight.

Ma chuckled, "You shouldn' ought to worry her."

"She likes it," said Tom.

"I know she likes it, but it worries her, too. And she's a-mournin' for Connie."

"Well, she might's well give him up. He's prob'ly studyin' to be President of the United States by now."

"Don't worry her," Ma said. "She ain't got no easy row to hoe."

Willie Eaton moved near, and he grinned and said, "You Tom Joad?"

"Yeah."

"Well, I'm Chairman the Entertainment Committee. We gonna need you. Fella tol' me 'bout you."

"Sure, I'll play with you," said Tom. "This here's Ma."

"Howdy," said Willie.

"Glad to meet ya."

Willie said, "Gonna put you on the gate to start, an' then on the floor. Want ya to look over the guys when they come in, an' try to spot 'em. You'll be with another fella. Then later I want ya to dance an' watch."

"Yeah! I can do that awright," said Tom.

Ma said apprehensively, "They ain't no trouble?"

"No, ma'am," Willie said. "They ain't gonna be no trouble."

"None at all," said Tom. "Well, I'll come 'long. See you at the dance, Ma." The two young men walked quickly away toward the main gate.

Ma piled the washed dishes on a box. "Come on out," she called, and when there was no answer, "Rosasharn, you come out."

The girl stepped from the tent, and she went on with the dish-wiping.

"Tom was on'y jollyin' ya."

"I know. I didn't mind; on'y I hate to have folks look at me."

"Ain't no way to he'p that. Folks gonna look. But it makes folks happy to see a girl in a fambly way—makes folks sort of giggly an' happy. Ain't you a-goin' to the dance?"

"I was—but I don' know. I wisht Connie was here." Her voice rose. "Ma, I wisht he was here. I can't hardly stan' it."

Ma looked closely at her. "I know," she said. "But, Rosasharn—don' shame your folks."

"I don' aim to, Ma."

"Well, don't you shame us. We got too much on us now, without no shame."

The girl's lip quivered. "I—I ain' goin' to the dance. I couldn'—Ma—he'p me!" She sat down and buried her head in her arms.

Ma wiped her hands on the dish towel and she squatted down in front of her daughter, and she put her two hands on Rose of Sharon's hair. "You're a good girl," she said. "You always was a good girl. I'll take care a you. Don't you fret." She put an interest in her tone. "Know what you an' me's gonna do? We're a-goin' to that dance, an' we're a-gonna set there an' watch. If anybody says to come dance—why, I'll say you ain't strong enough. I'll say you're poorly. An' you can hear the music an' all like that."

Rose of Sharon raised her head. "You won't let me dance?"

"No, I won't."

"An' don' let nobody touch me."

"No, I won't."

The girl sighed. She said desperately, "I don' know what I'm a-gonna do, Ma. I jus' don' know. I don' know."

Ma patted her knee. "Look," she said. "Look here at me. I'm a-gonna tell ya. In a little while it ain't gonna be so bad. In a little while. An' that's true. Now come on. We'll go get washed up, an' we'll put on our nice dress an' we'll set by the dance." She led Rose of Sharon toward the sanitary unit.

Pa and Uncle John squatted with a group of men by the porch of the office. "We nearly got work today," Pa said. "We was jus' a few minutes late. They awready got two fellas. An', well, sir, it was a funny thing. They's a straw boss there, an' he says, 'We jus' got some two-bit men. 'Course we could use twenty-cent men. We can use a lot a twenty-cent men. You go to your camp an' say we'll put a lot a fellas on for twenty cents.' "

The squatting men moved nervously. A broad-shouldered man, his face completely in the shadow of a black hat, spatted his knee with his palm. "I know it, goddamn it!" he cried. "An' they'll git men. They'll git hungry men. You can't feed your fam'ly on twenty cents an hour, but you'll take anything. They got you goin' an' comin'. They jes' auction a job off. Jesus Christ, pretty soon they're gonna make us pay to work."

"We would of took her," Pa said. "We ain't had no job. We sure would a took her, but they was them guys in there, an' the way they looked, we was scairt to take her."

Black Hat said, "Get crazy thinkin'! I been workin' for a fella, an' he can't pick his crop. Cost more jes' to pick her than he can git for her, an' he don' know what to do."

"Seems to me—" Pa stopped. The circle was silent for him. "Well—I jus' thought, if a fella had a acre. Well, my woman she could raise a little truck an' a couple pigs an' some chickens. An' us men could get out an' find work, an' then go back. Kids could maybe go to school. Never seen sech schools as out here."

"Our kids ain't happy in them schools," Black Hat said.

"Why not? They're pretty nice, them schools."

"Well, a raggedy kid with no shoes, an' them other kids with socks on, an' nice pants, an' them a-yellin' 'Okie.' My boy went to school. Had a fight evr' day. Done good, too. Tough little bastard. Ever' day he got to fight. Come home with his clothes tore an' his nose bloody. An' his ma'd whale him. Made her stop that. No need ever'body beatin' the hell outa him, poor little fella. Jesus! He give some a them kids a goin'-over, though—them nice-pants sons-a-bitches. I dunno. I dunno."

Pa demanded, "Well, what the hell am I gonna do? We're outa money. One of my boys got a short job, but that won't feed us. I'm a-gonna go an' take twenty cents. I got to."

Black Hat raised his head, and his bristled chin showed in the light, and his stringy neck where the whiskers lay flat like fur. "Yeah!" he said bitterly. "You'll do that. An' I'm a two-bit man. You'll take my job for twenty cents. An' then I'll git hungry an' I'll take my job back for fifteen. Yeah! You go right on an' do her."

"Well, what the hell can I do?" Pa demanded. "I can't starve so's you can get two bits."

Black Hat dipped his head again, and his chin went into the shadow. "I dunno," he said. "I jes' dunno. It's bad enough to work twelve hours a day an' come out jes' a little bit hungry, but we got to figure all a time, too. My kid ain't gettin' enough to eat. I can't think all the time, goddamn it! It drives a man crazy." The circle of men shifted their feet nervously.

Tom stood at the gate and watched the people coming in to the dance. A floodlight shone down into their faces. Willie Eaton said, "Jes' keep your eyes open. I'm sendin' Jule Vitela over. He's half Cherokee. Nice fella. Keep your eyes open. An' see if you can pick out the ones."

"O.K.," said Tom. He watched the farm families come in, the girls with braided hair and the boys polished for the dance. Jule came and stood beside him.

"I'm with you," he said.

Tom looked at the hawk nose and the high brown cheek bones and the slender receding chin. "They says you're half Injun. You look all Injun to me."

"No," said Jule. "Jes' half. Wisht I was a full-blood. I'd have my lan' on the reservation. Them full-bloods got it pretty nice, some of 'em."

"Look a them people," Tom said.

The guests were moving in through the gateway, families from the farms, migrants from the ditch camps. Children straining to be free and quiet parents holding them back.

Jule said, "These here dances done funny things. Our people got nothing, but jes' because they can ast their frien's to come here to the dance, sets 'em up an' makes 'em proud. An' the folks respects 'em 'count of these here dances. Fella got a little place where I was a-workin'. He come to a dance here. I ast him myself, an' he come. Says we got the only decent dance in the county, where a man can take his girls an' his wife. Hey! Look."

Three young men were coming through the gate—young working men in jeans. They walked close together. The guard at the gate questioned them, and they answered and passed through.

"Look at 'em careful," Jule said. He moved to the guard. "Who ast them three?" he asked.

"Fella named Jackson, Unit Four."

Jule came back to Tom. "I think them's our fellas."

"How ya know?"

"I dunno how. Jes' got a feelin'. They're kinda scared. Foller 'em an' tell Willie to look 'em over, an' tell Willie to check with Jackson, Unit Four. Get him to see if they're all right. I'll stay here."

Tom strolled after the three young men. They moved toward the dance floor and took their positions quietly on the edge of the crowd. Tom saw Willie near the band and signaled him.

"What cha want?" Willie asked.

"Them three—see—there?"

"Yeah."

"They say a fella name' Jackson, Unit Four, ast 'em."

Willie craned his neck and saw Huston and called him over. "Them three fellas," he said. "We better get Jackson, Unit Four, an' see if he ast 'em."

Huston turned on his heel and walked away; and in a few moments he was back with a lean and bony Kansan. "This here's Jackson," Huston said. "Look, Jackson, see them three young fellas—?"

"Yeah."

"Well, did you ast 'em?"

"No."

"Ever see 'em before?"

Jackson peered at them. "Sure. Worked at Gregorio's with 'em."

"So they knowed your name."

"Sure. I worked right beside 'em."

"Awright," Huston said. "Don't you go near 'em. We ain't gonna th'ow 'em out if they're nice. Thanks, Mr. Jackson."

"Good work," he said to Tom. "I guess them's the fellas."

"Jule picked 'em out," said Tom.

"Hell, no wonder," said Willie. "His Injun blood smelled 'em. Well, I'll point 'em out to the boys."

A sixteen-year-old boy came running through the crowd. He stopped, panting, in front of Huston. "Mista Huston," he said. "I been like you said. They's a car with six men parked down by the euc'lyptus trees, an' they's one with four men up that north-side road. I ast 'em for a match. They got guns. I seen 'em."

Huston's eyes grew hard and cruel. "Willie," he said, "you sure you got ever'thing ready?"

Willie grinned happily. "Sure have, Mr. Huston. Ain't gonna be no trouble."

"Well, don't hurt 'em. 'Member now. If you kin, quiet an' nice, I kinda like to see 'em. Be in my tent."

"I'll see what we kin do," said Willie.

Dancing had not formally started, but now Willie climbed onto the platform. "Choose up your squares," he called. The music stopped. Boys and girls, young men and women, ran about until eight squares were ready on the big floor, ready and waiting. The girls held their hands in front of them and squirmed their fingers. The boys tapped their feet restlessly. Around the floor the old folks sat, smiling slightly, holding the children back from the floor. And in the distance the Jesus-lovers sat with hard condemning faces and watched the sin.

Ma and Rose of Sharon sat on a bench and watched. And as each boy asked Rose of Sharon as partner, Ma said, "No, she ain't well." And Rose of Sharon blushed and her eyes were bright.

The caller stepped to the middle of the floor and held up his hands. "All ready? Then let her go!"

The music snarled out "Chicken Reel," shrill and clear, fiddle skirling, harmonicas nasal and sharp, and the guitars booming on the bass strings. The caller named the turns, the squares moved. And they danced forward and back, hands 'round, swing your lady. The caller, in a frenzy, tapped his feet, strutted back and forth, went through the figures as he called them.

"Swing your ladies an' a dol ce do. Join han's roun' an'

away we go." The music rose and fell, and the moving shoes beating in time on the platform sounded like drums. "Swing to the right an' a swing to lef'; break, now—break—back to—back," the caller sang the high vibrant monotone. Now the girls' hair lost the careful combing. Now perspiration stood out on the foreheads of the boys. Now the experts showed the tricky inter-steps. And the old people on the edge of the floor took up the rhythm, patted their hands softly, and tapped their feet; and they smiled gently and then caught one another's eyes and nodded.

Ma leaned her head close to Rose of Sharon's ear. "Maybe you wouldn' think it, but your Pa was as nice a dancer as I ever seen, when he was young." And Ma smiled. "Makes me think of ol' times," she said. And on the faces of the watchers the smiles were of old times.

"Up near Muskogee twenty years ago, they was a blin' man with a fiddle——"

"I seen a fella oncet could slap his heels four times in one jump."

"Swedes up in Dakota—know what they do sometimes? Put pepper on the floor. Gits up the ladies' skirts an' makes 'em purty lively—lively as a filly in season. Swedes do that sometimes."

In the distance, the Jesus-lovers watched their restive children. "Look on sin," they said. "Them folks is ridin' to hell on a poker. It's a shame the godly got to see it." And their children were silent and nervous.

"One more roun' an' then a little res'," the caller chanted. "Hit her hard, 'cause we're gonna stop soon." And the girls were damp and flushed, and they danced with open mouths and serious reverent faces, and the boys flung back their long hair and pranced, pointed their toes, and clicked their heels. In and out the squares moved, crossing, backing, whirling, and the music shrilled.

Then suddenly it stopped. The dancers stood still, panting with fatigue. And the children broke from restraint, dashed on the floor, chased one another madly, ran, slid, stole caps, and pulled hair. The dancers sat down, fanning themselves with their hands. The members of the band got up and stretched themselves and sat down again. And the guitar players worked softly over their strings.

Now Willie called, "Choose again for another square, if you can." The dancers scrambled to their feet and new dancers plunged forward for partners. Tom stood near the three young men. He saw them force their way through, out on the floor, toward one of the forming squares. He waved his hand at Willie, and Willie spoke to the fiddler. The fiddler squawked his bow across the strings. Twenty young men lounged slowly across the floor. The three reached the square. And one of them said, "I'll dance with this here."

A blond boy looked up in astonishment. "She's my partner."

"Listen, you little son-of-a-bitch——"

Off in the darkness a shrill whistle sounded. The three were walled in now. And each one felt the grip of hands. And then the wall of men moved slowly off the platform.

Willie yelped, "Le's go!" The music shrilled out, the caller intoned the figures, the feet thudded on the platform.

A touring car drove to the entrance. The driver called, "Open up. We hear you got a riot."

The guard kept his position. "We got no riot. Listen to that music. Who are you?"

"Deputy sheriffs."

"Got a warrant?"

"We don't need a warrant if there's a riot."

"Well, we got no riots here," said the gate guard.

The men in the car listened to the music and the sound of the caller, and then the car pulled slowly away and parked in a crossroad and waited.

In the moving squad each of the three young men was pinioned, and a hand was over each mouth. When they reached the darkness the group opened up.

Tom said, "That sure was did nice." He held both arms of his victim from behind.

Willie ran over to them from the dance floor. "Nice work," he said. "On'y need six now. Huston wants to see these here fellers."

Huston himself emerged from the darkness. "These the ones?"

"Sure," said Jule. "Went right up an' started it. But they didn' even swing once."

"Let's look at 'em." The prisoners were swung around to face him. Their heads were down. Huston put a flashlight beam in each sullen face. "What did you wanta do it for?" he asked. There was no answer. "Who the hell tol' you to do it?"

"Goddarn it, we didn' do nothing. We was jes' gonna dance."

"No, you wasn't," Jule said. "You was gonna sock that kid."

Tom said, "Mr. Huston, jus' when these here fellas moved in, somebody give a whistle."

"Yeah, I know! The cops come right to the gate." He turned back. "We ain't gonna hurt you. Now who tol' you to come bus' up our dance?" He waited for a reply. "You're our own folks," Huston said sadly. "You belong with us. How'd you happen to come? We know all about it," he added.

"Well, goddamn it, a fella got to eat."

"Well, who sent you? Who paid you to come?"

"We ain't been paid."

"An' you ain't gonna be. No fight, no pay. Ain't that right?"

One of the pinioned men said, "Do what you want. We ain't gonna tell nothing."

Huston's head sank down for a moment, and then he said softly, "O.K. Don't tell. But looka here. Don't knife your own folks. We're tryin' to get along, havin' fun an' keepin' order. Don't tear all that down. Jes' think about it. You're jes' harmin' yourself.

"Awright, boys, put 'em over the back fence. An' don't hurt 'em. They don't know what they're doin'."

The squad moved slowly toward the rear of the camp, and Huston looked after them.

Jule said, "Le's jes' take one good kick at 'em."

"No, you don't!" Willie cried. "I said we wouldn'."

"Jes' one nice little kick," Jule pleaded. "Jes' loft 'em over the fence."

"No, sir," Willie insisted.

"Listen, you," he said, "we're lettin' you off this time. But you take back the word. If'n ever this here happens again, we'll jes' natcherally kick the hell outa whoever comes; we'll bust ever' bone in their body. Now you tell your boys that. Huston says you're our kinda folks—maybe. I'd hate to think it."

They neared the fence. Two of the seated guards stood up

and moved over. "Got some fellas goin' home early," said Willie. The three men climbed over the fence and disappeared into the darkness.

And the squad moved quickly back toward the dance floor. And the music of "Ol' Dan Tucker" skirled and whined from the string band.

Over near the office the men still squatted and talked, and the shrill music came to them.

Pa said, "They's change a-comin'. I don' know what. Maybe we won't live to see her. But she's a-comin'. They's a res'less feelin'. Fella can't figger nothin' out, he's so nervous."

And Black Hat lifted his head up again, and the light fell on his bristly whiskers. He gathered some little rocks from the ground and shot them like marbles, with his thumb. "I don' know. She's a-comin' awright, like you say. Fella tol' me what happened in Akron, Ohio. Rubber companies. They got mountain people in 'cause they'd work cheap. An' these here mountain people up an' joined the union. Well, sir, hell jes' popped. All them storekeepers and legioners an' people like that, they get drillin' an' yellin', 'Red!' An' they're gonna run the union right outa Akron. Preachers git a-preachin' about it, an' papers a-yowlin', an' they's pick handles put out by the rubber companies, an' they're a-buyin' gas. Jesus, you'd think them mountain boys was reg'lar devils!" He stopped and found some more rocks to shoot. "Well, sir—it was las' March, an' one Sunday five thousan' of them mountain men had a turkey shoot outside a town. Five thousan' of 'em jes' marched through town with their rifles. An' they had their turkey shoot, an' then they marched back. An' that's all they done. Well, sir, they ain't been no trouble sence then. These here citizens committees give back the pick handles, an' the storekeepers keep their stores, an' nobody been clubbed nor tarred an' feathered, an' nobody been killed." There was a long silence, and then Black Hat said, "They're gettin' purty mean out here. Burned that camp an' beat up folks. I been thinkin'. All our folks got guns. I been thinkin' maybe we ought to git up a turkey shootin' club an' have meetin's ever' Sunday."

The men looked up at him, and then down at the ground, and their feet moved restlessly and they shifted their weight from one leg to the other.

Chapter Twenty-Five

THE spring is beautiful in California. Valleys in which the fruit blossoms are fragrant pink and white waters in a shallow sea. Then the first tendrils of the grapes, swelling from the old gnarled vines, cascade down to cover the trunks. The full green hills are round and soft as breasts. And on the level vegetable lands are the mile-long rows of pale green lettuce and the spindly little cauliflowers, the gray-green unearthly artichoke plants.

And then the leaves break out on the trees, and the petals drop from the fruit trees and carpet the earth with pink and white. The centers of the blossoms swell and grow and color: cherries and apples, peaches and pears, figs which close the flower in the fruit. All California quickens with produce, and the fruit grows heavy, and the limbs bend gradually under the fruit so that little crutches must be placed under them to support the weight.

Behind the fruitfulness are men of understanding and knowledge and skill, men who experiment with seed, endlessly developing the techniques for greater crops of plants whose roots will resist the million enemies of the earth: the molds, the insects, the rusts, the blights. These men work carefully and endlessly to perfect the seed, the roots. And there are the men of chemistry who spray the trees against pests, who sulphur the grapes, who cut out disease and rots, mildews and sicknesses. Doctors of preventive medicine, men at the borders who look for fruit flies, for Japanese beetle, men who quarantine the sick trees and root them out and burn them, men of knowledge. The men who graft the young trees, the little vines, are the cleverest of all, for theirs is a surgeon's job, as tender and delicate; and these men must have surgeons' hands and surgeons' hearts to slit the bark, to place the grafts, to bind the wounds and cover them from the air. These are great men.

Along the rows, the cultivators move, tearing the spring grass and turning it under to make a fertile earth, breaking the ground to hold the water up near the surface, ridging the ground in little pools for the irrigation, destroying the weed roots that may drink the water away from the trees.

And all the time the fruit swells and the flowers break out in long clusters on the vines. And in the growing year the warmth grows and the leaves turn dark green. The prunes lengthen like little green bird's eggs, and the limbs sag down against the crutches under the weight. And the hard little pears take shape, and the beginning of the fuzz comes out on the peaches. Grape blossoms shed their tiny petals and the hard little beads become green buttons, and the buttons grow heavy. The men who work in the fields, the owners of the little orchards, watch and calculate. The year is heavy with produce. And men are proud, for of their knowledge they can make the year heavy. They have transformed the world with their knowledge. The short, lean wheat has been made big and productive. Little sour apples have grown large and sweet, and that old grape that grew among the trees and fed the birds its tiny fruit has mothered a thousand varieties, red and black, green and pale pink, purple and yellow; and each variety with its own flavor. The men who work in the experimental farms have made new fruits: nectarines and forty kinds of plums, walnuts with paper shells. And always they work, selecting, grafting, changing, driving themselves, driving the earth to produce.

And first the cherries ripen. Cent and a half a pound. Hell, we can't pick 'em for that. Black cherries and red cherries, full and sweet, and the birds eat half of each cherry and the yellowjackets buzz into the holes the birds made. And on the ground the seeds drop and dry with black shreds hanging from them.

The purple prunes soften and sweeten. My God, we can't pick them and dry and sulphur them. We can't pay wages, no matter what wages. And the purple prunes carpet the ground. And first the skins wrinkle a little and swarms of flies come to feast, and the valley is filled with the odor of sweet decay. The meat turns dark and the crop shrivels on the ground.

And the pears grow yellow and soft. Five dollars a ton. Five dollars for forty fifty-pound boxes; trees pruned and sprayed, orchards cultivated—pick the fruit, put it in boxes, load the trucks, deliver the fruit to the cannery—forty boxes for five dollars. We can't do it. And the yellow fruit falls heavily to the ground and splashes on the ground. The yellowjackets dig into the soft meat, and there is a smell of ferment and rot.

Then the grapes—we can't make good wine. People can't buy good wine. Rip the grapes from the vines, good grapes, rotten grapes, wasp-stung grapes. Press stems, press dirt and rot.

But there's mildew and formic acid in the vats.

Add sulphur and tannic acid.

The smell from the ferment is not the rich odor of wine, but the smell of decay and chemicals.

Oh, well. It has alcohol in it, anyway. They can get drunk.

The little farmers watched debt creep up on them like the tide. They sprayed the trees and sold no crop, they pruned and grafted and could not pick the crop. And the men of knowledge have worked, have considered, and the fruit is rotting on the ground, and the decaying mash in the wine vats is poisoning the air. And taste the wine—no grape flavor at all, just sulphur and tannic acid and alcohol.

This little orchard will be a part of a great holding next year, for the debt will have choked the owner.

This vineyard will belong to the bank. Only the great owners can survive, for they own the canneries too. And four pears peeled and cut in half, cooked and canned, still cost fifteen cents. And the canned pears do not spoil. They will last for years.

The decay spreads over the State, and the sweet smell is a great sorrow on the land. Men who can graft the trees and make the seed fertile and big can find no way to let the hungry people eat their produce. Men who have created new fruits in the world cannot create a system whereby their fruits may be eaten. And the failure hangs over the State like a great sorrow.

The works of the roots of the vines, of the trees, must be destroyed to keep up the price, and this is the saddest, bitterest thing of all. Carloads of oranges dumped on the ground. The people came for miles to take the fruit, but this could not be. How would they buy oranges at twenty cents a dozen if they could drive out and pick them up? And men with hoses squirt kerosene on the oranges, and they are angry at the crime, angry at the people who have come to take the fruit. A million people hungry, needing the fruit—and kerosene sprayed over the golden mountains.

And the smell of rot fills the country.

Burn coffee for fuel in the ships. Burn corn to keep warm, it makes a hot fire. Dump potatoes in the rivers and place guards along the banks to keep the hungry people from fishing them out. Slaughter the pigs and bury them, and let the putrescence drip down into the earth.

There is a crime here that goes beyond denunciation. There is a sorrow here that weeping cannot symbolize. There is a failure here that topples all our success. The fertile earth, the straight tree rows, the sturdy trunks, and the ripe fruit. And children dying of pellagra must die because a profit cannot be taken from an orange. And coroners must fill in the certificates—died of malnutrition—because the food must rot, must be forced to rot.

The people come with nets to fish for potatoes in the river, and the guards hold them back; they come in rattling cars to get the dumped oranges, but the kerosene is sprayed. And they stand still and watch the potatoes float by, listen to the screaming pigs being killed in a ditch and covered with quicklime, watch the mountains of oranges slop down to a putrefying ooze; and in the eyes of the people there is the failure; and in the eyes of the hungry there is a growing wrath. In the souls of the people the grapes of wrath are filling and growing heavy, growing heavy for the vintage.

Chapter Twenty-Six

IN THE Weedpatch camp, on an evening when the long, barred clouds hung over the set sun and inflamed their edges, the Joad family lingered after their supper. Ma hesitated before she started to do the dishes.

"We got to do somepin," she said. And she pointed at Winfield. "Look at 'im," she said. And when they stared at the little boy, "He's a-jerkin' an' a-twistin' in his sleep. Lookut his color." The members of the family looked at the earth again in shame. "Fried dough," Ma said. "One month we been here. An' Tom had five days' work. An' the rest of you scrabblin' out ever' day, an' no work. An' scairt to talk. An' the money gone. You're scairt to talk it out. Ever' night you jus' eat, an' then you get wanderin' away. Can't bear to talk it out. Well, you got to. Rosasharn ain't far from due, an' lookut her color. You got to talk it out. Now don't none of you get up till we figger somepin out. One day' more grease an' two days' flour, an' ten potatoes. You set here an' get busy!"

They looked at the ground. Pa cleaned his thick nails with his pocket knife. Uncle John picked at a splinter on the box he sat on. Tom pinched his lower lip and pulled it away from his teeth.

He released his lip and said softly, "We been a-lookin', Ma. Been walkin' out sence we can't use the gas no more. Been goin' in ever' gate, walkin' up to ever' house, even when we knowed they wasn't gonna be nothin'. Puts a weight on ya. Goin' out lookin' for somepin you know you ain't gonna find."

Ma said fiercely, "You ain't got the right to get discouraged. This here fambly's goin' under. You jus' ain't got the right."

Pa inspected his scraped nail. "We gotta go," he said. "We didn' wanta go. It's nice here, an' folks is nice here. We're feared we'll have to go live in one a them Hoovervilles."

"Well, if we got to, we got to. First thing is, we got to eat."

Al broke in. "I got a tankful a gas in the truck. I didn' let nobody get into that."

Tom smiled. "This here Al got a lot of sense along with he's randy-pandy."

"Now you figger," Ma said. "I ain't watchin' this here fambly starve no more. One day' more grease. That's what we got. Come time for Rosasharn to lay in, she got to be fed up. You figger!"

"This here hot water an' toilets—" Pa began.

"Well, we can't eat no toilets."

Tom said, "They was a fella come by today lookin' for men to go to Marysville. Pickin' fruit."

"Well, why don' we go to Marysville?" Ma demanded.

"I dunno," said Tom. "Didn' seem right, somehow. He was so anxious. Wouldn' say how much the pay was. Said he didn' know exactly."

Ma said, "We're a-goin' to Marysville. I don' care what the pay is. We're a-goin'."

"It's too far," said Tom. "We ain't got the money for gasoline. We couldn' get there. Ma, you say we got to figger. I ain't done nothin' but figger the whole time."

Uncle John said, "Feller says they's cotton a-comin' in up north, near a place called Tulare. That ain't very far, the feller says."

"Well, we got to git goin', an' goin' quick. I ain't a-settin' here no longer, no matter how nice." Ma took up her bucket and walked toward the sanitary unit for hot water.

"Ma gets tough," Tom said. "I seen her a-gettin' mad quite a piece now. She jus' boils up."

Pa said with relief, "Well, she brang it into the open, anyways. I been layin' at night a-burnin' my brains up. Now we can talk her out, anyways."

Ma came back with her bucket of steaming water. "Well," she demanded, "figger anything out?"

"Jus' workin' her over," said Tom. "Now s'pose we jus' move up north where that cotton's at. We been over this here country. We know they ain't nothin' here. S'pose we pack up an' shove north. Then when the cotton's ready, we'll be there. I kinda like to get my han's aroun' some cotton. You got a full tank, Al?"

"Almos'—'bout two inches down."

"Should get us up to that place."

Ma poised a dish over the bucket. "Well?" she demanded.

Tom said, "You win. We'll move on, I guess. Huh, Pa?"

"Guess we got to," Pa said.

Ma glanced at him. "When?"

"Well—no need waitin'. Might's well go in the mornin'."

"We got to go in the mornin'. I tol' you what's lef'."

"Now, Ma, don' think I don' wanta go. I ain't had a good gutful to eat in two weeks. 'Course I filled up, but I didn' take no good from it."

Ma plunged the dish into the bucket. "We'll go in the mornin'," she said.

Pa sniffled. "Seems like times is changed," he said sarcastically. "Time was when a man said what we'd do. Seems like women is tellin' now. Seems like it's purty near time to get out a stick."

Ma put the clean dripping tin dish out on a box. She smiled down at her work. "You get your stick, Pa," she said. "Times when they's food an' a place to set, then maybe you can use your stick an' keep your skin whole. But you ain't a-doin' your job, either a-thinkin' or a-workin'. If you was, why, you could use your stick, an' women folks'd sniffle their nose an' creep-mouse aroun'. But you jus' get you a stick now an' you ain't lickin' no woman; you're a-fightin', 'cause I got a stick all laid out too."

Pa grinned with embarrassment. "Now it ain't good to have the little fellas hear you talkin' like that," he said.

"You get some bacon inside the little fellas 'fore you come tellin' what else is good for 'em," said Ma.

Pa got up in disgust and moved away, and Uncle John followed him.

Ma's hands were busy in the water, but she watched them go, and she said proudly to Tom, "He's all right. He ain't beat. He's like as not to take a smack at me."

Tom laughed. "You jus' a-treadin' him on?"

"Sure," said Ma. "Take a man, he can get worried an' worried, an' it eats out his liver, an' purty soon he'll jus' lay down and die with his heart et out. But if you can take an' make 'im mad, why, he'll be awright. Pa, he didn' say nothin', but he's mad now. He'll show me now. He's awright."

Al got up. "I'm gonna walk down the row," he said.

"Better see the truck's ready to go," Tom warned him.

"She's ready."

"If she ain't, I'll turn Ma on ya."

"She's ready." Al strolled jauntily along the row of tents.

Tom sighed. "I'm a-gettin' tired, Ma. How 'bout makin' me mad?"

"You got more sense, Tom. I don' need to make you mad. I got to lean on you. Them others—they're kinda strangers, all but you. You won't give up, Tom."

The job fell on him. "I don' like it," he said. "I wanta go out like Al. An' I wanta get mad like Pa, an' I wanta get drunk like Uncle John."

Ma shook her head. "You can't, Tom. I know. I knowed from the time you was a little fella. You can't. They's some folks that's just theirself an' nothin' more. There's Al—he's jus' a young fella after a girl. You wasn't never like that, Tom."

"Sure I was," said Tom. "Still am."

"No you ain't. Ever'thing you do is more'n you. When they sent you up to prison I knowed it. You're spoke for."

"Now, Ma—cut it out. It ain't true. It's all in your head."

She stacked the knives and forks on top of the plates. "Maybe. Maybe it's in my head. Rosasharn, you wipe up these here an' put 'em away."

The girl got breathlessly to her feet and her swollen middle hung out in front of her. She moved sluggishly to the box and picked up a washed dish.

Tom said, "Gettin' so tightful it's a-pullin' her eyes wide."

"Don't you go a-jollyin'," said Ma. "She's doin' good. You go 'long an' say goo'-by to anybody you wan'."

"O.K.," he said. "I'm gonna see how far it is up there."

Ma said to the girl, "He ain't sayin' stuff like that to make you feel bad. Where's Ruthie an' Winfiel'?"

"They snuck off after Pa. I seen 'em."

"Well, leave 'em go."

Rose of Sharon moved sluggishly about her work. Ma inspected her cautiously. "You feelin' pretty good? Your cheeks is kinda saggy."

"I ain't had milk like they said I ought."

"I know. We jus' didn' have no milk."

Rose of Sharon said dully, "Ef Connie hadn' went away, we'd a had a little house by now, with him studyin' an' all. Would a got milk like I need. Would a had a nice baby. This here baby ain't gonna be no good. I ought a had milk." She reached in her apron pocket and put something into her mouth.

Ma said, "I seen you nibblin' on somepin. What you eatin'?"

"Nothin'."

"Come on, what you nibblin' on?"

"Jus' a piece a slack lime. Foun' a big hunk."

"Why, tha's jus' like eatin' dirt."

"I kinda feel like I wan' it."

Ma was silent. She spread her knees and tightened her skirt. "I know," she said at last. "I et coal oncet when I was in a fambly way. Et a big piece a coal. Granma says I shouldn'. Don' you say that about the baby. You got no right even to think it."

"Got no husban'! Got no milk!"

Ma said, "If you was a well girl, I'd take a whang at you. Right in the face." She got up and went inside the tent. She came out and stood in front of Rose of Sharon, and she held out her hand. "Look!" The small gold earrings were in her hand. "These is for you."

The girl's eyes brightened for a moment, and then she looked aside. "I ain't pierced."

"Well, I'm a-gonna pierce ya." Ma hurried back into the

tent. She came back with a cardboard box. Hurriedly she threaded a needle, doubled the thread and tied a series of knots in it. She threaded a second needle and knotted the thread. In the box she found a piece of cork.

"It'll hurt. It'll hurt."

Ma stepped to her, put the cork in back of the ear lobe and pushed the needle through the ear, into the cork.

The girl twitched. "It sticks. It'll hurt."

"No more'n that."

"Yes, it will."

"Well, then. Le's see the other ear first." She placed the cork and pierced the other ear.

"It'll hurt."

"Hush!" said Ma. "It's all done."

Rose of Sharon looked at her in wonder. Ma clipped the needles off and pulled one knot of each thread through the lobes.

"Now," she said. "Ever' day we'll pull one knot, and in a couple weeks it'll be all well an' you can wear 'em. Here— they're your'n now. You can keep 'em."

Rose of Sharon touched her ears tenderly and looked at the tiny spots of blood on her fingers. "It didn' hurt. Jus' stuck a little."

"You oughta been pierced long ago," said Ma. She looked at the girl's face, and she smiled in triumph. "Now get them dishes all done up. Your baby gonna be a good baby. Very near let you have a baby without your ears was pierced. But you're safe now."

"Does it mean somepin?"

"Why, 'course it does," said Ma. " 'Course it does."

Al strolled down the street toward the dancing platform. Outside a neat little tent he whistled softly, and then moved along the street. He walked to the edge of the grounds and sat down in the grass.

The clouds over the west had lost the red edging now, and the cores were black. Al scratched his legs and looked toward the evening sky.

In a few moments a blond girl walked near; she was pretty and sharp-featured. She sat down in the grass beside him and did not speak. Al put his hand on her waist and walked his fingers around.

"Don't," she said. "You tickle."

"We're goin' away tomorra," said Al.

She looked at him, startled. "Tomorra? Where?"

"Up north," he said lightly.

"Well, we're gonna git married, ain't we?"

"Sure, sometime."

"You said purty soon!" she cried angrily.

"Well, soon is when soon comes."

"You promised." He walked his fingers around farther. "Git away," she cried. "You said we was."

"Well, sure we are."

"An' now you're goin' away."

Al demanded, "What's the matter with you? You in a fambly way?"

"No, I ain't."

Al laughed. "I jus' been wastin' my time, huh?"

Her chin shot out. She jumped to her feet. "You git away from me, Al Joad. I don' wanta see you no more."

"Aw, come on. What's the matter?"

"You think you're jus'—hell on wheels."

"Now wait a minute."

"You think I got to go out with you. Well, I don't! I got lots a chances."

"Now wait a minute."

"No, sir—you git away."

Al lunged suddenly, caught her by the ankle, and tripped her. He grabbed her when she fell and held her and put his hand over her angry mouth. She tried to bite his palm, but he cupped it out over her mouth, and he held her down with his other arm. And in a moment she lay still, and in another moment they were giggling together in the dry grass.

"Why, we'll be a-comin' back purty soon," said Al. "An' I'll have a pocketful a jack. We'll go down to Hollywood an' see the pitchers."

She was lying on her back. Al bent over her. And he saw the bright evening star reflected in her eyes, and he saw the black cloud reflected in her eyes. "We'll go on the train," he said.

"How long ya think it'll be?" she asked.

"Oh, maybe a month," he said.

The evening dark came down and Pa and Uncle John squatted with the heads of families out by the office. They studied the night and the future. The little manager, in his white clothes, frayed and clean, rested his elbows on the porch rail. His face was drawn and tired.

Huston looked up at him. "You better get some sleep, mister."

"I guess I ought. Baby born last night in Unit Three. I'm getting to be a good midwife."

"Fella oughta know," said Huston. "Married fella got to know."

Pa said, "We're a-gittin' out in the mornin'."

"Yeah? Which way you goin'?"

"Thought we'd go up north a little. Try to get in the first cotton. We ain't had work. We're outa food."

"Know if they's any work?" Huston asked.

"No, but we're sure they ain't none here."

"They will be, a little later," Huston said. "We'll hold on."

"We hate to go," said Pa. "Folks been so nice here—an' the toilets an' all. But we got to eat. Got a tank of gas. That'll get us a little piece up the road. We had a bath ever' day here. Never was so clean in my life. Funny thing—use ta be I on'y got a bath ever' week an' I never seemed to stink. But now if I don't get one ever' day I stink. Wonder if takin' a bath so often makes that?"

"Maybe you couldn't smell yourself before," the manager said.

"Maybe. I wisht we could stay."

The little manager held his temples between his palms. "I think there's going to be another baby tonight," he said.

"We gonna have one in our fambly 'fore long," said Pa. "I wisht we could have it here. I sure wisht we could."

Tom and Willie and Jule the half-breed sat on the edge of the dance floor and swung their feet.

"I got a sack of Durham," Jule said. "Like a smoke?"

"I sure would," said Tom. "Ain't had a smoke for a hell of a time." He rolled the brown cigarette carefully, to keep down the loss of tobacco.

"Well, sir, we'll be sorry to see you go," said Willy. "You folks is good folks."

Tom lighted his cigarette. "I been thinkin' about it a lot. Jesus Christ, I wisht we could settle down."

Jule took back his Durham. "It ain't nice," he said. "I got a little girl. Thought when I come out here she'd get some schoolin'. But hell, we ain't in one place hardly long enough. Jes' gits goin' an' we got to drag on."

"I hope we don't get in no more Hoovervilles," said Tom. "I was really scairt, there."

"Deputies push you aroun'?"

"I was scairt I'd kill somebody," said Tom. "Was on'y there a little while, but I was a-stewin' aroun' the whole time. Depity come in an' picked up a frien', jus' because he talked outa turn. I was jus' stewin' all the time."

"Ever been in a strike?" Willie asked.

"No."

"Well, I been a-thinkin' a lot. Why don' them depities get in here an' raise hell like ever' place else? Think that little guy in the office is a-stoppin' 'em? No, sir."

"Well, what is?" Jule asked.

"I'll tell ya. It's 'cause we're all a-workin' together. Depity can't pick on one fella in this camp. He's pickin' on the whole darn camp. An' he don't dare. All we got to do is give a yell an' they's two hunderd men out. Fella organizin' for the union was a-talkin' out on the road. He says we could do that any place. Jus' stick together. They ain't raisin' hell with no two hunderd men. They're pickin' on one man."

"Yeah," said Jule, "an' suppose you got a union? You got to have leaders. They'll jus' pick up your leaders, an' where's your union?"

"Well," said Willie, "we got to figure her out some time. I been out here a year, an' wages is goin' right on down. Fella can't feed his fam'ly on his work now, an' it's gettin' worse all the time. It ain't gonna do no good to set aroun' an' starve. I don' know what to do. If a fella owns a team a horses, he don't raise no hell if he got to feed 'em when they ain't workin'. But if a fella got men workin' for him, he jus' don't give a damn. Horses is a hell of a lot more worth than men. I don' understan' it."

"Gets so I don' wanta think about it," said Jule. "An' I got to think about it. I got this here little girl. You know how purty she is. One week they give her a prize in this camp 'cause she's so purty. Well, what's gonna happen to her? She's gettin' spindly. I ain't gonna stan' it. She's so purty. I'm gonna bust out."

"How?" Willie asked. "What you gonna do—steal some stuff an' git in jail? Kill somebody an' git hung?"

"I don' know," said Jule. "Gits me nuts thinkin' about it. Gets me clear nuts."

"I'm a-gonna miss them dances," Tom said. "Them was some of the nicest dances I ever seen. Well, I'm gonna turn in. So long. I'll be seein' you someplace." He shook hands.

"Sure will," said Jule.

"Well, so long." Tom moved away into the darkness.

In the darkness of the Joad tent Ruthie and Winfield lay on their mattress, and Ma lay beside them. Ruthie whispered, "Ma!"

"Yeah? Ain't you asleep yet?"

"Ma—they gonna have croquet where we're goin'?"

"I don' know. Get some sleep. We want to get an early start."

"Well, I wisht we'd stay here where we're sure we got croquet."

"Sh!" said Ma.

"Ma, Winfiel' hit a kid tonight."

"He shouldn' of."

"I know. I tol' 'im, but he hit the kid right in the nose an', Jesus, how the blood run down!"

"Don' talk like that. It ain't a nice way to talk."

Winfield turned over. "That kid says we was Okies," he said in an outraged voice. "He says he wasn't no Okie 'cause he come from Oregon. Says we was goddamn Okies. I socked him."

"Sh! You shouldn'. He can't hurt you callin' names."

"Well, I won't let 'im," Winfield said fiercely.

"Sh! Get some sleep."

Ruthie said, "You oughta seen the blood run down—all over his clothes."

Ma reached a hand from under the blanket and snapped Ruthie on the cheek with her finger. The little girl went rigid for a moment, and then dissolved into sniffling, quiet crying.

In the sanitary unit Pa and Uncle John sat in adjoining compartments. "Might's well get in a good las' one," said Pa. "It's sure nice. 'Member how the little fellas was so scairt when they flushed 'em the first time?"

"I wasn't so easy myself," said Uncle John. He pulled his overalls neatly up around his knees. "I'm gettin' bad," he said. "I feel sin."

"You can't sin none," said Pa. "You ain't got no money. Jus' sit tight. Cos' you at leas' two bucks to sin, an' we ain't got two bucks amongst us."

"Yeah! But I'm a-thinkin' sin."

"Awright. You can think sin for nothin'."

"It's jus' as bad," said Uncle John.

"It's a whole hell of a lot cheaper," said Pa.

"Don't you go makin' light of sin."

"I ain't. You jus' go ahead. You always gets sinful jus' when hell's a-poppin'."

"I know it," said Uncle John. "Always was that way. I never tol' half the stuff I done."

"Well, keep it to yaself."

"These here nice toilets gets me sinful."

"Go out in the bushes then. Come on, pull up ya pants an' le's get some sleep." Pa pulled his overall straps in place and snapped the buckle. He flushed the toilet and watched thoughtfully while the water whirled in the bowl.

It was still dark when Ma roused her camp. The low night lights shone through the open doors of the sanitary units. From the tents along the road came the assorted snores of the campers.

Ma said, "Come on, roll out. We got to be on our way. Day's not far off." She raised the screechy shade of the lantern and lighted the wick. "Come on, all of you."

The floor of the tent squirmed into slow action. Blankets and comforts were thrown back and sleepy eyes squinted blindly at the light. Ma slipped on her dress over the underclothes she wore to bed. "We got no coffee," she said. "I got a few biscuits. We can eat 'em on the road. Jus' get up now, an' we'll load the truck. Come on now. Don't make no noise. Don' wanta wake the neighbors."

It was a few moments before they were fully aroused. "Now don' you get away," Ma warned the children. The family dressed. The men pulled down the tarpaulin and loaded up the truck. "Make it nice an' flat," Ma warned them. They piled the mattress on top of the load and bound the tarpaulin in place over its ridge pole.

"Awright, Ma," said Tom. "She's ready."

Ma held a plate of cold biscuits in her hand. "Awright. Here. Each take one. It's all we got."

Ruthie and Winfield grabbed their biscuits and climbed up on the load. They covered themselves with a blanket and went back to sleep, still holding the cold hard biscuits in their hands. Tom got into the driver's seat and stepped on the starter. It buzzed a little, and then stopped.

"Goddamn you, Al!" Tom cried. "You let the battery run down."

Al blustered, "How the hell was I gonna keep her up if I ain't got gas to run her?"

Tom chuckled suddenly. "Well, I don' know how, but it's your fault. You got to crank her."

"I tell you it ain't my fault."

Tom got out and found the crank under the seat. "It's my fault," he said.

"Gimme that crank." Al seized it. "Pull down the spark so she don't take my arm off."

"O.K. Twist her tail."

Al labored at the crank, around and around. The engine caught, spluttered, and roared as Tom choked the car delicately. He raised the spark and reduced the throttle.

Ma climbed in beside him. "We woke up ever'body in the camp," she said.

"They'll go to sleep again."

Al climbed in on the other side. "Pa 'n' Uncle John got up top," he said. "Goin' to sleep again."

Tom drove toward the main gate. The watchman came out of the office and played his flashlight on the truck. "Wait a minute."

"What ya want?"

"You checkin' out?"

"Sure."

"Well, I got to cross you off."

"O.K."

"Know which way you're goin'?"

"Well, we're gonna try up north."

"Well, good luck," said the watchman.

"Same to you. So long."

The truck edged slowly over the big hump and into the road. Tom retraced the road he had driven before, past Weedpatch and west until he came to 99, then north on the great paved road, toward Bakersfield. It was growing light when he came into the outskirts of the city.

Tom said, "Ever' place you look is restaurants. An' them places all got coffee. Lookit that all-nighter there. Bet they got ten gallons a coffee in there, all hot!"

"Aw, shut up," said Al.

Tom grinned over at him. "Well, I see you got yaself a girl right off."

"Well, what of it?"

"He's mean this mornin', Ma. He ain't good company."

Al said irritably, "I'm goin' out on my own purty soon. Fella can make his way lot easier if he ain't got a fambly."

Tom said, "You'd have yaself a fambly in nine months. I seen you playin' aroun'."

"Ya crazy," said Al. "I'd get myself a job in a garage an' I'd eat in restaurants——"

"An' you'd have a wife an' kid in nine months."

"I tell ya I wouldn'."

Tom said, "You're a wise guy, Al. You gonna take some beatin' over the head."

"Who's gonna do it?"

"They'll always be guys to do it," said Tom.

"You think jus' because you——"

"Now you jus' stop that," Ma broke in.

"I done it," said Tom. "I was a-badgerin' him. I didn' mean no harm, Al. I didn' know you liked that girl so much."

"I don't like no girls much."

"Awright, then, you don't. You ain't gonna get no argument out of me."

The truck came to the edge of the city. "Look a them hotdog stan's—hunderds of 'em," said Tom.

Ma said, "Tom! I got a dollar put away. You wan' coffee bad enough to spen' it?"

"No, Ma. I'm jus' foolin'."

"You can have it if you wan' it bad enough."

"I wouldn' take it."

Al said, "Then shut up about coffee."

Tom was silent for a time. "Seems like I got my foot in it all the time," he said. "There's the road we run up that night."

"I hope we don't never have nothin' like that again," said Ma. "That was a bad night."

"I didn' like it none either."

The sun rose on their right, and the great shadow of the truck ran beside them, flicking over the fence posts beside the road. They ran on past the rebuilt Hooverville.

"Look," said Tom. "They got new people there. Looks like the same place."

Al came slowly out of his sullenness. "Fella tol' me some a them people been burned out fifteen-twenty times. Says they jus' go hide down the willows an' then they come out an' build 'em another weed shack. Jus' like gophers. Got so use' to it they don't even get mad no more, this fella says. They jus' figger it's like bad weather."

"Sure was bad weather for me that night," said Tom. They moved up the wide highway. And the sun's warmth made them shiver. "Gettin' snappy in the mornin'," said Tom. "Winter's on the way. I jus' hope we can get some money 'fore it comes. Tent ain't gonna be nice in the winter."

Ma sighed, and then she straightened her head. "Tom," she said, "we gotta have a house in the winter. I tell ya we got to. Ruthie's awright, but Winfiel' ain't so strong. We got to have a house when the rains come. I heard it jus' rains cats aroun' here."

"We'll get a house, Ma. You res' easy. You gonna have a house."

"Jus' so's it's got a roof an' a floor. Jus' to keep the little fellas off'n the groun'."

"We'll try, Ma."

"I don' wanna worry ya now."

"We'll try, Ma."

"I jus' get panicky sometimes," she said. "I jus' lose my spunk."

"I never seen you when you lost it."

"Nights I do, sometimes."

There came a harsh hissing from the front of the truck. Tom grabbed the wheel tight and he thrust the brake down to the floor. The truck bumped to a stop. Tom sighed. "Well, there she is." He leaned back in the seat. Al leaped out and ran to the right front tire.

"Great big nail," he called.

"We got any tire patch?"

"No," said Al. "Used it all up. Got patch, but no glue stuff."

Tom turned and smiled sadly at Ma. "You shouldn' a tol' about that dollar," he said. "We'd a fixed her some way." He got out of the car and went to the flat tire.

Al pointed to a big nail protruding from the flat casing. "There she is!"

"If they's one nail in the county, we run over it."

"Is it bad?" Ma called.

"No, not bad, but we got to fix her."

The family piled down from the top of the truck. "Puncture?" Pa asked, and then he saw the tire and was silent.

Tom moved Ma from the seat and got the can of tire patch from underneath the cushion. He unrolled the rubber patch and took out the tube of cement, squeezed it gently. "She's almos' dry," he said. "Maybe they's enough. Awright, Al. Block the back wheels. Le's get her jacked up."

Tom and Al worked well together. They put stones behind the wheels, put the jack under the front axle, and lifted the weight off the limp casing. They ripped off the casing. They found the hole, dipped a rag in the gas tank and washed the tube around the hole. And then, while Al held the tube tight over his knee, Tom tore the cement tube in two and spread the little fluid thinly on the rubber with his pocket knife. He scraped the gum delicately. "Now let her dry while I cut a patch." He trimmed and beveled the edge of the blue patch. Al held the tube tight while Tom put the patch tenderly in place. "There! Now bring her to the running board while I tap her with a hammer." He pounded the patch carefully, then stretched the tube and watched the edges of the patch. "There she is! She's gonna hold. Stick her on the rim an' we'll pump her up. Looks like you keep your buck, Ma."

Al said, "I wisht we had a spare. We got to get us a spare, Tom, on a rim an' all pumped up. Then we can fix a puncture at night."

"When we get money for a spare we'll get us some coffee an' side-meat instead," Tom said.

The light morning traffic buzzed by on the highway, and the sun grew warm and bright. A wind, gentle and sighing, blew in puffs from the southwest, and the mountains on both sides of the great valley were indistinct in a pearly mist.

Tom was pumping at the tire when a roadster, coming from the north, stopped on the other side of the road. A brown-faced man dressed in a light gray business suit got out and walked across to the truck. He was bareheaded. He smiled, and his teeth were very white against his brown skin. He wore a massive gold wedding ring on the third finger of his left hand. A little gold football hung on a slender chain across his vest.

"Morning," he said pleasantly.

Tom stopped pumping and looked up. "Mornin'."

The man ran his fingers through his coarse, short, graying hair. "You people looking for work?"

"We sure are, mister. Lookin' even under boards."

"Can you pick peaches?"

"We never done it," Pa said.

"We can do anything," Tom said hurriedly. "We can pick anything there is."

The man fingered his gold football. "Well, there's plenty of work for you about forty miles north."

"We'd sure admire to get it," said Tom. "You tell us how to get there, an' we'll go a-lopin'."

"Well, you go north to Pixley, that's thirty-five or -six

miles, and you turn east. Go about six miles. Ask anybody where the Hooper ranch is. You'll find plenty of work there."

"We sure will."

"Know where there's other people looking for work?"

"Sure," said Tom. "Down at the Weedpatch camp they's plenty lookin' for work."

"I'll take a run down there. We can use quite a few. Remember now, turn east at Pixley and keep straight east to the Hooper ranch."

"Sure," said Tom. "An' we thank ya, mister. We need work awful bad."

"All right. Get along as soon as you can." He walked back across the road, climbed into his open roadster, and drove away south.

Tom threw his weight on the pump. "Twenty apiece," he called. "One—two—three—four—" At twenty Al took the pump, and then Pa and then Uncle John. The tire filled out and grew plump and smooth. Three times around, the pump went. "Let 'er down an' le's see," said Tom.

Al released the jack and lowered the car. "Got plenty," he said. "Maybe a little too much."

They threw the tools into the car. "Come on, le's go," Tom called. "We're gonna get some work at last."

Ma got in the middle again. Al drove this time.

"Now take her easy. Don't burn her up, Al."

They drove on through the sunny morning fields. The mist lifted from the hilltops and they were clear and brown, with black-purple creases. The wild doves flew up from the fences as the truck passed. Al unconsciously increased his speed.

"Easy," Tom warned him. "She'll blow up if you crowd

her. We got to get there. Might even get in some work today."

Ma said excitedly, "With four men a-workin' maybe I can
get some credit right off. Fust thing I'll get is coffee, 'cause
you been wanting that, an' then some flour an' bakin' powder
an' some meat. Better not get no side-meat right off. Save
that for later. Maybe Sat'dy. An' soap. Got to get soap.
Wonder where we'll stay." She babbled on. "An' milk. I'll
get some milk 'cause Rosasharn, she ought to have milk. The
lady nurse says that."

A snake wriggled across the warm highway. Al zipped
over and ran it down and came back to his own lane.

"Gopher snake," said Tom. "You oughtn't to done that."

"I hate 'em," said Al gaily. "Hate all kinds. Give me the
stomach-quake."

The forenoon traffic on the highway increased, salesmen
in shiny coupés with the insignia of their companies painted
on the doors, red and white gasoline trucks dragging clink-
ing chains behind them, great square-doored vans from
wholesale grocery houses, delivering produce. The country
was rich along the roadside. There were orchards, heavy
leafed in their prime, and vineyards with the long green
crawlers carpeting the ground between the rows. There
were melon patches and grain fields. White houses stood in
the greenery, roses growing over them. And the sun was
gold and warm.

In the front seat of the truck Ma and Tom and Al were
overcome with happiness. "I ain't really felt so good for a
long time," Ma said. " 'F we pick plenty peaches we might
get a house, pay rent even, for a couple months. We got to
have a house."

Al said, "I'm a-gonna save up. I'll save up an' then I'm

a-goin' in a town an' get me a job in a garage. Live in a room an' eat in restaurants. Go to the movin' pitchers ever' damn night. Don' cost much. Cowboy pitchers." His hands tightened on the wheel.

The radiator bubbled and hissed steam. "Did you fill her up?" Tom asked.

"Yeah. Wind's kinda behind us. That's what makes her boil."

"It's a awful nice day," Tom said. "Use' ta work there in McAlester an' think all the things I'd do. I'd go in a straight line way to hell an' gone an' never stop nowheres. Seems like a long time ago. Seems like it's years ago I was in. They was a guard made it tough. I was gonna lay for 'im. Guess that's what makes me mad at cops. Seems like ever' cop got his face. He use' ta get red in the face. Looked like a pig. Had a brother out west, they said. Use' ta get fellas paroled to his brother, an' then they had to work for nothin'. If they raised a stink, they'd get sent back for breakin' parole. That's what the fellers said."

"Don' think about it," Ma begged him. "I'm a-gonna lay in a lot a stuff to eat. Lot a flour an' lard."

"Might's well think about it," said Tom. "Try to shut it out, an' it'll whang back at me. They was a screwball. Never tol' you 'bout him. Looked like Happy Hooligan. Harmless kinda fella. Always was gonna make a break. Fellas all called him Hooligan." Tom laughed to himself.

"Don' think about it," Ma begged.

"Go on," said Al. "Tell about the fella."

"It don't hurt nothin', Ma," Tom said. "This fella was always gonna break out. Make a plan, he would; but he couldn' keep it to hisself an' purty soon ever'body knowed it, even the warden. He'd make his break an' they'd take 'im by the han' an' lead 'im back. Well, one time he drawed a plan where he's goin' over. 'Course he showed it aroun', an' ever'body kep' still. An' he hid out, an' ever'body kep' still. So he's got himself a rope somewheres, an' he goes over the wall. They's six guards outside with a great big sack, an' Hooligan comes quiet down the rope an' they jus' hol' the sack out an' he goes right inside. They tie up the mouth an' take 'im back inside. Fellas laughed so hard they like to died. But it busted Hooligan's spirit. He jus' cried an' cried, an' moped aroun' an' got sick. Hurt his feelin's so bad. Cut his wrists with a pin an' bled to death 'cause his feelin's was hurt. No harm in 'im at all. They's all kinds a screwballs in stir."

"Don' talk about it," Ma said. "I knowed Purty Boy Floyd's ma. He wan't a bad boy. Jus' got drove in a corner."

The sun moved up toward noon and the shadow of the truck grew lean and moved in under the wheels.

"Mus' be Pixley up the road," Al said. "Seen a sign a little back." They drove into the little town and turned eastward on a narrower road. And the orchards lined the way and made an aisle.

"Hope we can find her easy," Tom said.

Ma said, "That fella said the Hooper ranch. Said anybody'd tell us. Hope they's a store near by. Might get some credit, with four men workin'. I could get a real nice supper if they'd gimme some credit. Make up a big stew maybe."

"An' coffee," said Tom. "Might even get me a sack a Durham. I ain't had no tobacca of my own for a long time."

Far ahead the road was blocked with cars, and a line of white motorcycles was drawn up along the roadside. "Mus' be a wreck," Tom said.

As they drew near a State policeman, in boots and Sam

Browne belt, stepped around the last parked car. He held up his hand and Al pulled to a stop. The policeman leaned confidentially on the side of the car. "Where you going?"

Al said, "Fella said they was work pickin' peaches up this way."

"Want to work, do you?"

"Damn right," said Tom.

"O.K. Wait here a minute." He moved to the side of the road and called ahead. "One more. That's six cars ready. Better take this batch through."

Tom called, "Hey! What's the matter?"

The patrol man lounged back. "Got a little trouble up ahead. Don't you worry. You'll get through. Just follow the line."

There came the splattering blast of motorcycles starting. The line of cars moved on, with the Joad truck last. Two motorcycles led the way, and two followed.

Tom said uneasily, "I wonder what's a matter."

"Maybe the road's out," Al suggested.

"Don' need four cops to lead us. I don' like it."

The motorcycles ahead speeded up. The line of old cars speeded up. Al hurried to keep in back of the last car.

"These here is our own people, all of 'em," Tom said. "I don' like this."

Suddenly the leading policemen turned off the road into a wide graveled entrance. The old cars whipped after them. The motorcycles roared their motors. Tom saw a line of men standing in the ditch beside the road, saw their mouths open as though they were yelling, saw their shaking fists and their furious faces. A stout woman ran toward the cars, but a roaring motorcycle stood in her way. A high wire gate swung open. The six old cars moved through and the gate closed behind them. The four motorcycles turned and sped back in the direction from which they had come. And now that the motors were gone, the distant yelling of the men in the ditch could be heard. Two men stood beside the graveled road. Each one carried a shotgun.

One called, "Go on, go on. What the hell are you waiting for?" The six cars moved ahead, turned a bend and came suddenly on the peach camp.

There were fifty little square, flat-roofed boxes, each with a door and a window, and the whole group in a square. A water tank stood high on one edge of the camp. And a little grocery store stood on the other side. At the end of each row of square houses stood two men armed with shotguns and wearing big silver stars pinned to their shirts.

The six cars stopped. Two bookkeepers moved from car to car. "Want to work?"

Tom answered, "Sure, but what is this?"

"That's not your affair. Want to work?"

"Sure we do."

"Name?"

"Joad."

"How many men?"

"Four."

"Women?"

"Two."

"Kids?"

"Two."

"Can all of you work?"

"Why—I guess so."

"O.K. Find house sixty-three. Wages five cents a box. No bruised fruit. All right, move along now. Go to work right away."

The cars moved on. On the door of each square red house a number was painted. "Sixty," Tom said. "There's sixty. Must be down that way. There, sixty-one, sixty-two— There she is."

Al parked the truck close to the door of the little house. The family came down from the top of the truck and looked about in bewilderment. Two deputies approached. They looked closely into each face.

"Name?"

"Joad," Tom said impatiently. "Say, what is this here?"

One of the deputies took out a long list. "Not here. Ever see these here? Look at the license. Nope. Ain't got it. Guess they're O.K."

"Now you look here. We don't want no trouble with you. Jes' do your work and mind your own business and you'll be all right." The two turned abruptly and walked away. At the end of the dusty street they sat down on two boxes and their position commanded the length of the street.

Tom stared after them. "They sure do wanta make us feel at home."

Ma opened the door of the house and stepped inside. The floor was splashed with grease. In the one room stood a rusty tin stove and nothing more. The tin stove rested on four bricks and its rusty stovepipe went up through the roof. The room smelled of sweat and grease. Rose of Sharon stood beside Ma. "We gonna live here?"

Ma was silent for a moment. "Why, sure," she said at last. "It ain't so bad once we wash it out. Get her mopped."

"I like the tent better," the girl said.

"This got a floor," Ma suggested. "This here wouldn' leak when it rains." She turned to the door. "Might as well unload," she said.

The men unloaded the truck silently. A fear had fallen on them. The great square of boxes was silent. A woman went by in the street, but she did not look at them. Her head was sunk and her dirty gingham dress was frayed at the bottom in little flags.

The pall had fallen on Ruthie and Winfield. They did not dash away to inspect the place. They stayed close to the truck, close to the family. They looked forlornly up and down the dusty street. Winfield found a piece of baling wire and he bent it back and forth until it broke. He made a little crank of the shortest piece and turned it around and around in his hands.

Tom and Pa were carrying the mattresses into the house when a clerk appeared. He wore khaki trousers and a blue shirt and a black necktie. He wore silver-bound eyeglasses, and his eyes, through the thick lenses, were weak and red, and the pupils were staring little bull's eyes. He leaned forward to look at Tom.

"I want to get you checked down," he said. "How many of you going to work?"

Tom said, "They's four men. Is this here hard work?"

"Picking peaches," the clerk said. "Piece work. Give five cents a box."

"Ain't no reason why the little fellas can't help?"

"Sure not, if they're careful."

Ma stood in the doorway. "Soon's I get settled down I'll come out an' help. We got nothin' to eat, mister. Do we get paid right off?"

"Well, no, not money right off. But you can get credit at the store for what you got coming."

"Come on, let's hurry," Tom said. "I want ta get some meat an' bread in me tonight. Where do we go, mister?"

"I'm going out there now. Come with me."

Tom and Pa and Al and Uncle John walked with him down the dusty street and into the orchard, in among the peach trees. The narrow leaves were beginning to turn a pale yellow. The peaches were little globes of gold and red on the branches. Among the trees were piles of empty boxes. The pickers scurried about, filling their buckets from the branches, putting the peaches in the boxes, carrying the boxes to the checking station; and at the stations, where the piles of filled boxes waited for the trucks, clerks waited to check against the names of the pickers.

"Here's four more," the guide said to a clerk.

"O.K. Ever picked before?"

"Never did," said Tom.

"Well, pick careful. No bruised fruit, no windfalls. Bruise your fruit an' we won't check 'em. There's some buckets."

Tom picked up a three-gallon bucket and looked at it. "Full a holes on the bottom."

"Sure," said the near-sighted clerk. "That keeps people from stealing them. All right—down in that section. Get going."

The four Joads took their buckets and went into the orchard. "They don't waste no time," Tom said.

"Christ Awmighty," Al said. "I ruther work in a garage."

Pa had followed docilely into the field. He turned suddenly on Al. "Now you jus' quit it," he said. "You been a-hankerin' an' a-complainin' an' a-bullblowin'. You get to work. You ain't so big I can't lick you yet."

Al's face turned red with anger. He started to bluster.

Tom moved near to him. "Come on, Al," he said quietly. "Bread an' meat. We got to get 'em."

They reached for the fruit and dropped them in the buckets. Tom ran at his work. One bucket full, two buckets. He dumped them in a box. Three buckets. The box was full. "I jus' made a nickel," he called. He picked up the box and walked hurriedly to the station. "Here's a nickel's worth," he said to the checker.

The man looked into the box, turned over a peach or two. "Put it over there. That's out," he said. "I told you not to bruise them. Dumped 'em outa the bucket, didn't you? Well, every damn peach is bruised. Can't check that one. Put 'em in easy or you're working for nothing."

"Why—goddamn it——"

"Now go easy. I warned you before you started."

Tom's eyes drooped sullenly. "O.K." he said. "O.K." He went quickly back to the others. "Might's well dump what you got," he said. "Yours is the same as mine. Won't take 'em."

"Now, what the hell!" Al began.

"Got to pick easier. Can't drop 'em in the bucket. Got to lay 'em in."

They started again, and this time they handled the fruit gently. The boxes filled more slowly. "We could figger somepin out, I bet," Tom said. "If Ruthie an' Winfiel' or Rosasharn jus' put 'em in the boxes, we could work out a system." He carried his newest box to the station. "Is this here worth a nickel?"

The checker looked them over, dug down several layers. "That's better," he said. He checked the box in. "Just take it easy."

Tom hurried back. "I got a nickel," he called. "I got a nickel. On'y got to do that there twenty times for a dollar."

They worked on steadily through the afternoon. Ruthie

and Winfield found them after a while. "You got to work," Pa told them. "You got to put the peaches careful in the box. Here, now, one at a time."

The children squatted down and picked the peaches out of the extra bucket, and a line of buckets stood ready for them. Tom carried the full boxes to the station. "That's seven," he said. "That's eight. Forty cents we got. Get a nice piece of meat for forty cents."

The afternoon passed. Ruthie tried to go away. "I'm tar'd," she whined. "I got to rest."

"You got to stay right where you're at," said Pa.

Uncle John picked slowly. He filled one bucket to two of Tom's. His pace didn't change.

In mid-afternoon Ma came trudging out. "I would a come before, but Rosasharn fainted," she said. "Jes' fainted away."

"You been eatin' peaches," she said to the children. "Well, they'll blast you out." Ma's stubby body moved quickly. She abandoned her bucket quickly and picked into her apron. When the sun went down they had picked twenty boxes.

Tom set the twentieth box down. "A buck," he said. "How long do we work?"

"Work till dark, long as you can see."

"Well, can we get credit now? Ma oughta go in an' buy some stuff to eat."

"Sure. I'll give you a slip for a dollar now." He wrote on a strip of paper and handed it to Tom.

He took it to Ma. "Here you are. You can get a dollar's worth of stuff at the store."

Ma put down her bucket and straightened her shoulders. "Gets you, the first time, don't it?"

"Sure. We'll all get used to it right off. Roll on in an' get some food."

Ma said, "What'll you like to eat?"

"Meat," said Tom. "Meat an' bread an' a big pot a coffee with sugar in. Great big piece a meat."

Ruthie wailed, "Ma, we're tar'd."

"Better come along in, then."

"They was tar'd when they started," Pa said. "Wild as rabbits they're a-gettin'. Ain't gonna be no good at all 'less we can pin 'em down."

"Soon's we get set down, they'll go to school," said Ma. She trudged away, and Ruthie and Winfield timidly followed her.

"We got to work ever' day?" Winfield asked.

Ma stopped and waited. She took his hand and walked along holding it. "It ain't hard work," she said. "Be good for you. An' you're helpin' us. If we all work, purty soon we'll live in a nice house. We all got to help."

"But I got so tar'd."

"I know. I got tar'd too. Ever'body gets wore out. Got to think about other stuff. Think about when you'll go to school."

"I don't wanta go to no school. Ruthie don't, neither. Them kids that goes to school, we seen 'em, Ma. Snots! Calls us Okies. We seen 'em. I ain't a-goin'."

Ma looked pityingly down on his straw hair. "Don' give us no trouble right now," she begged. "Soon's we get on our feet, you can be bad. But not now. We got too much, now."

"I et six of them peaches," Ruthie said.

"Well, you'll have the skitters. An' it ain't close to no toilet where we are."

The company's store was a large shed of corrugated iron. It had no display window. Ma opened the screen door and went in. A tiny man stood behind the counter. He was completely bald, and his head was blue-white. Large, brown eyebrows covered his eyes in such a high arch that his face seemed surprised and a little frightened. His nose was long and thin, and curved like a bird's beak, and his nostrils were blocked with light brown hair. Over the sleeves of his blue shirt he wore black sateen sleeve protectors. He was leaning on his elbows on the counter when Ma entered.

"Afternoon," she said.

He inspected her with interest. The arch over his eyes became higher. "Howdy."

"I got a slip here for a dollar."

"You can get a dollar's worth," he said, and he giggled shrilly. "Yes, sir. A dollar's worth. One dollar's worth." He moved his hand at the stock. "Any of it." He pulled his sleeve protectors up neatly.

"Thought I'd get a piece of meat."

"Got all kinds," he said. "Hamburg, like to have some hamburg? Twenty cents a pound, hamburg."

"Ain't that awful high? Seems to me hamburg was fifteen las' time I got some."

"Well," he giggled softly, "yes, it's high, an' same time it ain't high. Time you go on in town for a couple poun's of hamburg, it'll cos' you 'bout a gallon gas. So you see it ain't really high here, 'cause you got no gallon a gas."

Ma said sternly, "It didn' cos' you no gallon a gas to get it out here."

He laughed delightedly. "You're lookin' at it bass-ackwards," he said. "We ain't a-buyin' it, we're a-sellin' it. If we was buyin' it, why, that'd be different."

Ma put two fingers to her mouth and frowned with thought. "It looks all full a fat an' gristle."

"I ain't guaranteein' she won't cook down," the storekeeper said. "I ain't guaranteein' I'd eat her myself; but they's lots of stuff I wouldn' do."

Ma looked up at him fiercely for a moment. She controlled her voice. "Ain't you got some cheaper kind a meat?"

"Soup bones," he said. "Ten cents a pound."

"But them's jus' bones."

"Them's jes' bones," he said. "Make nice soup. Jes' bones."

"Got any boilin' beef?"

"Oh, yeah! Sure. That's two bits a poun'."

"Maybe I can't get no meat," Ma said. "But they want meat. They said they wanted meat."

"Ever'body wants meat—needs meat. That hamburg is purty nice stuff. Use the grease that comes out a her for gravy. Purty nice. No waste. Don't throw no bone away."

"How—how much is side-meat?"

"Well, now you're gettin' into fancy stuff. Christmas stuff. Thanksgivin' stuff. Thirty-five cents a poun'. I could sell you turkey cheaper, if I had some turkey."

Ma sighed. "Give me two pounds hamburg."

"Yes, ma'am." He scooped the pale meat on a piece of waxed paper. "An' what else?"

"Well, some bread."

"Right here. Fine big loaf, fifteen cents."

"That there's a twelve-cent loaf."

"Sure, it is. Go right in town an' get her for twelve cents. Gallon a gas. What else can I sell you, potatoes?"

"Yes, potatoes."

"Five pounds for a quarter."

Ma moved menacingly toward him. "I heard enough from you. I know what they cost in town."

The little man clamped his mouth tight. "Then go git 'em in town."

Ma looked at her knuckles. "What is this?" she asked softly. "You own this here store?"

"No. I jus' work here."

"Any reason you got to make fun? That help you any?" She regarded her shiny wrinkled hands. The little man was silent. "Who owns this here store?"

"Hooper Ranches, Incorporated, ma'am."

"An' they set the prices?"

"Yes, ma'am."

She looked up, smiling a little. "Ever'body comes in talks like me, is mad?"

He hesitated for a moment. "Yes, ma'am."

"An' that's why you make fun?"

"What cha mean?"

"Doin' a dirty thing like this. Shames ya, don't it? Got to act flip, huh?" Her voice was gentle. The clerk watched her, fascinated. He didn't answer. "That's how it is," Ma said finally. "Forty cents for meat, fifteen for bread, quarter for potatoes. That's eighty cents. Coffee?"

"Twenty cents the cheapest, ma'am."

"An' that's the dollar. Seven of us workin', an' that's supper." She studied her hand. "Wrap 'em up," she said quickly.

"Yes, ma'am," he said. "Thanks." He put the potatoes in a bag and folded the top carefully down. His eyes slipped to Ma, and then hid in his work again. She watched him, and she smiled a little.

"How'd you get a job like this?" she asked.

"A fella got to eat," he began; and then, belligerently, "A fella got a right to eat."

"What fella?" Ma asked.

He placed the four packages on the counter. "Meat," he

said. "Potatoes, bread, coffee. One dollar, even." She handed him her slip of paper and watched while he entered the name and the amount in a ledger. "There," he said. "Now we're all even."

Ma picked up her bags. "Say," she said. "We got no sugar for the coffee. My boy Tom, he wants sugar. Look!" she said. "They're a-workin' out there. You let me have some sugar an' I'll bring the slip in later."

The little man looked away—took his eyes as far from Ma as he could. "I can't do it," he said softly. "That's the rule. I can't. I'd get in trouble. I'd get canned."

"But they're a-workin' out in the field now. They got more'n a dime comin'. Gimme ten cents' of sugar. Tom, he wanted sugar in his coffee. Spoke about it."

"I can't do it, ma'am. That's the rule. No slip, no groceries. The manager, he talks about that all the time. No, I can't do it. No, I can't. They'd catch me. They always catch fellas. Always. I can't."

"For a dime?"

"For anything, ma'am." He looked pleadingly at her. And then his face lost its fear. He took ten cents from his pocket and rang it up in the cash register. "There," he said with relief. He pulled a little bag from under the counter, whipped it open and scooped some sugar into it, weighed the bag, and added a little more sugar. "There you are," he said. "Now it's all right. You bring in your slip an' I'll get my dime back."

Ma studied him. Her hand went blindly out and put the little bag of sugar on the pile in her arm. "Thanks to you," she said quietly. She started for the door, and when she reached it, she turned about. "I'm learnin' one thing good," she said. "Learnin' it all a time, ever' day. If you're in trouble or hurt or need—go to poor people. They're the only ones that'll help—the only ones." The screen door slammed behind her.

The little man leaned his elbows on the counter and looked after her with his surprised eyes. A plump tortoise-shell cat leaped up on the counter and stalked lazily near to him. It rubbed sideways against his arms, and he reached out with his hand and pulled it against his cheek. The cat purred loudly, and the tip of its tail jerked back and forth.

Tom and Al and Pa and Uncle John walked in from the orchard when the dusk was deep. Their feet were a little heavy against the road.

"You wouldn' think jus' reachin' up an' pickin'd get you in the back," Pa said.

"Be awright in a couple days," said Tom. "Say, Pa, after we eat I'm a-gonna walk out an' see what all that fuss is outside the gate. It's been a-workin' on me. Wanta come?"

"No," said Pa. "I like to have a little while to jus' work an' not think about nothin'. Seems like I jus' been beatin' my brains to death for a hell of a long time. No, I'm gonna set awhile, an' then go to bed."

"How 'bout you, Al?"

Al looked away. "Guess I'll look aroun' in here, first," he said.

"Well, I know Uncle John won't come. Guess I'll go her alone. Got me all curious."

Pa said, "I'll get a hell of a lot curiouser 'fore I'll do anything about it—with all them cops out there."

"Maybe they ain't there at night," Tom suggested.

"Well, I ain't gonna find out. An' you better not tell

Ma where you're a-goin'. She'll jus' squirt her head off worryin'."

Tom turned to Al. "Ain't you curious?"

"Guess I'll jes' look aroun' this here camp," Al said.

"Lookin' for girls, huh?"

"Mindin' my own business," Al said acidly.

"I'm still a-goin'," said Tom.

They emerged from the orchard into the dusty street between the red shacks. The low yellow light of kerosene lanterns shone from some of the doorways, and inside, in the half-gloom, the black shapes of people moved about. At the end of the street a guard still sat, his shotgun resting against his knee.

Tom paused as he passed the guard. "Got a place where a fella can get a bath, mister?"

The guard studied him in the half-light. At last he said, "See that water tank?"

"Yeah."

"Well, there's a hose over there."

"Any warm water?"

"Say, who in hell you think you are, J. P. Morgan?"

"No," said Tom. "No, I sure don't. Good night, mister."

The guard grunted contemptuously. "Hot water, for Christ's sake. Be wantin' tubs next." He stared glumly after the four Joads.

A second guard came around the end house. "'S'matter, Mack?"

"Why, them goddamn Okies. 'Is they warm water?' he says."

The second guard rested his gun butt on the ground. "It's them gov'ment camps," he said. "I bet that fella been in a gov'ment camp. We ain't gonna have no peace till we wipe them camps out. They'll be wantin' clean sheets, first thing we know."

Mack asked, "How is it out at the main gate—hear anything?"

"Well, they was out there yellin' all day. State police got it in hand. They're runnin' the hell outa them smart guys. I heard they's a long lean son-of-a-bitch spark-pluggin' the thing. Fella says they'll get him tonight, an' then she'll go to pieces."

"We won't have no job if it comes too easy," Mack said.

"We'll have a job, all right. These goddamn Okies! You got to watch 'em all the time. Things get a little quiet, we can always stir 'em up a little."

"Have trouble when they cut the rate here, I guess."

"We sure will. No, you needn' worry about us havin' work —not while Hooper's snubbin' close."

The fire roared in the Joad house. Hamburger patties splashed and hissed in the grease, and the potatoes bubbled. The house was full of smoke, and the yellow lantern light threw heavy black shadows on the walls. Ma worked quickly about the fire while Rose of Sharon sat on a box resting her heavy abdomen on her knees.

"Feelin' better now?" Ma asked.

"Smell a cookin' gets me. I'm hungry, too."

"Go set in the door," Ma said. "I got to have that box to break up anyways."

The men trooped in. "Meat, by God!" said Tom. "And coffee. I smell her. Jesus, I'm hungry! I et a lot of peaches, but they didn' do no good. Where can we wash, Ma?"

"Go down to the water tank. Wash down there. I jus' sent Ruthie an' Winfiel' to wash." The men went out again.

"Go on now, Rosasharn," Ma ordered. "Either you set in the door or else on the bed. I got to break that box up."

The girl helped herself up with her hands. She moved heavily to one of the mattresses and sat down on it. Ruthie and Winfield came in quietly, trying by silence and by keeping close to the wall to remain obscure.

Ma looked over at them. "I got a feelin' you little fellas is lucky they ain't much light," she said. She pounced at Winfield and felt his hair. "Well, you got wet, anyway, but I bet you ain't clean."

"They wasn't no soap," Winfield complained.

"No, that's right. I couldn' buy no soap. Not today. Maybe we can get soap tomorra." She went back to the stove, laid out the plates, and began to serve the supper. Two patties apiece and a big potato. She placed three slices of bread on each plate. When the meat was all out of the frying pan she poured a little of the grease on each plate. The men came in again, their faces dripping and their hair shining with water.

"Leave me at her," Tom cried.

They took the plates. They ate silently, wolfishly, and wiped up the grease with the bread. The children retired into the corner of the room, put their plates on the floor, and knelt in front of the food like little animals.

Tom swallowed the last of his bread. "Got any more, Ma?"

"No," she said. "That's all. You made a dollar, an' that's a dollar's worth."

"That?"

"They charge extry out here. We got to go in town when we can."

"I ain't full," said Tom.

"Well, tomorra you'll get in a full day. Tomorra night—we'll have plenty."

Al wiped his mouth on his sleeve. "Guess I'll take a look around," he said.

"Wait, I'll go with you." Tom followed him outside. In the darkness Tom went close to his brother. "Sure you don' wanta come with me?"

"No. I'm gonna look aroun' like I said."

"O.K.," said Tom. He turned away and strolled down the street. The smoke from the houses hung low to the ground, and the lanterns threw their pictures of doorways and windows into the street. On the doorsteps people sat and looked out into the darkness. Tom could see their heads turn as their eyes followed him down the street. At the street end the dirt road continued across a stubble field, and the black lumps of haycocks were visible in the starlight. A thin blade of moon was low in the sky toward the west, and the long cloud of the milky way trailed clearly overhead. Tom's feet sounded softly on the dusty road, a dark patch against the yellow stubble. He put his hands in his pockets and trudged along toward the main gate. An embankment came close to the road. Tom could hear the whisper of water against the grasses in the irrigation ditch. He climbed up the bank and looked down on the dark water, and saw the stretched reflections of the stars. The State road was ahead. Car lights swooping past showed where it was. Tom set out again toward it. He could see the high wire gate in the starlight.

A figure stirred beside the road. A voice said, "Hello—who is it?"

Tom stopped and stood still. "Who are you?"

A man stood up and walked near. Tom could see the gun in his hand. Then a flashlight played on his face. "Where you think you're going?"

"Well, I thought I'd take a walk. Any law against it?"

"You better walk some other way."

Tom asked, "Can't I even get out of here?"

"Not tonight you can't. Want to walk back, or shall I whistle some help an' take you?"

"Hell," said Tom, "it ain't nothin' to me. If it's gonna cause a mess, I don't give a darn. Sure, I'll go back."

The dark figure relaxed. The flash went off. "Ya see, it's for your own good. Them crazy pickets might get you."

"What pickets?"

"Them goddamn reds."

"Oh," said Tom. "I didn' know 'bout them."

"You seen 'em when you come, didn' you?"

"Well, I seen a bunch a guys, but they was so many cops I didn' know. Thought it was a accident."

"Well, you better git along back."

"That's O.K. with me, mister." He swung about and started back. He walked quietly along the road a hundred yards, and then he stopped and listened. The twittering call of a raccoon sounded near the irrigation ditch and, very far away, the angry howl of a tied dog. Tom sat down beside the road and listened. He heard the high soft laughter of a night hawk and the stealthy movement of a creeping animal in the stubble. He inspected the skyline in both directions, dark frames both ways, nothing to show against. Now he stood up and walked slowly to the right of the road, off into the stubble field, and he walked bent down, nearly as low as the haycocks. He moved slowly and stopped occasionally to listen. At last he came to the wire fence, five strands of taut barbed wire. Beside the fence he lay on his back, moved his head under the lowest strand, held the wire up with his hands and slid himself under, pushing against the ground with his feet.

He was about to get up when a group of men walked by on the edge of the highway. Tom waited until they were far ahead before he stood up and followed them. He watched the side of the road for tents. A few automobiles went by. A stream cut across the fields, and the highway crossed it on a small concrete bridge. Tom looked over the side of the bridge. In the bottom of the deep ravine he saw a tent and a lantern was burning inside. He watched it for a moment, saw the shadows of people against the canvas walls. Tom climbed a fence and moved down into the ravine through brush and dwarf willows; and in the bottom, beside a tiny stream, he found a trail. A man sat on a box in front of the tent.

"Evenin'," Tom said.

"Who are you?"

"Well—I guess, well—I'm jus' goin' past."

"Know anybody here?"

"No. I tell you I was jus' goin' past."

A head stuck out of the tent. A voice said, "What's the matter?"

"Casy!" Tom cried. "Casy! For Chris' sake, what you doin' here?"

"Why, my God, it's Tom Joad! Come on in, Tommy. Come on in."

"Know him, do ya?" the man in front asked.

"Know him? Christ, yes. Knowed him for years. I come west with him. Come on in, Tom." He clutched Tom's elbow and pulled him into the tent.

Three other men sat on the ground, and in the center of the tent a lantern burned. The men looked up suspiciously. A dark-faced, scowling man held out his hand. "Glad to meet ya," he said. "I heard what Casy said. This the fella you was tellin' about?"

"Sure. This is him. Well, for God's sake! Where's your folks? What you doin' here?"

"Well," said Tom, "we heard they was work this-a-way. An' we come, an' a bunch a State cops run us into this here ranch an' we been a-pickin' peaches all afternoon. I seen a bunch a fellas yellin'. They wouldn' tell me nothin', so I come out here to see what's goin' on. How'n hell'd you get here, Casy?"

The preacher leaned forward and the yellow lantern light fell on his high pale forehead. "Jail house is a kinda funny place," he said. "Here's me, been a-goin' into the wilderness like Jesus to try find out somepin. Almost got her sometimes, too. But it's in the jail house I really got her." His eyes were sharp and merry. "Great big ol' cell, an' she's full all a time. New guys come in, and guys go out. An' 'course I talked to all of 'em."

" 'Course you did," said Tom. "Always talk. If you was up on the gallows you'd be passin' the time a day with the hangman. Never seen sech a talker."

The men in the tent chuckled. A wizened little man with a wrinkled face slapped his knee. "Talks all the time," he said. "Folks kinda likes to hear 'im, though."

"Use' ta be a preacher," said Tom. "Did he tell that?"

"Sure, he told."

Casy grinned. "Well, sir," he went on, "I begin gettin' at things. Some a them fellas in the tank was drunks, but mostly they was there 'cause they stole stuff; an' mostly it was stuff they needed an' couldn' get no other way. Ya see?" he asked.

"No," said Tom.

"Well, they was nice fellas, ya see. What made 'em bad was they needed stuff. An' I begin to see, then. It's need that makes all the trouble. I ain't got it worked out. Well, one day they give us some beans that was sour. One fella started yellin', an' nothin' happened. He yelled his head off. Trusty come along an' looked in an' went on. Then another fella yelled. Well, sir, then we all got yellin'. And we all got on the same tone, an' I tell ya, it jus' seemed like that tank bulged an' give and swelled up. By God! Then somepin happened! They come a-runnin', and they give us some other stuff to eat—give it to us. Ya see?"

"No," said Tom.

Casy put his chin down on his hands. "Maybe I can't tell you," he said. "Maybe you got to find out. Where's your cap?"

"I come out without it."

"How's your sister?"

"Hell, she's big as a cow. I bet she got twins. Gonna need wheels under her stomach. Got to holdin' it with her han's, now. You ain' tol' me what's goin' on."

The wizened man said, "We struck. This here's a strike."

"Well, fi' cents a box ain't much, but a fella can eat."

"Fi' cents?" the wizened man cried. "Fi' cents! They payin' you fi' cents?"

"Sure. We made a buck an' a half."

A heavy silence fell in the tent. Casy stared out the entrance, into the dark night. "Lookie, Tom," he said at last. "We come to work there. They says it's gonna be fi' cents. They was a hell of a lot of us. We got there an' they says they're payin' two an' a half cents. A fella can't even eat on that, an' if he got kids— So we says we won't take it. So they druv us off. An' all the cops in the worl' come down on us. Now they're payin' you five. When they bust this here strike—ya think they'll pay five?"

"I dunno," Tom said. "Payin' five now."

"Lookie," said Casy. "We tried to camp together, an' they druv us like pigs. Scattered us. Beat the hell outa fellas. Druv us like pigs. They run you in like pigs, too. We can't las' much longer. Some people ain't et for two days. You goin' back tonight?"

"Aim to," said Tom.

"Well—tell the folks in there how it is, Tom. Tell 'em they're starvin' us an' stabbin' theirself in the back. 'Cause sure as cowflops she'll drop to two an' a half jus' as soon as they clear us out."

"I'll tell 'em," said Tom. "I don' know how. Never seen so many guys with guns. Don' know if they'll even let a fella talk. An' folks don' pass no time of day. They jus' hang down their heads an' won't even give a fella a howdy."

"Try an' tell 'em, Tom. They'll get two an' a half, jus' the minute we're gone. You know what two an' a half is—that's one ton of peaches picked an' carried for a dollar." He dropped his head. "No—you can't do it. You can't get your food for that. Can't eat for that."

"I'll try to get to tell the folks."

"How's your ma?"

"Purty good. She liked that gov'ment camp. Baths an' hot water."

"Yeah—I heard."

"It was pretty nice there. Couldn' find no work, though. Had a leave."

"I'd like to go to one," said Casy. "Like to see it. Fella says they ain't no cops."

"Folks is their own cops."

Casy looked up excitedly. "An' was they any trouble? Fightin', stealin', drinkin'?"

"No," said Tom.

"Well, if a fella went bad—what then? What'd they do?"

"Put 'im outa the camp."

"But they wasn' many?"

"Hell, no," said Tom. "We was there a month, an' on'y one."

Casy's eyes shone with excitement. He turned to the other men. "Ya see?" he cried. "I tol' you. Cops cause more trouble than they stop. Look, Tom. Try an' get the folks in there to come on out. They can do it in a couple days. Them peaches is ripe. Tell 'em."

"They won't," said Tom. "They're a-gettin' five, an' they don' give a damn about nothin' else."

"But jus' the minute they ain't strikebreakin' they won't get no five."

"I don' think they'll swalla that. Five they're a-gettin'. Tha's all they care about."

"Well, tell 'em anyways."

"Pa wouldn' do it," Tom said. "I know 'im. He'd say it wasn't none of his business."

"Yes," Casy said disconsolately. "I guess that's right. Have to take a beatin' 'fore he'll know."

"We was outa food," Tom said. "Tonight we had meat. Not much, but we had it. Think Pa's gonna give up his meat on account a other fellas? An' Rosasharn oughta get milk. Think Ma's gonna wanta starve that baby jus' 'cause a bunch a fellas is yellin' outside a gate?"

Casy said sadly, "I wisht they could see it. I wisht they could see the on'y way they can depen' on their meat— Oh, the hell! Get tar'd sometimes. God-awful tar'd. I knowed a fella. Brang 'im in while I was in the jail house. Been tryin' to start a union. Got one started. An' then them vigilantes bust it up. An' know what? Them very folks he been tryin' to help tossed him out. Wouldn' have nothin' to do with 'im. Scared they'd get saw in his comp'ny. Says, 'Git out. You're a danger on us.' Well, sir, it hurt his feelin's purty bad. But then he says, 'It ain't so bad if you know.' He says, 'French Revolution—all them fellas that figgered her out got their heads chopped off. Always that way,' he says. 'Jus' as natural as rain. You didn' do it for fun no way. Doin' it 'cause you have to. 'Cause it's you. Look a Washington,' he says. 'Fit the Revolution, an' after, them sons-a-bitches turned on him. An' Lincoln the same. Same folks yellin' to kill 'em. Natural as rain.' "

"Don't soun' like no fun," said Tom.

"No, it don't. This fella in jail, he says, 'Anyways, you do what you can. An',' he says, 'the on'y thing you got to look at is that ever' time they's a little step fo'ward, she may slip back a little, but she never slips clear back. You can prove that,' he says, 'an' that makes the whole thing right. An' that means they wasn't no waste even if it seemed like they was.' "

"Talkin'," said Tom. "Always talkin'. Take my brother Al. He's out lookin' for a girl. He don't care 'bout nothin' else. Couple days he'll get him a girl. Think about it all day an' do it all night. He don't give a damn 'bout steps up or down or sideways."

"Sure," said Casy. "Sure. He's jus' doin' what he's got to do. All of us like that."

The man seated outside pulled the tent flap wide. "God-damn it, I don' like it," he said.

Casy looked out at him. "What's the matter?"

"I don' know. I jus' itch all over. Nervous as a cat."

"Well, what's the matter?"

"I don' know. Seems like I hear somepin, an' then I listen an' they ain't nothin' to hear."

"You're jus' jumpy," the wizened man said. He got up and went outside. And in a second he looked into the tent. "They's a great big ol' black cloud a-sailin' over. Bet she's got thunder. That's what's itchin' him—'lectricity." He ducked out again. The other two men stood up from the ground and went outside.

Casy said softly, "All of 'em's itchy. Them cops been sayin' how they're gonna beat the hell outa us an' run us outa the county. They figger I'm a leader 'cause I talk so much."

The wizened face looked in again. "Casy, turn out that lantern an' come outside. They's somepin."

Casy turned the screw. The flame drew down into the slots and popped and went out. Casy groped outside and Tom followed him. "What is it?" Casy asked softly.

"I dunno. Listen!"

There was a wall of frog sounds that merged with silence. A high, shrill whistle of crickets. But through this background came other sounds—faint footsteps from the road, a crunch of clods up on the bank, a little swish of brush down the stream.

"Can't really tell if you hear it. Fools you. Get nervous," Casy reassured them. "We're all nervous. Can't really tell. You hear it, Tom?"

"I hear it," said Tom. "Yeah, I hear it. I think they's guys comin' from ever' which way. We better get outa here."

The wizened man whispered, "Under the bridge span— out that way. Hate to leave my tent."

"Le's go," said Casy.

They moved quietly along the edge of the stream. The black span was a cave before them. Casy bent over and moved through. Tom behind. Their feet slipped into the water. Thirty feet they moved, and their breathing echoed from the curved ceiling. Then they came out on the other side and straightened up.

A sharp call, "There they are!" Two flashlight beams fell on the men, caught them, blinded them. "Stand where you are." The voices came out of the darkness. "That's him. That shiny bastard. That's him."

Casy stared blindly at the light. He breathed heavily. "Listen," he said. "You fellas don' know what you're doin'. You're helpin' to starve kids."

"Shut up, you red son-of-a-bitch."

A short heavy man stepped into the light. He carried a new white pick handle.

Casy went on, "You don' know what you're a-doin'."

The heavy man swung with the pick handle. Casy dodged down into the swing. The heavy club crashed into the side of his head with a dull crunch of bone, and Casy fell sideways out of the light.

"Jesus, George. I think you killed him."

"Put the light on him," said George. "Serve the son-of-a-bitch right." The flashlight beam dropped, searched and found Casy's crushed head.

Tom looked down at the preacher. The light crossed the heavy man's legs and the white new pick handle. Tom leaped silently. He wrenched the club free. The first time he knew he had missed and struck a shoulder, but the second time his crushing blow found the head, and as the heavy man sank down, three more blows found his head. The lights danced about. There were shouts, the sound of running feet, crashing through brush. Tom stood over the prostrate man. And then a club reached his head, a glancing blow. He felt the stroke like an electric shock. And then he was running along the stream, bending low. He heard the splash of footsteps following him. Suddenly he turned and squirmed up into the brush, deep into a poison-oak thicket. And he lay still. The footsteps came near, the light beams glanced along the stream bottom. Tom wriggled up through the thicket to the top. He emerged in an orchard. And still he could hear the calls, the pursuit in the stream bottom. He bent low and ran over the cultivated earth; the clods slipped and rolled under his feet. Ahead he saw the bushes that bounded the field, bushes along the edges of an irrigation ditch. He slipped through the fence, edged in among vines and blackberry bushes. And then he lay still, panting hoarsely. He felt his numb face and nose. The nose was crushed, and a trickle of blood dripped from his chin. He lay still on his stomach until his mind came back. And then he crawled slowly over the edge of the ditch. He bathed his face in the cool water, tore off the tail of his blue shirt and dipped it and held it against his torn cheek and nose. The water stung and burned.

The black cloud had crossed the sky, a blob of dark against the stars. The night was quiet again.

Tom stepped into the water and felt the bottom drop from under his feet. He threshed the two strokes across the ditch and pulled himself heavily up the other bank. His clothes clung to him. He moved and made a slopping noise; his shoes squished. Then he sat down, took off his shoes and emptied them. He wrung the bottoms of his trousers, took off his coat and squeezed the water from it.

Along the highway he saw the dancing beams of the flashlights, searching the ditches. Tom put on his shoes and moved cautiously across the stubble field. The squishing noise no longer came from his shoes. He went by instinct toward the other side of the stubble field, and at last he came to the road. Very cautiously he approached the square of houses.

Once a guard, thinking he heard a noise, called, "Who's there?"

Tom dropped and froze to the ground, and the flashlight beam passed over him. He crept silently to the door of the Joad house. The door squalled on its hinges. And Ma's voice, calm and steady and wide awake:

"What's that?"

"Me. Tom."

"Well, you better get some sleep. Al ain't in yet."

"He must a foun' a girl."

"Go on to sleep," she said softly. "Over under the window."

He found his place and took off his clothes to the skin. He lay shivering under his blanket. And his torn face awakened from its numbness, and his whole head throbbed.

It was an hour more before Al came in. He moved cautiously near and stepped on Tom's wet clothes.

"Sh!" said Tom.

Al whispered, "You awake? How'd you get wet?"

"Sh," said Tom. "Tell you in the mornin'."

Pa turned on his back, and his snoring filled the room with gasps and snorts.

"You're col'," Al said.

"Sh. Go to sleep." The little square of the window showed gray against the black of the room.

Tom did not sleep. The nerves of his wounded face came back to life and throbbed, and his cheek bone ached, and his broken nose bulged and pulsed with pain that seemed to toss him about, to shake him. He watched the little square window, saw the stars slide down over it and drop from sight. At intervals he heard the footsteps of the watchmen.

At last the roosters crowed, far away, and gradually the window lightened. Tom touched his swollen face with his fingertips, and at his movement Al groaned and murmured in his sleep.

The dawn came finally. In the houses, packed together, there was a sound of movement, a crash of breaking sticks, a little clatter of pans. In the graying gloom Ma sat up suddenly. Tom could see her face, swollen with sleep. She looked at the window, for a long moment. And then she threw the blanket off and found her dress. Still sitting down, she put it over her head and held her arms up and let the dress slide down to her waist. She stood up and pulled the dress down around her ankles. Then, in bare feet, she stepped carefully to the window and looked out, and while she stared at the growing light, her quick fingers unbraided her hair and smoothed the strands and braided them up again. Then she clasped her hands in front of her and stood motionless for a moment. Her face was lighted sharply by the window. She turned, stepped carefully among the mattresses, and found the lantern. The shade screeched up, and she lighted the wick.

Pa rolled over and blinked at her. She said, "Pa, you got more money?"

"Huh? Yeah. Paper wrote for sixty cents."

"Well, git up an' go buy some flour an' lard. Quick, now."

Pa yawned. "Maybe the store ain't open."

"Make 'em open it. Got to get somepin in you fellas. You got to get out to work."

Pa struggled into his overalls and put on his rusty coat. He went sluggishly out the door, yawning and stretching.

The children awakened and watched from under their blanket, like mice. Pale light filled the room now, but colorless light, before the sun. Ma glanced at the mattresses. Uncle John was awake, Al slept heavily. Her eyes moved to Tom. For a moment she peered at him, and then she moved quickly to him. His face was puffed and blue, and the blood was dried black on his lips and chin. The edges of the torn cheek were gathered and tight.

"Tom," she whispered, "what's the matter?"

"Sh!" he said. "Don't talk loud. I got in a fight."

"Tom!"

"I couldn' help it, Ma."

She knelt down beside him. "You in trouble?"

He was a long time answering. "Yeah," he said. "In trouble. I can't go out to work. I got to hide."

The children crawled near on their hands and knees, staring greedily. "What's the matter'th him, Ma?"

"Hush!" Ma said. "Go wash up."

"We got no soap."

"Well, use water."

"What's the matter'th Tom?"

"Now you hush. An' don't you tell nobody."

They backed away and squatted down against the far wall, knowing they would not be inspected.

Ma asked, "Is it bad?"

"Nose busted."

"I mean the trouble?"

"Yeah. Bad!"

Al opened his eyes and looked at Tom. "Well, for Chris' sake! What was you in?"

"What's a matter?" Uncle John asked.

Pa clumped in. "They was open all right." He put a tiny

bag of flour and his package of lard on the floor beside the stove. "'S'a matter?" he asked.

Tom braced himself on one elbow for a moment, and then he lay back. "Jesus, I'm weak. I'm gonna tell ya once. So I'll tell all of ya. How 'bout the kids?"

Ma looked at them, huddled against the wall. "Go wash ya face."

"No," Tom said. "They got to hear. They got to know. They might blab if they don' know."

"What the hell is this?" Pa demanded.

"I'm a-gonna tell. Las' night I went out to see what all the yellin' was about. An' I come on Casy."

"The preacher?"

"Yeah, Pa. The preacher, on'y he was a-leadin' the strike. They come for him."

Pa demanded, "Who come for him?"

"I dunno. Same kinda guys that turned us back on the road that night. Had pick handles." He paused. "They killed 'im. Busted his head. I was standin' there. I went nuts. Grabbed the pick handle." He looked bleakly back at the night, the darkness, the flashlights, as he spoke. "I—I clubbed a guy."

Ma's breath caught in her throat. Pa stiffened. "Kill 'im?" he asked softly.

"I—don't know. I was nuts. Tried to."

Ma asked, "Was you saw?"

"I dunno. I dunno. I guess so. They had the lights on us."

For a moment Ma stared into his eyes. "Pa," she said, "break up some boxes. We got to get breakfas'. You got to go to work. Ruthie, Winfiel'. If anybody asts you—Tom is sick—you hear? If you tell—he'll—get sent to jail. You hear?"

"Yes, ma'am."

"Keep your eye on 'em, John. Don' let 'em talk to no-body." She built the fire as Pa broke the boxes that had held the goods. She made her dough, put a pot of coffee to boil. The light wood caught and roared its flame in the chimney.

Pa finished breaking the boxes. He came near to Tom. "Casy—he was a good man. What'd he wanta mess with that stuff for?"

Tom said dully, "They come to work for fi' cents a box."

"That's what we're a-gettin'."

"Yeah. What we was a-doin' was breakin' strike. They give them fellas two an' a half cents."

"You can't eat on that."

"I know," Tom said wearily. "That's why they struck. Well, I think they bust that strike las' night. We'll maybe be gettin' two an' a half cents today."

"Why, the sons-a-bitches——"

"Yeah! Pa. You see? Casy was still a—good man. Goddamn it, I can't get that pitcher outa my head. Him layin' there—head jus' crushed flat an' oozin'. Jesus!" He covered his eyes with his hand.

"Well, what we gonna do?" Uncle John asked.

Al was standing up now. "Well, by God, I know what I'm gonna do. I'm gonna get out of it."

"No, you ain't, Al," Tom said. "We need you now. I'm the one. I'm a danger now. Soon's I get on my feet I got to go."

Ma worked at the stove. Her head was half turned to hear. She put grease in the frying pan, and when it whispered with heat, she spooned the dough into it.

Tom went on, "You got to stay, Al. You got to take care a the truck."

"Well, I don' like it."

"Can't help it, Al. It's your folks. You can help 'em. I'm a danger to 'em."

Al grumbled angrily. "I don' know why I ain't let to get me a job in a garage."

"Later, maybe." Tom looked past him, and he saw Rose of Sharon lying on the mattress. Her eyes were huge—opened wide. "Don't worry," he called to her. "Don't you worry. Gonna get you some milk today." She blinked slowly, and didn't answer him.

Pa said, "We got to know, Tom. Think ya killed this fella?"

"I don' know. It was dark. An' somebody smacked me. I don' know. I hope so. I hope I killed the bastard."

"Tom!" Ma called. "Don' talk like that."

From the street came the sound of many cars moving slowly. Pa stepped to the window and looked out. "They's a whole slew a new people comin' in," he said.

"I guess they bust the strike, awright," said Tom. "I guess you'll start at two an' a half cents."

"But a fella could work at a run, an' still he couldn' eat."

"I know," said Tom. "Eat win'fall peaches. That'll keep ya up."

Ma turned the dough and stirred the coffee. "Listen to me," she said. "I'm gettin' cornmeal today. We're a-gonna eat cornmeal mush. An' soon's we get enough for gas, we're movin' away. This ain't a good place. An' I ain't gonna have Tom out alone. No, sir."

"Ya can't do that, Ma. I tell you I'm jus' a danger to ya."

Her chin was set. "That's what we'll do. Here, come eat this here, an' then get out to work. I'll come out soon's I get washed up. We got to make some money."

They ate the fried dough so hot that it sizzled in their mouths. And they tossed the coffee down and filled their cups and drank more coffee.

Uncle John shook his head over his plate. "Don't look like we're a-gonna get shet of this here. I bet it's my sin."

"Oh, shut up!" Pa cried. "We ain't got the time for your sin now. Come on now. Le's get out to her. Kids, you come he'p. Ma's right. We got to go outa here."

When they were gone, Ma took a plate and a cup to Tom. "Better eat a little somepin."

"I can't, Ma. I'm so darn sore I couldn' chew."

"You better try."

"No, I can't, Ma."

She sat down on the edge of his mattress. "You got to tell me," she said. "I got to figger how it was. I got to keep straight. What was Casy a-doin'? Why'd they kill 'im?"

"He was jus' standin' there with the lights on' 'im."

"What'd he say? Can ya 'member what he says?"

Tom said, "Sure. Casy said, 'You got no right to starve people.' An' then this heavy fella called him a red son-of-a-bitch. An' Casy says, 'You don' know what you're a-doin'.' An' then this guy smashed 'im."

Ma looked down. She twisted her hands together. "Tha's what he said—'You don' know what you're doin' '?"

"Yeah!"

Ma said, "I wisht Granma could a heard."

"Ma—I didn' know what I was a-doin', no more'n when you take a breath. I didn' even know I was gonna do it."

"It's awright. I wisht you didn' do it. I wisht you wasn' there. But you done what you had to do. I can't read no fault on you." She went to the stove and dipped a cloth in the heating dishwater. "Here," she said. "Put that there on your face."

He laid the warm cloth over his nose and cheek, and winced at the heat. "Ma, I'm a-gonna go away tonight. I can't go puttin' this on you folks."

Ma said angrily, "Tom! They's a whole lot I don' un'erstan'. But goin' away ain't gonna ease us. It's gonna bear us down." And she went on, "They was the time when we was on the lan'. They was a boundary to us then. Ol' folks died off, an' little fellas come, an' we was always one thing—we was the fambly—kinda whole and clear. An' now we ain't clear no more. I can't get straight. They ain't nothin' keeps us clear. Al—he's a-hankerin' an' a-jibbitin' to go off on his own. An' Uncle John is jus' a-draggin' along. Pa's lost his place. He ain't the head no more. We're crackin' up, Tom. There ain't no fambly now. An' Rosasharn—" She looked around and found the girl's wide eyes. "She gonna have her baby an' they won't be no fambly. I don' know. I been a-tryin' to keep her goin'. Winfiel'—what's he gonna be, this-a-way? Gettin' wild, an' Ruthie too—like animals. Got nothin' to trus'. Don' go, Tom. Stay an' help."

"O.K.," he said tiredly. "O.K. I shouldn', though. I know it."

Ma went to her dishpan and washed the tin plates and dried them. "You didn' sleep."

"No."

"Well, you sleep. I seen your clothes was wet. I'll hang 'em by the stove to dry." She finished her work. "I'm goin' now. I'll pick. Rosasharn, if anybody comes, Tom's sick, you hear? Don' let nobody in. You hear?" Rose of Sharon nodded. "We'll come back at noon. Get some sleep, Tom.

Maybe we can get outa here tonight." She moved swiftly to him. "Tom, you ain't gonna slip out?"

"No, Ma."

"You sure? You won't go?"

"No, Ma. I'll be here."

"Awright. 'Member, Rosasharn." She went out and closed the door firmly behind her.

Tom lay still—and then a wave of sleep lifted him to the edge of unconsciousness and dropped him slowly back and lifted him again.

"You—Tom!"

"Huh? Yeah!" He started awake. He looked over at Rose of Sharon. Her eyes were blazing with resentment. "What you want?"

"You killed a fella!"

"Yeah. Not so loud! You wanta rouse somebody?"

"What da I care?" she cried. "That lady tol' me. She says what sin's gonna do. She tol' me. What chance I got to have a nice baby? Connie's gone, an' I ain't gettin' good food. I ain't gettin' milk." Her voice rose hysterically. "An' now you kill a fella. What chance that baby got to get bore right? I know—gonna be a freak—a freak! I never done no dancin'."

Tom got up. "Sh!" he said. "You're gonna get folks in here."

"I don' care. I'll have a freak! I didn' dance no hug-dance."

He went near to her. "Be quiet."

"You get away from me. It ain't the first fella you killed, neither." Her face was growing red with hysteria. Her words blurred. "I don' wanta look at you." She covered her head with her blanket.

Tom heard the choked, smothered cries. He bit his lower

lip and studied the floor. And then he went to Pa's bed. Under the edge of the mattress the rifle lay, a lever-action Winchester .38, long and heavy. Tom picked it up and dropped the lever to see that a cartridge was in the chamber. He tested the hammer on half-cock. And then he went back to his mattress. He laid the rifle on the floor beside him, stock up and barrel pointing down. Rose of Sharon's voice thinned to a whimper. Tom lay down again and covered himself, covered his bruised cheek with the blanket and made a little tunnel to breathe through. He sighed, "Jesus, oh, Jesus!"

Outside, a group of cars went by, and voices sounded.

"How many men?"

"Jes' us—three. Whatcha payin'?"

"You go to house twenty-five. Number's right on the door."

"O.K., mister. Whatcha payin'?"

"Two and a half cents."

"Why, goddamn it, a man can't make his dinner!"

"That's what we're payin'. There's two hundred men coming from the South that'll be glad to get it."

"But, Jesus, mister!"

"Go on now. Either take it or go on along. I got no time to argue."

"But——"

"Look. I didn' set the price. I'm just checking you in. If you want it, take it. If you don't, turn right around and go along."

"Twenty-five, you say?"

"Yes, twenty-five."

Tom dozed on his mattress. A stealthy sound in the room awakened him. His hand crept to the rifle and tightened on

the grip. He drew back the covers from his face. Rose of
Sharon was standing beside his mattress.

"What you want?" Tom demanded.

"You sleep," she said. "You jus' sleep off. I'll watch the
door. They won't nobody get in."

He studied her face for a moment. "O.K.," he said, and he
covered his face with the blanket again.

In the beginning dusk Ma came back to the house. She
paused on the doorstep and knocked and said, "It's me," so
that Tom would not be worried. She opened the door and
entered, carrying a bag. Tom awakened and sat up on his
mattress. His wound had dried and tightened so that the
unbroken skin was shiny. His left eye was drawn nearly shut.
"Anybody come while we was gone?" Ma asked.

"No," he said. "Nobody. I see they dropped the price."

"How'd you know?"

"I heard folks talkin' outside."

Rose of Sharon looked dully up at Ma.

Tom pointed at her with his thumb. "She raised hell, Ma.
Thinks all the trouble is aimed right smack at her. If I'm
gonna get her upset like that I oughta go 'long."

Ma turned on Rose of Sharon. "What you doin'?"

The girl said resentfully, "How'm I gonna have a nice
baby with stuff like this?"

Ma said, "Hush! You hush now. I know how you're
a-feelin', an' I know you can't he'p it, but you jus' keep your
mouth shut."

She turned back to Tom. "Don't pay her no mind, Tom.
It's awful hard, an' I 'member how it is. Ever'thing is a-
shootin' right at you when you're gonna have a baby, an'
ever'thing anybody says is a insult, an' ever'thing's against

you. Don't pay no mind. She can't he'p it. It's jus' the way she feels."

"I don' wanta hurt her."

"Hush! Jus' don' talk." She set her bag down on the cold stove. "Didn' hardly make nothin'," she said. "I tol' you, we're gonna get outa here. Tom, try an' wrassle me some wood. No—you can't. Here, we got on'y this one box lef'. Break it up. I tol' the other fellas to pick up some sticks on the way back. Gonna have mush an' a little sugar on."

Tom got up and stamped the last box to small pieces. Ma carefully built her fire in one end of the stove, conserving the flame under one stove hole. She filled a kettle with water and put it over the flame. The kettle rattled over the direct fire, rattled and wheezed.

"How was it pickin' today?" Tom asked.

Ma dipped a cup into her bag of cornmeal. "I don' wanta talk about it. I was thinkin' today how they use' to be jokes. I don' like it, Tom. We don't joke no more. When they's a joke, it's a mean bitter joke, an' they ain't no fun in it. Fella says today, 'Depression is over. I seen a jackrabbit, an' they wasn't nobody after him.' An' another fella says, 'That ain't the reason. Can't afford to kill jackrabbits no more. Catch 'em and milk 'em an' turn 'em loose. One you seen prob'ly gone dry.' That's how I mean. Ain't really funny, not funny like that time Uncle John converted an Injun an' brang him home, an' that Injun et his way clean to the bottom of the bean bin, an' then backslid with Uncle John's whisky. Tom, put a rag with col' water on your face."

The dusk deepened. Ma lighted the lantern and hung it on a nail. She fed the fire and poured cornmeal gradually into the hot water. "Rosasharn." she said, "can you stir the mush?"

Outside there was a patter of running feet. The door burst open and banged against the wall. Ruthie rushed in. "Ma!" she cried. "Ma. Winfiel' got a fit!"

"Where? Tell me!"

Ruthie panted, "Got white an' fell down. Et so many peaches he skittered hisself all day. Jus' fell down. White!"

"Take me!" Ma demanded. "Rosasharn, you watch that mush."

She went out with Ruthie. She ran heavily up the street behind the little girl. Three men walked toward her in the dusk, and the center man carried Winfield in his arms. Ma ran up to them. "He's mine," she cried. "Give 'im to me."

"I'll carry 'im for you, ma'am."

"No, here, give 'im to me." She hoisted the little boy and turned back; and then she remembered herself. "I sure thank ya," she said to the men.

"Welcome, ma'am. The little fella's purty weak. Looks like he got worms."

Ma hurried back, and Winfield was limp and relaxed in her arms. Ma carried him into the house and knelt down and laid him on a mattress. "Tell me. What's the matter?" she demanded. He opened his eyes dizzily and shook his head and closed his eyes again.

Ruthie said, "I tol' ya, Ma. He skittered all day. Ever' little while. Et too many peaches."

Ma felt his head. "He ain't fevered. But he's white and drawed out."

Tom came near and held the lantern down. "I know," he said. "He's hungered. Got no strength. Get him a can a milk an' make him drink it. Make 'im take milk on his mush."

"Winfiel'," Ma said. "Tell how ya feel."

"Dizzy," said Winfield, "jus' a-whirlin' dizzy."

"You never seen sech skitters," Ruthie said importantly.

Pa and Uncle John and Al came into the house. Their arms were full of sticks and bits of brush. They dropped their loads by the stove. "Now what?" Pa demanded.

"It's Winfiel'. He needs some milk."

"Christ Awmighty! We all need stuff!"

Ma said, "How much'd we make today?"

"Dollar forty-two."

"Well, you go right over'n get a can a milk for Winfiel'."

"Now why'd he have to get sick?"

"I don't know why, but he is. Now you git!" Pa went grumbling out the door. "You stirrin' that mush?"

"Yeah." Rose of Sharon speeded up the stirring to prove it.

Al complained, "God Awmighty, Ma! Is mush all we get after workin' till dark?"

"Al, you know we got to git. Take all we got for gas. You know."

"But, God Awmighty, Ma! A fella needs meat if he's gonna work."

"Jus' you sit quiet," she said. "We got to take the bigges' thing an' whup it fust. An' you know what that thing is."

Tom asked, "Is it about me?"

"We'll talk when we've et," said Ma. "Al, we got enough gas to go a ways, ain't we?"

" 'Bout a quarter tank," said Al.

"I wisht you'd tell me," Tom said.

"After. Jus' wait."

"Keep a-stirrin' that mush, you. Here, lemme put on some coffee. You can have sugar on your mush or in your coffee. They ain't enough for both."

Pa came back with one tall can of milk. " 'Leven cents," he said disgustedly.

"Here!" Ma took the can and stabbed it open. She let the thick stream out into a cup, and handed it to Tom. "Give that to Winfiel'."

Tom knelt beside the mattress. "Here, drink this."

"I can't. I'd sick it all up. Leave me be."

Tom stood up. "He can't take it now, Ma. Wait a little."

Ma took the cup and set it on the window ledge. "Don't none of you touch that," she warned. "That's for Winfiel'."

"I ain't had no milk," Rose of Sharon said sullenly. "I oughta have some."

"I know, but you're still on your feet. This here little fella's down. Is that mush good an' thick?"

"Yeah. Can't hardly stir it no more."

"Awright, le's eat. Now here's the sugar. They's about one spoon each. Have it on ya mush or in ya coffee."

Tom said, "I kinda like salt an' pepper on mush."

"Salt her if you like," Ma said. "The pepper's out."

The boxes were all gone. The family sat on the mattresses to eat their mush. They served themselves again and again, until the pot was nearly empty. "Save some for Winfiel'," Ma said.

Winfield sat up and drank his milk, and instantly he was ravenous. He put the mush pot between his legs and ate what was left and scraped at the crust on the sides. Ma poured the rest of the canned milk in a cup and sneaked it to Rose of Sharon to drink secretly in a corner. She poured the hot black coffee into the cups and passed them around.

"Now will you tell what's goin' on?" Tom asked. "I wanta hear."

Pa said uneasily, "I wisht Ruthie an' Winfiel' didn' hafta hear. Can't they go outside?"

Ma said, "No. They got to act growed up, even if they

ain't. They's no help for it. Ruthie—you an' Winfiel' ain't
ever to say what you hear, else you'll jus' break us to pieces."

"We won't," Ruthie said. "We're growed up."

"Well, jus' be quiet, then." The cups of coffee were on the
floor. The short thick flame of the lantern, like a stubby but-
terfly's wing, cast a yellow gloom on the walls.

"Now tell," said Tom.

Ma said, "Pa, you tell."

Uncle John slupped his coffee. Pa said, "Well, they
dropped the price like you said. An' they was a whole slew a
new pickers so goddamn hungry they'd pick for a loaf a
bread. Go for a peach, an' somebody'd get it first. Gonna get
the whole crop picked right off. Fellas runnin' to a new tree.
I seen fights—one fella claims it's his tree, 'nother fella wants
to pick off'n it. Brang these here folks from as far's El Centro.
Hungrier'n hell. Work all day for a piece a bread. I says to
the checker, 'We can't work for two an' a half cents a box,'
an' he says, 'Go on, then, quit. These fellas can.' I says,
'Soon's they get fed up they won't.' An' he says, 'Hell, we'll
have these here peaches in 'fore they get fed up.'" Pa
stopped.

"She was a devil," said Uncle John. "They say they's two
hunderd more men comin' in tonight."

Tom said, "Yeah! But how about the other?"

Pa was silent for a while. "Tom," he said, "looks like you
done it."

"I kinda thought so. Couldn' see. Felt like it."

"Seems like the people ain't talkin' 'bout much else," said
Uncle John. "They got posses out, an' they's fellas talkin' up
a lynchin'—'course when they catch the fella."

Tom looked over at the wide-eyed children. They seldom
blinked their eyes. It was as though they were afraid some-

thing might happen in the split second of darkness. Tom said, "Well—this fella that done it, he on'y done it after they killed Casy."

Pa interrupted, "That ain't the way they're tellin' it now. They're sayin' he done it fust."

Tom's breath sighed out, "Ah-h!"

"They're workin' up a feelin' against us folks. That's what I heard. All them drum-corpse fellas an' lodges an' all that. Say they're gonna get this here fella."

"They know what he looks like?" Tom asked.

"Well—not exactly—but the way I heard it, they think he got hit. They think—he'll have——"

Tom put his hand up slowly and touched his bruised cheek.

Ma cried, "It ain't so, what they say!"

"Easy, Ma," Tom said. "They got it cold. Anything them drum-corpse fellas say is right if it's against us."

Ma peered through the ill light, and she watched Tom's face, and particularly his lips. "You promised," she said.

"Ma, I—maybe this fella oughta go away. If—this fella done somepin wrong, maybe he'd think, 'O.K. Le's get the hangin' over. I done wrong an' I got to take it.' But this fella didn' do nothin' wrong. He don' feel no worse'n if he killed a skunk."

Ruthie broke in, "Ma, me an' Winfiel' knows. He don' have to go this-fella'in' for us."

Tom chuckled. "Well, this fella don' want no hangin', 'cause he'd do it again. An' same time, he don't aim to bring trouble down on his folks. Ma—I got to go."

Ma covered her mouth with her fingers and coughed to clear her throat. "You can't," she said. "They wouldn' be no way to hide out. You couldn' trus' nobody. But you can trus' us. We can hide you, an' we can see you get to eat while your face gets well."

"But, Ma——"

She got to her feet. "You ain't goin'. We're a-takin' you. Al, you back the truck against the door. Now, I got it figgered out. We'll put one mattress on the bottom, an' then Tom gets quick there, an' we take another mattress an' sort of fold it so it makes a cave, an' he's in the cave; and then we sort of wall it in. He can breathe out the end, ya see. Don't argue. That's what we'll do."

Pa complained, "Seems like the man ain't got no say no more. She's jus' a heller. Come time we get settled down, I'm a-gonna smack her."

"Come that time, you can," said Ma. "Roust up, Al. It's dark enough."

Al went outside to the truck. He studied the matter and backed up near the steps.

Ma said, "Quick now. Git that mattress in!"

Pa and Uncle John flung it over the end gate. "Now that one." They tossed the second mattress up. "Now—Tom, you jump up there an' git under. Hurry up."

Tom climbed quickly, and dropped. He straightened one mattress and pulled the second on top of him. Pa bent it upwards, stood it sides up, so that the arch covered Tom. He could see out between the side-boards of the truck. Pa and Al and Uncle John loaded quickly, piled the blankets on top of Tom's cave, stood the buckets against the sides, spread the last mattress behind. Pots and pans, extra clothes, went in loose, for their boxes had been burned. They were nearly finished loading when a guard moved near, carrying his shotgun across his crooked arm.

"What's goin' on here?" he asked.

"We're goin' out," said Pa.

"What for?"

"Well—we got a job offered—good job."

"Yeah? Where's it at?"

"Why—down by Weedpatch."

"Let's have a look at you." He turned a flashlight in Pa's face, in Uncle John's, and in Al's. "Wasn't there another fella with you?"

Al said, "You mean that hitch-hiker? Little short fella with a pale face?"

"Yeah. I guess that's what he looked like."

"We jus' picked him up on the way in. He went away this mornin' when the rate dropped."

"What did he look like again?"

"Short fella. Pale face."

"Was he bruised up this mornin'?"

"I didn' see nothin'," said Al. "Is the gas pump open?"

"Yeah, till eight."

"Git in," Al cried. "If we're gonna get to Weedpatch 'fore mornin' we gotta ram on. Gettin' in front, Ma?"

"No, I'll set in back," she said. "Pa, you set back here too. Let Rosasharn set in front with Al an' Uncle John."

"Give me the work slip, Pa," said Al. "I'll get gas an' change if I can."

The guard watched them pull along the street and turn left to the gasoline pumps.

"Put in two," said Al.

"You ain't goin' far."

"No, not far. Can I get change on this here work slip?"

"Well—I ain't supposed to."

"Look, mister," Al said. "We got a good job offered if we get there tonight. If we don't, we miss out. Be a good fella."

"Well, O.K. You sign her over to me."

Al got out and walked around the nose of the Hudson. "Sure I will," he said. He unscrewed the water cap and filled the radiator.

"Two, you say?"

"Yeah, two."

"Which way you goin'?"

"South. We got a job."

"Yeah? Jobs is scarce—reg'lar jobs."

"We got a frien'," Al said. "Job's all waitin' for us. Well, so long." The truck swung around and bumped over the dirt street into the road. The feeble headlight jiggled over the way, and the right headlight blinked on and off from a bad connection. At every jolt the loose pots and pans in the truck-bed jangled and crashed.

Rose of Sharon moaned softly.

"Feel bad?" Uncle John asked.

"Yeah! Feel bad all a time. Wisht I could set still in a nice place. Wisht we was home an' never come. Connie wouldn' a went away if we was home. He would a studied up an' got someplace." Neither Al nor Uncle John answered her. They were embarrassed about Connie.

At the white painted gate to the ranch a guard came to the side of the truck. "Goin' out for good?"

"Yeah," said Al. "Goin' north. Got a job."

The guard turned his flashlight on the truck, turned it up into the tent. Ma and Pa looked stonily down into the glare. "O.K." The guard swung the gate open. The truck turned left and moved toward 101, the great north-south highway.

"Know where we're a-goin'?" Uncle John asked.

"No," said Al. "Jus' goin', an' gettin' goddamn sick of it."

"I ain't so tur'ble far from my time," Rose of Sharon said threateningly. "They better be a nice place for me."

The night air was cold with the first sting of frost. Beside the road the leaves were beginning to drop from the fruit trees. On the load, Ma sat with her back against the truck side, and Pa sat opposite, facing her.

Ma called, "You all right, Tom?"

His muffled voice came back, "Kinda tight in here. We all through the ranch?"

"You be careful," said Ma. "Might git stopped."

Tom lifted up one side of his cave. In the dimness of the truck the pots jangled. "I can pull her down quick," he said. " 'Sides, I don' like gettin' trapped in here." He rested up on his elbow. "By God, she's gettin' cold, ain't she?"

"They's clouds up," said Pa. "Fellas says it's gonna be an early winter."

"Squirrels a-buildin' high, or grass seeds?" Tom asked. "By God, you can tell weather from anythin'. I bet you could find a fella could tell weather from a old pair of underdrawers."

"I dunno," Pa said. "Seems like it's gittin' on winter to me. Fella'd have to live here a long time to know."

"Which way we a-goin'?" Tom asked.

"I dunno. Al, he turned off lef'. Seems like he's goin' back the way we come."

Tom said, "I can't figger what's best. Seems like if we get on the main highway they'll be more cops. With my face this-a-way, they'd pick me right up. Maybe we oughta keep to back roads."

Ma said, "Hammer on the back. Get Al to stop."

Tom pounded the front board with his fist; the truck

pulled to a stop on the side of the road. Al got out and walked to the back. Ruthie and Winfield peeked out from under their blanket.

"What ya want?" Al demanded.

Ma said, "We got to figger what to do. Maybe we better keep on the back roads. Tom says so."

"It's my face," Tom added. "Anybody'd know. Any cop'd know me."

"Well, which way you wanta go? I figgered north. We been south."

"Yeah," said Tom, "but keep on back roads."

Al asked, "How 'bout pullin' off an' catchin' some sleep, goin' on tomorra?"

Ma said quickly, "Not yet. Le's get some distance fust."

"O.K." Al got back in his seat and drove on.

Ruthie and Winfield covered up their heads again. Ma called, "Is Winfiel' all right?"

"Sure, he's awright," Ruthie said. "He been sleepin'."

Ma leaned back against the truck side. "Gives ya a funny feelin' to be hunted like. I'm gittin' mean."

"Ever'body's gittin' mean," said Pa. "Ever'body. You seen that fight today. Fella changes. Down that gov'ment camp we wasn' mean."

Al turned right on a graveled road, and the yellow lights shuddered over the ground. The fruit trees were gone now, and cotton plants took their place. They drove on for twenty miles through the cotton, turning, angling on the country roads. The road paralleled a bushy creek and turned over a concrete bridge and followed the stream on the other side. And then, on the edge of the creek the lights showed a long line of red boxcars, wheelless; and a big sign on the edge of the road said, "Cotton Pickers Wanted." Al slowed down.

Tom peered between the side-bars of the truck. A quarter of a mile past the boxcars Tom hammered on the car again. Al stopped beside the road and got out again.

"Now what ya want?"

"Shut off the engine an' climb up here," Tom said.

Al got into the seat, drove off into the ditch, cut lights and engine. He climbed over the tail gate. "Awright," he said.

Tom crawled over the pots and knelt in front of Ma. "Look," he said. "It says they want cotton pickers. I seen that sign. Now I been tryin' to figger how I'm gonna stay with you, an' not make no trouble. When my face gets well, maybe it'll be awright, but not now. Ya see them cars back there. Well, the pickers live in them. Now maybe they's work there. How about if you get work there an' live in one of them cars?"

"How 'bout you?" Ma demanded.

"Well, you seen that crick, all full a brush. Well, I could hide in that brush an' keep outa sight. An' at night you could bring me out somepin to eat. I seen a culvert, little ways back. I could maybe sleep in there."

Pa said, "By God, I'd like to get my hands on some cotton! There's work, I un'erstan'."

"Them cars might be a purty place to stay," said Ma. "Nice an' dry. You think they's enough brush to hide in, Tom?"

"Sure. I been watchin'. I could fix up a little place, hide away. Soon's my face gets well, why, I'd come out."

"You gonna scar purty bad," said Ma.

"Hell! Ever'body got scars."

"I picked four hunderd poun's oncet," Pa said. " 'Course it was a good heavy crop. If we all pick, we could get some money."

"Could get some meat," said Al. "What'll we do right now?"

"Go back there, an' sleep in the truck till mornin'," Pa said. "Git work in the mornin'. I can see them bolls even in the dark."

"How 'bout Tom?" Ma asked.

"Now you jus' forget me, Ma. I'll take me a blanket. You look out on the way back. They's a nice culvert. You can bring me some bread or potatoes, or mush, an' just leave it there. I'll come get it."

"Well!"

"Seems like good sense to me," said Pa.

"It is good sense," Tom insisted. "Soon's my face gets a little better, why, I'll come out an' go to pickin'."

"Well, awright," Ma agreed. "But don' you take no chancet. Don' let nobody see you for a while."

Tom crawled to the back of the truck. "I'll jus' take this here blanket. You look for that culvert on the way back, Ma."

"Take care," she begged. "You take care."

"Sure," said Tom. "Sure I will." He climbed the tail board, stepped down the bank. "Good night," he said.

Ma watched his figure blur with the night and disappear into the bushes beside the stream. "Dear Jesus, I hope it's awright," she said.

Al asked, "You want I should go back now?"

"Yeah," said Pa.

"Go slow," said Ma. "I wanta be sure an' see that culvert he said about. I got to see that."

Al backed and filled on the narrow road, until he had reversed his direction. He drove slowly back to the line of box-cars. The truck lights showed the cat-walks up to the wide car doors. The doors were dark. No one moved in the night. Al shut off his lights.

"You and Uncle John climb up back," he said to Rose of Sharon. "I'll sleep in the seat here."

Uncle John helped the heavy girl to climb up over the tail board. Ma piled the pots in a small space. The family lay wedged close together in the back of the truck.

A baby cried, in long jerking cackles, in one of the box-cars. A dog trotted out, sniffing and snorting, and moved slowly around the Joad truck. The tinkle of moving water came from the streambed.

Chapter Twenty-Seven

COTTON Pickers Wanted—placards on the road, handbills out, orange-colored handbills—Cotton Pickers Wanted.

Here, up this road, it says.

The dark, green plants stringy now, and the heavy bolls clutched in the pod. White cotton spilling out like popcorn.

Like to get our hands on the bolls. Tenderly, with the fingertips.

I'm a good picker.

Here's the man, right here.

I aim to pick some cotton.

Got a bag?

Well, no, I ain't.

Cost ya a dollar, the bag. Take it out o' your first hunderd and fifty. Eighty cents a hunderd first time over the field. Ninety cents second time over. Get your bag there. One dollar. 'F you ain't got the buck, we'll take it out of your first hunderd and fifty. That's fair, and you know it.

Sure it's fair. Good cotton bag, last all season. An' when she's wore out, draggin', turn 'er aroun', use the other end. Sew up the open end. Open up the wore end. And when both ends is gone, why, that's nice cloth! Makes a nice pair a summer drawers. Makes nightshirts. And well, hell—a cotton bag's a nice thing.

Hang it around your waist. Straddle it, drag it between your legs. She drags light at first. And your fingertips pick out the fluff, and the hands go twisting into the sack between your legs. Kids come along behind; got no bags for the kids —use a gunny sack or put it in your ol' man's bag. She hangs heavy, some, now. Lean forward, hoist 'er along. I'm a good hand with cotton. Finger-wise, boll-wise. Jes' move along talkin', an' maybe singin' till the bag gets heavy. Fingers go right to it. Fingers know. Eyes see the work—and don't see it.

Talkin' across the rows——

They was a lady back home, won't mention no names— had a nigger kid all of a sudden. Nobody knowed before. Never did hunt out the nigger. Couldn' never hold up her head no more. But I started to tell—she was a good picker.

Now the bag is heavy, boost it along. Set your hips and tow it along, like a work horse. And the kids pickin' into the old man's sack. Good crop here. Gets thin in the low places, thin and stringy. Never seen no cotton like this here California cotton. Long fiber, bes' damn cotton I ever seen. Spoil the lan' pretty soon. Like a fella wants to buy some cotton lan'— Don' buy her, rent her. Then when she's cottoned on down, move someplace new.

Lines of people moving across the fields. Finger-wise. Inquisitive fingers snick in and out and find the bolls. Hardly have to look.

Bet I could pick cotton if I was blind. Got a feelin' for a cotton boll. Pick clean, clean as a whistle.

Sack's full now. Take her to the scales. Argue. Scale man says you got rocks to make weight. How 'bout him? His scales is fixed. Sometimes he's right, you got rocks in the sack. Sometimes you're right, the scales is crooked. Sometimes both; rocks an' crooked scales. Always argue, always fight. Keeps your head up. An' his head up. What's a few rocks? Jus' one, maybe. Quarter pound? Always argue.

Back with the empty sack. Got our own book. Mark in the weight. Got to. If they know you're markin', then they don't cheat. But God he'p ya if ya don' keep your own weight.

This is good work. Kids runnin' aroun'. Heard 'bout the cotton-pickin' machine?

Yeah, I heard.

Think it'll ever come?

Well, if it comes—fella says it'll put han' pickin' out.

Come night. All tired. Good pickin', though. Got three dollars, me an' the ol' woman an' the kids.

The cars move to the cotton fields. The cotton camps set up. The screened high trucks and trailers are piled high with white fluff. Cotton clings to the fence wires, and cotton rolls in little balls along the road when the wind blows. And clean white cotton, going to the gin. And the big, lumpy bales standing, going to the compress. And cotton clinging to your clothes and stuck to your whiskers. Blow your nose, there's cotton in your nose.

Hunch along now, fill up the bag 'fore dark. Wise fingers seeking in the bolls. Hips hunching along, dragging the bag. Kids are tired, now in the evening. They trip over their feet in the cultivated earth. And the sun is going down.

Wisht it would last. It ain't much money, God knows, but I wisht it would last.

On the highway the old cars piling in, drawn by the handbills.

Got a cotton bag?

No.

Cost ya a dollar, then.

If they was on'y fifty of us, we could stay awhile, but they's five hunderd. She won't last hardly at all. I knowed a fella never did git his bag paid out. Ever' job he got a new bag, an' ever' fiel' was done 'fore he got his weight.

Try for God's sake ta save a little money! Winter's comin' fast. They ain't no work at all in California in the winter. Fill up the bag 'fore it's dark. I seen that fella put two clods in.

Well, hell. Why not? I'm jus' balancin' the crooked scales. Now here's my book, three hunderd an' twelve poun's.

Right!

Jesus, he never argued! His scales mus' be crooked. Well, that's a nice day anyways.

They say a thousan' men are on their way to this field. We'll be fightin' for a row tomorra. We'll be snatchin' cotton, quick.

Cotton Pickers Wanted. More men picking, quicker to the gin.

Now into the cotton camp.

Side-meat tonight, by God! We got money for side-meat! Stick out a han' to the little fella, he's wore out. Run in ahead an' git us four poun' of side-meat. The ol' woman'll make some nice biscuits tonight, ef she ain't too tired.

Chapter Twenty-Eight

THE boxcars, twelve of them, stood end to end on a little flat beside the stream. There were two rows of six each, the wheels removed. Up to the big sliding doors slatted planks ran for cat-walks. They made good houses, water-tight and draftless, room for twenty-four families, one family in each end of each car. No windows, but the wide doors stood open. In some of the cars a canvas hung down in the center of the car, while in others only the position of the door made the boundary.

The Joads had one end of an end car. Some previous occupant had fitted up an oil can with a stovepipe, had made a hole in the wall for the stovepipe. Even with the wide door open, it was dark in the ends of the car. Ma hung the tarpaulin across the middle of the car.

"It's nice," she said. "It's almost nicer than anything we had 'cept the gov'ment camp."

Each night she unrolled the mattresses on the floor, and each morning rolled them up again. And every day they went into the fields and picked the cotton, and every night they had meat. On a Saturday they drove into Tulare, and they bought a tin stove and new overalls for Al and Pa and Winfield and Uncle John, and they bought a dress for Ma and gave Ma's best dress to Rose of Sharon.

"She's so big," Ma said. "Jus' a waste of good money to get her a new dress now."

The Joads had been lucky. They got in early enough to have a place in the boxcars. Now the tents of the late-comers filled the little flat, and those who had the boxcars were old-timers, and in a way aristocrats.

The narrow stream slipped by, out of the willows, and back into the willows again. From each car a hard-beaten path went down to the stream. Between the cars the clothes lines hung, and every day the lines were covered with drying clothes.

In the evening they walked back from the fields, carrying their folded cotton bags under their arms. They went into the store which stood at the crossroads, and there were many pickers in the store, buying their supplies.

"How much today?"

"We're doin' fine. We made three and a half today. Wisht she'd keep up. Them kids is gettin' to be good pickers. Ma's worked 'em up a little bag for each. They couldn' tow a growed-up bag. Dump into ours. Made bags outa a couple old shirts. Work fine."

And Ma went to the meat counter, her forefinger pressed against her lips, blowing on her finger, thinking deeply. "Might get some pork chops," she said. "How much?"

"Thirty cents a pound, ma'am."

"Well, lemme have three poun's. An' a nice piece a boilin' beef. My girl can cook it tomorra. An' a bottle a milk for my girl. She dotes on milk. Gonna have a baby. Nurse-lady tol' her to eat lots a milk. Now, le's see, we got potatoes."

Pa came close, carrying a can of sirup in his hands. "Might get this here," he said. "Might have some hotcakes."

Ma frowned. "Well—well, yes. Here, we'll take this here. Now—we got plenty lard."

Ruthie came near, in her hands two large boxes of Cracker

Jack, in her eyes a brooding question, which on a nod or a shake of Ma's head might become tragedy or joyous excitement. "Ma?" She held up the boxes, jerked them up and down to make them attractive.

"Now you put them back——"

The tragedy began to form in Ruthie's eyes. Pa said, "They're on'y a nickel apiece. Them little fellas worked good today."

"Well——" The excitement began to steal into Ruthie's eyes. "Awright."

Ruthie turned and fled. Halfway to the door she caught Winfield and rushed him out the door, into the evening.

Uncle John fingered a pair of canvas gloves with yellow leather palms, tried them on and took them off and laid them down. He moved gradually to the liquor shelves, and he stood studying the labels on the bottles. Ma saw him. "Pa," she said, and motioned with her head toward Uncle John.

Pa lounged over to him. "Gettin' thirsty, John?"

"No, I ain't."

"Jus' wait till cotton's done," said Pa. "Then you can go on a hell of a drunk."

" 'Tain't sweatin' me none," Uncle John said. "I'm workin' hard an' sleepin' good. No dreams nor nothin'."

"Jus' seen you sort of droolin' out at them bottles."

"I didn' hardly see 'em. Funny thing. I wanta buy stuff. Stuff I don't need. Like to git one a them safety razors. Thought I'd like to have some a them gloves over there. Awful cheap."

"Can't pick no cotton with gloves," said Pa.

"I know that. An' I don't need no safety razor, neither. Stuff settin' out there, you jus' feel like buyin' it whether you need it or not."

Ma called, "Come on. We got ever'thing." She carried a bag. Uncle John and Pa each took a package. Outside Ruthie and Winfield were waiting, their eyes strained, their cheeks puffed and full of Cracker Jack.

"Won't eat no supper, I bet," Ma said.

People streamed toward the boxcar camp. The tents were lighted. Smoke poured from the stovepipes. The Joads climbed up their cat-walk and into their end of the boxcar. Rose of Sharon sat on a box beside the stove. She had a fire started, and the tin stove was wine-colored with heat. "Did ya get milk?" she demanded.

"Yeah. Right here."

"Give it to me. I ain't had any sence noon."

"She thinks it's like medicine."

"That nurse-lady says so."

"You got potatoes ready?"

"Right there—peeled."

"We'll fry 'em," said Ma. "Got pork chops. Cut up them potatoes in the new fry pan. And th'ow in a onion. You fellas go out an' wash, an' bring in a bucket a water. Where's Ruthie an' Winfiel'? They oughta wash. They each got Cracker Jack," Ma told Rose of Sharon. "Each got a whole box."

The men went out to wash in the stream. Rose of Sharon sliced the potatoes into the frying pan and stirred them about with the knife point.

Suddenly the tarpaulin was thrust aside. A stout perspiring face looked in from the other end of the car. "How'd you all make out, Mis' Joad?"

Ma swung around. "Why, evenin', Mis' Wainwright. We done good. Three an' a half. Three fifty-seven, exact."

"We done four dollars."

"Well," said Ma. " 'Course they's more *of* you."

"Yeah. Jonas is growin' up. Havin' pork chops, I see."

Winfield crept in through the door. "Ma!"

"Hush a minute. Yes, my men jus' loves pork chops."

"I'm cookin' bacon," said Mrs. Wainwright. "Can you smell it cookin'?"

"No—can't smell it over these here onions in the potatoes."

"She's burnin'!" Mrs. Wainwright cried, and her head jerked back.

"Ma," Winfield said.

"What? You sick from Cracker Jack?"

"Ma—Ruthie tol'."

"Tol' what?"

" 'Bout Tom."

Ma stared. "Tol'?" Then she knelt in front of him. "Winfiel', who'd she tell?"

Embarrassment seized Winfield. He backed away. "Well, she on'y tol' a little bit."

"Winfiel'! Now you tell what she said."

"She—she didn' eat all her Cracker Jack. She kep' some, an' she et jus' one piece at a time, slow, like she always done, an' she says, 'Bet you wisht you had some lef'."

"Winfiel'!" Ma demanded. "You tell now." She looked back nervously at the curtain. "Rosasharn, you go over talk to Mis' Wainwright so she don' listen."

"How 'bout these here potatoes?"

"I'll watch 'em. Now you go. I don' want her listenin' at that curtain." The girl shuffled heavily down the car and went around the side of the hung tarpaulin.

Ma said, "Now, Winfiel', you tell."

"Like I said, she et jus' one little piece at a time, an' she bust some in two so it'd las' longer."

"Go on, hurry up."

"Well, some kids come aroun', an' 'course they tried to get some, but Ruthie, she jus' nibbled an' nibbled, an' wouldn' give 'em none. So they got mad. An' one kid grabbed her Cracker Jack box."

"Winfiel', you tell quick about the other."

"I am," he said. "So Ruthie got mad an' chased 'em, an' she fit one, an' then she fit another, an' then one big girl up an' licked her. Hit 'er a good one. So then Ruthie cried, an' she said she'd git her big brother, an' he'd kill that big girl. An' that big girl said, Oh, yeah? Well, she got a big brother too." Winfield was breathless in his telling. "So then they fit, an' that big girl hit Ruthie a good one, an' Ruthie said her brother'd kill that big girl's brother. An' that big girl said how about if her brother kil't our brother. An' then—an' then, Ruthie said our brother already kil't two fellas. An'— an'—that big girl said, 'Oh, yeah! You're jus' a little smarty liar.' An' Ruthie said, Oh, yeah? Well, our brother's a-hidin' right now from killin' a fella, an' he can kill that big girl's brother too. An' then they called names an' Ruthie throwed a rock, an' that big girl chased her, an' I come home."

"Oh, my!" Ma said wearily. "Oh! My dear sweet Lord Jesus asleep in a manger! What we goin' to do now?" She put her forehead in her hand and rubbed her eyes. "What we gonna do now?" A smell of burning potatoes came from the roaring stove. Ma moved automatically and turned them.

"Rosasharn!" Ma called. The girl appeared around the curtain. "Come watch this here supper. Winfiel', you go out an' you fin' Ruthie an' bring her back here."

"Gonna whup her, Ma?" he asked hopefully.

"No. This here you couldn' do nothin' about. Why, I

wonder, did she haf' to do it? No. It won't do no good to whup her. Run now, an' find her an' bring her back."

Winfield ran for the car door, and he met the three men tramping up the cat-walk, and he stood aside while they came in.

Ma said softly, "Pa, I got to talk to you. Ruthie tol' some kids how Tom's a-hidin'."

"What?"

"She tol'. Got in a fight an' tol'."

"Why, the little bitch!"

"No, she didn' know what she was a-doin'. Now look, Pa. I want you to stay here. I'm goin' out an' try to fin' Tom an' tell him. I got to tell 'im to be careful. You stick here, Pa, an' kinda watch out for things. I'll take 'im some dinner."

"Awright," Pa agreed.

"Don' you even mention to Ruthie what she done. I'll tell her."

At that moment Ruthie came in, with Winfield behind her. The little girl was dirtied. Her mouth was sticky, and her nose still dripped a little blood from her fight. She looked shamed and frightened. Winfield triumphantly followed her. Ruthie looked fiercely about, but she went to a corner of the car and put her back in the corner. Her shame and fierceness were blended.

"I tol' her what she done," Winfield said.

Ma was putting two chops and some fried potatoes on a tin plate. "Hush, Winfiel'," she said. "They ain't no need to hurt her feelings no more'n what they're hurt."

Ruthie's body hurtled across the car. She grabbed Ma around the middle and buried her head in Ma's stomach, and her strangled sobs shook her whole body. Ma tried to loosen her, but the grubby fingers clung tight. Ma brushed the hair on the back of her head gently, and she patted her shoulders. "Hush," she said. "You didn' know."

Ruthie raised her dirty, tear-stained, bloody face. "They stoled my Cracker Jack!" she cried. "That big son-of-a-bitch of a girl, she belted me—" She went off into hard crying again.

"Hush!" Ma said. "Don' talk like that. Here. Let go. I'm a-goin' now."

"Whyn't ya whup her, Ma? If she didn't git snotty with her Cracker Jack 'twouldn' a happened. Go on, give her a whup."

"You jus' min' your business, mister," Ma said fiercely. "You'll git a whup yourself. Now leggo, Ruthie."

Winfield retired to a rolled mattress, and he regarded the family cynically and dully. And he put himself in a good position of defense, for Ruthie would attack him at the first opportunity, and he knew it. Ruthie went quietly, heart-brokenly to the other side of the car.

Ma put a sheet of newspaper over the tin plate. "I'm a-goin' now," she said.

"Ain't you gonna eat nothin' yourself?" Uncle John demanded.

"Later. When I come back. I wouldn' want nothin' now." Ma walked to the open door; she steadied herself down the steep, cleated cat-walk.

On the stream side of the boxcars, the tents were pitched close together, their guy ropes crossing one another, and the pegs of one at the canvas line of the next. The lights shone through the cloth, and all the chimneys belched smoke. Men and women stood in the doorways talking. Children ran feverishly about. Ma moved majestically down the line of tents. Here and there she was recognized as she went by.

"Evenin', Mis' Joad."

"Evenin'."

"Takin' somepin out, Mis' Joad?"

"They's a frien'. I'm takin' back some bread."

She came at last to the end of the line of tents. She stopped and looked back. A glow of light was on the camp, and the soft overtone of a multitude of speakers. Now and then a harsher voice cut through. The smell of smoke filled the air. Someone played a harmonica softly, trying for an effect, one phrase over and over.

Ma stepped in among the willows beside the stream. She moved off the trail and waited, silently, listening to hear any possible follower. A man walked down the trail toward the camp, boosting his suspenders and buttoning his jeans as he went. Ma sat very still, and he passed on without seeing her. She waited five minutes and then she stood up and crept on up the trail beside the stream. She moved quietly, so quietly that she could hear the murmur of the water above her soft steps on the willow leaves. Trail and stream swung to the left and then to the right again until they neared the highway. In the gray starlight she could see the embankment and the black round hole of the culvert where she always left Tom's food. She moved forward cautiously, thrust her package into the hole, and took back the empty tin plate which was left there. She crept back among the willows, forced her way into a thicket, and sat down to wait. Through the tangle she could see the black hole of the culvert. She clasped her knees and sat silently. In a few moments the thicket crept to life again. The field mice moved cautiously over the leaves. A skunk padded heavily and unself-consciously down the trail, carrying a faint effluvium with him. And then a wind stirred the willows delicately, as though it tested them, and a shower of golden leaves coasted down to the ground. Suddenly a gust boiled in and racked the trees, and a cricking downpour of leaves fell. Ma could feel them on her hair and on her shoulders. Over the sky a plump black cloud moved, erasing the stars. The fat drops of rain scattered down, splashing loudly on the fallen leaves, and the cloud moved on and unveiled the stars again. Ma shivered. The wind blew past and left the thicket quiet, but the rushing of the trees went on down the stream. From back at the camp came the thin penetrating tone of a violin feeling about for a tune.

Ma heard a stealthy step among the leaves far to her left, and she grew tense. She released her knees and straightened her head, the better to hear. The movement stopped, and after a long moment began again. A vine rasped harshly on the dry leaves. Ma saw a dark figure creep into the open and draw near to the culvert. The black round hole was obscured for a moment, and then the figure moved back. She called softly, "Tom!" The figure stood still, so still, so low to the ground that it might have been a stump. She called again, "Tom, oh, Tom!" Then the figure moved.

"That you, Ma?"

"Right over here." She stood up and went to meet him.

"You shouldn' of came," he said.

"I got to see you, Tom. I got to talk to you."

"It's near the trail," he said. "Somebody might come by."

"Ain't you got a place, Tom?"

"Yeah—but if—well, s'pose somebody seen you with me—whole fambly'd be in a jam."

"I got to, Tom."

"Then come along. Come quiet." He crossed the little

stream, wading carelessly through the water, and Ma followed him. He moved through the brush, out into a field on the other side of the thicket, and along the plowed ground. The blackening stems of the cotton were harsh against the ground, and a few fluffs of cotton clung to the stems. A quarter of a mile they went along the edge of the field, and then he turned into the brush again. He approached a great mound of wild blackberry bushes, leaned over and pulled a mat of vines aside. "You got to crawl in," he said.

Ma went down on her hands and knees. She felt sand under her, and then the black inside of the mound no longer touched her, and she felt Tom's blanket on the ground. He arranged the vines in place again. It was lightless in the cave.

"Where are you, Ma?"

"Here. Right here. Talk soft, Tom."

"Don't worry. I been livin' like a rabbit some time."

She heard him unwrap his tin plate.

"Pork chops," she said. "And fry potatoes."

"God Awmighty, an' still warm."

Ma could not see him at all in the blackness, but she could hear him chewing, tearing at the meat and swallowing.

"It's a pretty good hide-out," he said.

Ma said uneasily, "Tom—Ruthie tol' about you." She heard him gulp.

"Ruthie? What for?"

"Well, it wasn' her fault. Got in a fight, an' says her brother'll lick that other girl's brother. You know how they do. An' she tol' that her brother killed a man an' was hidin'."

Tom was chuckling. "With me I was always gonna get Uncle John after 'em, but he never would do it. That's jus' kid talk, Ma. That's awright."

"No, it ain't," Ma said. "Them kids'll tell it aroun' an'

then the folks'll hear, an' they'll tell aroun', an' pretty soon, well, they liable to get men out to look, jus' in case. Tom, you got to go away."

"That's what I said right along. I was always scared somebody'd see you put stuff in that culvert, an' then they'd watch."

"I know. But I wanted you near. I was scared for you. I ain't seen you. Can't see you now. How's your face?"

"Gettin' well quick."

"Come clost, Tom. Let me feel it. Come clost." He crawled near. Her reaching hand found his head in the blackness and her fingers moved down to his nose, and then over his left cheek. "You got a bad scar, Tom. An' your nose is all crooked."

"Maybe tha's a good thing. Nobody wouldn't know me, maybe. If my prints wasn't on record, I'd be glad." He went back to his eating.

"Hush," she said. "Listen!"

"It's the wind, Ma. Jus' the wind." The gust poured down the stream, and the trees rustled under its passing.

She crawled close to his voice. "I wanta touch ya again, Tom. It's like I'm blin', it's so dark. I wanta remember, even if it's on'y my fingers that remember. You got to go away, Tom."

"Yeah! I knowed it from the start."

"We made purty good," she said. "I been squirrelin' money away. Hol' out your han', Tom. I got seven dollars here."

"I ain't gonna take ya money," he said. "I'll get 'long all right."

"Hol' out ya han', Tom. I ain't gonna sleep none if you got no money. Maybe you got to take a bus, or somepin. I want you should go a long ways off, three-four hunderd miles."

"I ain't gonna take it."

"Tom," she said sternly. "You take this money. You hear me? You got no right to cause me pain."

"You ain't playin' fair," he said.

"I thought maybe you could go to a big city. Los Angeles, maybe. They wouldn' never look for you there."

"Hm-m," he said. "Lookie, Ma. I been all day an' all night hidin' alone. Guess who I been thinkin' about? Casy! He talked a lot. Used ta bother me. But now I been thinkin' what he said, an' I can remember—all of it. Says one time he went out in the wilderness to find his own soul, an' he foun' he didn' have no soul that was his'n. Says he foun' he jus' got a little piece of a great big soul. Says a wilderness ain't no good, 'cause his little piece of a soul wasn't no good 'less it was with the rest, an' was whole. Funny how I remember. Didn' think I was even listenin'. But I know now a fella ain't no good alone."

"He was a good man," Ma said.

Tom went on, "He spouted out some Scripture once, an' it didn' soun' like no hell-fire Scripture. He tol' it twicet, an' I remember it. Says it's from the Preacher."

"How's it go, Tom?"

— "Goes, 'Two are better than one, because they have a good reward for their labor. For if they fall, the one will lif' up his fellow, but woe to him that is alone when he falleth, for he hath not another to help him up.' That's part of her."

"Go on," Ma said. "Go on, Tom."

"Jus' a little bit more. 'Again, if two lie together, then they have heat: but how can one be warm alone? And if one prevail against him, two shall withstand him, and a three-fold cord is not quickly broken.' "

"An' that's Scripture?"

"Casy said it was. Called it the Preacher."

"Hush—listen."

"On'y the wind, Ma. I know the wind. An' I got to thinkin', Ma—most of the preachin' is about the poor we shall have always with us, an' if you got nothin', why, jus' fol' your hands an' to hell with it, you gonna git ice cream on gol' plates when you're dead. An' then this here Preacher says two get a better reward for their work."

"Tom," she said. "What you aimin' to do?"

He was quiet for a long time. "I been thinkin' how it was in that gov'ment camp, how our folks took care a theirselves, an' if they was a fight they fixed it theirself; an' they wasn't no cops wagglin' their guns, but they was better order than them cops ever give. I been a-wonderin' why we can't do that all over. Throw out the cops that ain't our people. All work together for our own thing—all farm our own lan'."

"Tom," Ma repeated, "what you gonna do?"

"What Casy done," he said.

"But they killed him."

"Yeah," said Tom. "He didn' duck quick enough. He wasn' doing nothin' against the law, Ma. I been thinkin' a hell of a lot, thinkin' about our people livin' like pigs, an' the good rich lan' layin' fallow, or maybe one fella with a million acres, while a hunderd thousan' good farmers is starvin'. An' I been wonderin' if all our folks got together an' yelled, like them fellas yelled, only a few of 'em at the Hooper ranch——"

Ma said, "Tom, they'll drive you, an' cut you down like they done to young Floyd."

"They gonna drive me anyways. They drivin' all our people."

"You don't aim to kill nobody, Tom?"

"No. I been thinkin', long as I'm a outlaw anyways, maybe I could— Hell, I ain't thought it out clear, Ma. Don' worry me now. Don' worry me."

They sat silent in the coal-black cave of vines. Ma said, "How'm I gonna know 'bout you? They might kill ya an' I wouldn' know. They might hurt ya. How'm I gonna know?"

Tom laughed uneasily, "Well, maybe like Casy says, a fella ain't got a soul of his own, but on'y a piece of a big one—an' then——"

"Then what, Tom?"

"Then it don' matter. Then I'll be all aroun' in the dark. I'll be ever'where—wherever you look. Wherever they's a fight so hungry people can eat, I'll be there. Wherever they's a cop beatin' up a guy, I'll be there. If Casy knowed, why, I'll be in the way guys yell when they're mad an'—I'll be in the way kids laugh when they're hungry an' they know supper's ready. An' when our folks eat the stuff they raise an' live in the houses they build—why, I'll be there. See? God, I'm talkin' like Casy. Comes of thinkin' about him so much. Seems like I can see him sometimes."

"I don' un'erstan'," Ma said. "I don' really know."

"Me neither," said Tom. "It's jus' stuff I been thinkin' about. Get thinkin' a lot when you ain't movin' aroun'. You got to get back, Ma."

"You take the money then."

He was silent for a moment. "Awright," he said.

"An', Tom, later—when it's blowed over, you'll come back. You'll find us?"

"Sure," he said. "Now you better go. Here, gimme your han'." He guided her toward the entrance. Her fingers clutched his wrist. He swept the vines aside and followed her out. "Go up to the field till you come to a sycamore on the edge, an' then cut acrost the stream. Good-by."

"Good-by," she said, and she walked quickly away. Her eyes were wet and burning, but she did not cry. Her footsteps were loud and careless on the leaves as she went through the brush. And as she went, out of the dim sky the rain began to fall, big drops and few, splashing on the dry leaves heavily. Ma stopped and stood still in the dripping thicket. She turned about—took three steps back toward the mound of vines; and then she turned quickly and went back toward the boxcar camp. She went straight out to the culvert and climbed up on the road. The rain had passed now, but the sky was overcast. Behind her on the road she heard footsteps, and she turned nervously. The blinking of a dim flashlight played on the road. Ma turned back and started for home. In a moment a man caught up with her. Politely, he kept his light on the ground and did not play it in her face.

"Evenin'," he said.

Ma said, "Howdy."

"Looks like we might have a little rain."

"I hope not. Stop the pickin'. We need the pickin'."

"I need the pickin' too. You live at the camp there?"

"Yes, sir." Their footsteps beat on the road together.

"I got twenty acres of cotton. Little late, but it's ready now. Thought I'd go down and try to get some pickers."

"You'll get 'em awright. Season's near over."

"Hope so. My place is only a mile up that way."

"Six of us," said Ma. "Three men an' me an' two little fellas."

"I'll put out a sign. Two miles—this road."

"We'll be there in the mornin'."

"I hope it don't rain."

"Me too," said Ma. "Twenty acres won' las' long."

"The less it lasts the gladder I'll be. My cotton's late. Didn' get it in till late."

"What you payin', mister?"

"Ninety cents."

"We'll pick. I hear fellas say nex' year it'll be seventy-five or even sixty."

"That's what I hear."

"They'll be trouble," said Ma.

"Sure. I know. Little fella like me can't do anything. The Association sets the rate, and we got to mind. If we don't— we ain't got a farm. Little fella gets crowded all the time."

They came to the camp. "We'll be there," Ma said. "Not much pickin' lef'." She went to the end boxcar and climbed the cleated walk. The low light of the lantern made gloomy shadows in the car. Pa and Uncle John and an elderly man squatted against the car wall.

"Hello," Ma said. "Evenin', Mr. Wainwright."

He raised a delicately chiseled face. His eyes were deep under the ridges of his brows. His hair was blue-white and fine. A patina of silver beard covered his jaws and chin. "Evenin', ma'am," he said.

"We got pickin' tomorra," Ma observed. "Mile north. Twenty acres."

"Better take the truck, I guess," Pa said. "Get in more pickin'."

Wainwright raised his head eagerly. "S'pose we can pick?"

"Why, sure. I walked a piece with the fella. He was comin' to get pickers."

"Cotton's nearly gone. Purty thin, these here seconds. Gonna be hard to make a wage on the seconds. Got her pretty clean the fust time."

"Your folks could maybe ride with us," Ma said. "Split the gas."

"Well—that's frien'ly of you, ma'am."

"Saves us both," said Ma.

Pa said, "Mr. Wainwright—he's got a worry he come to us about. We was a-talkin' her over."

"What's the matter?"

Wainwright looked down at the floor. "Our Aggie," he said. "She's a big girl—near sixteen, an' growed up."

"Aggie's a pretty girl," said Ma.

"Listen 'im out," Pa said.

"Well, her an' your boy Al, they're a-walkin' out ever' night. An' Aggie's a good healthy girl that oughta have a husban', else she might git in trouble. We never had no trouble in our family. But what with us bein' so poor off, now, Mis' Wainwright an' me, we got to worryin'. S'pose she got in trouble?"

Ma rolled down a mattress and sat on it. "They out now?" she asked.

"Always out," said Wainwright. "Ever' night."

"Hm. Well, Al's a good boy. Kinda figgers he's a dung-hill rooster these days, but he's a good steady boy. I couldn' want for a better boy."

"Oh, we ain't complainin' about Al as a fella! We like him. But what scares Mis' Wainwright an' me—well, she's a growed-up woman-girl. An' what if we go away, or you go away, an' we find out Aggie's in trouble? We ain't had no shame in our family."

Ma said softly, "We'll try an' see that we don't put no shame on you."

He stood up quickly. "Thank you, ma'am. Aggie's a growed-up woman-girl. She's a good girl—jes' as nice an' good. We'll sure thank you, ma'am, if you'll keep shame from us. It ain't Aggie's fault. She's growed up."

"Pa'll talk to Al," said Ma. "Or if Pa won't, I will."

Wainwright said, "Good night, then, an' we sure thank ya." He went around the end of the curtain. They could hear him talking softly in the other end of the car, explaining the result of his embassy.

Ma listened a moment, and then, "You fellas," she said. "Come over an' set here."

Pa and Uncle John got heavily up from their squats. They sat on the mattress beside Ma.

"Where's the little fellas?"

Pa pointed to a mattress in the corner. "Ruthie, she jumped Winfiel' an' bit 'im. Made 'em both lay down. Guess they're asleep. Rosasharn, she went to set with a lady she knows."

Ma sighed. "I foun' Tom," she said softly. "I—sent 'im away. Far off."

Pa nodded slowly. Uncle John dropped his chin on his chest. "Couldn' do nothin' else," Pa said. "Think he could, John?"

Uncle John looked up. "I can't think nothin' out," he said. "Don't seem like I'm hardly awake no more."

"Tom's a good boy," Ma said; and then she apologized, "I didn' mean no harm a-sayin' I'd talk to Al."

"I know," Pa said quietly. "I ain't no good any more.

Spen' all my time a-thinkin' how it use' ta be. Spen' all my time thinkin' of home, an' I ain't never gonna see it no more."

"This here's purtier—better lan'," said Ma.

"I know. I never even see it, thinkin' how the willow's los' its leaves now. Sometimes figgerin' to mend that hole in the south fence. Funny! Woman takin' over the fambly. Woman sayin' we'll do this here, an' we'll go there. An' I don' even care."

"Woman can change better'n a man," Ma said soothingly. "Woman got all her life in her arms. Man got it all in his head. Don' you mind. Maybe—well, maybe nex' year we can get a place."

"We got nothin', now," Pa said. "Comin' a long time—no work, no crops. What we gonna do then? How we gonna git stuff to eat? An' I tell you Rosasharn ain't so far from due. Git so I hate to think. Go diggin' back to a ol' time to keep from thinkin'. Seems like our life's over an' done."

"No, it ain't," Ma smiled. "It ain't, Pa. An' that's one more thing a woman knows. I noticed that. Man, he lives in jerks—baby born an' a man dies, an' that's a jerk—gets a farm an' loses his farm, an' that's a jerk. Woman, it's all one flow, like a stream, little eddies, little waterfalls, but the river, it goes right on. Woman looks at it like that. We ain't gonna die out. People is goin' on—changin' a little, maybe, but goin' right on."

"How can you tell?" Uncle John demanded. "What's to keep ever'thing from stoppin'; all the folks from jus' gittin' tired an' layin' down?"

Ma considered. She rubbed the shiny back of one hand with the other, pushed the fingers of her right hand between the fingers of her left. "Hard to say," she said. "Ever'thing we do—seems to me is aimed right at goin' on. Seems that way to me. Even gettin' hungry—even bein' sick; some die, but the rest is tougher. Jus' try to live the day, jus' the day."

Uncle John said, "If on'y she didn' die that time——"

"Jus' live the day," Ma said. "Don' worry yaself."

"They might be a good year nex' year, back home," said Pa.

Ma said, "Listen!"

There were creeping steps on the cat-walk, and then Al came in past the curtain. "Hullo," he said. "I thought you'd be sleepin' by now."

"Al," Ma said. "We're a-talkin'. Come set here."

"Sure—O.K. I wanta talk too. I'll hafta be goin' away pretty soon now."

"You can't. We need you here. Why you got to go away?"

"Well, me an' Aggie Wainwright, we figgers to get married, an' I'm gonna git a job in a garage, an' we'll have a rent' house for a while, an'—" He looked up fiercely. "Well, we are, an' they ain't nobody can stop us!"

They were staring at him. "Al," Ma said at last, "we're glad. We're awful glad."

"You are?"

"Why, 'course we are. You're a growed man. You need a wife. But don' go right now, Al."

"I promised Aggie," he said. "We got to go. We can't stan' this no more."

"Jus' stay till spring," Ma begged. "Jus' till spring. Won't you stay till spring? Who'd drive the truck?"

"Well——"

Mrs. Wainwright put her head around the curtain. "You heard yet?" she demanded.

"Yeah! Jus' heard."

"Oh, my! I wisht—I wisht we had a cake. I wisht we had—a cake or somepin."

"I'll set on some coffee an' make up some pancakes," Ma said. "We got sirup."

"Oh, my!" Mrs. Wainwright said. "Why—well. Look, I'll bring some sugar. We'll put sugar in them pancakes."

Ma broke twigs into the stove, and the coals from the dinner cooking started them blazing. Ruthie and Winfield came out of their bed like hermit crabs from shells. For a moment they were careful; they watched to see whether they were still criminals. When no one noticed them, they grew bold. Ruthie hopped all the way to the door and back on one foot, without touching the wall.

Ma was pouring flour into a bowl when Rose of Sharon climbed the cat-walk. She steadied herself and advanced cautiously. "What's a matter?" she asked.

"Why, it's news!" Ma cried. "We're gonna have a little party 'count a Al an' Aggie Wainwright is gonna get married."

Rose of Sharon stood perfectly still. She looked slowly at Al, who stood there flustered and embarrassed.

Mrs. Wainwright shouted from the other end of the car, "I'm puttin' a fresh dress on Aggie. I'll be right over."

Rose of Sharon turned slowly. She went back to the wide door, and she crept down the cat-walk. Once on the ground, she moved slowly toward the stream and the trail that went beside it. She took the way Ma had gone earlier—into the willows. The wind blew more steadily now, and the bushes whished steadily. Rose of Sharon went down on her knees and crawled deep into the brush. The berry vines cut her face and pulled at her hair, but she didn't mind. Only when she felt the bushes touching her all over did she stop. She stretched out on her back. And she felt the weight of the baby inside of her.

In the lightless car, Ma stirred, and then she pushed the blanket back and got up. At the open door of the car the gray starlight penetrated a little. Ma walked to the door and stood looking out. The stars were paling in the east. The wind blew softly over the willow thickets, and from the little stream came the quiet talking of the water. Most of the camp was still asleep, but in front of one tent a little fire burned, and people were standing about it, warming themselves. Ma could see them in the light of the new dancing fire as they stood facing the flames, rubbing their hands; and then they turned their backs and held their hands behind them. For a long moment Ma looked out, and she held her hands clasped in front of her. The uneven wind whisked up and passed, and a bite of frost was in the air. Ma shivered and rubbed her hands together. She crept back and fumbled for the matches, beside the lantern. The shade screeched up. She lighted the wick, watched it burn blue for a moment and then put up its yellow, delicately curved ring of light. She carried the lantern to the stove and set it down while she broke the brittle dry willow twigs into the fire box. In a moment the fire was roaring up the chimney.

Rose of Sharon rolled heavily over and sat up. "I'll git right up," she said.

"Whyn't you lay a minute till it warms?" Ma asked.

"No, I'll git."

Ma filled the coffee pot from the bucket and set it on the stove, and she put on the frying pan, deep with fat, to get hot for the pones. "What's over you?" she said softly.

"I'm a-goin' out," Rose of Sharon said.

"Out where?"

"Goin' out to pick cotton."

"You can't," Ma said. "You're too far along."

"No, I ain't. An' I'm a-goin'."

Ma measured coffee into the water. "Rosasharn, you wasn't to the pancakes las' night." The girl didn't answer. "What you wanta pick cotton for?" Still no answer. "Is it 'cause of Al an' Aggie?" This time Ma looked closely at her daughter. "Oh. Well, you don' need to pick."

"I'm goin'."

"Awright, but don' you strain yourself."

"Git up, Pa! Wake up, git up!"

Pa blinked and yawned. "Ain't slep' out," he moaned. "Musta been on to eleven o'clock when we went down."

"Come on, git up, all a you, an' wash."

The inhabitants of the car came slowly to life, squirmed up out of the blankets, writhed into their clothes. Ma sliced salt pork into her second frying pan. "Git out an' wash," she commanded.

A light sprang up in the other end of the car. And there came the sound of the breaking of twigs from the Wainwright end. "Mis' Joad," came the call. "We're gettin' ready. We'll be ready."

Al grumbled, "What we got to be up so early for?"

"It's on'y twenty acres," Ma said. "Got to get there. Ain't much cotton lef'. Got to be there 'fore she's picked." Ma rushed them dressed, rushed the breakfast into them. "Come on, drink your coffee," she said. "Got to start."

"We can't pick no cotton in the dark, Ma."

"We can *be* there when it gets light."

"Maybe it's wet."

"Didn' rain enough. Come on now, drink your coffee. Al, soon's you're through, better get the engine runnin'."

She called, "You near ready, Mis' Wainwright?"

"Jus' eatin'. Be ready in a minute."

Outside, the camp had come to life. Fires burned in front of the tents. The stovepipes from the boxcars spurted smoke.

Al tipped up his coffee and got a mouthful of grounds. He went down the cat-walk spitting them out.

"We're awready, Mis' Wainwright," Ma called. She turned to Rose of Sharon. She said, "You got to stay."

The girl set her jaw. "I'm a-goin'," she said. "Ma, I got to go."

"Well, you got no cotton sack. You can't pull no sack."

"I'll pick into your sack."

"I wisht you wouldn'."

"I'm a-goin'."

Ma sighed. "I'll keep my eye on you. Wisht we could have a doctor." Rose of Sharon moved nervously about the car. She put on a light coat and took it off. "Take a blanket," Ma said. "Then if you wanta res', you can keep warm." They heard the truck motor roar up behind the boxcar. "We gonna be first out," Ma said exultantly. "Awright, get your sacks. Ruthie, don' you forget them shirts I fixed for you to pick in."

Wainwrights and Joads climbed into the truck in the dark. The dawn was coming, but it was slow and pale.

"Turn lef'," Ma told Al. "They'll be a sign out where we're goin'." They drove along the dark road. And other cars followed them, and behind, in the camp, the cars were being started, the families piling in; and the cars pulled out on the highway and turned left.

A piece of cardboard was tied to a mailbox on the right-hand side of the road, and on it, printed with blue crayon, "Cotton Pickers Wanted." Al turned into the entrance and drove out to the barnyard. And the barnyard was full of cars already. An electric globe on the end of the white barn lighted a group of men and women standing near the scales, their bags rolled under their arms. Some of the women wore the bags over their shoulders and crossed in front.

"We ain't so early as we thought," said Al. He pulled the truck against a fence and parked. The families climbed down and went to join the waiting group, and more cars came in from the road and parked, and more families joined the group. Under the light on the barn end, the owner signed them in.

"Hawley?" he said. "H-a-w-l-e-y? How many?"

"Four. Will——"

"Will."

"Benton——"

"Benton."

"Amelia——"

"Amelia."

"Claire——"

"Claire. Who's next? Carpenter? How many?"

"Six."

He wrote them in the book, with a space left for the weights. "Got your bags? I got a few. Cost you a dollar." And the cars poured into the yard. The owner pulled his sheep-lined leather jacket up around his throat. He looked at the driveway apprehensively. "This twenty isn't gonna take long to pick with all these people," he said.

Children were climbing into the big cotton trailer, digging their toes into the chicken-wire sides. "Git off there," the

owner cried. "Come on down. You'll tear that wire loose."
And the children climbed slowly down, embarrassed and
silent. The gray dawn came. "I'll have to take a tare for
dew," the owner said. "Change it when the sun comes out.
All right, go out when you want. Light enough to see."

The people moved quickly out into the cotton field and
took their rows. They tied the bags to their waists and they
slapped their hands together to warm stiff fingers that had to
be nimble. The dawn colored over the eastern hills, and the
wide line moved over the rows. And from the highway the
cars still moved in and parked in the barnyard until it was
full, and they parked along the road on both sides. The wind
blew briskly across the field. "I don't know how you all
found out," the owner said. "There must be a hell of a grape-
vine. The twenty won't last till noon. What name? Hume?
How many?"

The line of people moved out across the field, and the
strong steady west wind blew their clothes. Their fingers
flew to the spilling bolls, and flew to the long sacks growing
heavy behind them.

Pa spoke to the man in the row to his right. "Back home
we might get rain out of a wind like this. Seems a little mite
frosty for rain. How long you been out here?" He kept his
eyes down on his work as he spoke.

His neighbor didn't look up. "I been here nearly a year."

"Would you say it was gonna rain?"

"Can't tell, an' that ain't no insult, neither. Folks that lived
here all their life can't tell. If the rain can git in the way of a
crop, it'll rain. Tha's what they say out here."

Pa looked quickly at the western hills. Big gray clouds
were coasting over the ridge, riding the wind swiftly. "Them
looks like rain-heads," he said.

His neighbor stole a squinting look. "Can't tell," he said. And all down the line of rows the people looked back at the clouds. And then they bent lower to their work, and their hands flew to the cotton. They raced at the picking, raced against time and cotton weight, raced against the rain and against each other—only so much cotton to pick, only so much money to be made. They came to the other side of the field and ran to get a new row. And now they faced into the wind, and they could see the high gray clouds moving over the sky toward the rising sun. And more cars parked along the roadside, and new pickers came to be checked in. The line of people moved frantically across the field, weighed at the end, marked their cotton, checked the weights into their own books, and ran for new rows.

At eleven o'clock the field was picked and the work was done. The wire-sided trailers were hooked on behind wire-sided trucks, and they moved out to the highway and drove away to the gin. The cotton fluffed out through the chicken wire and little clouds of cotton blew through the air, and rags of cotton caught and waved on the weeds beside the road. The pickers clustered disconsolately back to the barnyard and stood in line to be paid off.

"Hume, James. Twenty-two cents. Ralph, thirty cents. Joad, Thomas, ninety cents. Winfield, fifteen cents." The money lay in rolls, silver and nickels and pennies. And each man looked in his own book as he was being paid. "Wainwright, Agnes, thirty-four cents. Tobin, sixty-three cents." The line moved past slowly. The families went back to their cars, silently. And they drove slowly away.

Joads and Wainwrights waited in the truck for the driveway to clear. And as they waited, the first drops of rain began to fall. Al put his hand out of the cab to feel them. Rose of Sharon sat in the middle, and Ma on the outside. The girl's eyes were lusterless again.

"You shouldn' of came," Ma said. "You didn' pick more'n ten-fifteen pounds." Rose of Sharon looked down at her great bulging belly, and she didn't reply. She shivered suddenly and held her head high. Ma, watching her closely, unrolled her cotton bag, spread it over Rose of Sharon's shoulders, and drew her close.

At last the way was clear. Al started his motor and drove out into the highway. The big infrequent drops of rain lanced down and splashed on the road, and as the truck moved along, the drops became smaller and closer. Rain pounded on the cab of the truck so loudly that it could be heard over the pounding of the old worn motor. On the truck bed the Wainwrights and Joads spread their cotton bags over their heads and shoulders.

Rose of Sharon shivered violently against Ma's arm, and Ma cried, "Go faster, Al. Rosasharn got a chill. Gotta get her feet in hot water."

Al speeded the pounding motor, and when he came to the boxcar camp, he drove down close to the red cars. Ma was spouting orders before they were well stopped. "Al," she commanded, "you an' John an' Pa go into the willows an' c'lect all the dead stuff you can. We got to keep warm."

"Wonder if the roof leaks."

"No, I don' think so. Be nice an' dry, but we got to have wood. Got to keep warm. Take Ruthie an' Winfiel' too. They can get twigs. This here girl ain't well." Ma got out, and Rose of Sharon tried to follow, but her knees buckled and she sat down heavily on the running board.

Fat Mrs. Wainwright saw her. "What's a matter? Her time come?"

"No, I don' think so," said Ma. "Got a chill. Maybe took col'. Gimme a han', will you?" The two women supported Rose of Sharon. After a few steps her strength came back—her legs took her weight.

"I'm awright, Ma," she said. "It was jus' a minute there."

The older women kept hands on her elbows. "Feet in hot water," Ma said wisely. They helped her up the cat-walk and into the boxcar.

"You rub her," Mrs. Wainwright said. "I'll get a far' goin'." She used the last of the twigs and built up a blaze in the stove. The rain poured now, scoured at the roof of the car.

Ma looked up at it. "Thank God we got a tight roof," she said. "Them tents leaks, no matter how good. Jus' put on a little water, Mis' Wainwright."

Rose of Sharon lay still on a mattress. She let them take off her shoes and rub her feet. Mrs. Wainwright bent over her. "You got pain?" she demanded.

"No. Jus' don' feel good. Jus' feel bad."

"I got pain killer an' salts," Mrs. Wainwright said. "You're welcome to 'em if you want 'em. Perfec'ly welcome."

The girl shivered violently. "Cover me up, Ma. I'm col'." Ma brought all the blankets and piled them on top of her. The rain roared down on the roof.

Now the wood-gatherers returned, their arms piled high with sticks and their hats and coats dripping. "Jesus, she's wet," Pa said. "Soaks you in a minute."

Ma said, "Better go back an' get more. Burns up awful quick. Be dark purty soon." Ruthie and Winfield dripped in and threw their sticks on the pile. They turned to go again. "You stay," Ma ordered. "Stan' up close to the fire an' get dry."

The afternoon was silver with rain, the roads glittered with water. Hour by hour the cotton plants seemed to blacken and shrivel. Pa and Al and Uncle John made trip after trip into the thickets and brought back loads of dead wood. They piled it near the door, until the heap of it nearly reached the ceiling, and at last they stopped and walked toward the stove. Streams of water ran from their hats to their shoulders. The edges of their coats dripped and their shoes squished as they walked.

"Awright, now, get off them clothes," Ma said. "I got some nice coffee for you fellas. An' you got dry overhalls to put on. Don' stan' there."

The evening came early. In the boxcars the families huddled together, listening to the pouring water on the roofs.

Chapter Twenty-Nine

OVER the high coast mountains and over the valleys the gray clouds marched in from the ocean. The wind blew fiercely and silently, high in the air, and it swished in the brush, and it roared in the forests. The clouds came in brokenly, in puffs, in folds, in gray crags; and they piled in together and settled low over the west. And then the wind stopped and left the clouds deep and solid. The rain began with gusty showers, pauses and downpours; and then gradually it settled to a single tempo, small drops and a steady beat, rain that was gray to see through, rain that cut midday light to evening. And at first the dry earth sucked the moisture down and blackened. For two days the earth drank the rain, until the earth was full. Then puddles formed, and in the low places little lakes formed in the fields. The muddy lakes rose higher, and the steady rain whipped the shining water. At last the mountains were full, and the hillsides spilled into the streams, built them to freshets, and sent them roaring down the canyons into the valleys. The rain beat on steadily. And the streams and the little rivers edged up to the bank sides and worked at willows and tree roots, bent the willows deep in the current, cut out the roots of cottonwoods and brought down the trees. The muddy water whirled along the bank sides and crept up the banks until at last it spilled over, into the fields, into the orchards, into the cotton patches where the black stems stood. Level fields became lakes, broad and gray, and the rain whipped up the surfaces. Then the water poured over the highways, and cars moved slowly, cutting the water ahead, and leaving a boiling muddy wake behind. The earth whispered under the beat of the rain, and the streams thundered under the churning freshets.

When the first rain started, the migrant people huddled in their tents, saying, It'll soon be over, and asking, How long's it likely to go on?

And when the puddles formed, the men went out in the rain with shovels and built little dikes around the tents. The beating rain worked at the canvas until it penetrated and sent streams down. And then the little dikes washed out and the water came inside, and the streams wet the beds and the blankets. The people sat in wet clothes. They set up boxes and put planks on the boxes. Then, day and night, they sat on the planks.

Beside the tents the old cars stood, and water fouled the ignition wires and water fouled the carburetors. The little gray tents stood in lakes. And at last the people had to move. Then the cars wouldn't start because the wires were shorted; and if the engines would run, deep mud engulfed the wheels. And the people waded away, carrying their wet blankets in their arms. They splashed along, carrying the children, carrying the very old, in their arms. And if a barn stood on high ground, it was filled with people, shivering and hopeless.

Then some went to the relief offices, and they came sadly back to their own people.

They's rules—you got to be here a year before you can git relief. They say the gov'ment is gonna help. They don' know when.

And gradually the greatest terror of all came along.

They ain't gonna be no kinda work for three months.

In the barns, the people sat huddled together; and the terror came over them, and their faces were gray with terror. The children cried with hunger, and there was no food.

Then the sickness came, pneumonia, and measles that went to the eyes and to the mastoids.

And the rain fell steadily, and the water flowed over the highways, for the culverts could not carry the water.

Then from the tents, from the crowded barns, groups of sodden men went out, their clothes slopping rags, their shoes muddy pulp. They splashed out through the water, to the towns, to the country stores, to the relief offices, to beg for food, to cringe and beg for food, to beg for relief, to try to steal, to lie. And under the begging, and under the cringing, a hopeless anger began to smolder. And in the little towns pity for the sodden men changed to anger, and anger at the hungry people changed to fear of them. Then sheriffs swore in deputies in droves, and orders were rushed for rifles, for tear gas, for ammunition. Then the hungry men crowded the alleys behind the stores to beg for bread, to beg for rotting vegetables, to steal when they could.

Frantic men pounded on the doors of the doctors; and the doctors were busy. And sad men left word at country stores for the coroner to send a car. The coroners were not too busy. The coroners' wagons backed up through the mud and took out the dead.

And the rain pattered relentlessly down, and the streams broke their banks and spread out over the country.

Huddled under sheds, lying in wet hay, the hunger and the fear bred anger. Then boys went out, not to beg, but to steal; and men went out weakly, to try to steal.

The sheriffs swore in new deputies and ordered new rifles;

and the comfortable people in tight houses felt pity at first, and then distaste, and finally hatred for the migrant people.

In the wet hay of leaking barns babies were born to women who panted with pneumonia. And old people curled up in corners and died that way, so that the coroners could not straighten them. At night the frantic men walked boldly to hen roosts and carried off the squawking chickens. If they were shot at, they did not run, but splashed sullenly away; and if they were hit, they sank tiredly in the mud.

The rain stopped. On the fields the water stood, reflecting the gray sky, and the land whispered with moving water. And the men came out of the barns, out of the sheds. They squatted on their hams and looked out over the flooded land. And they were silent. And sometimes they talked very quietly.

No work till spring. No work.

And if no work—no money, no food.

Fella had a team of horses, had to use 'em to plow an' cultivate an' mow, wouldn' think a turnin' 'em out to starve when they wasn't workin'.

Them's horses—we're men.

The women watched the men, watched to see whether the break had come at last. The women stood silently and watched. And where a number of men gathered together, the fear went from their faces, and anger took its place. And the women sighed with relief, for they knew it was all right—the break had not come; and the break would never come as long as fear could turn to wrath.

Tiny points of grass came through the earth, and in a few days the hills were pale green with the beginning year.

Chapter Thirty

IN THE boxcar camp the water stood in puddles, and the rain splashed in the mud. Gradually the little stream crept up the bank toward the low flat where the boxcars stood.

On the second day of the rain Al took the tarpaulin down from the middle of the car. He carried it out and spread it on the nose of the truck, and he came back into the car and sat down on his mattress. Now, without the separation, the two families in the car were one. The men sat together, and their spirits were damp. Ma kept a little fire going in the stove, kept a few twigs burning, and she conserved her wood. The rain poured down on the nearly flat roof of the boxcar.

On the third day the Wainwrights grew restless. "Maybe we better go 'long," Mrs. Wainwright said.

And Ma tried to keep them. "Where'd you go an' be sure of a tight roof?"

"I dunno, but I got a feelin' we oughta go along." They argued together, and Ma watched Al.

Ruthie and Winfield tried to play for a while, and then they too relapsed into sullen inactivity, and the rain drummed down on the roof.

On the third day the sound of the stream could be heard above the drumming rain. Pa and Uncle John stood in the open door and looked out on the rising stream. At both ends of the camp the water ran near to the highway, but at the camp it looped away so that the highway embankment surrounded the camp at the back and the stream closed it in on the front. And Pa said, "How's it look to you, John? Seems to me if that crick comes up, she'll flood us."

Uncle John opened his mouth and rubbed his bristling chin. "Yeah," he said. "Might at that."

Rose of Sharon was down with a heavy cold, her face flushed and her eyes shining with fever. Ma sat beside her with a cup of hot milk. "Here," she said. "Take this here. Got bacon grease in it for strength. Here, drink it!"

Rose of Sharon shook her head weakly. "I ain't hungry."

Pa drew a curved line in the air with his finger. "If we was all to get our shovels an' throw up a bank, I bet we could keep her out. On'y have to go from up there down to there."

"Yeah," Uncle John agreed. "Might. Dunno if them other fellas'd wanta. They'd maybe ruther move somewheres else."

"But these here cars is dry," Pa insisted. "Couldn' find no dry place as good as this. You wait." From the pile of brush in the car he picked a twig. He ran down the cat-walk, splashed through the mud to the stream and he set his twig upright on the edge of the swirling water. In a moment he was back in the car. "Jesus, ya get wet through," he said.

Both men kept their eyes on the little twig on the water's edge. They saw the water move slowly up around it and creep up the bank. Pa squatted down in the doorway. "Comin' up fast," he said. "I think we oughta go talk to the other fellas. See if they'll help ditch up. Got to git outa here if they won't." Pa looked down the long car to the Wainwright end. Al was with them, sitting beside Aggie. Pa walked into their precinct. "Water's risin'," he said. "How about if we throwed up a bank? We could do her if ever'body helped."

Wainwright said, "We was jes' talkin'. Seems like we oughta be gettin' outa here."

Pa said, "You been aroun'. You know what chancet we got a gettin' a dry place to stay."

"I know. But jes' the same——"

Al said, "Pa, if they go, I'm a-goin' too."

Pa looked startled. "You can't, Al. The truck— We ain't fit to drive that truck."

"I don' care. Me an' Aggie got to stick together."

"Now you wait," Pa said. "Come on over here." Wainwright and Al got to their feet and approached the door. "See?" Pa said, pointing. "Jus' a bank from there an' down to there." He looked at his stick. The water swirled about it now, and crept up the bank.

"Be a lot a work, an' then she might come over anyways," Wainwright protested.

"Well, we ain't doin' nothin', might's well be workin'. We ain't gonna find us no nice place to live like this. Come on, now. Le's go talk to the other fellas. We can do her if ever'-body helps."

Al said, "If Aggie goes, I'm a-goin' too."

Pa said, "Look, Al, if them fellas won't dig, then we'll all hafta go. Come on, le's go talk to 'em." They hunched their shoulders and ran down the cat-walk to the next car and up the walk into its open door.

Ma was at the stove, feeding a few sticks to the feeble flame. Ruthie crowded close beside her. "I'm hungry," Ruthie whined.

"No, you ain't," Ma said. "You had good mush."

"Wisht I had a box a Cracker Jack. There ain't nothin' to do. Ain't no fun."

"They'll be fun," Ma said. "You jus' wait. Be fun purty soon. Git a house an' a place, purty soon."

"Wisht we had a dog," Ruthie said.

"We'll have a dog; have a cat, too."

"Yella cat?"

"Don't bother me," Ma begged. "Don't go plaguin' me now, Ruthie. Rosasharn's sick. Jus' you be a good girl a little while. They'll be fun." Ruthie wandered, complaining, away.

From the mattress where Rose of Sharon lay covered up there came a quick sharp cry, cut off in the middle. Ma whirled and went to her. Rose of Sharon was holding her breath and her eyes were filled with terror.

"What is it?" Ma cried. The girl expelled her breath and caught it again. Suddenly Ma put her hand under the covers. Then she stood up. "Mis' Wainwright," she called. "Oh, Mis' Wainwright!"

The fat little woman came down the car. "Want me?"

"Look!" Ma pointed at Rose of Sharon's face. Her teeth were clamped on her lower lip and her forehead was wet with perspiration, and the shining terror was in her eyes.

"I think it's come," Ma said. "It's early."

The girl heaved a great sigh and relaxed. She released her lip and closed her eyes. Mrs. Wainwright bent over her.

"Did it kinda grab you all over—quick? Open up an' answer me." Rose of Sharon nodded weakly. Mrs. Wainwright turned to Ma. "Yep," she said. "It's come. Early, ya say?"

"Maybe the fever brang it."

"Well, she oughta be up on her feet. Oughta be walkin' aroun'."

"She can't," Ma said. "She ain't got the strength."

"Well, she oughta." Mrs. Wainwright grew quiet and stern with efficiency. "I he'ped with lots," she said. "Come

on, le's close that door, nearly. Keep out the draf'." The two
women pushed on the heavy sliding door, boosted it along
until only a foot was open. "I'll git our lamp, too," Mrs.
Wainwright said. Her face was purple with excitement.
"Aggie," she called. "You take care of these here little
fellas."

Ma nodded, "Tha's right. Ruthie! You an' Winfiel' go
down with Aggie. Go on now."

"Why?" they demanded.

" 'Cause you got to. Rosasharn gonna have her baby."

"I wanta watch, Ma. Please let me."

"Ruthie! You git now. You git quick." There was no argument against such a tone. Ruthie and Winfield went reluctantly down the car. Ma lighted the lantern. Mrs. Wainwright brought her Rochester lamp down and set it on the
floor, and its big circular flame lighted the boxcar brightly.

Ruthie and Winfield stood behind the brush pile and
peered over. "Gonna have a baby, an' we're a-gonna see,"
Ruthie said softly. "Don't you make no noise now. Ma won't
let us watch. If she looks this-a-way, you scrunch down
behin' the brush. Then we'll see."

"There ain't many kids seen it," Winfield said.

"There ain't no kids seen it," Ruthie insisted proudly.
"On'y us."

Down by the mattress, in the bright light of the lamp, Ma
and Mrs. Wainwright held conference. Their voices were
raised a little over the hollow beating of the rain. Mrs. Wainwright took a paring knife from her apron pocket and
slipped it under the mattress. "Maybe it don't do no good,"
she said apologetically. "Our folks always done it. Don't do
no harm, anyways."

Ma nodded. "We used a plow point. I guess anything

sharp'll work, long as it can cut birth pains. I hope it ain't gonna be a long one."

"You feelin' awright now?"

Rose of Sharon nodded nervously. "Is it a-comin'?"

"Sure," Ma said. "Gonna have a nice baby. You jus' got to help us. Feel like you could get up an' walk?"

"I can try."

"That's a good girl," Mrs. Wainwright said. "That *is* a good girl. We'll he'p you, honey. We'll walk with ya." They helped her to her feet and pinned a blanket over her shoulders. Then Ma held her arm from one side, and Mrs. Wainwright from the other. They walked her to the brush pile and turned slowly and walked her back, over and over; and the rain drummed deeply on the roof.

Ruthie and Winfield watched anxiously. "When's she goin' to have it?" he demanded.

"Sh! Don't draw 'em. We won't be let to look."

Aggie joined them behind the brush pile. Aggie's lean face and yellow hair showed in the lamplight, and her nose was long and sharp in the shadow of her head on the wall.

Ruthie whispered, "You ever saw a baby bore?"

"Sure," said Aggie.

"Well, when's she gonna have it?"

"Oh, not for a long, long time."

"Well, how long?"

"Maybe not 'fore tomorrow mornin'."

"Shucks!" said Ruthie. "Ain't no good watchin' now, then. Oh! Look!"

The walking women had stopped. Rose of Sharon had stiffened, and she whined with pain. They laid her down on the mattress and wiped her forehead while she grunted and clenched her fists. And Ma talked softly to her. "Easy," Ma said. "Gonna be all right—all right. Jus' grip ya han's. Now, then, take your lip inta your teeth. Tha's good—tha's good." The pain passed on. They let her rest awhile, and then helped her up again, and the three walked back and forth, back and forth between the pains.

Pa stuck his head in through the narrow opening. His hat dripped with water. "What ya shut the door for?" he asked. And then he saw the walking women.

Ma said, "Her time's come."

"Then—then we couldn' go 'f we wanted to."

"No."

"Then we got to buil' that bank."

"You got to."

Pa sloshed through the mud to the stream. His marking stick was four inches down. Twenty men stood in the rain. Pa cried, "We got to build her. My girl got her pains." The men gathered about him.

"Baby?"

"Yeah. We can't go now."

A tall man said, "It ain't our baby. We kin go."

"Sure," Pa said. "You can go. Go on. Nobody's stoppin' you. They's only eight shovels." He hurried to the lowest part of the bank and drove his shovel into the mud. The shovelful lifted with a sucking sound. He drove it again, and threw the mud into the low place on the stream bank. And beside him the other men ranged themselves. They heaped the mud up in a long embankment, and those who had no shovels cut live willow whips and wove them in a mat and kicked them into the bank. Over the men came a fury of work, a fury of battle. When one man dropped his shovel, another took it up. They had shed their coats and hats. Their shirts and trousers clung tightly to their bodies, their shoes were shapeless blobs of mud. A shrill scream came from the Joad car. The men stopped, listened uneasily, and then plunged to work again. And the little levee of earth extended until it connected with the highway embankment on either end. They were tired now, and the shovels moved more slowly. And the stream rose slowly. It edged above the place where the first dirt had been thrown.

Pa laughed in triumph. "She'd come over if we hadn' a built up!" he cried.

The stream rose slowly up the side of the new wall, and tore at the willow mat. "Higher!" Pa cried. "We got to git her higher!"

The evening came, and the work went on. And now the men were beyond weariness. Their faces were set and dead. They worked jerkily, like machines. When it was dark the women set lanterns in the car doors, and kept pots of coffee handy. And the women ran one by one to the Joad car and wedged themselves inside.

The pains were coming close now, twenty minutes apart. And Rose of Sharon had lost her restraint. She screamed fiercely under the fierce pains. And the neighbor women looked at her and patted her gently and went back to their own cars.

Ma had a good fire going now, and all her utensils, filled with water, sat on the stove to heat. Every little while Pa looked in the car door. "All right?" he asked.

"Yeah! I think so," Ma assured him.

As it grew dark, someone brought out a flashlight to work by. Uncle John plunged on, throwing mud on top of the wall.

"You take it easy," Pa said. "You'll kill yaself."

"I can't he'p it. I can't stan' that yellin'. It's like—it's like when——"

"I know," Pa said. "But jus' take it easy."

Uncle John blubbered, "I'll run away. By God, I got to work or I'll run away."

Pa turned from him. "How's she stan' on the last marker?"

The man with the flashlight threw the beam on the stick. The rain cut whitely through the light. "Comin' up."

"She'll come up slower now," Pa said. "Got to flood purty far on the other side."

"She's comin' up, though."

The women filled the coffee pots and set them out again. And as the night went on, the men moved slower and slower, and they lifted their heavy feet like draft horses. More mud on the levee, more willows interlaced. The rain fell steadily. When the flashlight turned on faces, the eyes showed staring, and the muscles on the cheeks were welted out.

For a long time the screams continued from the car, and at last they were still.

Pa said, "Ma'd call me if it was bore." He went on shoveling the mud sullenly.

The stream eddied and boiled against the bank. Then, from up the stream there came a ripping crash. The beam of the flashlight showed a great cottonwood toppling. The men stopped to watch. The branches of the tree sank into the water and edged around with the current while the stream dug out the little roots. Slowly the tree was freed, and slowly it edged down the stream. The weary men watched, their mouths hanging open. The tree moved slowly down. Then a branch caught on a stump, snagged and held. And very slowly the roots swung around and hooked themselves on the new embankment. The water piled up behind. The tree moved and tore the bank. A little stream slipped through. Pa threw himself forward and jammed mud in the break. The water piled against the tree. And then the bank washed quickly down, washed around ankles, around knees. The men broke and ran, and the current worked smoothly into the flat, under the cars, under the automobiles.

Uncle John saw the water break through. In the murk he could see it. Uncontrollably his weight pulled him down. He went to his knees, and the tugging water swirled about his chest.

Pa saw him go. "Hey! What's the matter?" He lifted him to his feet. "You sick? Come on, the cars is high."

Uncle John gathered his strength. "I dunno," he said apologetically. "Legs give out. Jus' give out." Pa helped him along toward the cars.

When the dike swept out, Al turned and ran. His feet moved heavily. The water was about his calves when he reached the truck. He flung the tarpaulin off the nose and jumped into the car. He stepped on the starter. The engine turned over and over, and there was no bark of the motor. He choked the engine deeply. The battery turned the sodden motor more and more slowly, and there was no cough. Over and over, slower and slower. Al set the spark high. He felt under the seat for the crank and jumped out. The water was higher than the running board. He ran to the front end. Crank case was under water now. Frantically he fitted the crank and twisted around and around, and his clenched hand on the crank splashed in the slowly flowing water at each turn. At last his frenzy gave out. The motor was full of water, the battery fouled by now. On slightly higher ground two cars were started and their lights on. They floundered in the mud and dug their wheels down until finally the drivers cut off the motors and sat still, looking into the headlight beams. And the rain whipped white streaks through the lights. Al went slowly around the truck, reached in, and turned off the ignition.

When Pa reached the cat-walk, he found the lower end floating. He stepped it down into the mud, under water. "Think ya can make it awright, John?" he asked.

"I'll be awright. Jus' go on."

Pa cautiously climbed the cat-walk and squeezed himself in the narrow opening. The two lamps were turned low. Ma sat on the mattress beside Rose of Sharon, and Ma fanned her still face with a piece of cardboard. Mrs. Wainwright poked dry brush into the stove, and a dank smoke edged out around the lids and filled the car with a smell of burning tissue. Ma looked up at Pa when he entered, and then quickly down.

"How—is she?" Pa asked.

Ma did not look up at him again. "Awright, I think. Sleepin'."

The air was fetid and close with the smell of the birth. Uncle John clambered in and held himself upright against the side of the car. Mrs. Wainwright left her work and came to Pa. She pulled him by the elbow toward the corner of the car. She picked up a lantern and held it over an apple box in the corner. On a newspaper lay a blue shriveled little mummy.

"Never breathed," said Mrs. Wainwright softly. "Never was alive."

Uncle John turned and shuffled tiredly down the car to the dark end. The rain whished softly on the roof now, so softly that they could hear Uncle John's tired sniffling from the dark.

Pa looked up at Mrs. Wainwright. He took the lantern from her hand and put it on the floor. Ruthie and Winfield were asleep on their own mattress, their arms over their eyes to cut out the light.

Pa walked slowly to Rose of Sharon's mattress. He tried to squat down, but his legs were too tired. He knelt instead. Ma fanned her square of cardboard back and forth. She looked at Pa for a moment, and her eyes were wide and staring, like a sleepwalker's eyes.

Pa said, "We—done—what we could."

"I know."

"We worked all night. An' a tree cut out the bank."

"I know."

"You can hear it under the car."

"I know. I heard it."

"Think she's gonna be all right?"

"I dunno."

"Well—couldn' we—of did nothin'?"

Ma's lips were stiff and white. "No. They was on'y one thing to do—ever—an' we done it."

"We worked till we dropped, an' a tree— Rain's lettin' up some." Ma looked at the ceiling, and then down again. Pa went on, compelled to talk. "I dunno how high she'll rise. Might flood the car."

"I know."

"You know ever'thing."

She was silent, and the cardboard moved slowly back and forth.

"Did we slip up?" he pleaded. "Is they anything we could of did?"

Ma looked at him strangely. Her white lips smiled in a

dreaming compassion. "Don't take no blame. Hush! It'll be awright. They's changes—all over."

"Maybe the water—maybe we'll have to go."

"When it's time to go—we'll go. We'll do what we got to do. Now hush. You might wake her."

Mrs. Wainwright broke twigs and poked them in the sodden, smoking fire.

From outside came the sound of an angry voice. "I'm goin' in an' see the son-of-a-bitch myself."

And then, just outside the door, Al's voice, "Where you think you're goin'?"

"Goin' in to see that bastard Joad."

"No, you ain't. What's the matter'th you?"

"If he didn't have that fool idear about the bank, we'd a got out. Now our car is dead."

"You think ours is burnin' up the road?"

"I'm a-goin' in."

Al's voice was cold. "You're gonna fight your way in."

Pa got slowly to his feet and went to the door. "Awright, Al. I'm comin' out. It's awright, Al." Pa slid down the cat-walk. Ma heard him say, "We got sickness. Come on down here."

The rain scattered lightly on the roof now, and a new-risen breeze blew it along in sweeps. Mrs. Wainwright came from the stove and looked down at Rose of Sharon. "Dawn's a-comin' soon, ma'am. Whyn't you git some sleep? I'll set with her."

"No," Ma said. "I ain't tar'd."

"In a pig's eye," said Mrs. Wainwright. "Come on, you lay down awhile."

Ma fanned the air slowly with her cardboard. "You been frien'ly," she said. "We thank you."

The stout woman smiled. "No need to thank. Ever'body's in the same wagon. S'pose we was down. You'd a give us a han'."

"Yes," Ma said, "we would."

"Or anybody."

"Or anybody. Use' ta be the fambly was fust. It ain't so now. It's anybody. Worse off we get, the more we got to do."

"We couldn' a saved it."

"I know," said Ma.

Ruthie sighed deeply and took her arm from over her eyes. She looked blindly at the lamp for a moment, and then turned her head and looked at Ma. "Is it bore?" she demanded. "Is the baby out?"

Mrs. Wainwright picked up a sack and spread it over the apple box in the corner.

"Where's the baby?" Ruthie demanded.

Ma wet her lips. "They ain't no baby. They never was no baby. We was wrong."

"Shucks!" Ruthie yawned. "I wisht it had a been a baby."

Mrs. Wainwright sat down beside Ma and took the cardboard from her and fanned the air. Ma folded her hands in her lap, and her tired eyes never left the face of Rose of Sharon, sleeping in exhaustion. "Come on," Mrs. Wainwright said. "Jus' lay down. You'll be right beside her. Why, you'd wake up if she took a deep breath, even."

"Awright, I will." Ma stretched out on the mattress beside the sleeping girl. And Mrs. Wainwright sat on the floor and kept watch.

Pa and Al and Uncle John sat in the car doorway and watched the steely dawn come. The rain had stopped, but the sky was deep and solid with cloud. As the light came, it was reflected on the water. The men could see the current of the stream, slipping swiftly down, bearing black branches of trees, boxes, boards. The water swirled into the flat where the boxcars stood. There was no sign of the embankment left. On the flat the current stopped. The edges of the flood were lined with yellow foam. Pa leaned out the door and placed a twig on the cat-walk, just above the water line. The men watched the water slowly climb to it, lift it gently and float it away. Pa placed another twig an inch above the water and settled back to watch.

"Think it'll come inside the car?" Al asked.

"Can't tell. They's a hell of a lot of water got to come down from the hills yet. Can't tell. Might start up to rain again."

Al said, "I been a-thinkin'. If she come in, ever'thing'll get soaked."

"Yeah."

"Well, she won't come up more'n three-four feet in the car 'cause she'll go over the highway an' spread out first."

"How you know?" Pa asked.

"I took a sight on her, off the end of the car." He held his hand. " 'Bout this far up she'll come."

"Awright," Pa said. "What about it? We won't be here."

"We got to be here. Truck's here. Take a week to get the water out of her when the flood goes down."

"Well—what's your idear?"

"We can tear out the side-boards of the truck an' build a kinda platform in here to pile our stuff 'an to set up on."

"Yeah? How'll we cook—how'll we eat?"

"Well, it'll keep our stuff dry."

The light grew stronger outside, a gray metallic light. The second little stick floated away from the cat-walk. Pa placed another one higher up. "Sure climbin'," he said. "I guess we better do that."

Ma turned restlessly in her sleep. Her eyes started wide open. She cried sharply in warning, "Tom! Oh, Tom! Tom!"

Mrs. Wainwright spoke soothingly. The eyes flicked closed again and Ma squirmed under her dream. Mrs. Wainwright got up and walked to the doorway. "Hey!" she said softly. "We ain't gonna git out soon." She pointed to the corner of the car where the apple box was. "That ain't doin' no good. Jus' cause trouble an' sorra. Couldn' you fellas kinda—take it out an' bury it?"

The men were silent. Pa said at last, "Guess you're right. Jus' cause sorra. 'Gainst the law to bury it."

"They's lots a things 'gainst the law that we can't he'p doin'."

"Yeah."

Al said, "We oughta git them truck sides tore off 'fore the water comes up much more."

Pa turned to Uncle John. "Will you take an' bury it while Al an me git that lumber in?"

Uncle John said sullenly, "Why do I got to do it? Why don't you fellas? I don' like it." And then, "Sure. I'll do it. Sure, I will. Come on, give it to me." His voice began to rise. "Come on! Give it to me."

"Don' wake 'em up," Mrs. Wainwright said. She brought

the apple box to the doorway and straightened the sack decently over it.

"Shovel's standin' right behin' you," Pa said.

Uncle John took the shovel in one hand. He slipped out the doorway into the slowly moving water, and it rose nearly to his waist before he struck bottom. He turned and settled the apple box under his other arm.

Pa said, "Come on, Al. Le's git that lumber in."

In the gray dawn light Uncle John waded around the end of the car, past the Joad truck; and he climbed the slippery bank to the highway. He walked down the highway, past the boxcar flat, until he came to a place where the boiling stream ran close to the road, where the willows grew along the road side. He put his shovel down, and holding the box in front of him, he edged through the brush until he came to the edge of the swift stream. For a time he stood watching it swirl by, leaving its yellow foam among the willow stems. He held the apple box against his chest. And then he leaned over and set the box in the stream and steadied it with his hand. He said fiercely, "Go down an' tell 'em. Go down in the street an' rot an' tell 'em that way. That's the way you can talk. Don' even know if you was a boy or a girl. Ain't gonna find out. Go on down now, an' lay in the street. Maybe they'll know then." He guided the box gently out into the current and let it go. It settled low in the water, edged sideways, whirled around, and turned slowly over. The sack floated away, and the box, caught in the swift water, floated quickly away, out of sight, behind the brush. Uncle John grabbed the shovel and went rapidly back to the boxcars. He sloshed down into the water and waded to the truck, where Pa and Al were working, taking down the one-by-six planks.

Pa looked over at him. "Get it done?"

"Yeah."

"Well, look," Pa said. "If you'll he'p Al, I'll go down the store an' get some stuff to eat."

"Get some bacon," Al said. "I need some meat."

"I will," Pa said. He jumped down from the truck and Uncle John took his place.

When they pushed the planks into the car door, Ma awakened and sat up. "What you doin'?"

"Gonna build up a place to keep outa the wet."

"Why?" Ma asked. "It's dry in here."

"Ain't gonna be. Water's comin' up."

Ma struggled up to her feet and went to the door. "We got to git outa here."

"Can't," Al said. "All our stuff's here. Truck's here. Ever'thing we got."

"Where's Pa?"

"Gone to get stuff for breakfas'."

Ma looked down at the water. It was only six inches down from the floor by now. She went back to the mattress and looked at Rose of Sharon. The girl stared back at her.

"How you feel?" Ma asked.

"Tar'd. Jus' tar'd out."

"Gonna get some breakfas' into you."

"I ain't hungry."

Mrs. Wainwright moved beside Ma. "She looks all right. Come through it fine."

Rose of Sharon's eyes questioned Ma, and Ma tried to avoid the question. Mrs. Wainwright walked to the stove.

"Ma."

"Yeah? What you want?"

"Is—it—all right?"

Ma gave up the attempt. She kneeled down on the mattress. "You can have more," she said. "We done ever'thing we knowed."

Rose of Sharon struggled and pushed herself up. "Ma!"

"You couldn' he'p it."

The girl lay back again, and covered her eyes with her arms. Ruthie crept close and looked down in awe. She whispered harshly, "She sick, Ma? She gonna die?"

" 'Course not. She's gonna be awright. Awright."

Pa came in with his armload of packages. "How is she?"

"Awright," Ma said. "She's gonna be awright."

Ruthie reported to Winfield. "She ain't gonna die. Ma says so."

And Winfield, picking his teeth with a splinter in a very adult manner, said, "I knowed it all the time."

"How'd you know?"

"I won't tell," said Winfield, and he spat out a piece of the splinter.

Ma built the fire up with the last twigs and cooked the bacon and made gravy. Pa had brought store bread. Ma scowled when she saw it. "We got any money lef'?"

"Nope," said Pa. "But we was so hungry."

"An' you got store bread," Ma said accusingly.

"Well, we was awful hungry. Worked all night long."

Ma sighed. "Now what we gonna do?"

As they ate, the water crept up and up. Al gulped his food and he and Pa built the platform. Five feet wide, six feet long, four feet above the floor. And the water crept to the edge of the doorway, seemed to hesitate a long time, and then moved slowly inward over the floor. And outside, the rain began again, as it had before, big heavy drops splashing on the water, pounding hollowly on the roof.

Al said, "Come on now, let's get the mattresses up. Let's put the blankets up, so they don't git wet." They piled their possessions up on the platform, and the water crept over the floor. Pa and Ma, Al and Uncle John, each at a corner, lifted Rose of Sharon's mattress, with the girl on it, and put it on top of the pile.

And the girl protested, "I can walk. I'm awright." And the water crept over the floor, a thin film of it. Rose of Sharon whispered to Ma, and Ma put her hand under the blanket and felt her breast and nodded.

In the other end of the boxcar, the Wainwrights were pounding, building a platform for themselves. The rain thickened, and then passed away.

Ma looked down at her feet. The water was half an inch deep on the car floor by now. "You, Ruthie—Winfiel'!" she called distractedly. "Come get on top of the pile. You'll get cold." She saw them safely up, sitting awkwardly beside Rose of Sharon. Ma said suddenly, "We got to git out."

"We can't," Pa said. "Like Al says, all our stuff's here. We'll pull off the boxcar door an' make more room to set on."

The family huddled on the platforms, silent and fretful. The water was six inches deep in the car before the flood spread evenly over the embankment and moved into the cotton field on the other side. During that day and night the men slept soddenly, side by side on the boxcar door. And Ma lay close to Rose of Sharon. Sometimes Ma whispered to her and sometimes sat up quietly, her face brooding. Under the blanket she hoarded the remains of the store bread.

The rain had become intermittent now—little wet squalls

and quiet times. On the morning of the second day Pa splashed through the camp and came back with ten potatoes in his pockets. Ma watched him sullenly while he chopped out part of the inner wall of the car, built a fire, and scooped water into a pan. The family ate the steaming boiled potatoes with their fingers. And when this last food was gone, they stared at the gray water; and in the night they did not lie down for a long time.

When the morning came they awakened nervously. Rose of Sharon whispered to Ma.

Ma nodded her head. "Yes," she said. "It's time for it." And then she turned to the car door, where the men lay. "We're a-gettin' outa here," she said savagely, "gettin' to higher groun'. An' you're comin' or you ain't comin', but I'm takin' Rosasharn an' the little fellas outa here."

"We can't!" Pa said weakly.

"Awright, then. Maybe you'll pack Rosasharn to the highway, anyways, an' then come back. It ain't rainin' now, an' we're a-goin'."

"Awright, we'll go," Pa said.

Al said, "Ma, I ain't goin'."

"Why not?"

"Well—Aggie—why, her an' me——"

Ma smiled. " 'Course," she said. "You stay here, Al. Take care of the stuff. When the water goes down—why, we'll come back. Come quick, 'fore it rains again," she told Pa. "Come on, Rosasharn. We're goin' to a dry place."

"I can walk."

"Maybe a little, on the road. Git your back bent, Pa."

Pa slipped into the water and stood waiting. Ma helped Rose of Sharon down from the platform and steadied her across the car. Pa took her in his arms, held her as high as he could, and pushed his way carefully through the deep water, around the car, and to the highway. He set her down on her feet and held onto her. Uncle John carried Ruthie and followed. Ma slid down into the water, and for a moment her skirts billowed out around her.

"Winfiel', set on my shoulder. Al—we'll come back soon's the water's down. Al—" She paused. "If—if Tom comes—tell him we'll be back. Tell him be careful. Winfiel'! Climb on my shoulder—there! Now, keep your feet still." She staggered off through the breast-high water. At the highway embankment they helped her up and lifted Winfield from her shoulder.

They stood on the highway and looked back over the sheet of water, the dark red blocks of the cars, the trucks and automobiles deep in the slowly moving water. And as they stood, a little misting rain began to fall.

"We got to git along," Ma said. "Rosasharn, you feel like you could walk?"

"Kinda dizzy," the girl said. "Feel like I been beat."

Pa complained, "Now we're a-goin', where' we goin'?"

"I dunno. Come on, give your han' to Rosasharn." Ma took the girl's right arm to steady her, and Pa her left. "Goin' someplace where it's dry. Got to. You fellas ain't had dry clothes on for two days." They moved slowly along the highway. They could hear the rushing of the water in the stream beside the road. Ruthie and Winfield marched together, splashing their feet against the road. They went slowly along the road. The sky grew darker and the rain thickened. No traffic moved along the highway.

"We got to hurry," Ma said. "If this here girl gits good an' wet—I don't know what'll happen to her."

"You ain't said where-at we're a-hurryin' to," Pa reminded her sarcastically.

The road curved along beside the stream. Ma searched the land and the flooded fields. Far off the road, on the left, on a slight rolling hill a rain-blackened barn stood. "Look!" Ma said. "Look there! I bet it's dry in that barn. Le's go there till the rain stops."

Pa sighed. "Prob'ly get run out by the fella owns it."

Ahead, beside the road, Ruthie saw a spot of red. She raced to it. A scraggly geranium gone wild, and there was one rain-beaten blossom on it. She picked the flower. She took a petal carefully off and stuck on her nose. Winfield ran up to see.

"Lemme have one?" he said.

"No, sir! It's all mine. I foun' it." She stuck another red petal on her forehead, a little bright-red heart.

"Come on, Ruthie! Lemme have one. Come on, now." He grabbed at the flower in her hand and missed it, and Ruthie banged him in the face with her open hand. He stood for a moment, surprised, and then his lips shook and his eyes welled.

The others caught up. "Now what you done?" Ma asked. "Now what you done?"

"He tried to grab my fl'ar."

Winfield sobbed, "I—on'y wanted one—to—stick on my nose."

"Give him one, Ruthie."

"Leave him find his own. This here's mine."

"Ruthie! You give him one."

Ruthie heard the threat in Ma's tone, and changed her tactics. "Here," she said with elaborate kindness. "I'll stick on one for you." The older people walked on. Winfield held his nose near to her. She wet a petal with her tongue and jabbed it cruelly on his nose. "You little son-of-a-bitch," she said softly. Winfield felt for the petal with his fingers, and pressed it down on his nose. They walked quickly after the others. Ruthie felt how the fun was gone. "Here," she said. "Here's some more. Stick some on your forehead."

From the right of the road there came a sharp swishing. Ma cried, "Hurry up. They's a big rain. Le's go through the fence here. It's shorter. Come on, now! Bear on, Rosasharn." They half dragged the girl across the ditch, helped her through the fence. And then the storm struck them. Sheets of rain fell on them. They plowed through the mud and up the little incline. The black barn was nearly obscured by the rain. It hissed and splashed, and the growing wind drove it along. Rose of Sharon's feet slipped and she dragged between her supporters.

"Pa! Can you carry her?"

Pa leaned over and picked her up. "We're wet through anyways," he said. "Hurry up. Winfiel'—Ruthie! Run on ahead."

They came panting up to the rain-soaked barn and staggered into the open end. There was no door in this end. A few rusty farm tools lay about, a disk plow and a broken cultivator, an iron wheel. The rain hammered on the roof and curtained the entrance. Pa gently set Rose of Sharon down on an oily box. "God Awmighty!" he said.

Ma said, "Maybe they's hay inside. Look, there's a door." She swung the door on its rusty hinges. "They is hay," she cried. "Come on in, you."

It was dark inside. A little light came in through the cracks between the boards.

"Lay down, Rosasharn," Ma said. "Lay down an' res'. I'll try to figger some way to dry you off."

Winfield said, "Ma!" and the rain roaring on the roof drowned his voice. "*Ma!*"

"What is it? What you want?"

"Look! In the corner."

Ma looked. There were two figures in the gloom; a man who lay on his back, and a boy sitting beside him, his eyes wide, staring at the newcomers. As she looked, the boy got slowly up to his feet and came toward her. His voice croaked. "You own this here?"

"No," Ma said. "Jus' come in outa the wet. We got a sick girl. You got a dry blanket we could use an' get her wet clothes off?"

The boy went back to the corner and brought a dirty comfort and held it out to Ma.

"Thank ya," she said. "What's the matter'th that fella?"

The boy spoke in a croaking monotone. "Fust he was sick —but now he's starvin'."

"What?"

"Starvin'. Got sick in the cotton. He ain't et for six days."

Ma walked to the corner and looked down at the man. He was about fifty, his whiskery face gaunt, and his open eyes were vague and staring. The boy stood beside her. "Your pa?" Ma asked.

"Yeah! Says he wasn' hungry, or he jus' et. Give me the food. Now he's too weak. Can't hardly move."

The pounding of the rain decreased to a soothing swish on the roof. The gaunt man moved his lips. Ma knelt beside him and put her ear close. His lips moved again.

"Sure," Ma said. "You jus' be easy. He'll be awright. You jus' wait'll I get them wet clo'es off'n my girl."

Ma went back to the girl. "Now slip 'em off," she said. She held the comfort up to screen her from view. And when she was naked, Ma folded the comfort about her.

The boy was at her side again explaining, "I didn' know. He said he et, or he wasn' hungry. Las' night I went an' bust a winda an' stoled some bread. Made 'im chew 'er down. But he puked it all up, an' then he was weaker. Got to have soup or milk. You folks got money to git milk?"

Ma said, "Hush. Don' worry. We'll figger somepin out."

Suddenly the boy cried, "He's dyin', I tell you! He's starvin' to death, I tell you."

"Hush," said Ma. She looked at Pa and Uncle John standing helplessly gazing at the sick man. She looked at Rose of Sharon huddled in the comfort. Ma's eyes passed Rose of Sharon's eyes, and then came back to them. And the two women looked deep into each other. The girl's breath came short and gasping.

She said "Yes."

Ma smiled. "I knowed you would. I knowed!" She looked down at her hands, tight-locked in her lap.

Rose of Sharon whispered, "Will—will you all—go out?" The rain whisked lightly on the roof.

Ma leaned forward and with her palm she brushed the tousled hair back from her daughter's forehead, and she kissed her on the forehead. Ma got up quickly. "Come on, you fellas," she called. "You come out in the tool shed."

Ruthie opened her mouth to speak. "Hush," Ma said. "Hush and git." She herded them through the door, drew the boy with her; and she closed the squeaking door.

For a minute Rose of Sharon sat still in the whispering barn. Then she hoisted her tired body up and drew the comfort about her. She moved slowly to the corner and stood looking down at the wasted face, into the wide, frightened eyes. Then slowly she lay down beside him. He shook his head slowly from side to side. Rose of Sharon loosened one side of the blanket and bared her breast. "You got to," she said. She squirmed closer and pulled his head close. "There!" she said. "There." Her hand moved behind his head and supported it. Her fingers moved gently in his hair. She looked up and across the barn, and her lips came together and smiled mysteriously.

II

The Social Context

Fact and Fiction

This piece appeared in the issue of *Fortune* for the month in which *The Grapes of Wrath* was published, and it was obviously researched simultaneously without either Steinbeck or the *Fortune* writer knowing of the other's work. The article was published without a byline, as were all of *Fortune*'s articles during this period, but it is interesting to note that Archibald MacLeish was one of *Fortune*'s staff writers at the time.

"I Wonder Where We Can Go Now"

The migrants are familiar enough to anyone who has traveled much through California's interior. On the roads, where you can see them in numbers, they take on a kind of patchwork pattern. They come along in wheezy old cars with the father or one of the older boys driving. The mother and the younger children sit in back; and around them, crammed inside and overflowing to the running boards, the front and rear bumpers, the top and sides, they carry along everything they own. A galvanized iron washtub is tied to the rear, a dirty, patched tent lashed to a fender. There is a cast-iron stove, a mattress, some boxes full of old dishes, extra clothing, and a few staple groceries like flour, lard, and potatoes. You see, at odd angles, the protruding handle of a broom, part of a paint-flaked bedstead, perhaps even an old phonograph or radio. You notice the faces of the people in these cars. There is worry, but also something more: they are the faces of people afraid of hunger; completely dispossessed, certain only of being harried along when their immediate usefulness is over. As one boy said, "When they need us they call us migrants. When we've picked their crop, we're bums and we got to get out."

It is worth while to study these people closely. They have

---

become California's sorest social problem. More, they are one of the major social problems of the U.S. Probably you have heard of them. They are the itinerant agricultural laborers about whom John Steinbeck wrote his *Of Mice and Men* and *In Dubious Battle*, and who have made disturbing headline news when they and the growers and the deputy sheriffs came to blows and bricks and bullets at Salinas and the Imperial Valley. California's agricultural system could not exist without them—that is, without some of them. But there are far, far more of them than the system can utilize. Like certain of the state's homegrown products, they represent glut, depreciation, and decay.

They live under physical conditions ranging from the fairly tolerable to the terriby bad. Most of California's growers supply either tent space or permanent shelter on their own land, and it is noteworthy that they spent some $3,000,000 in the last two years, largely at the insistence of the Associated Farmers, a growers' pressure group of which more will be seen later. Some growers' camps are well built and equipped, but the average is poor. The last reports of the state Division of Immigration and Housing, which since 1933 has had only three full-time inspectors for the job of examining over 8,000 public and private camps, rate almost a third of them as "bad"—i.e., either poorly equipped or poorly policed. A typical big grower's camp, not a "bad" one, consists of frame cabins arranged in rows, with a water line between every two rows. There would be communal bathhouses, perhaps flush toilets or perhaps a few earth-pit privies. The cabins rent for from $1 to $10 a month, and are furnished typically with a wood- or gas-burning stove, cots or pallets, and a water pail. But not even the big growers provide housing for more than part of their peak labor load. Many of the migrants live in dirty roadside tourist camps, labor contractors' camps, or privately run tenting grounds, where the rents may be as high or higher but the equipment is more primitive. Some live in squatter camps. Conditions in these shelters are notoriously squalid, particularly in the Imperial Valley, which offers the absolute low for the entire state. The following report on the Imperial, by a group of California investigators, would be on the whole as apt today as when it was filed:[1]

"In Imperial County, many families were found camping out by the side of irrigation ditches, with little or no shelter. One such family consisted of the father, mother, and eight children. The father hoped there would be some work in the valley later in the year. The mother had tuberculosis and pellagra and it was because of her health that the family came to California. One of the children had active tuberculosis. The family had no home but a 1921 Ford. The mother was trying to chop some wood for the fire . . . A meat and vegetable stew was being cooked in a large, rusty tin can over a grate supported by four other cans. A cupboard and a table had been constructed of boxes. There were no toilet facilities, Nature's needs being attended to behind bushes. Some water was brought from the ice plant in El Centro for drinking purposes, but for cooking and washing, water from the irrigation ditches was used. The family had been sleeping on the ground. The blankets were kept during the daytime in the car. There was no possible shelter. . . . The mother told the worker on the survey that she had been known as the best housekeeper in her home town. . . .

"Many of the families camping along the irrigation ditches were using the ditchwater for drinking purposes as well as using the side of the ditch as a toilet. In February a child from one of these families was taken to the County Hospital with spinal meningitis. There had been no quarantine and the other members of the family were mixing with their neighbors. Children dressed in rags, their hands encrusted with dirt, complexions pasty white, their teeth quite rotted, were observed in these camps.

"One blind baby was not able to sit up. The mother said,

---

[1] Transients in California, *a report of the Division of Special Surveys and Studies, State Relief Administration of California,* 1936.

'We've never had enough money for doctors. I don't know what's the matter with baby or why she's blind. She certainly is poorly. I don't know what the relief will do. We're transients. My husband does farming or anything. We picked cotton in Arizona for a little while after we left Oklahoma but didn't earn much. We thought if we came to California we would be able to pick peas, but when we arrived all the company camps were full and they wouldn't let us in. We have been here a month and my husband hasn't had a thing to do yet. Now the health doctor gave us notice to move no later than today. I wonder where we can go. . . . '"

Briefly and in its grimmest aspects, this is the tragedy in California. As a single state's problem of coping with an unwanted glut of humanity, it would warrant serious study. But it concerns us here in an even larger sense, i.e., as the most aggravated effect of a national situation—a situation so grave that President Roosevelt in February ordered an attack upon it by a committee headed by WPA Administrator F. C. Harrington. California is generally supposed to harbor 150,000 to 250,000 of the estimated million-odd agricultural migrants including families in the U.S.—many more than any other state. But the most important reasons for that lie outside California's control. They lie specifically at the heart of the national migrant problem, and to understand them it is necessary to look across the plains with a long focus.

The migrations of distressed people are, of course, as old as history itself. When things look a little better somewhere else, you move on; the only static population is the population of the cemeteries. Movement, relocation, far from being deplorable, are in fact essential to an active economy, the demands of which can be compared to the pressure areas on a barometric map. Masses of workers shift like air currents from high- to low-pressure areas, but with a difference. The air currents obey physical laws, while the currents of foot-loose humanity, theoretically governed by the neat laws of classical economics, move too often on rumor, sentiment, hope, and malicious deception. . . .

THE LONG ROAD

There are two kinds of agricultural migrants. One group can be thought of as "habitual" migrants, which means that they have followed migratory life for years and will probably go on following it until they grow too old to work. The others are "removal" migrants, which means that they have been forced into migratory life by dispossession from land or job; most of them have been on the road only a few months or a few years, most of them are family units, and nearly all of them would settle permanently if they could. . . .

The habitual migrants, mostly single men, are much the smaller group. Two years ago they were estimated conservatively at between 200,000 and 350,000, and there are probably as many today.

The habitual migrant, however underpaid, underfed, and underemployed, has the dignity of a way of life. It is even possible to think of him romantically. But there is no romance in the "removal" migrant families. They are the truly dispossessed, unequipped for the hazards of the road, searching only for a place to stop and take root.

Removal migrants have taken to the road from distressed areas all over the U.S., but mostly from the South and Midwest. The causes of their distress are embedded deep in the whole tragic history of American agriculture, dating from the earliest misuse of the soil. (For what happened in the Great Plains, see *Fortune's* story on "The Grasslands," November, 1935.) The intervening chapters are familiar—land speculation, recurrent depressions and droughts, reduction of industrial outlets to surplus farm population, power farming, soil erosion, all leading up to the climax of the disastrous droughts and dust storms in the 1930's. With that final calamity, the thin stream of dispossessed families from the Great Plains states erupted in full force into a mass upheaval in 1934. Since then more than 200,000 persons have left the drought area, and others are leaving every day. Rains and federal aid have slowed the migration in some areas.

But neither temporary rain nor government money can reverse the fact that large sections of the Great Plains cannot afford a decent living for even their present population. According to land economists, the minimum desirable amount of reconversion to grazing would probably displace another 250,000 to 400,000 people. If the pattern of the last few years can be taken as a guide, many of them would pile their family goods and kin into secondhand automobiles, set out with a few dollars, and drive west to join the overflowing stream of migratory farm workers.

Everybody knows about the so-called Dust Bowl migration; its spectacular effects have made vivid copy in the press. But there has been another distress force at work, far more insidious yet potentially even more drastic: the spread of power farming. This trend to mechanization, chiefly in the form of the all-purpose tractor, is general and, from the growers' standpoint, necessary; but its impact on the life of the farm worker has been most devastating in the cotton belt, where it is throwing thousands out of work.

From 1930 to 1937 farm tractor sales in the U.S. increased 50 per cent. In the same time sales in ten cotton states increased 90 per cent. Some conception of the labor displacement involved can be had from the case of the Mississippi planter who bought twenty-two tractors and thirteen four-row cultivators, evicted 130 of his 160 cropper families, and kept only thirty for day laborers. The change is well under way in some areas—most notably in the western dry areas of Texas and Oklahoma, and in the Arkansas and Mississippi deltas—and is incipient in others.

A common procedure is for a landowner to throw several tenant-operated farms into one operating unit, evict the tenant families, and hire a tractor driver by the day. Usually it is impossible for the evicted tenant to get another place: he must go into the towns and live on relief, or hire himself out for whatever day labor the farms require, or move away and try for a new start somewhere else. Tens of thousands have already been displaced, and it is the sober conclusion of economists that if the present trend continues, a majority of the South's 1,800,000 tenants will be added to the nation's landless and jobless. If and when the mechanical cotton picker is finally perfected, these people will have not even the seasonal recourse of cotton picking.

It is an ironical sidelight that the government's crop-control program has abetted the dispossession. Crop restriction in itself reduces the labor need, and therefore causes some eviction. But more important, the benefit payments have furnished landowners with the capital to buy tractors. In addition, though the law requires that benefit checks be divided between owner and tenant, owners in many cases have secured the whole amount for themselves by dismissing the tenants and rehiring them as wageworkers. The disturbances in southeastern Missouri last January, when some 300 tenant-cropper families camped on the highways in public protest, were partly directed against this practice. But such isolated acts of treachery, however cruel, are merely incidental to the forces that are crowding the southern farm workers by the thousands off the land and into the army of migrants.

It should now be clear that the migrant problem is twofold in form. There is the problem of basic conditions that cause people to become migrants in the first place, i.e., the distress that makes life unlivable where they came from. And there is society's problem of coping with a drifting populace of landless, generally jobless humans, who must eat, sleep, fight off sickness, and maintain the decent forms of family life. Both problems are national, but the second is most acute on the Pacific Coast. The routes of most of the habitual migrants lead west, where they are attracted by the work prospects of the great variety of crops and the long growing seasons. The removal migrants trend west for the same reason, and also because of the mild climate and the physical opulence of the country. The two streams meet and ferment in California.

THE LAND OF PLENTY

The best-informed authorities place the number of men, women, and children in California who follow the crops during some part of the year at between 150,000 and 250,000. Roughly speaking, it is probable that except during the peak season there are about two or three migrants for every job available to them. Their employment span is about four to six months a year of more or less intermittent work. Their average income *per family* is somewhere between $350 and $450 a year. Out of this must come gas, oil, and repairs for their old cars. And since the average family probably contains four members, the remainder leaves well under $100 a year for the physical needs of each person—less than half the amount the California Relief Administration estimates to be necessary for living on a subsistence level.

To get even this amount the migrant must be alert to the possibilities of his trade. Most of California's growing areas have different crops, and each crop has a somewhat different growing season. With some experience in the field, the migrant learns the most likely spots to look for work at any season. The natural migratory current begins in the South in the Imperial Valley, with the lettuce and peas and cantaloupe, and courses north with the crops to the fruit harvests in the Sacramento Valley; an eddy reaches beyond to the apple, berry, and hop crops of Washington and Oregon. The current comes back down again following the late harvests, the pruning, thinning, and hoeing, and another eddy goes on into the cotton and truck crops of Arizona. The movement is most active from August through October, just before and during the peak harvest season. It slows and stagnates toward spring, when only about a third or even a fourth as many jobs are available. Not many migrants make this full circuit. If they can find work in any of the big valleys, they stay until it gives out. But probably a fifth of them each year travel at least from the Imperial Valley to the Sacramento, a distance of about 600 miles.

Now, a supply of migrant workers has long been essential to California's kind of agriculture, which is highly intensive, with peak demands for hand labor far in excess of any local supply. Intensive crops like fruits and vegetables increased from 6.6 per cent of total crop values in 1869 to 78.4 per cent in 1929. This intensive farming has been made possible by heavy investments in irrigation, farm machinery, and other equipment that only well-heeled individuals or corporations could afford. Such investments are profitable only when applied to large acreages. Hence, with intensive farming has come an increase in the size of the growing unit, and an increased concentration of land ownership.

To an outsider, with ideas about agriculture derived from the East or Middle West, that intensity of California agriculture is fairly visible. The "farms," particularly in the Imperial Valley, are more like big food factories, with every device of scientific farming used to secure maximum output from the soil. Instead of farmhouses with barns and outbuildings, there are mostly long rows of shacks along the ditchbanks and in the eucalyptus groves. The "farmers" of much of the land are absentee owners, with offices in the cities, who do their farming through local managers. Even the managers are likely to live in town. The crops and terrain and acreages vary through the state, but the pattern of high-pressure land use prevails. California's agriculture is not "farming" in the traditional sense. It is industry as much as lumbering and oil are industries.

Figures make the point clear. In California today less than one-tenth of the farms produce more than one-half of the crops, while the small farmers (41.4 per cent) produce only 6 per cent. One-third of all U.S. large-scale farms (annual crop value of $30,000) are in California. The trend has been to corporate farming under absentee ownership, with a decrease in independent family-size farms.

To work these farms, with their violently fluctuating labor demands, landowners in the past encouraged heavy immigration of low-wage workers from abroad—Chinese, Japanese, a few

Hindus, thousands of Filipinos. More important than any of these races, however, were the Mexicans who began arriving in large numbers about 1910 and thereafter supplied the bulk of the migrant forces for two decades. The Mexicans brought complications. Unlike the other migrants, they traveled with their families, and when their slim earnings gave out they "squatted" in southern California subsisting on local charity. But they suited the growers fine. They were stolid and strong, inured to heat, hard labor, and low pay, and when the federal government put up bars to further Mexican immigration in 1929, the growers protested loudly. But through the immigration law, and also because the free-land policy of the Mexican Government after 1934 attracted many back to their homeland, the Mexican migrants have become a much diminished force.

Throughout all these years there were, of course, some thousands of white native-born citizens among the migrants. A few traveled in family groups, but customarily they were single men, harvest followers of the kind who worked in the wheat harvests of the grain states. After 1930 the whole character of the California migrants began to change. Numbers of semi-urban unemployed Californians went into the fields to replace the departed Mexicans. Then single unemployed workers, both urban and rural, streamed into California from all over the country—a serious addition to the chronic oversupply. And finally, beginning in 1935, came the Dust Bowl hordes and the dispossessed southern tenants—far more than the farm economy could absorb, and an ordinary labor situation became an acute sociological problem.

Plant quarantine stations along the state's borders counted 285,000 refugees (including some duplications) "in need of manual employment" in the period from mid-1935 to January 1, 1939, besides 59,000 returning Californians of the same type. So alarming in size and suddenness was this mass migration that the Los Angeles Chamber of Commerce attempted briefly—and quite illegally—to shunt it aside by means of a "bum blockade" on main highways at the state borders. The total number of refugees since 1930 is unknown, but it may well reach 350,000. Naturally not all of these people have become migratory farm laborers; some have returned home, some have become resident laborers, a few have settled on small subsistence farms, and probably most of the pre-1935 single migrants have gone into the cities to join the ranks of the casually employed or unemployed. But the results so far as migrant farm labor is concerned are these: the racial characteristic has changed from predominantly foreign to predominantly white American, the single migrant has given way to the family group, and the number of migrants has swelled to an army that California agriculture cannot conceivably support.

ON THE PLAINS OF HEAVEN

The consequence of low income and privation is social unrest, and there is plenty of social unrest among California's migrants. But until recently there was surprisingly little articulate protest. On the surface, the situation would seem susceptible to union agitation, but it contains special elements: the migrants have no money to pay dues, and they move about so often and so far that it is difficult to weld them into a militant, closely knit group. Moreover, the traditional craft setup of American unionism offered no place to the unskilled worker, and consequently none to the farm laborer. The I.W.W. did heavy duty after 1913, year of the bloody Wheatland hop riots, but fell apart in the early twenties. The A. F. of L. made several feeble attempts at organizing on a craft basis between 1909 and 1915, and again in the early thirties, but not much came of it. The Mexican and Filipino workers had their private organizations and occasionally caused the growers trouble. It remained for a Communist-led union, the Cannery and Agricultural Workers' Industrial Union, to organize the first effective drive among the migrants.

This group appeared in California in 1930 but didn't get fully under way until 1933. In the spring and early summer of that year it followed the crops as they ripened, organizing in peas, lettuce, strawberries, and peaches, and having its most notable success in a nine-county cotton pickers' strike that affected 12,000 workers. By the middle of the 1934 working season, the union had led about fifty strikes involving some 50,000 workers. Its leaders claim that at its height it had a membership of around 21,000, and that it raised the basic hourly field wage from an average of 15 to 17.5 cents an hour in 1932 to an average of 27.5 cents in 1934. In the summer of 1934, however, the union was broken up by the anti-Red activities of employers and state authorities. Its last stand was an apricot pickers' strike in June, 1934, on the Balfour, Guthrie ranches near Brentwood. Deputies herded 200 strikers into a cattle pen, arrested some of their leaders, and convoyed the rest out of the county. In the trials following the big California Red scare of 1934, the union's president and secretary, along with six of their associates, were convicted of treason under the criminal-syndicalism law. Five of the eight prisoners were later paroled and the remaining three were liberated when an appellate court reversed all the convictions in 1937.

After the demise of the C. & A.W.I.U., the Communist party in California gave most of its attention to the industrial situation in San Francisco. Now, however, it is understood to be concentrating again on agricultural workers. The international party "line" changed in 1934 from a tactic of parallel unionism to one of united-front collaboration, so the Communists work through the C.I.O.'s United Cannery, Agricultural, Packing, and Allied Workers of America, which was formed in 1937. This new group has the arena pretty much to itself, since the A. F. of L. has preferred to give most of its time to the canneries, where the packers have welcomed it as a bulwark against the hated C.I.O. Possibly because so much of its energy has been drawn off in the cannery battle, the C.I.O. has not made an impressive showing among the field and shed workers, claiming only 5,000 of them in the California district. It has led nine of the fourteen field workers' strikes of the last year and a half (employers charge the union with instigation; the union says the strikes were spontaneous). Eight of the nine union-led strikes ended in union victory or compromise.

Though the union's membership is small its mere existence as a strike threat fills California's growers with panic. Harvesting can't wait on negotiation. Crops must be picked within a few days of ripening or not at all; and if not at all, the result may be financial ruin. This has created a situation of which thoughtful Californians are far from proud. Vigilante activity against strikers and organizers since 1932 has been bloody and direct. Scores of workers have been injured and so have a number of strikebreakers and deputized townspeople and farmers. California's industrialized farming can exhibit all the customary weapons of industrial warfare including tear gas, finks, goon squads, propaganda, bribery, and espionage.

Spearhead of the growers in this unhappy situation is the Associated Farmers. Composed mainly of small or medium-scale farm operators, this organization is dominated by the big growers, packers, utilities, banks, and other absentee landlords who are all-important in the state's farm system. Now the A.F.'s stated objectives are thoroughly worthy. And it will be recalled that A.F. engineered the growers' expenditure of $3,000,000 to improve the housing of migrants. But its tactics in labor disputes are infinitely less enlightened. It claims to be "not anti-union or anti-labor," but it takes pride in having helped enact antipicketing ordinances in the majority of California's fifty-eight counties. A.F. members were in the thick of the worst recent strikes. In the particularly bloody Salinas lettuce strike, the county head of the A.F. himself convoyed the lettuce trucks and led the battle against the strikers. In the Stockton cannery strike, it was the organization's Pacific Coast President who brought in a thousand deputized farmers to see that the spinach was canned. From labor's point of view, the Associated Farmers is a thinly camouflaged strikebreaking agency. To the big grower, it is a strong-arm defense against the menace of Communist agitation. The small grower's view is less clear-cut, but he often finds it healthier to join the Associated Farmers than not, if he wants to get crop loans from the banks. Incidentally, investigation of the A.F. was next on the docket of the La Follette Civil Liberties Committee when that body was allowed to expire last January.

Vigilanteism is an alarming and dangerous thing in a democracy, but it is not uncommon. It is, in fact, a characteristic of industrial warfare whether the locale be Michigan, Pennsylvania, or Mohawk Valley. But California's worker-grower relationship contains something more than physical violence. On the side of the growers it often contains an antipathy amounting almost to hatred, and this may seem odd in view of the fact that the growers could not exist without the aid of the migrants. The reasons are of two kinds, one emotional, the other economic. The first kind can be summed up in a composite grower statement—with many exceptions among individuals, of course—that runs about like this:

"We didn't ask these Okies and Arkies [so called because so many are from Oklahoma and Arkansas] to come out here. They were failures where they lived, and they came because our relief payments are about the biggest in the country. Most of them aren't the kind of people who make good citizens. They're naturally dirty, ignorant, immoral, and superstitious. If you do anything for them they don't appreciate it, and if you let them on your ground they dirty it up and destroy property —they're used to living like trash. They've been inbreeding for so long that they're low-grade stock. After they've been here a year or two and learned how to handle our crops they make good workers, maybe the best we've ever had, but you can't depend on them. They're too damn independent; they won't take orders like a Mexican or a Jap, and they're not satisfied with the wages we can afford to pay. They're easy bait for the Red organizers. They're not satisfied with what they have, and yet if you gave them a hundred-acre farm and all the equipment they'd go bankrupt again inside of five years."

There is some fact in this view, but a great deal more fiction.

From experienced sociologists who have worked among the migrants* and from *Fortune*'s own observation a more accurate general statement would be this:

"The majority of the migrants are ordinary Americans who have been dispossessed mostly by forces outside their control. Most of them are unskilled farm laborers, though there are workmen and tradespeople among them—mechanics, construction workers, miners, salesmen, and so on. They haven't had much schooling but they are intelligent enough. They are anxious to work and they don't like to take relief. They appreciate what is done for them. They are mildly religious, their moral standards are fair. Their standards of cleanliness are normal under decent conditions, but they tend to succumb to the effects of squalid surroundings. They are stand-offish, and they don't work well together. Some of them have become so far demoralized by long unemployment and substandard living that possibly they can never be rehabilitated; they have even lost ambition. But for the most part they are potentially self-supporting citizens who want only a chance to make a new start."

That, then, is the emotional argument over the migrant. In the economic argument the growers have better reason for short tempers. It is imperative that the growers have enough mobile labor to meet their peak seasonal demand of some 175,000 workers, but afterward many of that number become sheer surplus, and the growers feel no more obligation toward them than a New York department-store owner, for example, might feel toward part-time clerks laid off after a rush season. While they acknowledge their dependence upon the 175,000, growers nevertheless argue that an employer cannot be held responsible for the year-round maintenance of workers needed only for a few weeks or months. And since agriculture supplies a considerable share of California's productive wealth, some

---

* One of the most eminent authorities in the U.S. on agricultural migrant labor is Dr. Paul S. Taylor of the University of California.

believe it reasonable that the workers be subsidized during slack seasons by relief payments—but no relief to the uninvited surplus workers. Furthermore, as the growers vehemently point out, California's farm-labor wage rates are among the highest in the nation. If it were possible to give the migrants steady work their incomes would be above national average for unskilled labor. Obviously steady work is impossible because: (1) the work is seasonal, (2) jobs are widely separated and time must be lost on the road, and (3) lacking accurate information, migrants move about on hope and rumor, with a consequent inefficient distribution of workers to available jobs. . . .

WHAT TO DO?

Yet the migrants remain, and the question remains as to what should be done about them. There have been palliatives. California's settlement laws require three years' residence in the state and one in the county without receipt of "any public or private relief from friends, charitable organizations, or relatives other than legally responsible relatives"—before eligibility for full assistance is established. In practice, however, the state has found a way to cut the waiting period down to one year, at the end of which the migrant may receive about $16 per month. During the wait, however, the migrants may be in serious distress. The State Relief Administration will give them temporary aid until their settlement in some other state is verified, and then provide for transportation back home. But their home states receive them coldly. State relief officials put up various barriers against their return, and state legislators have even juggled settlement laws in order to escape responsibility.

For example a migratory South Dakotan, thirty days after leaving that state, loses his right to South Dakota relief. It will be at least twelve months before he can qualify for relief in California—and three years in some other states, and even five in others. Such a wholesale abandonment is one of the most alarming aspects of the whole migrant problem; readers will be reminded of Raymond Leslie Buell's analysis of the tendency toward national disunion through state tax policies ("Death by Tariff," *Fortune*, August, 1938). The majority choose to scrape along until they have established California settlement and a right to aid from public funds.

In the interim some may be able to get dried skim milk, flour, and other so-called "surplus" foods from the Surplus Commodities Corporation, and perhaps a direct grant from the Farm Security Administration. Drawing on its emergency funds, the FSA last year allotted $750,000 for relief grants, most of which has gone to nonresident migrants, and has so far aided some 20,000 families. The FSA has been much abused by California pressure groups. The result, they say, will only be to increase the state's relief burden by enabling the migrants to hang on until they become legal residents. FSA officials reply simply that the thousands of distressed cannot be permitted to starve.

Of all government agencies, the FSA stands alone in its effort to effect a genuine (if admittedly partial) solution to the migrant problem. The FSA's program has taken a number of directions. Four years ago construction was begun on sanitary, government-supervised camps, some permanently located in heavy work areas, others capable of being moved along with the crops. Five mobile camps were experimented with last year. The permanent camps, of which ten are in operation in California, furnish solid tent bases, an isolation unit, a clinic, assembly hall and nursery, incinerator, pump house, laundry tubs, shower baths, and sanitary toilets—all for a per family cost of about $400. Administration of the camps is in the hands of the migrants themselves under FSA supervision, and the camp charge is only ten cents a week or two hours' labor on camp maintenance; the "rents" go into an entertainment and emergency fund. Plans also call for from twenty to forty-eight small frame houses to be erected at each location, each house to have a small piece of ground attached. These places will be rented—for $8.20 per month—to hand-picked migrant families, who can work in the surrounding countryside and spend their spare time raising food for their own use.

Another undertaking financed by the FSA is the Agricultural Workers Health and Medical Association. Nonresident families in California are disqualified from free medical care as well as from ordinary relief, and with a few notable exceptions like Dr. Joe Smith of Kern County, county health authorities pay little attention to them except in acute emergencies. Until the Association was established early last year distress was naturally great. Dr. R. C. Williams, FSA physician largely responsible for setting up the Association, found that a great part of the sickness he observed was the result of malnutrition. For this the obvious prescription was food rather than medicine, so Association doctors were given authority to sign grocery orders. The Association now has on its panel local doctors and nurses throughout the area, and has done an excellent job of caring for nonresident families who apply. Its facilities are not, however, extended to migrants who have attained residence. And despite the efforts of the state Health Department, conditions among the vast majority continue to be deplorable. Epidemics of smallpox, typhoid, and malaria are common. Infant mortality is high. A common cause is malnutrition, since the mothers' diet will not produce adequate milk. The older children get milk infrequently if at all, and most of them have deficiency ailments of one kind or another.

From the old Resettlement Administration, FSA inherited an extensive program of rural rehabilitation, and this it has carried on and expanded. A few of the drought-area migrants come west with enough capital to buy cutover timberland or low-grade farmland. To some of these families FSA has made crop, seed, and equipment loans sufficient to put them on their feet and give them a good start toward success. Similarly, a few migrants with no capital but with a desire to settle are sharing in the benefits of industrialized farming on the FSA's big coöperative farms. Only two such farms are in operation now, however—one in California and one in Arizona. Though FSA officials are pleased with the results of the program and hope to extend it, they face several obstacles: not much good land is available at reasonable prices; in addition, private owners shout "Socialism!" whenever coöperative farming is mentioned; and finally, the migrants themselves are slow to learn the meaning of coöperation. They are rugged individualists, and more than anything else they want "a piece of ground" where they can work out their own destiny. . . .

What the final solution must be it is no part of the journalist's function to say. Left-wingers believe there is no way out short of land nationalization combined with a broad resettlement program. Reactionary growers have been heard to speak of "a permanent peon class." The problem has been investigated by both government and private agencies, and various cures have been offered for specific details—bad housing, insufficient medical aid, inconsistent settlement laws, relief troubles, and so on. Bills introduced by Congressman Jerry Voorhis seek to extend medical and financial provisions of Social Security to migrants, and also recommend changes in the U.S. Employment Service, under which the Farm Placement Service operates. Except in Texas, where it has done excellent work, the Service has been criticized by employers and workers alike, especially in California. Growers complain that it has worked out no way of registering migrants so that they will be available when needed; further, that it refuses to send as many men as the growers request, with the result that local labor shortages occur and workers are able to demand higher wages. Labor leaders insist to the contrary that the Service has coöperated with unscrupulous owners in flooding the labor market, thereby lowering wages, and that it has sometimes served in effect as a strikebreaking agency. The Service finds itself in a delicate position. The total evidence suggests, however, that it has been remiss in its main job, which is to keep workers informed about the employment market. If migrants knew exactly where to look for work their waste motion would be less, and their incomes correspondingly higher.

A possible attack on the migrant problem is suggested by the widely publicized Tagus Ranch, owned by the Merritt family. Manager "Clint" Merritt Jr. has been able to diversify crops and varieties of planting on the 7,000-acre tract so that work is comparatively steady throughout the year. Seven hundred families are housed on the ranch in cottages that rent for from $2 to $3 a month. The men work about eight months in the year, and a bare minimum of migrants are needed at the season's peak. Sociologists look askance at Tagus because of its company store, brass checks, and other devices of excessive paternalism. But the Merritts' crop system shows that the migrant-labor problem is not wholly insoluble.

On the more immediate problem of providing work for the surplus migrants and the potential migrants, not many feasible ideas have been developed. FSA officials believe that much could be done through a national forestry program. Forest Service studies show that there are 630,000,000 acres of forest land in the U.S.; that an annual expenditure of $504,000,000 would provide year-round work for (1) 315,000 men at going wages, or (2) 710,000 men at WPA wages, or (3) 1,260,000 men at a wage of $400 a year.

In the meantime the migrants continue to be a national problem. California's situation has been dealt with here at length. It is more acute than the situation of other states for reasons noted, but it is representative of conditions in a number of other states, and of conditions perhaps soon to be found in more. Yet, except for the efforts of the FSA, very little had been done until February, when President Roosevelt ordered the investigation of the migrant-labor situation by WPA Administrator Harrington. Colonel Harrington's work was to be concerned with the handling of migrant families already on the road. It might be equally wise to investigate causes. For it is certain that the migratory farm-labor problem, going back as it does into the basic forces of power farming, land depletion, and the other dislocating factors in our agriculture, is not a problem that resolves itself quietly.

FRANK J. TAYLOR

Frank J. Taylor has been a newspaperman on several West Coast papers and the San Francisco Bureau of the Associated Press. He has been assistant manager of the *New York Globe* and manager of the Washington Bureau of the Scripps-Howard newspapers. Since 1924 he has devoted his time to writing books and doing articles for nationally known magazines.

California's *Grapes of Wrath*

Californians are wrathy over *The Grapes of Wrath*, John Steinbeck's best-selling novel of migrant agricultural workers. Though the book is fiction, many readers accept it as fact.

By implication, it brands California farmers with unbelievable cruelty in their dealings with refugees from the "dust bowl." It charges that they deliberately lured a surplus of workers westward to depress wages, deputized peace officers to hound the migrants ever onward, burned the squatters' shacktowns, stomped down gardens and destroyed surplus foods in a conspiracy to force the refugees to work for starvation wages, allowed children to hunger and mothers to bear babies unattended in squalor. It implies that hatred of the migrants is fostered by the land barons who use the "Bank of the West" (obviously the Bank of America) and the "Farmers Association" (the Associated Farmers) to gobble up the lands of the small farmers and concentrate them in a few large holdings.

These are a few of the sins for which Steinbeck indicts California farmers. It is difficult to rebut fiction, which requires no proof, with facts, which do require proof.

The experiences of the Joad family, whose misfortunes in their trek from Oklahoma to California Steinbeck portrays so

Originally published in *Forum*, CII (November 1939), 232–238.

graphically, are not typical of those of the real migrants I found in the course of two reportorial tours of the agricultural valleys. I made one inquiry during the winter of 1937–38, following the flood which Steinbeck describes; I made another at the height of the harvest this year.

Along three thousand miles of highways and byways, I was unable to find a single counterpart of the Joad family. Nor have I discovered one during fifteen years of residence in the Santa Clara Valley (the same valley where John Steinbeck now lives), which is crowded each summer with transient workers harvesting the fruit crops. The lot of the "fruit tramp" is admittedly no bed of roses, but neither is it the bitter fate described in *The Grapes of Wrath*.

NO JOADS HERE

The Joad family of nine, created by Steinbeck to typify the "Okie" migrants, is anything but typical. A survey made for the Farm Security Administration revealed that thirty was the average age of migrant adults, that the average family had 2.8 children.

Steinbeck's Joads, once arrived in the "land of promise," earned so little that they faced slow starvation. Actually, no migrant family hungers in California unless it is too proud to accept relief. Few migrants are.

There is no red tape about getting free food or shelter.

The FSA maintains warehouses in eleven strategically located towns, where the grant officer is authorized to issue 15 days' rations to any migrant who applies, identifies himself by showing his driver's license, and answers a few simple questions about his family, his earnings, and his travels. In emergencies, the grant officer may issue money for clothing, gasoline, or medical supplies. The food includes standard brands of a score of staple products, flour, beans, corn meal, canned milk and tomatoes, dried fruit, and other grocery items. Before the 15 days are up, the grant officer or his assistant visits the migrant family in camp, and, if the need still exists, the ration is renewed repeatedly until the family finds work.

Shelter is provided by the FSA (a unit of the Federal Resettlement Administration) at model camps which Steinbeck himself represents as satisfactory. The one at Shafter is typical. A migrant family is assigned to a wooden platform on which a tent may be pitched; if the family lacks a tent, the camp has some to lend. The rent is a dime a day, and the migrant who wants to save the money can work it out by helping to clean up camp. The dime goes into a community benefit fund, administered by a committee. Camp facilities include toilets, showers and laundry tubs, with hot and cold running water, a community house. These thirteen camps cost around $190,000 apiece, and each accommodates some three hundred families. Last summer there were vacant platforms, though in winter there is a shortage of space.

Various relief organizations divide the responsibility of providing food and shelter for California's migrants. Federal authorities, working through the FSA, assume the burden for the first year. After a migrant family has been in the State a year, it becomes eligible for State relief. After three years, it becomes a county charge. State relief for agricultural workers averages $51 a month in California, as compared with $21 in Oklahoma, less for several neighboring States. The U.S. Farm Placement Service notes that WPA wages in California are $44 per month, in Oklahoma $32. California old-age pensions are $32 per month, Oklahoma's $20. These are U.S. Social Security Board figures. Records of the FSA grant offices indicate that many migrants earned under $200 a year back home—or less than one third the relief allowance in California. Thus thousands of Okies, having discovered this comparative bonanza, urge their kinsfolk to join them in California, where the average migrant family earns $400 during the harvest season and is able, after the first lean year, to draw an equal sum for relief during eight months of enforced idleness.

WAGES, HEALTH CONDITIONS

The advantages of life in California for migrant workers are not limited to the salubrious climate and largess.

When the harvest is on, the base wage for agricultural workers on California farms is $2.10 per day with board, as compared to $1.00 in Oklahoma, $1.35 in Texas, and 65 cents in Arkansas. These figures are from the U.S. Bureau of Agricultural Economics. Cotton pickers in California's San Joaquin Valley are paid 90 cents per 100 pounds. In Oklahoma, the pay is 65 cents a hundred, in Arkansas and Texas 60 cents. California has 180 separate crops to harvest, and some crop is ripening somewhere in the State every month of the year. A fortunate migrant may work eight to ten months each year. Back home he was lucky to work three months.

Another advantage of life in California is the free medical service. Few of the migrants had ever seen the inside of a hospital or employed a doctor, dentist, or nurse before they came to California. Each FSA camp has a full-time nurse and a part-time doctor to serve the migrant families without charge. Medical supplies, too, are free.

At the Shafter camp, I asked how many babies had been born in camp this year.

"None," the manager replied. "The mothers all go to Kern General Hospital."

At the hospital, supported by Kern County, I learned that, of 727 children born to migrant mothers in the County during the first 5 months of this year, 544 were delivered in the hospital, without charge. In fact, under State law, no general hospital may refuse a mother in labor. Yet in the Steinbeck book a camp manager is obliged to act as midwife.

It is a fortunante break, not only for the migrants but for the Californians as well, that the incoming streams of dilapidated "jalopies," piled high with beds and utensils, converge at Bakersfield, seat of Kern County. As large as Massachusetts (and wealthy, thanks to oil), Kern County maintains a remarkable health service under the direction of Dr. Joe Smith, who believes that an ill person is a menace to others and that it is the County's duty to make him well. Dr. Smith's eighteen nurses, each with a car, spend most of their time in schools and labor camps, checking the health and diet of children. Any migrant family needing medical service can have it free at Kern General, and some with contagious diseases receive it against their will.

Kern County, strategically located, is California's front-line defense against epidemics. Few migrant families manage to cross the huge area without at least one examination. Other counties to the north likewise employ nurses to visit the migrant camps, but they are not as selfishly altruistic as is Kern. Though resisting the nurses' attentions at first, the migrants are now eager for them.

One of the accusations in the Steinbeck novel is that State and county peace officers hound the migrants from camp to camp, to push them into strikebreaking jobs. But inquiry reveals that officers invade camps only when appealed to by health officials.

The health officer of Madera County found a group of migrants camped atop a huge manure pile. "It's warmer here," they protested, when he ordered them to move. Only when he invoked police authority would they budge.

One health deputy discovered a case of smallpox in a camp. Telling the family to stay indoors, he hurried to town for vaccine. When he came back, the entire camp had evaporated into the night, and, before all the exposed migrants could be traced and rounded up into isolation camps, health officers of the neighboring counties had to cope with over six hundred cases of smallpox.

Investigating a typhus outbreak, a health officer found that several families had chopped holes in their cabin floors for toilets, without digging pits. In Santa Clara County, migrants were found camping around a polluted well. One of them explained, "The folks that was here before us used it," and they stayed on until deputy sheriffs removed them forcibly.

Outside nearly every agricultural community, from El Centro

on the Mexican border to Redding near the Oregon line, is a shantytown or squatter camp. These are frightful places in which to live, devoid of adequate sanitation, often without pure water. Local authorities can do little about these rural slums, because they are outside city limits.

The most unsanitary squatter camp was that in the river bottom just north of Bakersfield, where squatters had made themselves at home on property of the Kern County Land Company, one of the State's major land "barons." The land company offered no objection to the squatter camp, but the citizens of Bakersfield did when the migrants' children came over the line to school and epidemics of flu, skin diseases, chicken pox, and other ailments depleted the classrooms. There were threats of vigilante action from irate parents, but what happened was quite different. Deputies from the county health office surveyed the camp, discovered that most of the occupants were employed and could afford to rent homes, that some of them had been there seven years. After six months of patient persuasion, all but twenty-six families were induced to move to town. When the twenty-six refused to budge, the health officer had their flimsy shacks moved to higher ground. They are still there. The vacated shacks were pushed into a pile and burned by order of the health department. That is the prosaic story behind the lurid burning of Bakersfield's "Hooverville," as dramatized in The Grapes of Wrath (p. 382).

THE GREAT MIGRATION

The great flood of the winter of 1937–38, with which Steinbeck drowned the last hopes of the Joad family, hit the migrants hardest in Madera County, where thousands of them worked in the cotton fields. Near Firebaugh, the San Joaquin River rose in its rampage to wash out eight hundred campers. It was after dark one Saturday night when a deputy sheriff reported the plight of these unfortunates to Dr. Lee A. Stone, the wiry old health officer, an ex-Southerner formerly on the staff of the U.S. Public Health Service. Dr. Stone mobilized all the trucks and cars he could find, hurried to the scene, moved the eight hundred refugees thirty miles through the blinding rain to the little city of Madera, and sheltered them in the schools. Then he raised funds by phone for temporary quarters.

Discovering that most of his unexpected guests had but recently come to California, he hit on the idea of returning them to their kinsfolk in Oklahoma, Arkansas, and Texas. When he had raised the necessary funds to buy railroad tickets, he hurried over with the news.

They listened in stony silence.

Finally, one of the men spoke up. "Thanks, Doc," he drawled. "Here we be and here we stay and we ain't a gonna leave the promised land."

"No sirree, we ain't a gonna leave California," chorused the rest. And they didn't.

Almost all the counties in the San Joaquin and Sacramento Valleys have standing offers of free transportation back home for any migrant family. Not one family in a hundred has accepted.

No one knows how many migrants have poured into California since the last census was taken, because the count was not started until 1935, when the State Department of Agriculture instructed the plant-quarantine inspectors at the border to check and report incoming farm workers. To date, 285,000 of them have been reported, but the count is incomplete because many thousands have ridden in on freight trains.

The migrants' trek dates back to 1925, when cotton first became a major crop in California. Some authorities think that almost a hundred thousand families have moved into the State, mostly from the dust-bowl area. This would mean half a million individuals, a migration exceeding the gold rush of pioneer days. Others who have studied the trek of the Okies— so called because forty-two out of every hundred migrants come from Oklahoma—place the figure at three hundred thousand.

In either case, it is a tremendous lump of impoverished population for the people of the Great Interior Valley to assimilate. It is as if the entire population of Cincinnati were to visit Cleveland and, once there, decide to remain indefinitely as star boarders. And it has taken the combined resources of the State, the counties, the federal government, and the individual farmers to meet the emergency. Madera County, for instance, which had 15,000 residents when the invasion started, now has double that population; and most of the newcomers are public charges part of each year. Kern County has a population of 130,000 persons, of whom 35,000 are on relief. The County hospital budget has increased from $100,000 in 1926 to the present figure of $970,000, all of which except some $8,000, contributed by the federal government for the aid of crippled children, is paid by Kern's taxpayers.

CALIFORNIA'S SPECIAL PROBLEM

Owing to the peculiarities of agriculture in the Far West, the farmers of California are as hopelessly dependent on the migrant workers as the migrants are dependent on the farmers for jobs. For California agriculture differs from farming elsewhere in several ways.

Most California crops are so extremely perishable that they must be harvested on the day of ripening—not a day earlier or a day later. This is true of fresh fruits, such as peaches, apricots, and pears, which must be picked, packed, iced, and shipped to the hour. It is true also of field crops like lettuce, tomatoes, melons. Asparagus is actually harvested twice a day. Timely and uninterrupted handling of these perishables means the difference between a $300,000,000 yearly income and a multi-million expense for intensive planting, cultivating, irrigating, spraying, thinning, and harvesting. Most of the California farmers' customers live two to three thousand miles distant, beyond two mountain ranges, and it costs as much to deliver the foodstuffs to them in good condition as it does to battle the perennial droughts, the insects, the vagaries of soil and atmosphere in the struggle to grow the crops. Including nonperishables, the annual take from the soil totals around $600,000,000 and is the State's main livelihood.

Another peculiarity of California agriculture is the manner in which it is broken up into "deals," to use the local term for crops. There are about 180 deals in all, and they, too, are often migrant. The lettuce deal begins in midwinter in Imperial Valley, near the Mexican border; it migrates first to Arizona, then to the Salinas Valley, which from April to November is the country's salad bowl. Melon, tomato, spinach, fresh-pea deals likewise follow the sun north each spring and summer. Navel oranges ripen in midwinter south of the Tehachapi range, Valencias in midsummer north of these mountains. The peach deal trails the apricot deal; then comes the prune deal, the grape deal, and finally cotton.

California is a long, slender State, broken up into a score of agricultural "islands." In the San Diego island, the growers concentrate on avocados and bulbs. The Santa Clara Valley is the prune and apricot island. The Sacramento Valley produces nine tenths of the country's canned peaches. There are three grape islands, two lettuce islands, an asparagus island behind the dikes of the delta country—a sort of little Netherlands. There is a cotton belt in the San Joaquin Valley. In all these highly specialized, intensively cultivated regions, harvest time comes with a vengeance.

For generations, transient workers have appeared by the thousands at harvest time.

The Mexicans pitched their tents in orchards or made camp in rude summertime shelters. They picked the fruit, collected their wages, and faded over the horizon to the next crop. They were good workers, with an instinctive touch for ripening fruit and melons, and better help than the Orientals who preceded them. In 1934, the migrations of these Mexican workers ended abruptly, as their new agrarian government back home offered each returning family a slice of a confiscated estate.

The exodus of the Mexicans coincided with the influx of

dust-bowl refugees. For a time, the Okies were the answer to the farmers' prayers. They still are, for that matter, except that there are now too many of them for the available jobs and they have brought with them serious social problems.

Three years ago the University of California assigned Dr. R. L. Adams, Professor of Agricultural Economics, to survey the State's farm-labor requirements. Dr. Adams says the crops require 144,700 workers in the peak months, over and above the year-round hired hands. By midwinter this demand has fallen off to 59,000. In May, it is back to a hundred thousand; in August it is 134,000. Thus there are at times nearly 86,000 more workers than jobs, even if there is no labor surplus. To-day there is a surplus of fifty to seventy thousand workers, even at the harvest peak. Early this year the influx was tapering off, but in June 1,600 more agricultural workers were at the border than in June a year earlier.

HOUSING: A STUMBLING BLOCK

Unlike the Mexicans, the Okies do not disappear over the horizon at the end of each harvest. They linger on in the flimsy shelters intended only for the rainless California summer. When rains come, in the fall, the camp sites are seas of mud; rubbish and filth accumulate; and the farmers are taken to task for the facilities provided for their unwelcome guests. Hence the migrant-worker problem is essentially a housing problem

The FSA has sought a solution in low-price cottages, costing $1,000 to $1,500 per unit and renting for $8.20 per month, including heat, light, and water. Each is surrounded by a half-acre of land for a garden. These cottages are snapped up as soon as they are completed, but there are not enough of them, and they are usable only for workers who have ceased to be migrants. FSA has another answer, a portable motorized camp—platforms, Diesel-powered electric plant, laundry tubs and showers—so designed that it may be loaded on trucks and shifted with the crops and the demand for harvest hands. First tried out this summer, it may be the migrant camp of the future.

The farmers, who have added ten thousand cabins to the shelters provided for migrant workers in the last three years, look askance at the FSA camps. Because of the perishable nature of their crops, California farmers live in terror of strikes. The federal camps are feared as hotbeds of radical activities, a fear that dates back to 1931, when communists undertook to organize the fruit workers and dispatched squads of agitators to drag workers from their ladders and intimidate their families. I found no evidence to justify this alarm. The Okies I talked with were oblivious to class struggle; all they asked was more work.

On many of the larger farms, such as the Tagus, the Hoover, the DiGiorgio ranches, the owners provide housing as good as FSA demonstration communities and for less.

On the Tagus Ranch, H. C. Merritt offers two hundred permanent families neat little cottages for $3.00 to $5.00 per month, including a plot of ground for a garden. Some of the first white migrants chopped up the partitions between the rooms and used them for firewood, although free wood was provided for the chopping. When he protested, the Okies explained they preferred to live in one-room houses. Now Tagus families are graduated from one-room to three-room houses as they qualify for them.

Mr. Merritt's attitude toward federal camps is typical. "If my workmen live on the ranch and I tell them to be on hand at eight in the morning to pick peaches, they're on hand," he said. "If they're in a federal camp, I don't know whether they'll be here or not. While I'm looking for other pickers, the peaches drop on the ground, and a year's work is gone."

STUBBORN INDIVIDUALISTS

An inference of *The Grapes of Wrath* is that most of the California farmlands are in great holdings, operated by corporations or land "barons." The State has 6,732,390 acres devoted to crops, and the 1935 census shows that 1,738,906 are in farms less than 100 acres in extent, 3,068,742 are in farms of 100 to 1,000 acres, and 1,924,742 are in farms of over 1,000.

An insinuation of *The Grapes of Wrath* is that wages are forced down by the Associated Farmers and the Bank of America, acting in conspiracy. Actually, neither the Association nor the Bank concerns itself with wages. Rates of pay are worked out through the farmer co-operatives in each crop or through local groups, such as the San Joaquin Regional Council, which agrees each spring on a base wage. California farmers pay higher wages than those of any State but Connecticut, according to the U.S. Farm Placement Bureau.

This same federal organization conducted an inquiry into the charge, aired in *The Grapes of Wrath*, that California farmers had distributed handbills through the dust-bowl area, offering jobs to lure a surplus of migrant labor to the State. Only two cases were unearthed, one by a labor contractor in Santa Barbara County, another by an Imperial Valley contractor. The licenses of both have since been revoked. At the Associated Farmers head office in San Francisco, I saw hundreds of clippings from Midwest newspapers—publicity inspired by the Association—advising migrants *not* to come to California.

The problem of connecting migrant workers who want jobs with farmers who need help is serious. A rumor will sweep like wildfire through migrant camps, of jobs in some valley hundreds of miles distant. Two days later that valley is swamped with so many workers that the harvest which ordinarily would last a month is finished in a week. The U.S. Department of Labor, working with the State Employment Office, now maintains job-information services in eighty-one towns and cities. At any of these offices, migrant workers may check on job prospects in any other area. But most workers still prefer to take a chance.

California's big question—what is going to happen to these people—is still unanswered.

East of Visalia, the FSA is attempting an experiment in co-operative farming. On the 530-acre Mineral King ranch, purchased with federal funds, twenty above-average migrant families were set to work raising cotton, alfalfa, and poultry and running a dairy. At the end of the first year, the farm showed a profit of $900 per family, more than twice the average family's earning from following the crops.

At Casa Grande, Arizona, the FSA has another co-operative farm, of 4,000 acres, with sixty families working it.

Co-operative farms, directed by trained men from universities, produce good crops and good livings; but the Okies are rugged individualists. "I'm not going to have any damn government telling me what I'm going to plant," exploded one of the Mineral King farmers, as he packed his family in the car and took to the road again. And so, in spite of the good intentions of the Farm Security Administration, the Governor's Committee on Unemployment, the Simon J. Lubin Society, the John Steinbeck Committee, and other organizations, the highly individualistic newcomers probably will work out their own destiny in their own way.

For a glimpse of how they may do it, visit Salinas, in the lettuce island, which saw its first invasion eight years ago. The first Okies in the area squatted in squalor outside the town until an enterprising wheat farmer divided his ranch into half-acre lots, which he offered at $250 apiece, $5.00 down, $5.00 a month. The Okies snapped them up and strutted around, proud of their property ownership. Today, in Little Oklahoma City, as the community is called, one can envisage the whole process of assimilation—the ancient trailer resting on its axles, a lean-to or tent alongside it, in the front a wooden shack and, sometimes, a vine-covered cottage. Off to the south, some of the Okies are living in neat little three- to five-room cottages. The Okies of Little Oklahoma City are fortunate. They muscled into the lettuce-packing game and now have virtually a monopoly around Salinas, earning from 50 to 60 cents an hour for eight or nine months of the year. In that one community, three thousand migrants have achieved a respectable standard of living. Their children are intermarrying with the natives. Outwardly, they are Californians.

What they have done can be done by others. Their accomplishment is a challenge to shiftless Okies and an answer to the broad accusations hurled so heedlessly in *The Grapes of Wrath*.

CAREY McWILLIAMS

Carey McWilliams has practiced law, served as Commissioner of Immigration and Housing for the State of California, and is now the editor of *The Nation*. In addition to publishing a biography of Ambrose Bierce, he has written in-depth investigations of American socio-economic issues in *Factories in the Field, Ill Fares the Land, Brothers Under the Skin, Witchhunt: The Revival of Heresy*, and many others.

California Pastoral

On December 6, 1939, the LaFollette Committee hearings opened in San Francisco in an atmosphere of tension, defiance, and considerable truculence. No sooner had Senator LaFollette announced that the committee was in session than Phil Bancroft, Associated Farmers leader, arose and demanded that the Senator cease "giving aid and comfort to the Communists," and that he return to Wisconsin and mind his own business. During the first week that the committee was in session, the Associated Farmers held their annual convention at Stockton, with over 2,000 members in attendance. Open defiance of the committee was voiced throughout the convention. John Steinbeck was warmly denounced as the arch-enemy, defamer, and slanderer of migratory farm labor in California, while I was tenderly referred to as "Agricultural Pest No. 1 in California, outranking pear blight and boll weevil."

The impact of the "dust bowl" migration upon the rural economy of California was graphically outlined in an opening statement to the committee prepared by Henry H. Fowler, its chief counsel. Between January 1, 1933, and June 1, 1939—the years of greatest migration to California—approximately 180 agricultural strikes had occurred in the state. Strikes had taken

Reprinted from *Antioch Review*, II (March 1942), 103–121.

place in 34 out of the 58 counties of California—in every important agricultural county and in connection with every major crop. The national significance of these strikes can perhaps best be appraised in light of the realization that California produces about 40 per cent of the fruits and vegetables consumed in the United States.

In concluding his statement, Mr. Fowler pointed out that "California agriculture has and is suffering from employer-employee strife far out of proportion to the number of workers employed in comparison with the remainder of the country." Comparative figures amply justify this conclusion. Normally employing only 4.4 per cent of the nation's agricultural workers, California has been the scene of from 34.3 to 100 per cent of the annual strikes among agricultural workers. The importance of the strikes themselves can be variously illustrated. Approximately 89,276 workers were involved in 113 out of the total of 180 strikes recorded during this period. Civil and criminal disturbances occurred in connection with 65 out of 180 strikes; arrests of one type or another were reported in 39 strikes; property damage occurred in 11; evictions and deportations were noted in 15. The year 1937, which marked the height of the dust-bowl migration, was also the year during which 14 so-called "violent" strikes occurred. During their first years in California, the Joads did not contribute notably to the tranquility of the state. As bearing on the favorite question of whether *The Grapes of Wrath* accurately described conditions in California, I have selected three typical "incidents" investigated by the LaFollette Committee. The facts are, in each case, all recorded in the transcript of the hearing. These vignettes of "rural life in California," in the years from 1933 to 1939, tell the story of the reception accorded Tom Joad and his fellow migrants in California. The Associated Farmers of California are still smarting from the inconsiderate manner in which the LaFollette Committee came along in 1939 and verified the general picture of conditions in the state as set forth in *The Grapes of Wrath* and *Factories in the Field*. Let the record, then, speak for itself.

THE OKIES PICK 'COTS

Yolo and Solano counties lie in the Sacramento Valley, in northern California. There are no large towns or population centers in either county. For years migrants have trooped into the area each season to work in the apricot orchards around Winters—a small stream of migrants in April to thin the groves, a river of migrants for the harvest period which begins in July and lasts for about thirty days. Not only is the picking season short, but the 'cots are a precarious crop. In the morning they are likely to be "a bit on the green tinge," but by afternoon or the next morning they may be too ripe to pick. For the shippers and canners are fastidious, and with a market pretty thoroughly controlled, they can deal with the growers in an arbitrary and high-handed manner. If the market happens to be glutted, they simply refuse to receive any more apricots that day and the crop rots in the field.

In the early summer of 1937, about 3,500 or 4,000 migrants, most of them recent recruits from the dust bowl, were camped in the Winters district. Some of them had moved into the growers' camps; others were camped along the highways; a large group were huddled together in a squatter camp. Most of them were living in roadside camps with a "good many people sleeping out on the roads." One large grower had occasion to visit the major migrant camp in the community. "Conditions," he testified, "were awful. There were many families there. There were broken-down cars and there were pieces of tents, and they were going to march on the town." Robert Blum, a reporter for the Oakland *Tribune*, also visited the camp. "I wouldn't want to live there myself," was his comment. Everyone agreed that there was a surplus of workers in the area; perhaps 200 or 250 more families had moved in than could possibly hope to find employment.

"Trouble" had been anticipated. The growers had been "tipped off" that Henry Wells and Donald Bingham, organizers for Local 20241, Agricultural Workers Union, affiliated at that time with the American Federation of Labor, were about to invade the district. Before any union demands were presented, however, the machinery had been set in motion "to control the situation." In the month of June, 1937, 47 persons were sworn in as deputy sheriffs in Yolo County and 27 of these were deputized on June 7—weeks before the strike occurred. In Solano County twelve deputies were sworn in, making an emergency force, for the two counties, of 59 men. The funds to pay for the salaries and supplies of this improvised force naturally came from the general funds of the two counties. Units of the Associated Farmers had existed in both counties since 1934; but because of the fact that the apricot district overlapped their boundaries, an emergency organization, known as the Yosolano Associated Farmers, was formed.

On June 21, 1937 the growers of the district met in the American Legion hall, in Winters, to fix the rate for picking. The practice of joint action among growers on wage rates is, of course, quite common throughout California. At this meeting a union organizer appeared and presented the demands of the workers: 40 cents an hour; union recognition; job stewards; and yearly vacations for permanent employees. It must be remembered that 4,000 people had moved into the district for the season. No one knows from what distances they had traveled; some of them, however, had driven 400 or 500 miles. These workers had not only paid their own transportation expenses but, as usually happens, they had arrived some weeks in advance of the season. Nor were they to be blamed for having anticipated the season, for no one can tell in advance the precise day or week when the 'cots will be ripe. After traveling considerable distances and waiting days and even weeks for the season to start, these workers could anticipate about three weeks employment. Naturally they wanted to make as much as they could during this brief period.

The demand for a nickel an hour increase was denied and the rate for the season was fixed at 35 cents an hour. The demand, according to the union organizer, was "turned down flat." Out of 4,000 workers, the union had a paid-up membership of about 500, a total membership of perhaps a thousand.

For a few days prior to June 22, the union had been holding meetings on the property of Mr. John Storland, a small grower. Typical of many small growers in California, Mr. Storland was inclined to sympathize with the workers; he even had the quaint notion that they had a right to hold public meetings. To make possible the exercise of this right, he had donated a corner of his property for union meetings. But his fellow-growers in the community did not agree with Mr. Storland. They sent two delegations to interview him. On the first visit, they protested gently but firmly against the use of his property for strike meetings; on their second call, they protested "more forcibly, more vigorously," and informed Mr. Storland that he would have "to take the consequences" if further meetings were permitted.

On June 22, 1937, the strike started. Picket lines were established at one or two of the orchards and the appearance of these pickets was the signal for the Associated Farmer machine to swing into action. On that day a total of 16 strikers were arrested. Those who were arrested were told that the action against them would be dismissed if they would agree "to leave this locality for a least a distance of twenty miles" and not return. A large delegation of fruit growers then called upon the Board of Supervisors of Solano County and demanded action. The chairman of the Board was, as might be expected, an officer and director of the Associated Farmers of Solano County. The growers got instant and double-barrelled action: first, an emergency anti-camping ordinance was adopted; and second, an apricot patrol of deputy sheriffs was created. Prior to the time the patrol was established and on the day when the first special deputies were sworn in, the Board of Supervisors of Yolo County had adopted an interesting resolution:

Whereas, the County of Yolo has already exceeded the amount budgeted for relief of employable and unemployable indigents; therefore be it,
Resolved: That from this date no relief will be given unemployed employables or transient indigents in the county.

The suspension and cessation of relief during the apricot picking season was designed, of course, to insure acceptance of the wage rate previously established by the growers. Taking advantage of the ordinance against public camping, the sheriff, accompanied by his hastily recruited army of deputies, moved on the migrant camp and told the workers that "they would have to get out—it was the order of the Board." And move they did, in all directions. In many instances the county had to provide gasoline, out of public funds, to enable the stranded migrants "to move on."

In the meantime, general headquarters had been established in the city hall at Winters. No one seems to have raised any question or to have even considered the propriety of using public property for a strike-breaking center. Not only was the apricot patrol policing the orchards during all this time, but martial law, in effect, had been decreed throughout the area. Let Mr. Blum, a reporter for the Oakland *Tribune*, describe what he observed:

Throughout the morning of the 23d, groups of special deputies—that is, nonuniformed deputies—were patrolling the town of Winters, the main street and adjacent streets and along the railroad tracks, in groups of two or three; questioning persons whom they might have encountered along the sidewalks or walking along the roadways, and I was close to several of these groups. They would stop these people and ask them what they were doing, and if they were looking for work. If they said they were looking for work, they would walk back with them to the City Hall, where this employment committee or employment headquarters was located. If they said they weren't looking for work or could not explain their presence in town satisfactorily, they were told that if they did not leave town or accept work they would be faced with being jailed.

Mr. L. M. Ireland, an insurance salesman, was one of the special deputy sheriffs. "At that time," said Mr. Ireland, "the fruit was just about ready to fall on the ground, and we knew—I had lived in Winters all my life—and I knew that if this fruit did fall on the ground it wasn't going to hurt the farmers but the whole business community as well." So Mr. Ireland, insurance salesman, joined up with the vigilantes. One morning while he was acting as a deputy, a farmer came to town and asked help in getting some pickers. Mr. Ireland and another deputy got busy at once. They interviewed several stragglers on Main Street and marched them off to G.H.Q. and then called at the home of a prospective worker. Asked if he wanted to work, he answered: "Who the hell's business is it?" For this unforgivable piece of *lèse majesté*, he was promptly placed under arrest and taken to the calaboose. Mr. Ireland thought that the whole affair had been handled with remarkable decorum and propriety, since the sheriff had cautioned the deputies "to be exceptionally careful about hurting any person or trying not to make anybody peeved."

While the strike was in progress, Mr. John T. Dudley, secretary of the Industrial Union Council of Sacramento, was asked to visit Winters, observe conditions, and report back to the Council. By the time Mr. Dudley arrived on the scene, the strike was virtually at an end and the migrants were being evicted from their camp. Realizing that there was nothing much to be accomplished in Winters, Mr. Dudley and his committee started to return to Sacramento. But as they were leaving, the sheriff and his posse picked them up and took them to the courthouse. A crowd of three or four hundred people quickly gathered, and stared through the windows into the room where the sheriff was quizzing Mr. Dudley. Members of the mob, at the open windows and the doors, swung ropes about and shouted: "Bring 'em out! We'll tar and feather them! Let's get them out and hang them!" When Mr. Dudley asked permission to use the telephone, "some big heavy-set fellow with a deputy sheriff's badge yelled very loudly: 'Don't let that bastard use the phone!'" The sheriff refused to accord the party a safe escort out of the county and decided to lock them up in jail overnight. Fearing a possible suit for false arrest, he managed the next morning to browbeat Mr. Dudley into pleading guilty to a charge of vagrancy and then released him. I would merely emphasize that this little episode occurred in the county courthouse, in the presence of the sheriff and of the chairman of the Board of Supervisors.

The strike was broken; the migrants were scattered; the 'cots were picked. But the victory had to be officially reported, solemnly memorialized, and formally chronicled. The scene of the victory rites was the annual meeting of the Associated Farmers of California, December 6, 1937, at which the president of the Yolo County unit, praising the action in the 'cots, said that "the strength of any army depends upon what happens under fire. Yolo County unit proved itself this year during the apricot strike at Winters." *Business Week*, in its issue of July 17, 1937, neatly summed up the situation as follows:

Yolo County has an ordinance which forbids picketing. Solano County hurriedly enacted an ordinance forbidding itinerant pickers to camp on public property, for reasons of public health. Since the only camp ground available is on the property of the farmers, unemployed pickers could only move on. And the deputy sheriffs saw to it that they did just that, even providing enough gasoline, in some cases, to take them out of the two counties. The strike faded, the apricots were picked, and the farmers were delighted to have found an effective method to break strikes.

Tom Joad had had his first taste of industrialized agriculture; glorious Yosolano had triumphed over 4,000 destitute pickers; peace was restored.

Despite its usual acumen, *Business Week* neglected to praise one aspect of this action—its cheapness. Through the good work of the staff of the LaFollette Committee, it is possible to set forth an accounting:

Expended by the City of Winters for telephone calls, meals for special officers, and "sundries"	$ 135.10
Expended by the County of Yolo for special deputies during the scrimmage	667.48
Expended by the County of Solano for the same purpose	1,187.25
Expended by the County of Solano for gas and oil used as part of the technique to evict migrants	46.26
TOTAL	$2,036.09

In addition to the public funds spent in breaking this strike, the growers themselves contributed a niggardly pittance of $185.36; otherwise the entire cost of the action fell upon the general taxpayers of the community. But if the nickel an hour increase had been granted, it would have cost the growers, for the season, about $66,600. The saving was, therefore, substantial; the community itself had been taxed to support the vigilantism of the Associated Farmers. It will also be noted that the scrimmage itself was not at all unlike a somewhat similar episode described in *The Grapes of Wrath*.

STORM TROOPERS IN STANISLAUS

The principal town in Stanislaus County, in the San Joaquin Valley, is Modesto. It is a pleasant little place with urban pretensions. There are nice homes on well shaded streets; a junior college; a highly developed civic life. There are good stores; good hotels; a good newspaper. There are six important canneries, any number of dry-yards, and an airport in Modesto. Okies and Arkies began to drift into the community around 1933 and 1934, but they found it difficult to settle in the town itself. So they moved out near the airport and attempted to shift for themselves. There a large land company subdivided a tract of land near the airport and sold tiny lots to migrants. Soon there were two thriving communities: Little Oklahoma on one side of a canal bank, and Little Arkansas on the other. The two settlements today constitute a good-sized community. But the migrants are not a part of Modesto; they even have their own shopping center. Visiting Little Oklahoma one can see the migrant settlement pattern in its several phases: first the tent or trailer parked on a lot; then a lean-to or shack on the rear of the lot (later to be used as a garage); and finally the little one- or two-room frame shack built by the occupants. Here the "folks" have settled. On some of the streets in Little Oklahoma all the residents are from the same county or small town in Oklahoma. The settlement is something of a mess but the inhabitants have done their best to make it a decent community and to invest it with even a few of the airs of a typical California town.

Here, in Little Oklahoma, lives my friend, Mrs. Lawler—a kind, hospitable, friendly woman. Her husband used to be a farmer, and later an oil worker in Oklahoma. The Lawlers have three children, a boy and a girl and an older daughter now happily married to a "Californian." The first year they were in Little Oklahoma, the daughter was returning home from school one afternoon when a neighbor boy, passing her on a bicycle, shouted: "Get out of the way, you damned Okie!" This made the girl feel "right bad." For the boy was himself an Okie, only he had lived in California for several years and this made him a kind of Californian—a native son by adoption. Mrs. Lawler, like most of the women in Little Oklahoma, works in the canneries at night. Standing at the vats or bins during the warm humid mid-summer nights, it gets pretty suffocating. The atmosphere is thick and soggy; the foreladies keep pushing the help hard. But once the Lawlers had a break. A movie company on location near Modesto needed some extras for the filming of *Dodge City*. Mr. and Mrs. Lawler and some of their neighbors got bit-parts in the picture. If you have seen the picture, you will remember Mrs. Lawler. She is the woman who stands at the street corner and, as the herd of wild steers comes stampeding through the town, rushes out in front of the herd, picks up a youngster, and dashes to cover. "Not a bit afraid of cattle," she was so cool and daring in the picture that she gave the cameraman the thrill of his life. For she waited until the very last second before making her famous dash to save the child. It was the big moment in the picture and Mrs. Lawler made $50 out of her brief but endlessly exciting career as an actress. When the picture was shown in Modesto, Mrs. Lawler and her neighbors were there to see it; they were also present when *The Grapes of Wrath* was shown. Mrs. Lawler liked it almost as much as *Dodge City*, only "the little hurts are the worst and I could have told them so much about that."

Most of the families in Little Oklahoma and Little Arkansas are on relief, or working on WPA projects, part of the year. There just isn't enough work. You can't make a living in the canneries and it is "a killing and back-breaking" job anyway.

I have other friends in Modesto but I had better not mention their names. They are the kind of people who want to see you at night, "but not downtown." They are always eager to tell what they know; what they have observed; to furnish names and dates. They are as furtive as Negroes in the Deep South. They will talk above a whisper, but they don't want to be quoted. They are teachers, and lawyers, and housewives, and janitors, and clerks. If any of them were to say publicly what they have told me in private, they would have to leave Modesto. They all remember the excitement when Fred Hogue, of the Associated Farmers, organized a private army. Senator LaFollette and Senator Thomas heard about this episode and were truly amazed. I mentioned it during the course of a Town Meeting of the Air broadcast in March, 1940, but not many people would believe that such an episode had occurred.

The Associated Farmers had organized in Stanislaus County in 1936. Most of the money for the organization had come from the banks, hotels, oil companies, farm implement houses, and the canneries. There had been a riot of cannery workers in Stockton during 1937 and Stockton is only thirty miles or so from Modesto. The Associated Farmers were afraid that the Okie women might decide to join the union. So they decided to stage a "mobilization." Three thousand people assembled in the football stadium at the junior college and at the conclusion of the meeting rose and repeated the following pledge: "We pledge ourselves for law and order and the right to work." The speakers at the meeting included the sheriff, the city attorney, an official of the Associated Farmers, the president of the Retail Merchants Association, the president of the Chamber of Commerce, the president of one of the canneries, and representing "the farmers," Roy Pike, manager of the El Solyo Ranch—one of the largest farm-factories in California. But no one spoke on behalf of labor; no one spoke on behalf of the Okies, although the meeting was being held for their benefit. The meeting was quite successful for, as Mr. Pike observed, "the hangers-on around several of the canneries in Modesto, who have been present for over a week in relation to the threatened strike, were absent the next morning." The leading citizens had mobilized; the little people were put in their place.

Senator Thomas questioned Mr. Hogue about this meeting and also about the plans for a citizens' army which had been prepared by the Associated Farmers. The Associated Farmers were to raise an army of 600 men; the business interests in Modesto were to raise and to drill a similar force. Both groups were organized in such a way that they could be mobilized on two hours' notice. The "third order of business" in the Manual of Instructions was as follows:

Organize Drill Squads and arrange to meet with them twice a week for at least three weeks until all hands become accustomed to the things expected of them because of their volunteering for and undertaking the important responsibility of their enrollment as Special Deputies under the Sheriff of Stanislaus County.

Another portion of the Manual stated:

Each Captain in charge of Four Sergeants; each Sergeant in charge of four Corporals; and each Corporal in charge of four Privates.

Here is Senator Thomas' comment, at the conclusion of this part of the investigation:

Mr. Hogue, I have never seen a military organization put down on paper any more definitely than that plan which you have provided here.

In reporting on the work of the Associated Farmers of Stanislaus County, at the annual convention on December 6, 1937, Mr. Hogue was quoted as follows:

The Associated Farmers have 700 contributing members in the county and their assessment to the State organization has been paid.

No labor difficulties. Approximately 6,000 cannery workers are employed in the county and the canneries are run on the "open-shop" basis. Due to the work of the Associated Farmers, labor organizers coming in were unable to make headway.

The officials of the Associated Farmers testified before Senator LaFollette that this army of 1,200 men had never actually been drilled. My Modesto friends, who were in a position to know the facts, later told me that the armies—the businessmen's unit and the "farmer" unit—drilled for several weeks at the junior college.

THE JOADS ON STRIKE

Madera is one of the principal "cotton counties" in the San Joaquin Valley. Although California produces only about 3 per cent of the cotton grown in the United States, the crop is one of the most profitable products raised in the state. California cotton growers, in 1938, received about $23,476,000, with some $3,350,000 additional in the form of A.A.A. benefit payments. Cotton in California is an irrigated crop: its yields are about three times as great as the national average yield per acre. Cotton can be grown in California for less cost per pound than elsewhere in the United States and commands a somewhat better price by reason of its long fibre quality. A hundred pounds of seed cotton in California contain more lint than the same amount of cotton grown elsewhere. Most of the cotton grown' in the state used to be shipped to Japan. Despite the obvious advantages which cotton growers in California enjoy over those in other areas, they receive the same Triple A subsidies. As a consequence, cotton is a "racket" crop in California; it is grown for the Triple A payments. In 1938, $3,356,361 in Triple A payments were divided among 8,700 cotton growers in the state. Of these cotton growers, 204 members of the Associated Farmers received $1,107,544.72. To state it another way, 2.34 per cent of the cotton growers received 33 per cent of the total benefit payments. The people in the San Joaquin Valley will tell you that cotton is the curse of the valley. It exhausts the soil, makes for an unbalanced farm economy, and breeds poverty. But it is a highly profitable crop for a few hundred growers.

It takes 35,000 workers to pick the cotton crop in California. There are few single men or single women in the fields; large families are always preferred. The beginning of the dust-bowl migration to California can be traced back to the early '20's when cotton became an important crop. As long as cotton has been grown in the state, families have come west each fall from Oklahoma, Texas, and Arkansas to work in the fields. The cotton growers, however, preceded the cotton pickers, from the South to California. Many former Texas, Georgia, and Mississippi growers moved west to California when it was discovered that cotton could be grown there with such marked advantages. Once re-established in California, they naturally sent back to Texas and Oklahoma for their labor. They also brought their prejudices with them when they moved to California. One grower, testifying at the LaFollette hearings, told the Senator:

I am a southerner, born in Georgia, and when a big buck nigger gets up on a platform and walks backward and forward and says, "I haven't worked for a year, I have eat jail food, and have been in the fighting and can do it," that kind of gets under my skin.

Most of these large cotton growers are, of course, migrants themselves. But this circumstance has not predisposed them as a group to regard the plight of the Joads in California with any particular sympathy.

In March and April, 1939, I was in the San Joaquin Valley, inspecting labor camps. There are some 470 cotton camps in the valley. According to a formula used by the growers, each cabin in a cotton camp is theoretically supposed to account for 800 pounds of cotton a day during the picking season. Since the average worker can only pick about 200 pounds a day, it follows that each cabin must contain about four active pickers. Overcrowding is inevitable. The cabins are all one-room frame shacks and I have frequently found as many as eight and ten people living in one cabin. Some of the cotton camps are quite large; as many as 2,000 pickers will sometimes be found in a single camp. There are Negro camps, Mexican camps, and White-American camps. In some of the camps, particularly those operated by Mexican labor contractors, it is not uncommon to see open gambling, cock fights, and occasionally, to discover a contractor who is operating a *bagnio* with six or seven bedraggled Mexican prostitutes. Most of the camps should ordinarily be vacant in March or April since the cotton picking is over by January. But in the spring of 1939 the camps were 40 per cent occupied. Most of the occupants told me that they had been stranded at the end of the season and had to stay on in the camp. With scarcely an exception, they were all on relief, and in many cases the growers were getting $5 a month rent for the cabins from the State Relief Administration. Most of the large cotton camps are located miles away from the nearest major highway, and some of them, in the winter and spring, are islands in a sea of mud and water. There is a characteristic odor about a cotton camp that defies description. For days after an inspection trip of this kind, I could still imagine that the odor of the camps somehow clung to my clothes.

One day in May, 1939, I received a long distance telephone call from Governor Culbert L. Olson. Workers in Madera County were threatening to picket the offices of the State Relief Administration in protest against a rate of 20 cents an hour which had been established by the growers as the prevailing wage for cotton chopping. Prior to the time that Governor Olson was elected, the State Relief Administration followed the practice of denying relief whenever employment was available in the fields, regardless of what wage might be offered. The Governor, in this case, had promised the workers a hearing to determine whether they should be forced off relief to chop cotton at 20 cents an hour. He asked me to conduct the hearing. Two days later I opened the hearing in the Memorial Hall in Madera. Workers swarmed all over the place: they packed the hall; they stood in the doorways; they sat perched on the window ledges. Shortly after I arrived, a delegation of eight or ten cotton growers entered the hall. When they walked into the already crowded hall, a path was opened for them like that through which Moses crossed the Red Sea. I have never felt, before or since, such a sharply drawn class line. The growers were disdainful and contemptuous; the workers ominously quiet. The very idea of the hearing was anathema to the growers; the workers, on the other hand, enjoyed every moment of the hearing and listened intently to the testimony. Throughout the hearing—the first of its kind ever conducted in California— perfect order was maintained, with the workers showing a tendency to laugh good-naturedly at the description of their own sorry plight.

The story they had to tell was undeniably impressive. Working ten hours a day in the fields chopping cotton, they had to pay their own transportation expenses to and from work, sometimes commuting ten and fifteen miles each way. For the miserable shacks in which most of them lived, rents averaged about $8 or $10 a month. Utility charges were high; food was high. Under these circumstances, no man could support a family on 20 cents an hour. Average earnings for the season, at this rate, would actually be less than the meager allowances they received on relief. All of the growers who testified agreed that the rate was too low, but they contended it was the most they could afford to pay. At the conclusion of the hearing, I recommended to the Governor that no worker should be cut off relief unless afforded 27½ cents an hour in fields of "clean" cotton, or 30 cents an hour in fields of "dirty" cotton. The rates recommended were meager, but a strike was avoided at the time. It was quite apparent to me then that, with feeling running high among the migrants, there would be trouble in the fall when cotton picking started. Seldom have the Associated Farmers of California been as wild with rage as they were over the wage-rate hearing in Madera. The Governor's office was bombarded with letters, telegrams, and petitions of protest. Meetings were held throughout the state to condemn the idea of wage-rate hearings. An increase of 7½ cents an hour was enough to convince the Associated Farmers that I intended, alone and single-handed, to "sovietize" California agriculture.

One of the reasons that this incident had occurred in Madera County was the fact that dust-bowl migrants had been pouring into the county since 1933. The population of the county had nearly doubled—between 1935 and 1938. Migrants discovered, of course, that there was no place for them in the rural economy of the region except as farm workers. There were no homesteads to be claimed, no free lands awaiting settlement. The price of good farm land in the county was utterly beyond the reach of the average migrant family. Stranded in the community, migrants had to seek relief. Resentment between "residents" and "newcomers" rapidly developed. A great portion of the population of the county actually came from the same areas in the South and Southwest; they were all citizens, all farmers, all "White-Americans." They shared to a considerable degree the same prejudices, the same taboos, the same aspirations. Yet the residents vehemently contended that they were "the people of Madera County"; and by inference that the Okies were "aliens." This feeling was so pronounced that in the summer of 1939 a sign appeared in the foyer of a motion picture theatre in a San Joaquin Valley town, reading: "Negroes and Okies Upstairs."

Basically the social antagonism that divided Madera County into two warring camps—about equal in numbers but with the "residents" in almost exclusive possession of the symbols of authority and prestige—can be traced to the economic relationships involved in large-scale cotton operations in California. Over 50 per cent of the large-scale cotton farms in the United States are located in Arizona and California. There is one company, in California, which operates, through lessees, 10,000 acres of cotton land. Industrialized agriculture frequently involves a division of tasks or of functions. As Professor Clark Kerr has pointed out, a six-fold division of functions may be found in cotton production in California: ownership, financing, custom-work, supervision, labor, and management. Most of the operators are lessees; the land owners are banks, insurance companies, large land companies. Financing is handled through the cotton-ginning companies to a large extent. Custom-work implies that the "operator" or "lessee" may, and frequently does, contract with a "custom contractor" to supply the machinery needed for certain operations. Supervision is supplied by foremen, superintendents, or labor contractors. The actual manual labor is performed by migrant workers. Management may be obtained through a general farm manager who may supervise or manage several different operations at the same time. It frequently happens, therefore, that the land owner is far removed from actual farm operations and that even the operator or lessee has no interest, other than a purely speculative interest, in the land itself. Under this pattern of operations, the operator or lessee can usually be found sitting behind a desk in an air-cooled office in the nearest town.

The "controls" of a system of this kind are usually traceable to the cotton-ginning company, which stands behind the cotton grower. In California one concern, Anderson, Clayton and Company, gins about 35 per cent of the total cotton production. The company operates 46 cotton-ginning plants in the San Joaquin Valley, 28 in Arizona. Needless to say, the company has long been one of the patron saints of the Associated Farmers. The company has its affiliates and subsidiaries: Western Production Company, The Interstate Cotton and Oil Company, and the San Joaquin Cotton and Oil Company. The company made loans in 1939 totaling more than $6,500,000 to approximately 1,986 California cotton growers. When a cotton operator desires a loan, the company exercises a direct control over the budget. If a particular budget is "out of line" on labor costs, the company simply refuses to make a loan until the item in question is corrected. The amount of the loan is advanced in a series of installments or allotments. The chattel mortgage used to secure the loan provides that the money to be advanced by the com-

pany is to be used by the mortgagor as the company at its
exclusive discretion shall direct. The grower must agree to gin
his crop at one of the company's gins; he must also agree to sell
his cotton seed to the company as well as the cotton oil. When
the all-important matter of securing an advance to cover picking
costs arises, the grower must negotiate with the company to the
best of his ability. The company will want to know what rate
the grower intends to pay for cotton-picking labor. If this rate
is out of line, he will not get an advance. The actual relationship is not that of 1,986 independent cotton growers, but of
1,986 operators raising cotton for Anderson, Clayton and Company. The control that the cotton-ginning companies exercise
over wage rates was clearly brought out during the LaFollette
Committee hearings:

Senator LaFollette: Now, then, suppose a farmer or a grower desired
to pay higher wages than that set by the bureau, what would be the
policy as far as the request for advancing money was concerned?

Mr. Jensen [of Anderson, Clayton and Company]: Well, if such a
grower—I really don't know—we don't encounter that, that I know
of, Senator.

To understand the role that the cotton-ginning companies play
in this situation it is necessary to remember that they are only
incidentally interested in the price of cotton. They make money
out of ginning rates, warehouse rates; out of the by-products,
the seed, the oil, the cotton-cake. But they must induce others
to raise cotton and they must recruit workers to pick cotton.
The only reason Anderson, Clayton and Company does not
raise most of the cotton in California, is simply that it is cheaper
for them to get someone else to do it. They are willing to allow a margin of profit for the grower—most of which is
squeezed out of labor—provided the genuinely lucrative phases
of the business remain their exclusive prerogative.

Disregarding the organized action of the workers in the
spring, the cotton growers met in August, 1939 and fixed a uniform rate of 75 cents a hundred pounds for cotton picking.

Immediately workers began to hold protest meetings throughout the San Joaquin Valley. They had not been consulted about this rate; nor were they given an opportunity to express their views on the fairness of the rate before it was established. Thus once again Governor Olson decided to intervene. A committee of seven was appointed to hold a hearing and to recommend a fair rate. The hearing this time was held in Fresno. The growers were not in attendance; they had decided to boycott the hearing. Witness after witness paraded to the stand to tell us why he could not make a living on "75 cents a hundred." Bert Wilson, who farmed for forty years in Oklahoma, told us that "a man cain't make a living under $1.25 a hundred. Groceries is too high. We sleep on the ground, put our babies on the ground, and these farmers will ask us to pick for eighty cents and we cain't do it. I have a little cabin that rents for $4 a month, about 12 x 12, and six in the family—we just cain't bed up like dogs." John Stevens had raised cotton in Oklahoma for twenty years before coming to California in 1938. An elderly man, he had a wife and six children to support. For weeks before the hearing, the family had been living on "a little meat, some gravy, light bread and coffee," and camping in a tent. When he arrived in California, in April, 1938, Stevens "went to picking peas. Then I went to the cherries over east of Stockton. Then I came back over to Hollister to the fruit and couldn't get in there. Too many people there. Worked then in the garlic and then back to Sacramento for the hops, and then the tomatoes and then back to the hops and the peas, and then the cotton." The previous year, 1938, he had managed to get about 30 days work "in the cotton. You would go into the field where there's 160 acres and there would be a man for every row from the start. It don't last long and you are all the time moving. You can't make nothing—there are too many people and it keeps you on the move."

Here in brief is what we discovered at this hearing: thousands of migrant families, stranded throughout the San Joaquin Valley, hopefully regarded the cotton-picking season, from

September to January, as the one employment opportunity by which they might earn enough to keep off relief during the winter. Without consulting these workers, *all* of the cotton growers of the valley had agreed upon a wage rate. Insofar as the growers were concerned, they were practicing collective bargaining— among themselves. But this same right they refused to concede to others. Professor Clark Kerr has some pointed comments to make about this method of determining wage rates:

The effectiveness of fixing the rates is increased by the inelasticity of the supply curve of labor. There is little alternate employment immediately available and channels for relief are partly closed. The supply curve in part of its range apparently also may be a backward sloping one. Farmers and government officials consistently report that raising the wages means that the workers quit earlier in the day and do not bring their children with them, and thus it takes longer to get the work done. A supply curve with this negative slope invites wage fixation and at comparatively low levels, *since lowering the rate may actually increase, rather than decrease,* the supply of labor. Also, the labor supply is constantly composed of new workers coming into the area for reasons in addition to the prospective level of wages offered there and having little connection with those who went before or who came after. Individual employers likewise may never face the same workers again. [Italics added by McWilliams.]

Nothing so strikingly illustrates the cul-de-sac into which the migrants had drifted in California, than the curious circumstance that a lowered wage rate, in this case, might possibly attract more workers than a rate fixed at a subsistence level. The more migrants, the less work; the lower the rate, the more migrants in the field.

Since our board had no power to enforce its recommendations, it had merely the effect of delaying for a week or so the strike of cotton pickers that had already been voted. Headquarters for the strike were established in Madera and there, in the city park, the strikers assembled nearly every night. There was little formal organization about the strike and practically no experienced leadership. With about 30,000 workers involved, the maximum that were out on strike was never more than 8,000 or 10,000 workers. But in certain counties, such as Madera, the strike was amazingly effective. The production of cotton began to decline rapidly. Within a week after the strike was called, it had become about 90 per cent effective in Madera County. Since the LaFollette Committee investigators had, by October, 1939, arrived in California there was little violence at the outset of the strike. But, when the strike began to be effective, the growers, in the words of one of their spokesmen, "decided to squeeze the core out of the boil."

On the morning of October 21, 1939, an army began to converge from all directions upon the public park in Madera. Wearing arm bands with the letters "AFC" (Associated Farmers of California), over six hundred men, armed with clubs, pick handles, rubber hose, and auto cranks, rushed into the park and proceeded to break up an orderly strike meeting. Standing on the edge of the park and obviously enjoying the affray was Sheriff W. O. Justice ("With Out" Justice, the migrants called him) of Madera County. Scores of strikers were injured and were treated at the hospital; among those receiving a minor injury was an investigator of the LaFollette Committee! Called as witness before the LaFollette Committee, the sheriff freely admitted that assaults were committed in his presence and that he had made not a single arrest. At first he testified that he could not identify the assailants. But Senator LaFollette then produced a photograph, taken at the time, which showed the sheriff in company with the ringleaders of the mob. With the utmost reluctance, the sheriff was then forced to identify, one after another, eight or ten people in the picture. Having forced him to admit then that he did know who the leaders of the mob were, the Senator then asked him if he intended to arrest them. The answer was a prompt and unequivocal "No." Yet before the strike was over, he had arrested 142 strikers for purely technical offenses, such as peaceful picketing and parading without a permit. Bail had been fixed in these cases as high as $2,500. Not a single grower was arrested although admittedly they had paraded without a permit, committed assaults, and fomented a riot. The record of this incident, in the LaFollette Committee transcript (Volume 51), is as clear a case of the unequal enforcement of the law as that committee ever exposed.

After the riot on October 21, the strike soon collapsed. Governor Olson sent personal representatives to Madera to address later strike meetings and these meetings were not disturbed. But the strike itself had, in the meantime, been broken. Gradually the Joads drifted into the fields to pick cotton at six-bits a hundred; the gins were soon running at full capacity; and a bumper crop was harvested.

These notes by no means exhaust the LaFollette Committee transcript, but they will serve to illustrate, perhaps, the fact that Mr. Steinbeck, in *The Grapes of Wrath*, was not relying upon his imagination. One of the incidents I have described took place *after* the publication of the novel at a time when the Associated Farmers, by every resource at their disposal, were attempting to convince the public that there was not a shred of truth in the book. Had some of the leaders of the organization been trying out for parts in the picture, they could not have acted more in character than they did.

MARTIN SHOCKLEY

Martin S. Shockley has taught at The Citadel, the University of Oklahoma, Carleton College, Evansville College, and North Texas State College. He is co-author of *Reading and Writing*, and editor of *Southwest Writers Anthology*. His articles have appeared in *Studies in Philology*, *American Literature*, and *College English*.

The Reception of *The Grapes of Wrath* in Oklahoma

Most of us remember the sensational reception of *The Grapes of Wrath* (1939), Mr. Westbrook Pegler's column about the vile language of the book, Raymond Clapper's column recommending the book to economic royalists, Mr. Frank J. Taylor's article in the *Forum* attacking factual inaccuracies, and the editorial in *Collier's* charging communistic propaganda. Many of us also remember that the Associated Farmers of Kern County, California, denounced the book as "obscene sensationalism" and "propaganda in its vilest form," that the Kansas City Board of Education banned the book from Kansas City libraries, and that the Library Board of East St. Louis banned it and ordered the librarian to burn the three copies which the library owned. These items were carried in the Oklahoma press. The *Forum*'s article was even reprinted in the Sunday section of the Oklahoma City *Daily Oklahoman* on October 29, 1939, with the editor's headnote of approval.

With such publicity, *The Grapes of Wrath* sold sensationally in Oklahoma bookstores. Most stores consider it their best seller, excepting only *Gone With the Wind*. One bookstore in Tulsa reported about one thousand sales. Mr. Hollis Russell of Stevenson's Bookstore in Oklahoma City told me, "People

---

Reprinted from *American Literature*, XV (January 1944), 351–61. By permission of the publisher.

who looked as though they had never read a book in their lives came in to buy it."

Of thirty libraries answering my letter of inquiry, only four, including one state college library, do not own at least one copy of the book, and the Tulsa Public Library owns twenty-eight copies. Most libraries received the book soon after publication in the spring of 1939. Librarians generally agreed that the circulation of *The Grapes of Wrath* was second only to that of *Gone With the Wind*, although three librarians reported equal circulation for the two books, and one (Oklahoma Agricultural and Mechanical College) reported *The Grapes of Wrath* their most widely circulated volume. The librarians often added that many private copies circulated widely in their communities, and some called attention to the extraordinary demand for rental copies. A few libraries restricted circulation to "adults only." About half the libraries mentioned long waiting lists, Miss Sue Salmon of the Duncan Public Library reporting that "Even as late as the spring of 1940 we counted 75 people waiting." Mrs. Virginia Harrison of A. and M. College stated that the four copies there "were on waiting list practically the entire time up to March 19, 1941." After over two hundred students had signed the waiting list for the two copies in the University of Oklahoma library, faculty members donated several additional copies to the library.

The Grapes of Wrath was reviewed throughout Oklahoma to large and curious audiences. A high-school English teacher wrote that he had reviewed the book three times, at a ladies' culture club, at a faculty tea, and at a meeting of the Junior Chamber of Commerce, receiving comments ranging from one lady's opinion that Ma Joad was a "magnificent character," to a lawyer's remark that "Such people should be kept in their place." When Professor J. P. Blickensderfer reviewed the book in the library at the University of Oklahoma, so many people were turned away for lack of standing room that he repeated the review two weeks later, again to a packed audience.

Much of what has passed in Oklahoma for criticism of *The Grapes of Wrath* has been little or nothing more than efforts to prove or to disprove the factual accuracy of Steinbeck's fiction. One of the minority supporters of the truth of Steinbeck's picture of the Okies has been Professor O. B. Duncan, Head of the Department of Sociology at A. and M. College. In an interview widely printed in Oklahoma newspapers, Professor Duncan discussed the economic and social problems which are involved.

The farm migrant as decribed in Steinbeck's *Grapes of Wrath*, Duncan said, was the logical consequence of privation, insecurity, low income, inadequate standards of living, impoverishment in matters of education and cultural opportunities and a lack of spiritual satisfaction.

"I have been asked quite often if I could not dig up some statistics capable of refuting the story of the *Grapes of Wrath*," Duncan related. "It cannot be done, for all the available data proved beyond doubt that the general impression given by Steinbeck's book is substantially reliable."[1]

Billed as "The one man, who above all others, should know best the farm conditions around Sallisaw," Mr. Houston Ward, county agent for Sequoyah County, of which Sallisaw is the county seat, spoke over radio station WKY in Oklahoma City on March 16, 1940, under the sponsorship of the State Agriculture Department. Under the headline "Houston B. Ward 'Tells All' About *The Grapes of Wrath*," the press quoted Mr. Ward on these inaccuracies:

"Locating Sallisaw in the dust bowl region; having Grandpaw Joad yearning for enough California grapes to squish all over his face when in reality Sallisaw is in one of the greatest grape growing regions in the nation; making the tractor as the cause of the farmer's dispossession when in reality there are only 40 tractors in all Sequoyah county. . . . People in Sequoyah county are so upset by these obvious errors in the book and picture, they are inclined to overlook the moral lesson the book teaches," Ward said.[2]

---

[1] Oklahoma City *Times*, Feb. 5, 1940.
[2] *Ibid.*, March 16, 1940.

Numerous editorials in Oklahoma newspapers have refuted or debunked Steinbeck by proving that not all Oklahomans are Joads, and that not all Oklahoma is dust bowl. The following editorial, headed "GRAPES OF WRATH? OBSCENITY AND INACCURACY," is quoted from the Oklahoma City *Times*, May 4, 1939:

How book reviewers love to have their preconceived notions about any given region corroborated by a morbid, filthily-worded novel! It is said that *Grapes of Wrath*, by John Steinbeck, shows symptoms of becoming a best seller, by kindness of naive, ga-ga reviewers. It pictures Oklahoma with complete and absurd untruthfulness, hence has what it takes. That American literary tradition is still in its nonage . . . is amply proved by the fact that goldfish-swallowing critics who know nothing about the region or people pictured in a novel accept at face value even the most inaccurate depiction, by way of alleged regional fiction. No, the writer of these lines has not read the book. This editorial is based upon hearsay, and that makes it even, for that is how Steinbeck knows Oklahoma.

Mr. W. M. Harrison, editor of the Oklahoma City *Times*, devoted his column, "The Tiny Times," to a review of the book on May 8, 1939. He wrote:

Any reader who has his roots planted in the red soil will boil with indignation over the bedraggled, bestial characters that will give the ignorant east convincing confirmation of their ideas of the people of the southwest. . . . If you have children, I'd advise against leaving the book around home. It has *Tobacco Road* looking as pure as Charlotte Brontë, when it comes to obscene, vulgar, lewd, stable language.

Usually the editors consider the book a disgrace to the state, and when they do not deny its truth they seek compensation. One editor wrote:

Oklahoma may come in for some ridicule in other states because of such movie mistakes as *Oklahoma Kid* and such literature as the current *Grapes of Wrath*. Nationally we may rank near the bottom in the number of good books purchased, and in the amount we pay our teachers. But when the biggest livestock and Four H club show comes along each year the nation finds out that somebody amounts to something in Oklahoma.[3]

On September 25, 1941, during the Oklahoma State Fair, the *Daily Oklahoman,* of Oklahoma City, carried a large cartoon showing the Oklahoma farmer proudly and scornfully reclining atop a heap of corn, wheat, and pumpkins, jeering at a small and anguished Steinbeck holding a copy of *The Grapes of Wrath.* The caption: "Now eat every gol-durn word of it."

Considerable resentment toward the state of California was felt in Oklahoma because California had stigmatized Oklahoma by calling all dust bowl migrants—even those from Arkansas and Texas—"Okies." One lengthy newspaper editorial was headed "So California Wants Nothing But Cream"[4] and another "It's Enough to Justify a Civil War."[5] On June 13, 1939, the *Daily Oklahoman* carried under a streamer headline a long article on the number of Californians on Oklahoma's relief rolls. In Tulsa, employees of the Mid Continent Petroleum Company organized the Oklahoma's California Hecklers Club, the stated purpose being to "make California take back what she's been dishing out." The club's motto was "A heckle a day will keep a Californian at bay." A seven-point program was adopted, beginning, "Turn the other cheek, but have a raspberry in it," and ending, "Provide Chamber of Commerce publicity to all Californians who can read."[6] The Stillwater *Gazette* in editorial approval wrote of the club: "*The Grapes of Wrath* have soured and this time it's the Californians who'll get indigestion."[7]

Numerous letters from subscribers have appeared in newspapers throughout Oklahoma. Some are apologetic, some bitter, some violent. A few have defended Steinbeck, sympathized with

[3] *Ibid.*, Dec. 5, 1939.
[4] *Ibid.*, Nov. 28, 1938.
[5] *Ibid.*, Aug. 6, 1938.
[6] Stillwater *Gazette*, April 26, 1940.
[7] *Ibid.*

the Joads, and praised *The Grapes of Wrath*. Some take the book as text for economic, social, or political preachments. Miss Mary E. Lemon, of Kingfisher, wrote:

To many of us John Steinbeck's novel, *The Grapes of Wrath*, has sounded the keynote of our domestic depression, and put the situation before us in an appealing way. When the small farmers and home owners—the great masses upon which our national stability depends—were being deprived of their homes and sent roaming about the country, knocking from pillar to post; when banks were bursting with idle money, and insurance companies were taking on more holdings and money than they knew what to do with, Steinbeck attempted a sympathetic exposition of this status.[8]

Mr. P. A. Oliver, of Sallisaw, wrote no less emphatically:

The Grapes of Wrath was written to arouse sympathy for the millions of poor farmers and tenants who have been brought to miserable ruin because of the development of machinery. . . . The people are caught in the inexorable contradiction of capitalism. As machinery is more and more highly developed, more and more workers are deprived of wages, of buying power. As buying power is destroyed, markets are destroyed. As the millions of workers are replaced by machinery in the industrial centers, the markets over the world collapse. The collapse of world markets destroyed the market for the cotton and vegetables produced by the poor farmers and tenants of Sequoyah county. Sequoyah county is a part of the world and hence suffered along with the rest of the capitalistic world in the collapse of capitalistic business. The day of free enterprise is done. The day of the little farmer is done. Had it not been for government spending, every farmer in the United States, every banker, every lawyer, every doctor, and all other professional workers and wage earners would long since have joined the Joads on the trail of tears. Better do some serious thinking before you ridicule the Joads.[9]

From September 22 to 25, 1940, a Congressional committee headed by Representative Tolan of California held hearings in

---

[8] Oklahoma City *Times*, Dec. 22, 1939.
[9] Sallisaw *Democrat-American*, March 28, 1940.

Oklahoma's capitol investigating the problem of migratory workers. Apparently Oklahoma viewed with suspicion this intrusion, for as early as August 16, a newspaper editorial stated that

Anticipating an attempt to "smear" Oklahoma, Governor Phillips is marshalling witnesses and statistics to give the state's version of the migration. He has called on Dr. Henry G. Bennett and faculty members of the Oklahoma A. and M. college to assist in the presentation. Oklahoma has a right to resent any undue reflections on the state. If the hearing develops into a mud-slinging contest, Oklahoma citizens have a few choice puddles from which to gather ammunition for an attack on the ham-and-egg crackpot ideas hatched on the western coast.[10]

On September 9 the *Daily Oklahoman* of Oklahoma City carried a story giving the names of the members of the committee which the governor had appointed to prepare his report. The paper stated that "Governor Phillips announced his intention to refute the 'Okies' story when the committee of congressmen come here to study conditions causing the migration." During the hearings, front-page stories kept Oklahomans alert to Steinbeck's guilt. On September 20 the *Daily Oklahoman* reported with apparent relief that "The fictional Joad family of *The Grapes of Wrath* could be matched by any state in the union, according to testimony." Next morning the same paper's leading editorial on "Mechanized Farms and 'Okies'" stated that mechanized farming was not responsible for conditions represented in *The Grapes of Wrath*. The editorial concluded, "It is a disagreeable fact, but one that cannot be ignored by men earnestly seeking the truth wherever found, that two of the chief factors that produce 'Okies' are AAA and WPA."

Under the heading "'Grapes' Story Arouses Wrath of Governor," the Oklahoma City *Times* on October 2, 1939, printed the story of a correspondence between His Excellency Leon C. Phillips, Governor of Oklahoma, and an unnamed physician of

---

[10] *Payne County News* (Stillwater), Aug. 16, 1940.

Detroit, Michigan. The unnamed physician wrote, as quoted in the paper:

"Is it at all conceivable that the state of Oklahoma, through its corporations and banks, is dispossessing farmers and sharecroppers . . . ? I am wondering whether you, my dear governor, have read the book in question." To which the governor warmly replied: "I have not read the thing. I do not permit myself to get excited about the works of any fiction writer. In Oklahoma we have as fine citizens as even your state could boast. . . . I would suggest you go back to reading detective magazines. . . ."

The following news item is quoted from the Stillwater *Gazette* of March 23, 1940:

Thirty-six unemployed men and women picketed Oklahoma's state capitol for two hours Saturday calling on Governor Phillips to do something about conditions portrayed in John Steinbeck's novel, *The Grapes of Wrath*. One of their signs stated "Steinbeck told the truth." Eli Jaffee, president of the Oklahoma City Workers' Alliance, said that "we are the Okies who didn't go to California, and we want jobs." Phillips refused to talk with the group. He said that he considered that the novel and the movie version of the book presented an exaggerated and untrue picture of Oklahoma's tenant farmer problems as well as an untruthful version of how migrants are received in California.

If His Excellency the Governor had been reticent as a critic of literature, the Honorable Lyle Boren, Congressman from Oklahoma, was no way abashed. The following speech, reprinted from the *Congressional Record,* was published in the *Daily Oklahoman*, January 24, 1940:

Mr. Speaker, my colleagues, considerable has been said in the cloakrooms, in the press and in various reviews about a book entitled *The Grapes of Wrath*. I cannot find it possible to let this dirty, lying, filthy manuscript go heralded before the public without a word of challenge or protest.

I would have my colleagues in Congress, who are concerning themselves with the fundamental economic problems of America, know that Oklahoma, like other States in the Union, has its economic problems, but that no Oklahoma economic problem has been portrayed in the low and vulgar lines of this publication. As a citizen of Oklahoma, I would have it known that I resent, for the great State of Oklahoma, the implications in that book. . . .

I stand before you today as an example in my judgment, of the average son of the tenant farmer of America. If I have in any way done more in the sense of personal accomplishment than the average son of the tenant farmer of Oklahoma, it has been a matter of circumstance, and I know of a surety that the heart and brain and character of the average tenant farmer of Oklahoma cannot be surpassed and probably not equalled by any other group.

Today, I stand before this body as a son of a tenant farmer, labeled by John Steinbeck as an "Okie." For myself, for my dad and my mother, whose hair is silvery in the service of building the State of Oklahoma, I say to you, and to every honest, square-minded reader in America, that the painting Steinbeck made in his book is a lie, a black, infernal creation of a twisted, distorted mind.

Some have blasphemed the name of Charles Dickens by making comparisons between his writing and this. I have no doubt but that Charles Dickens accurately portrayed certain economic conditions in his country and in his time, but this book portrays only John Steinbeck's unfamiliarity with facts and his complete ignorance of his subject. . . .

Take the vulgarity out of this book and it would be blank from cover to cover. It is painful to me to further charge that if you take the obscene language out, its author could not sell a copy. . . .

I would have you know that there is not a tenant farmer in Oklahoma that Oklahoma needs to apologize for. I want to declare to my nation and to the world that I am proud of my tenant-farmer heritage, and I would to Almighty God that all citizens of America could be as clean and noble and fine as the Oklahomans that Steinbeck labeled "Okies." The only apology that needs to be made is by the State of California for being the parent of such offspring as this author. . . .

Just nine days after Congressman Boren's speech had appeared in print, a long reply by Miss Katharine Maloney, of Coalgate, appeared on the Forum page of the Oklahoma City *Times*. I quote a few brief excerpts from Miss Maloney's letter:

If Boren read *The Grapes of Wrath*, which I have cause to believe he did not, he would not label John Steinbeck a "damnable liar." John Steinbeck portrayed the characters in his book just as they actually are. . . . Why, if Boren wants to bring something up in congress, doesn't he do something to bring better living conditions to the tenant farmer? . . . This would make a better platform for a politician than the book. . . .

Not only politics, but the pulpit as well were moved by the book. One minister in Wewoka was quoted as praising it as a "truthful book of literary as well as social value, resembling in power and beauty of style the King James version of the Bible."[11] His was decidedly a minority opinion. The other extreme may be represented by the Reverend W. Lee Rector, of Ardmore, who considered *The Grapes of Wrath* a "heaven-shaming and Christ-insulting book." As reported in the press, the Reverend Mr. Rector stated:

"The projection of the preacher of the book into a role of hypocrisy and sexuality discounts the holy calling of God-called preachers. . . . The sexual roles that the author makes the preacher and young women play is so vile and misrepresentative of them as a whole that all readers should revolt at the debasement the author makes of them." The pastor complained that the book's masterly handling of profanity tends to "popularize iniquity" and that the book is "100 percent false to Christianity. We protest with all our heart against the Communistic base of the story. . . . As does Communism, it shrewdly inveighs against the rich, the preacher, and Christianity. Should any of us Ardmore preachers attend the show which advertises this infamous book, his flock should put him on the spot, give him his walking papers, and ask God to forgive his poor soul."[12]

Other Oklahomans resented the filming of the story. Mr. Reo M'Vickn wrote the following letter, which was published in the Oklahoma City *Times* on January 26, 1940:

---

[11] Letter in my possession.
[12] Oklahoma City *Times*, March 30, 1940.

After reading the preview of *Grapes of Wrath* (*Look*, January 16) I think the state of Oklahoma as a whole should take definite steps to prevent the use of the name of our state in such a production. They are trying to disgrace Oklahoma and I for one am in favor of stopping them before they get started.

Oklahoma Chambers of Commerce had already tried to stop the filming of the picture. The following story is taken from the Oklahoma City *Times*, August 7, 1939:

Neither Stanley Draper, secretary-manager of the Oklahoma City Chamber of Commerce, nor Dr. J. M. Ashton, research director of the State Chamber of Commerce, wants Twentieth Century Fox Corporation to make *Grapes of Wrath* in the "dust bowl." . . . Enough fault was found with the facts in Joseph [*sic*] Steinbeck's book on the "okies." . . . So the two Chamber of Commerce men think someone should protest the inaccurate and unfair treatment the state seems to be about to receive in the filming of the picture. Draper is going to suggest the mayor of Oklahoma City protest, and Ashton will ask the governor to do likewise. . . .

On September 1, 1941, the *Daily Oklahoman* carried a four-column headline, "Lions to Attack 'Okie' Literature." The news story described the nature of the attack:

Those who write smart and not so complimentary things about Oklahoma and Okies had better watch out, because the 3-A district governor of Oklahoma Lions clubs and his cabinet, at their first session here Sunday, discussed an all-out counter-offensive. . . . The district governor and a dozen members of his cabinet agreed in their meeting at the Skirvin hotel that something should be done to offset *Grapes of Wrath* publicity. . . .[13]

The opinions and incidents which I have presented are representative, by no means inclusive. There are, I should say, two main bodies of opinion, one that this is an honest, sympathetic, and artistically powerful presentation of economic, social, and

---

[13] The governor of district 3-A of the Lions clubs of Oklahoma is Dr. Joseph H. Marshburn, Professor of English in the University of Oklahoma.

human problems; the other, the great majority, that this is a vile, filthy book, an outsider's malicious attempt to smear the state of Oklahoma with outrageous lies. The latter opinion, I may add, is frequently accompanied by the remark: "I haven't read a word of it, but I know it's all a dirty lie."

The reception of *The Grapes of Wrath* in Oklahoma suggests many interesting problems, particularly pertinent to contemporary regional literature in America. Any honest literary interpretation of a region seems to offend the people of that region. Ellen Glasgow, though herself a Virginian, has been received in her native state with a coolness equal to the warmth with which Virginians have welcomed Thomas Nelson Page. Romanticizers of the Old South are local literary lions, while authors who treat contemporary problems are renegades who would ridicule their own people for the sake of literary notoriety.

A tremendous provincial self-consciousness expresses itself in fierce resentment of "outsiders who meddle in our affairs." One consistent theme in the writings of Oklahomans who attacked *The Grapes of Wrath* was that this book represents us unfairly; it will give us a lot of unfavorable publicity, and confirm the low opinion of us that seems to prevail outside the state. Rarely did someone say, "We should do something about those conditions; we should do something to help those people." Generally they said, "We should deny it vigorously; all Oklahomans are not Okies."

Properly speaking, *The Grapes of Wrath* is not a regional novel; but it has regional significance; it raises regional problems. Economic collapse, farm tenantry, migratory labor are not regional problems; they are national or international in scope, and can never be solved through state or regional action. But the Joads represent a regional culture which, as Steinbeck shows us, is now rapidly disintegrating as the result of extra-regional forces. It may well be that powerful extra-regional forces operating in the world today foreshadow the end of cultural regionalism as we have known it in America.

III

✦❀✦❀✦❀✦❀✦❀✦❀✦❀✦❀✦❀✦❀✦❀✦❀✦❀✦❀✦❀✦❀✦❀✦❀✦❀✦

The Critical Context

Art and Philosophy

EDITOR'S INTRODUCTION:
THE PATTERN OF CRITICISM

The hysterical reaction that *The Grapes of Wrath* aroused in part of the American public, and notably in its politicians and self-appointed guardians of morality, was reflected in book reviews and literary essays. Most of these were emotional reactions to the social message of the novel. Curiously, as public excitement over the novel subsided, so too did literary interest, and there would be fewer critical essays on *The Grapes of Wrath* for the next fifteen years. To be sure, the novel was not ignored in literary histories and in surveys of American fiction, some of which contain valuable insights: for example, Harry Thornton Moore's chapter in his pioneer study of Steinbeck (1939), the twenty pages in Joseph Warren Beach's *American Fiction, 1920-1940*, and the briefer considerations by Harry Slochower, Floyd Stovall, and others.[1] But the current standing of a piece of literature is indicated to a large extent by its ability to sustain a dialogue among critics. It is therefore significant that in those first fifteen years there appeared in literary journals fewer than half a dozen essays devoted to a critical analysis of *The Grapes of Wrath*. Only two of these, by Frederic Carpenter and by Chester E. Eisinger, made a measurable contribution to our understanding of the novel. By contrast, in the equal space of time between 1954 and 1969 there appeared at least forty essays, short and long, on *The Grapes of Wrath*, most

---

This essay, in a slightly different form, was presented at the University of Connecticut conference on *The Grapes of Wrath*, May 3, 1969. It is printed here for the first time.

[1] For complete bibliographical information about materials mentioned in the Introduction, consult the Bibliography at the end of this volume.

of which considered some technical aspect of the novel. For these and other reasons to be made clear, 1954 is a useful point of demarcation in an account of how the novel was received by critics.

One of the most striking aspects of critical writing about *The Grapes of Wrath* in its first fifteen years was its assertive nature. There was little analysis or detailed explication. This was true whether the topic of discussion was the novel's total impact, its use of interchapters, the nature of its social message, or whatever. The assertions concerning the characters' credibility and effectiveness were particularly extreme. There was Malcolm Cowley's statement that "in the Joad family, everyone from Grampa—'full a' piss an' vinegar,' as he says of himself— down to the two brats, Ruthie and Winfield, is a distinct and living person." And, there was Edmund Wilson's statement that "it is as if human sentiments and speeches had been assigned to a flock of lemmings on their way to throw themselves into the sea." It is toward one of these two poles that almost all assertions gravitated. Thus Joseph Warren Beach: ". . . it is notable as a work of fiction by virtue of the fact that all social problems are so effectively dramatized in individual situations and characters." But the great majority of commentators agreed with Wilson. Harry Thornton Moore, who published the first book on Steinbeck the same year as *The Grapes of Wrath*, found Casy the most real character in the book, yet even Casy was "nevertheless . . . something of a contrivance, a sounding board." Arthur Hobson Quinn, as late as 1951, found all but Ma Joad to be "puppets with differentiating traits." Alfred Kazin, who thought Steinbeck's people in general were at least "always on the verge of becoming human," withheld this charity from the Joads, whom he called "symbolic marionettes." Similar assertions were made by Max Eastman, John S. Kennedy, W. M. Frohock, and Kenneth Burke, to name only well-known figures.

The voices of moderation were few. Harry Slochower said simply that Steinbeck was "more successful in his picture of the general forces that surround his people than in the creation of characters who react to them." And those attempting to understand the particular nature and purpose of Steinbeck's characterization were even fewer. Kenneth Burke, alone, among those critics agreeing with Wilson, offered a rationale for his opinion: ". . . most of the characters derive their role, which is to say their personality, purely from their relationship to the basic situation." Reacting to Wilson's strong statements, Stanley Edgar Hyman suggested that by the same logic one could prove that "because Shakespeare packed *Hamlet* with images of disease and decay he thought of all people as diseased." Hyman went on to point toward a thematic use of these images in *The Grapes of Wrath*. Leon Whipple observed that ". . . on the whole Steinbeck is interested in people as symbols in his design" and "of necessity he makes inarticulate people articulate, but within the conventions we must grant a novelist."

This same pattern of polarity, with few opinions in between, is observed in another aspect of the novel to receive much critical attention—its interchapters. As late as 1951, Frederick J. Hoffman, a well-known and respected scholar, stated that these interchapters in *The Grapes of Wrath* are "perhaps some of the most wretched violations of aesthetic taste observable in modern American fiction. . . . A study of the style, rhetoric, and intellectual content of the fifteen chapters reveals Steinbeck's writing at its worst and his mind at its most confused. . . ." Although this judgment was not unique, no other commentator of significance quite reached this height of invective. Malcolm Cowley simply found most of the interchapters "too shrill, too evangelistic." At the other pole, we have such statements as Harry Thornton Moore's, that the interchapters are, in some respect, the best parts of the book, and Joseph Warren Beach's approval of them as, in the most part, "ingenious and effective means of dramatizing the thought of a whole group of people." Although Beach did not use the word, he described some of these interchapters in terms of cinematic montage techniques. Howard Baker found these chapters a "brilliant structural effect," imposing form on an "intrinsically formless narrative." Slochower found them necessary "because his characters by themselves, *do not know* and therefore cannot 'tell' the wider meaning of their story."

Incomplete as these attempts were, at least, unlike the opinions about the characters, they sometimes moved towards analytic understanding. Certainly not all critics stopped with Bernard de Voto, who found these interchapters "necessary because no one could have stood the painfulness of the story without some tranquilizing relief"!

It may be noted in passing that not all qualified readers found *The Grapes of Wrath* so moving. Harry Thornton Moore observed that the novel lacked the "compulsion of participation" necessary; that Steinbeck had assembled "all the ingredients for a great book, and then failed to provide it with a proportioned and intensified drama." Maxwell Geismar thought the novel lacked the art and realism of certain previous Steinbeck books and was a return to glamour and theatrics, that it was sentimental and distorted. And Arthur Hobson Quinn, in 1951, recorded that "the final impression left by the novel is not of the author's indignation so much as of his cleverness as a contriver of effects." Puzzled by the novel's continuing popularity in the face of what he took to be true opinions like those above, Bernard Bowron set out to solve this mystery. He discovered that the novel's appeal lay not in its social message, or its characters, or its techniques (which he dismissed as "calculated crudities"), but in the simple fact that *The Grapes of Wrath* was another example of the "Wagons West" romance, complete with tarpaulin-covered trucks, campfires, natural hazards, and hostile Indians cleverly disguised as state troopers and deputized vigilantes. The novel, said Bowron, "appeals to any grown man who just wants to go camping," and it was finally dismissed as "a triumph of literary engineering."

As might be expected, the vehement polarity of opinion concerning another aspect of the novel, its sociological message, gradually subsided as the proletarian thirties gave way to the national unity of the forties. Also, the excellent article by Carey McWilliams, "California Pastoral," based on the LaFollette committee investigations, put a permanent lid on potboiling attempts to discredit the novel by an attack on its facts. One need quote only from Elizabeth Monroe to recall the kind of reaction which was soon to disappear, although it broke out briefly again in one essay as late as 1959. Miss Monroe objected to *The Grapes of Wrath* particularly because it is a novel "that preaches class warfare and hate," and because the only sin the novel recognizes is "the desire to possess" things. In the less extreme terms of another reviewer, Steinbeck was "arousing the poor . . . to courage, endurance, organization and revolt." The full weight of such statements cannot be appreciated unless it is kept in mind that in that era such terms were impossible to dissociate from international Communism.

In this context of opinion about the novel's sociological message, the very early essay by Frederic I. Carpenter (1941), "The Philosophical Joads," takes on real significance. Carpenter's analysis made two important points. First, that *The Grapes of Wrath* is not spontaneously irresponsible in its observations about American life, but has sure roots in our native American tradition: the mystical transcendentalism of Emerson, the earthy democracy of Whitman, and the pragmatic instrumentalism of William James. Carpenter leaned heavily on this. "To repeat," he said: "this group idea of *The Grapes of Wrath* is that of American Transcendentalism. . . . For the first time in history, *The Grapes of Wrath* brings together and makes real three great skeins of American thought." Secondly, and this is more implicit in the essay than explicit, Carpenter suggested that the novel's form and technique are intimately related to this content—the "imaginative realization of these old ideas in new and concrete forms."

Six years later, Chester E. Eisinger found a fourth "skein of American thought" in the novel—Jeffersonian agrarianism. It is interesting that Eisinger's perception of this element in *The Grapes of Wrath* led him to question the novel's accomplishment. "It remains to inquire," he summed up, "if agrarianism, its form and substance, is the part of the Jeffersonian tradition that we should preserve." And he went on to suggest that technological progress had made agrarianism impractical and undesirable. Eisinger's analysis, although it overstates somewhat, and Carpenter's essay were the most valuable contributions made in fifteen years to our understanding of the novel's social content.

In these same fifteen years there appeared no essays of comparable value analyzing the technical or formal aspects of *The Grapes of Wrath*. B. R. McElderry's essay in 1944 was a valiant attempt to give the novel critical respectability, but the method could not succeed. To bring short passages from a variety of critical essays by a variety of writers on drama, poetry, and fiction into momentary contact with the novel as if they were touchstones was not to examine "*The Grapes of Wrath* in the Light of Modern Critical Theory," but to light a match in the Marabar caves. For example, he quoted from Edmund Wilson's essay describing *The Grapes of Wrath* as "mere sentimental optimism" and then went on to say that although this is a valid charge, "I do not believe it is a very important one."

Finally, it is curious that although some reviewers and several subsequent critics made general remarks concerning certain similarities of the novel to the Bible, no essay appeared in which this similarity was explored further. In his study of Steinbeck, Moore remarked in passing that "the exodus of the dispossessed looking for their promised land" had a familiar ring, and suggested that Tom Joad may be "the Joshua to come." Moore also noted the biblical flavor of the prose style, but concluded lamely, "It may have been partly deliberate in a general way (certainly there is no intricate matching of episode with episode)." Except for some observations concerning the symbolism of the novel's ending, no critic pushed beyond this point. Yet it was precisely with an exploration of this symbolism that productive analysis of *The Grapes of Wrath* was to begin its second fifteen years in the winepress of criticism.

This period began in 1955 with Warren French's spirited attack on Bowron's thesis that *The Grapes of Wrath* owed its popularity to its exploitation of the "Wagons West" romance. French disposed of the superficial similarities judged so significant by Bowron and also pointed out in detail the basic differences, suggesting that both *The Grapes of Wrath* and the "Wagons West" romances were examples of an older, journey motif which included such variants as the Hebrew *Exodus*, the *Odyssey*, and *Pilgrim's Progress*. This observation was elaborated by subsequent critics.

A year later Martin Shockley's ground-breaking essay, "Christian Symbolism in *The Grapes of Wrath*," provoked a flurry of attacks and counterattacks to the number of eight exchanges over a six-year period. Reacting against the denial of Casy as a Christ figure by novelist Alan Paton and theologian Liston Pope, Shockley stated: "I propose an interpretation of *The Grapes of Wrath* in which Casy represents a contemporary adaptation of the Christ image, and in which the meaning of the book is revealed through a sequence of Christian symbols." Earlier critics had pointed to some possible parallels to the Bible, usually the Old Testament, but Shockley was the first to make so bold and inclusive a statement. Actually, his observations on the novel's biblical language and the western exodus do not add much to what Moore had pointed out sixteen years earlier. But the similarities he drew between Christ and Casy in terms of words and deeds were central and well supported. He also saw Tom Joad as a disciple and pointed to Rosasharn's last action as representing the "resurrective aspect of Christ," the "multifoliate rose" image of T. S. Eliot.

Unfortunately, although Shockley had declared that Casy is a Christ "innocent of Paulism, of Catholicism, of Puritanism," he had to resort to Unitarianism and Albert Schweitzer to make a "Christian" statement out of Casy's words, "All that lives is holy" and "Maybe all men got one big soul ever'body's a part of." It may have been this weakness in his argument which prompted Eric W. Carlson's attack. "In *The Grapes of Wrath*," said Carlson, "a few loose biblical analogies may be identified, but these are not primary to the structure of the novel, and to contend that they give it an 'essentially and thoroughly Christian' meaning is to distort Steinbeck's intention and its primary framework of *non*-Christian symbolism." The theme of the novel, said Carlson, is not specifically Christian because: a) it is not an expression of humility and resignation; b) it has its origins in the people, not a body of religious concepts and beliefs. The social theme can resemble Christianity only "after doctrine, dogma, sacrament, ritual, miracle, and theism itself have been stripped away, leaving only the idealized brotherhood of man and the Unitarian Oversoul. . . . Christianity without Christ is hardly Christianity." The ideas of "resurrection and redemption are conspicuously absent." According to Carlson, not even the ending of the novel is Christian symbolism, but a culminating expression of "the main theme of the novel: the prime function of life is to nourish life." Finally, the novel's "epic naturalism is neither romantic, nor mystic, nor Christian. . . . it is a humanistic integration of the knowledge of man made available by modern science, philosophy, and art."

Shockley and Carlson, along with the present editor in his "*The Grapes of Wrath* as Fiction," proposed the central arguments which were to be elaborated and qualified by several subsequent critics. Some, such as de Schweinitz, attempted to mediate by pointing out that one side was using the word "Christian" less rigidly than the other; that the novel is not an "*illustration*" of Hebraism or Christianity but "strongly and pervasively *recalls* them." But Walter F. Taylor in 1959 insisted that the novel was not only *not* Christian or Hebraic, but positively anti-religious: "He has only hijacked part of the Christian story in order to turn it to the illustration of profoundly non-Christian meanings." Two years earlier, George Bluestone had also questioned the novel's supposed "Christian" theme, but with more pertinence and less hysteria. He had pointed out that throughout the novel there is "suspicion of a theology not rooted in ordinary human needs," and that Ma Joad, who is most furious at the religious fanatics, "represents the state of natural grace to which Casy aspires." Bluestone also pointed out the ironic implications of little Ruthie's prayer, as it is recalled by Granma: "Now I lay me down to sleep. I pray the Lord my soul to keep. An' when she got there the cupboard was bare, an' so the poor dog got none."

Others, for example Crockett, Moseley, Dougherty, Dunn, Browning, Slade, Pollock and Cannon, came to Shockley's aid. Some brought with them more flexible interpretations of the Bible to fit the words and actions of Tom and Casy. Others brought new parallels, such as Tom's being a Moses figure or even a St. Paul, or the number of Joads corresponding to the 12 disciples, or 12 tribes of Israel, or Ma Joad's being a Deborah, or Casy's being really an Aaron figure, or Rosasharn's milk being a symbol not of communion but of the manna which the Jews ate in the wilderness. Etcetera!

This growing wild flood of biblical criticism crested in 1963 with the appearance of Joseph Fontenrose's chapter on the novel and J. P. Hunter's essay, "Steinbeck's Wine of Affirmation in *The Grapes of Wrath*." Fontenrose provided such a wealth of detailed, convincing parallels with both the Old and New Testament as to make any further doubt about their organic relationship to the novel irresponsible. Fontenrose further provided a larger scheme within which these symbols and references could be assimilated. He proposed that the book's "concluding theme that family interests must be subordinate to the common welfare, that all individual souls are part of one great soul, corresponds to Jesus' rejection of family ties for the kingdom of heaven's sake: 'For whosoever shall do the will of my father which is in heaven, the same is my brother, and sister, and mother.'" "In no Steinbeck novel," said Fontenrose, "do the biological and mythical strands fit so neatly together as in *The Grapes of Wrath*." And, going beyond the biblical parallels, "Jesus is a dying god, and the dying god is the year spirit, the rituals of whose cult are entwined in this novel with rituals of migration and colony-founding."

To this, J. P. Hunter added even more specific biblical parallels, such as, for example, the Joads climbing into the truck two by two while Noah stands on the ground watching. He further strengthened the observation made by myself, French, and Fontenrose that the book's major theme is the "conversion to a wider concern" which is emphasized by a pattern of Old and New Testament references. Thus the ending of the novel becomes truly organic because it is Rosasharn, who had been the most self-centered, who now, out of necessity, adopts the human race as her family. For Hunter the book's ending telescopes the Old Testament deluge, the New Testament stable, and the continuing act of communion; Mount Ararat, Bethlehem, and California.

The culmination to which these two critics bring this material is so impressive that it is difficult to see what could follow them in this vein. And it is precisely this impasse which is admitted in Agnes Donohue's " 'The Endless Journey to No End' ": "Enough has been made," she says, "of the biblical analogues in *The Grapes of Wrath*. . . . What Steinbeck suggests is richly symbolic, a mixture of myth and scripture." She sees the journey motif "as a complex symbol of fallen man's compulsive but doomed search for Paradise and ritual reenactment of the Fall. More than an historical, biblical, or sociological exodus, the journey of the Joads is a deeply mythical hegira of the human spirit in a fallen world. . . ."

This changing conception of the book's action, from social document to "Wagons West" romance to biblical analogue to "deeply mythical hegira of the human spirit," is reflected also in corresponding changes at other critical points. The present editor's essay on *The Grapes of Wrath* pointed out some of the techniques whereby the interchapters are closely knit into the fiber of the novel. Hunter and French supported this attempt through their discussions of these chapters' thematic contribution to the whole. Through the work of Bluestone and Griffin and Freedman, criticism has moved from the mere repetition of Wilson's charge about Steinbeck's "animalism" to a careful analysis of the symbolic meaning and thematic function of the animals and animal tropes in the novel. Bluestone in 1957 carefully noted not only the wide range of themes which are "accompanied by, or expressed in terms of, zoological images," but also he plotted a curve of their incidence and matched this neatly to the curve of the novel's plot. Working together on the assumption that "dominant motifs are of central importance in the form and meaning of certain works of fiction" (an assumption critics had made very infrequently about the work of Steinbeck), Griffin and Freedman classified the various tropes and put them into categories according to their function; for example, "metonymic" and "epitome." Their work demonstrated, in fact, that certain parts of *The Grapes of Wrath* cannot be understood without some analysis of the particular animal imagery involved, which often creates and not merely illustrates meaning. The two critics concluded that "Steinbeck's intricate and masterful manipulation of the various references to machines and animals is an essential factor in the stature of *The Grapes of Wrath* as one of the monuments of twentieth-century American literature."

Concerning the novel's themes, French, in his 1961 study of Steinbeck, demonstrated in detail an earlier thesis that the main theme is "the education of the heart," the movement of the Joads from regarding themselves as a "self-important family unit" to their regarding themselves "as a part of a vast human family." In this respect, French rightly compared Steinbeck to Hawthorne, for in this light *The Grapes of Wrath* is not a political or sociological novel, but a moral one, substantially more than "a period piece about a troublesome past era." More recently, in articles published here for the first time, Pascal Covici, Jr. ("Work and the Timeliness of *The Grapes of Wrath*"), Betty Perez ("House and Home: Thematic Symbols in *The Grapes of Wrath*"), and John R. Reed ("*The Grapes of Wrath* and the Esthetics of Indigence") add substantially to our understanding of the further implications and contributions of these themes to the novel's matrix of meanings. Steinbeck does indeed reassert, and in a novel depicting real physical hunger, that man cannot live by bread alone; but it is perhaps unexpected that the spiritual butter for which he asks is work: "The last clear definite function of a man—muscles aching to work. . . ." Perez enlarges the meaning of home in the novel from the purely physical house which the turtle carries with him to the aura which emanates from Ma Joad, Casy, and finally Rosasharn. Reed points out how masterfully Steinbeck transforms the naturalistic and even vulgar details of poverty into esthetically effective contributions.

But it must not be assumed from these last examples that recognition of the technical and thematic accomplishment of Steinbeck's greatest novel has proceeded smoothly for the last fifteen years. On the occasion of Steinbeck's being awarded the Nobel Prize for Literature in 1962, Arthur Mizener objected to this award, repeating that even *The Grapes of Wrath*, his best book, is "watered down by tenth-rate philosophizing," "sentimentality," and "thoroughly unbelievable, manipulated characters." The most methodical effort to deny the accomplishment of this great novel came in an article by Walter Fuller Taylor, who found many pernicious ideas which are "not organically necessary to the social message" of the novel. "For under cover of a pious social objective a number of other and quite different meanings are slipped past the reader's guard: those of hostility, bitterness, and contempt toward the middle classes, of antagonism toward religion in its organized forms, of the enjoyment of a Tobacco-Road sort of slovenliness, of an easy-going promiscuity and animalism in sex, of Casy's curious transcendental mysticism [apparently on a par with the other vices], of a tolerance that at first seems all-inclusive but that actually extends only so far as Steinbeck's personal preferences." Worse yet, perhaps, the novel is rife with "vulgarity in deed and word."

Clearly, as Taylor's arguments demonstrate, such attempts to discredit the novel are hysterical. Slowly at first, but more and more surely, utilizing the work of their predecessors, literary critics have added to our understanding and appreciation of what is certainly one of the great American novels. This process is not yet complete. Each time the present editor has discussed *The Grapes of Wrath* with students he has come away with something new and valuable, some fresh observation made possible through the different knowledge and experience of their own time and age. As you read the following essays, perhaps you will find that some particular point significant in your own understanding of the novel seems not to have been noticed by these critics. That will be the beginning of your own contribution.

FREDERIC I. CARPENTER

Frederic I. Carpenter has taught at the University of Chicago and
the University of California at Berkeley. He has been Editorial
Advisor for *College English* and Editor of *New England Quarterly*.
His publications include *Emerson Handbook, American Literature
and the Dream, The American Myth* and books on Robinson
Jeffers and Eugene O'Neill for the Twayne Authors Series.

The Philosophical Joads

A popular heresy has it that a novelist should not discuss ideas
—especially not abstract ideas. Even the best contemporary reviewers concern themselves with the entertainment value of a
book (will it please their readers?), and with the impression of
immediate reality which it creates. *The Grapes of Wrath,* for
instance, was praised for its swift action and for the moving
sincerity of its characters. But its mystical ideas and the moraliz-
ing interpretations intruded by the author between the narrative chapters were condemned. Presumably the book became a
best seller in spite of these; its art was great enough to overcome its philosophy.

But in the course of time a book is also judged by other
standards. Aristotle once argued that poetry should be more
"philosophical" than history; and all books are eventually
weighed for their content of wisdom. Novels that have become
classics do more than tell a story and describe characters; they
offer insight into men's motives and point to the springs of
action. Together with the moving picture, they offer the criticism of life.

Although this theory of art may seem classical, all important
modern novels—especially American novels—have clearly suggested an abstract idea of life. *The Scarlet Letter* symbolized
"sin," *Moby Dick* offered an allegory of evil. *Huck Finn* de-

Reprinted from *College English*, II (January 1941), 315–325. By permission of the National Council of Teachers of English and Frederic I.
Carpenter.

scribed the revolt of the "natural individual" against "civiliza-
tion," and *Babbitt* (like Emerson's "Self-reliance") denounced
the narrow conventions of "society." Now *The Grapes of Wrath*
goes beyond these to preach a positive philosophy of life and to
damn that blind conservatism which fears ideas.

I shall take for granted the narrative power of the book and
the vivid reality of its characters: modern critics, both professional and popular, have borne witness to these. The novel is a
best seller. But it also has ideas. These appear abstractly and
obviously in the interpretative interchapters. But more important is Steinbeck's creation of Jim Casy, "the preacher," to
interpret and to embody the philosophy of the novel. And consummate is the skill with which Jim Casy's philosophy has been
integrated with the action of the story, until it motivates and
gives significance to the lives of Tom Joad, and Ma, and Rose of
Sharon. It is not too much to say that Jim Casy's ideas determine and direct the Joads's actions.

Beside and beyond their function in the story, the ideas of
John Steinbeck and Jim Casy possess a significance of their own.
They continue, develop, integrate, and realize the thought of
the great writers of American history. Here the mystical transcendentalism of Emerson reappears, and the earthy democracy
of Whitman, and the pragmatic instrumentalism of William
James and John Dewey. And these old philosophies grow and
change in the book until they become new. They coalesce into
an organic whole. And, finally, they find embodiment in character and action, so that they seem no longer ideas, but facts.
The enduring greatness of *The Grapes of Wrath* consists in its
imaginative realization of these old ideas in new and concrete
forms. Jim Casy translates American philosophy into words of
one syllable, and the Joads translate it into action.

I

"Ever know a guy that said big words like that?" asks the
truck driver in the first narrative chapter of *The Grapes of
Wrath*. "Preacher," replies Tom Joad. "Well, it makes you mad

to hear a guy use big words. Course with a preacher it's all right because nobody would fool around with a preacher anyway." But soon afterward Tom meets Jim Casy and finds him changed. "I was a preacher," said the man seriously, "but not no more." Because Casy has ceased to be an orthodox minister and no longer uses big words, Tom Joad plays around with him. And the story results.

But although he is no longer a minister, Jim Casy continues to preach. His words have become simple and his ideas unorthodox. "Just Jim Casy now. Ain't got the call no more. Got a lot of sinful idears—but they seem kinda sensible" (p. 27). A century before, this same experience and essentially these same ideas had occurred to another preacher: Ralph Waldo Emerson had given up the ministry because of his unorthodoxy. But Emerson had kept on using big words. Now Casy translates them: "Why do we got to hang it on God or Jesus? Maybe it's all men an' all women we love; maybe that's the Holy Sperit—the human sperit—the whole shebang. Maybe all men got one big soul ever'body's a part of" (pp. 32–33). And so the Emersonian oversoul comes to earth in Oklahoma.

Unorthodox Jim Casy went into the Oklahoma wilderness to save his soul. And in the wilderness he experienced the religious feeling of identity with nature which has always been the heart of transcendental mysticism: "There was the hills, an' there was me, an' we wasn't separate no more. We was one thing. An' that one thing was holy." Like Emerson, Casy came to the conviction that holiness, or goodness, results from this feeling of unity: "I got to thinkin' how we was holy when we was one thing, an' mankin' was holy when it was one thing."

Thus far Jim Casy's transcendentalism has remained vague and apparently insignificant. But the corollary of this mystical philosophy is that any man's self-seeking destroys the unity or "holiness" of nature: "An' it [this one thing] on'y got unholy when one mis'able little fella got the bit in his teeth, an' run off his own way. . . . Fella like that bust the holiness" (p. 110). Or, as Emerson phrased it, while discussing Nature: "The world lacks unity because man is disunited with himself. . . . Love is its demand." So Jim Casy preaches the religion of love.

He finds that this transcendental religion alters the old standards: "Here's me that used to give all my fight against the devil 'cause I figured the devil was the enemy. But they's some-pin worse'n the devil got hold a the country" (p. 175). Now, like Emerson, he almost welcomes "the dear old devil." Now he fears not the lusts of the flesh but rather the lusts of the spirit. For the abstract lust of possession isolates a man from his fellows and destroys the unity of nature and the love of man. As Steinbeck writes: "The quality of owning freezes you forever into 'I,' and cuts you off forever from the 'we'" (p. 206). Or, as the Concord farmers in Emerson's poem "Hamatreya" had exclaimed: "'Tis mine, my children's and my name's," only to have "their avarice cooled like lust in the chill of the grave." To a preacher of the oversoul, possessive egotism may become the unpardonable sin.

If a society has adopted "the quality of owning" (as typified by absentee ownership) as its social norm, then Protestant nonconformity may become the highest virtue, and even resistance to authority may become justified. At the beginning of his novel Steinbeck had suggested this, describing how "the faces of the watching men lost their bemused perplexity and became hard and angry and resistant. Then the women knew that they were safe . . . their men were whole" (pp. 6–7). For this is the paradox of Protestantism: when men resist unjust and selfish authority, they themselves become "whole" in spirit.

But this American ideal of nonconformity seems negative: how can men be sure that their Protestant rebellion does not come from the devil? To this there has always been but one answer—faith: faith in the instincts of the common man, faith in ultimate social progress, and faith in the direction in which democracy is moving. So Ma Joad counsels the discouraged Tom: "Why, Tom, we're the people that live. They ain't gonna wipe us out. Why, we're the people—we go on" (p. 383). And so Steinbeck himself affirms a final faith in progress: "When theories change and crash, when schools, philosophies . . . grow and disintegrate, man reaches, stumbles forward. . . . Having stepped forward, he may slip back, but only half a step, never the full step back" (pp. 204–205). Whether this be democratic faith, or mere transcendental optimism, it has always been the motive force of our American life and finds reaffirmation in this novel.

II

Upon the foundation of this old American idealism Steinbeck has built. But the Emersonian oversoul had seemed very vague and very ineffective—only the individual had been real, and he had been concerned more with his private soul than with other people. *The Grapes of Wrath* develops the old idea in new ways. It traces the transformation of the Protestant individual into the member of a social group—the old "I" becomes "we." And it traces the transformation of the passive individual into the active participant—the idealist becomes pragmatist. The first development continues the poetic thought of Walt Whitman; the second continues the philosophy of William James and John Dewey.

"One's-self I sing, a simple separate person," Whitman had proclaimed. "Yet utter the word Democratic, the word En-Masse." Other American writers had emphasized the individual above the group. Even Whitman celebrated his "comrades and lovers" in an essentially personal relationship. But Steinbeck now emphasizes the group above the individual and from an impersonal point of view. Where formerly American and Protestant thought has been separatist, Steinbeck now faces the problem of social integration. In his novel the "mutually repellent particles" of individualism begin to cohère.

"This is the beginning," he writes, "from 'I' to 'we.' " This is the beginning, that is, of reconstruction. When the old society has been split and the Protestant individuals wander aimlessly about, some new nucleus must be found, or chaos and nihilism will follow. "In the night one family camps in a ditch and another family pulls in and the tents come out. The two men squat on their hams and the women and children listen. Here is the node." Here is the new nucleus. "And from this first 'we,' there grows a still more dangerous thing: 'I have a little food' plus 'I have none.' If from this problem the sum is 'We have a little food,' the thing is on its way, the movement has direction" (p. 206). A new social group is forming, based on the word "en masse." But here is no socialism imposed from above; here is a natural grouping of simple separate persons.

By virtue of his wholehearted participation in this new group the individual may become greater than himself. Some men, of course, will remain mere individuals, but in every group there must be leaders, or "representative men." A poet gives expression to the group idea, or a preacher organizes it. After Jim Casy's death, Tom is chosen to lead. Ma explains: "They's some folks that's just theirself, an' nothin' more. There's Al [for instance] he's jus' a young fella after a girl. You wasn't never like that, Tom" (p. 482). Because he has been an individualist, but through the influence of Casy and of his group idea has become more than himself, Tom becomes "a leader of the people." But his strength derives from his increased sense of participation in the group.

From Jim Casy, and eventually from the thought of Americans like Whitman, Tom Joad has inherited this idea. At the end of the book he sums it up, recalling how Casy "went out in the wilderness to find his own soul, and he found he didn't have no soul that was his'n. Says he foun' he jus' got a little piece of a great big soul. Says a wilderness ain't no good 'cause his little piece of a soul wasn't no good 'less it was with the rest, an' was whole" (p. 570). Unlike Emerson, who had said goodbye to the proud world, these latterday Americans must live in the midst of it. "I know now," concludes Tom, "a fella ain't no good alone."

To repeat: this group idea is American, not Russian; and stems from Walt Whitman, not Karl Marx. But it does include some elements that have usually seemed sinful to ortho-dox Anglo-Saxons. "Of physiology from top to toe I sing," Whitman had declared, and added a good many details that his friend Emerson thought unnecessary. Now the Joads frankly discuss anatomical details and joke about them. Like most com-mon people, they do not abscond or conceal. Sometimes they seem to go beyond the bounds of literary decency: the unbut-toned antics of Grandpa Joad touch a new low in folk-comedy. The movies (which reproduced most of the realism of the book) could not quite stomach this. But for the most part they preserved the spirit of the book, because it was whole and healthy.

In Whitman's time almost everyone deprecated this physio-logical realism, and in our own many readers and critics still deprecate it. Nevertheless, it is absolutely necessary—both ar-tistically and logically. In the first place, characters like the Joads do act and talk that way—to describe them as genteel would be to distort the picture. And, in the second place, Whit-man himself had suggested the necessity of it: just as the litera-ture of democracy must describe all sorts of people, "en masse," so it must describe all of the life of the people. To exclude the common or "low" elements of individual life would be as false as to exclude the common or low elements of society. Either would destroy the wholeness of life and nature. There-fore, along with the dust-driven Joads, we must have Grandpa's dirty drawers.

But beyond this physiological realism lies the problem of sex. And this problem is not one of realism at all. Throughout this turbulent novel an almost traditional reticence concerning the details of sex is observed. The problem here is rather one of fundamental morality, for sex had always been a symbol of sin. *The Scarlet Letter* reasserted the authority of an orthodox morality. Now Jim Casy questions that orthodoxy. On this first meeting with Tom he descirbes how, after sessions of preach-ing, he had often lain with a girl and then felt sinful afterward. This time the movies repeated his confession, because it is central to the motivation of the story. Disbelief in the sinfulness of sex converts Jim Casy from a preacher of the old morality to a practitioner of the new.

But in questioning the old morality Jim Casy does not deny morality. He doubts the strict justice of Hawthorne's code: "Maybe it ain't a sin. Maybe it's just the way folks is. Maybe we been whippin' the hell out of ourselves for nothin'" (p. 31). But he recognizes that love must always remain responsible and purposeful. Al Joad remains just "a boy after a girl." In place of the old, Casy preaches the new morality of Whitman, which uses sex to symbolize the love of man for his fellows. Jim Casy and Tom Joad have become more responsible and more purposeful than Pa Joad and Uncle John ever were: they love people so much that they are ready to die for them. Formerly the only unit of human love was the family, and the family remains the fundamental unit. The tragedy of *The Grapes of Wrath* consists in the breakup of the family. But the new moral of this novel is that the love of all people—if it be unselfish— may even supersede the love of family. So Casy dies for his people, and Tom is ready to, and Rose of Sharon symbolically transmutes her maternal love to a love of all people. Here is a new realization of "the word democratic, the word en-masse."

III

"An' I got to thinkin', Ma—most of the preachin' is about the poor we shall have always with us, an' if you got nothin', why, jus' fol' your hands an' to hell with it, you gonna git ice cream on gol' plates when you're dead. An' then this here Preacher says two get a better reward for their work" (p. 571).

Catholic Christianity had always preached humility and passive obedience. Protestantism preached spiritual nonconformity, but kept its disobedience passive. Transcendentalism sought to save the individual but not the group. ("Are they *my* poor?" asked Emerson.) Whitman sympathized more deeply with the common people and loved them abstractly, but trusted that

God and democracy would save them. The pragmatic philoso-
phers first sought to implement American idealism by making
thought itself instrumental. And now Steinbeck quotes scripture to urge popular action for the realization of the old ideals.

In the course of the book Steinbeck develops and translates
the thought of the earlier pragmatists. "Thinking," wrote John
Dewey, "is a kind of activity which we perform at specific
need." And Steinbeck repeats: "Need is the stimulus to concept, concept to action" (p. 207). The cause of the Okies' migration is their need, and their migration itself becomes a kind
of thinking—an unconscious groping for the solution to a half-
formulated problem. Their need becomes the stimulus to
concept.

In this novel a kind of pragmatic thinking takes place before
our eyes: the idea develops from the predicament of the characters, and the resulting action becomes integral with the
thought. The evils of absentee ownership produce the mass
migration, and the mass migration results in the idea of group
action: "A half-million people moving over the country. . . .
And tractors turning the multiple furrows in the vacant land"
(p. 207).

But what good is generalized thought? And how is future action to be planned? Americans in general, and pragmatists in
particular, have always disagreed in answering these questions.
William James argued that thought was good only in so far as it
satisfied a particular need and that plans, like actions, were
"plural"—and should be conceived and executed individually.
But Charles Sanders Peirce, and the transcendentalists before
him, had argued that the most generalized thought was best,
provided it eventually resulted in effective action. The problems of mankind should be considered as a unified whole,
monistically.

Now Tom Joad is a pluralist—a pragmatist after William
James. Tom said, "I'm still layin' my dogs down one at a time."
Casy replied: "Yeah, but when a fence comes up at ya, ya gonna
climb that fence." "I climb fences when I got fences to climb,"

said Tom. But Jim Casy believes in looking far ahead and seeing the thing as a whole: "But they's different kinda fences.
They's folks like me that climbs fences that ain't even strang up
yet" (p. 237). Which is to say that Casy is a kind of transcendental pragmatist. His thought seeks to generalize the problems
of the Okies and to integrate them with the larger problem of
industrial America. His solution is the principle of group action
guided by conceptual thought and functioning within the
framework of democratic society and law.

And at the end of the story Tom Joad becomes converted to
Jim Casy's pragmatism. It is not important that the particular
strike should be won, or that the particular need should be
satisfied; but it is important that men should think in terms of
action, and that they should think and act in terms of the whole
rather than the particular individual. "For every little beaten
strike is proof that the step is being taken" (p. 205). The value
of an idea lies not in its immediate but in its eventual success.
That idea is good which works—in the long run.

But the point of the whole novel is that action is an absolute
essential of human life. If need and failure produce only fear,
disintegration follows. But if they produce anger, then reconstruction may follow. The grapes of wrath must be trampled to
make manifest the glory of the Lord. At the beginning of the
story Steinbeck described the incipient wrath of the defeated
farmers. At the end he repeats the scene. "And where a number of men gathered together, the fear went from their faces,
and anger took its place. And the women sighed with relief . . .
the break would never come as long as fear could turn to
wrath" (p. 592). Then wrath could turn to action.

IV

To sum up: the fundamental idea of *The Grapes of Wrath*
is that of American transcendentalism: "Maybe all men got one
big soul ever'body's a part of" (p. 33). From this idea it follows
that every individual will trust those instincts which he shares

with all men, even when these conflict with the teachings of orthodox religion and of existing society. But his self-reliance will
not merely seek individual freedom, as did Emerson. It will
rather seek social freedom or mass democracy, as did Whitman.
If this mass democracy leads to the abandonment of genteel
taboos and to the modification of some traditional ideas of morality, that is inevitable. But whatever happens, the American
will act to realize his ideals. He will seek to make himself whole
—i.e., to join himself to other men by means of purposeful actions for some goal beyond himself.

But at this point the crucial question arises—and it is "crucial" in every sense of the word. What if this self-reliance lead
to death? What if the individual is killed before the social
group is saved? Does the failure of the individual action invali-
date the whole idea? "How'm I gonna know about you?" Ma
asks. "They might kill ya an' I wouldn't know."

The answer has already been suggested by the terms in which
the story has been told. If the individual has identified himself
with the oversoul, so that his life has become one with the life
of all men, his individual death and failure will not matter.
From the old transcendental philosophy of identity to Tom
Joad and the moving pictures may seem a long way, but even
the movies faithfully reproduced Tom's final declaration of
transcendental faith: "They might kill ya," Ma had objected.

"Tom laughed uneasily, 'Well, maybe like Casy says, a fella
ain't got a soul of his own, but on'y a piece of a big one—an'
then—'

" 'Then what, Tom?'

" 'Then it don' matter. Then I'll be aroun' in the dark. I'll
be ever'where—wherever you look. Wherever they's a fight so
hungry people can eat, I'll be there. Wherever they's a cop
beating up a guy, I'll be there. If Casy knowed, why, I'll be in
the way guys yell when they're mad, an'—I'll be in the way kids
laugh when they're hungry an' they know supper's ready. An'
when our folks eat the stuff they raise an' live in the houses
they build—why, I'll be there. See?' " (p. 572).

For the first time in history, *The Grapes of Wrath* brings together and makes real three great skeins of American thought. It begins with the transcendental oversoul, Emerson's faith in the common man, and his Protestant self-reliance. To this it joins Whitman's religion of the love of all men and his mass democracy. And it combines these mystical and poetic ideas with the realistic philosophy of pragmatism and its emphasis on effective action. From this it develops a new kind of Christianity—not otherworldly and passive, but earthly and active. And Oklahoma Jim Casy and the Joads think and do all these philosophical things.

$$\diamond$$

CHESTER E. EISINGER

Chester E. Eisinger has taught at the University of Michigan and Purdue University. His publications include two books on the 1940s, *Fiction of the Forties* and *The 1940's: Profile of a Nation in Crisis*, as well as various essays on American literature and culture.

Jeffersonian Agrarianism in
The Grapes of Wrath

In a brilliant and provocative essay written in 1941,[1] Frederic I. Carpenter found three significant American ideas running through John Steinbeck's novel, *The Grapes of Wrath*: the transcendentalism of Emerson, the democracy of Whitman, and the pragmatic instrumentalism of James and Dewey. To this distinguished company of thinkers and doctrines that molded Steinbeck's thought and attitudes I should like to add the agrarianism of Jefferson. The philosophic ideas considered by Carpenter are conveyed to the reader through Jim Casy's talk and the Joads' actions. Casy, however, has nothing to do with the agrarianism in the novel. It emanates from the Joads and other dispossessed farmers, from the people. It is theirs and Steinbeck's; and it is a noble, traditionally popular ideal, standing as an anachronism in the midst of the machine-made culture of twentieth century America—a culture sick and foundering in depression when Steinbeck wrote this novel.

A discussion of the agrarianism in *The Grapes of Wrath*

---

[1] Reprinted in this book, pp. 708–719.—ED.

Reprinted from *The University of Kansas City Review*, XIV (Winter 1947), 149–154. By permission of the publisher and Chester E. Eisinger.

does not pretend to serve as an interpretation of the entire novel. Nevertheless, it is my conviction that this doctrine is no less important than the other ideologies dramatized in the novel. As a matter of fact, agrarianism is closely associated with what was apparently one of the primary motives for writing the book, the desire to protest against the harsh inequities of the financial-industrial system that had brought chaos to America in the thirties. At times Steinbeck, with his curious combination of humanism and mysticism, seems to propose the substitution of agrarianism for industrialism as an antidote for what ailed the country.

During the disastrous thirties there were others who saw flaws in our economic system and had a similar solution. The manner, almost purposefulness, with which a financial-industrial society had encouraged moral and cultural aridity, even when successful in terms of production, prompted twelve Southerners to publish in 1930 *I'll Take My Stand*, a clarion call issued on a shepherd's pipe, summoning us back to the land and the somewhat feudal and gentlemanly traditions of the plantation days. In short, the Southern Agrarians were offering a positive program to place over against finance capitalism even before the full effects of the depression had been felt, and they continued their agitation in *The American Review*, a journal that flourished in this decade. This period saw also the growth of the back-to-the-farm movement and the proliferation of books guaranteeing independence, and even security, on five acres.

I am not suggesting that Steinbeck was influenced by the Southerners or anyone else, but only that in this period of crumbling faiths many men turned to agrarianism as others turned to the Townsend Plan or Huey Long. Naturally, the men in the agrarian group had much in common, and certainly all of them drew upon Jeffersonian agrarianism. Because he had faith in the common man and thus gave his thinking a broad popular basis, Steinbeck was closer to Jeffersonianism than were the Southern Agrarians, who sought to resurrect not only an agricultural way of life but also the traditional cultural values of Europe. Steinbeck was concerned with democracy, and looked upon agrarianism as a way of life that would enable us to realize the full potentialities of the creed. Jefferson, of course, held the same belief.

In order to clarify the full impact of Jeffersonian thought on Steinbeck, it is necessary at least to adumbrate the nature of eighteenth century agrarianism in America. This was a doctrine informed by the spirit and principles of Jefferson. Basic to it is the belief that landed property held in freehold must be available to everyone. Jefferson took seriously his middle-class heritage from Locke, placing great faith in property and the property holder. To him, equalitarian democracy meant a country made up of small farmers, and in fighting for the abolition of entail and primogeniture in Virginia he tried to achieve a commonwealth dominated by precisely this group. Although Jefferson himself never went so far, many Jeffersonians agreed that if a man could not get legal title to landed property, he could claim ownership to land he occupied and tilled by virtue of a natural right. Possession of his own land gave the small farmer control of the means of production. It followed therefore that such a man could be economically independent, for he would be obligated to no man, he could reap what he sowed, and his agricultural way of life would make for a relatively high degree of self-sufficiency. It also followed that such a man would be politically independent, inasmuch as no one held a coercive power over him; no part of his way of life or his security was threatened by an outside force. The independent freehold farmer was a complete individualist, so the Jeffersonian myth goes, who acted in accordance with his own instincts or desires and rose or fell by virtue of his own efforts. Mostly he rose because he was a moral man; God had made his breast "His peculiar deposit for substantial and genuine virtue." History does not record the corruption of an agricultural people. In other words, agrarianism has a sprinkling of primitivism. Close contact with nature and with God makes and

keeps men pure. By contrast the city is a cesspool of evil.
Immorality thrives there, alongside of business and finance.
These latter rob the common man of economic and political
independence and destroy the dominant position of the farmer
in the affairs of the state. Jeffersonian agrarianism, then,
was essentially democratic: it insisted on the widespread ownership of property, on political and economic independence, on
individualism; it created a society in which every individual
had status; it made the dignity of man something more than a
political slogan.[2]

II

Seven books preceded *The Grapes of Wrath*, but in only one
of them do we have any foretaste of Steinbeck's predilection for
agrarianism. True, in *The Pastures of Heaven, To a God Unknown*, and *The Long Valley* he had dealt with tillers of the
soil and with ranchers, but in these books he was preoccupied
with psychological analysis, and the tone was mystical and
nostalgic. Although dealing with agricultural workers, *In Dubious Battle* is concerned essentially with a strike and a scientist.
But *Of Mice and Men* shows clearly Steinbeck's interest in
agrarianism, even though he is still haunted by psychological
abnormality.

In this latter book we have the disenchanted and disinherited
if not the dispossessed of *The Grapes of Wrath*. Lennie and
George, migratory workers in the California fields, cherish the
dream of a little farm of their own where, as Lennie's refrain
has it, they can *"live off the fatta the lan'."* George yearns for
his own place where he could bring in his own crops, where
he could get what comes up out of the ground. He wants the
full reward of his own labor. He wants the independence that
ownership can give him. Nobody could fire him if the farm

---

[2] What has been summarized here as the Jeffersonian myth and Jeffer-
sonian agrarianism has been dealt with more thoroughly in the author's
"The Freehold Concept in Eighteenth-Century American Letters," *The
William and Mary Quarterly*, 3rd ser., IV (Jan. 1947), 42–59.

were his. If someone came he didn't like, he could say, " 'Get the hell out,' and by God he's got to do it." They would produce all they could eat, and then: "We'd jus' live there. We'd belong there. . . . We'd have our own place where we belonged and not sleep in no bunk house." A stake in society and status in society—these give men the dignity that is rightfully theirs in a democracy. Productive property, Steinbeck seems to suggest, is a real restorative. Even Candy, the used up sweeper, and Crooks, the misshapen Negro, are reinvigorated by the prospect of ownership and stability.

Of Mice and Men, however, was a sentimental and slight book. Three years later, in The Grapes of Wrath, Steinbeck was able to present a fuller exposition of his agrarian views. Early in the novel he introduces the conflict between the farmer and the financial-industrial interests of the city. The truck driver remarks to Tom that the tractors are pushing the croppers off the land. The full significance of this observation is not apparent until we come to the fifth chapter. Here Steinbeck makes clear that the tractors are the instruments of a mysterious financial system, just as some men represent that system. These men are deprived of will and personality by the system and its machine. When they must tell the croppers to get off the land, they shed their humanity and take refuge in the cold mathematics of the system. From now on there will be a tractor and a superintendent on the land, not the people. And the land will be raped methodically, without passion. It will be productive because it yields a crop, but it will be sterile too because no one loves or hates it and because it will bear under iron and die under iron. The sterility of machine culture is emphasized by Steinbeck's comment, much later in the book, on the languid, heat-raddled ladies, parasites on that culture, whose sexual intercourse is safe, odorless, and unproductive (pp. 210–211). The animosity to the city is emphasized in the bitter attitude toward business ethics, summed up best perhaps in the incident of the tire with the broken casing. "You go steal that tire an' you're a thief, but he tried to steal your four dollars for a busted tire. They call that sound business" (p. 164). Finally, Steinbeck remarks how the business men farmers, those who keep books but never follow the plow, buy up the canneries in California, cut off the small farmer's market, and eventually take the property away from him (p. 387). Chiefly in negative terms Steinbeck is showing us that the farmer is the productive, healthy member of society. He suggests a primitivistic conception of nature: that the farmer draws spiritual strength as well as sustenance from the soil. Antithetical to these notions is the aridity of the city-bred rich woman, the dishonesty of business, and the essentially inhuman and unproductive nature of the machine age.

Precisely what was it that this sick business culture was destroying? Very briefly it was a way of life that was based on the retention of the land. The Okies had their roots deep in the land, and they didn't want to be shoved off it. Grampa took up the land, and Pa was born here, and we were born here. It's our land. "We measured it and broke it up. We were born on it, and we got killed on it, died on it. Even if it's no good, it's still ours. That's what makes it ours—being born on it, working it, dying on it. That makes ownership, not a paper with numbers on it" (p. 45). The Okies argue, in other words, that occupying the land and devoting one's labor to it are the criteria of ownership, and that these transcend the legal right to the land represented by the title. These two criteria are the backbone of the natural right argument current in the eighteenth century: men had a natural right to as much land as they could profitably use. This natural right assumption gave sanction to the squatter whose heritage passed down into the nineteenth century, and even into the twentieth. For when the Okies want to work a little patch of ground lying fallow, the California police chase them off. "You goddamned squatters. Pretty soon you'd think you owned it. You'd be sore as hell. Think you owned it. Get off now . . . the cop was right. A crop raised—why, that makes ownership" (p. 321).

When you are shoved off the land and can exercise neither a

legal nor a natural right to possess land, then you have lost status and your life has lost meaning. There is a kind of mystic exaltation in the ownership of property which the farmer experiences. Crévecœur called it "the bright idea of property." Steinbeck's anonymous tenant knows it too. " 'If a man owns a little property, that property is him, it's part of him, and it's like him. If he owns property only so he can walk on it and handle it and be sad when it isn't doing well, and feel fine when the rain falls on it, that property is him, and some way he's bigger because he owns it' " (p. 50). So, then, is he smaller when he loses it? When the tractor knocked over the elder Tom's house and drove him from the land, it took something out of him; he was never the same. Grampa can't survive the loss of the homestead. At the last moment he refuses to leave. " 'This country ain't no good, but it's my country' " (p. 152). When he dies en route to California, Casy says shrewdly, " 'An' Grampa didn' die tonight. He died the minute you took 'im off the place' " (p. 199). If Grampa could not survive being torn up by the roots, at least he escaped the indignities that the others must endure because they are landless. They are called bums by the proprietor of a camping ground; Pa mildly protests. "It's dirt hard for folks to tear up an' go. Folks like us that had our place. We ain't shif'less. Till we got tractored off, we was people with a farm" (p. 256). We were cropping, but we used to own the land. Pa must remind himself and the others that nobody calls a freehold farmer a shiftless bum. He is a broken man who must find solace in the past. Ma, too, recalls the dignity of the Joad heritage. "We don't look up to nobody. Grampa's grampa, he fit in the Revolution. We was farm people till the debt. And then—them people. They done somepin to us . . . made me feel mean. Made me feel ashamed" (p. 420). They—the California police, the owners of the orchards—had worked on the spirit of the Okies and worn it down. The pride of the freeholder withers after dispossession, and his function in life disappears.

The way of life normal to the farmer is the productive life. Fallow land, when men are starving, is a sin. The uniform impulse among the Okies is to get hold of an acre and make something grow on it. In this way they hope to gain some slight measure of security. Unfortunately, the California land has all been "stolen" by the early American settlers who took it from the Mexicans. "They put up houses and barns, they turned the earth and planted crops. And these things were possession, and possession was ownership" (p. 315). Those who were now the great owners had exercised a natural right to get the land, and now they held it, aware that "when property accumulates in too few hands it is taken away" (p. 324). In a dynamic American society, the feverish Americans who had utilized a radical doctrine to gain the land had now become the conservative, stable element while a new radical group arose, the dispossessed Okies. Now these latter wanted the land. The Okies are Steinbeck's protagonists in a kind of revolutionary social action which is as American as Jefferson's successful efforts to abolish entail and primogeniture; and this action would yield the same results—a wider distribution of property. Thus it is that when Tom takes his last leave of Ma, going forth to carry on the work of Casy, who has died a martyr to the cause of social justice, he reflects on the Okie-run government camp where there was better order than the police had ever been able to establish in areas of their jurisdiction. "I been awonderin' why we can't do that all over. Throw out the cops that ain't our people. All work together for our own thing—all farm our own lan'." But what are you going to do? demands the practical Ma. "I been thinkin' a hell of a lot, thinkin' about our people livin' like pigs, an' the good rich lan' layin' fallow, or maybe one fella with a million acres, while a hundred thousan' good farmers is starvin'. An' I been wonderin' if all our folks got together an' yelled, like them fellas yelled, only a few of 'em at the Hooper ranch . . ." (p. 571). The democratic way for Steinbeck is to achieve through collective action the individual security on the land that Jefferson prized so highly. When men farm their own land they will run their own society.

III

It is clear, I think, that Steinbeck has much in common with Jeffersonian agrarianism and that he is attracted to the doctrine because he has the same humanistic interest in democracy that Jefferson had. It remains to inquire if agrarianism, its form and substance, is the part of the Jeffersonian tradition that we should preserve. Certainly we could use today many of the virtues attributed to the independent yeoman by Jefferson. But I fear that we cannot use and cannot achieve agrarianism as a formal way of life. Its champions of the thirties have apparently realized the futility of running counter to the temper of the times. *The American Review* is dead, and pretty well buried in the libraries. Many of the Southern Agrarians have turned their backs on social problems and have become engrossed in an authoritarian kind of aesthetics.

Steinbeck himself, if we are to judge by *Cannery Row* and *The Wayward Bus*, has abandoned any serious consideration of the problems of political economy.

The bankruptcy of Jefferson's ideal is only too well illustrated in the fact that the family size farm continues to disappear from the American scene. It would seem that the survival of an idea, or even its resurrection in troubled times, is no proof of its validity. In the great war just passed we have seen the triumph of American capitalism (Louis Hacker's phrase) and of American industrial strength. The machine age, or the atomic age, is fastened upon us and growing apace. Almost alone now, Louis Bromfield is repeating the axioms of the Physiocrats and calling us back to the land. Nobody listens.

We must seek another road to the independence and security and dignity that we expect from democracy.

PETER LISCA

Peter Lisca has taught at the Woman's College of the University of North Carolina, the University of Washington, and the University of Florida. He is the author of *The Wide World of John Steinbeck* and numerous articles appearing in *PMLA, Modern Fiction Studies, Twentieth Century Literature,* and various collections of essays.

The Grapes of Wrath as Fiction

When *The Grapes of Wrath* was published in April of 1939 there was little likelihood of its being accepted and evaluated as a piece of fiction. Because of its nominal subject, it was too readily confused with such high-class reporting as Ruth McKenny's *Industrial Valley,* the WPA collection of case histories called *These Are Our Lives,* and Dorothea Lange and Paul S. Taylor's *An American Exodus.* The merits of *The Grapes of Wrath* were debated as social documentation rather than fiction. In addition to incurring the disadvantages of its historical position, coming as a kind of climax to the literature of the Great Depression, Steinbeck's novel also suffered from the perennial vulnerability of all social fiction to an attack on its facts and intentions.

The passage of eighteen years has done very little to alter this initial situation. Except for scattered remarks, formal criticism of *The Grapes of Wrath* is still pretty much limited to a chapter by Joseph Warren Beach, a chapter by Harry Thornton Moore, a few paragraphs by Kenneth Burke, part of a chapter by the French critic Claude-Edmonde Magny, and an essay by

Reprinted from *PMLA*, LXXII (March 1957), 296–309. By permission of the Modern Language Association. Copyright © 1957 by the Modern Language Association.

B. R. McElderry, Jr. In a period of such intensive analysis of the techniques of fiction as the past fifteen years, the dearth of critical material on *The Grapes of Wrath* must indicate an assumption on the part of critics that this novel cannot sustain such analysis. The present paper is an attempt to correct this assumption by exploring some of the techniques by which John Steinbeck was able to give significant form to his sprawling materials and prevent his novel of social protest from degenerating into propaganda.

The ideas and materials of *The Grapes of Wrath* presented Steinbeck with a problem of structure similar to that of Tolstoy's in writing *War and Peace*. Tolstoy's materials were, roughly, the adventures of the Bezukhov, Rostov, and Bolkonski families on the one hand, and the Napoleonic Wars on the other. And while the plot development brought these two blocks of material together, there was enough about the Napoleonic Wars left over so that the author had to incorporate it in separate philosophic interchapters. Steinbeck's materials were similar. There were the adventures of the Joads, the Wilsons, and the Wainwrights; there was also the Great Depression. And like Tolstoy, he had enough material left over to write separate philosophic interchapters.

In the light of this basic analogy, Percy Lubbock's comments on the structural role of these two elements in *War and Peace* become significant for an understanding of structure in *The Grapes of Wrath*: "I can discover no angle at which the two stories will appear to unite and merge in a single impression. Neither is subordinated to the other, and there is nothing above them . . . to which they are both related. Nor are they placed together to illustrate a contrast; nothing *results* from their juxtaposition. Only from time to time, upon no apparent principle and without a word of warning, one of them is dropped and the other is resumed."[1] In these few phrases Lubbock has defined the aesthetic conditions not only for *War*

---

[1] *The Craft of Fiction* (New York: Peter Smith, 1945), p. 33.

and Peace but for any other piece of fiction whose strategies include an intercalary construction—*The Grapes of Wrath,* for example. The test is whether anything *results* from this kind of structure.

Counting the opening description of the drought and the penultimate chapter on the rains, pieces of straightforward description allowable even to strictly "scenic" novels (Lubbock's term for materials presented entirely from the reader's point of view), there are in *The Grapes of Wrath* sixteen interchapters, making up a total of just under a hundred pages— almost one sixth of the book. In none of these chapters do the Joads, Wilsons, or Wainwrights appear.

These interchapters have two main functions. First, by presenting the social background they serve to amplify the pattern of action created by the Joad family. Thus, for example, Chapter i presents in panoramic terms the drought which forces the Joads off their land; Chapters vii and ix depict, respectively, the buying of jalopies for the migration and the selling of household goods; Chapter xi describes at length a decaying and deserted house which is the prototype of all the houses abandoned in the Dust Bowl. In thirteen such chapters almost every aspect of the Joads's adventures is enlarged and seen as part of the social climate. The remaining interchapters have the function of providing such historical information as the development of land ownership in California, the consequent development of migrant labor, and certain economic aspects of the social lag. These three informative chapters make up only nineteen of the novel's six hundred-odd pages. Scattered through the sixteen interchapters are occasional paragraphs whose purpose is to present, with choric effect, the philosophy or social message to which the current situation gives rise. For the most part these paragraphs occur in four chapters—ix, xi, xiv, and xix.

While all of these various materials are obviously ideologically related to the longer narrative section of the novel (five hundred pages), there remains the problem of their aesthetic integration with the book as a whole. Even a cursory reading will show that there is a general correspondence between the material of each interchapter and that of the current narrative portion. The magnificent opening description of the drought sets forth the condition which gives rise to the novel's action; Highway 66 is given a chapter as the Joads begin their trek on that historic route; the chapters dealing with migrant life appear interspersed with the narrative of the Joads's actual journey; the last interchapter, xxix, describes the rain in which the action of the novel ends.

A more careful reading will make evident that this integration of the interchapters into a total structure goes far beyond this merely complementary juxtaposition. There is in addition an intricate interweaving of specific details. Like the anonymous house in the interchapter (v), one corner of the Joad house has been knocked off its foundation by a tractor (pp. 52–53, 54). The man who in the interchapter threatens the tractor driver with his rifle becomes Grampa Joad, except that whereas the anonymous tenant does not fire, Grampa shoots out both headlights (pp. 53, 62). The tractor driver in the interchapter, Joe Davis, is a family acquaintance of the anonymous tenants, as Willy is an acquaintance of the Joads in the narrative chapter (pp. 50, 62). The jalopy sitting in the Joads's front yard is the same kind of jalopy described in the used-car lot of Chapter vii. Chapter viii ends with Al Joad driving off to sell a truckload of household goods. Chapter ix is an interchapter describing anonymous farmers selling such goods, including many items which the Joads themselves are selling—pumps, farming tools, furniture, a team and wagon for ten dollars. In the following chapter Al Joad returns with an empty truck, having sold everything for eighteen dollars—including ten dollars for a team and wagon. Every interchapter is tied into the book's narrative portion by this kind of specific cross reference, which amplifies the Joads's typical actions to the level of a communal experience.

Often, this interlocking of details becomes thematic or symbolic. The dust which is mentioned twenty-seven times in three pages of Chapter i comes to stand not only for the land itself but also for the basic situation out of which the novel's action develops. Everything which moves on the ground, from insects to trucks, raises a proportionate amount of dust: "a walking man lifted a thin layer as high as his waist" (p. 4). When Tom returns home after four years in prison and gets out of the truck which had given him a ride, he steps off the highway and performs the symbolic ritual of taking off his new, prison-issue shoes and carefully working his bare feet into the dust. He then moves off across the land, "making a cloud that hung low to the ground behind him" (p. 23).

One of the novel's most important symbols, the turtle, is presented in what is actually the first interchapter (iii). And while this chapter is a masterpiece of realistic description (often included as such in Freshman English texts), it is also obvious that the turtle is symbolic and its adventures prophetic allegory. "Nobody can't keep a turtle though," says Jim Casy. "They work at it and work at it, and at last one day they get out and away they go . . ." (p. 28). The indomitable life force that drives the turtle drives the Joads, and in the same direction—southwest. As the turtle picks up seeds in its shell and drops them on the other side of the road, so the Joads pick up life in Oklahoma and carry it across the country to California. (As Grandfather in "The Leader of the People" puts it, "We carried life out here and set it down the way those ants carry eggs.") As the turtle survives the truck's attempts to smash it on the highway and as it crushes the red ant which runs into its shell, so the Joads endure the perils of their journey.

This symbolic value is retained and further defined when the turtle enters specifically into the narrative. Its incident with the red ant is echoed two hundred and seventy pages later when another red ant runs over "the folds of loose skin" on Granma's neck and she reaches up with her "little wrinkled claws"; Ma Joad picks it off and crushes it (p. 286). In Chapter iii the turtle is seen "dragging his high-domed shell across the grass." In the next chapter, Tom sees "the high-domed back of a land turtle" and picking up the turtle, carries it with him (p. 24). It is only when he is convinced that his family has left the land that he releases the turtle, which travels "southwest as it had been from the first," a direction which is repeated in the next two sentences. The first thing which Tom does after releasing the turtle is to put on his shoes, which he had taken off when he left the highway and stepped onto the land (p. 60). Thus, not only the turtle but also Tom's connection with it is symbolic, as symbolic as Lennie's appearance in *Of Mice and Men* with a dead mouse in his pocket.

In addition to this constant knitting together of the two kinds of chapters, often the interchapters are further assimilated into the narrative portion by incorporating in themselves the techniques of fiction. The general conflict between small farmers and the banks, for example, is presented as an imaginary dialogue, each speaker personifying the sentiments of his group. And although neither speaker is a "real" person, both are dramatically differentiated and their arguments embody details particular to the specific social condition. This kind of dramatization is also evident in such chapters as those concerning the buying of used cars, the selling of household goods, the police intimidation of migrants, and others.

Because Steinbeck's subject in *The Grapes of Wrath* is not the adventures of the Joad family so much as the social conditions which occasion them, these interchapters serve a vital purpose. As Percy Lubbock has pointed out, the purely "scenic" technique "is out of the question . . . whenever the story is too big, too comprehensive, too widely ranging to be treated scenically, with no opportunity for general and panoramic survey. . . . These stories, therefore, which will not naturally accommodate themselves to the reader's point of view, and the reader's alone, we regard as rather pictorial than dramatic—meaning that they call for some narrator, somebody who *knows*, to contemplate the facts and create an impression of them [pp. 254–255]."

Steinbeck's story certainly is "big," "comprehensive," and "wide ranging." But although he tried to free his materials by utilizing what Lubbock calls "pictorial" as well as "scenic" techniques, he also took pains to keep these techniques from breaking the novel in two parts. The cross reference of detail, the interweaving symbols, and the dramatization are designed to make the necessary "pictorial" sections of the novel tend toward the "scenic." Conversely, an examination of the narrative portion of *The Grapes of Wrath* will reveal that its techniques make the "scenic" tend toward the "pictorial." Steinbeck worked from both sides to make the two kinds of chapters approach each other and fuse into a single impression.

That the narrative portion of *The Grapes of Wrath* tends toward the "pictorial" can be seen readily if the book is compared to another of Steinbeck's social novels, *In Dubious Battle*, which has a straightforward plot development and an involving action. Of course things happen in *The Grapes of Wrath*, and what happens not only grows out of what has gone before but grows into what will happen in the future. But while critics have perceived that plot is not the organizational principle of the novel, they have not attempted to relate this face to the novel's materials as they are revealed through other techniques, assuming instead that this lack of plot constitutes one of the novel's major flaws. Actually, this lack of an informing plot is instrumental in at least two ways. It could reasonably be expected that the greatest threat to the novel's unity would come from the interchapters' constant breaking up of the narrative line of action. But the very fact that *The Grapes of Wrath* is *not* organized by a unifying plot works for absorbing these interchapters smoothly into its texture. A second way in which this tendency of the "scenic" toward the "pictorial" is germane to the novel's materials becomes evident when it is considered that Steinbeck's subject is not an action so much as a situation. Description, therefore, must often substitute for narration.

This substitution of the static for the dynamic also gives us an insight into the nature and function of the novel's characters, who often have been called "puppets," "symbolic marion-

ettes," and "symbols," but seldom real people. While there are
scant objective grounds for determining whether a novel's characters are "real," one fruitful approach is to consider fictional
characters not only in relation to life but in relation to the *rest* of
the fiction of which they are a part.

In his Preface to *The Forgotten Village*, which immediately
followed *The Grapes of Wrath*, Steinbeck comments on just
these relationships.

A great many documentary films have used the generalized method,
that is, the showing of a condition or an event as it affects a group
of people. The audience can then have a personalized reaction from
imagining one member of that group. I have felt that this was the
more difficult observation from the audience's viewpoint. It means
very little to know that a million Chinese are starving unless you
know one Chinese who is starving. In *The Forgotten Village* we reversed the usual process. Our story centered on one family in one
small village. We wished our audience to know this family very well,
and incidentally to like it, as we did. Then, from association with
this little personalized group, the larger conclusion concerning the
racial group could be drawn with something like participation.[2]

This is precisely the strategy in *The Grapes of Wrath*. Whatever value the Joads have as individuals is "incidental" to their
primary function as a "personalized group." Kenneth Burke
has pointed out that "most of the characters derive their role,
which is to say their personality, purely from their relationship
to the basic situation." But what he takes to be a serious
weakness is actually one of the book's greatest accomplishments. The characters are so absorbed into the novel's "basic
situation" that the reader's response goes beyond sympathy
for individuals to moral indignation about their social condition. This is, of course, precisely Steinbeck's intention. And
certainly the Joads are admirably suited for this purpose. This
conception of character is parallel to the fusing of the "scenic"
and "pictorial" techniques in the narrative and interchapters.

---

[2] New York: The Viking Press, 1941.

Although the diverse materials of *The Grapes of Wrath* made organization by a unifying plot difficult, nevertheless the novel does have structural form. The action progresses through three successive movements, and its significance is revealed by an intricate system of themes and symbols.

The Grapes of Wrath is divided into thirty consecutive chapters with no larger grouping; but even a cursory reading reveals that the novel is made up of three major parts: the drought, the journey, and California. The first section ends with Chapter x (p. 156). It is separated from the second section, the journey, by *two* interchapters. The first of these chapters presents a final picture of the deserted land—"The houses were left vacant on the land, and the land was vacant because of this." The second interchapter is devoted to Highway 66. It is followed by Chapter xiii which begins the Joads's journey on that historic highway—"The ancient overloaded Hudson creaked and grunted to the highway at Sallisaw and turned west, and the sun was blinding" (p. 167). The journey section extends past the geographical California border, across the desert to Bakersfield (pp. 167–314). This section ends with Chapter xviii—"And the truck rolled down the mountain into the great valley"—and the next chapter begins the California section by introducing the reader to labor conditions in that state. Steinbeck had this tripartite division in mind as early as September of 1937, when he told one interviewer that he was working on "the first of three related longer novels."[3]

This structure has its roots in the Old Testament. The novel's three sections correspond to the oppression in Egypt, the exodus, and the sojourn in the land of Canaan, which in both accounts is first viewed from the mountains. The parallel is not worked out in detail, but the grand design is there: the plagues (erosion), the Egyptians (banks), the exodus (journey), and the hostile tribes of Canaan (Californians).

This Biblical structure is supported by a continuum of sym-

---

[3] Joseph Henry Jackson, "John Steinbeck: A Portrait," *Sat. Rev. of Lit.*, xvi (Sept. 25, 1937), 18.

bols and symbolic actions. The most pervasive symbolism is that of grapes. The novel's title, taken from "The Battle Hymn of the Republic" ("He is trampling out the vintage where the grapes of wrath are stored"), is itself a reference to Revelation: "And the angel thrust in his sickle into the earth, and gathered the vine of the earth, and cast it into the great winepress of the wrath of God" (xiv.19). Similarly in Deuteronomy: "Their grapes are grapes of gall, their clusters are bitter. Their wine is the poison of serpents" (xxxii.32); in Jeremiah: "The fathers have eaten sour grapes, and their children's teeth are set on edge" (xxxi.29). Sometimes these aspects of the symbol are stated in the novel's interchapters: "In the souls of the people the grapes of wrath are filling and growing heavy, heavy for the vintage" (pp. 388, 477).

But Steinbeck also uses grapes for symbols of plenty, as the one huge cluster of grapes which Joshua and Oshea bring back from their first excursion into the rich land of Canaan, a cluster so huge that "they bare it between two on a staff" (Num. xiii.23). It is this meaning of grapes that is frequently alluded to by Grampa Joad: "Gonna get me a whole big bunch of grapes off a bush, or whatever, an' I'm gonna squash 'em on my face an' let 'em run offen my chin" (p. 112). Although Grampa dies long before the Joads get to California, he is symbolically present through the anonymous old man in the barn (stable), who is saved from starvation by Rosasharn's breasts: "This thy stature is like to a palm tree, and thy breasts to clusters of grapes" (Cant. vii.7).[7] Rosasharn's giving of new life to the old man is another reference to the orthodox interpretation of Canticles: "I [Christ] am the rose of Sharon, and the lily of the valleys" (ii.1); and to the Gospels: "take, eat; this is my body." Still another important Biblical symbol is Jim Casy (Jesus Christ), who will be discussed in another connection.

---

[4] One of the oddest interpretations of this scene is that of Harry Sloch-ower, who uses this incident to explain the novel's title: "The grapes have turned to 'wrath,' indicated by the fact that the first milk of the mother is said to be bitter."

Closely associated with this latter symbolic meaning of grapes and the land of Canaan is Ma Joad's frequent assertion that "We are the people." She has not been reading Carl Sandburg; she has been reading her Bible. As Sairy tells Tom when he is looking for a suitable verse to bury with Grampa, "Turn to Psalms, over further. You kin always get somepin outa Psalms" (p. 195). And it is from Psalms that Ma gets her phrase: "For he is our God; and we are the people of his pasture, and the sheep of his hand" (xcv.7). They are the people who pick up life in Oklahoma (Egypt) and carry it to California (Canaan) as the turtle picks up seeds and as the ants pick up their eggs in "The Leader of the People." These parallels to the Hebrews of Exodus are all brought into focus when, near the end of the novel, Uncle John sets Rose of Sharon's stillborn child in an old apple crate (like Moses in the basket), sets the box in a stream "among the willow stems" and floats it toward the town saying, "Go down an' tell 'em" (p. 609).

As the Israelites developed a code of laws in their exodus, so do the migrants: "The families learned what rights must be observed—the right of privacy in the tent . . . the right of the hungry to be fed; the right of the pregnant and the sick to transcend all other rights" (p. 265). Chapter xvii can be seen as the "Deuteronomy" of *The Grapes of Wrath*. It is this kind of context which makes of the Joads's journey "out west" an archetype of mass migration.[5]

The novel's Biblical structure and symbolism are supported by Steinbeck's skillful use of an Old Testament prose. The extent to which he succeeded in re-creating the epic dignity of this prose can be demonstrated by arranging a typical passage from the novel according to phrases, in the manner of the Bates Bible, leaving the punctuation intact except for capitals.

[5] Bernard Bowron fails to perceive this larger significance of the Joads's journey and attempts to make far too much out of some obvious similarities to the Covered Wagon genre.

> The tractors had lights shining,
> For there is no day and night for a tractor
> And the disks turn the earth in the darkness
> And they glitter in the daylight.
>
> And when a horse stops work and goes into the barn
> There is a life and a vitality left,
> There is a breathing and a warmth,
> And the feet shift on the straw,
> And the jaws champ on the hay,
> And the ears and the eyes are alive.
> There is a warmth of life in the barn,
> And the heat and smell of life.
>
> But when the motor of a tractor stops,
> It is as dead as the ore it came from.
> The heat goes out of it
> Like the living heat that leaves a corpse. (p. 157)

The parallel grammatical structure of parallel meanings, the simplicity of diction, the balance, the concrete details, the summary sentences, the reiterations—all are here. Note also the organization: four phrases for the tractor, eight for the horse, four again for the tractor. Except for the terms of machinery, this passage might be one of the psalms.

It is this echo—more, this pedal point—evident even in the most obviously "directed" passages, which supports their often simple philosophy, imbuing them with a dignity which their content alone could not sustain. The style gives them their authority:

Burn coffee for fuel in the ships. Burn corn to keep warm, it makes a hot fire. Dump potatoes in the rivers and place guards along the banks to keep the hungry people from fishing them out. Slaughter the pigs and bury them, and let the putrescence drip down into the earth.

There is a crime here that goes beyond denunciation. There is a sorrow here that weeping cannot symbolize. There is a failure here that topples all our success. The fertile earth, the straight tree rows, the sturdy trunks, and the ripe fruit. And children dying of pellagra must die because a profit cannot be taken from an orange. (p. 477)

These passages are not complex philosophy, but they may well be profound. The Biblical resonance which gives them authority is used discreetly, is never employed on the trivial and particular, and its recurrence has a cumulative effect.

There are many other distinct prose styles in the interchapters of *The Grapes of Wrath*, and each is just as functional in its place. There is, for example, the harsh, staccato prose of Chapter vii, which is devoted to the sale of used cars.

Cadillacs, La Salles, Buicks, Plymouths, Packards, Chevvies, Fords, Pontiacs. Row on row, headlights glinting in the afternoon sun. Good Used Cars.

Soften 'em up Joe. Jesus, I wisht I had a thousand jalopies! Get 'em ready to deal, and I'll close 'em.

Goin' to California? Here's jus' what you need. Looks shot, but they's thousan's of miles in her.

Lined up side by side. Good Used Cars. Bargains. Clean runs good. (p. 89)

A good contrast to this prose style is offered by Chapter ix, which presents the loss and despair of people forced to abandon their household goods. Here the prose style itself takes on their dazed resignation.

The women sat among the doomed things, turning them over and looking past them and back. This book. My father had it. He liked a book. *Pilgrim's Progress*. Used to read it. Got his name in it. And his pipe—still smells rank. And this picture—an angel. I looked at that before the fust three come—didn't seem to do much good. Think we could get this china dog in? Aunt Sadie brought it from the St. Louis Fair. See? Wrote right on it. No, I guess not. Here's a letter my brother wrote the day before he died. Here's an old-time hat. These feathers—never got to use them. No, there isn't room. (p. 120)

At times, as in the description of a folk dance in Chapter xxiii, the prose style becomes a veritable chameleon: "Look at that Texas boy, long legs loose, taps four times for ever' damn step. Never see a boy swing aroun' like that. Look at him swing that Cherokee girl, red in cheeks and her toe points out" (p. 449). No other American novel has succeeded in forging and making instrumental so many prose styles.

This rapid shifting of prose style and technique has value as Americana and contributes to a "realism" far beyond that of literal reporting. Also, this rapid shifting is important because it tends to destroy any impression that these interchapters are, as a group, a separate entity. They are a group only in that they are not a direct part of the narrative. They have enough individuality of subject matter, prose style, and technique to keep the novel from falling into two parts, and to keep the reader from feeling that he is now reading "the other part."

In addition to the supporting Biblical structure and context, the interchapters and narrative section are held together by an interweaving of two opposing themes which make up the "plot" of *The Grapes of Wrath*. One of these, the negative one, concerns itself with the increasingly straitened circumstances of the Joads. At the beginning of their journey they have $154, their household goods, two barrels of pork, a serviceable truck, and their good health. As the novel progresses they become more and more impoverished until at the end they are destitute, without food, sick, their truck and goods abandoned in the mud, without shelter, and without hope of work. This economic decline is paralleled by a disintegration of the family's morale. The Joads start off as a cheerful group full of hope and will power and by the end of the novel are spiritually bankrupt. As Steinbeck had noted about the migrants around Bakersfield three years earlier, they "feel that paralyzed dullness with which the mind protects itself against too much sorrow and too much pain."[6] When the Joads enter their first Hooverville they catch a glimpse of the deterioration which lies ahead of them. They see filthy tin and rug shacks littered with

[6] "The Harvest Gypsies."

trash, the children dirty and diseased, the heads of families "bull-simple" from being roughed-up too often, all spirit gone and in its place a whining, passive resistance to authority. Although the novel ends before the Joads come to this point, in the last chapter they are well on their way.

And as the family group declines morally and economically, so the family unit itself breaks up. Grampa dies before they are out of Oklahoma and lies in a nameless grave; Granma is buried a pauper; Noah deserts the family; Connie deserts Rosasharn; the baby is born dead; Tom becomes a fugitive; Al is planning to leave as soon as possible; Casy is killed; and they are forced to abandon the Wilsons.

These two negative or downward movements are balanced by two positive or upward movements. Although the primitive family unit is breaking up, the fragments are going to make up a larger group. The sense of a communal unit grows steadily through the narrative—the Wilsons, the Wainwrights—and is pointed to again and again in the interchapters: "One man, one family driven from the land; this rusty car creaking along the highway to the west. I lost my land, a single tractor took my land. I am alone and I am bewildered. And in the night one family camps in a ditch and another family pulls in and the tents come out. The two men squat on their hams and the women and children listen. . . . For here 'I lost my land' is changed; a cell is split and from its splitting grows the thing you [owners] hate—'We lost *our* land' " (p. 206). Oppression and intimidation only serve to strengthen the social group; the relief offered by a federal migrant camp only gives them a vision of the democratic life they can attain by cooperation, which is why the local citizens are opposed to these camps.

Another of the techniques by which Steinbeck develops this theme of unity can be illustrated by the Joads's relationship with the Wilson family of Kansas, which they meet just before crossing the Oklahoma border. This relationship is developed not so much by explicit statement, as in the interchapters, as by symbols. Grampa Joad, for example, dies in the Wilsons' tent and is buried in one of the Wilsons' blankets. Furthermore, the epitaph which is buried with Grampa (in Oklahoma soil) is written on a page torn from the Wilsons' Bible—that page usually reserved for family births, marriages, and deaths. In burying this page with Grampa the Wilsons symbolize not only their adoption of the Joads, but their renouncing of hope for continuing their own family line. Also, note it is the more destitute Wilson family which embraces the Joads. Steinbeck makes of the two families' relationship a microcosm of the migration's total picture, its human significance.

This growing awareness on the part of the people en masse is paralleled by the education and conversion of Tom and Casy. At the beginning of the book, Tom's attitude is individualistic. He is looking out for himself. As he puts it, "I'm still laying my dogs down one at a time," and "I climb fences when I got fences to climb" (p. 237). His first real lesson comes when Casy strikes out against the trooper to save his friend and then gives himself up in his place (p. 361). The section immediately following is that of the family's stay in a federal migrant camp, and here Tom's education is advanced still further. By the time Casy is killed, Tom is ready for his conversion, which he seals by revenging his mentor. While Tom is hiding out in the cave after having struck the vigilante, he has time to think of Casy and his message, so that in his last meeting with his mother, in which he asserts his spiritual unity with all men, it is evident that he has moved from material and personal resentment to ethical indignation, from particulars to principles. It is significant that this last meeting between mother and son should take place under conditions reminiscent of the prenatal state. The entrance to the cave is covered with black vines and the interior is damp and completely dark, so that the contact of mother and son is actually physical rather than visual; she gives him food. When Tom comes out of the cave after announcing his conversion it is as though he were reborn. When Tom says, "An' when our folks eat the stuff they raise an' live in the houses they build—why I'll be there" (p. 572), he is paraphrasing Isaiah: "And they shall build houses and inhabit them, they shall not build and another inhabit; they shall not plant and another eat" (LXV, 21–22).

The development of Jim Casy is similar to that of Tom. He moves from Bible-belt evangelism to social prophecy. At the beginning of the book he has already left preaching and has returned from "in the hills, thinkin', almost you might say like Jesus went into the wilderness to think His way out of a mess of troubles" (p. 109). But although Casy is already approaching his revelation of the Over-Soul, it is only through his experiences with the Joads that he is able to complete his vision. As Tom moves from material resentment to ethical indignation, so Casy moves from the purely speculative to the pragmatic. Both move from stasis to action. Casy's Christlike development is complete when he dies saying, "You don' know what you're a doin'" (p. 527). Those critics are reading superficially who, like Elizabeth N. Monroe, think that Steinbeck "expects us to admire Casy, an itinerant preacher, who, over-excited from his evangelistic revivals, is in the habit of taking one or another of the girls in his audience to lie in the grass." Actually, Casy himself perceives the incongruity of this behavior, which is why he goes "into the wilderness" and renounces his Bible-belt evangelism for a species of social humanism, and his congregation for the human race. His development, like that of Tom, is symbolic of the changing social condition which is the novel's essential theme, paralleling the development of the Joad family as a whole, which is, again, but a "personalized group." Casy resembles Ralph Waldo Emerson more than he does Lewis' Elmer Gantry or Caldwell's Semon Dye. For like Emerson, Casy discovers the Over-Soul through intuition and rejects his congregation in order to preach to the world.[7]

Because these themes of education and conversion are not the central, involving action of the novel, but grow slowly out of a

---

[7] Further parallels between Casy and Christ: see Martin Shockley's "Christian Symbolism in *The Grapes of Wrath*."

rich and solid context, the development of Tom and Casy achieves an authority lacking in most proletarian fiction. The novel's thematic organization also makes it possible for Steinbeck successfully to incorporate the widest variety of materials and, with the exception of romantic love, to present a full scale of human emotions.

This ability of Steinbeck's thematic structure to absorb incidents organically into its context is important for an understanding of the novel's last scene, of which there has been much criticism. The novel's materials do make a climactic ending difficult. The author faced three pitfalls: a *deus ex machina* ending; a summing up, moral essay; and simply a new level of horror. But the novel's thematic treatment of material made it possible for Steinbeck to end on a high point, to bring his novel to a symbolic climax without doing violence to credulity, structure, or theme.

This climax is prepared for by the last interchapter, which parallels in terms of rain the opening description of the drought. The last paragraphs of these chapters are strikingly similar:

The women studied the men's faces secretly. . . . After a while the faces of the watching men lost their bemused perplexity and became hard and angry and resistant. Then the women knew that they were safe and that there was no break. (p. 6)

The women watched the men, watched to see whether the break had come at last. . . . And where a number of men gathered together, the fear went from their faces, and anger took its place. And the women sighed with relief, for they knew it was all right—the break had not come. (p. 592)

With this latter paragraph, a recapitulation of the novel's two main themes as they are worked out in three movements, *The Grapes of Wrath* is brought full circle. The last chapter compactly reenacts the whole drama of the Joads's journey in one uninterrupted continuity of suspense. The rain continues to fall; the little mud levee collapses; Rosasharn's baby is born dead; the boxcar must be abandoned; they take to the highway in search of food and find instead a starving man. Then the miracle happens. As Rose of Sharon offers her breast to the old man the novel's two counter themes are brought together in a symbolic paradox. Out of her own need she gives life; out of the profoundest depth of despair comes the greatest assertion of faith.[8]

Steinbeck's great achievement in *The Grapes of Wrath* is that while minimizing what seem to be the most essential elements of fiction—plot and character—he was able to create a well-made and emotionally compelling novel out of materials which in most other hands have resulted in sentimental propaganda.

---

[8] For parallels to this scene see Maupassant's "Idylle"; Byron's *Childe Harold*, Can. iv, St. 148–151; Rubens' painting of old Cimon taking milk from the breast of Pero; and an 18th-century play called *The Grecian's Daughter*, discussed in Maurice W. Disher's *Blood and Thunder* (London: Frederick Muller Ltd., 1949), p. 23. See also Celeste T. Wright.

ERIC W. CARLSON

Eric W. Carlson has taught at Portland Junior College, Boston University, Babson Institute and the University of Connecticut. He has written *The Recognition of Edgar Allan Poe, Introduction to Poe* and articles which have appeared in *College English* and *American Literature*.

Symbolism in *The Grapes of Wrath*

In his "Christian Symbolism in *The Grapes of Wrath*" Martin Shockley shows a commendable freedom from the usual critical stereotypes about this novel as a "propaganda tract" of the Thirties or as an example of "sociological naturalism" in fiction. In disagreeing with Paton and Pope he holds that Casy is a true Christ-symbol and that "the meaning of the book is revealed through a sequence of Christian symbols"; in agreeing with F. I. Carpenter ("The Philosophical Joads"),[1] he nevertheless finds a "further, stronger, more direct relation to the Bible." Qualified only by the remark that Casy's religion is "innocent of Paulism, of Catholicism, of Puritanism," Shockley's interpretation of Casy identifies him "simply and directly with Christ" from the evidence of his new-found religion, his deeds, and his death, and from Tom's discipleship and Rosasharn's sacramental gift of herself in the final scene of the novel. In short, the major intended meaning, it is claimed, is "essentially and thoroughly Christian."

Now all this may seem plausible and in itself innocent

---

[1] Reprinted in this book, pp. 708–719.—Ed.

Reprinted from *College English*, XIX, 2 (January 1958), 172–75. By permission of the National Council of Teachers of English and Eric W. Carlson.

enough. A closer examination of the novel as a whole, however, will lead to rather different conclusions, namely: (1) the
Christian symbols and Biblical analogies function at best in a
secondary capacity within a context of meaning that is so unorthodox as to be the opposite of what is generally considered
"Christian"; (2) the primary symbolic structure, as well as
meaning, is naturalistic and humanistic, not Christian; (3) the
main theme reflects not only this foreground of natural symbolism but also the author's philosophic perspective of scientific
humanism. In other words, in *The Grapes of Wrath* a few loose
Biblical analogies may be identified, but these are not primary
to the structure and theme of the novel, and to contend that
they give it an "essentially and thoroughly Christian" meaning
is to distort Steinbeck's intention and its primary framework of
non-Christian symbolism.

In the first place, several of the Biblical analogies are really
so tenuous as to depend entirely on other, major parallels for
validity. Tom Joad as the Prodigal Son, for instance, hardly
makes for a strong and direct analogy: Tom is quite unrepent-
ant, having killed in self-defense, and Tom's homecoming is
described in a most moving fashion, without benefit of analogy.
Other of the cited analogies can be invoked only as the loosest
sort of parallels, hardly metaphoric, much less symbolic. For
example, to speak of the Joads and other migrants as wandering, like the Israelites, in a wilderness of hardships while they
seek the Promised Land is but to point up by conventional metaphor the general emotional pattern of the trek westward and
the long-awaited sight of California. Even when the Joads make
their dramatic entrance into California, as described in Ch. 18,
that fact is subordinate to the significance of Ma's stoicism
(only she has known of Grandma's death), her concern for the
unity of the family, Tom's idealism, etc. As for Noah's going
down the river, Shockley chooses not to "press" this point,
major examples being enough. But if major examples suffice,
why speak of the truck drivers' generous tips (in Ch. 15) as
constituting Mae's reward for "casting her bread upon the

waters"? Wouldn't it be far simpler to say, without recourse to Biblical allusion, that this incident dramatizes a simple human fact: kindness breeds kindness? The strongest and most direct relationship of this incident is not to Christ but to Mae's earlier reluctance to sell the loaf of bread and, by an even more emphatic contrast, to the penny-pinching tourist couples—both suggestive of how the hard shell of economic exploitation inhibits natural sympathy and generosity. In fact, Ch. 15 is but one of a number of carefully interrelated chapters that develop the social theme of mutualism and its negative counterpart, possessive egoism, out of a pattern of human experience that is realized pragmatically, not theistically, and distilled into natural, social and epic symbols.

The title-phrase "*Grapes of Wrath*" is a good case in point. According to Shockley, it is "a direct Christian allusion, suggesting the glory of the coming of the Lord, revealing that the story exists in Christian context, indicating that we should expect to find some Christian meaning." One grants that the "Battle Hymn of the Republic" expresses the spirit of militant Christianity, the sacrificial idealism and the retribution associated with the Calvinist legacy of the South. But except for fanatics like Grandma Joad and the Jehovites, the specifically Christian association of "the grapes of wrath" has disappeared among the migrants, even as Casy had abandoned his old-style revivalism in search of something better. From the first chapter to the last, the "grapes of wrath" theme represents the indomitable spirit of man—that spirit which remains whole by resisting despair and resignation in the face of the drought of life, physical privation, exploitation, persecution, the tyranny of name-calling, and the uprooting of the very way of life itself. Out of these shared miseries there grows a spirit of resistance to the "possessive egotism" (Carpenter's term) of absentee ownership—"'a bad thing made by men, and by God that's something we can change'" (p. 52); out of this nonconformity comes a sense of shared purpose and group action. Or, in the words of one of the interchapters, "From need to concept to action" (p. 207).

In brief, then, the "grapes of wrath" theme is not specifically Christian for two reasons: it is not an expression of Christian humility and resignation; and, if one grants that the Christian spirit may on occasion be assertive and militant, here the title theme has its origin in the chaarcter and the experience of the people rather than in a body of religious concepts and beliefs. As Barker Fairley has made clear, with special reference to the style of this novel, *The Grapes of Wrath* has behind it a long American "democratic tradition" which is embodied in its "epic form" and in its "epic tendency" of style, as well as in its folkways and philosophy.

Jim Casy belongs to this deeply rooted American liberal-democratic tradition. Like Emerson, Casy gives up the church and becomes a humble free-thinking seeker of the truth, relying on observation, shared experience, natural sympathy, and natural introspection and insight. When the revelation of his new calling comes to Casy, it comes as a result of his having lived among the migrants, sharing their hardships, miseries, and hopes. His new faith grows out of an experiential understanding and love of his fellow man. As articulated by Casy, his new faith has four major beliefs: (1) a belief in the brotherhood of man, manifesting itself as "love"—i.e., good will, compassion and mutualism; (2) a belief in the spirit-of-man as the oversoul or Holy Spirit shared by all men in their outgoing love; (3) a belief in the unity of man and nature; and (4) an acceptance of all life as an expression of spirit. To Casy these beliefs are ideal spiritual values and therefore "holy"; he seems to doubt that the word "holy" has any other valid meaning, really, and that there is holiness enough in the ideal unity of common purpose (spirit) when men strive together toward a worthy goal in harmony with nature (the way of life). Here we have the social theme again, with religious overtones associated by some readers with Christianity—or at least that core Christianity which remains after doctrine, dogma, sacrament, ritual, miracle, and theism itself have been stripped away, leaving only the idealized brotherhood of man and the unitarian

Over-Soul. " 'I figgered about the Holy Sperit and the Jesus road,' Casy explained. 'I figgered, "Why do we got to hang it on God or Jesus? Maybe," I figgered, "maybe it's all men an' all women we love; maybe that's the Holy Sperit—the human sperit—the whole shebang. Maybe all men got one big soul ever'body's a part of." Now I sat there thinkin' it, an' all of a suddent—I knew it. I knew it so deep down that it was true, and I still know it' " (pp. 32–33). Like Emerson's Brahma, this is not the God of Christ—at least not to Casy and Steinbeck; and it is dubious semantics to insist on labeling "Christian" so unorthodox a creed. Christianity without Christ is hardly Christianity. And although Carpenter concludes that "a new kind of Christianity—not otherworldly and passive, but earthly and active"—is developed from Steinbeck's integration of "three great skeins of American thought" (Emersonianism, Whitman's democratic religion, and pragmatism), that integration is less a product and characteristic of Christianity than it is of the humanist tendency and character of the American experience and the modern climate of opinion.

But if Casy's beliefs are not characteristically Christian, there is still a striking similarity to Christ in Casy's initials and his dying words. In those final words—"You don't know what you're a-doin' "—the ideas of resurrection and redemption are conspicuously absent, however. His death is not the death of a redeeming Christ, any more than the death of Jim Conklin in *The Red Badge of Courage* is such a death, even if both have names beginning with J and C. Casy does not seek death, nor is he resigned to it when it comes, though in his last words he seems to forgive his enemies. Apart from dramatizing the brutality of exploitative capitalism (not capitalism as such, necessarily), the significance of Casy's death lies in its indication of his love of man, a love that risked death even as Tom assumes Casy's mission at the same risk. This love of man, channeled by a democratic sense of social justice and a realistic sense of pragmatic action, explains Casy's compulsion to serve his fellow man, and his willingness to take the blame, after striking down the deputy, in order to save Tom from arrest. Sacrificial in appearance, this latter action is motivated by a pragmatic social idealism.

After Casy's death, Tom consciously accepts the mission of Casy's practical humanitarianism as more inspiring and realistic than Christian resignation to circumstance and the promise of heavenly reward.

The strained quality of Shockley's thesis is most apparent, however, in his interpretation of the final scene, where Rosasharn gives her breast milk to save the life of the starving old man. Here an attempt is made to cram a stark, primal symbol into the mold of orthodox Christian symbolism and doctrine. Having identified Casy's gospel as "innocent of Paulism, Catholicism, and of Puritanism," Shockley now identifies Rosasharn's symbolic action with Communion or Mass and with the "resurrective aspect of Christ"! How much simpler is Carpenter's remark that in this scene Rosasharn "symbolically transmutes her maternal love to a love of all people." As implied by her smile and hair-stroking gesture, Rosasharn, whose maternal instinct has been frustrated, feels a momentary satisfaction. But the beauty and the significance of this scene derive chiefly from its symbolizing the main theme of the novel: the prime function of life is to nourish life. Throughout most of the novel Rosasharn has been a weak, silly, and sentimental woman—an ironic contrast to the idealized Rose of Sharon of the "Song of Solomon." And yet in this closing scene common biology and psychology are transcended and transformed by a symbolic meaning that grows out of the natural, right, and compassionate quality of the action itself and out of the already developed structure of symbolism and meaning. In fact, I can think of no more impressive example of what William Sansom recently (*NYTBR*, 30 Dec. 1956) termed the *round* ending, one "that truly 'rounds off' the book, completing as a broad and living thing—an egg, if you like, rather than a straight thin line between arbitrary points. Round indeed as the final chords of a symphony—whose quality is not only finality but also a balanced suggestion that the music really continues . . . an ending must suggest the continuance of life, and, by definition, of that which makes life continuable and endurable, hope: the end thus must be a statement of beginning."

That this "roundness" and significance lies not in any specifically Christian symbolism can be seen in Steinbeck's careful preparation of the primary symbolic structure of the novel, a body of symbolism which, in keeping with the theme, is both naturalistic and experiential. Ch. 1, for instance, describes the way the elemental forces in nature turn into dust and death. In the last paragraph of this chapter the men attempt to think through their frustration as they face this drought of life. Here, at the outset, is implied the universal interdependence or ecological balance of man and nature. In Ch. 3, the second of a series of symbolic interchapters, the turtle is a remarkable example of creative nature symbolism, further developing the idea of interdependence and introducing the central theme, the primal drive of life. The former is implied by the description of the seeds in the opening paragraph, and of the way the head of oats caught by the turtle's leg is dropped and covered with earth by the turtle's shell. The latter theme is symbolized by the turtle's dogged movement forward, the way all life naturally seeks to go somewhere through an instinctive urge to self-realization. In Ch. 4 Tom picks up the turtle, strokes the smooth, clean, creamy yellow underside with his finger and then rolls it up in his coat, as if identifying himself with its sensitivity, previously described by the turtle's sudden reaction when a red ant irritated the soft skin under the shell. A few pages further on in this chapter and also in Ch. 6 Tom and Casy find in the turtle's fixed sense of direction and purpose—briefly re-enforced by the sight of the shepherd dog trotting fast down the road, heedless of Tom's whistle—a point of common meaning for the idea that people too have a right to "go someplace."

This sort of nature symbolism recurs throughout the novel but, as these first chapters have illustrated, the nature symbols tend increasingly to relate to human situations and events that themselves have symbolic values. Among these we might note the tractor and its driver (5), Muley (6), the second-hand car dealer (7), Highway 66, the Joads' truck, the empty abandoned houses (11), the federal camp, the Hooverville camp, Noah's departure, the death and burial of Grampa, Casy's death, and the flood. Along with the main characters, these events are presented with such vividness and representative value as to become dramatic symbols of basic attitudes, conflicts and purposes in life—some social, others universal or epic. The social truths implied range from the tyranny of words (the handbills), the crime of monopoly (the evils of absentee ownership), economic exploitation, and the tragedy of direct action, to the positive values of folk fellowship, folk morality (the new Law of the Road) developed out of the migration (17), group action and democracy-in-process (22). But the most significant level is the epic level of the universally human: man's dependence on the primal elements (water, sun, fire, land), and the epic nature of sex, womanhood, family life, death, mutualism of spirit, and the epic idea of the race of man. The final though separate identifications with humanity of both Tom and Rosasharn underscore the epic idea that all men are brothers because all men belong to the Race of Man. This emphasis on the transcendent yet real unity of spirit is clearly more than a "biological approach to ethics" (Hyman).

The Grapes of Wrath is epic in form as well as theme, mainly through the skillful interweaving of the interchapters and the narrative chapters. It is undoubtedly this basic structure that Steinbeck had in mind when he described the structure of this novel as "very carefully worked out."

Many critics have found in Steinbeck's work an element of the mystical, the mysterious, or the religious. But as Steinbeck's search for spiritual values looks inside human experience, nature, and the life process, it is teleological only in the scientific (not the metaphysical) sense of the term. Steinbeck's naturalism goes beyond both the mechanistic determinism of

Dreiser and the mystic dualism of traditional Christianity. Steinbeck lifts the biology of stimulus-response to the biology of spirit, much as Edmund W. Sinnott has done in his studies of cell and psyche. His epic naturalism is neither romantic, nor mystic, nor Christian; it is an experiential discovery of the process by which "physiological man" becomes the "whole man" (*Sea of Cortez*, p. 87). As such it is a humanistic integration of the knowledge of man made available by modern science, philosophy, and art.

❖◆

WALTER FULLER TAYLOR

Walter Fuller Taylor has served as Professor of English and Dean
at Blue Mountain College, Mississippi. He has published *History
of American Letters*, *The Economic Novel in America*, and *The
Story of American Letters*.

The Grapes of Wrath Reconsidered

John Steinbeck's *The Grapes of Wrath* is, of course, vintage of
1939; and now that the wine has aged for twenty years it reveals
underlying flavors that in the first flush of discovery were overlooked. Since some of these flavors have a noticeable acerbity,
suggestive less of grape than of green persimmon, and since
they have undoubtedly been there from the beginning, it is a
bit surprising that they should have been so long neglected.
Yet the flavor, the "meaning" of a book is not absolute or un-
alterable. The residue of experience that a reader brings away
now from *The Grapes of Wrath* may be, must be, different
from that in 1939, when the naturalism of Zola and Frank
Norris still carried prestige, and when the memory of the
evils of the Great Depression focused in brilliant bitter light
Steinbeck's indictment of social injustice.

The Grapes of Wrath still fulfills, of course, its original
twofold function as naturalistic novel and social tract. In the
former function, it subjects its people (in Frank Norris's words)
to "terrible things," from Tom Joad's return to an abandoned
home to the stillbirth of Rosasharn's "blue shriveled little
mummy." In the latter, it dramatizes the terrible plight of
tenant families who have been "tractored out"; it exposes a sys-

---

Reprinted from *Mississippi Quarterly*, XII (Summer 1959), 136–144. By
permission.

tem of land monopoly as destructive as any set forth in *Progress and Poverty*; it holds our gaze unsparingly on the tragic attrition of the Joads as a family unity. Truly, "there is a crime here that goes beyond denunciation. There is a sorrow here that weeping cannot symbolize. There is a failure here that topples all our successes."

Now a book meant to expose a "crime . . . that goes beyond denunciation" is likely to be, in the biblical sense, a parable. Its events are made to happen not as they might happen actually, but as they may best carry conviction for the author's case. Its people, while they sometimes act as individuals, at other times act as types or symbols, as do the figures in a medieval morality play. In much of Steinbeck's story, Tom Joad is just the individual man Tom Joad; toward the close he becomes an embodiment—a self-conscious, highly articulate embodiment—of the workingman's resistance to injustice everywhere. *The Grapes of Wrath* is not, then, a realistic novel, though it makes occasional use of the techniques of realism. It is a parable; and toward the reader's full realization of the meanings of that parable are directed Steinbeck's unusual talents as a maker of myth.

I have purposely said "meanings," not "meaning," since *The Grapes of Wrath* is in intent not single but multiple. It is more than a naturalistic novel, more than a social tract; it is anything but "simple and uncomplicated," as an early critic incautiously called it. Its social idealism, even, appears sometimes as only an outer layer, the exterior label on a package whose inner core is something else entirely; and in the making of books there is of course no pure-food-and-drug act to require that the contents correspond to the label. Along with its concern for social justice, *The Grapes of Wrath* actually imparts significances that have nothing at all to do with social justice, but that nevertheless remain with the reader as part of his residue of experience. With the aid of twenty years' perspective, we can, and should, inquire just what are these interior meanings.

Among these meanings—meanings, let us repeat, not organically necessary to the social message of the novel—is the illustration of a kind of secular religion, whose Messiah is the ex-Holinist preacher Jim Casy. Casy, of course, modestly disclaims Messiahship, but his very disclaimer is ingeniously made to set forth Steinbeck's own Messianic intention in creating him. "I ain't sayin' I'm like Jesus . . . ," Casy is made to observe (p. 110). "But I got tired like Him, an' I got mixed up like Him, an' I went into the wilderness like Him." Though Steinbeck is misreporting the New Testament story when he refers to Jesus as "mixed up," the thrice-stated parallel is of course emphatic enough. The same parallel extends through Casy's offering himself in place of Tom Joad to the law, and even to the words Casy speaks to his killers: "You don' know what you're a-doin' " (p. 527).

If in Jim Casy Steinbeck makes use of the story of the Christ, the theology and ethic of Casy's religion have little enough to do with Christianity. Contrary to Christian dualism, man and man's world are looked on, Transcendental fashion, as part of one great Soul, universally holy except when some "mis'able little fella" acts in arrogant self-assertion to "bust the holiness" (p. 110). Contrary to the Christian attitudes of moral selectiveness and self-discipline, in Steinbeck's secular religion there is no need for self-control; all is permitted. To act ethically, men have only to act naturally. They have only to forget the illusion of sin, practice a universal tolerance, and obey that impulse. According to the newly tolerant Casy, "There ain't no sin and there ain't no virtue. There's just stuff people do" (p. 32). And according to his interpreter Ma Joad, "What people does is right to do" (pp. 289–290).

Steinbeck's secular religion is not, to put it mildly, much turned toward self-discipline. It sanctions any simple, easy, and natural indulgence. His Casy plans to cuss and swear and to "lay in the grass, open an' honest" (p. 128), with anybody that will have him. His folk find their pleasurable indulgences in storytelling, in an occasional movie, in dancing, in folk music made by fiddle and guitar and harmonica, in the softened, dreamlike world of a gentle drunkenness. They find them, above all, in sex, a simple natural appetite that involves no responsibilities for possible children or for the feelings of one's sexual partner. Once, to be sure, Steinbeck does waver in his uncompromising stand for sexual irresponsibility. According to the customs spontaneously formed in the roadside "worlds" of the migrants, "a man might not have one girl one night and another the next" (p. 266), for that would endanger the "worlds." But this falling-off from consistency is minor. Later, in his genial attitude toward Al Joad's promiscuity, Steinbeck makes it clear enough that a man may properly have one girl one *week* and another the next.

Sex, then, in the Steinbeckian ethic, means simply promiscuity in its simplest and easiest expression. Sexual behaviour with which Steinbeck is sympathetic is that of Tom Joad, who came out of prison "smokin'," found a "hoor girl," and "run her down . . . like she was a rabbit" (p. 233). Or it is that of Grampa's brother, who, if he got "any kids, cuckoo'd 'em, an' somebody else is a-raisin' 'em" (p. 126). Or it is that of Al Joad, whose tomcatting is described with humorous tolerance. The inevitable result of sexual maturity is not, of course, marriage; it is fornication. "It ain't Aggie's fault," says her father, of her relations with Al Joad. "She's growed up" (p. 576).

Now this picture of human mating, curiously simple and sometimes unintentionally humorous, is not employed by Steinbeck as mere shock material, or as a new version of the pleasant rascalities of the picaresque novel, still less as a realistic study of Sex among the Okies. It is part of a persistently held philosophy, according to which the only values lie in the experiences of the moment, the only valid end of living is the continued renewing of the life of the life cells. The same nonteleological outlook appears, for example, in books as different otherwise as *Tortilla Flat* and *The Wayward Bus*; and it glows into unusual sharpness in *Burning Bright*, which sanctions the murder of a man who has fulfilled his seminal function. Looked at from this nonteleological viewpoint, the experiencing of sex unavoidably loses its special human meanings and becomes, not merely primitive, not merely promiscuous, but simply animal.

Now a few of Steinbeck's critics, notably John S. Kennedy, have observed his fondness for animalism: the majority have missed it entirely—a failure of perception the more conspicuous for the fact that Steinbeck took pains to write into *The Grapes of Wrath* a brief subparable of free and natural sex behaviour:

A committee of dogs had met in the road, in honor of a bitch. Five males, shepherd mongrels, collie mongrels, dogs whose breeds had been blurred by a freedom of social life, were engaged in complimenting the bitch. For each dog sniffed daintily and then stalked to a cotton stalk on stiff legs. . . . Joad laughed joyously. "By God!" he said. "By God!" . . . One dog mounted and, now that it was accomplished, the others gave way and watched with interest, and their tongues were out, and their tongues dripped. (pp. 93–94).

A reader who really "buys" *The Grapes of Wrath* has bought, it would seem, something besides a plea for social justice. He has in fact bought an elaborately illustrated and reiterated philosophy of casual sex indulgence. He has also bought, along with a concept of sexual promiscuity, a humorous tolerance of the Tobacco-Road way of life once enjoyed by the Joads in Oklahoma. The reader's affections are to embrace Granma, who in a fit of religious ecstasy has ripped one of her husband's buttocks nearly off with a shotgun blast. They are to embrace even more warmly Grampa, who insists on going about with his fly open, and who, choked at table, sprays into his lap a "mouthful of paste." They are to embrace a social group where it is natural enough for a woman "in a family way" to go raving, because the pig got in the house and "et the baby."

The reader's affections are to embrace also a language employed, not precisely for vulgarity, but for apparently calculated effects of shock and revulsion. Now the mere amount and proportion of obscene language in *The Grapes of Wrath* are not, to be sure, especially high. Pungent Saxon monosyllables are much scarcer there than in the casual talk of schoolboys, where the same words are taken for granted and make little or no impression. But in *The Grapes of Wrath* these identical words *seem* more objectionable because the writer's imagination has so joined fact and idea, and image and word, as to startle the reader into aversion or even nausea. When Tom Joad is hungry he is given—as an appetizer?—the line, "My guts is yellin' bloody murder" (p. 66). Irritated by a truck-driver's curiosity, he is made to express his annoyance by saying, "You're wettin' your pants to know what I done" (p. 18).

To this vulgarity in deed and word the reader of *The Grapes of Wrath* has been expected, for twenty years, to grant approval or at least entire tolerance. Yet the pertinent critical questions suggested by it have hardly been asked, still less answered. It hardly seems in point to ask whether Steinbeck's dialogue is really the language of the California migrants, since after all his book is not realism but social parable. It would be more in point to ask whether the vulgarity contributes anything to the parable—anything, that is, beyond the linking of the book with the established popularity of the *Tobacco Road* theme. It would be more in point to inquire, apropos of Steinbeck's pungent language, into our different mental responses to a certain act, to the *spoken* word that designates it, and to the *written* word; for acts that are in themselves natural and inoffensive may be brought into offensive prominence by the connotations of a spoken word or by the bold black and white of the printed page. And if the act itself is repellent, the spoken word may be pointlessly nauseating. It is one thing to have the reader know that Tom Joad has killed a man in self defense; it is quite another—especially for any reader who has witnessed violent death—to have Tom observe with relish that he knocked the man's head "plumb to squash."

Now if reader and critic have largely overlooked these questions, and if they have really taken at face value Steinbeck's tolerant instruction that "what people does is right to do," and if they then take a good, straight, hard look at Steinbeck, some things are not "right" at all; to find, instead, that his pages are sown with emotionally charged moral judgments and sometimes virulent with hatred. Among the things that are emphatically not "right" is the practice of religion, specifically of Christianity. Although no such presentation is needful for Steinbeck's social ends, Christianity appears in *The Grapes of Wrath* only in the dubious form of certain Holinist sects; and even these are made visible only through a poisonous aura of hostile connotation.

For religion, as Steinbeck allows his readers to see it, is the ridiculous thing that causes Pa Joad to hurt his leg "Jesus-jumpin'," or that wrings out of Granma her shrill and terrible cry, "Pu-raise Gawd for vittory." It is the malignant force that drives the howling Mrs. Sandry to try to break Rosasharn's spirit, that impels preachers to make their people "grovel and whine on the ground." It is the source-spring of the intolerance which, when the dance is held at the government labor camp, makes the "Jesus lovers" sit with "hard condemning faces" and "watch the sin." Nowhere in *The Grapes of Wrath*, either in these episodes or elsewhere, does Steinbeck reveal any genuine knowledge of Christianity or any other of the great world religions. His approach to religion cannot therefore be that of the informed unbeliever or the genuine intellectual. Instead, he attacks religion by attaching to it belittling labels and emotion-triggering stimuli. He undercuts it by associating it with psychological illness, with morbid sexuality, with the practice of fanatical absurdities. He employs, in brief, the methods of the political demagogue, oblivious of the fact that demagoguery is no less demagogic for using the printed page instead of the political platform.

Apparently, after all, not *everything* that people do is right to do. Some things, such as keeping up any organized forms of religion, are quite seriously wrong; and one evil, especially, is the most seriously wrong of all. To Steinbeck, the deadliest of the deadly sins is simply being a typical American citizen—that is, a member of the middle classes. Hatred of the middle classes is in fact, according to Steinbeck's secretary Toni Seixas, one of the main "clues" to the understanding of his fiction. But quite apart from her testimony, the fiction itself carries abundant evidence of Steinbeck's feeling. Repeatedly it attacks the middle class not by direct invective or rational illustration, but by the insidious propaganda devices of epithet, innuendo, and hostile connotation.

To illustrate:—In *The Grapes of Wrath* a child is killed on Highway 66 by a recklessly driven Cadillac (p. 215). Prosperous owners of Cadillacs, Steinbeck implies, have a way of killing small children, whereas the Okie driver of a battered pick-up only tries, unsuccessfully, to run down a cat. Proletarian talk— that about the woman back home who "had a nigger kid all of a sudden"—is presented as natural and wholesomely robust. Capitalists' talk—that about the movie actress with a venereal disease—is presented as unwholesome gossip. The middle-class stooge who sells under-par hamburger to Ma Joad is presented as a neurotic who "giggled softly." Salesmen in a used-car lot, watching their victim-customers with "small, intent" eyes, are "neat" and "deadly." A California landholder is a "fat, sof' fella with little mean eyes. . . ." California deputies, servants of the middle class, are "fat-assed men with guns slung on fat hips."

Of this insidious denigration of the middle classes, the core is the description of the people who ride the "big cars" on Highway 66. The women, who to another writer would be just women, become in Steinbeck's imagination "languid, heat-raddled ladies," who require a thousand accoutrements to freshen their faces, to move their bowels, and to keep their sexual life "safe and unproductive": ladies who in the midst of all these luxuries remain weary, discontented, and sullen. Their companions, suitable mates, are "little, pot-bellied men . . . , clean, pink men with puzzled, worried eyes," men whose business amounts only to "curious ritualized thievery" and whose lives consist only of "thin, tiresome routines" (p. 211). Such people are naturally looked on with contempt by Steinbeck's fine proletarian truck drivers and by his roadside waitress Mae, who speaks of them with obscene contempt.

Such writing obviously presents no reasoned anti-middle-class philosophy; it offers no illustrated or imaginatively realized case; it does not grow, even, out of the fine old Bohemian tradition of flaying the bourgeoisie. It suggests, rather, a motivation deeply personal, an emotional drive so powerful as to cause Steinbeck to bypass his reader's intellect and to trigger quite irrational responses. By wrapping the middle classes in connotations of physical weakness, worry, sexual sterility, bafflement, and fear, Steinbeck would waken toward them feelings of revulsion and hate. And if we turn from *The Grapes of Wrath* to other books of Steinbeck—to *Cannery Row* or *The Wayward Bus*—we turn there only to discover the same obsessive hatred of the same class, the same insidious propagandist method, the same skillful aesthetic demagoguery. For many American readers, this discovery could be disconcerting, since they are themselves so likely to be, consciously or unconsciously, members of the middle class. Now it is not disconcerting to deal with an author's hatred of an idea, a particular person, party, or even one of his own characters. But surely it is disconcerting to find that the author hates you, the reader, with a powerful, compulsive hatred; that the tolerance he speaks of so smoothly is in fact never extended to *you*; and that just in having been born on the right side of the tracks you have committed the one unpardonable sin.

Even so brief a look into these interior meanings of *The Grapes of Wrath* suggests how incomplete is the customary view of Steinbeck's masterpiece—the view, namely, that the book is a naturalistic novel aimed at the exposure of social injustice. For under cover of a pious social objective a number of other and quite different meanings are slipped past the reader's guard: those of hostility, bitterness, and contempt toward the middle classes, of antagonism toward religion in its organized forms, of the enjoyment of a Tobacco-Road sort of slovenliness, of an easygoing promiscuity and animalism in sex, of Casy's curious Transcendental mysticism, of a tolerance that at first seems all-inclusive but that actually extends only so far as Steinbeck's personal preferences.

Now some of these accessory meanings of *The Grapes of*

Wrath have been defined by certain of Steinbeck's critics, especially Blake Nevius and John S. Kennedy. But with Steinbeck, as with Faulkner, there has been on the whole a tremendous divergence between the "matter" of the author and the "matter" of the critical studies about him. Divergence has even passed at times into contradiction. Steinbeck has been taken at times as a social idealist in the traditional, democratic sense; but such idealism consorts ill with his calculated release of hatred toward much of the American public. He has been taken as Christian; but actually he has only hijacked—if I may borrow for a moment his unscrupulous way with language—he has only hijacked part of the Christian story in order to turn it to the illustration of profoundly non-Christian meanings.

How then has it come about, in an age of criticism such as ours, that an important novelist has been so incompletely perceived? Not, in all likelihood, out of any merely personal limitations on the part of his critics, but rather out of the amorphous state of our general culture. For a half-century and more, that culture has been shaken by certain deep-seated conflicts in ideology—conflicts, that is to say, in systems of value; and these conflicts have been so powerful that they could easily bend out of focus any clear vision of what we and our writers actually are. One such conflict pits an idea of society rooted in our traditional democratic idealism, with its bent toward the reconciliation of class differences, against the hard-boiled Marxian attitude of class struggle, with its corollary of releasing all the hatreds needful for breaking an opposing class. Another conflict, concerned if anything even more deeply with the nature of man, pits the humanism of classical and Christian tradition, with its stress on man as a rational and moral being, against the naturalism of recent times, with its stress on man as a nonrational, instinct-driven cog within a mechanical cosmos.

Now it might be reasonably held that much of the deeper tension of our age comes not just from the Machine or just from the stresses of metropolitan living, but rather from the difficulty of choosing between these dilemmas about the nature of society and the nature of man; or, if not of choosing, at least of finding some tenable median point between the two. The sheer difficulty of these choices has seemed to scant some of our intellectuals of clearly seen and firmly held values, and to leave them with only an uncritical acceptance of the ideas that happen to be in vogue at any given moment. This too-ready acceptance of the current intellectual mode has tended of course to blur critical vision; critical perception has depended on what "truths" were in or out of favor. With Steinbeck, this responsiveness to intellectual fashion has afforded a curious sort of protective coloration. Some of his primary meanings were at first all but invisible, so completely was *The Grapes of Wrath* toned in with the intellectual hues of the latter nineteen-thirties.

For on the eve of World War II it was still intellectually fashionable to advocate Marxism, and to clothe that philosophy with its appropriate garments of propaganda. It was fashionable to display one's freedom from the Victorian proprieties; indeed, to go as far toward one extreme as the Victorians had gone toward another. And it was fashionable also to assume a kind of secular religion and ethic, not fully defined even yet, but certainly committed to some such formula as "Sex made easy." Since Steinbeck's earlier critics took these attitudes so much for granted, they naturally turned the discussion of *The Grapes of Wrath* in other directions, upon other issues. Yet these attitudes, these "values," were not such as might endure forever, knowing no change of hue or form under the eye of eternity. Already they have been undermined by the cataclysm of World War II, the rise of neo-orthodoxy, and the rediscovery of the need for self-discipline; in this new climate of opinion a reader may be, and quite certainly *should* be, confused or even confounded by the difference between what the critics say is in *The Grapes of Wrath*, and what he himself intuitively feels to be there.

The experience conveyed by such fiction is one thing, the critical treatment of that same fiction quite another; and the discrepancy between the two suggests a possible function of criticism at the present time—a function not too different from that suggested a century ago by Matthew Arnold. That is the function of defining precisely the great idea-patterns that have furnished the dynamics of so much of our recent literature; of defining them, and then of interpreting that literature in the light of its relation to these currents of thought. With regard to Steinbeck, such a body of criticism would discourage obscurantist talk about his "Christian symbolism" and his unifying of "three great skeins" of traditional American thought (Carpenter) and would lend aid and comfort to the critical minority who have steadily told the truth about his nonteleological naturalism and his contribution to interclass hatreds.

In essaying this difficult reappraisal of recent literature in the light of its dynamic idea-patterns, perhaps we might hope for some outcome beyond the immediate one of the elucidation of works of art. For does not part of the fascination of criticism, as of creation, lie in just this—that the immediate outcome is never the total one? The task is never finished, and therefore keeps perpetually the excitement of pioneering. In perception, as in exploration, the horizon continually changes; always, in the distance, loom other ranges of blue mountains, remote and unexplored. We shall never wholly chart them, but in our partial efforts we may make some ascent from confusion toward clarity, and gain the release from tension that comes of fuller understanding. For in genuinely knowing our recent authors, and the major ideas that have moved them, we may reasonably hope to grow into a more nearly adequate knowledge of what we as human beings are, and of what is, *now, for us,* the human condition.

❀◈

ROBERT J. GRIFFIN AND
WILLIAM A. FREEDMAN

Robert J. Griffin has taught at Yale University and California State
College at Hayward. He has written an essay on Sinclair Lewis pub-
lished in *American Winners of the Nobel Prize*, edited *Twentieth
Century Interpretations of Arrowsmith*, and published various arti-
cles in *College English, Studies in English Literature, Kansas City
Review*, and *The Nation*.

William A. Freedman has taught at Brooklyn College of the City of
New York and the University of Jerusalem in Haifa, Israel. He has
published poems and articles in a variety of journals and little magazines including *Shenandoah, Novel, Modern Fiction Studies, Chicago
Review* and *Tennessee Studies in Literature*.

Machines and Animals:
Pervasive Motifs in *The Grapes of Wrath*

Once the hubbub over John Steinbeck's "propaganda tract"
began to die down—there are still those who refuse to let it die
completely—critics began to pay serious attention to *The
Grapes of Wrath* as a work of art.[1] Such aspects of the novel as
its characterization (whether or not the Joads are "cardboard

---

[1] For discussion of the criticism about Steinbeck's work, see Peter Lisca,
The Wide World of John Steinbeck, and E. W. Tedlock, Jr., and C. V.
Wicker, *Steinbeck and His Critics*. Lisca's treatment of the criticism serves
as his introductory chapter and centers on the lamentable preoccupation
with Steinbeck's social and philosophical attitudes and the consequent neglect of his artistry. Tedlock and Wicker's is likewise introductory and
similarly oriented, closing with the hopeful conviction that "future critics
will find him to be an artist with an artist's intentions, methods, and stature" (p. xli). The most recent comprehensively excellent study of the
novels is Warren French, *John Steinbeck* (New York, 1961).

Reprinted from *Journal of English and Germanic Philology,* LXII (April
1963), 569–580. By permission of the publisher.

figures"), the prose style (actually the several prose styles, but particularly the poetic effectiveness of the descriptive passages), and the interrelationship of the different kinds of chapters[2] have been discussed at some length. In this paper we should like to concentrate on two pervasive motifs in the novel, namely, the crucially important motifs of *machines* and *animals* which contribute considerably to structure and thematic content. We may call these two the "dominant motifs," but we must remember that extracting these elements is necessarily an act of oversimplification; it is only through their complex relationships with subsidiary motifs and devices, and with the more straightforward narration and exposition and argumentation, that they provide major symbols integral to the art and substance of the novel.[3] With this qualification in mind, we may proceed to a consideration of machines and animals as sources of tropes, as signs and underscoring devices, and ultimately as persistent symbols.

Very few of the tropes of the novel—the metaphors, similes, and allusions—make use of machinery as such. "Tractored out" is of course a prominent figure of speech repeated several times to express the Okies' plight in being forced from their plots of land by the mechanical monstrosity of industrialized farming ("tractored off" also appears a couple of times). But otherwise about the only instance of a metaphorical use of machinery is a single simile late in the novel: the weary men trying to build a bank of earth to hold back the flood "worked jerkily, like machines" (p. 600). There are a good many metaphors applied

---

[2] See Lisca (pp. 732–735 of this volume) for discussion of Steinbeck's success at integrating different kinds of chapters into a unified though complex structure.

[3] A really thorough exegesis of the novel would have to describe the many secondary devices interwoven with the major motifs: the significance of clothing, e.g., particularly hats—the gradual metamorphosis of the cheap new cap Tom gets on leaving prison, Uncle John's defacement of his old hat as he prepares to lose himself in drink, etc. The Biblical allusions— though not a "motif" in our sense—are of course an essential part of the novel.

to mechanical apparatuses—that is, tropes in which machinery is characterized by some nonmechanical phenomenon as the vehicle of the metaphor. Generally this metaphorical characterization of machines emphasizes animalism or the bestial side of human affairs, as the seeders are said to rape the land. Fundamentally these metaphors appear designed to contribute to a general sense of tragedy or disaster indicated by such secondary motifs as the blood tropes—"the sun was as red as ripe new blood" (p. 6), "the earth was bloody in [the sun's] setting light" (p. 129)—and the frequent recurrence of "cut"—"the sun cut into the shade" (p. 10), "the road was cut with furrows" (p. 23).

While there are very few machine tropes, animal tropes abound. Often animals are used to characterize the human sex drive: Muley Graves (whose name is not inappropriate here) refers to himself during his first experience as "snortin' like a buck deer, randy as a billygoat" (p. 69); young, virile Al Joad has been "a-billygoatin' aroun' the country. Tom-cattin' hisself to death" (p. 111). And the sexuality of animals several times appears as the vehicle of a metaphor: Casy refers to a participant in a revival meeting as "jumpy as a stud horse in a box stall" (p. 38). Animal tropes frequently serve to denote violence or depravity in human behavior: fighting "like a couple of cats" (p. 27); a tractor hitting a share-cropper's cabin "give her a shake like a dog shakes a rat" (p. 62); Muley used to be "mean like a wolf" but now is "mean like a weasel" (p. 78); and Ma Joad describes Purty Boy Floyd's career as comparable to a maddened animal at bay—"they shot at him like a varmint, an' he shot back, an' then they run him like a coyote, an' him a-snappin' an' a-snarlin', mean as a lobo" (p. 103). Animal tropes may simply indicate a harmless playfulness or swagger: Winfield Joad is "kid-wild and calfish" (p. 129), and Al acts like "a dung-hill rooster" (p. 575). But the most frequent and significant use of the numerous animal tropes is to characterize the Okies' plight: the Joads are forced off their forty acres, forced to live "piled in John's house like gophers in a winter burrow" (p. 63); then they begin an abortive trip toward what they hope will prove to be a "New Canaan" in California, and Casy uses this tacit analogy to describe the impersonal, industrial economy from which they are fleeing:

Ever see one a them Gila monsters take hold, mister? Grabs hold, an' you chop him in two an' his head hangs on. Chop him at the neck an' his head hangs on. Got to take a screw-driver an' pry his head apart to git him loose. An' while he's layin' there, poison is drippin' an' drippin' into the hole he's made with his teeth. (p. 175)

Casy argues that the wrong results from men not staying "harnessed" together in a common effort ("mankin' was holy when it was one thing"); one man can get "the bit in his teeth an' run off his own way, kickin' an' draggin' an' fightin'" (p. 110). Consequently the roads to California are "full of frantic people running like ants" (p. 324—the "ants" simile appears again, for instance, on p. 388). In California the Okies work, when they can get work, "like draft horses" (p. 601); they are driven "like pigs" (p. 523) and forced to live "like pigs" (p. 571). Casy has been observing and listening to the Okies in their misfortunes, and he knows their fear and dissatisfaction and restlessness: "I hear 'em an' feel 'em; an' they're beating their wings like a bird in a attic. Gonna bust their wings on a dusty winda tryin' ta get out" (p. 340).

It should be noted that the animalistic references to people are not as a rule unfavorable ("randy as a billygoat" is scarcely a pejorative in Steinbeck's lusty lexicon). The few derogatory animal tropes are almost all applied to the exploiters (banks, land companies, profiteers) and not to the exploited (the Joads and the other Okies). That these latter must behave like the lower animals is not their fault. Their animalism is the result of the encroachments of the machine economy. Machines, then, are frequently depicted as evil objects: they "tear in and shove the croppers out" (p. 13); "one man on a tractor can take the place of twelve or fourteen families" (p. 44); so the Okies must take to the road, seeking a new home, lamenting, "I lost my land, a single tractor took my land" (p. 206). Farming has become a mechanized industry, and Steinbeck devotes an entire chapter (nineteen) to the tragic results:

The tractors which throw men out of work, the belt lines which carry loads, the machines which produce, all were increased; and more and more families scampered on the highways, looking for crumbs from the great holdings, lusting after the land beside the roads. The great owners formed associations for protection and they met to discuss ways to intimidate, to kill, to gas. (p. 325)

The Okies are very aware of the evils brought about by mechanization. Reduced to picking cotton for bare-subsistence wages, they realize that even this source of income may soon go. One asks, "Heard 'bout the new cotton-pickin' machine?" (p. 556).

The Joads find themselves living—trying to live—in an age of machinery. Machines or mechanized devices quite naturally play important roles in the symbolism of the novel. ("Symbolism" is here understood to mean the employment of concrete images—objects and events—to embody or suggest abstract qualities or concepts.) Some machines serve as "interior" symbols; they are, that is, recognized as symbolic by characters in the novel. Still others, largely because of the frequency with which or crucial contexts in which they appear, can be seen by the careful reader to take on symbolic significance. The "huge red transport truck" of chapter two, for example, can be seen as a sort of epitome of the mechanical-industrial economy—the bigness, the newness, the mobility, the massive efficiency, even the inhumanity (*No Riders*) and lack of trust—"a brass padlock stood straight out from the hasp on the big back doors" (p. 8). It is a mobile era in which one must accommodate to the mass mechanization in order to survive. Farmers can no longer hope to get by with a team and a wagon. And Steinbeck finds in the used-car business (chapter seven), preying on the need to move out and move quickly, an apt representation for the exploitation of those who have not yet been able to accommodate:

"In the towns, on the edges of the towns, in fields, in vacant lots, the used-car yards, the wreckers' yards, the garages with blazoned signs—Used Cars, Good Used Cars, Cheap transportation" (p. 83). The Joads' makeshift truck aptly represents their predicament—their need to move, their inability to move efficiently or in style, their over-all precariousness: "The engine was noisy, full of little clashings, and the brake rods banged. There was a wooden creaking from the wheels, and a thin jet of steam escaped through a hole in the top of the radiator cap" (p. 133).[4] Steinbeck makes overt the symbolic nature of this truck; when the members of the family meet for their final council before migrating, they meet near the truck: "The house was dead, and the fields were dead; but this truck was the active thing, the living principle" (p. 135). Here, as throughout the novel, the Joads' predicament is a representative instance of the predicaments of thousands. Highway 66 is the "main migrant road" (chapter twelve), and on this "long concrete path" move the dispossessed, the "people in flight": "In the day ancient leaky radiators sent up columns of steam, loose connecting rods hammered and pounded. And the men driving the trucks and the overloaded cars listened apprehensively. How far between towns? It is a terror between towns. If something breaks—well, if something breaks we camp right here while Jim walks to town and gets a part and walks back" (p. 161). Along this route the dispossessed farmers find that they are not alone in their troubles. The independent, small-scale service station operator is being squeezed out of his livelihood just as the farmers have been; Tom tells the poor operator that he too will soon be a part of the vast moving (p. 174). And the various types of vehicles moving along Route 66 are obvious

---

[4] Of course it is inevitable that the poor condition of the Joads' truck parallels their own predicament; they cannot afford anything better. But the point is that the truck becomes so accurate an index that the author can use it for metonymic expression of the owners' plight; deterioration of the truck expresses deterioration of the family. A symbol is not the less a symbol because it functions well at the literal level.

status symbols. Some have "class an' speed"; these are the insolent chariots of the exploiters. Others are the beat-up, overloaded conveyors of the exploited in search of a better life. The reactions of those who are better-off to the sad vehicles of the Okies are representative of their lack of understanding and sympathy:

"Jesus, I'd hate to start out in a jalopy like that."
"Well, you and me got sense. Them goddamn Okies got no sense and no feeling. They ain't human. A human being wouldn't live like they do. A human being couldn't stand it to be so dirty and miserable. They ain't a hell of a lot better than gorillas." (p. 301)

The Okies are conscious of vehicles as status symbols and automatically distrust anyone in a better car. When a new Chevrolet pulls into the laborers' camp, the laborers automatically know that it brings trouble. Similarly the condition of the Okies' vehicles provides perfect parallels for their own sad state. As the Joads are trying to move ahead without being able to ascertain exactly where they are headed—"even if we got to crawl"—so their truck's "dim lights felt along the broad black highway ahead" (p. 384). As the Joads' condition worsens, so naturally does that of their truck (e.g., "the right head light blinked on and off from a bad connection"—p. 548). In the development of the novel their vehicles are so closely identified with the Okies that a statement of some damage to the vehicles becomes obviously symbolic of other troubles for the owners. When the disastrous rains come, "beside the tents the old cars stood, and water fouled the ignition wires and water fouled the carburetors" (p. 590). The disastrousness of the ensuing flood is quite clearly signaled by mention of the "trucks and automobiles deep in the slowly moving water" (p. 614).

As the Okies' vehicles provide an accurate index to their circumstances, so do the animals they own, particularly their pets. The deserted cat that Tom and Casy find when they survey the Joads' deserted farm represents the forlorn state of the dispossessed (see pp. 57–60—the cat actually foreshadows the

appearance of Muley Graves with his tales of lonely scavenger-
ing). The dogs that appear when Tom and Casy reach Uncle
John's place are indicative of human behavior in the face of
new circumstances (one sniffs cautiously up to examine the
strangers, while the other seeks some adequate excuse for
avoiding the possible danger—p. 98). After the company's
tractors move in and the share-croppers are "shoved off" their
land, the pets that they left behind must fend for themselves
and thus gradually revert to the primitive state of their ancestors—a reversion not unlike the desperate measures that the
Okies are driven to by adversity and animosity: "The wild cats
crept in from the fields at night, but they did not mew at the
doorstep any more. They moved like shadows of a cloud across
the moon, into the rooms to hunt the mice" (p. 159). The
Joads take a dog with them on their flight to California, but he
is not prepared to adjust to the new, fast, mechanized life thrust
upon him; when his owners stop for gas and water, he wanders
out to the great highway—"A big swift car whisked near, tires
squealed. The dog dodged helplessly, and with a shriek, cut off
in the middle, went under the wheels" (p. 177). The owner of
the dilapidated independent service station comments on the
sad scene, "A dog jus' don' last no time near a highway. I had
three dogs run over in a year. Don't keep none, no more" (p.
177). After the Joads have been in California for a while and
discover the grim facts of life for them there, they move on to
another "Hooverville" camp of migrants. They find their fellow job-seekers hungry, fearful, and distrustful; the single pet
there vividly expresses the general attitude or atmosphere of
the place: "A lean brown mongrel dog came sniffing around
the side of the tent. He was nervous and flexed to run. He
sniffed close before he was aware of the two men, and then
looking up he saw them, leaped sideways, and fled, ears back,
bony tail clamped protectively" (p. 341). Yet having pets is
indicative of the love and sympathy of which man is capable
when in favorable circumstances. The simple, "natural" Joads
never lose their appreciation for pets. When their fortunes are

at their lowest ebb, Ma still holds hopes for a pleasant future: " 'Wisht we had a dog,' Ruthie said. [Ma replied] 'We'll have a dog; have a cat too' " (p. 596).

Pets, then, serve as symbolic indices to human situations; and other animal symbols are used to excellent advantage. One of Steinbeck's favorite devices is the use of epitome—the description of some object or event, apart from the main movement of the narrative, which symbolically sums up something central to the meaning of the narrative. Toward the end of *The Grapes of Wrath* the migrants are gathered about a fire, telling stories, and one of them recounts an experience of a single Indian brave whom they were forced to shoot—epitomizing the indomitability and dignity of man, and foreshadowing Casy's fate.[5]

We have already noted the use of animals for symbolic foreshadowing (for instance, the dispossessed cat and Muley Graves).[6] Probably Steinbeck's most famous use of the symbolic epitome is the land turtle.[7] The progress of the Okies, representative of the perseverance of "Manself," is neatly foreshadowed in the description of the turtle's persistent forward movement: he slowly plods his way, seeking to prevail in the face of adversities, and he succeeds in spite of insects, such obstacles as the highway, motorists' swerving to hit him (though some swerve to avoid hitting him), Tom's imprisoning

---

[5] "They was a brave on a ridge, against the sun. Knowed he stood out. Spread his arms an' stood." Finally the soldiers are prevailed upon to shoot him down. "An' he wasn' big—he'd looked so grand—up there. All tore to pieces an' little. Ever see a cock pheasant, stiff and beautiful, ever' feather drawed an' painted, an' even his eyes drawed in pretty? An' bang! You pick him up—bloody and twisted, an' you spoiled somepin better'n you; . . . you spoiled somepin in yaself, an' you can't never fix it up" (p. 445).

[6] There are in *Grapes* numerous instances of foreshadowing which do not participate in either of the dominant motifs. For example, Rose of Sharon's gesture of human sharing at the end of the novel is foreshadowed in Tom's first meal in the government camp: a mother breast-feeding her child invites him to share the breakfast she is cooking (p. 395).

[7] Kenneth Burke has called the turtle a "mediating material object for tying together Tom, Casy, and the plot, a kind of externalizing vessel, or 'symbol.' "

him for a while in his coat, the attacks of a cat, and so on. Stein-beck does not leave discernment of the rich parallels wholly to the reader's imagination. There are, for instance, similarities be-tween Tom's progress along the dirt road and the turtle's: "And as the turtle crawled on down the embankment, its shell dragged dirt over the seeds . . . drawing a wavy shallow trench in the dust with its shell" (p. 22); and "Joad plodded along, dragging his cloud of dust behind him . . . dragging his heels a little in the dust" (p. 24—at this point in the novel Tom has not yet begun to sow the seeds of new growth among the down-trodden Okies). Casy remarks on the indomitability of the turtle, and its similarity to himself: "Nobody can't keep a turtle though. They work at it and work at it, and at last one day they get out and away they go—off somewheres. It's like me" (p. 28). But at this point in the novel Casy is not alto-gether like the turtle, for he has not yet discovered the goal to which he will devote himself unstintingly· " 'Goin' someplace,' he repeated. 'That's right, he's goin' someplace. Me—I don't know where I'm goin' ' " (p. 29).[8]

Animal epitomes, such as the turtle and the "lean gray cat," occur several times at crucial points. And frequently a person's character will be represented by his reaction to or treatment of lower animals. As Tom and Casy walk along the dusty road a gopher snake wriggles across their path; Tom peers at it, sees that it is harmless, and says, "Let him go" (p. 93). Tom is not cruel or vicious, but he does recognize the need to prevent or put down impending disaster. Later, a "rattlesnake crawled across the road and Tom hit it and broke it and left it squirm-ing" (p. 314). The exploitation of the Okies is symbolized by

---

[8] The case of the turtle is an excellent example of the intricate interrela-tionships of the Joads' story and the interchapters (i.e., those which do not deal directly with the Joad plot). All of chapter three is devoted to descrip-tions of the turtle's slow, apparently unwitting but nonetheless definite progress. Yet, under analysis this chapter, like that on the used-car lots, for instance, proves to be an integral part of the "symbolic structure" of the novel.

the grossly unfair price paid a share-cropper for the matched pair of bay horses he is forced to sell. In this purchase of the bays, the exploiters are buying a part of the croppers' history, their loves and labors; and a swelling bitterness is part of the bargain: "You're buying years of work, toil in the sun; you're buying a sorrow that can't talk. But watch it, mister" (p. 118).

Animals convey symbolic significance throughout the novel. When the Okies are about to set out on what they are aware will be no pleasure jaunt to California—though they scarcely have any idea how dire will be the journey and the life at the end of it—an ominous "shadow of a buzzard slid across the earth, and the family all looked up at the sailing black bird" (p. 227). In the light of the more obvious uses of animals as epitomes or omens, it is easy to see that other references to animals, which might otherwise seem incidental, are intentionally parallel to the actions or troubles of people. Here is a vivid parallel for the plight of the share-cropper, caught in the vast, rapid, mechanized movement of the industrial economy (the great highway is persistently the bearer of symbolic phenomena):

A jackrabbit got caught in the lights and he bounced along ahead, cruising easily, his great ears flopping with every jump. Now and then he tried to break off the road, but the wall of darkness thrust him back. Far ahead bright headlights appeared and bore down on them. The rabbit hesitated, faltered, then turned and bolted toward the lesser lights of the Dodge. There was a small soft jolt as he went under the wheels. The oncoming car swished by. (p. 252)

As the weary Okies gather in a Hooverville to try to find some way out of the disaster they have flown into, moths circle frantically about the single light: "A lamp bug slammed into the lantern and broke itself, and fell into darkness" (p. 255). While the wary mongrel at the camp represents the timorous doubts of the Okies, the arrogant skunks that prowl about at night are reminiscent of the imperious deputies and owners who intimidate the campers. The Okies are driven like ani-

mals, forced to live like animals, and frequently the treatment they receive from their short-term employers is not as
good as that given farm animals:

> Fella had a team of horses, had to use 'em to plow an' cultivate
> an' mow, wouldn' think a turnin' 'em out to starve when they
> wasn't workin'.
> Them's horses—we're men. (p. 592)

We have seen that both machines and animals serve as effective symbolic devices in *The Grapes of Wrath*. Frequently the
machine and animal motifs are conjoined to afford a doubly
rich imagery or symbolism. Thus the banks are seen as monstrous animals, but *mechanical* monsters: "the banks were machines and masters all at the same time" (p. 43). The men for
whom the share-croppers formerly worked disclaim responsibility: "It's the monster. The bank isn't like a man" (p. 45). The
tractors that the banks send in are similarly monstrous—
"snub-nosed monsters, raising the dust and sticking their snouts
into it, straight down the country, across the country, through
fences, through dooryards, in and out of gullies in straight
lines" (p. 47). And the man driving the tractor is no longer a
man; he is "a part of the monster, a robot in the seat" (p. 48).
Their inability to stop these monsters represents the frantic
frustration of the dispossessed; Grampa Joad tries to shoot a
tractor, and does get one of its headlights, but the monster
keeps on moving across their land (p. 62). The new kind of
mechanical farming is contrasted with the old kind of personal
contact with the land. The new kind is easy and efficient: "So
easy that the wonder goes out of work, so efficient that the
wonder goes out of land and the working of it, and with the
wonder the deep understanding and the relation" (p. 157).

We have seen that machines are usually instruments or indices of misfortune in Steinbeck's novel. But to assume that
machinery is automatically or necessarily bad for Steinbeck
would be a serious mistake. Machines are *instruments*, and in
the hands of the right people they can be instruments of good

fortune. When the turtle tries to cross the highway, one driver tries to smash him, while another swerves to miss him (p. 22);[9] it depends on who is behind the wheel. Al's relationship with the truck is indicative of the complex problems of accommodating in a machine age. He knows about motors, so he can take care of the truck and put it to good use. He is admitted to a place of responsibility in the family council because of his up-to-date ability. He becomes "the soul of the car" (p. 167). The young people are more in tune with the machines of their times, whereas the older ones are not prepared to accommodate to the exigencies of the industrial economy:

Casy turned to Tom. "Funny how you fellas can fix a car. Jus' light right in an' fix her. I couldn't fix no car, not even now when I seen you do it."

"Got to grow into her when you're a little kid," Tom said. "It ain't jus' knowin'. It's more'n that. Kids now can tear down a car 'thout even thinkin' about it." (p. 252)

The tractors that shove the croppers off their land are not inherently evil; they are simply the symptoms of unfair exploitation. In one of the interchapters (fourteen) Steinbeck expresses the thought that the machines are in themselves of neutral value:

Is a tractor bad? Is the power that turns the long furrows wrong? If this tractor were ours it would be good—not mine, but ours. If our tractor turned the long furrows of our land, it would be good. Not my land, but ours. We could love that tractor then as we have loved this land when it was ours. But this tractor does two things—it turns the land and turns us off the land. There is little difference between this tractor and a tank. The people are driven, intimidated, hurt by both. (pp. 205–206)

Machinery, like the science and technology that can develop bigger and better crops (see pp. 473–477), is not enough for

[9] Steinbeck makes frequent use of such contrasts or juxtapositions. The cheerfulness of the Saturday night dance at the government camp, for example, is effectively juxtaposed with the harsh grumbling of the hyper-religious campers who do not attend (p. 450).

progress; there must be human understanding and cooperation. The Okies—through a fault not really their own—have been unable to adjust to the machinery of industrialization. Toward the very last of the novel Ma pleads with Al not to desert the family, because he is the only one left qualified to handle the truck that has become so necessary a part of their lives. As the flood creeps up about the Joads, the truck is inundated, put out of action. But the novel ends on a hopeful note of human sharing, and we may surmise that the Okies (or at least their children) can eventually assimilate themselves into a machine-oriented society.

Some critics have noted Steinbeck's preoccupation with animal images and symbols, and labeled his view of man as "biological."[10] This label is a gross oversimplification, responsible for a good deal of misreading of Steinbeck's work. The animal motif in Grapes does not at all indicate that man is or ought to be exactly like the lower animals. The Okies crawl across the country like ants, live like pigs, and fight amongst themselves like cats, mainly because they have been forced into this animalistic existence. Man can plod on in his progress like the turtle, but he can also become conscious of his goals and deliberately employ new devices in attaining those goals. Man's progress need not be blind; for he can couple human knowledge with human love, and manipulate science and technology to make possible the betterment of himself and all his fellows. Steinbeck does not present a picture of utopia in his novel, but the dominant motifs do indicate that such a society is possible.

It has been a fundamental assumption of this study that dominant motifs are of central importance in the form and meaning of certain works of fiction. In this particular case we would contend that Steinbeck's intricate and masterful manip-

---

[10] See e.g., Edmund Wilson. Peter Lisca (*The Wide World of John Steinbeck*) has tried to dispel this misconception of Steinbeck's biologism—as has Frederick Bracher. While there are still those who prefer to view *Grapes* as a primarily sociological document, the oversimplification of Steinbeck's "biological view" has been pretty well quashed in recent criticism.

ulation of the various references to machines and animals is an essential factor in the stature of *The Grapes of Wrath* as one of the monuments of twentieth-century American literature. By their very pervasiveness—the recurrence of the components that constitute the motifs—the references contribute significantly to the unity of the work; they help, for instance, to bind together the Joad chapters with those which generalize the meaning that the Joads' story illustrates. Certain animals and machines play important parts on the literal level of the story, and these and others serve to underscore principal developments or "themes" in the novel. Certain animals and machines are recognizably symbolic within the context of the story, and still others (the epitomes for example) can be discerned as much more meaningful than their overt, apparently incidental mention might at first seem to indicate. Both the interior and the more subtle symbols—as reinforced by the recurrence of related allusions or figures of speech—are interwoven and played off against one another to such an extent that the overall meaning is not merely made more vivid: it is considerably enriched. A consideration of these motifs does not begin to exhaust the richness of the book; but this discussion can, we hope, contribute to a fuller understanding of Steinbeck's novel as a consummate complex work of art.

JOSEPH FONTENROSE

Joseph Fontenrose has taught at Cornell University, the University of Oregon, and the University of California, where he has been Professor of Classics. He has published several books on mythology, including *The Ritual Theory of Myth, Python: A Study of Delphic Myth and Its Origin*, and *The Cult and Myth of Pyrrhos at Delphi*, as well as numerous articles in philological and archeological journals.

The Grapes of Wrath

The Grapes of Wrath has little plot in the ordinary sense; there is no complex involvement of character with character, no mesh of events. The story of the Joads could be the true story of a real family. But there is character development, as Tom Joad, "jus' puttin' one foot in front a the other" (p. 236) at first, gradually reaches an understanding of Casy's message and takes up Casy's mission. And the Joads as a whole progress from an exclusive concern for family interests to a broader vision of cooperation with all oppressed people. Lisca has pointed out that the plot consists of two downward movements balanced by two upward movements. As the Joad family's fortunes decline, the family morale declines, too: the family loses members and is threatened with dissolution. But as the family grows weaker, the communal unit of united workers, which came to birth in the roadside camps on the westward trek, grows stronger, and this upward movement is accompanied by the growth of Casy and Tom Joad in understanding of the forces at work. We can put the process another way: the family unit, no longer viable, fades into the communal unit, which receives from it the family's strength and values.

Collective persons are important characters in this novel too, since the plot movement must be expressed in group terms. It can be read as a story of conflicts and interactions among several group organisms: the Joad family (representative of all Okie families), the Shawnee Land and Cattle Company (representative of all Oklahoma land companies), the California Farmers' Association (the organization of big California agricultural corporations, controlled by the Bank of the West), and the workers' union, still immature as the story ends. The Joad family is a democratic, cooperative organism; it is a cohesive group, and yet no member loses his individual character in the group. When the Joads act as a family, they act as a unit: "And without any signal the family gathered by the truck, and the congress, the family government, went into session." It met beside the truck, "the active thing, the living principle," for it was now "the new hearth, the living center of the family" (pp. 135–136). The Oklahoma land company is another sort of organism entirely. It is one of the monsters of Chapter Five which "don't breathe air, don't eat side-meat." Such creatures "breathe profits; they eat the interest on money. If they don't get it, they die the way you die without air, without side-meat. It is a sad thing, but it is so." "The bank is something else than men. It happens that every man in a bank hates what the bank does, and yet the bank does it." As Doc Burton said in *In Dubious Battle*, a group's ends may be entirely different from the ends of its individual members. The monster is the sort of organism that absorbs its members, drains them of their individualities, and makes them into organization men. The tractor is the monster visible: "Snub-nosed monsters, raising the dust and sticking their snouts into it, straight down the country, across the country, through fences, through dooryards, in and out of gullies in straight lines." As the bank officer to the bank, so the driver to the tractor:

The man sitting in the iron seat did not look like a man; gloved, goggled, rubber dust mask over nose and mouth, he was a part of the monster, a robot in the seat. . . . A twitch at the controls could swerve the cat', but the driver's hands could not twitch because the monster that built the tractor, the monster that sent the tractor out, had somehow got into the driver's hands, into his brain and muscle, had goggled him and muzzled him—goggled his mind, muzzled his speech, goggled his perception, muzzled his protest [p. 48].

He had no feeling for the land that he plowed and planted. It was nothing to him whether the sown seeds germinated or not. "He ate without relish" a lunch of "sandwiches wrapped in waxed paper, . . . [and] a piece of pie branded like an engine part" (p. 49).

The monster is in fact Leviathan. In discussing *In Dubious Battle* I alluded to the relation of the group organism to Thomas Hobbes's symbol for the state as collective person, "that great LEVIATHAN, or rather, to speak more reverently, . . . that *mortal god*, to which we owe under the *immortal God*, our peace and defence." Steinbeck's monster is as despotic as Hobbes's Leviathan, but hardly as beneficial to man. He is rather the original Leviathan of Isaiah 27 and Psalm 74, enemy of the Lord. When Casy saw what the tractor had done to the Joad farm, he said, "If I was still a preacher I'd say the arm of the Lord had struck. But now I don't know what happened." He soon discovered the true culprit: "Here's me that used to give all my fight against the devil 'cause I figured the devil was the enemy. But they's somepin worse'n the devil got hold a the country, an' it ain't gonna let go till it's chopped loose. Ever see one a them Gila monsters take hold, mister?" (p. 55). If this monster is a mortal god, he is seemingly invulnerable: "Maybe there's nobody to shoot." But we have seen him, a visible god, in the tractor with its "shining disks, cutting the earth with blades—not plowing but surgery . . . And pulled behind the disks, the harrows combing with iron teeth . . ." (pp. 48–49). Thus, as a participant in the action, the group organism, like the individual characters, takes on a mythical role, derived from the Biblical substructure of the novel.

The Joad family fled the Oklahoma Leviathan, only to run into his brother, the California Leviathan—the Farmers' Association and its typical member, the Hooper ranch, a veritable prison with its barbed-wire fences and armed guards—much the same sort of creature, but even meaner. It is the Growers' Association of *In Dubious Battle*, and its image is not the tractor, but the fat-rumped deputy carrying a gun in holster on his hip. In legend and folktale it makes little difference whether the hero faces a dragon or an ogre.

Leviathan made easy prey of the little fishes, the separate family units. But these units became the gametes of a larger organism, a union of all migrant workers. On the road one family met another:

And in the night one family camps in a ditch and another family pulls in and the tents come out. The two men squat on their hams and the women and children listen. Here is the node, you who hate change and fear revolution. Keep these two squatting men apart; . . . Here is the anlage of the thing you fear. This is the zygote. For here "I lost my land" is changed; a cell is split and from its splitting grows the thing you hate—"We lost *our* land." . . . And from this first "we" there grows a still more dangerous thing: "I have a little food" plus "I have none." If from this problem the sum is "We have a little food," the thing is on its way, the movement has direction. Only a little multiplication now, and this land, this tractor are ours [p. 206].

In just this way the Joads and Wilsons met on the road; the Joads shared their little money and food with the Wilsons, repaired the Wilsons' car, and joined forces with them for the journey westward.

Then several families came together in roadside camps. Perhaps twenty families would camp together at a suitable place. "In the evening a strange thing happened: the twenty families became one family, the children were the children of all. The loss of home became one loss, and the golden time in the West was one dream" (p. 264). A world was created every evening and dissolved every morning, and was then re-created the next evening, complete with government and laws. And the members, being group-men in a new kind of group, were changed accordingly: "They were not farm men any more, but migrant men. . . . That man whose mind had been bound with acres lived with narrow concrete miles" (pp. 267–268). In Archibald MacLeish's words he now had only "the narrow acre of the road."

The democracy, self-government, and fraternity of the road-side camps blossomed more perfectly in the government camps, where men were orderly and harmonious without police. And the government camps, in which a minority of the migrants lived, were the model for the future commune of all workers. When Tom went away, near the end of the book, he said to his mother,

I been thinkin' how it was in that gov'ment camp, how our folks took care a theirselves, an' if they was a fight they fixed it theirself; an' they wasn't no cops wagglin' their guns, but they was better order than them cops ever give. I been a-wonderin' why we can't do that all over. Throw out the cops that ain't our people. All work together for our own thing—all farm our own lan' [p. 571].

Shortly after lamenting that the family was breaking up, Ma Joad, soul of the Joad family, attained the larger vision, agreeing with Mrs. Wainwright that the Joads would help the Wainwrights if they needed help: "Or anybody. Use' ta be the fambly was fust. It ain't so now. It's anybody. Worse off we get, the more we got to do" (p. 606). At the end of the book the new collective organism is still in its infancy. This is the child that has been born, not Rose of Sharon's that was conceived of the self-fish Connie Rivers; and her final act symbolizes this truth. It is a ritual act: she who cannot be mother of a family adopts the newly born collective person as represented by one of "the people [who] sat huddled together" in the barns when winter storms came (p. 591). It is the family unity and strength imparted to the larger unit. In primitive adoption rituals the adopting mother offers her breast to the adopted child.

The conflict of organisms is necessarily an ecological struggle, a disturbance of an ecological cycle. In Sea of Cortez Steinbeck describes a potentially perfect ecological cycle. At Cape San Lucas in Lower California the fishermen catch tuna and bring their catch to the cannery; the entrails and other waste are thrown back into the water; small fish come in to eat this refuse and are caught for bait; the bait is used to catch tuna. But the cormorants "are the flies in a perfect ecological ointment"; for they prey on the bait-fish and tend to keep them away from the cannery shore. So the natives hate the cormorants as subversives. Just such a cycle operated in California agriculture, and the migrants, driven from their homes, were absorbed into it. The agricultural corporations and big growers need pickers in great numbers to harvest their manifold crops. In the thirties they advertised everywhere for pickers with the object of bringing in more job-seekers than they needed; with too many men on hand they could lower wages and increase profits. When one crop was picked, the workers had to hurry on to another crop, if they were to make a bare subsistence. They never stayed long enough in one county to qualify for relief, and so the growers were saved higher taxes. When the time for the next harvest approached, the growers advertised again for pickers, sending handbills everywhere to bring workers back in great numbers. But there were flies in this ointment too: labor leaders, radical agitators, socialists, made the pickers dissatisfied with wages and working conditions, organized them in unions, promoted strikes, and were cordially hated by the growers.

Critics, of course, have noticed the biological features of *The Grapes of Wrath*, but without realizing how literally the monster, the family unit, and the workers' commune are meant to be real organisms. In fact, the biological and organismic side of the novel has been slighted, if not ignored. The mythical side, however, has been much more fortunate, in marked contrast to the neglect of mythical themes and structure in earlier novels. The title suggests a Biblical parallel, since Julia Ward Howe's "vintage where the grapes of wrath are stored" obviously alludes to Revelation 14:19, "the great winepress of the wrath of God." Peter Lisca has accurately pointed to the principal mythical model: the exodus of the Hebrews from Egypt to Canaan. He shows that the novel's three well-marked divisions—drought (Chapters 1–10), journey (11–18), and sojourn in California (19–30)—correspond to oppression in Egypt, exodus, and settlement in Canaan: the drought and erosion are the plagues of Egypt; the banks and land companies are Pharaoh and the Egyptian oppressors; California is Canaan, a land flowing with milk and honey; and the Californians, like the Canaanites, are hostile to the immigrants. Lisca also indicates several specific parallels: the symbolism of grapes to indicate either abundance (Numbers 13:23) or wrath and vengeance (Deuteronomy 32:32) ; the migrants are "the people," and Ma Joad's words, "we're the people—we go on" (p. 383), suggest a chosen people; in the roadside camps the migrants, like the Hebrews, formulated codes of laws to govern themselves; finally, among the willows by a stream John Joad set Rose of Sharon's stillborn child afloat in an apple box, as the infant Moses was placed in a basket among flags in the river.

There are other parallels that Lisca does not mention. The name *Joad*, I am sure, is meant to suggest *Judah*. The Joads had lived in Oklahoma peacefully since the first settlement, as the Hebrews had lived in Egypt since Joseph's time. But "there arose up a new king over Egypt, which knew not Joseph" (Exodus 1:8); and the monster, representing a changed economic order, and quite as hard-hearted as Pharaoh, knew not the Joads and their kin. In Oklahoma the dust filtered into every house and settled on everything, as in one of the Egyptian plagues the dust became lice which settled on man and beast (Exodus 8:17); plants were covered, as the locusts devoured every green thing in Egypt (Exodus 10:15); the dust ruined the corn, as hail ruined the Egyptians' flax and barley (Exodus 9:31); and it made the night as black as the plague of darkness in Egypt (Exodus 10:22 f.). On the eve of departure the Joads slaughtered two pigs, more likely victims in Oklahoma than the lambs sacrificed by the Hebrews on Passover (Exodus

12). But whereas the Hebrews despoiled the Egyptians of jewels before leaving (Exodus 12:35 f.), the Joads and other Okies were despoiled of goods and money by sharp businessmen in the land that they left.

On the journey the Joads crossed the Colorado (Red) River (Steinbeck does not mention their crossing the North Fork of the Red River on Highway 66, although he refers several times to the red country of Oklahoma) and the desert. Grampa and Granma Joad, like the elder Israelites, died on the way. Connie Rivers complained about the conditions into which the Joads had led him, and finally deserted them: the Hebrews continually murmured against their leaders on the ground that they were worse off in the desert than in Egypt, and Korah rebelled (Numbers 16). The migrants' fried dough was the unleavened bread of the Israelites, and both peoples longed for meat. The laws of the roadside camp, like the Mosaic law, forbade murder, theft, adultery, rape, and seduction; and they too included rules of sanitation, privacy, and hospitality. In the camps "a man might have a willing girl if he stayed with her, if he fathered her children and protected them," as in Exodus 22:16, "And if a man entice a maid that is not betrothed, and lie with her, he shall surely endow her to be his wife." The migrant lawbreaker was banished from all camps; the Hebrew lawbreaker was either banished or stoned. Steinbeck's repeated "It is unlawful" echoes the "Thou shalt not" of the Decalogue.

On the road west the Joads met men who were going back to Oklahoma from California. These men reported that although California was a lovely and rich country the residents were hostile to the migrant workers, treated them badly, and paid them so poorly that many migrants starved to death in slack periods. In Numbers 13, scouts whom Moses sent ahead into Canaan came back with the report that "surely it floweth with milk and honey"; nevertheless they made "an evil report of the land which they had searched unto the children of Israel, saying, The land . . . is a land that eateth up the inhabitants thereof"; and the natives were giants who looked upon the

Hebrews as locusts. Yet the Joads, like Joshua and Caleb, were determined to enter the land. The meanness of California officers at the border, the efforts to turn back indigent migrants, the refusal of cities and towns to let migrant workers enter, except when their labor was needed—in all this we may see the efforts of the Edomites, Moabites, and Amorites to keep the Israelites from entering their countries.

In spite of the Canaanites' hostility the Israelites persisted and took over the promised land. The Book of Joshua ends with victory and conquest. But *The Grapes of Wrath* ends at a low point in the fortunes of the Joads, as if the Exodus story had ended with the Hebrews' defeat at Ai (Joshua 7), when the Canaanites routed an army of 3,000 Israelites and killed a number of them, "wherefore the hearts of the people melted, and became as water. And Joshua rent his clothes, and fell to the earth upon his face . . ." The defeat came upon Israel because Achan had "taken of the accursed thing," that is, from Canaanite spoils which belonged to the Lord he had taken silver, gold, and fine raiment. The migrant Okies met defeat because they had not learned to give up selfish desires for money and possessions: still too many wanted to undercut the pay of fellow-workers and had no feeling of a common cause. But they would accomplish nothing if they did not stand together. The issue is left there, and a happy ending depends on an "if": if the migrants should realize their strength in union. Casy, Tom, and Pa Joad predict a change that is coming, a better time for the people, when they will take matters into their own hands and set them right. And the author foresees doom for the oppressors: "Every little means, every violence, every raid on a Hooverville, every deputy swaggering through a ragged camp put off the day a little and cemented the inevitability of the day" (p. 325). Only future events will tell us how the story ends: it had not ended in 1939.

Perhaps the most striking episodic parallel to Exodus occurs near the end of the novel. When Tom killed the vigilante who struck Casy down and left the region when it looked as if he would be found out, he acted as Moses had done. For "when Moses was grown" he saw an Egyptian beating a Hebrew laborer, and he killed the Egyptian and hid his body in the sand. The next day when he reproved a Hebrew for striking another, the angry offender said, ". . . intendest thou to kill me, as thou killedst the Egyptian?" And Moses, seeing that his deed was known, "fled from the face of Pharaoh, and dwelt in the land of Midian." In the Pentateuch this happened in Egypt before the Exodus; in *The Grapes of Wrath* it happened in California after the migration. It is another Steinbeck myth inversion. The "house of bondage" is in the new land; in the old land the people had lived in patriarchal contentment until they were forced to leave. It was more like Israel's earlier migration from Palestine to Egypt. Just after reaching California, Tom said to Casy, ". . . this ain't no lan' of milk an' honey like the preachers say. They's a mean thing here" (p. 342). So Moses' task of delivering his people from bondage is just beginning, not ending; it is now that he strikes the first blow. The migrants have gained nothing by merely exchanging one land for another; they must still deal with the "mean thing."

Hence a stillborn child is set adrift upon a stream at the end of the story, rather than a living child at the beginning. It was a "blue shriveled little mummy" (p. 603). This time the firstborn of the oppressed had died; yet it was a sign to the oppressors. John Joad said, "Go down and tell 'em. Go down in the street an' rot an' tell 'em that way. That's the way you can talk" (p. 609). What message? It is given in Chapter Twenty-Five: oranges, corn, potatoes, pigs, are destroyed to keep prices up, though millions of people need them. "And children dying of pellagra must die because a profit cannot be taken from an orange."

Tom Joad becomes the new Moses who will lead the oppressed people, succeeding Jim Casy, who had found One Big Soul in the hills, as Moses had found the Lord on Mount Horeb. As a teacher of a social gospel Casy is more like Jesus than like Moses, and nearly as many echoes of the New Testament as of the Old are heard in *The Grapes of Wrath*. Peter

Lisca and Martin Shockley have listed several parallels between the Joad story and the gospel story. Jim Casy's initials are JC, and he retired to the wilderness to find spiritual truth ("I been in the hills . . . like Jesus went into the wilderness . . .") and came forth to teach a new doctrine of love and good works (p. 109). One of the vigilantes who attacked him pointed him out with the words, "That's him. That shiny bastard"; and just before the mortal blow struck him Casy said, "You don' know what you're a-doin'" (p. 527). And Casy sacrificed himself for others when he surrendered himself as the man who had struck a deputy at Hooverville. Two Joads were named Thomas, and one became Casy's disciple, who would carry on his teaching. Tom told his mother, "I'm talkin' like Casy," after saying that he would be present everywhere, though unseen, "If Casy knowed," echoing Jesus' words, "Lo, I am with you always, . . ." (p. 572). Lisca and Shockley have also perceived the Eucharist in Rose of Sharon's final act, when she gave her nourishment (the body and blood) to save the life of a starving man.

The correspondences between the gospel story and Steinbeck's novel go still deeper than these critics have indicated. Thirteen persons started west, Casy and twelve Joads, who, as we have seen, also represent Judea (Judah) whom Jesus came to teach. Not only were two Joads named Thomas, but another was John; Casy's name was James, brother and disciple of Jesus. One of the twelve, Connie Rivers, was not really a Joad; he is Judas, for not only did he desert the Joads selfishly at a critical moment, but just before he did so he told his wife that he would have done better to stay home "an' study 'bout tractors. Three dollars a day they get, an' pick up extra money, too" (pp. 343–344). The tractor driver of Chapter Five got three dollars a day, and the extra money was a couple of dollars for "[caving] the house in a little." Three dollars are thirty pieces of silver—remember Sinclair Lewis' Elmer Gantry, who received thirty dimes after his betrayal of the old teacher of Greek and Hebrew at the seminary. We should notice too the crowing of roosters on the night when Casy was killed—the only passage, I believe, where this is mentioned—and this at a time when the Joads had to deny Tom.

Casy taught as one with authority: "the sperit" was strong in him. His gospel coincided in certain respects with Jesus' doctrine: love for all men, sympathy for the poor and oppressed, realization of the gospel in active ministry, subordination of formal observances to men's real needs and of property to humanity, and toleration of men's weaknesses and sensual desires. When Casy said, "An' I wouldn' pray for a ol' fella that's dead. He's awright" (p. 197), he was saying in Okie speech, "Let the dead bury their dead" (Luke 9:60).

Casy's doctrine, however, went beyond Christ's. He had rejected the Christianity which he once preached, much as Jesus, starting out as John the Baptist's disciple, abandoned and transformed John's teachings. In *The Grapes of Wrath* John Joad, Tom's uncle, represents John the Baptist, who had practiced asceticism and emphasized remission of sins. John Joad, of course, has almost no literal resemblance to John the Baptist; but he did live a lonely, comfortless life in a spiritual desert, and he was guilt-ridden, obsessed with sin. He was a pious man, a Baptist in denomination; and we hear about his baptism "over to Polk's place. Why, he got to plungin' an' jumpin'. Jumped over a feeny bush as big as a piana. Over he'd jump, an' back he'd jump, howlin' like a dog-wolf in moon time" (p. 39). John, trying to atone for his "sins," was good to children, and they "thought he was Jesus Christ Awmighty." He was, however, the forerunner: for one greater than he had come. When Casy gave himself up to the officers to save Tom, then John realized how unworthy he was beside Casy: "He done her so easy. Jus' stepped up there an' says, 'I done her'" (p. 367).

It is John Joad's Christianity that Casy rejected. After worrying about his sexual backslidings, Casy came to the conclusion that

Maybe it ain't a sin. Maybe it's just the way folks is. . . . There ain't no sin and there ain't no virtue. There's just stuff people do. It's all part of the same thing. And some of the things folks do is

nice, and some ain't nice, but that's as far as any man got a right
to say [pp. 31–32].

His doctrine of sin led to his positive doctrine of love: ". . .
maybe it's all men an' all women we love; maybe that's the
Holy Sperit—the human sperit—the whole shebang. Maybe all
men got one big soul ever'body's a part of" (p. 33). And so he
arrived at the doctrine of the Oversoul. "All that lives is holy"
(p. 196), he said, and this meant that he should be with other
men: "a wilderness ain't no good, 'cause his little piece of a soul
wasn't no good 'less it was with the rest, an' was whole" (p.
570). In a California jail his doctrine took complete shape as a
social gospel, and Casy's ministry became the organizing of farm
workers into unions.

In colloquial language Casy and Tom express the book's doctrine: that not only is each social unit—family, corporation,
union, state—a single organism, but so is mankind as a whole,
embracing all the rest. It is, in effect, a transcendental version
of the social-organism theory: Comte's religion of humanity
with an Emersonian content, as Woodburn Ross has pointed
out. The wine of this new gospel is poured into the old bottle
of Christian scripture. Through echoes of the evangelists the
author wants to make clear that this is the evangel for our
times. The passage quoted above, on the two squatting men
who are the anlage and zygote of the new communal organism,
recalls Matthew 18:20: "For where two or three are gathered
together in my name, there am I in the midst of them." The
"crime . . . that goes beyond denunciation," "a failure . . . that
topples all our success"—want and hunger in the midst of
plenty—that is the sin against the Holy Ghost. The large tracts
of uncultivated land that landless farmers could work, and the
prophecies that the absentee owners, grown soft, will lose those
lands to the dispossessed, strong in adversity and in union, recall the parable of the vineyard: the wicked husbandmen will
be destroyed and the vineyard let to other husbandmen who
will produce as they should (Matthew 21:33–41). Such owners
are like the Scribes and Pharisees, who do not go into the king-

dom of heaven themselves, and refuse to let anyone else go in (Matthew 23:13); instead they bind heavy burdens on men's shoulders (Matthew 23:4). Finally, the concluding theme, that family interests must be subordinate to the common welfare, that all individual souls are part of one great soul, corresponds to Jesus' rejection of family ties for the kingdom of heaven's sake: "For whosoever shall do the will of my Father which is in heaven, the same is my brother, and sister, and mother" (Matthew 12:50).

Tom, Casy's disciple, is a Christ figure, too. He seems at first just another Okie, a man quick to wrath who had killed another man in a brawl at a dance, often rough of speech, and not always kind to others. But we gradually become aware that he is different from his kinsmen. His mother said to him, "I knowed from the time you was a little fella. . . . Ever'thing you do is more'n you. When they sent you up to prison I knowed it. You're spoke for" (p. 482). In prison he had received a Christmas card from his grandmother, and on it was the verse "Jesus meek and Jesus mild"; thereafter his cell-block mates called him Jesus Meek. The Messianic succession was complete when Tom said farewell to his mother, announcing his intention of taking up Casy's work and trying to induce "our people . . . [to] work together for our own thing" (p. 571), to take over all "the good rich lan' layin' fallow" ("he hath anointed me to preach the gospel to the poor, . . . to set at liberty them that are bruised": Luke 4:18, quoting Isaiah). Though he would vanish from his parents' sight and they would not know where he was, yet, if Casy was right, if a man has no soul of his own, but only a fragment of the one big soul,

"Then it don' matter. Then I'll be all aroun' in the dark. I'll be ever'where—wherever you look. Wherever they's a fight so hungry people can eat, I'll be there. Wherever they's a cop beatin' up a guy, I'll be there. If Casy knowed, why, I'll be in the way guys yell when they're mad an'—I'll be in the way kids laugh when they're hungry an' they know supper's ready. An' when our folks eat the stuff they raise an' live in the houses they build—why, I'll be there [p. 572].

It is not only "Lo, I am with you always" but also "where two or three are gathered together . . . there am I in the midst of them," and it is identity with the hungry, thirsty, sick, naked, and imprisoned, as expressed in Matthew 25:35–45. This means also no hate even for the wrongdoers: "The other side is made of men" too, as Doc Burton said in *In Dubious Battle*. When Tom Joad reproved the one-eyed man who reviled his employer, he was in effect saying, "And why beholdest thou the mote that is in thy brother's eye, but considerest not the beam that is in thine own eye?" (Matthew 7:3).

Jesus is a dying god, and the dying god is the year spirit, the rituals of whose cult are entwined in this novel with rituals of migration and colony-founding. The sunset was red "and the earth was bloody in its setting light" on the eve of the Joads' departure for California in summer drought; then the family congress went into session, and just after that two pigs were slaughtered. The slaughter is described in detail, as was the slaughter of cows in *In Dubious Battle*. The migrants were leaving the graves of their ancestors behind them, personified in Muley Graves. He was stubborn, as his nickname indicates, and he refused to leave the country, although he had no house to live in: ". . . There ain't nobody can run a guy name of Graves outa this country," he said, and "I'm jus' wanderin' aroun' like a damn ol' graveyard ghos'." "Like a ol' graveyard ghos' goin' to neighbors' houses in the night" (pp. 69, 70). Then Grampa died before the Joads were out of Oklahoma, and he was buried in his own country's soil. Granma died in the night that followed their arrival in California. The new venture is not for the ancestors; but the pauper's grave that Granma received in California links the old country to the new and the Joad family to another land: this is now their home. Finally, Casy made the supreme sacrifice at a moment when the Joads were down and out. It was already fall; the nights were now chilly (the Hooper ranch must have had a very late peach crop). The Joads moved to the cotton fields and settled in the camp where the winter rains overtook them. The storms were destructive and yet harbingers of the new year: "Tiny points of grass came through the earth, and in a few days the hills were pale green with the beginning year" (p. 592). The migration and the year are one thing.

In no Steinbeck novel do the biological and mythical strands fit so neatly together as in *The Grapes of Wrath*. The Oklahoma land company is at once monster, Leviathan, and Pharaoh oppressing the tenant farmers, who are equally monster's prey and Israelites. The California land companies are Canaanites, Pharisees, Roman government, and the dominant organism of an ecological community. The family organisms are forced to join together into a larger collective organism; the Hebrews' migration and sufferings weld them into a united nation; the poor and oppressed receive a Messiah who teaches them unity in the Oversoul. The Joads are equally a family unit, the twelve tribes of Israel, and the twelve disciples. Casy and Tom are both Moses and Jesus as leaders of the people and guiding organs in the new collective organism. Each theme—organismic, ecological, mythical; and each phase of the mythical: Exodus, Messiah, Leviathan, ritual sequence—builds up to a single conclusion: the unity of all mankind.

To liken the Okies to the Israelites—this too may seem incongruous. Yet the parallel is really close. The oppressed laborers in Egypt were as much despised by their masters as the migrant workers in California. Moses was certainly a labor agitator, and Jesus appealed to the poor and lowly and called rude fishermen and tax-gatherers to his company. Again the mythical structure imparts a cosmic meaning to the tale. These contemporary events, says Steinbeck, are as portentous for the future as was the Hebrews' migration from Egypt, and for the same reasons.

The myth is accompanied by symbolic images. As the title would lead us to expect, the imagery of grapes, vineyards, and vintage is abundant. As Lisca has pointed out, the grapes mean abundance at first and then bitterness, which turns to wrath as abundant harvests are deliberately destroyed: "In the souls of the people the grapes of wrath are filling and growing heavy, growing heavy for the vintage" (p. 477). The turtle of the early chapters that persistently kept to his southwestward course has been noticed by nearly every reviewer and critic who has discussed *The Grapes of Wrath*. The snakes in this novel have received less attention. After their first view of the fertile California valley from Tehachapi, the Joads went down the road into it, and on the way down they ran over a rattlesnake (Tom was driving), which the wheel broke and left squirming in the road (p. 314). This is an omen which betokens fulfillment of the behest spoken in the "Battle Hymn of the Republic": "Let the Hero, born of woman, crush the serpent with his heel." The snake represents the agricultural system of California, which the immigrants are destined to crush. Later Al Joad deliberately ran over a gopher snake; when Tom reproved him, Al gaily said, "I hate 'em . . . Hate all kinds" (p. 499). The Okies do not yet know who their friends are.

Steinbeck left the conclusion of his story to events. How did it turn out? On September 1, 1939, fewer than five months after *The Grapes of Wrath* was published, Hitler invaded Poland and began the war which interrupted the course of events that Steinbeck foresaw. In 1940 America began to prepare for war and was in it before the end of 1941. This meant an end of unemployment. The Okies and Arkies came to work in the shipyards of San Francisco and San Pedro bays; they replaced enlisted men in industries and businesses everywhere; and many, of course, were enlisted, too. They found houses to live in, settled down, and remained employed when the war was over. Mexicans and Orientals once more harvested California's crops, and "wetbacks" became a problem. So did *The Grapes of Wrath* never find a conclusion, cut off by the turn of events? Had the owners learned their lesson and improved conditions? Disquieting reports have been coming from the fields: more Americans are now employed in migratory farm labor than a few years ago, pay is low, and conditions are bad. Perhaps the story has not ended yet.

J. P. HUNTER

J. P. Hunter has taught at the University of Florida, Williams College, the University of California at Riverside and Emory University. His publications include a book on *Robinson Crusoe*, a critical edition of *Moll Flanders*, and articles in *Review of English Studies* and *The Journal of English and Germanic Philology*.

Steinbeck's Wine of Affirmation in *The Grapes of Wrath*

I

Almost everyone agrees that *The Grapes of Wrath* is Steinbeck's most important early work, and it may well be that his critical reputation will ultimately stand or fall on that one book. Those who do not like the novel contend that it exemplifies Steinbeck's most blatant artistic weaknesses: lack of character development, imperfect conception of structure, careless working out of theme, and sentimentality. The last two chapters of the novel have been considered especially illustrative of these weaknesses, for they are said to demonstrate the final inability of Steinbeck to come to grips, except in a superficial way, with the ideological and artistic problems posed in the novel. The final scene has drawn the sharpest criticism of all, for here Steinbeck is charged with a sensational, shocking, and therefore commercial substitute for an artistic solution. The charges are not new ones, but they have a peculiar urgency at a time when the reputation of Steinbeck's early work is in danger of eclipse. And they constitute a basal attack on Steinbeck

Reprinted from *Essays in Modern American Literature*, edited by Richard E. Langford, Guy Owen and William E. Taylor. Deland, Florida: Stetson University Press, 1963. By permission of copyright owner, Everett/Edwards, Inc., Deland, Florida.

as artist, for if it is true that his most important book is inadequately conceived and imperfectly worked out, Steinbeck's claim to a place among significant novelists is seriously impaired.

The inadequacy of the ending of *The Grapes of Wrath*, is, however, more apparent than real. When the events of the last two chapters (and particularly the final scene in the barn) are examined in relation to the novel's total structure, they demonstrate a careful working out of theme in fictional terms. At the end, the Joads who remain (only six of the original twelve) seem to have a grim physical future; as they hover in a dry barn while the deluge continues and the waters rise, they face the prospect of a workless winter in a hostile world. But even though their promised land has turned out to be "no lan' of milk and honey" (p. 342) but instead a battleground stained with the blood of Jim Casy, the Joads are at last able to come to grips with their world. Instead of idealists who dream of white houses and clusters of plenty they have become people of action who translate the prophecy of Jim Casy into the realities of wrath.

II

Under the old order in Oklahoma, the Joads were a proud people, individualists who asked nothing from anyone and who were content with their family-size world as long as they had a home surrounded by land which they could caress into fertility. Like the early Tom, they believed in "Just puttin' one foot in front a the other" (p. 237), and their thoughts did not stray beyond the limits of their families and their land. When the change comes, when they find themselves in captivity on land they have known as their own, and finally when the captor banks insult their dignity by driving them like nomads away from their homes, they do not understand the change, and they are helpless to oppose it. A few, like Muley Graves, may try, pitifully, to fight back with a sniper's bullet or a harassing laugh from parched fields, but the majority only know that the old is gone, and that they are powerless to fight against the new. As the dust covers the land and the burrowing machines cut their swath of progress through fields and houses, the men stand figuring in the dust, unbroken by events, but powerless to change them.

In their powerlessness, the Joads and their neighbors first choose the road of illusion, and they pursue their particular Western version of the American dream across Route 66. In their heads dance visions of plenty in California—their Canaan of the Golden West—but their map is an orange handbill, and soon their luxurious dreams of ripe fruit and white houses are changed to nightmares of hunger and Hoovervilles. Even in California, the Joads are merely individuals driven by forces they do not understand until, in wrath, they learn their lesson.

The lesson they learn forms the thematic base of *The Grapes of Wrath*, and although the Joads do not accept it fully until the end of the novel, the solution has been suggested quite early in the narrative. This theme—that strength can be achieved through a selfless unity of the entire community of Dispossessed—is first suggested when Tom and Jim Casy meet Muley Graves, a kind of mad prophet, on the old Joad place, and Muley is asked whether he will share his food. " 'I ain't got no choice in the matter,' " Muley says, then explains:

"That ain't like I mean it. That ain't. I mean"—he stumbled— "what I mean, if a fella's got somepin to eat an' another fella's hungry—why, the first fella ain't got no choice. I mean, s'pose I pick up my rabbits an' go off somewheres an' eat 'em. See?"

"I see," said Casy. "I can see that. Muley sees somepin there, Tom. Muley's got a-holt of somepin and it's too big for him, an' it's too big for me" [p. 66].

Though he still doesn't understand the concept fully, Casy has already incorporated Muley's prophetic wisdom into his own wilderness philosophy when, during his breakfast "grace" (two chapters later), he tells of his insights:

"I got thinkin' how . . . mankin' was holy when it was one thing. An' it on'y got unholy when one mis'able little fella got the bit in his teeth an' run off his own way, kickin' an' draggin' and fightin'. Fella like that bust the holiness. But when they're all workin' together, not one fella for another fella, but one fella kind of harnessed to the whole shebang—that's right, that's holy" [p. 110].

Later Casy develops the idea and translates it into action, ultimately even sacrificing himself for it. But at first he finds few hearers. At breakfast, Ma is the only one who seems to notice the unusual "prayer," and she watches Casy "as though he were suddenly a spirit, not human any more, a voice out of the ground" (pp. 111, 126). The other Joads listen to Casy, but they do not hear him for a long time.

III

Casy's role is central to the structure of *The Grapes of Wrath*, for in him the narrative structure and the thematic structure are united. This role is best seen when set against the Biblical background which informs both types of structure in the novel. Peter Lisca has noted that the novel reflects the three-part division of the Old Testament exodus account (captivity, journey, promised land), but that the "parallel is not worked out in detail." Actually, the lack of detailed parallel seems to be deliberate, for Steinbeck is reflecting a broader background of which the exodus story is only a part.

Steinbeck makes the incidents in his novel suggest a wide range of Old and New Testament stories. As the twelve Joads (corresponding to the twelve tribes of Israel) embark on their journey (leaving the old order behind), they mount the truck in ark fashion, two by two:

. . . the rest swarmed up on top of the load, Connie and Rose of Sharon, Pa and Uncle John, Ruthie and Winfield, Tom and the preacher. Noah stood on the ground looking up at the great load of them sitting on top of the truck [p. 155].

Grampa (like Lot's wife) is unable to cope with the thought of a new life, and his wistful look at the past brings his death—a parallel emphasized by the scripture verse (quoting Lot) which Tom picks out to bury with Grampa. Uncle John (like Ananias) withholds money from the common fund, in order to satisfy his selfish desires. The list could be lengthened extensively, and many allusions are as isolated and apparently unrelated to the context as the ones cited here. Looked at in one way, these allusions seem patternless, for they refer to widely separated sections of Biblical history. However, the frequency of allusion suggests the basic similarity between the plight of the Joads and that of the Hebrew people. Rather than paralleling a single section of Biblical history, the novel reflects the broader history of the chosen people from their physical bondage to their spiritual release by means of a messiah.

If the reader approaches *The Grapes of Wrath* searching for too exact a parallel, he will be disappointed, for just when it seems as if a one-to-one ratio exists, Steinbeck breaks the pattern. Tom, for example, is a Moses-type leader of his people as they journey toward the promised land. Like Moses, he has killed a man and has been away for a time before rejoining his people and becoming their leader. Like Moses, he has a younger brother (Aaron-Al) who serves as a vehicle for the leader (spokesman-truck driver). And shortly before reaching the destination, he hears and rejects the evil reports of those who have visited the land (Hebrew "spies"—Oklahomans going back). But soon the parallel ends. Carried out carefully at the beginning, it does not seem to exist once the journey is completed. Granma, not Tom, dies just before the new land is reached, and Tom remains the leader of the people until finally (and here a different parallel is suggested) he becomes a disciple of Casy's gospel. This, in the miniature of one character, is what continually happens in *The Grapes of Wrath*. The scene changes, the parallel breaks; and gradually the context shifts from a basically Old Testament one to a New Testament one.

Steinbeck makes his allusions suggestive, rather than exhaustive, and he implies certain parallels without calling for too rigid an allegorical reading. In *East of Eden* Steinbeck also uses the method of suggestive allusion, and Adam's sons are not named Cain and Abel, but Caleb and Aaron (note the initials game again). This is no mere puzzle or covering of tracks, for the method serves to nullify too literal a reading, while at the same time drawing in a whole new range of suggestions. Instead of only Abel, the reader is asked to recall also the Biblical characteristics of another No. 2 brother. In *The Grapes of Wrath*, the method gives Steinbeck the freedom to skirt the particularly vexing time problem, for in the background myth the changes in the Hebrew people take place over centuries, while similar ideological changes in Steinbeck's characters occur within one year. In effect, Steinbeck collapses several hundred years of Hebrew history into the single year of his story; the entire history of man (according to the Judeo-Christian tradition) is reflected in the long hungry summer of one persecuted family.

This span of centuries is focused in Casy, whose ideas bridge the gap from Old to New Testament (according to the Christian concept of Biblical thought as developmental). Parallels between the life of Jim Casy and the messiah whose initials he bears are plentiful. He embarks upon his mission after a long period of meditation in the wilderness; he corrects the old ideas of religion and justice; he selflessly sacrifices himself for his cause, and when he dies he tells his persecutors, "You don' know what you're a-doin'" (p. 527). Less obvious perhaps, but equally important, is the role of the old Casy, before his wilderness experience, for he must ultimately be considered in messianic rather than Christological terms. Casy had been a typical hell-and-damnation evangelist who emphasized the rigidity of the old moral law and who considered himself ultimately doomed because human frailty prevented his achieving the purity demanded by the law. His conversion to a social gospel represents a movement from Old Testament to New Testament thought, an expanded horizon of responsibility. The annunciation of Casy's message and mission sets the ideological direction of the novel before the journey begins (just as the messiah concept influences Jewish thought for centuries before New Testament times), but only gradually does Casy make an impression upon a people (Jews-Joads) used to living under the old dispensation. Over Route 66 he rides quietly—a guest, a thirteenth —and only as time passes does the new idea blossom and the new order emerge; and the outsider—the thirteenth—becomes spiritual leader of a people to whom he had been a convention, a grace before meals.

Steinbeck's canvas is, on the surface, a painting of broad modern strokes, but its scenes are sketched along the outlines of the Judeo-Christian myth, a sort of polyptych depicting man's sojourn in a hostile world. The background is often faded, sometimes erased, and occasionally distorted, but structurally and ideologically it provides depth for Steinbeck's modern microcosm. In *The Grapes of Wrath* the background ideology becomes secularized and transcendentalized, but the direction of thought is still recognizable: a widening of concern. After the dispersion, there is still a saving remnant whose compassion begins to extend beyond its own familial or tribal group.

Steinbeck's method is perhaps not uniformly successful, and in some work done in this manner (such as *East of Eden* and *Burning Bright*) the fusion of the particular and the mythic seems, if not less perfectly conceived, less carefully wrought. But in *The Grapes of Wrath* the modern and mythic are peculiarly at one, and the story of a family which, in the values of its contemporary society, is hardly worth a jod, is invested with meaning when viewed against a history of enduring significance.

I V

Casy's gospel is reinforced thematically in *The Grapes of Wrath* by the panoramic intercalary chapters, which translate the plight of the Joad family into larger terms. Structurally, these chapters usually anticipate (in general terms) the particular actions which follow, and stylistically they often recall the King James Bible, particularly the prophetic books such as Isaiah and Jeremiah. Thematically, the most significant of these essays is Chapter 14, which begins:

The western land nervous under the beginning change. The Western States, nervous as horses before a thunder storm. The great owners, nervous, sensing a change, knowing nothing of the nature of the change.

Later the nature of the change is described:

One man, one family driven from the land; this rusty car creaking along the highway to the west. I lost my land, a single tractor took my land. I am alone and I am bewildered. And in the night one family camps in a ditch and another family pulls in and the tents come out. The two men squat on their hams and the women and children listen. . . . Here "I lost my land" is changed; a cell is split and from its splitting grows . . . "we lost *our* land." . . . Two men are not as lonely and perplexed as one. And from this first "we" there grows a still more dangerous thing: "I have a little food" plus "I have none." If from this problem the sum is "We have a little food," the thing is on its way, the movement has direction. Only a little multiplication now, and this land, this tractor are ours. . . . This is the beginning—from "I" to "we" [p. 206].

The intercalary chapters record this movement in the novel's action; similar passages in Chapters 1 and 29 (as Lisca has suggested) emphasize the change from family units to larger groupings:

1: The people came out of their houses. . . . Men stood by their fences. . . . The men were silent and they did not move often. And the women came out of the houses to stand beside their men—to feel whether this time the men would break. The women studied the men's faces secretly. . . . After a while the faces of the watching men lost their bemused perplexity and became hard and angry and resistant. Then the women knew they were safe and that there was no break.

29: The women watched the men, watched to see whether the break had come at last. The women stood silently and watched. And *where a number of men gathered together,* the fear went from their faces, and anger took its place. And the women sighed with relief, for they knew it was all right—the break had not come; and the break would never come as long as fear could turn to wrath. (Italics mine)

Though the movement from "I" to "we" is imaged several times throughout *The Grapes of Wrath,* the Joads do not really commit themselves to the new mode of thought until very late in the novel. Before their belated commitment, they show their limited view in many ways. Al cannot understand the men's cooperation in job-hunting: "Wouldn' it be better," he asks, "if one fella went alone? Then if they was one piece of work a fella'd get it,' " and he is told:

You ain't learned. . . . Takes gas to get roun' the country. Gas costs fifteen cents a gallon. Them four fellas can't take four cars. So each of 'em puts in a dime an' they get gas. You got to learn [p. 350].

Rose of Sharon and Connie think only of themselves and of how they will break from the group, and when difficulties arise Connie wishes that he had stayed in Oklahoma to man a tractor driving the people from the land. Later, alone, Rose of Sharon complains of her plight and frets about the coming child, and instead of sharing the family responsibility she adds to family worries. Uncle John is similarly preoccupied with his guilt and his personal problems and is almost useless to the group, picking cotton at only half the rate of the other men. Both he and Al withhold money from the family treasury. Noah, thoughtless of the others, wanders away. Connie, leaving a pregnant wife, also deserts. Even the children show a teasing selfishness. Ruthie eats her crackerjacks slowly so that she can taunt the other children when theirs are gone, and at croquet she ignores the rules and tries to play by herself.

Even though Ma, Pa, and Tom are less individualistic than

the others, their concern is limited to the family group. Ma's one aim is keeping the family together, and when she says "This here fambly's goin' under," she is lamenting the disintegration of her entire world. While not a dynamic leader, Pa does his best to fulfill his patriarchal responsibility. Tom shows that he values the family over himself by breaking parole to make the journey with them, and he frequently demonstrates his dedication to them. Once, Tom wishes he could act like Al, but he is unable to forget his responsibility. Ma describes him well: "Everything you do is more'n you," she says (p. 482).

Conversion to a wider concern comes rapidly toward the end of *The Grapes of Wrath*. Tom is the first Joad to extend his vision. In wrath, he moves to commitment beside the broken body of Jim Casy. A few days later, when he meets Ma in the dark cave, his dedication is complete. By contrast with Muley Graves (whose womb-like cave is an escape, a place where he feels "like nobody can come at me," p. 82) Tom does not plan to stay in his refuge. He tells Ma of his meditations about Casy and recites a passage Casy had quoted from Ecclesiastes (The Preacher):

Two are better than one, because they have a good reward for their labor. For if they fall, the one will lif' up his fellow, but woe to him that is alone when he falleth, for he hath not another to help him up. . . . Again, if two lie together, then they have heat; but how can one be warm alone? And if one prevail against him, two shall withstand him, and a three-fold cord is not quickly broken [pp. 570–571].

Tom has to leave the family to protect them, but by now he also has a more important reason. He has seen the folly of a narrow family devotion like that of tractor-driver Willy Feely ("Fust an' on'y thing I got to think about is my own folks. What happens to other folks is their look-out," p. 75) and plans to work for a cause transcending family lines:

"Tom," [Ma] said. "What you aimin' to do?"
He was quiet for a long time. . . .

"Tom," Ma repeated, "what you gonna do?"
"What Casy done," he said [p. 571].

Ma does not fully comprehend Tom's intention, but she has moved from a rigid defense of family unity during the journey (refusing to allow the family to split into two parts: "All we got is the family unbroke") to acceptance of new ideas in a new order. And after she leaves Tom she is tempted to reach backward—she takes "three steps toward the mound of vines"— but then quickly returns to the camp. Back in the boxcar, Pa talks wistfully of the past times ("spen' all my time a thinkin' how it use' ta be"), but Ma is acclimated to the difference now. "This here's purtier—better lan'," says Ma. Women, she observes, can adapt themselves to change. Earlier, before her meeting with Tom, she had lamented the breakup of the family; now she has a broader perspective: " '*People* is goin' on— changin' a little maybe, but goin' right on.' " Later, she is even more explicit. "Use ta be the fambly was fust. It ain't so now. It's anybody" (pp. 577, 606).

At the time of the birth, the larger unity is demonstrated. Pa (who had said earlier that he would work for twenty cents an hour even if it cost someone else his job) suddenly becomes a leader of men, conscious of the strength of organized effort:

"Water's risin'," he said. "How about if we throwed up a bank? We could do her if ever'body helped" [p. 594].

The dam is for the Joads, of course, but it is also for the others; all the families face the same danger, and each can flee—alone— or work together for their salvation, and they decide to stay:

Over the men came a fury of work, a fury of battle. When one man dropped his shovel, another took it up [p. 599].

Uncle John, choosing between desertion and devotion, works so hard that Pa has to caution him: "You take it easy. You'll kill yaself." And later, asked to dispose of the baby's body, Uncle John hesitates, then accedes:

"Why do I got to do it? Why don't you fellas? I don' like it." And then, "Sure, I'll do it. Sure, I will. Come on give it to me." His voice began to rise. "Come on! Give it to me" [p. 608].

Al, whose only concern had been a good time, also moves toward what is, for him, an acceptance of larger responsibility (marriage to Aggie). Even Ruthie, on a child level, shows a change. On the way to the barn, she refuses to share the petals of her flower with Winfield, and, commanded to share, cruelly jabs one petal on his nose; but in her childish way she also senses that times are different:

Ruthie felt how the fun was gone. "Here," she said. "Here's some more. Stick some on your forehead" [p. 616].

And, then, in Rose of Sharon, the final change.

V

Rose of Sharon's sacrificial act represents the final breakdown of old attitudes, and climaxes the novel's thematic movement. The final bastion of the old order, Rose of Sharon had been the most selfish of the remaining Joads; her concern had never extended beyond herself and her immediate family (Connie and the expected child). In giving life to the stranger (symbolically, she gives body and wine: Song of Songs 7:7— "Thy breasts [are like] to clusters of grapes"), she accepts the larger vision of Jim Casy, and her commitment fulfills the terms of salvation according to Casy's plan. In their hesitancy and confusion in the old times, the Joads had been powerless to change their fate. Unlike the turtle who dragged through the dust and planted the seeds of the future, they had drawn figures in the dust impotently with sticks. Now, however, they too are purposeful and share the secret of giving life.

The Biblical myth informs the final scene through a cluster of symbols which emphasize the change and affirm the new order. As the Joads hover in the one dry place in their world—a barn —the Bible's three major symbols of a purified order are suggested: the Old Testament deluge, the New Testament stable, and the continuing ritual of communion. In the fusion of the three, the novel's mythic background, ideological progression, and modern setting are brought together; Mt. Ararat, Bethlehem, and California are collapsed into a single unit of time, and life is affirmed in a massive symbol of regeneration.

The novel's final picture—a still life of Rose of Sharon holding the old man—combines the horror with the hope. Its imitation of the madonna and child (one face mysteriously smiling; the other wasted, and with wide, frightened eyes) is a grotesque one, for it reflects a grotesque world without painless answers, a world where men are hit by axe handles and children suffer from skitters. Steinbeck does not promise Paradise for the Joads. Their wildest dreams image not golden streets, but indoor plumbing. Dams will continue to break—babies will continue to be stillborn. But the people will go on: "this is the beginning—from 'I' to 'we.'" The grapes of wrath have ripened, and in trampling out the vintage the Dispossessed have committed themselves (like Casy) to die to make men free. In despair they learn the lesson; in wrath they share the rich red wine of hope.

PASCAL COVICI, JR.

Pascal Covici, Jr., son of Steinbeck's long-time editor and friend
at The Viking Press, teaches at Southern Methodist University.
He has published *Mark Twain's Humor*, edited the revised *Viking
Portable Steinbeck* (1971), and written articles for *Southwest Review* and *The Mississippi Quarterly*.

Work and the Timeliness of
The Grapes of Wrath

John Steinbeck's Okies are desperate to survive in a way foreign
to the experience of most readers of *The Grapes of Wrath* today. The immediate object of their desperation is the getting of
jobs. The luxury of looking for the "right" job, a preoccupation of the young in an affluent society, cannot be theirs, for
they absolutely have to find work—any sort of work—if they are
going to eat. This most obvious motif in the action suggests,
paradoxically, more about the book's continuing popularity
than may at first be apparent. Certainly, however, one dismisses
the implication on the back cover of the Bantam Books edition
that "the book still lives on, as it always will," because it is
"the epic chronicle of man's struggle against injustice and inhumanity." The social problems around which the story is organized can indeed remind us, if we want them to, of the war on
poverty, or perhaps of the divisive issue of prejudice, the judging of a man's worth and qualities simply on the basis of the
group one arbitrarily identifies him with: as Californians pre-
judged "Okies," so do whites and blacks pre-judge each other.
The social questions probed by the novel are certainly still with

---

This essay, in slightly different form, was presented at the University of
Connecticut's conference on *The Grapes of Wrath*, May 3, 1969. Printed
here for the first time by permission of the author.

814

us, although the specifically issue-, or question-, orientation of the book makes the least of its impacts today.

Also important are the images of man's existence made vivid through the novel. Tom Joad's journey toward social maturity, climaxed by Tom's rebirth as the successor to Preacher Casy, grips the imagination of most readers. Tom, becoming a man, transcends the simple practicality of his father and sees, as Casy saw, the large implications of corporate ownership as it cancels out considerations of human need and human feeling. Even more to our contemporary point may be Casy's sense—to which Tom also comes—of mankind as "one big soul" (pp. 33, 572, *passim*), a kind of at-one-ment that anticipates the ideal behind the recent Haight-Ashbury community, and others like it. This is real, and worth looking at, but the clearest pattern of the book's action concerns the journey and the struggle of the Joads, and all the others, to go to California because they want to find work. Let us, then, consider the force of "work" in the novel.

Although the problems of young people—and older ones, too—as they try to find a place for themselves in the labor market have a certain contemporary relevance, the huge differences between depression-torn Okies, uneducated and poor, and the affluent, middle-class college students (affluent, at least, in comparison) who form so large a part of the reading public for *The Grapes of Wrath* today, seem to constitute total disparity. The Okies absolutely have got to have money. The simplest, most obvious, force that work takes on in the novel is, therefore, that of basic human necessity: the fundamental need and preoccupation of the people is not sex, or meaning, but a job of work to do. When Casy wonders (p. 236), "Well—s'pose all these here folks an' ever'body—s'pose they can't get no jobs out there?" he is voicing the impossible fear. A few pages later (pp. 256–261), the Joads meet a man on his way back from the coast, going back in order to starve in familar surroundings rather than among strangers. His haunted description of the jobless nightmare that befell him—no work to be had at any price, and his family starving—arouses fears so deep that blank incomprehension and then fury greet him. Pa Joad can only reaffirm his innocent willingness to work, as if sheer will could conquer the immeasurable evil implicit in conditions that would deny man satisfaction of his basic need.

So many passages concern themselves with reiterating this need that documentation is unnecessary. Beyond the need itself lies the fate of those whose need is exploited or exaggerated by circumstances, or by the conniving of others. Those in need of work—desperate need—are demeaned by their desperation; "like ants scurrying for work" (p. 317), the Okies spread out over California. With no work, they cannot pay their debts (p. 431); they feel shame at failing to find work, even when there is no work to be found (p. 440). And behind the disgrace lies terror, "the greatest terror of all" (p. 590), at the possibility of continued joblessness. Today, lack of self-respect still accompanies lack of work, and thousands of people become ant-like in their frantic determination to find a job, but the problem affects a smaller percentage of the population, and may even seem of relatively slight concern to those who read books.

Frustration, as all first-year psychology students know, and as even college presidents are learning, leads to aggression, and this may be part of the book's present voice: "on the highways the people moved like ants and searched for work, for food. And the anger began to ferment" (p. 388). A reader's response here involves more than the fat cat's fear of the hungry. The element of wrath as it grows from the frustration of need shapes the book's whole movement, from the calm, pastoral despair of the opening chapters, through the crescendo of the flight westward, culminating in the violence of the strike ("Mus' be a wreck" [p. 501], says Tom, sensing the tone before he knows the facts) and the killing of Casy, and concluding with the reestablishment of a pastoral quietness, this time in hope and promise, as Rose of Sharon nurses the starving man, and the new grass colors the hills "pale green with the beginning year" (p. 592).

The intensity of the Okies' need for work not only provides the psychic, or aesthetic, force behind the wrath that breaks out late in the novel but also enables the author to explore one realization of work itself that contrasts with an ideal of what work can be. The need for work demeans the people who must "scurry" over the countryside in search of a job and demeans as well the job thus acquired. Even the honest work of picking cotton takes on a "frantic" quality as "the line of people" (p. 585) scrabble in the field in a manner reminiscent of the ant-like activity evoked earlier. The worker can become a mere extension of the job, a "robot," like the tractor-drivers who drive through farmhouses and over wells at the novel's beginning. Their work makes them part of their machines; it dehumanizes them (p. 48). In the act of farming by means of a piece of gasoline-powered metal, all connection between man and the land is lost; relationship between work and the human being who does it vanishes. The job becomes "so easy that the wonder goes out of work" (p. 157), and the work itself becomes simply three dollars a day, a soul-destroying, if belly-filling, wage. In the final degradation of work, the selling of used cars at exorbitant prices on the basis of exorbitant claims, work becomes merely exploitation, a ritual of deception played out to the chant of "Sock it to 'em!" (p. 83).

If work and the worker can be degraded so that the reader feels shame when confronted by the hungry cotton-pickers, uneasiness before the goggled tractor-drivers, and anger at the used-car salesmen, then one knows that the author has so engineered the force of work in the book that the reader is forced to measure the degradation against a norm that includes more qualities than those of basic human activity and elemental need. In *The Grapes of Wrath*, work encompasses this activity and this need, and much more besides. Work provides a stabilizing force, not simply in economic terms but psychologically and sociologically, too. When Ma trembles in anticipation of a visit from the ladies' committee of the Weedpatch Community, she turns to her work of putting the Joads' tent to rights, and snaps some starch into the crumbling Rose of Sharon by insisting that she, too, involve herself in obligations beyond her own self-concern. Guilt-ridden Uncle John, whose life is a continual pendulum-swing between guilt and attempted atonement over his wife's death through appendicitis, rejoices, for a while, that he's "workin' hard and sleepin' good" (p. 560); and when Rose of Sharon's impending delivery reminds John of his wife's travail, he throws himself with fury into the building of a dam to hold back flood waters, for "I got to work or I'll run away" (p. 601). Building the dam, futile though it turns out to be against the tangible flood, provides a welcome psychological alternative to "doin' nothin'" (p. 595), or panicking.

As Ma moves to take over the direction of the family, she sees that lack of a job has cost Pa his traditional role. Pa doesn't like it: "Seems like it's purty near time to get out a stick," he threatens. But Ma knows he's only bluffing. "Ma put the clean dripping tin dish out on a box. She smiled down at her work. 'You get your stick, Pa,' she said. 'Times when they's food an' a place to set, then maybe you can use your stick an' keep your skin whole. But you ain't a-doin' your job, either a-thinkin' or a-workin'. If you was, why, you could use your stick, an' women folks'd sniffle their nose an' creep-mouse aroun'. But you jus' get you a stick now an' you ain't lickin' no woman; you're a-fightin', 'cause I got a stick all laid out too'" (p. 481).

"A place to set" suggests another aspect of the implications behind the fact of work—or of "no work." Repeatedly, work is linked to the dream articulated in *Of Mice and Men*, the dream of one day having "a little lan'" of one's own (pp. 280, 571, *passim*). Such work is "steady work"; it implies a stability different from the shiftiness implicit in having to "scrabble for your dinner ever' day" (p. 280). "Steady" work on the one hand, the need to "scrabble" on the other: this contrast comes up again and again. The frantic connotations of "scrabbling" suggest both the dehumanization of humans caused by the over-whelming nature of their need, and the fury brought on by the frustration of need. And the need goes beyond the merely physical, important though this be. To work is to do well; the very roots of a man's self-respect lie in his capacity to find, perform, and keep on performing a job of useful work. Young Connie, Rose of Sharon's husband, strikes us favorably when first he appears; "he was a good hard worker and would make a good husband" (p. 130), we are told. But Connie sinks slowly in our estimation, finally vanishing from sight, abandoning his wife and unborn child. Conditions, one infers, have turned out to be too much for him; his desertion is the desertion of a good man, a man with high potential, who is driven beyond his capacity to respond manfully. One feels that when Connie's identity as a "good hard worker" slips away, not much of Connie can remain.

This high evaluation of the capacity to work does suggest a kind of "work ethic"—in the sense of Weber's Protestant, compulsive uptightness—but, in the context of the novel, it suggests a great deal more, and something a great deal more valuable, and relevant, today: briefly put, it suggests Veblen's "instinct of the craftsman," the sense of work as a source of self-respect through self-fulfillment. Not that this "instinct" eliminates the realistic concern for cash: the anonymous cotton-picker of Chapter 27 defines his day's work as "good pickin'" because he "got three dollars, me an' the ol' woman an' the kids" (p. 556). But more than money is at stake, clearly enough. "Like to get our hands on the bolls. Tenderly, with the fingertips" (p. 554). And "I'm a good hand with cotton. Finger-wise, boll-wise. Jes' move along talkin', an' maybe singin' till the bag gets heavy. Fingers go right to it. Fingers know. Eyes see the work—and don't see it" (p. 555). Pa Joad, after the frustrations of peach-picking, a job new to him, at which he is unskilled, hears of the chance to pick cotton and jumps at more than the possibility of the dollars: "By God, I'd like to get my hands on some cotton! There's work I un'erstan'" (p. 551).

Give a man work he understands, work he can do as well as he thinks it should be done, and he's a satisfied man. Tom Joad, parole-breaker with no "security" so far as the future is concerned, gets a pick in his hands and, "Jumping Jesus! If she don't feel good!" (p. 405). And later in the morning, "Damn it," he said, "a pick is a nice tool (*umph*), if you don' fight it (*umph*). You an' the pick (*umph*) workin' together (*umph*)" (p. 407). Earlier, the omniscient narrator of the generalizing interchapters had spelled out the large implications of which these concrete scenes are the application. Chapter 14, beginning with "the western land, nervous under the beginning change" (p. 204), tries to pinpoint the nature and cause of the change, isolating two phenomena. There is the response to intimidation and hurt that welds individuals into a collective body: " 'I have a little food' plus 'I have none.' If from this problem the sum is 'We have a little food,' the thing is on its way . . ." (p. 206). And second, the root cause of the hurt, and of anger:

muscles and mind aching to grow, to work, to create, multiplied a million times. The last clear definite function of man—muscles aching to work, minds aching to create beyond the single need—this is man. To build a wall, to build a house, a dam, and in the wall and house and dam to put something of Manself, and to Manself take back something of the wall, the house, the dam; to take hard muscles from the lifting, to take the clear lines and form from receiving. For man, unlike any other thing organic or inorganic in the universe, grows beyond his work, walks up the stairs of his accomplishments (p. 204).

Or—put more directly, if less articulately—"Jumping Jesus! If she don't feel good!"

Work feels good; take away the chance to have this good feeling, and the grapes of wrath begin their fermentation. Work enables people to share, and not only to share their material goods but also to participate in mutual dreams and in the fellowship of satisfying activity. All of these elements implicit in the "matter" of work in *The Grapes of Wrath* emerge, sharply focused, in one of the most lyrically satisfying passages in the novel, a passage originally published as "Breakfast" in *The Long Valley*, with only small changes (apart from the shift from first-person to third-person narrative) in the novel. At the start of Chapter 22, the Joads pull into the Weedpatch Camp and find, for the only time in California, a place where their humanity is respected. But they must find, in addition to respect, work. Still, respect is nice, too, and Tom goes to sleep chuckling happily after teasing Ma about how nice she will find things here. Rather than quote the whole passage (pp. 394–397), I shall assume the reader's familiarity with it and simply mention, in totally inadequate summary, that Tom awakens in the cold morning to the clank of a rusty stove and encounters a young woman—"a girl," the narrator calls her—making breakfast while nursing a baby. She is joined by two men, the younger presumably her husband (although we never know; perhaps her brother) and the older one explicitly the father of the younger. Tom accepts their invitation to join them; they enjoy their breakfast and casual conversation, through which we learn that the family has been working for twelve days, eating well and dressing adequately. After the meal, the men wonder if Tom wants to join them in their work of laying pipe. He eagerly assents.

Considering what twelve days of work has done for this small family group of three generations, it's no wonder that Tom "wants." The "quick gracefulness" of the girl's movements as she tends to her own particular "work"—preparing the meal, managing the fire, nursing the baby—contributes as much to the episode's import as the non-prying yet welcoming taciturnity of the family and the pride made possible by twelve days of working and eating and even wearing new clothes. The reflection of the mountain, and of the light coming over it, in the men's eyes adds no more to their stature than does the capacity that work has given them to share their meal, the warmth of their fire and of their fellowship, with Tom. But the two elements of the episode that make it so much more striking in the novel than it is by itself in *The Long Valley*, are the shared context and the offer of shared work. The narrator in "Breakfast" comes upon a tent in a valley, a tent apparently all by itself. The world of the narrator and the world of the group he joins have no visible links of connection beyond a shared humanity that the reader must take on faith. In response to the question, "Picking cotton?" the narrator responds with a minimal "No." At the end of "Breakfast," "The younger turned to me. ' 'Fyou want to pick cotton, we could maybe get you on.' " The narrator—whom one tends to equate with John Steinbeck, out making notes for the newspaper series he was doing on the plight of the Okies—answers, " 'No. I got to go along. Thanks for breakfast.' The older man waved his hand in a negative. 'O.K. Glad to have you.' They walked away together. The air was blazing with light at the eastern skyline. And I walked away down the country road."

The separation between the narrator and the working family contrasts sharply with Tom Joad's participation in a common experience. The assertion of a common humanity in the poetically rendered scene of "Breakfast" remains primarily an assertion rather than a presentation; it does not become an aesthetically realized emotion. What emerges from the same scene in the novel does so largely through the reader's sense of the impact that having work to do has upon the feelings and action of the nameless people with whom Tom breakfasts. In their willingness to share even their work with Tom, they demonstrate the same reflexive turning from "I" to "We" that lies behind the nervousness of "beginning change." Work is scarce; the handbills have lied;

"An' wages is comin' down all a time. I git so goddam tired jus' figgerin' how to eat."

"You got work now," Tom suggested.

"Yeah, but it ain't gonna las' long. Workin' for a nice fella. Got a little place. Works 'longside of us. But, hell—it ain't gonna las' no time."

Tom said, "Why in the hell you gonna git me on? I'll make it shorter. What you cuttin' your own throat for?" (pp. 400–401).

There is no answer to this, only a slow shake of the head and an, "I dunno. Got no sense, I guess. We figgered to get us each a hat. Can't do it, I guess." The sharing of work that deprives the breakfast-family of part of their own job puts Tom Joad behind that pick that feels so good to him. More than the meal, more than the friendship and caring implicit both in the meal and in the sharing of work, the work itself enables Tom Joad to feel like a happy man.

Casual entertainment, the pleasure of a movie or a song, counts; sex and love count; family ties count; but work, and the lack of work, define and delimit the satisfactions latent in these other sorts of cohesion and activity. Before he leaves for good, Tom quotes Casy's quoting of "The Preacher": "Two are better than one, because they have a good reward for their labor. For if they fall, the one will lif' up his fellow, but woe to him that is alone when he falleth, for he hath not another to help him up" (p. 570). And Tom wonders about the future, and about what he can do to make it match his vision of a world where "All work together for our own thing" (p. 571), a tangibly solid vision, to be sure, like the dream of Lennie and George for a place of their own, in *Of Mice and Men*, and like Ma's repeated wish for a little white house on its own land of good acres to fill; an agrarian image, essentially, where good farmers will be allowed to farm the millions of acres now lying fallow; and therefore, superficially considered, a sentimental, or at best an anachronistic, vision, for to define a social ideal for the twentieth century in terms that were outdated in 1785 when Jefferson propounded them in *Notes on the State of Virginia* smacks of a Luddite perspective especially irrelevant to a nation that exists by technology and whose population is continually leaping beyond any given last year's sense of how many people the land can support.

But the impact of the novel lies not in the specific image of social felicity it refers to—the white cottage surrounded by a few acres of well-farmed land—but, rather, in the quality of life that the image embodies. "The last clear definite function of man—muscles aching to work, minds aching to create beyond the single need" (p. 204) defines itself, finally, not as any particular job of work that a man, like any other tool, may perform; not simply as an extension of man-the-instrument, of man as a means to an objectively visible end; but as a paradigm of man's subjective condition, of man's deepest interiority. The work a man does is the man himself. The robots who drive the machines that evict Okies from their land; the manipulators and exploiters who "sock it to 'em" at the used-car lots—these are men in name only, not in inner being. And the people like Connie, the "good hard workers" who have it in them to be good husbands, good men, good human beings, lose this state of humanness when they lose the chance to do work.

The ache to work and the ache to create may well turn out to be culturally conditioned needs, but there has been no culture anywhere, no matter how idyllically South Seas it may be, whose people have not produced beyond the demands of simple animal need. Leisure is not enough, nor is mere drudgery at a high wage. The Grapes of Wrath "lives on, as it always will," not primarily because it speaks to the pressing social dilemma of jobless Americans in the 1930's, but because—through the artistry exemplified by the breakfast passage—it makes vividly real the satisfactions men derive from work, satisfactions that an affluent society will have to provide or else see all its wealth turn to a dust as arid as that which inundated "the red country and part of the gray country" (p. 3), and drove the Okies to their vintage. In presenting the terrible need of the Okies to find food to eat, John Steinbeck makes poignantly vivid this other, equally pressing, need. Economically, psychologically, socially, and—as in the Weedpatch Camp—politically, doing a job of work is the difference between living like a man and existing like an animal. Man cannot live by bread alone: he must have work.

❀◆

JOHN R. REED

John R. Reed has taught at the University of Cincinnati, the University of Connecticut, and Wayne State University. He has published a book on the public schools in British literature, and articles in *The University of Toronto Quarterly*, *Journal of English Literary History*, and *Victorian Poetry*.

The Grapes of Wrath and the Esthetics of Indigence

The representative from Oklahoma, Lyle H. Boren, addressing the 76th Congress of the United States in 1940, angrily dismissed *The Grapes of Wrath* as a false and foul novel. "Take the vulgarity out of this book," he said, "and it would be blank from cover to cover."[1] For a time, much of the criticism of Steinbeck's most popular novel pointed to the unsavoriness of its details and the crudeness of its speech. In recent years, however, few critics have concerned themselves with what now appears as rather tame language. But Steinbeck's use of rough language and his descriptions of some crude features of indigent life are thematically important.

Walter Fuller Taylor described *The Grapes of Wrath* as a "parable" rather than a realistic novel. He felt that any reader who accepted the novel, accepted "a concept of sexual promiscuity, a humorous tolerance of the Tobacco-Road way of life." For Taylor, the pernicious philosophy behind the novel was that "the only values lie in the experiences of the moment, the

---

[1] Part of Boren's speech is reproduced on pp. 687–688 of this book.—Ed.

This essay, in slightly different form, was presented at the University of Connecticut's conference on *The Grapes of Wrath*, May 3, 1969. Printed here for the first time by permission of the author.

only valid end of living is the continued renewing of the life of cells" (p. 760). Edmund Wilson, too, had seen Steinbeck's philosophy as essentailly biological with nothing to oppose the "vision of man's hating and destroying himself except an irreducible faith in life."

A series of critics have, however, traced a broader and more organized moral purpose in the imagery, allusions, and motifs of *The Grapes of Wrath*. These various approaches do not all agree, and so Agnes McNeill Donohue concludes that "as a storyteller with an American Puritan background Steinbeck seems to be mixing freely Old and New Testament imagery, Hebraic, Christian, archetypal and mythic symbols to enrich, fertilize, and extend his meaning." For her, Steinbeck's meaning is that man is a fallen creature journeying to a false Eden that reveals only his own corrupt heart.

My interest is not with such extensions of Steinbeck's meaning, but with the methods by which he was able to transform the image of the poor by associating their earthy life of the soil with emerging ideals and the abstractions and broad hopes that those ideals bring. Steinbeck himself, in accepting the Nobel Prize for Literature in 1962, said that the writer "is charged with exposing our many grievous faults and failures, with dredging up to the light our dark and dangerous dreams, for the purpose of improvement." But he added that a writer must also "celebrate man's proven capacity for greatness of heart and spirit," and he asserted: "I hold that a writer who does not passionately believe in the perfectibility of man has no dedication nor any membership in literature."[2]

It is my feeling that *The Grapes of Wrath* does not represent, as Maxwell Geismer has it (*Writers in Crisis*), "the dubious nuptials of 'Tobacco Road' with the *Ladies' Home Journal*," but signifies instead a marriage of man's "faults and failures" with his own "greatness of heart and spirit." It is in the use of

---

[2] Reprinted in *The Viking Portable Steinbeck* (revised edition), pp. 690–692.

indigence and its concomitants that Steinbeck makes evident man's capacity for moral transformation.

Early in *The Grapes of Wrath* the truck driver who gives Tom Joad a ride observes Tom's work-glazed hands, commenting, "I notice all stuff like that. Take a pride in it" (p. 13). Whether or not we can take this as Steinbeck's conscious clue to be on the alert for revelatory details, we certainly will recall the author's own observation of Tom's hands only a few pages before when he described them as "hard, with broad fingers and nails as thick and ridged as little clam shells. The space between thumb and forefinger and the hams of his hands were shiny with callus" (p. 9). We may remember this description soon after when we learn of the land turtle with "high-domed shell" who creeps determinedly forward on "hard legs and yellow-nailed feet" and who has "brows like fingernails" (p. 20). Such alerts to the association of simple details can, I believe, be taken as hints for the proper reading of Steinbeck's novel. Details which seem gratuitous at the beginning of the novel are gradually transformed to meaningful adjuncts of a higher mode of existence. This transformation results from a growing emphasis upon human dignity and an increasingly broad and symbolic fictional context.

When Tom first encounters Casy their manners and conversation are a peculiar combination of vulgarity and elevation. Steinbeck observes that Tom does not wipe the whiskey bottle after Casy has taken his swallow, but explains that Tom refrained from this hygienic gesture out of "politeness" (p. 28). Steinbeck decribes Casy's "gob of spit" in detail while the ex-preacher marvels at how "the more grace a girl got in her, the quicker she wants to go out in the grass" (p. 30). Yet these superficially crude musings mask an inchoate nobility that reveals itself when Casy says "There ain't no sin and there ain't no virtue. There's just stuff people do. It's all part of the same thing" (p. 32). And that thing is what Casy calls "the Holy Sperit—the human sperit" when he wonders if "maybe all men got one big soul ever'body's a part of" (p. 33).

Notwithstanding the Reverend Mr. W. Lee Rector's assertion
that the novel "tends to 'popularize iniquity,' "[3] Casy and
Tom's concerns become less personal and more universal as
their energies are channeled away from sensual gratification toward the achievement of an ideal. In fact, there is little actual
description of sexual activity in *The Grapes of Wrath*, and
when it occurs, it is discreet. Steinbeck is not writing a mere
apology for the sensuous life. Primarily he is opposing the full-
bloodedness of the Joads to the mechanical existence against
which they must struggle.

The vitality of the Okies is demonstrated in their faults,
but more nobly in their love for the land, which has ancestral
and personal value. "Places where folks live is them folks,"
Muley says, refusing to leave the land that is, by law, no longer
his (p. 71). Unlike the Okies, the tractor operator "could not
see the land as it was, he could not smell the land as it smelled;
his feet did not stamp the clods or feel the warmth and power
of the earth" (p. 48). Perhaps in their attachment to the earth
and their preservation of primary emotions the Okies are vulgar,
but the vulgarity that led Casy to sport in the grass with con-
senting girls filled with the Holy Sperit, is perhaps nobler than
the machines that come onto the land, "orgasms set by gears,
raping methodically, raping without passion" (p. 49). In contrast
to the Okies, the landowners in California had lost their passion
for the earth "and all their love was thinned with money, and all
their fierceness dribbled away in interest until they were no
longer farmers at all" (p. 316). One dispossessed farmer provides us with Steinbeck's meaning. "If a man owns a little
property," he says, "that property is him, it's part of him, and
it's like him," and "even if he isn't successful he's big with his
property." "But let a man get property he doesn't see" and the
property becomes stronger than the man "and he is small, not
big" (pp. 50, 51). There is dignity in love, not in volume or
power.

[3] Reported in Shockley's essay, p. 689 of this book.—ED.

Steinbeck is not romanticizing the passions of the Okies, as the constant animal imagery indicates; he is simply demonstrating that they retain a sensuous and vital force that has gone out of the business and managerial classes. Like Thoreau, Steinbeck believes that the less encumbered a man is by possessions, the more easily will he find his own soul. Possessions, for Steinbeck, are accretions that smother the spiritual life, as his often-quoted picture of middle-class tourists indicates. It is worth quoting again. "Languid, heat-raddled ladies, small nucleuses about whom revolve a thousand accouterments: creams, ointments to grease themselves, coloring matter in phials—black, pink, red, white, green, silver—to change the color of hair, eyes, lips, nails, brows, lashes, lids. Oils, seeds, and pills to make the bowels move. A bag of bottles, syringes, pills, powders, fluids, jellies to make their sexual intercourse safe, odorless, and unproductive" (pp. 210–211). The "little pot-bellied" husbands of these women are associated less with failures of the sensuous life and more with failures of the spirit, for their many organizations and societies are born of anxiety and designed to "reassure themselves that business is noble and not the curious ritualized thievery they know it is" (p. 211).

These representatives of the acquisitive middle class do not display the crude faults of the Okies, but neither do they reveal a capacity for the greatness of heart and spirit that Steinbeck confers on his ostensibly ignoble migrants. It is Casy who expresses the traditional paradox emerging from this contrast. If a man "needs a million acres to make him feel rich," he says, "seems to me he needs it 'cause he feels awful poor inside hisself," and no amount of land will make him "rich like Mis' Wilson was when she give her tent when Grampa died" (p. 282).

It is safe to charge that Steinbeck used crude language in *The Grapes of Wrath*. But it is worth noticing that this language is used colorfully and acutely by the migrants, less precisely, but just as crudely, by small business people, and cruelly and colorlessly by the secure community. The Joads and other

migrants use raw language in the form of conventional expletives or as metaphor—for example, one disillusioned migrant's
description of a certain millionaire as a "fat, sof' fella with little
mean eyes an' a mouth like a ass-hole" (p. 281). This language appears in the novel because it is the migrants' idiom as
Casy realizes when he justifies his own forms of speech.
"Maybe you wonder about me using bad words. Well, they ain't
bad to me no more. They're jus' words folks use, an' they don't
mean nothing bad with 'em" (p. 32).[4]

This kind of language is humorous, splenetic, even fierce
without being vicious; it is direct and forceful. More reprehen-
sible is the subtlety and cruelty of the secure community's foul
language. The police and associates of the dominant classes use
the same crude expletives as the migrants, but their community
at large has viler pejoratives. Soon after arriving in California
the Joads learn what Okies are. "Well, Okie use' ta mean you
was from Oklahoma. Now it means you're a dirty son-of-a-
bitch. Okie means you're scum. Don't mean nothing itself, it's
the way they say it" (p. 280). Language means less than the
spirit in which it is used. Casy sees the innocence of the Okies'
raw talk, while we are forced to recognize the malice of their
antagonists. Earthy speech, under these circumstances, becomes
an insignia of honor.

Whereas the language of the Okies remains largely the same
(though with an increasing use of words like "holy," "love," and
"dignity") and only our attitude toward it changes, the quality
of migrant life, as well as our attitude toward it, changes. Early
in the novel the character of indigent life is indicated by Tom's
anecdotes about Grampa (pp. 38, 59), Uncle John (p. 39), and
Willy's heifer (p. 94), and incidents like the time "the pig got

---

[4] Later, when he has decided to join the Joads heading for California, Casy
explains that he wants to learn what the people are all about. "Gonna lay
in the grass, open an' honest with anybody that'll have me. Gonna cuss an'
swear an' hear the poetry of folks talkin'. All that's holy, all that's what I
didn' understan'. All them things is the good things" (p. 128). The same
sentiment would probably apply to the waitress Mae's term for tourists.
"She calls them shitheels" (p. 212).

in over to Jacobs' an' et the baby" (p. 56). But these references to an earthy way of life do not remain mere random details. Instead they assume their place in a broad pattern of transformation. Occasional shocking details occur later in the novel—as in one man's description of how his brother was killed when a harrow ran over him "an' the points dug into his guts an' his stomach, an' they pulled his face off an'—God almighty!" (p. 271). But when they appear, these later details no longer indicate a crude and earthy attitude toward life so much as the hardships that men who work the soil must endure. From being offensive details, they become evidence of strength.

Just as derogatory language becomes more vile in the mouths of the middle class than among the migrants, so unpleasant details are more savage in the established community. The man who was run over by a harrow died for his land and his brother in telling the story is appalled by the details; Tom knocked a man's head "plumb to squash," but it was in self-defense (p. 35). The deputy sheriff who fired his pistol at Floyd Knowles, however, showed no consideration for the human life around him. When he shot, "a woman in front of a tent screamed and then looked at a hand which had no knuckles. The fingers hung on strings against her palm, and the torn flesh was white and bloodless" (p. 361). This is an unpleasant detail, but its purpose is considerably different from the others. This detail is an indictment.

Steinbeck was not using the details of indigent and oppresssd existence in order to gain an effect by shock. He had already done that in a series of articles written for the *San Francisco News* and later published with an added epilogue as a pamphlet entitled *Their Blood Is Strong*. Peter Lisca remarks that "actually, the extremes of poverty, injustice, and suffering depicted in these articles are nowhere equaled in *The Grapes of Wrath*."[5] And indeed nowhere in *The Grapes of Wrath* is there a description so disgusting and moving as one in *Their Blood Is Strong* that pictures a three-year-old child with "a

---

[5] *The Wide World of John Steinbeck*, p. 145.

gunny sack tied about his middle for clothing" suffering "the swollen belly caused by malnutrition. . . . He sits on the ground in the sun in front of the house, and the little black fruit flies buzz in circles and land on his closed eyes and crawl up his nose until he weakly brushes them away. They try to get at the mucus in the eye-corners. This child seems to have the reactions of a baby much younger. The first year he had a little milk, but he has had none since." In his novel, Steinbeck modified such details and carefully selected those that he used. Because such details are judiciously spaced, Rose of Sharon's "blue shrivelled little mummy" (p. 603) has more impact, and the conditions that produced it appear more unjust and repulsive.

Other details are presented with equal economy and with the same sort of accretive transformation. They reveal the movement of mind among the Joads and the Okies from self-concern to a broader, more exalted consciousness. Early in the novel, the hard-pressed Oklahoma farmers speculate on the future. "Maybe next year will be a good year. God knows how much cotton next year. And with all the wars—God knows what price cotton will bring. Don't they make explosives out of cotton? And uniforms? Get enough wars and cotton'll hit the ceiling" (p. 44). It is evident that these people are not above profiting from the sufferings of others, though they themselves will soon confront the uniforms and explosives their cotton goes to produce. Like their exploiters, they find it easy to overlook the consequences for others of their own prosperity. That is because they are not forced to experience the terror of war, just as the rich are not obliged to experience the anguish of poverty. It requires a sharp and painful uprooting to expand the consciousness of the poor. Steinbeck warns that "the quality of owning freezes you forever into 'I' and cuts you off forever from the 'We'" (p. 206). The migrants, having lost everything, inadvertently discover the meaning of their transformation from I to We, and in this transformation they achieve their highest dignity, for they become aware of abstractions that bind together lives that are otherwise squalid and debased.

It is in Chapter Ten, the chapter in which the Joads actually set out on their journey, that the transforming process becomes evident. Grampa's consistent vulgarity is touched by sentiment when he declares that he will not leave the land (pp. 151–152). The simple migration to the West is touched by glory in Casy's ambition to learn what the people really are (p. 128). The first hint of movement from I to We is signaled in the Joads' admitting Casy as a member of the family, though he has nothing more than his spirit to offer. But Ma already senses what Casy stands for. Hearing Casy explain how he "got thinkin' how we was holy when we was one thing, an' mankin' was holy when it was one thing," Ma feels he is "suddenly a spirit, not human any more, a voice out of the ground" (pp. 110, 111). Casy, the wandering, homeless preacher, becomes the attendant spirit of these wandering and homeless people, and it is this human spirit of idealism that will leaven and transform commonplace people like the Joads. Now the ancient Hudson truck becomes not merely a conveyance, but a "living principle" (p. 135); it is "the new hearth, the living center of the family" (p. 136). Given this sanctification of the truck, Steinbeck's elaborate descriptions of how to select vehicles (p. 137) and how to fix them (p. 234) become more than repair manual entries for migrants. The commonplace details of indigent life magnify in importance because of their consequences. "Eyes watched the tires, ears listened to the clattering motors, and minds struggled with oil, with gasoline, with the thinning rubber between air and road. Then a broken gear was tragedy" (p. 268). Similarly, death and killing are transformed in value. When Casy and Tom share Muley's rabbits, the elaborate description of how Tom skins and prepares the animals may appear unnecessary and even offensive (p. 67), but not much later a similar description of the killing and preparing of two pigs is of crucial importance, since survival of the Joad family will depend upon this activity (p. 141). Suddenly the anecdote of Uncle John's wasteful consumption of pork takes on ominous significance (pp. 39–40). Food is no longer a subject for jokes. From Tom's homicidal act of defense, to the killing of rabbits and pigs, and to Casy's advice to Muley not to kill anyone if he can help it (p. 72), death is generally associated with survival among the migrants.[6]

Still, on both large and small scale, the migrants' attitude toward death is more considerate than the attitude of the classes above them. Compare, for example, the crime of murder that put Tom in jail with the crime of the California landowners. "There is a crime here that goes beyond denunciation. There is a sorrow here that weeping cannot symbolize. There is a failure here that topples all our success. The fertile earth, the straight tree rows, the sturdy trunks, and the ripe fruit. And children dying of pellagra must die because a profit cannot be taken from an orange. And coroners must fill in the certificates —died of malnutrition—because the food must rot, must be forced to rot" (p. 477). When the vigilantes murder Casy, it is difficult not to observe that "Casy's crushed head" (p. 527) resembles Herb Turnbull's head that Tom had knocked "plumb to squash." Tom once more reacts defensively when he strikes down Casy's murderer. The identical act that was initially an unfortunate event in Tom's case, becomes an outright premeditated murder on the part of the vigilante, and is instantly transformed to a gesture of liberation by Tom. As with other details in the novel, all value is conferred by the meaning that surrounds them.

The difference in attitudes toward death is particularized in the death of the Joad dog. The animal is killed by "a big swift car," which slows momentarily after the accident and then speeds away, apparently because the occupants are indifferent to, or ashamed of, "the blot of blood and tangled, burst intestines" kicking slowly in the road (p. 177). Like the crime of the great landowners, this involves a pointless extinguishing of life. As Winfield remarks, "It ain't like killin' pigs" (p. 179).

---

[6] Al Joad, however, the person least capable of recognizing the consequences of his own acts, purposely swerves the truck to try to kill a cat on the road (p. 248).

In *Their Blood Is Strong*, Steinbeck regarded the destruction of dignity as one of the most regrettable results of the migrant's life. "A man herded about, surrounded by armed guards, starved, and forced to live in filth, loses his dignity; that is, he loses his valid position in regard to society, and consequently his whole ethics toward society." Dignity is also a central question in *The Grapes of Wrath*. As the vulgar details of their way of life assume a part in a developing pattern and are exalted by identification with an ideal, so references to pride and dignity among the Okies become more prominent.

The shift of emphasis from physical to spiritual concerns becomes obvious with the death of the earthy old Grampa. The family does not want to take charity and have Grampa buried by the State. On the other hand, they cannot afford the expense of a burial. Pa laments the time when a son could bury his parents "in dignity," and decides that the family will bury Grampa themselves, because "sometimes the law can't be foller'd no way . . . not in decency, anyways" (pp. 190–191). Even "Granma moved with dignity and held her head high" when Grampa died (p. 188). The clumsy and sometimes humorous details of the burial are dignified by Casy's clear identification of Grampa with the land the Joads are leaving. His death becomes a symbolic gesture and, significantly enough, it is at this point that the Joads and the Wilsons decide to combine their forces and travel together, taking another large step from I to We.

Gradually the movement West is enlarged and ennobled. Just before Grampa's death, the ennoblement had been signaled by Steinbeck's questions, "Where does the courage come from? Where does the terrible faith come from?" (p. 165). But after Grampa's death the concern for unity of purpose, preservation of the individual will, and maintenance of dignity become dominant and the Okies are no longer mere travelers, but "a moving, questing people" (p. 385). They have "changed their social life—changed as in the whole universe only man can change" (p. 267).

It is important then that men maintain their dignity and

pride and that they be able to transform the meanness of their lives—the indignities and humiliations of poverty and abuse—into something larger and more significant. Consequently, Steinbeck praises the government camps because they encourage dignity, pride and decency. The Hoovervilles and company camps make men feel debased, but, as Pa reflects later, "Down in that gov'ment camp we wasn' mean" (p. 550).[7]

Bearing upon this issue is another very important aspect of the novel. If it is assumed that men must, at any cost, maintain their dignity, then it is worthwhile to consider what the cost may be. At the end of the first chapter, the women of families that are being driven off the land find consolation in the "hard and angry and resistant" look that replaces the "bemused perplexity" of their men and they realize that they are "safe and that there was no break" (p. 6). And near the end of the novel, the women again "sighed with relief, for they knew it was all right—the break had not come; and the break would never come as long as fear could turn to wrath" (p. 592). It is man's capacity to transform perplexity and fear to wrath and resistance that Steinbeck means to describe through his selection of apparently unconnected details of indigent life.

The Okies are not strangers to violence. Tom's crime, for example, is not shameful, but honored by his brother Al (p. 115), and Pa Joad declares, "When Tom here got in trouble we could hold up our heads" (p. 190). Steinbeck constantly refers to the essentially violent attitudes of the Okies. The first reaction of the dispossessed farmers is to ask who they can kill to protect themselves. "The tenants cried, Grampa killed Indians, Pa killed snakes for the land. Maybe we can kill banks—they're worse than Indians and snakes" (pp. 45–46). Even Ma, who is first described as being "remote and faultless in judgment as a goddess" whose "imperturbability could be depended upon" (p. 100), declares that only by force will she tolerate the separa-

---

[7] See also *The Grapes of Wrath*, p. 420, for an amplification of this sentiment.

tion of her family (p. 230). Moreover, Ma is tempted to hit a policeman (p. 293), threatens to strike Mrs. Sandry, who has been tormenting Rose of Sharon (p. 438), and generally manifests a tendency to "boil up" as Tom puts it (p. 480).[8]

Steinbeck carefully shows that the Okies live in a climate of toughness and violence and are prepared to respond violently to protect themselves. It is worth recalling the title of Steinbeck's pamphlet, *Their Blood Is Strong*, in which he notes that the migrants are only "gypsies by force of circumstance." More correctly, "they are descendants of men who crossed into the Middle West, who won their lands by fighting." In *The Grapes of Wrath*, Steinbeck describes these migrants as "the new barbarians" who, unlike the Californians, were "hardened, intent, and dangerous" and "wanted only two things—land and food." Accordingly, the owners hated the migrants for perhaps they "had heard from their grandfathers how easy it is to steal land from a soft man if you are fierce and hungry and armed" (p. 318). But the migrants become still more dangerous if they can preserve and venerate their dignity; what Steinbeck calls their Manself, and which he defines as the capacity to "suffer and die for a concept"—important because "this one quality is man, distinctive in the universe" (p. 205). Even intimations of violence can be ennobled. It is not mere familiarity with and acceptance of violence as a remedy that the dominant class must fear from the migrants, but their elevation of that violence to a controlled, disciplined and idealized weapon.

Just as crudities of behavior are transformed to noble simplicities, and banal details are transformed to life-and-death essentials; and just as killing a rabbit to satisfy a brief hunger becomes killing pigs to sustain a family, thereby foreshadowing the severe needs to come; so Tom's crime and the random violence of the migrants are transformed to righteous anger, a power ready for disciplined use. Tom feels shamed when Ma

---

[8] According to an earlier passage (pp. 64–65), Ma has been given to violent behavior in previous incidents.

prevents him from responding violently to the insolent bully-
ing of vigilantes (p. 382), but Ma has learned the important
lesson of containing force until it can be effectively used. When
Tom kicks a deputy sheriff to prevent him from shooting Floyd
Knowles, Casy insists upon assuming the blame. This is an act
of serious importance, for it represents the substitution of an
idea for a response and of one I for another—the largest step
toward disciplining the powers of the people. And Casy knows
what his act signifies: "Between his guards Casy sat proudly,
his head up and the stringy muscles of his neck prominent.
On his lips there was a faint smile and on his face a curious
look of conquest" (p. 364). Casy has both preserved his dignity and achieved a higher end; moreover, occurring at a moment of jeopardy, his act assumes greater significance. Yet it is
only one of several important preparations for the final cancel-
lation of I in favor of We. When Rose of Sharon witnesses a
similar jeopardy, she discards outmoded notions of shame and
self in favor of a selfless dignity by offering what she can of herself for another, and, like Casy, "her lips came together and
smiled mysteriously" (p. 619). It is the smile of an even higher
conquest.

Peter Lisca was correct in emphasizing the essentially integrated nature of *The Grapes of Wrath*, but this integration
surely does not depend upon a Biblical structure. I do not feel
that *The Grapes of Wrath* requires the network of Hebraic,
Christian, archetypal and mythic allusions and symbols that can
be found in it to convey its meaning. If that were so, Steinbeck might be guilty of what Alfred Kazin described as the left-
wing writer's folly, which "was to assume that artistry was something *added* to the concern" for social questions. If Biblical
allusion, in itself, were an important artistic feature, popular
rewritings of the Twenty-third Psalm that appeared during the
Thirties might be valued as noble poems rather than cutting
satires.

Depression is my shepherd; I am in want.
He maketh me to lie down on park benches; He leadeth me beside
    still factories.

He restoreth the bread lines; He leadeth me in the paths of destruction for his Party's sake.

Yea, though I walk through the Valley of Unemployment, I fear every evil; for thou art with me; the Politicians and Profiteers they frighten me.

Thou preparest a reduction in mine salary before me in the presence of mine creditors; Thou anointest mine income with taxes; my expenses runneth over mine income.

Surely unemployment and poverty will follow me all the days of the Republican administration; and I shall dwell in a mortgaged house forever.[9]

Rose of Sharon's act, though dignified by various religious and mythic allusions, needs only its own power to demonstrate nobility. The transformation of her nature in a moment of crisis merely epitomizes the general movement of the novel from concerns of the flesh to concerns of the spirit.

It is easy to agree with Eric Carlson, who claims that "Steinbeck's search for spiritual values looks inside human experience, nature, and the life process," and that his "naturalism goes beyond both the mechanistic determinism of Dreiser and the mystic dualism of traditional Christianity" and "lifts the biology of stimulus-response to the biology of spirit" (pp. 755–756). *The Grapes of Wrath*, which was denounced as filthy, crude, and ill-made, is in fact none of these. It is not ill-made because Steinbeck, through selection and restraint,[10] transformed the potentially offensive details of indigent life into an esthetically sound artistic creation. Details develop and expand in meaning and function to achieve a thematic ecology, and the final, emblematic tableau, arrested at the moment between life and death, unites animal necessity with the high achievements of the human spirit.

---

[9] Quoted in Donald W. Whisenhunt's "The Bard in the Depression: Texas Style," *Journal of Popular Culture* (Winter 1968), pp. 375–76.

[10] Steinbeck rewrote the novel, feeling that he had been too severe on the landowners and big companies. He sought to be fair in his rendering of the situation and apparently this attempt at restraint had an effect upon his style.

BETTY PEREZ

Betty Perez recently received her Ph.D. from the University of Florida, where she worked with Professor Peter Lisca. Her dissertation examined the content, structure, and form of *Sea of Cortez* in the light of new information about Edward F. Ricketts' collaborative role.

House and Home:
Thematic Symbols in *The Grapes of Wrath*

As Griffin and Freedman convincingly demonstrate, details and images which have only passing interest individually may form patterns throughout the course of the novel and, symbolically, contribute to the total structure and thematic content. Refraining from exaggerating the importance of the motifs which they extract for examination or from suggesting that these are the only patterns, Griffin and Freedman state clearly that "it is only through their complex relationships with subsidiary motifs and devices, and with the more straightforward narration and exposition and argumentation, that they [the motifs of animals and machines] provide major symbols integral to the art and substance of the novel" (p. 770). This essay will investigate the development of another such pattern—that of house and home —which not only gives additional support to the recognized theme of community in *The Grapes of Wrath*, but also reveals the significance of many details which have received little attention or which have been made a part of other discussions.

The seeds of the symbolic use of house and home, like the prefigurement of many events and situations in the novel, are

---

found in the description of the turtle—whose symbolic importance in *The Grapes of Wrath* has been recognized by many interpretations. Griffin and Freedman call the turtle episode a "symbolic epitome" and state that "the progress of the Okies, representative of the perseverance of 'Manself,' is neatly foreshadowed in the description of the turtle's persistent forward movement: he slowly plods his way, seeking to prevail in the face of adversities, and he succeeds in spite of insects, such obstacles as the highway, motorists' swerving to hit him (though some swerve to avoid hitting him), Tom's imprisoning him for a while in his coat, the attacks of a cat, and so on" (pp. 777–778). They find that similar descriptions are given of the turtle dragging its shell and of Tom dragging his heels in the dust and further note that Casy specifically remarks on the indomitability of the turtle in likening it to himself. "Nobody can't keep a turtle though. They work at it and work at it, and at last one day they get out and away they go—off somewheres. It's like me" (p. 28). Peter Lisca in "*The Grapes of Wrath* as Fiction" terms this tenacious quality "the indomitable life force" and the turtle's adventures "prophetic allegory."

The indomitable life force that drives the turtle drives the Joads, and in the same direction—southwest. As the turtle picks up seeds in its shell and drops them on the other side of the road, so the Joads pick up life in Oklahoma and carry it across the country to California. . . . As the turtle survives the truck's attempt to smash it on the highway and as it crushes the red ant which runs into its shell, so the Joads endure the perils of their journey (p. 733).

These observations are appropriate and enlightening, but there is yet another likeness between the turtle and the collective people on the move which may be developed: the turtle, like the migrants, takes its home along with it. Steinbeck stresses this similarity in his treatment of the relationship between the turtle and its shell. He consistently suggests that the shell is not simply a part of the turtle, like a leg for example, but rather that it is almost something external, something extra, something brought along. The first reference to the turtle runs thus: "And over the grass at the roadside a land turtle crawled, turning aside for nothing, dragging his high-domed shell over the grass" (p. 20). Subsequent descriptions employ similar language: "boosting and dragging his shell along"; "the hind legs kicked his shell along"; "the hind legs pushed the shell against the wall"; "the shell boosted along, waggling from side to side." The shell is the home or house of the turtle and boosting it along he is like the Okies who take all they can with them on a truck which becomes their house and home.

Because a turtle lives in its shell, the shell is quite literally its house or home. However, as Griffin and Freedman remind us, "a symbol is not the less a symbol because it functions well at the literal level" (p. 774n.), and through his use of the turtle Steinbeck evokes comparisons of symbolic value which would not be possible had he chosen some other southwestern animal. Several critics have mentioned that, like the migrants, the turtle meets and survives several obstacles, but they have not remarked on the fact that in each case it is the turtle's shell which saves it from trouble or harm. The dried grasses and potent seeds—armed with "twisting darts," "little spears," and "balls of tiny thorns"—are not bothersome to the turtle as they are to dogs, horses, and sheep. "The barley beards slid off his shell, and the clover burrs fell on him and rolled to the ground. . . . He came over the grass leaving a beaten trail behind him" (p. 20). The red ant is crushed within his shell, and his shell also protects him from the vehicles on the road and, later, from attacks of the gray cat. Thus the shell is also the turtle's home in the sense that it is a protection from danger, a retreat from the threats of the environment. The images of house and home are thus intrinsically present in the treatment of an object whose symbolic use and importance has already been established. It remains now to see exactly how house and home become thematic symbols in The Grapes of Wrath and to detail the shift in meaning from the denotation of simple shelter or security to a special sense of "home" which will be more clearly defined later, but which is basically a concern for human dignity and a reliance on certain forms of behavior.

Without attempting to maintain the conventional distinction between house as a structure[1] and home as a spirit of community, it is convenient to begin an examination of house and home symbolism in *The Grapes of Wrath* with the most concrete use of the term house in the novel. The first chapter focuses attention on the house as a shelter from the dust and the wind. "Men and women huddled in their houses. . . . Houses were shut tight, and cloth wedged around doors and windows" (p. 5). Even after the "plague" passes, the people remain near the protection of the house as if only it could offer them security. "The women went into the houses to their work, and the children began to play. . . . The men sat in the doorways of their houses; their hands were busy with sticks and little rocks" (p. 7).

In Chapter Two, however, the meanings of house and home are not restricted to a protective shelter and the development of the image begins. Tom, who has been away from "home" (and all it represents of human feelings and companionship), is now returning. As Casy joins him, they speak of reaching home and our expectation of seeing the Joad house is built up by a discussion of its history almost as the entrance of an important character in a play is preceded by a discussion between minor characters. The house is presented almost as a live thing, capable of breeding.

Casy said, "Ol' Tom's house can't be more'n a mile from here. Ain't she over that third rise?"

---

[1] Paul McCarthy in "House and Shelter as Symbol in *The Grapes of Wrath*" (*South Dakota Review*, 1967, pp. 48–67) uses the house symbol in a different way. He sees the various descriptions of the different types of shelter as symbolically clarifying theme and character. He also works out three types of shelter symbols: 1) the cave of the lone man, 2) the house of the family, and 3) the shelter of collected individuals or families. These, he says, indicate different social attitudes.

"Sure," said Joad. " 'Less somebody stole it, like Pa stole it."

"Your pa stole it?"

"Sure, got it a mile an' a half east of here an' drug it. Was a family livin' there, an' they moved away. Gramps an' Pa an' my brother Noah like to took the whole house, but she wouldn' come. They only got part of her. That's why she looks so funny on one end. They cut her in two an' drug her over with twelve head of horses and two mules. They was goin' back for the other half an' stick her together again, but before they got there Wink Manley come with his boys and stole the other half. Pa an' Grampa was pretty sore, but a little later them an' Wink got drunk together an' laughed their heads off about it. Wink, he says his house is at stud, an' if we'll bring our'n over an' breed 'em we'll maybe get a litter of crap houses" (pp. 37–38).

The essential humanity of the house as a symbol of people's lives is also felt and expressed by Muley Graves, who tries to justify his existence as an "ol' graveyard ghost" by telling himself, "I'm lookin' after things so when all the folks come back it'll be all right" (p. 69). He believes that "place where folks live is them folks," and senses the life associations in the houses he visits. "Peters', Jacobs', Rance's, Joad's; an' the houses all dark, standin' like miser'ble ratty boxes, but they was good parties an' dancin'. An' there was meetin's and shoutin' glory. They was weddin's, all in them houses" (p. 70).

The emotional connection of the people to the land and to their possessions is fairly explicit in The Grapes of Wrath as in the interchapter on the selling of personal property which demonstrates that the associations and memories of the people are bound up with the things they have owned, used, loved. "Now, what'll you give for the team and wagon? Those fine bays, matched they are, matched in color, matched the way they walk, stride to stride. . . . I've got a girl. She likes to braid the manes and forelocks, puts little red bows on them. Likes to do it. Not any more. . . . How much? Ten dollars? For both? And the wagon—Oh, Jesus Christ! I'd shoot 'em for dog feed first. Oh, take 'em! Take 'em quick, mister. You're buying a little girl plaiting the forelocks, taking off her hair ribbon to make bows, standing back, head cocked, rubbing the soft noses with her cheek. You're buying years of work, toil in the sun; you're buying a sorrow that can't talk" (p. 118). This same sort of relationship is also established by people with their houses, with the rooms of births and deaths, of weddings and meetings. " 'I built it with my hands. Straightened old nails to put the sheathing on. Rafters are wired to the stringers with baling wire. It's mine. I built it. You bump it down—I'll be in the window with a rifle' " (p. 51). The houses, with their associations of life and vitality, are placed in direct contrast to the unfeeling machines, those men and tractors, which destroy them. The destruction of the houses, as well as the mechanical rape of the land, symbolizes the lack of human feeling in the powers behind the machines; the houses are assaulted with the same disdain and lack of concern with which the owners dispossess their tenants. "Across the dooryard the tractor cut, and the hard, foot-beaten ground was seeded field, and the tractor cut through again; the uncut space was ten feet wide. And back he came. The iron guard bit into the house-corner, crumbled the wall, and wrenched the little house from its foundation so that it fell sideways, crushed like a bug" (p. 52).

The personal feelings of the migrants for their houses are particularized in the case of the Joads. Muley describes for Tom the onslaught of the tractor. "Your grampa didn't wanta kill the guy drivin' that cat', an' that was Willy Feeley, an' Willy knew it, so he jus' come on, an' bumped the hell outa the house, an' give her a shake like a dog shakes a rat. Well, it took somepin outa Tom [senior]. Kinda got into 'im. He ain't been the same ever since" (p. 62). Ma Joad also attributes a change, a new hardness, in her attitude to having had her house pushed over (p. 104), and it is clear that when the tractors crush the tenant houses like bugs or shake them like rats, more than a simple physical structure is being attacked.

Tom's reaction to the destroyed Joad house is illustrative of this further development in the house-home symbolism; for what draws particular comment from him is not just the physical destruction, but the fact that certain types of behavior which denote home have been abandoned. Noticing that even "the dooryard . . . pounded hard by the bare feet of children and by stamping horses' hooves and by the broad wagon wheels" has been cultivated, Tom exclaims, " We never planted here. . . . We always kept this clear. Why, you can't get a horse in now without he tromps the cotton" (p. 55). On the following page of the novel, Tom and Casy examine the crushed and sagging house. "Joad stopped at the step, a twelve-by-twelve timber. 'Doorstep's here,' he said. 'But they're gone—or Ma's dead.' He pointed to the low gate across the front door. 'If Ma was anywheres about, that gate'd be shut and hooked. That's one thing she always done—seen that gate was shut.' His eyes were warm. . . . 'She never lef' that pig gate open 'less she was in the house herself. Never did forget. No—they're gone—or dead.' "

The association of the feeling of home with certain behavior will be developed throughout the novel and thus will receive more of our attention later, but the other aspect of Tom's reaction is also important—the association of Ma with the home. A close relationship between migrant women and their houses is established earlier in the novel in the chapter in which the men are dispossessed, which contains the following progression: "In the open doors the women stood looking out"; "In the doorways of the sun-beaten tenant houses, women sighed and then shifted feet"; "The women moved cautiously out of the doorways toward their men"; "And the women went quickly, quietly back into the houses and herded the children ahead of them." The association of Ma with the house and with a certain type of behavior which underlies Tom's comments quoted earlier leads very quickly to an identification of Ma with the idea of "home" as the migrants sever their ties with a permanent home structure. The bustle of life at Uncle John's house, which contrasts sharply with the deathlike atmosphere of the crushed Joad house with its "blind front windows," centers upon and is primarily caused by the presence of Ma. The difference between the two houses is so striking that in conversation "home" comes to mean Uncle John's house, or where "the folks" are, rather than the Joad house, which is called simply "the other place" (p. 98). Perhaps because of her position in the family and the role she must play in the changing concept of what "home" really is, Steinbeck devotes more authorial comment to introducing Ma's personality and particular attributes than to any other character. The qualities she displays (pp. 99–101), including a simple friendly manner, politeness to strangers, and a willingness to share, are the foundation of "home"-ness—all that will be left when the physical structure of the house has completely disappeared.

Although she is unaware of it until later, Ma is also an embodiment of the spiritual solace, the force which makes "home," about which Casy is thinking when he says that people on the road need some kind of home. The full significance of Casy's remark is not clear until the end of the novel, but as a development in the thematic use of house and home, its importance must be stressed. Like several other remarks by Casy, this speech is not related to the narrative movement of the novel and is neither addressed to any of the characters nor understood by them. In fact, much of what Casy says in the early part of *The Grapes of Wrath* is simply the result of thinking aloud. This does not detract from the importance of his statements—quite the contrary—but it does necessitate a rather close reading and some piecing together of related thoughts. Returning to the turtle passage for a moment, we notice that both Tom and Casy remark on the turtle's incessant movement. " 'Where the hell you s'pose he's goin'?' said Joad. 'I seen turtles all my life. They're always goin' someplace. They always seem to want to get there' " (p. 60). Casy remarks that he is like the turtle himself in wanting to be "goin' " but he admits that he, unlike the turtle, does not have a definite direction or destination.

To know where he is going and to be able to lead others is, however, exactly what Casy desires. As he puts it, "I got the call to lead the people, an' no place to lead 'em" (p. 29). Tom's suggestion, "Lead 'em around and around. . . . What the hell you want to lead 'em someplace for? Jus' lead 'em," takes Casy's statement too literally, for when Casy does assume leadership, the direction is toward commitment and the "home" to which he leads is not a physical place.

Against this carefully laid background, the language of Casy's decision to go west with the other migrants has a special meaning which could too easily be overlooked. "I think I got her now," he says, struggling to voice his feelings. "I don't know if I can say her. I guess I won't try to say her—but maybe there's a place for a preacher. Maybe I can preach again. Folks out lonely on the road, folks with no lan', no home to get to. They got to have some kind of home. Maybe—" (p. 76). Although he cannot yet fully articulate what he inwardly perceives, Casy recognizes that as the tie with the physical home, what we have been calling "house," is broken the need for some sort of spiritual "home"[2] is increased. This nonmaterial "home"—the bond of community formed by "two together"—becomes the destination toward which Casy "leads" and the sustaining "shelter" in the novel's final chapter. Casy, however, is precocious in his recognition of the true meaning of "home," and the Joads come to his fuller understanding only after experience teaches them the distinction between house—and all it symbolizes for them—and the sense of solidarity and human dignity which is not contingent on material possessions and which actually seems to increase when physical conditions deteriorate.

Whereas the Joads' understanding of "home" develops as *The Grapes of Wrath* progresses, their symbolic use of "house" is static, consistent, and fairly obvious. A house, particularly a "little white house," becomes their symbol for security, happiness, and the good life. Observe how Ma pictures California,

---

[2] It need hardly be pointed out that the "home" to which Casy wants to lead the people, while it is nonmaterial, is an earthly possibility and not a "heavenly mansion."

for example. "I like to think how nice it's gonna be, maybe, in California. Never cold. An' fruit ever'place, an' people just bein' in the nicest places, little white houses in among the orange trees. I wonder—that is, if we all get jobs an' all work—maybe we can get one of them little white houses. An' the little fellas go out an' pick oranges right off the tree" (p. 124). This formula for expressing their hopes and expectations of a new life in the promised land is readily accepted by Pa, who says, "We had hard times here. 'Course it'll be different out there—plenty work, an' ever'thing nice an' green, an' little white houses an' oranges growin' aroun'" (p. 149). Tom uses a similar image to tease his pregnant sister. "Gonna get 'im bore in a orange ranch, huh? In one a them white houses with orange trees all aroun'" (pp. 134–135). Both Pa and Tom mention that the idea of these white houses came from a picture and Tom's doubt regarding the possibility of such a place—"Get to thinkin' they ain't no such country" (p. 278)—is ironically true despite the physical existence of just such an environment as they had pictured. "The country was rich along the roadside. There were orchards, heavy leafed in their prime, and vineyards with the long green crawlers carpeting the ground between the rows. There were melon patches and grain fields. White houses stood in the greenery, roses growing over them. And the sun was gold and warm" (p. 499). The white houses do exist, but they are not for the migrants, and the desire for a house—which Ma usually voices, but which affects even Al—continues to motivate their search and shape their dreams of security. Near the end of the novel, however, the specifications have been lowered pathetically. "We got to have a house when the rains come," Ma tells Tom. "Jus' so's it's got a roof an' a floor. Jus' to keep the little fellas off'n the groun'" (p. 495).

The symbolic use of house is also emphasized in the fact that throughout *The Grapes of Wrath* the house, rather than any other necessary item such as clothing, is held out as a promise of better things to come. Even in the bitter desolation of the boxcars, Ma offers the dream to Ruthie, who complains that there "ain't no fun." "They'll be fun," Ma said. "You jus' wait. Be fun purty soon. Git a house an' a place, purty soon" (p. 596). More than a symbol of security—which, of course, it is —the hope, the need of a house serves to encourage slackers and to define the migrants' goal in concrete terms. When Winfield, the youngest, asks, "We got to work ever' day?" Ma tells him, "It ain't hard work. . . . Be good for you. An' you're helpin' us. If we all work, purty soon we'll live in a nice house. We all got to help" (p. 509). Similarly, Rose of Sharon tries to rebuild Connie's sense of responsibility toward her and the coming child by telling him ("fiercely"), "We got to have a house 'fore the baby comes. We ain't gonna have this baby in no tent" (p. 344).

Although the search for the little white house and the security promised by it fails, the Joads carry with them always their real "home" in the sense spoken of by Casy. Although they are only vaguely aware of its significance until later in the novel, this nonmaterial "home"—created by certain feelings, codes, beliefs, and traditions—is packed along by the Joads just as the turtle boosts along its shell. The essential elements of this "home" are found in the characteristics attributed to Ma (who becomes, as we have mentioned, the center and embodiment of "home") such as sociability, humility, pleasantness, imperturbability, dignity, and concern. When the truck becomes "the active thing, the living principle" (p. 135), "the new hearth, the living center of the family" around which the men squat in council, Pa asks Al, the family mechanic, about the physical workings of the engine, etc. But when the decision must be made as to whether Casy can go along, he does not see it as a mechanical problem and ask Al how much load the truck will carry. He asks Ma, the center and principle of the "home," and she answers, characteristically ignoring physical matters for those of the spirit, not with reason but with feeling. "As far as 'kin,' we can't do nothin', not go to California or nothin'; but as far as 'will,' why we'll do what we will—it's a long time our folks been here and east before, an' I never heerd tell of no

Joads or no Hazletts, neither, ever refusin' food an' shelter or a lift on the road to anybody that asked. . . . There ain't room for more'n six, an' twelve is goin' sure. One more ain't gonna hurt. . . . An' any time when we got two pigs an' over a hundred dollars, an' we wonderin' if we kin feed a fella—" (p. 139). This sense of "home" as sharing is established by Ma and it is this, rather than their possessions and belongings, which stays with them and sustains them even in the "rain-blackened barn."

Many incidents along the way emphasize the spirit of "home" which Casy recognized that the dispossessed people desperately need. "Home" is created by a spiritual fellowship of souls, but is often made concrete in physical sharing, as is illustrated in the much-quoted " 'I have a little food' plus 'I have none' " paragraph in Chapter Fourteen, which details the change "from 'I' to 'we.' "[3] For the Joads, "home" is created both when they accept Casy and when the Wilsons lend their tent. The security created by this "home" is expressed by Mrs. Wilson, who says, "I ain't felt so—safe in a long time" (p. 192).

In addition to sharing feelings and possessions, "home" is defined by certain codes and conventions of behavior. Tom was shocked by the plowed field in front of the doorway and by the open pig gate and recognized the loss of "home" in these violations. Conversely, certain courteous actions by the migrants reestablish "home" on the road. Besides the "rights" enumerated in Chapter Seventeen, there is actually a sort of decorum in the manner of the migrants, representative of their essential humanity, which is conspicuously absent from the behavior of the owners and law officers. For example, the Joads always request permission to camp beside another family, even though neither family owns the land. As Tom puts it, "Anyway you're here an' we ain't. You got a right to say if you wan' neighbors or not"

---

[3] The development of this sense of community in *The Grapes of Wrath*, as indicated in the change from "I" to "we," is dealt with in detail in a fifty-minute lecture by Peter Lisca which is published in *From Irving to Steinbeck: Studies in American Literature*, Gainesville: University of Florida Press, 1972.

(p. 183). This characteristic is so important and distinctive that it is also included in one of the generalizing interchapters.

The car pulled off the road and stopped, and because others were there first, certain courtesies were necessary. And the man, the leader of the family, leaned from the car.

Can we pull up here an' sleep?

Why, sure, be proud to have you. What State you from?

Come all the way from Arkansas.

They's Arkansas people down that fourth tent.

That so?

And the great question, How's the water?

Well, she don't taste so good, but they's plenty.

Well, thank ya.

No thanks to me.

But the courtesies had to be (pp. 268–269).

On the other hand, "the right of privacy in the tent," clearly recognized and respected by the migrants, is flagrantly violated by the unfeeling official with "a big silver star" who, in ignoring the privacy of the tent, negates the humanity of its occupants. "Who's in here?" he demands at the Joad tent. "I want to know who's in here" (pp. 290–291). He violates the sense of "home" which Ma carries with her and establishes at each of their camps. In contrast to his brutalized behavior, similar to the tractors' pushing over the croppers' cabins, is the courteous deference of the little manager at Weedpatch who employs the conventions of polite behavior and restores Ma's sense of dignity and "home" simply by drinking a cup of her sugarless coffee.

These conventions of behavior are preserved even in the boxcar and in the barn, the last "home" of the novel; and, whereas the codes of behavior may not be those of the middle class, they are firmly established and understood. Al's relationship to Aggie, for example, requires that he not leave her with an illegitimate child and thus bring "shame" on both families, but neither family attempts to restrain the young couple's natural sexual drives. The need of privacy is recognized even in the scene in the barn which has seemed shockingly base to some readers; all the group except Rose of Sharon go into the toolshed so that her act of mercy has no spectators. Likewise, some necessary privacy is maintained by the separating tarpaulin in the shared boxcar, but as the possessions of the physical home are depleted, the force and power of the kinship "home" grows. "On the second day of the rain Al took the tarpaulin down from the middle of the car. He carried it out and spread it on the nose of the truck, and he came back into the car and sat down on his mattress. Now, without the separation, the two families in the car were one" (p. 593). At this low ebb of material comforts, with Rose of Sharon's baby still-born, without hope of a white house or security, Ma returns to Casy's ideas of one big soul and of the hope engendered by two together. "Use' ta be the fambly was fust," she says. "It ain't so now. It's anybody. Worse off we get, the more we got to do" (p. 606). This sense of "home" expressed in the spirit of sharing is intensified in extremity and acts as a sustaining factor.

By the end of the novel, therefore, "home"—that spirit of community and solace spoken of by Casy—has become completely dissociated from material possessions and physical structure and is described as the "family." In this context, the final scene, always controversial and powerful, gains the accumulated significance of "home" which has been building and developing throughout *The Grapes of Wrath*. The "rain-blackened barn," little more than a shelter from the rain, may be a mockery of the "little white house" of the Joads' dreams, but it becomes a transfigured symbol of "home" through the human warmth and concern which Ma and Rose of Sharon share with the miserable occupants. The lingering, closing image of the book, Rose of Sharon's gift, not of material possessions but literally of herself, exemplifies the "home" to which Casy hoped to lead the people —that mutual support and concern which alone can protect the migrants from annihilation (like the turtle's shell) and offer them hope in the face of despair.

IV

Two Unpublished Documents

A Letter from Steinbeck to his Editor

On January 9, 1939, after reading the manuscript of *The Grapes of Wrath* (which reached New York just before Christmas), Steinbeck's friend and editor at The Viking Press, Pascal Covici, wrote him a very enthusiastic letter saying that two other readers and himself were left "emotionally exhausted." Nevertheless, despite their feeling that it would be "a sacrilege to suggest revisions in so grand a book," they thought they would not be good publishers if they failed to point out a possible weakness or fault—the ending:

> Your idea is to end the book on a great symbolic note, that life must go on and will go on with a greater love and sympathy and understanding for our fellowmen. The episode you use in the end is extremely poignant. Nobody could fail to be moved by the incident of Rose of Sharon giving her breast to the starving man yet, taken as the finale of such a book with all its vastness and surge, it struck us on reflection as being all too abrupt . . . As the end of the final episode it is perfect; as the end of the whole book not quite. It seems to us that the last few pages need building up. The incident needs leading up to, so that the meeting with the starving man is not so much an accident or chance encounter, but more an integral part of the saga of the Joad family.
>
> And it needs something else leading away from it so that the symbolism of the gesture is more apparent in relation to the book as a whole. . . .
>
> Again I repeat, all this seems like sacrilege. Now do as you think best.

He mentioned in a postscript that de Maupassant had used a similar incident.

As many subsequent reviewers and critics have repeated Covici's original objections, and as they have been answered by as many defenders of this ending for the novel, it is interesting to hear what Steinbeck himself had to say on the matter in the following letter, which he wrote immediately on receiving his editor's suggestions.

Dear Pat:

I have your letter today. And I'm sorry but I cannot change that ending. It is casual—there is no fruity climax, it is not more important than any other part of the book—if there is a symbol, it is a survival symbol not a love symbol, it must be an accident, it must be a stranger, and it must be quick. To build this stranger into the structure of the book would be to warp the whole meaning of the book. The fact that the Joads don't know him, don't care about him, have no ties to him—that is the emphasis. The giving of the breast has no more sentiment than the giving of a piece of bread. I'm sorry if that doesn't get over. It will maybe. I've been on this design and balance for a long time and I think I know how I want it. And if I'm wrong, I'm alone in my wrongness. As for the Maupassant story—I've never read it but I can't see that it makes much difference. There are no new stories and I wouldn't like them if there were. The incident of the earth mother feeding by the breast is older than literature.

You know that I've never been touchy about changes, but I have too many thousands of hours on this book, every incident has been too carefully chosen and its weight judged and fitted. The balance is there. One other thing—I am not writing a satisfying story. I've done my damndest to rip a reader's nerves to rags, I don't want him satisfied.

And still one more thing—I've tried to write this book the way lives are lived not the way books are written.

This letter sounds angry. I don't mean it to be. I know that books lead to a strong deep climax. This one doesn't except by implication, and the reader must bring the implication to it. If he doesn't, it wasn't a book for him to read. Throughout I've tried to make the reader participate in the actuality, what he takes from it will be scaled entirely on his own depth or shallowness. There are five layers in this book, a reader will find as many as he can and he won't find more than he has in himself.

I seem to be getting well slowly. The pain is going away.

Nerves still pretty tattered but rest will stop that before long. I fret pretty much at having to stay in bed. Guess I was pretty close to a collapse when I finally went to bed. I feel the results of it now.

Love to you all
John

Steinbeck's Suggestion for an Interview with Joseph Henry Jackson

After the publication of *The Grapes of Wrath*, Steinbeck found himself besieged with requests for guest appearances, speeches, and interviews. Being very shy and suspicious of the effects of publicity on the integrity of his work, he acceded to very few of these demands. When asked by his friend Joseph Henry Jackson of the *San Francisco Chronicle*, however, he sent the following suggestion for the kind of questions and answers he would prefer in such an interview.

QUESTION: Why did you choose the migration from the dust bowl to California as the theme for a novel?

ANSWER: Well, whether a writer knows it or not, or wants it or not, he simply sets down what the people of his own time are doing, thinking, wanting. He can't help that. It is all the writer knows. I have set down what a large section of our people are doing and wanting, and symbolically what all people of all time are doing and wanting. This migration is the outward sign of the want.

QUESTION: And what, in all time, are all people doing and wanting?

ANSWER: They use different symbols in different times but universally, people want comfort and security and out of these a relationship with one another. In the growth of our country the symbol of these things was new land. That was the security. The writer sets down the desire of his own time, the action of the people toward attaining that desire, the obstacles to attainment and the struggle to overcome the obstacles.

QUESTION: In the growing American literature there was no such cleavage between so called classes as seems to be at the core of present-day writing. Can you account for that?

ANSWER: Easily. Before the country was settled, the whole drive of the country by both rich and poor was to settle it. To this end they worked together. The menaces were Indians, weather, loneliness and the quality of the unknown. But this phase ended. When there was no longer unlimited land for everyone, then battles developed for what there was. And then as always, those few who had financial resources and financial brains had little difficulty acquiring the land in larger and larger blocks. I speak in terms of land, but the same applies of course to all resources, minerals, timber, etc. This condition left the great people in their original desire for the security symbol, land, but this time the menace (as they say in Hollywood) had changed. It was no longer Indians and weather and loneliness, it had become the holders of the land. In this discussion I am ignoring justice and law although it is pretty impossible to acquire half a million acres of land justly and lawfully. Now, since the people go on with their struggle, the writer still sets down that struggle and still sets down the opponents. The opponents or rather the obstacles to the desired end right now happen to be those individuals and groups of financiers who by the principle of ownership withhold security from the mass of the people. And since this is so, this is the material the writer deals in.

QUESTION: And do you think that by removing this principle of ownership, the people will gain their desire?

ANSWER: To a certain extent. But the greatness of the human lies in the fact that he never attains his desire. His desire keeps bounding ahead of his attainment and his search is endless. Out of this he has grown stronger slowly and constantly during the ages. There is little question in my mind that the principle of private ownership of means of production is not long with us. This is not in terms of what I think is right or wrong or good or bad, but in terms of what is inevitable. The province of the writer is to set down what is and what may come of it with as little confusion and as little nonsense as possible. The human like any other life form will tolerate an unhealthful condition for some time and then will either die or will overcome the condition either by mutation or by destroying the unhealthful condition. Since there seems little tendency for the human race to become extinct, and since one cannot through biological mutation overcome the necessity for eating, I judge that the final method will be the one chosen.

QUESTION: During the middle period of American writing, many books were written about owners and financiers, in a word about the controllers of financial destiny, the empire builders and such. Lately there are no such books. Books are written about the poor. Can you account for this?

ANSWER: Boileau said that kings, Gods, and Heroes only were fit subjects for literature. The writer can only write about what he admires. Present-day kings aren't very inspiring, the gods are on a vacation and about the only heroes left are the scientists and the poor. In the time you speak of, the time of the empire builders, those giants may have been outrageous but they had courage. When they did a thing they took the credit or the blame. Rockefeller at Leadville earned the hatred of the whole country for shooting miners. But at present there are no heroic giants. Ownership is hidden in interlocking directorates, labor spying and labor war is carried on by agents provocateurs, owners hide under the names of proxies and corporation titles. In a word, they have ceased being Heroes and have become cowardly and contemptible. And as such they have become, in Boileau's sense, unworthy of literature. But the poor are still in the open. When they make a struggle it is an heroic struggle with starvation, death or imprisonment the penalty if they lose. And since our race admires gallantry, the writer will deal with it where he finds it. He finds it in the struggling poor now. When the rich are hurt they show a tendency to jump off office buildings, or, as several doctors have assured me, to become sexually impotent.

QUESTION: Then you admire the migrant people you describe in this book? Will you tell me why?

ANSWER: I admire them intensely. Because they are brave, because although the technique of their life is difficult and complicated, they meet it with increasing strength, because they are kind, humorous and wise, because their speech has the metaphor and flavor and imagery of poetry, because they can resist and fight back and because I believe that out of those qualities will grow a new system and a new life which will be better than anything we have had before.

TOPICS FOR DISCUSSION
AND PAPERS

1. Read carefully the publishers' original criticism of the novel's ending (p. 857) and discuss the merits of their objections point for point. Is Steinbeck's justification in his return letter convincing? Where would you amplify or disagree? Look up a number of essays on the novel and keep a record of the various points they make about the ending. Among the material consulted beyond this edition, be sure to include the items found in the last section of the Bibliography under Chametzky, Crockett, De Schweinitz, Pollock, Shockley, and Wright. How do they compare with Steinbeck's arguments?

2. Although it is always interesting to have an author's statements about his own work, it would be uncritical to confuse these statements with the work itself. Choose one or two of Steinbeck's own questions and answers about his philosophy and intentions included in the list he sent to Joseph Henry Jackson (pp. 859–862), and examine the novel for the degree to which it embodies these statements.

3. If you were asked by someone who had not read the novel, "What is it about?" what would you write down in one sentence? Compare your sentence with those of others. If the sentences are strikingly different—as they are likely to be—how do you account for their diversity? Try to make a case for your sentence against those of others. Do your disagreements indicate a failure of communication on the part of the novel? What can you conclude about the novel from this experiment?

4. George Miron, in a pamphlet called *The Truth about John Steinbeck and the Migrants*, states that he can think "of no other novel which advances the idea of class war and promotes hatred of class against class . . . more than does *The Grapes of Wrath*." Is this the kind of impression the novel leaves with you? In opposition to the above statement, consider that of Stanley Edgar Hyman in "Some Notes on John Steinbeck": "Actually, as a care-

ful reading makes clear, the central message of *The Grapes of Wrath* is an appeal to the owning class to behave, to become enlightened, rather than to the working class to change its own conditions." Consider that the year before the publication of this novel Steinbeck had withdrawn from publication a completed, sixty-thousand-word novel, to be titled *Lettuceberg* or perhaps *Oklahoma*, because, as he wrote his agents, it wasn't completely honest, but tried to "cause hatred through partial understanding."

5. Compare the view of agricultural and migrant conditions in Frank J. Taylor's article with that in the articles by *Fortune* magazine and Carey McWilliams. Which is the more convincing? Why? Pursue this topic further in the following sources: Carey McWilliams, *Factories in the Field*; Paul S. Taylor, *An American Exodus: A Record of Human Erosion*; Leo Gurko, *The Angry Decade*; Salzman and Wallenstein, *Years of Protest*; Dixon Wector, *The Age of the Great Depression*.

6. In his Introduction, "The Pattern of Criticism," your editor states that "the hysterical reaction which *The Grapes of Wrath* aroused in part of the American public [as evidenced in Shockley's essay in this volume] was reflected in book reviews and literary essays." Consult the *Book Review Digest* and select some reviews which, judging from the excerpt presented there, promise to be "hysterical" and report on them. On what grounds was the book most objected to?

7. *The Grapes of Wrath* is sometimes compared to Harriet Beecher Stowe's *Uncle Tom's Cabin* in its immediate social repercussions. Discuss how the two books differ in the means by which they achieved this effect. Do you think that Stowe's book would be as effective today? Why or why not?

8. Steinbeck wrote two other novels in the 1930's dealing with migrant workers: *In Dubious Battle* and *Of Mice and Men*. The latter is very different from *The Grapes of Wrath* in that it deals much more with individuals, although of course they may be seen as representative. *In Dubious Battle* is a novel about a strike of migrant workers and resembles *The Grapes of Wrath* in its attention to large groups of men. Yet the two novels, although they share this trait, are very different in other respects—prose style, structure, characterization, use of symbolism, etc.—their total effect. Compare one or more aspects of both novels in some detail.

9. Assuming that the information in the essays by Carey Mc-Williams and *Fortune* magazine is correct, use these essays to "prove" or "disprove" as many facts, incidents, and conditions as you can in *The Grapes of Wrath*.

10. In his essay, "*The Grapes of Wrath* Reconsidered," Walter Fuller Taylor complains of the novel's "vulgarity in deed and word," and that Steinbeck so manages these vulgarities "as to startle the reader into aversion or even nausea." Was this your reading experience? Granted, that the book's use of language and depiction of intimate detail is considerably less bold than that encountered in more recent fiction, and inoffensive to readers of today. There still remains the problem of Steinbeck's deliberate use of such language and detail as he knew would be found shocking at that time. Make a list of such passages which might have been found offensive. Does there seem to be some effective purpose in each case? What is their cumulative contribution to the novel?

11. In his essay, "Work and the Timeliness of *The Grapes of Wrath*," Pascal Covici, Jr. gives one argument for the book's contemporary relevance. Are there others? Do you feel that this relevance to our own time is coincidental or that the novel has some universal or enduring qualities which will continue to keep it relevant to contemporary life? What are these qualities and how are they achieved?

12. What was your initial reaction to the interchapters in *The Grapes of Wrath*? Did they "interfere" with your reading of the novel, or did they contribute to your participation and enjoyment? If they interfered, do the arguments in your editor's essay, "*The Grapes of Wrath* as Fiction," convince you of their centrality to the novel or that you might enjoy them on a second reading of the book? If you enjoyed them, do that essay's arguments satisfactorily explain your enjoyment?

13. As noted in the Introduction to the critical essays, much discussion of the novel has revolved around its characters. Some reviewers and critics have found them to be mere puppets, animalistic, unreal; others have praised their human qualities. Where do you stand on this? What kinds of details can you present to support your opinion? Is it possible to logically argue this point at all? What kinds of evidence can be agreed on? Furthermore, it is clear that most contemporary readers have no difficulty in accepting the

book's characters as real, moving human beings. What might be some of the reasons for this shift in appreciation? Consider the total social context and the possible effects of mass communication media.

14. Assuming that The Grapes of Wrath is essentially accurate in its depiction of economic, political, sociological conditions in Oklahoma, en route, and in California, how fair is the novel in assigning blame for these conditions?

15. Commentators have made much of the book's biblical symbolism. How much of this was apparent to you on a first reading? Although it is impossible to question that this symbolism is ubiquitous in The Grapes of Wrath, what is the effect of its presence? Would the novel be appreciably diminished if the biblical symbolism were completely removed? How?

16. In 1936 Steinbeck wrote for the San Francisco News a series of eight articles on migrant labor in California. These were reprinted together with an epilogue by Steinbeck in 1938 by the Lubin Society of California in a pamphlet called Their Blood Is Strong. This pamphlet has been reprinted in French's A Companion to The Grapes of Wrath, generally available in college libraries. Also in 1936, Steinbeck wrote an essay for The Nation (September 13) called "Dubious Battle in California," again on the subject of migrant labor. Read one or both of these works and comment on the use of this material in The Grapes of Wrath. What observations did he not use in the novel? Why?

17. Compare Steinbeck's articles on migrant labor (detailed in the preceding question) with those by McWilliams, Fortune magazine, and Frank J. Taylor in this volume. Could Steinbeck have written The Grapes of Wrath without doing his own research?

18. It has been charged sometimes by critics that The Grapes of Wrath is "sentimental." Look up several definitions of the term in dictionaries and literary handbooks. Do you agree that this term can be applied to the novel's characters and plot? To the interchapters? Just what are the specific sentimental incidents and aspects of character in the novel? Is it possible to have these elements and still be a great novel?

19. Chester E. Eisinger in "Jeffersonian Agrarianism in The Grapes of Wrath" and Griffin and Freedman in "Machines and Animals: Pervasive Motifs in The Grapes of Wrath" point to the

novel's concern with mechanized agriculture. Gather evidence from the novel for a summary of Steinbeck's views on the subject. Is he really against mechanized agriculture *per se*? Is he really for a return to the horse and plow?

20. Most attention to the novel's characters focuses on the adults and their sometimes symbolic roles—Jim Casy, Tom, Granma, Grampa, and Ma Joad. There are in the novel, however, not only the Joad children but those of other migrants. Looking at the children in the novel, what can be said of their reality simply as children? What is their contribution to the novel's direction?

21. It is tempting when talking about a long and impressive novel to call it "epic." Look up the term in some literary handbooks. Does *The Grapes of Wrath* seem to embody any of these characteristics? Does it embody enough of them to be called an epic?

BIBLIOGRAPHY

Works by John Steinbeck

For information concerning articles, poems, letters, speeches, separate publication of short stories, etc., by Steinbeck, consult the Hayashi bibliography cited below. Those items marked with an asterisk are available in Viking Compass paperback editions; those with a dagger are available in Bantam paperbacks.

FICTION

† *Cup of Gold*. New York: Robert M. McBride & Co., 1929.

* *The Pastures of Heaven*. New York: Brewer, Warren & Putnam, 1932.

† *To a God Unknown*. New York: Robert O. Ballou, 1933.

* *Tortilla Flat*. New York: Covici-Friede, 1935.

* *In Dubious Battle*. New York: Covici-Friede, 1936.

* *The Red Pony*. New York: Covici-Friede, 1937; The Viking Press, 1945. [Included in *The Long Valley*, 1938.]

* *Of Mice and Men*. New York: Covici-Friede, 1937.

* *The Long Valley*. New York: The Viking Press, 1938.

* *The Grapes of Wrath*. New York: The Viking Press, 1939.

† *The Moon Is Down*. New York: The Viking Press, 1942.

* *Cannery Row*. New York: The Viking Press, 1945.

† *The Wayward Bus*. New York: The Viking Press, 1947.

* *The Pearl*. New York: The Viking Press, 1947.

† *Burning Bright*. New York: The Viking Press, 1950.

* *East of Eden*. New York: The Viking Press, 1952.

† *Sweet Thursday*. New York: The Viking Press, 1954.

† *The Short Reign of Pippin IV: A Fabrication*. New York: The Viking Press, 1957.

† *The Winter of Our Discontent*. New York: The Viking Press, 1961.

NONFICTION

Their Blood Is Strong (pamphlet). San Francisco: Simon J. Lubin Society of California, Inc., 1938. [Articles published in *San Francisco News*, October 5-12, 1936, as "The Harvest Gypsies."] Reprinted in French, *Companion*, pp. 53-92.

Sea of Cortez: A Leisurely Journal of Travel and Research (in collaboration with Edward F. Ricketts). New York: The Viking Press, 1941.

Bombs Away: The Story of a Bomber Team. New York: The Viking Press, 1942.

† *A Russian Journal* (with pictures by Robert Capa). New York: The Viking Press, 1948.

* *The Log from the Sea of Cortez.* New York: The Viking Press, 1951. [The narrative portion of *Sea of Cortez* and a tribute, "About Ed Ricketts."]

† *Once There Was a War.* New York: The Viking Press, 1958. [Steinbeck's wartime dispatches published in the New York *Herald Tribune*, June-December, 1943.]

* *Travels with Charley in Search of America.* New York: The Viking Press, 1962.

† *America and Americans.* New York: The Viking Press, 1966.

Journal of a Novel: The East of Eden *Letters* (posthumous). New York: The Viking Press, 1969.

PLAYS

Of Mice and Men. New York: Covici-Friede, 1937.

The Moon Is Down. New York: The Viking Press, 1943.

Burning Bright. New York: Dramatists Play Service, 1951.

Pipe Dream (musical comedy by Richard Rodgers and Oscar Hammerstein II based on *Sweet Thursday*). New York: The Viking Press, 1956.

FILM STORIES AND SCRIPTS

The Forgotten Village (documentary). Herbert Kline, Producer, 1941. Story and script. New York: The Viking Press, 1941.

Lifeboat. 20th Century–Fox Film Corp., 1944. Story. Unpublished.

A *Medal for Benny*. Paramount Studios, 1945. Story, with Jack Wagner. *Best Film Plays—1945*, ed. by John Gassner and Dudley Nichols. New York: Crown, 1946.

The Pearl (from his novel). RKO, 1947. Script. Unpublished.

The Red Pony (from his stories). Feldman Group Productions and Lewis Milestone Productions, 1949. Script. Unpublished.

Viva Zapata. 20th Century–Fox Film Corp., 1952. Story and script. *Argosy*, XXXIII (February, 1952), abridged.

Criticism

The following bibliography does not attempt to be complete, but the section on *The Grapes of Wrath* does contain most items of interest as well as the major sources of information and criticism. The most detailed and complete bibliography is Tetsumaro Hayashi's *John Steinbeck: A Concise Bibliography* (1930-1965), together with the supplements published in the *Steinbeck Quarterly* beginning with Volume I (September, 1968). The bibliography in *Modern Fiction Studies* XI (Spring, 1965), although selective, is more manageable for the student who is not pursuing the minutiae of literary notices and book reviews. Those items marked with an asterisk are reprinted in the present volume.

On Steinbeck, General

BOOKS

Astro, Richard and Hayashi, Tetsumaro, eds. *Steinbeck: The Man and His Work*. Corvallis: Oregon State University Press, 1971.

Beach, Joseph Warren. "John Steinbeck: Journeyman Artist." *American Fiction, 1920-1940*. New York: Macmillan, 1942. Pp. 307-327. Reprinted in Tedlock and Wicker, pp. 80-91.

Boynton, Percy. "John Steinbeck." *America in Contemporary Fiction*. University of Chicago Press, 1940. Pp. 241-257.

Burgum, Edwin Berry. "The Fickle Sensibility of John Steinbeck."

The Novel and the World's Dilemma. New York: Oxford University Press, 1947. Pp. 272-291. Reprinted as "The Sensibility of John Steinbeck," in Tedlock and Wicker, pp. 104-118.

Covici, Pascal, Jr. "John Steinbeck and the Language of Awareness." *The Thirties: Fiction, Poetry, Drama,* Warren French, ed. Deland, Florida: Everett Edwards Press, 1967. Pp. 47-54.

Davis, Robert Murray. *Steinbeck* (Twentieth Century Views). Englewood Cliffs, N.J.: Prentice-Hall, Inc., 1972.

Ditsky, John. "Faulkner Land and Steinbeck Country." Astro and Hayashi, pp. 11-23.

Fontenrose, Joseph. *John Steinbeck: An Introduction and Interpretation.* American Authors and Critics Series. New York: Barnes and Noble, 1963; New York: Holt, Rinehart and Winston, 1967.

French, Warren. *John Steinbeck.* Twayne's United States Authors Series. New York: Twayne, 1961.

———. "John Steinbeck." *Fifteen Modern American Authors,* Jackson R. Bryer, ed. Durham, North Carolina: Duke University Press, 1969. Pp. 369-387.

——— and Kidd, Walter E., eds. "John Steinbeck." *American Winners of the Nobel Literary Prize.* Norman: University of Oklahoma Press, 1968. Pp. 193-223.

Frohock, W. M. "John Steinbeck: The Utility of Wrath." *The Novel of Violence in America.* Revised edition. Dallas: Southern Methodist University Press, 1958. Pp. 124-143.

Geismar, Maxwell. "John Steinbeck." *American Moderns: From Rebellion to Conformity.* New York: Hill and Wang, 1958. Pp. 151-156, 164-167.

———. "John Steinbeck: Of Wrath and Joy." *Writers in Crisis: The American Novel Between Two Wars.* Boston: Houghton Mifflin, 1942. Pp. 237-270. Reprinted in Donohue, pp. 134-142.

Hayashi, Tetsumaro. *John Steinbeck: A Concise Bibliography.* Metuchen, New Jersey: Scarecrow Press, 1967.

Hedgepeth, Joel. "Philosophy on Cannery Row." Astro and Hayashi, pp. 89-129.

Hoffman, Frederick J. *The Modern Novel in America, 1900-1950.* Chicago: Henry Regnery, 1951. Pp. 146–153. Gateway edition, 1956. Pp. 160-168.

Howard, Leon. *Literature and the American Tradition.* Garden City, New York: Doubleday, 1960. Pp. 300-303.

Hyman, Stanley Edgar. "John Steinbeck: Of Invertebrates and Men" (1942). *The Promised End: Essays and Reviews, 1942-1962.* Cleveland and New York: World, 1963. Pp. 17-22.

Kazin, Alfred. *On Native Grounds: An Interpretation of Modern American Prose Literature.* New York: Harcourt, Brace, 1942. Pp. 393-399.

Kennedy, John S. "John Steinbeck: Life Affirmed and Dissolved." *Fifty Years of the American Novel: A Catholic Appraisal,* Harold C. Gardiner, ed. New York: Charles Scribner's Sons, 1951. Pp. 217-236. Reprinted in Tedlock and Wicker, pp. 119-134.

Lewis, Richard W. B. "John Steinbeck: The Fitful Daemon." *The Young Rebel in American Literature,* Carl Bode, ed. London: Heinemann, 1959. Pp. 121-141. Reprinted New York: Frederick A. Praeger, 1960, and *Modern American Fiction: Essays in Criticism,* A. Walton Litz, ed. New York: Oxford University Press, 1963. Pp. 265-277.

Lisca, Peter. "Escape and Commitment: Two Poles of the Steinbeck Hero." Astro and Hayashi, pp. 75-88.

————. "John Steinbeck: A Literary Biography." Tedlock and Wicker, pp. 3-22.

————. *The Wide World of John Steinbeck.* New Brunswick, New Jersey: Rutgers University Press, 1958.

Magny, Claude-Edmonde. "Steinbeck, or the Limits of the Impersonal Novel," trans. Françoise Gourier. Tedlock and Wicker, pp. 216-227.

Marks, Lester J. *Thematic Design in the Novels of John Steinbeck.* The Hague: Mouton, 1969.

Metzger, Charles. "Steinbeck's Mexican-Americans." Astro and Hayashi, pp. 141-155.

Moore, Harry T. *The Novels of John Steinbeck: A First Critical Study.* Chicago: Normandie House, 1939. Reprinted Port Washington, New York: Kennikat Press, 1968.

Pratt, John Clark. *John Steinbeck: A Critical Essay* (pamphlet). Grand Rapids, Michigan: William B. Eerdmans, 1970.

Prescott, Orville. "Squandered Talents." *In My Opinion.* Indianapolis: Bobbs-Merrill, 1952. Pp. 58-64.

Quinn, Arthur Hobson. "Steinbeck." *The Literature of the American People.* New York: Appleton-Century-Crofts, 1951. Pp. 958-961.

Ross, Woodburn O. "John Steinbeck: Earth and Stars." *University of Missouri Studies in Honor of A. H. R. Fairchild,* Charles T. Prouty, ed. Columbia: University of Missouri Press, 1946. Pp. 179-197. Reprinted in Tedlock and Wicker, pp. 167-182.

Scully, Frank. "Steinbeck." *Rogue's Gallery.* Hollywood: Murray and Gee, 1943. Pp. 37-55.

Slochower, Harry. "John Dos Passos and John Steinbeck: Contrasting Notions of the Communal Personality." *Byrdcliffe Afternoons.* Woodstock, New York: Overlook Press, January, 1940. Pp. 11-27.

————. "The Promise of America: John Steinbeck." *Literature and Philosophy Between Two World Wars: The Problem in a War Culture.* New York: Citadel Press, 1964. Pp. 299-306. (Same as *No Voice is Wholly Lost.* New York: Creative Age Press, 1945. Pp. 299-308.)

Snell, George. *The Shapers of American Fiction: 1798–1947.* New York: Dutton, 1947. Pp. 187-197.

Tedlock, E. W., Jr., and Wicker, C. V., eds. *Steinbeck and His Critics: a Record of Twenty-five Years.* Albuquerque, New Mexico: University of New Mexico Press, 1957.

Wagenknecht, Edward. *Cavalcade of the American Novel.* New York: Henry Holt, 1952. Pp. 443-448.

Walcutt, Charles C. *American Literary Naturalism, A Divided Stream.* Minneapolis: University of Minnesota Press, 1956. Pp. 258-270. Reprinted in Donohue, pp. 162-165.

Watt, F. W. *John Steinbeck.* Evergreen Pilot Books. New York: Grove Press, 1962.

Widmer, Kingsley. "John Steinbeck: Example of Sentimental Rebellions." *Literary Rebel.* Carbondale: Southern Illinois University Press, 1965. Pp. 114-129.

Whipple, Thomas K. "Steinbeck: Through a Glass, Though Brightly." *Study Out the Land.* Berkeley: University of California Press, 1943. Pp. 105-111.

PERIODICALS

Astro, Richard. "Steinbeck and Mainwaring: Two Californians for the Earth." *Steinbeck Quarterly,* III (Winter 1970), 3-11.

Baker, Carlos. "Steinbeck of California." *Delphian Quarterly,* XXIII (April 1940), 40-44.

Beebe, Maurice, and Bryer, Jackson R. "Criticism of John Stein-beck: A Selected Checklist." *Modern Fiction Studies*, XI (Spring 1965), 90-103.

Bracher, Frederick. "Steinbeck and the Biological View of Man." *Pacific Spectator*, II (Winter 1948), 14-29. Reprinted in Ted-lock and Wicker, pp. 183-196.

Brown, Daniel R. "A Monolith of Logic Against Waves of Non-sense." *Renascence*, XVI (Fall 1963), 48-51.

Calverton, V. F. "Steinbeck, Hemingway, and Faulkner." *Modern Quarterly*, XI (Fall 1939), 36-44.

Carpenter, Frederic I. "John Steinbeck: American Dreamer." *Southwest Review*, XXVI (Summer 1940), 454-467. Reprinted in Tedlock and Wicker, pp. 68-79.

Champney, Freeman. "John Steinbeck, Californian." *Antioch Review*, VII (Fall 1947), 345-362. Reprinted in Tedlock and Wicker, pp. 135-151.

Cousins, Norman. "Who Are the Real People?" *Saturday Review of Literature*, XXVII (March 17, 1945), 14.

Cowley, Malcolm. "American Tragedy." *The New Republic*, XCVIII (May 3, 1939), 382.

Eastman, Max. "John Steinbeck—Genevieve Tabouis." *The American Mercury*, LIV (June 1942), 754-756.

Fairley, Barker. "John Steinbeck and the Coming Literature." *Sewanee Review*, L (April 1942), 145-161.

Gannett, Lewis. "John Steinbeck: Novelist at Work." *Atlantic Monthly*, CLXXVI (December 1944), 55-60. Reprinted as "John Steinbeck's Way of Writing" in *The Viking Portable Steinbeck*, Pascal Covici, ed. New York: The Viking Press, 1958. Pp. vii-xviii. Also reprinted in Tedlock and Wicker, pp. 23-37.

Gibbs, Lincoln R. "John Steinbeck, Moralist." *Antioch Review*, II (Summer 1942), 172-184. Reprinted in Tedlock and Wicker, pp. 92-103.

Hester, Sister Mary. "Mr. Steinbeck? Frankly, No." *Today*, VII (May 1963), 23-26.

Hyman, Stanley Edgar. "Some Notes on John Steinbeck." *Antioch Review*, II (Summer 1942), 185-200. Reprinted in Tedlock and Wicker, pp. 152-166.

Jackson, Joseph Henry. "John Steinbeck: A Portrait." *Saturday Review of Literature*, XVI (September 25, 1937), 18.

Jones, Claude E. "Proletarian Writing and John Steinbeck." *Sewanee Review*, XLVIII (October 1940), 445-456.

Levidova, I. "The Post-War Books of John Steinbeck." *Soviet Review*, IV (Summer 1963), 3-13.

Lisca, Peter. "Steinbeck's Image of Man and His Decline as a Writer." *Modern Fiction Studies*, XI (Spring 1965), 3-10.

————. "Steinbeck and Hemingway: Suggestions for a Comparative Study." *Steinbeck Quarterly*, II (Spring 1969), 9-17.

Marshall, Margaret. "Writers in the Wilderness." *The Nation*, CXLIX (November 25, 1939), 576-579.

Mizener, Arthur. "Does a Moral Vision of the Thirties Deserve a Nobel Prize?" *New York Times Book Review* (December 9, 1962), 4, 43-45. Reprinted in Donohue, *Casebook*, pp. 267-272.

Moloney, Michael F. "Half-Faiths in Modern Fiction." *Catholic World*, CLXXI (August 1950), 344-350.

Nevius, Blake. "Steinbeck: One Aspect." *Pacific Spectator*, III (Summer 1949), 302-310. Reprinted in Tedlock and Wicker, pp. 197-205.

Nossen, Evon. "The Beast-Man Theme in the Works of Steinbeck." *Ball State University Forum*, 7 (Spring 1966), pp. 52-64.

Poulakidas, Andreas K. "Steinbeck, Kazantazakis and Socialism." *Steinbeck Quarterly*, III (Summer 1970), 62-72.

Rascoe, Burton. "John Steinbeck." *English Journal*, XXVII (March 1938), 205-216. Reprinted in Tedlock and Wicker, pp. 57-67.

Redman, Ben Ray. "The Case of John Steinbeck." *American Mercury*, LXIV (May 1947), 624-630.

Richards, Edmund C. "The Challenge of John Steinbeck." *North American Review*, CCXLIII (Summer 1957), 406-413.

Ricketts, Toni Jackson (Seixas, Antonia). "John Steinbeck and the Non-teleological Bus." *What's Doing on the Monterey Peninsula*, I (March 1947). Reprinted in Tedlock and Wicker, pp. 275-280.

Roane, Margaret C. "John Steinbeck as a Spokesman for the Mentally Retarded." *Wisconsin Studies in Contemporary Literature*, V (Summer 1964), 127-132.

Ross, Woodburn O. "John Steinbeck: Naturalism's Priest." *College English*, X (May 1949), 432-437. Reprinted in Tedlock and Wicker, pp. 206-215.

Rundell, Walter, Jr. "Steinbeck's Image of the West." *The American West*, I (Spring 1964), 4-17, 79.

Sartre, Jean-Paul. "American Novelists in French Eyes." *Atlantic Monthly*, CLXXVIII (August 1946), 114-118.

Seixas, Antonia. See Ricketts, Toni Jackson.

Taylor, Horace P., Jr. "The Biological Naturalism of John Steinbeck." *McNeese Review*, XII (Winter 1960-1961), 81-97.

Tuttleton, James W. "Steinbeck in Russia: The Rhetoric of Praise and Blame." *Modern Fiction Studies*, XI (Spring 1965), 79-89.

Van Gelder, Robert. "Interview with a Best Selling Author." *Cosmopolitan*, CXXII (April 1947), 123-125.

Weeks, Donald. "Steinbeck Against Steinbeck." *Pacific Spectator*, I (Autumn 1947), 447-457.

Wilson, Edmund. "The Californians: Storm and Steinbeck." *The New Republic*, CIII (December 9, 1940), 784-787. Reprinted in Donohue, pp. 151-158.

Woodress, James. "John Steinbeck: Hostage to Fortune." *South Atlantic Quarterly*, LXIII (Summer 1964), 385-397. Reprinted in Donohue, pp. 278-290.

On *The Grapes of Wrath*

BOOKS

Beach, Joseph Warren. "John Steinbeck: Art and Propaganda." *American Fiction, 1920-1940*. New York: Macmillan, 1942. Pp. 327-347. Reprinted in Tedlock and Wicker, pp. 250-265.

Bluestone, George. "*The Grapes of Wrath*." *Novels Into Film*. Baltimore: Johns Hopkins University Press, 1957. Pp. 147-169. Reprinted in Davis, *Steinbeck*, pp. 102-121.

Boynton, Percy. "John Steinbeck." *America in Contemporary Fiction*. University of Chicago Press, 1940. Pp. 251-257.

Burke, Kenneth. *The Philosophy of Literary Form*. Baton Rouge: Louisiana State University Press, 1941. P. 91 and *passim*.

*Covici, Pascal, Jr. "Work and the Timeliness of *The Grapes of Wrath*." Lisca, *Grapes*.

Donohue, Agnes McNeill, ed. *A Casebook on the Grapes of Wrath*. New York: Thomas Y. Crowell Company, 1968. Pp. 257-266.

———. " 'The Endless Journey to No End': Journey and Eden Symbolism in Hawthorne and Steinbeck." Donohue, pp. 257-266.

*Fontenrose, Joseph. "*The Grapes of Wrath*." *John Steinbeck: An Introduction and Interpretation*. American Authors and Critics

Series. New York: Barnes and Noble, 1963. Holt, Rinehart and Winston, 1967. Pp. 67-83.

French, Warren, ed. *A Companion to the Grapes of Wrath*. New York: The Viking Press, 1963.

———. "The Education of the Heart." *John Steinbeck*. New Haven, Connecticut: College and University Press, 1961. Pp. 95-112.

Frohock, W. M. "John Steinbeck: The Utility of Wrath." *The Novel of Violence in America*. Revised Edition. Dallas: Southern Methodist University Press, 1958. Pp. 129-133.

Geismar, Maxwell. "John Steinbeck: Of Wrath and Joy." *Writers in Crisis: The American Novel Between Two Wars*. Boston: Houghton Mifflin, 1942. Pp. 263-270. Reprinted in Donohue, pp. 134-142.

Goethals, Thomas R. *The Grapes of Wrath: A Critical Commentary*. New York: R. D. M. Corporation, 1963.

Gurko, Leo. "The Joads in California." *The Angry Decade*. New York: Dodd, Mead, 1947. Pp. 201-221. Reprinted in Donohue, pp. 63-67.

Hoffman, Frederick J. *The Modern Novel in America, 1900-1950*. Chicago: Henry Regnery, 1951. Pp. 146-153. Gateway Edition, 1956. Pp. 160-168.

*Hunter, J. P. "Steinbeck's Wine of Affirmation in *The Grapes of Wrath*." *Essays in Modern American Literature*, Richard E. Langford, Guy Owen, William Taylor, eds. Deland, Florida: Stetson University Press, 1963. Pp. 76-89.

Lisca, Peter. "The Dynamics of Community in *The Grapes of Wrath*." *From Irving to Steinbeck: Studies in American Literature*, Motley F. Deakin and Peter Lisca, eds. Gainesville: University of Florida Press, 1972.

*———. "Editor's Introduction: The Pattern of Criticism." *The Grapes of Wrath: Text and Criticism*, The Viking Critical Library Edition. New York: The Viking Press, 1972.

———. "The Grapes of Wrath." *The Wide World of John Steinbeck*. New Brunswick, New Jersey: Rutgers University Press, 1958. Pp. 144-177.

Lutwack, Leonard. *Heroic Fiction*. Carbondale: Southern Illinois University Press, 1971. Pp. 47-63.

Marks, Lester J. *Thematic Design in the Novels of John Steinbeck*. The Hague: Mouton, 1969. Pp. 66-82.

Miron, George Thomas. *The Truth about John Steinbeck and the Migrants.* Los Angeles: Haynes Corporation, 1939.

Monroe, Elizabeth N. *The Novel and Society.* Chapel Hill: University of North Carolina Press, 1941. Pp. 17-18 and *passim.*

Moore, Harry T. *The Novels of John Steinbeck: A First Critical Study.* Chicago: Normandie House, 1939. Pp. 53-72. Reprinted Port Washington, New York: Kennikat Press, 1968.

Moseley, Edwin M. "Christ as the Brother of Man: Steinbeck's *The Grapes of Wrath.*" *Pseudonyms of Christ in the Modern Novel: Motifs and Methods.* University of Pittsburgh Press, 1963. Pp. 163-175. Reprinted in Donohue, pp. 209-218.

Orlova, R. "Money Against Humanity: Notes on the Work of John Steinbeck," trans. Armin Moskovic. Reprinted in French, *Companion,* pp. 152-159.

*Perez, Betty. "House and Home: Thematic Symbols in *The Grapes of Wrath.*" Lisca, *Grapes.*

Pratt, John Clark. *John Steinbeck: A Critical Essay* (pamphlet). Grand Rapids, Michigan: William B. Eerdmans, 1970. Pp. 19-24.

*Reed, John R. "*The Grapes of Wrath* and the Esthetics of Indigence." Lisca, *Grapes.*

Snell, George. *The Shapers of American Fiction: 1798-1947.* New York: Dutton, 1947. Pp. 193-196.

Stovall, Floyd. *American Idealism.* Norman, Oklahoma: University of Oklahoma Press. Pp. 159-166.

Watt, F. W. *John Steinbeck.* Evergreen Pilot Books. New York: Grove Press, 1962. Pp. 63-75.

PERIODICALS

Aaron, Daniel. "The Radical Humanism of John Steinbeck: *The Grapes of Wrath* Thirty Years Later." *Saturday Review,* LI (September 28, 1968), 26-27, 55-56.

Baker, Howard. "In Praise of the Novel: The Fiction of Huxley, Steinbeck, & Others." *Southern Review,* V (1939-1940), 778-800.

Bowron, Bernard. "*The Grapes of Wrath*: A 'Wagons West' Romance." *Colorado Quarterly,* III (Summer 1954), 84-91. Reprinted in French, *Companion,* pp. 208-216.

Browning, Chris. "Grape Symbolism in *The Grapes of Wrath.*" *Discourse,* XI (Winter 1968), 129-140.

Cannon, Gerard. "The Pauline Apostleship of Tom Joad." *Col-*

lege English, XXIV (December 1962), 222-224. Reprinted in Donohue, pp. 118-122.

*Carlson, Eric W. "Symbolism in *The Grapes of Wrath*." *College English*, XIX (January 1958), 172-175.

*Carpenter, Frederic I. "The Philosophical Joads." *College English*, II (January 1941), 315-325.

Chametzky, Jules. "The Ambivalent Endings of *The Grapes of Wrath*." *Modern Fiction Studies*, XI (Spring 1965), 34-44. Reprinted in Donohue, pp. 232-244.

Crockett, H. Kelly. "The Bible and *The Grapes of Wrath*." *College English*, XXIV (December 1962), 193-198. Reprinted in Donohue, pp. 105-114.

De Schweinitz, George. "Steinbeck and Christianity." *College English*, XIX (May 1958), 369. Reprinted in Donohue, pp. 103-104.

De Voto, Bernard. "American Novels: 1939." *Atlantic Monthly*, CLXV (January 1940), 66-74.

Dougherty, Charles T. "The Christ-Figure in *The Grapes of Wrath*." *College English*, XXIV (December 1962), 224-226. Reprinted in Donohue, pp. 115-117.

Dunn, Thomas F. "*The Grapes of Wrath*." *College English*, XXIV (April 1963), 566-567. Reprinted in Donohue, pp. 123-125.

*Eisinger, Chester E. "Jeffersonian Agrarianism in *The Grapes of Wrath*." *The University of Kansas City Review*, XIV (Winter 1947), 149-154.

French, Warren. "Another Look at *The Grapes of Wrath*." *Colorado Quarterly*, III (Winter 1955), 337-343. Reprinted in his *Companion*, pp. 217-224.

*Griffin, Robert J., and Freedman, William A. "Machines and Animals: Pervasive Motifs in *The Grapes of Wrath*." *Journal of English and Germanic Philology*, LXII (April 1963), 569-580.

Hayashi, Tetsumaro. "The Function of the Joad Clan in *The Grapes of Wrath*." *Modern Review*, CXXIII (March 1968), 158, 161-162.

Klammer, Enno. "*The Grapes of Wrath*—A Modern Exodus Account." *Cresset*, XXV (February 1962), 8-11.

Kuhl, A. "Mostly of *The Grapes of Wrath*." *Catholic World*, CL (November 1939), 160-165.

*Lisca, Peter. "*The Grapes of Wrath* as Fiction." PMLA, LXXII (March 1957), 296-309. Enlarged and incorporated in his *The Wide World of John Steinbeck*, pp. 144-177.

McCarthy, Paul. "House and Shelter as Symbol in *The Grapes of Wrath*." *South Dakota Review* (1967), 48-67.

McElderry, B. R., Jr. "*The Grapes of Wrath* in the Light of Modern Critical Theory." *College English*, V (March 1944), 308-313. Reprinted in French, *Companion*, pp. 199-208.

*McWilliams, Carey. "California Pastoral," *Antioch Review*, II (March 1942), 103-121.

Paton, Alan, and Pope, Liston. "The Novelist and Christ." *Saturday Review*, XXXVII (December 4, 1954), 15-16, 56-59.

Pollock, Theodore. "On the Ending of *The Grapes of Wrath*." *Modern Fiction Studies*, IV (Summer 1958), 177-178. Reprinted in French, *Companion*, pp. 224-226.

Shockley, Martin S. "Christian Symbolism in *The Grapes of Wrath*." *College English*, XVIII (November 1956), 87-90. Reprinted in Tedlock and Wicker, pp. 231-240.

*———. "The Reception of *The Grapes of Wrath* in Oklahoma." *American Literature*, XV (January 1944), 351-361.

Slade, Leonard A. "The Use of Biblical Allusions in *The Grapes of Wrath*." *College Language Association Journal*, XI (March 1968), 241-247.

*Taylor, Frank J. "California's 'Grapes of Wrath.' " *Forum*, CII (November 1939), 232-238.

*Taylor, Walter Fuller. "*The Grapes of Wrath* Reconsidered." *Mississippi Quarterly*, XII (Summer 1959), 136-144.

Whipple, Leon. "Novels on Social Themes." *Survey Graphic*, XXVIII (June 1939), 401.

Wright, Celeste T. "Ancient Analogues of an Incident in John Steinbeck." *Western Folklore*, XIV (January 1955), 50-51. Reprinted in Donohue, pp. 159-161.